JUSTICE

Help! *Please help*."

The desperate cry came from much further down. A shiver ran up the back of Rix's neck as he peered into the shadowed depths. The crevasse widened below the bulge, then narrowed steadily as it went down, and far below he made out another three trapped soldiers. One fellow was alternately whimpering and moaning, a dreadful, hackle-raising sound. The second man was thrashing violently as if having a panic attack. The third soldier, the highest, made no sound, though the whites of his eyes were luminous in the gloom.

They were at least forty feet down. Rix's throat clamped at the thought of being trapped in such a place, either starving to death or slowly suffocating when the soil fell in on them. Or, most horrible of all, being slowly squeezed to jelly as the crack closed again . . .

How was he to get the injured men out when they could not help themselves? He probed the edge of the crevasse with one foot. The soil cracked; it would not support his weight.

Dozens of soldiers were gathering along the crevasse. "Get me three sturdy poles," said Rix, "six inches through and at least ten feet long. No, make it twelve feet long. Plus a hundred and fifty feet of rope and a block and tackle."

The soldiers looked past Rix, as if seeking confirmation of the order. Libbens was behind him, scowling. Libbens stamped a foot. The edge of the crevasse crumbled and he leapt backwards.

"It's not worth the risk," said Libbens. "Leave them."

JUSTICE

THE TAINTED REALM TRILOGY
BOOK THREE

IAN IRVINE

orbit

www.orbitbooks.net

ORBIT

First published in Great Britain in 2014 by Orbit
First published in Australia and New Zealand in 2013 by Orbit

Copyright © 2013 by Ian Irvine

Excerpt from *The Crown Tower* by Michael J. Sullivan
Copyright © 2013 by Michael J. Sullivan

The moral right of the author has been asserted.

A CIP catalogue record for this book
is available from the British Library.

ISBN 978-1-84149-830-0

Typeset in Garamond by M Rules
Printed and bound in Great Britain by
Clays Ltd, St Ives plc

Papers used by Orbit are from well-managed forests
and other responsible sources.

MIX
Paper from
responsible sources
FSC
www.fsc.org   FSC® C104740

Orbit
An imprint of
Little, Brown Book Group
100 Victoria Embankment
London EC4Y 0DY

An Hachette UK Company
www.hachette.co.uk

www.orbitbooks.net

To Laurie, webmaster supreme

CONTENTS

TO BLEDDIMIRE

GARRAMIDE
TOUCHSTONE
TIRNAN TWIL
THE THIRD PASS
NANDELOCH MOUNTAINS
SWIRE
TOGL
LAKE FUMEROUS
CAULDERON
THE VOMITS
CROWBUNG RANGE
RUTHERIN
THE CAPE
ESTERLYZ

N

0 MILES 10
5

GREATER
HIGHTSPALL

CENTRAL HIGHTSPALL

(THE ANCIENT REALM FORMERLY
KNOWN AS CYTHE)

NYRDLY

LAKELAND

REBROFF

SWIRE

BASTION BARR

RINKL RIVER

RESTIN

FENNERY

BOLSTIR

TINKER'S CLEFT

TOGL

LAKE BUNT

LIDDEN FIELD

FLUME

GORDION

REFFERING

GLIMMERING

MANOR ASSIDY

RED MESA

LAKE
FUMEROUS

LAKE YIZL

GRUME

CAULDERON

KLENG

SUTHLY

CYTHON
RAT-HOLE

GULLIHOE

THE VOMITS

MULCLAST

CROWBUNG RANGE

THE SEETHINGS

RIBROSE

TYDDERLEY

PRECIPITOUS CRAG

CATACOMBS
OF THE KINGS

N

MILES

0   5

LIST OF CHARACTERS

Benn: Glynnie's little brother, lost somewhere in Cauldron.

Errek First-King: The legendary inventor of king-magery, recreated as a spirit by Lyf.

Five Heroes, the: The Five Herovians who killed Lyf two thousand years ago. They were subsequently turned to opal and cast into the Abysm, but recently escaped and are bent on turning Hightspall into their Promised Realm.

Glynnie: A heroic maidservant who rescued Rix from Grandys. Benn's big sister.

Grandys, Axil: The first of the Five Heroes and the founder of Hightspall. A brilliant, brutal leader.

Grasbee: A general of Hightspall's army, sacked for incompetence.

Grolik: A gauntling in Lyf's service.

Holm: Tali's friend, an old man who was once a brilliant surgeon.

Hramm: Lyf's supreme commander, an acerbic, impatient man.

Jackery: A highly competent sergeant in Hightspall's army.

Krebb: A colonel of Hightspall's army, sacked by the former chancellor.

Libbens: A choleric general, sacked by the former chancellor.

Lirriam: One of the Five Heroes, an enigmatic woman and Grandys' bitter rival.

Lyf: Last king of Cythe, murdered by the Five Heroes. Now reincarnated from his ghostly wrythen, Lyf leads the Cythonian people in a war of vengeance.

Maloch: An enchanted sword wielded by Axil Grandys.

Moley Gryle: Lyf's adjutant, a striking young woman and a brilliant intuit.

Nuddell: Rix's sergeant at Fortress Garramide.

Radl: Commander of the Pale army. She has been Tali's enemy since childhood.

Rannilt: A little slave girl who escaped with Tali. She wants to be a healer.

Rix: Disgraced former heir to the vast estates of House Ricinus, now Lord of Fortress Garramide and reluctant commander of Hightspall's army. Also known as Deadhand.

Rufuss: One of the Five Heroes, a tall, gaunt man full of murderous rage.

Syrten: One of the Five Heroes, an inarticulate, golem-like warrior.

Tali: An escaped Pale slave who returned to Cython and led the slaves' rebellion. She loved Tobry.

Thom: A wood boy in Fortress Garramide.

Tobry: Rix's closest friend, now a mad, dying shifter.

Tonklin: A loyal sergeant, rescued from a crevasse by Rix.

Wil: A blind Cythonian, addicted to sniffing alkoyl, who interfered with the Engine

Wyverin, the: A legendary beast whose appearance is said to forecast the doom of Hightspall.

Yulia: One of the Five Heroes, she is sick with guilt at all they have done.

PRÉCIS OF VENGEANCE

In the underground city of Cython, a simple youth called WIL reads the forbidden but incomplete iron book, *The Consolation of Vengeance*. It burns his eyes out, but he also has a foreseeing about *the one*, a slave girl of the Pale who will grow up to challenge the Cythonians' legendary leader, King LYF. Wil should have told the matriarchs where to find *the one*, so they could have her killed, but he lies, and other girls are killed in her place.

Lyf, the creator of the iron book, was murdered two thousand years ago but still exists as a bodiless wrythen bent on two things: restoring his dispossessed people to the land above, and taking revenge on the Hightspallers who killed him and drove his people out.

TALI, an eight-year-old slave girl in Cython, is led, along with her mother IUSIA, on a secret escape route by TINYHEAD, a Cythonian. But Tinyhead betrays them, and in a gloomy cellar Iusia is caught by a masked man and woman. Though Tali has a gift for magery, she is unable to summon it in her mother's defence—using magery in Cython means instant death and she has been taught to suppress it.

While the terrified child watches from hiding, Iusia's captors hack something out of her head, killing her, then take her blood. After they have gone, Tali sees a richly dressed boy hiding on the other side of the cellar. He flees and she returns to her slave's existence, swearing to bring the killers to justice when she grows up.

In a cavern deep in the mountains, Lyf's wrythen is trying to bring his two-thousand-year-old plan to completion. To do so he has to recover his king-magery, the mighty healing force that was lost when he was murdered by the legendary Five Heroes at the behest of their leader, AXIL GRANDYS. But first, Lyf needs all five ebony pearls, powerful magical artefacts that only form in the heads of rare, female Pale slaves.

Lacking a body, Lyf cannot take the pearls himself, and long ago he forced the sorcerer DEROE to get each new pearl for him, possessing Deroe to make sure he complied. To escape the agony of possession, Deroe employed LORD and LADY RICINUS to take the second, third and fourth pearls for him, hoping thereby to drive Lyf out and kill him. For this service, Deroe made House Ricinus fabulously wealthy.

Now Lyf forms a long-term plan to get the fifth pearl—the master pearl—by compelling the Ricinus's son and heir, RIXIUM (RIX), via the great heatstone in Rix's room, to take the master pearl once the host slave girl comes of age.

Tali turns eighteen, discovers that three more of her direct female ancestors were also murdered at a young age, and knows that the killers will soon be hunting her. She has to escape Cython but does not know how—the Pale have been enslaved for a thousand years and in that time none have ever escaped. At the same time she begins to have terrible headaches, as though something is grinding against the inside of her skull. The master pearl is waking (though she does not know they exist).

The pain accentuates Tali's rebellious streak, but her attack on a vicious guard results in the execution of her only friend, MIA, by their overseer, BANJ. Stricken with guilt, Tali swears that one day she will save her enslaved people. Then she realises that Tinyhead is hunting her.

Tali also discovers that the Cythonians, who are masters of alchymie and have invented many alchymical weapons, are preparing to go to war on Hightspall, the land above, where Tali's ancestors came from. Tali feels sure that Hightspall is unprepared; she has to warn her country.

With the aid of a ten-year-old slave girl, RANNILT, who has an unfathomable gift for magery, and MIMOY, a foul-mouthed old woman who turns out to be Tali's ancestor, she escapes, beating Tinyhead and killing Banj with an uncontrollable burst of magery. For that crime, if the Cythonians catch her, she will suffer the most terrible death they can devise. Mimoy dies, but Tali and Rannilt get away and Tali sets off across Hightspall to try and find clues to the killers' identities.

In Palace Ricinus, Rix is about to come of age. Soon he will inherit one of the greatest fortunes in Hightspall. He's a trained warrior as well as a gifted artist, though some of his paintings are disturbingly divinatory. But Rix is troubled by nightmares about doom and destruction, the fall of his house, and his role in a future, terrible murder. He is supposed to be completing his father's portrait for Lord Ricinus's Honouring, which Rix's social-climbing mother, Lady Ricinus, plans to use to raise House Ricinus to the First Circle, the highest families of all.

Rix can't bear the hypocrisy, for his father is a disgusting drunk and his mother a cold, merciless woman without a good word for anyone. The Honouring will be a travesty and he has to get away. With his reckless and impoverished friend TOBRY, Rix goes off to the mountains, hunting, in the middle of the night. He takes MALOCH, a battered old sword that bears a protective enchantment, though on the way Maloch seems to be leading him.

Rix and Tobry are attacked by a caitsthe, a huge shifter cat, and only a brilliant attack by Rix drives the injured beast off. They pursue it into a deep cavern, but are forced to flee from Lyf's malevolent wrythen. Tobry is knocked out by a rock fall; Rix, after an almighty battle, kills the caitsthe but is immediately attacked by the wrythen, which is trying to possess Tobry. On driving it off, Rix discovers that the wrythen is afraid of Maloch, which it recognises as the sword Axil Grandys used to hack Lyf's feet off before he was murdered two thousand years ago.

Rix carries Tobry to safety. On the way home they realise that preparations they saw in the wrythen's caverns presage war, and head across the thermal wasteland of the Seethings to check on the Rat Hole, a shaft up to the surface used by the Cythonians.

Rix and Tobry encounter Tali and Rannilt in the Seethings. Tobry is immediately smitten by Tali, but Rix and Tali clash and, when he recognises her as a Pale, he rides off in a fury—in Hightspall the Pale are regarded as traitors for serving the enemy. Tobry apologises and goes after him. Once they're gone, Tali has a blinding revelation—Rix is the boy she saw in the murder cellar! He's her best clue to the killers' identities, and she has to go after him, though how can she ever trust him?

Tali's escape causes the Cythonians to bring forward their plans for war. They attack Hightspall, using devastating chymical weaponry and causing great destruction. Hordes of shifters go on the rampage; the great volcanoes known as the Vomits erupt violently; and from across the sea the ice sheets are closing in. It feels as though the land is rising up to cast the Hightspallers out.

After a series of captures, escapes and recaptures, Rix and Tobry rescue Tali from her Cythonian hunters, though even now Tali isn't sure she can trust Rix. She tells him about her mother's murder but he doesn't react—it's as if he doesn't remember, though she knows he was there.

Rix returns to the palace, in the capital city of Caulderon, to complete his father's portrait, a painting he loathes. Lady Ricinus is furious that he has neglected his responsibilities. The portrait must be completed by the Honouring—the future of House Ricinus depends on it—and she confines Rix to his rooms until it's completed.

Rix's nightmares and premonitions of doom return, stronger than ever. He works on the portrait as long as he can bear it, and also begins another painting that comes from his subconscious—a haunting cellar, a woman laid on a bench, two people standing by her and a wide-eyed child in the background. He can't paint their faces, nor work out why the scene fills him with such horror, for in a childhood illness he lost all memory of the murder he witnessed.

Tobry brings Tali and Rannilt to Caulderon and hides them, knowing that Lady Ricinus would never allow a despised Pale in the palace. Tali is also being hunted by the CHANCELLOR, the supreme ruler of Hightspall, since her knowledge of Cython will be invaluable to the war. Tali sneaks into the palace anyway; she has to pursue the clues to her mother's murder.

The Cythonians besiege Caulderon. Rix, more and more disturbed at what he's painting, goes to see his old nurse, LUZIA, to ask her about his childhood, but finds her murdered, presumably to stop her talking to him. Rix is shattered. And Rannilt, whom Tobry had left with Luzia, is missing.

Tali gets into Rix's rooms and sees the painting, which she recognises instantly as the murder scene. How can Rix not know? He goes on with it, working unconsciously, and to his horror Tali's face appears on the prone woman. It's his nightmare made real; is Tali the woman he's doomed to kill? He fights the compulsion with all he has.

The wrythen is pleased. His plans are finally back on track; soon he will tighten the compulsion on Rix and force him to cut the master pearl from Tali. Then he will dispose of Deroe and, with all five pearls, recover king-magery and exact his vengeance.

The war is going badly for Hightspall; the Cythonians are winning everywhere. The chancellor orders Palace Ricinus searched for Tali, and gives Lady Ricinus an ultimatum—find Tali, or House Ricinus will be crushed. She knows he'll do it, too, because the chancellor has always despised House Ricinus. Lady Ricinus plots the worst treason of all—to have him killed.

Rix and Tali discover the plot, separately, and Rix is torn by an impossible conflict. If he does not betray his mother, he too will be guilty of treason. But if he does betray her, how could he live with himself?

Rix redoes the cellar painting and to his horror, this time he sees what the two unidentified people by the bench are doing—gouging an ebony pearl from the dying woman's head. Then Tali confronts Rix, screaming at him, "That's my mother. You were there! How can you not know? And now Lyf wants you to do it to me."

The chancellor is an unpleasant, vengeful man but Tali can't stand by and see him killed. She tells him about the treason, though he does not say what he plans to do about it. He also holds Rannilt and has been interrogating her for her knowledge of Cython.

The following day Rix, tormented by his own conflict, also visits the chancellor, who forces the truth out of him. He throws Rix out, saying that he could never trust a man who would betray his own mother.

Rix, now utterly dishonoured, feels that he has only one way out. He completes his father's portrait then, in a drunken frenzy, repaints the cellar picture from scratch. But this time he paints the faces of the killers—Lord and Lady Ricinus. House Ricinus, and everything

Rix has, comes from the depraved, murderous trade in ebony pearls. He staggers up to the roof to cast himself off to his death, but slips, knocks himself out and only recovers as the Honouring is beginning. He'd promised to be there, and he plans to do this last duty before he dies.

Tali, in disguise, goes to the Honouring Ball with Tobry, and begins to feel that she loves him, though she tries to deny it. At the Honouring, Lady Ricinus's triumph is complete—the forged documents she presents are verified and House Ricinus is accepted into the First Circle. Then Rix unveils his portrait of Lord Ricinus, but to his horror someone has switched paintings, and he actually reveals the painting of the murder cellar, clearly showing both the killers' faces and the ebony pearl. The chancellor smiles; he's about to have his revenge.

Lady Ricinus is defiant, blaming everyone else, even her own son, but Lord Ricinus can't take any more. He confesses everything, revealing that Rix was taken down to witness the murder as a boy, to make him complicit in the family business. And they took Iusia's blood because it has healing powers.

House Ricinus is condemned, its assets confiscated, the servants cast out and the disembowelled lord and lady hung from the front gates. Rix survives because he's not yet of age, but is universally condemned for betraying his parents.

GLYNNIE, a young maidservant, begs refuge for herself and her little brother, BENN, and Rix takes them in. That night the three Vomits erupt at once, a sign of the fall of nations. Rix is plagued by murderous nightmares, sent by Lyf, and plans to take his own life in the morning. A colossal eruption causes a tidal wave in Lake Fumerous which washes the city walls away. Caulderon is defenceless and now the enemy attack.

Rix prepares to ride out and die. Tali begs Tobry to stop him, saying that she loves Rix, though this is a lie—she actually loves Tobry. Tobry, in despair, stops Rix.

Tali knows Lyf is coming, and Deroe too; he has been lured to the cellar by Lyf in pursuit of the master pearl. Tali plans to seize the three pearls from Deroe, but he turns the tables on her and prepares to cut out her master pearl for himself.

Lyf wakes the compulsion, using the heatstone, and forces Rix to go to the cellar to kill Tali. Rix fights the compulsion but cannot defeat it. Tobry realises what is happening and smashes the heatstone, which lets off a tremendous blast of force that knocks everyone down and frees Rix from the compulsion.

A horde of shifters attack, led by a caitsthe. The only way the allies can be saved is for Tobry to face his worst nightmare—to become a caitsthe himself. In despair at losing Tali, he does so and manages to hold the attack off.

During a battle in the cellar, Lyf's faithful servant, Tinyhead, goes for Rix, but Wil, now hopelessly addled from sniffing the alchymical solvent *alkoyl* to assuage his guilt, strangles Tinyhead and flees with Lyf's iron book.

Tali recovers and seizes the three pearls from Deroe, but Lyf breaks through and holds the lives of Rix, Tobry, Glynnie and Benn in his hands. Tali can still execute Lyf and gain justice for her mother, but only at the cost of her friends' lives. She can't do it. Lyf kills Deroe, seizes the three pearls to add to his own and calls his armies to attack the city.

They storm Cauld>eron and soon the city is doomed; Tali, Rix, Tobry, Rannilt, Glynnie and Benn are trapped in the palace. They are at the top of Rix's tower when the chancellor appears and orders Tobry killed, because he's a shifter. Tali realises that her own healing blood might be able to turn him back, and it seems to work. But the vengeful chancellor, who has always hated Tobry, has him cast off the tower to his death. He orders Rix's right hand severed with Maloch, then takes Tali and Rannilt prisoner for their healing blood, and flees Cauld`eron.

PRÉCIS OF REBELLION

Glynnie and Benn help Rix down into the labyrinthine passages below the palace. Rix is weak; despairing; dazed. In a dark crypt, Glynnie attempts to rejoin his amputated hand, using the last of Tali's healing blood. To her surprise and Rix's consternation, it works. He does a drawing on the wall of the crypt, however it shows himself and Tali about to murder Tobry. Rix's paintings have often been prophetic but what can this one mean—Tobry is dead.

Rix's reattached hand goes dead. They are pursued by Lyf's troops and a horde of jackal shifters. Eventually they find a submerged drainage channel and Rix takes Glynnie down into the lake, but when he returns for Benn there is no sign of him. He's either been captured or has drowned. Glynnie is distraught. Rix and Glynnie fight the enemy on the lake, and flee. Rix promises that one day they will return and try to find Benn.

Glynnie has fallen for Rix and feels that, now he's been dispossessed, the imbalance between lord and servant has been reduced; that she has a chance. But Rix still sees her as a girl who needs protection. He plans to find a safe house to leave her, then build an army and lead the fight-back for Hightspall; he feels sure he's going to die in this war. Glynnie is outraged by his presumption; she feels betrayed and lost.

But no safe house can be found, and Rix's enchanted sword, Maloch, points the way to the one place Rix still owns—Fortress Garramide, on a rain-drenched plateau high in the rugged Nandeloch Mountains. They head to Garramide through a land ruined by war.

Tali and Rannilt are taken west by the chancellor with the battered remnant of his army, to grim Fortress Rutherin on the west coast. Rannilt wants to be a healer but Tali points out that Lyf stole her gift. Rannilt denies this but Tali won't listen. She is determined to bring Lyf to justice for his part in her mother's murder, but can't because she's lost control of her magery.

The chancellor is bitter and desperate: news about the war is very bad. Hightspall's armies have lost every battle; more than half the country has fallen to Lyf's forces and the rest can't hold out long. Tali is weak, for her healing blood is being taken to heal people bitten by shifters. And she's desolate—it's her fault that Tobry, whom she loves, chose to become a shifter and was killed. Tali also fears the chancellor will discover that she carries the master pearl in her head, and cut it out of her.

Her other worry is that Lyf will realise the eighty thousand Pale slaves in Cython are a threat at the heart of his empire; that he will put them down. She cannot allow this to happen to her people but what can she do? After her bloody escape, she's terrified of going anywhere near Cython.

She realises that she's being watched by KRONI, an old clock attendant, and also by LIZUE, another prisoner in the cells. Rannilt reveals Tali's true identity and Lizue attacks, trying to cut the master pearl out of her head—she's one of Lyf's agents. Tali manages to escape and flees down to the old port of Rutherin. The chancellor's men are closing in when she is rescued by Kroni, taken onto his boat, and he sails out to sea into the pack ice.

Kroni's real name is HOLM but is he an ally, or does he want to sell her to the highest bidder? After a number of battles, including being attacked by Lizue from a gauntling (a flying shifter), Holm's boat being burned, and he and Tali taking refuge on an iceberg, she realises that this gentle, troubled man is on her side.

Wil, now mad and tormented by guilt, has gone all the way down to the Engine at the heart of the land, the Engine whose imbalance Cythonians believe causes all the quakes, eruptions and other disasters that plague Hightspall. The king's primary duty is to heal the land, that is to use king-magery to put the Engine back into balance, but king-magery was lost when Grandys killed Lyf 2000 years ago and now the land cannot be healed. Wil, suffering acute withdrawal from his alkoyl addiction, interferes with the Engine and sends it further out of balance.

Rix, now known as Deadhand, and Glynnie reach Garramide but

find that it has been taken over by a gigantic bandit, ARKYZ LEATHERHEAD, and his gang. Rix takes Leatherhead on and kills him, though his widow, the flamboyant BLATHY, swears revenge. Rix takes Garramide back, though his reputation has preceded him and he knows he's on trial. The castellan, SWELT, supports Rix and he sets out to build his power by a raid on an enemy-occupied fortress, but one of Rix's allies betrays him and the raid is a disaster.

Though Rix and Glynnie had been more than friends, their relationship is fractured; she acts as though they're servant and master again. Many of the people of the fortress are against him and now one of Lyf's battalions is marching to besiege Garramide.

Art is Rix's sole consolation, yet when he takes up his brushes his dead hand comes alive and he paints a screaming figure made from black opal. It is Axil Grandys, Maloch's original owner, whom Lyf's vengeful wrythen petrified and cast into the Abysm in ancient times, along with the other four Heroes. Rix is haunted by this figure, which seems to be changing, but he's also fascinated by it.

On the iceberg Tali falls, hits her head and relives one of her ancestors' deaths at the moment an ebony pearl was cut from her. Tali has had these nightmares before and feels sure she'll be the next one to die. She has to get her magery back and Holm helps her to do so, though he tells her that she can either use it for destruction or for healing, but not both—if she uses it destructively she will never be able to heal again.

Holm was once a brilliant young surgeon but, after a tragedy of his own making, gave it up forever. They reach shore and find themselves hunted and attacked. They eventually escape and head for the suspended tower of Tirnan Twil, where Axil Grandys' papers and personal effects are held. Tali hopes to find a clue that will help them to defeat Lyf.

The siege of Garramide reaches a climax, though Rix knows he cannot hold the enemy out. Then, in the middle of a bitter snowstorm, beyond his wildest hope Tobry reappears and they turn the enemy back.

When Tobry was hurled from the tower he landed in a pit of water, mud and corpses—he was badly injured but his shifter nature saved his life and he was nursed back to health by an enemy soldier, Salyk. Rix thinks that Tobry was healed by Tali's healing blood and Tobry does not tell him otherwise, though in fact he did not get enough healing blood and the shifter curse is getting worse.

Lyf has torn down much of old Caulderon, including Palace Ricinus; he has executed thousands of dissidents and Herovians, and is bent on rebuilding the old city as it was during his reign. However his people are increasingly troubled by the excessive bloodshed and destruction and, when the chancellor's envoys propose a peace conference, Lyf reluctantly agrees.

At Tirnan Twil Tali sees a curious self-portrait, done by Lyf when he was a young man, which shows him wearing a simple, woven metal headband. Tirnan Twil is fire-bombed by a flock of gauntlings, who want revenge on Tali because she killed Lizue and crippled her gauntling. Tali and Holm barely escape. They head for the closest refuge, Garramide, and Tali has a joyful reunion with Tobry, until he reveals his terrible secret: he's still a shifter, it's passed to the incurable stage, and he's going to go mad and die. He won't let Tali use healing magery on him. It's too risky for her.

Blathy is listening through the keyhole and spreads the news to the other dissidents in Garramide—that Rix has allowed a vicious shifter into their midst. They plan a mutiny.

Rix is furious that Tobry, his oldest friend, did not tell him. Morale is dreadful in Garramide now and Rix keeps dreaming about the furious, opalised man he painted. This gives him an idea—if he could recover Axil Grandys' petrified body from the Abysm and place it above the gates of Garramide, this symbol of the legendary founder of Hightspall would greatly boost his people's morale, and terrify Lyf's forces. Tali and Holm get wind of this reckless plan and stop Rix on the brink of the Abysm just in time—the enchanted sword, Maloch, is rattling furiously in its sheath, trying to get to Grandys.

Back in Garramide, Tali, in desperation, drugs Tobry and attempts to heal him with her healing blood, but when she takes the knife to him he *shifts* and goes for her, and only Holm's intervention saves her. This is too much for the mutineers, who attack in the middle of the night. Blathy almost succeeds in killing Rix but Glynnie saves his life; he counterattacks and the mutiny is defeated though at heavy cost. Many good people are dead, including Swelt. The following morning, envoys from Lyf and the chancellor appear, calling Rix to a peace conference at Glimmering.

The conference seethes with suspicion. Tali fears it's a stratagem by Lyf to get her master pearl. However the chancellor and Lyf agree on a truce and are about to sign the papers when the towering figure of Axil Grandys appears—returned from stone to human form! In a few minutes of shattering violence he wounds Lyf, steals two of his ebony pearls and drives him off, then wrests Maloch from Rix and *commands* him to follow and serve. Rix, who has no magery, is unable to break this command.

Lyf is badly shaken by the attack, for Grandys has wounded him with the very sword with which he amputated Lyf's feet in ancient times. But there's worse—Lyf has lost his ability to heal people. Does this mean he will never be able to heal his beloved land? Is Cython, which had victory within its reach, about to be defeated?

Grandys rescues the other four Heroes—RUFUSS, SYRTEN, LIRRIAM and YULIA—from the Abysm and turns them back from opal. He recruits an army of Herovians, his people, and such is his power, charisma and reputation that within days he has a force of thousands. He rampages across northern Hightspall, takes Lyf's strongest fortress after a savage siege and puts Rochlis, Lyf's greatest general to death. Soon Grandys holds the whole of northern Hightspall and is threatening the centre. Everyone knows he's after the greatest prize of all—to recover Lyf's lost king-magery.

The chancellor takes Tali and Rannilt to Garramide—he can't afford for Grandys to realise that Tali has the master pearl, the key to recovering king-magery, inside her. He sends envoys to Grandys, proposing an alliance against Lyf. Grandys sends the envoys' heads back in a bag. He wants it all for himself.

Tali is sick with fear—if Lyf is forced to retreat to Cython he may want to get rid of the Pale, and if that happens she will have no choice but to return and try to rouse them to rebellion ... though after a thousand years of slavery the Pale are cowed and docile, and she is not a natural leader.

Forced to fight beside Grandys, Rix soon comes to despise the man: Grandys may be a brilliant and charismatic warrior but he's also a bloodthirsty bully who kills prisoners for the fun of it, and he's bent on erasing all trace of both Hightspall and Cython so as to create the Herovians" Promised Realm. Rix fights Grandys and is defeated. He tries to break Grandys' command on him but it is too strong.

The chancellor calls his army from Rutherin and heads west to meet it; it's time to make a stand. His camp is attacked by the Five Heroes; Grandys wounds the chancellor in the arm with Maloch and abducts Glynnie. The chancellor's arm goes black and has to be amputated, but will not heal. He knows he's going to die.

Tali uses magery to spy on Lyf, for there's a key to using king-magery and she needs to know what it is. She hears mention of a circlet and realises it's the one Lyf was wearing in the self-portrait she saw in Tirnan Twil. Later she overhears Lyf discussing the planned genocide of the Pale in Cython. Now she has no choice; she has to go to their aid.

Tobry and Holm reluctantly agree to help and they get into Cython via a long-forgotten air shaft. Tobry tailors a spell to give them enough air for the flooded passage, but it exhausts his magery and brings on a shifter attack. If he can't control it he could turn shifter at the worst possible moment. After many obstacles Tali eventually reaches the Pale's Empound and enters, trying to look like any other slave.

But the Pale won't listen because she's no longer one of them. She is attacked by Radl, her enemy since childhood. Tali manages to convince Radl of the Pale's peril, and she bullies a few thousand of her people into rebelling. They attack but the small, poorly armed Pale are no match for the Cythonians, who lock the rest of the Pale in the Empound and attack. Soon the battle is going badly.

Tali sees, via her mage-glass, that Tobry is about to turn shifter. She runs after him with the potion that can reverse it, but is cut off by Lyf. He reveals that there was no plan for genocide—he knew she was spying on him and simply wanted to lure her here, but now that the Pale have rebelled he's justified in putting them down.

Tali kicks his crutches from under him and gets away, but finds the Pale in full retreat and dying in droves. She leads a retreat down to the forbidden chymical level of Cython, and there follows a colossal battle with many different kinds of chymical weaponry. But the enemy's numbers are too great. Defeat looks inevitable until Tali realises that there's only one way out—she must use her magery for destruction.

It has unintended consequences—part of the centre of Cython collapses, including the area where the Cythonian people dwell. Many are killed, including the three MATRIARCHS who rule the underground city, and the same collapse frees the rest of the Pale. They swarm out, overwhelm the Cythonians who then retreat, abandoning Cython.

The rebellion has succeeded but Tobry has relapsed badly; he will soon be taken by incurable shifter madness. They head north to Reffering to meet the dying chancellor, who is awaiting his army, though by the time it arrives only five thousand troops remain—the rest have been lost through disastrous leadership, and desertion.

Down at the Engine, Wil is in despair at the loss of Cython, which he loves more than anything. He's got to make up for it; he's got to destroy Cython's enemies. He pushes with the Engine further out of balance and the ground starts to quake.

In Reffering the situation is dire—Grandys is moving in an army of ten thousand battle-hardened fighters, while Lyf is bringing his army of fifty thousand north, determined to make up for the loss of Cython by wiping his enemies off the map.

Rix finally works out how to break Grandys' command. He plans to fight him hand to hand at the drunken feast after the next victory, then kill him with a concealed dagger. After Grandys takes Bastion Cowly, Rix makes his move but Grandys brings out a prisoner, Glynnie, and says she goes to the winner. Rix and Grandys fight a brutal battle but when Rix attempts to kill him his concealed dagger is gone—Grandys has seen through the ploy. Rix has lost and Glynnie is also doomed.

Grandys hurls Rix into an icy water cistern. The soldiers push him away from the edges, the drunken Herovians placing bets on how long it will take for Rix to drown.

The men of Bastion Cowly counterattack; little Glynnie smashes the drunken Grandys in the face with a length of timber and manages to get Rix onto a horse and away. They reach the chancellor's camp, where he expects a hostile welcome, but the chancellor sees in Rix the tough and courageous leader he's been looking for. He appoints Rix commander of Hightspall's army, to the outrage of the officers who were passed over. Rix doesn't think he's up to leading an army into battle against greatly superior foes, as early as tomorrow, but he has no choice.

The ground is shaking constantly now and the quakes are getting worse. And Tobry is declining by the hour. Tali wants to use her powerful magery to try and heal him but Holm says it's too late— she's already chosen the other path—destruction. Tobry suddenly falls into the slavering shifter madness that signals the end is close. Tali and Rix can't bear to see their dear friend in this state. They ignore Rannilt's absurd pleas that she can heal him and decide that there's only one thing to be done.

At dawn the following day they take Tobry out to a glade by a stream, chain him to a tree and prepare to put him down. Only then does Rix realise the truth of the mural he painted in the crypt below the palace three months ago.

PART ONE

INCARNATE

CHAPTER 1

Tali was holding the disembowelling knife so tightly that her knuckles ached. She looked into the eyes of the man she loved, the man she had to kill, and her heart gave a convulsive lurch. She tried to swallow but her throat was too tight.

"It has to be done," said Rix dully. "It's the only way."

"That doesn't make it any easier."

It was ten minutes past dawn and they were in a meadow by a pebble-bottomed stream, a pretty, peaceful place. A band of ancient trees clothed each bank, forming a winding green ribbon across the surrounding grassland. White flowers dotted the short meadow grass; in the distance, a range of snowy mountains ran from left to right. Behind them, on the plain beyond a low hill, four armies prepared for slaughter.

Their mad, ruined friend, Tobry, was chained to the largest tree, its trunk two yards through the middle. His shirt had been torn open, revealing a trace of reddish fur on his chest. His eyes were caitsthe yellow, the mark of the incurable shifter curse. To Tali's left a brazier blazed; beside it sat a paper-wrapped packet of powdered lead. The one sure way to kill a caitsthe was to burn its twin livers on a fire fuelled with that deadly substance.

"Now!" said Rix.

"I thought he'd died three months ago," Tali said softly, putting off the evil moment.

"We saw him thrown from the tower."

"I ached for Tobry, wept for him." She slipped her fingers into her short hair, caught a handful and clenched until her scalp stung. "And finally, I came to accept his death. Then he came back as a shifter, doomed to madness . . ."

"There was nothing to be done. No one's ever cured a full-blown shifter."

"He told me to turn away." Her voice went shrill. She moved closer to Rix. "Tobry knew he'd die a mindless beast, *and I couldn't accept it*." Tali's pale skin flushed to the roots of her golden blonde hair. "I did shameful things, trying to save him. Wicked things . . . "

"Out of love," said Rix uncomfortably.

He thrust his sword into the soft ground, bisecting a white daisy, and stepped away, scrubbing his dead hand across his eyes.

Tali looked up at Rix—she was a small woman and he stood head and shoulders above her. "He doesn't know us; he'll kill us if he gets the chance. He's got to be put down and *I . . . just . . . can't . . . bear . . . it*."

He put his good arm around her shoulders. The shifter snarled. Rix pulled away and, with a jerky movement, plucked his sword from the grass.

"He's a beast in torment. We have to do our duty by him."

"Yes," said Tali.

"Ready?" Rix's jaw locked.

"Yes," she whispered.

"It's hard to kill a shifter."

"I know."

"When I strike it'll probably *turn* him, and in caitsthe form he'll be three times stronger. A caitsthe can heal most injuries in seconds by partial *shifting*. You'll have to be quick."

"I know." Tali's fingers tightened around the hilt of the knife. She rubbed her knuckles with her left hand.

"Cut straight across the belly, left to right, then heave out—"

"Get on with it!" she screeched.

Rix swallowed audibly, rubbed a large signet ring on his middle finger, then raised the sword in a trembling hand. But before he could strike, someone came belting through the trees towards them. A pale, skinny girl, about ten years old.

"Stop!" she screamed. "*I can heal him*."

"Not in front of Rannilt," Tali hissed.

"What kind of a man do you think I am?" Rix snapped.

Tali dropped the knife and ran to grab Rannilt. Even chained, Tobry was too powerful, too dangerous. Rannilt stopped.

"You can't heal anyone," said Tali, spreading her arms wide. "You lost your healing gift when Lyf attacked you in the caves that day. He stole your magery, remember?"

"He didn't, he didn't!" cried Rannilt. "*You're lyin'.*"

She darted around Tali, under Rix's outstretched arm, and ran towards Tobry.

"Stop her!" said Tali.

Rannilt, a little, waif-like figure, reached out to Tobry. Her arms were scarred, her skinny fingers crooked from having been broken repeatedly when she'd been a bullied slave girl.

"I can heal you," Rannilt said softly, standing on tiptoes and gazing earnestly up at Tobry. The air between them seemed to smoulder. "*I got to heal.*"

Tobry made a small, yearning movement, as if allowing her to try, but came up against the chains and let out a roar. Rannilt jumped backwards, her thin chest heaving. After a few seconds she took a small step towards him.

"You got to let me try," she said to Tali. "Tobry's my friend."

"No one can heal him," said Tali. "Rix, grab her."

Rix sprang and tried to drag Rannilt away. She kicked him in the shins, drove her bony shoulder hard into Tali's breast, knocking her off her feet, and ducked past.

"You're not killin' him!"

Rannilt shoved the brazier over, scattering coals across the ground, then took hold of the packet of powdered lead and tried to tear it open. The tough paper did not give. She took it between her sharp little teeth.

"Put that down!" roared Rix. "It's deadly poison."

Rannilt spun on one foot and hurled the packet against a rock. It burst open, scattering lead dust everywhere.

"You're not murderin' Tobry," she shrieked.

The ground shook so violently that she fell to one knee. The quakes and tremors had been coming for days now but this one seemed different. Stronger. Tali turned to Rix.

"Was that—?"

"The Big One?"

The land heaved and a crack opened fifty yards away, squirting dust into the air like a fountain. Rannilt let out a squawk.

The earth gave forth an enormous, grinding groan. A wave passed through the ground, tossing the three of them off their feet. A larger wave followed, and a third, larger still. Tali was thrown backwards across the grass; her head cracked against a stone and dust filled her eyes and nose. A series of wrenching roars was followed by ground-shaking thumps. She opened her eyes but could not see.

The earth groaned like a giant in torment. Rannilt screamed and bolted.

Rix roared, "Look out!"

He heaved Tali into the air, carried her for four or five long strides, then dived with her as the ground shuddered one final time. Then came a colossal, thundering crash.

She wiped dust out of her eyes and looked around. Rix was on his knees a couple of yards away, gasping. Many of the trees along the stream had been toppled.

"That was too close," he said.

She sensed something behind them—huge, blocking the morning light. Tali turned slowly. The gigantic tree had been wrenched out by the roots and its trunk lay in a deep indentation in the soft ground only a few yards from her. Tobry's chains ran around the trunk and disappeared below it. The crown of the tree had been smashed and broken branches were scattered across a large area. Bees buzzed frantically around a dislodged hive. Rannilt was nowhere to be seen.

Tali wrapped her arms around herself and stared at the fatal spot. It had been so quick. She sagged.

"Do you think, even a shifter—?" she began, not looking at Rix. She was afraid to see the truth in his eyes.

"No," said Rix. "No chance at all."

An ache formed in her middle, a vast upwelling of loss that spread all through her. Her eyes stung. "It's for the best, isn't it?" But she wanted to scream and pound her fists into the dirt.

"He wouldn't have felt a thing."

Rix took her right hand with his good hand. It enveloped hers completely. They bowed their heads for a minute, remembering Tobry as he had been before the shifter curse took him.

Rannilt! "Where's Rannilt?" Tali pulled free, ran the length of the fallen trunk and clambered onto the highest branch, staring around her. Her voice rose. "Rix, I can't see her."

"She's safe."

"How do you know?"

"She ran that way as the tree fell." He pointed west across the grassland.

"I'll go after her . . ."

But Tali slid down and plodded back to Tobry's chains. Her legs felt so heavy it was an effort to walk. She stared at the chains as if her gaze could penetrate the ground to the body beneath. Her eyes filled with tears. She wiped them away. "You'd better get going—you've got an army to command."

Rix swallowed. "Assuming I can. I've never led more than fifty men before—and that ended in disaster."

"Rubbish! You led hundreds of people when Garramide was besieged—you saved the fortress."

"It's not the same as leading an army of five thousand into battle."

Before the chancellor died, last night, he had outraged his generals by giving the command of Hightspall's army to Rix.

"The chancellor despised me for betraying my own mother," Rix went on. "And rightly so."

"You had no choice. She committed high treason—and murder."

"And yet, she was my mother," Rix said bitterly. He paced across the grass, then whirled. "Why did he give *me* the command?"

Tali knew that Rix had always been troubled by self-doubt. He had to pull himself together, fast. "You earned his respect. He believed you were the only man with a hope of leading our army to victory."

"Then he was a fool!" Rix snapped. "Lyf's army is fifty thousand strong. Axil Grandys has ten thousand hardened veterans, and a genius for leadership. All I have is five thousand men who've known only defeat . . . and three failed commanders who hate my guts."

"The Pale are on our side."

"Five thousand former slaves, mostly small, undernourished, untrained and poorly armed."

"I'm also Pale," said Tali softly. "Also small, undernourished and untrained."

Rix managed a fleeting smile. "So you are—yet you led the slaves' rebellion in Cython, and won their freedom. You've changed our world. I have to be positive."

His grey right hand, from which he had gained the name Deadhand, twitched. He froze, his lips parted.

"What is it?" said Tali.

"I dreamed about the portrait last night . . . "

"The one you painted for your father's Honouring?"

"Yes . . . "

The portrait, which portrayed Lord Ricinus killing a wyverin—a winged beast like a two-legged dragon—had been intended to symbolise him vanquishing House Ricinus's enemies. But sometimes Rix's paintings held messages about the future, and the portrait had contained a hidden divination—that Rix's father and his house would fall.

The Honouring had begun in triumph. House Ricinus had been raised to the First Circle—the greatest and oldest families in Hightspall. But the night had ended in disaster, with Lord and Lady Ricinus condemned to death by the chancellor for high treason, the fall of House Ricinus, and Rix utterly disgraced.

"But in my dream the picture had changed," said Rix. "The wyverin was only pretending to be dead; it was rising to kill Father. And the Cythonians say . . . "

"What?" said Tali.

"When the wyverin rises, the world ends."

"Whose world—ours, or theirs?"

"I don't know. But there's more to the portrait than I ever intended. There's something I've missed . . . "

CHAPTER 2

Leaving Tali to find Rannilt, Rix ran for the army camp, which was a mile and a half away on the other side of the hill. He had to get ready for a battle he couldn't hope to win, yet had no option but to fight.

The sky had clouded over and a keen southerly drove scattered raindrops into his face. He reached the top of the hill, looked east towards his army, and stopped, panting. His stomach gave an anxious quiver. He rubbed his face with both hands, drew a deep breath and released it in a rush. What if he couldn't do it?

The sacked generals hated him. Rix could not guess how the troops felt, though every man would know he had betrayed his own mother. He'd had no choice—her conspiracy to have Hightspall's chancellor assassinated in wartime was high treason, the blackest crime in the register.

And yet, and yet . . . *his own mother* . . .

Rix's parents had died the cruel deaths ordained for traitors. Though the chancellor had spared Rix, he was forever tainted by their crimes and his own betrayal. In time the world might forget or forgive him, but Rix never would. It was too monstrous.

His stomach gave another flutter. He fought an urge to run the other way, and keep running. No, it was his duty to take command, to fight for his country and protect his troops. He had to find a way. He ran on, reached the camp and stopped, looking around in dismay.

The place was in chaos and the troops were milling around, leaderless; he couldn't see an officer anywhere. The quakes had toppled hundreds of tents, several were on fire, and a steaming crevasse ran through the middle, a roaring fan-geyser gushing up from its centre for a good fifty feet. Drifting plumes of steam obscured the part of the camp that lay beyond.

To Rix's left a fault scarp had lifted the ground by several feet. Further left, the pond from which the camp had drawn its water was an empty expanse of mud and dying eels, which the cooks were collecting in baskets. A hundred feet further on, a broad area of soil had liquefied to grey quick-mud. How the hell was he supposed to fight in country like this?

A weedy soldier slouched by, dragging a notched sword so blunt that he would have been hard pressed to cut an onion with it.

"Hoy!" said Rix.

The soldier ignored him.

"You, dragging the sword, *here*!"

He turned towards Rix, disinterestedly. Either he did not recognise his new commanding officer or he was too ill-disciplined to care.

"What news of the enemy?" said Rix.

The soldier shrugged.

"The Cythonians? Grandys' army?" said Rix.

"No one tells us nothin'."

Rix clenched his fist, thought better of it and thrust it in his pocket. "Get that sword sharpened."

Where was he to start? He was looking vainly for a familiar face among the five thousand milling men when a meaty hand caught him by the left shoulder and jerked him around. General Libbens!

"You're a bastard, Deadhand!" snarled the chancellor's former general, who had led his army to a crushing defeat in Rutherin several months ago, and blamed his officers for it. "A stinking traitor from a treasonous House, and you got only command by foul sorcery—"

Rix was used to this kind of abuse—he'd had it, one way or another, for months—though he wasn't taking it from his officers.

"I don't know any sorcery. I couldn't cast a spell to save my life." No, he must not sound apologetic. He had to take charge. "This camp is a shambles. Why haven't you pulled the men into line?"

"Our commanding officer was away, *communing with a mad shifter*."

"That's why we have a *chain* of command, you incompetent fool. No wonder the chancellor sacked you. Put the camp to rights, now!"

Libbens' red face darkened to a bruised purple. His right hand drifted towards the hilt of his sword.

"Draw on your commander and you hang," Rix said coldly.

Judging by Libbens' expression, he wanted to hack Rix's head from his shoulders and mutilate his corpse; he wanted it so badly he was shaking. He stalked off, bellowing at his officers.

Spiders hunted one another down Rix's spine. Then, from the far side of the camp, someone let out a long, agonised scream. A man's scream, followed by a high-pitched whinnying.

He squinted through the drifting steam but could not see man or horse. The ground quivered and the injured man let out a shrill, bubbling shriek of agony. Rix pinpointed the direction and ran, dodging around the collapsed tents. He leapt a foot-wide crevasse; his feet sank ankle-deep in a patch of soft earth; he drove on and, twenty yards ahead, saw it.

A second crevasse, a great tear in the ground, three feet across at its widest and a couple of hundred yards long. A horse's head and neck protruded out of it, thrashing back and forth. Rix could see the terror in its brown eyes. Half a dozen soldiers were standing around the crevasse, staring, though none made any attempt to help the trapped beast.

Rix skidded to a halt at the edge, leaned over, then sprang backwards. The crevasse cut through deep, crumbly soil and soft rock that could collapse at any moment. The horse was caught by the chest, trapped in a vertical position and kicking helplessly. One of its front legs was broken and it could not be saved. It would have to be put out of its agony.

"Help!" an unseen man groaned.

Rix went sideways until he could see past the horse. Two men were trapped further down, where the sides of the crevasse bulged in. The smaller fellow had blood around his mouth and nose, and the right side of his chest was bowed inwards as if the horse had kicked him. Broken ribs and a punctured lung, Rix judged—almost certainly a death sentence.

The ground shuddered and the horse kicked instinctively, *thud*. The man with the crushed chest let out another bubbling cry, fainter this time. The other man was supporting his right arm with his left, as if his collarbone was broken. With such an injury he had no chance of getting himself out.

"Help! *Please help*."

The desperate cry came from much further down. A shiver ran up the back of Rix's neck as he peered into the shadowed depths. The crevasse widened below the bulge, then narrowed steadily as it went down, and far below he made out another three trapped soldiers. One fellow was alternately whimpering and moaning, a dreadful, hackle-raising sound. The second man was thrashing violently as if having a panic attack. The third soldier, the highest, made no sound, though the whites of his eyes were luminous in the gloom.

They were at least forty feet down. Rix's throat clamped at the thought of being trapped in such a place, either starving to death or slowly suffocating when the soil fell in on them. Or, most horrible of all, being slowly squeezed to jelly as the crack closed again ...

How was he to get the injured men out when they could not help themselves? He probed the edge of the crevasse with one foot. The soil cracked; it would not support his weight.

Dozens of soldiers were gathering along the crevasse. "Get me three sturdy poles," said Rix, "six inches through and at least ten feet long. No, make it twelve feet long. Plus a hundred and fifty feet of rope and a block and tackle."

The soldiers looked past Rix, as if seeking confirmation of the order. Libbens was behind him, scowling. Libbens stamped a foot. The edge of the crevasse crumbled and he leapt backwards.

"It's not worth the risk," said Libbens. "Leave them."

Rix fought down his fury. "You're a coward as well as a fool, Libbens." He met the eyes of his troops. "I'm your commanding officer and the least of my men is worth the risk." He pointed to the nearest group of soldiers. "You! Fetch the gear, *now*."

After a momentary hesitation, they ran. Libbens walked away, stiff with outrage. Rix paced the length of the crevasse, looking for a safer way to reach the trapped men, but there was none. The best way was straight down, here where it was widest, but first the crippled horse had to be put down and hauled out.

The man with the crushed chest let out another scream. Rix looked around. "I need a volunteer ..."

The soldiers backed away. He cursed them under his breath. What kind of miserable army had he inherited?

"Come back here!" They returned, slowly. He took a deep breath, then roared, "Rope, *now*!"

A soldier came running with a coil of rope. Rix cut it in half and knotted an end of one length around his chest, under the arms. He pointed to the four most reliable-looking men, in turn, and tossed the coil to the nearest.

"You four, take hold of the rope and hold tight. Don't let it out until I tell you. Got it?"

"Yes, sir," said the leading man.

Rix backed to the most solid edge he could see, four feet from the horse's head. The ground began to crack underfoot. "Pay the rope out slowly as I go down. Don't let me drop, *all right*?"

"Yes, sir."

He stepped backwards over the edge, creating a shower of earth, but as soon as his weight came on the rope he dropped sharply.

"I said *hold it*!" he bellowed.

He stopped, hanging in the middle of the crevasse, facing the trapped horse. It lowered its head to his level; it was panting and foam-covered strands of saliva hung from its mouth. A lump of earth thudded onto its back. Its eyes rolled and it kicked backwards, connecting with a pulpy thud. The soldier with the crushed chest made a gurgling sound. Rix winced.

He stroked down the horse's long face. "Steady now," he said softly. "It's all right. The pain will be over in a minute."

It slowly quietened. Rix continued to stroke its nose and soothe it, feeling as though he was plotting the murder of a friend. *Another* friend, he thought grimly. He reached down, took his sword in his left hand and rotated on the rope. The job had to be done quickly, cleanly and as painlessly as possible, and that wasn't going to be easy in this confined space.

"Down, slowly!" he said to the rope men. "Two feet."

They dropped him four feet. Now he was well below the horse's neck. The ground trembled and dirt and small stones showered down on him. The horse whinnied. One of the men trapped in the depths cried out in terror.

"I'm sorry," Rix said to the noble beast.

With a quick, deep stroke, he cut its throat. Hot blood pumped out, gallons of it. He covered his face but there was nothing he could do to get out of the deluge; in seconds he was drenched. The horse thrashed its legs; its head rose and fell; it looked him in the eyes and he read betrayal there, then its head drooped.

"Up!" he yelled.

The soldiers raised him and he clambered out, dripping blood.

"Don't leave us!" cried one of the trapped men.

"I'm not going anywhere," Rix called down. "I'll get you out." Or die in the attempt, more than likely.

The horse took a long time to die.

A dozen men came staggering up, bearing three heavy poles and the other gear.

"Is anyone here a rigger?" said Rix.

A stocky man with a red birthmark on his forehead stepped forward. "I am."

"Rig up a tripod and tie the block and tackle under the top. Then swing one leg of the tripod across until the block and tackle is above the horse." Rix tossed him the other length of rope. "Run it down to me."

When it was ready Rix pulled the rope down from the block and tackle, and the soldiers lowered him down the blood-soaked crevasse. With some difficulty, he fastened the rope around the belly of the dead horse and, with a dozen men heaving, it was hauled out. He supposed the poor beast would end up on their dinner plates. An army could never get enough fresh meat.

He swung across to the two injured men. Astonishingly, the soldier with the crushed chest was still alive. He was shuddering with the pain, and every breath gurgled in his lungs as though they were partly filled with blood, but somehow he clung to life.

"End—it," he gasped. "No hope now."

Putting him out of his agony would have been the decent thing to do, but Rix couldn't do it. Not in front of a hostile army he had to win over.

"What's your name, fellow?"

"G-Gam. Common soldier."

"I'll soon have you up, Gam," said Rix. "Then Holm will look after you. He's the best surgeon I know." Though Rix doubted if even Holm could save a man with such injuries.

How to get him up? Rix couldn't tie a rope around Gam's crushed chest. He fashioned a harness around the soldier's hips and Gam was lifted out, groaning piteously.

The haul rope came back down in a shower of grit. Rix fixed it to his own rope and swung across to the soldier with the broken collarbone, a hard-faced bruiser with two front teeth missing. And the soldier surprised him.

"Tonklin's the name, sir. Sergeant Tonklin, and they're my men at the bottom. I'll be all right for a while. Go down for them before the crack closes. "

Rix's scalp crawled. The ground was still quivering, and a larger quake could close it as easily as it had opened it. He looked down at the trapped men and his right arm developed a tremor. He wanted out of this deadly crack, right now.

"The blokes up top can haul me out any time," said Tonklin.

"You're a good man," said Rix. His guts throbbed. He forced himself to ignore the pain. "Lower me until I say stop," he called. "Steadily."

They lowered him in a series of tooth-snapping jerks until, forty-five feet down, he was level with the highest of the three trapped soldiers. Though tall, he was a beardless boy of fifteen or sixteen, and his deep blue eyes were flicking wildly back and forth. He was biting his knuckles, fighting panic and the urge to scream. Rix knew how he felt. The crevasse had a malevolent feeling, as if it ached to crush them into oblivion, and the air reeked of the horse's blood. Rix reeked even worse.

"What's your name, lad?" he said.

"Harin. And that's Dessin." Harin indicated the lowest man, ten feet below them. "He's my father, and he's hurt bad. Can you—?"

"I'll get to him in a minute," said Rix. "You injured?" He untied the haul rope and began to fasten it around the chest of the boy.

"Just scratches. Please, look after Father first."

The ground shook, raining dirt down on their heads. The earth groaned and the crevasse narrowed several inches.

Dessin shrieked. "Pull me out! It's crushing my legs!"

"I'll get to you shortly," said Rix.

"You've got to come *now*."

Sensing a shadow above him, Rix glanced up. The crevasse had been spanned with boards and Libbens was standing on them, staring down at Rix—no, at his lifeline. Grubs inched down Rix's spine.

"You can help the boy any time!" wept Dessin. "If you don't get me out now, I'm a dead man."

Rix gave him a cold stare and continued.

"Please help Father," said the boy. "We need him bad."

"In a minute!" Rix snapped. "Sorry, soldier," he added. "There's only one way to do this, and that's to be methodical."

He finished the harness and called for the lad to be raised. When the rope came slithering down again in a splattering rain of mud and horse blood, Rix swung across and down another six feet to the second man.

"It's my turn, you mongrel!" screamed Dessin.

The second man was a small, black-haired fellow with a long, bloody graze up his right thigh and hip, and another on his shoulder. His teeth were gritted, his face bloodless. His hips were trapped in a narrow part of the crevasse and his legs hung oddly.

"Where does it hurt, soldier?" said Rix.

"Think my hip's busted," he said faintly. "Left leg, too."

Rix probed the red-raw area. It was worse than that—both his pelvis and his left thigh bone were broken and, judging by the swelling and his blanched appearance, he was bleeding internally. With all those broken bones, lifting him would cause him agony.

Rix set to work, fashioning the best harness he could. It was so warm and humid down here that sweat was running down his face. It was stifling; he gasped at the dead air as if he could not get enough. What if he ended up trapped here? What if the crevasse closed and squeezed him to death? He'd been a fool to come down. A leader had to lead, but only an idiot risked his life, and the fate of his army and country, playing the hero.

He fought an urge to abandon his men and flee hand over hand up the rope. The strong had a duty to help the weak. If no one else could do it, or would, he had to—leader or not.

"There's nothing I can do for you here," said Rix. Probably nothing anyone could do, even Holm, but you never knew.

"He's going to die anyway," sobbed Dessin. "And he's a lazy, useless bastard, no loss to anyone."

"I'll get to you in a minute, I said," Rix snapped.

Dessin twisted his upper body from side to side. "The crack's gonna snap closed and squash me like a tomato, and I've got six kids to feed. *Get—me—out!*"

Rix completed the harness and bawled for the injured man to be heaved up. He was moving down the four feet to Dessin when the ground shook violently and the crevasse narrowed by a couple of inches. The hair stood up on Rix's head—the gap on either side of him was only a couple of inches now. If he'd been side-on, the contraction would have broken both his collarbones.

Dessin howled, "It's pinching my legs off. Do something, you stupid mongrel!"

Rix edged his way down. The soldier's thighs were caught between ledges of harder rock jutting into the crevasse from either side, and when it had narrowed, the ledges had been forced into his flesh almost to the bones. He must be in agony. Blood was running down his legs . . . and if the crevasse narrowed any further . . .

Rix took hold of Dessin's right thigh and tried to work it free.

"You bastard! You're tearing my leg off."

"What would you have me do?" Rix snapped.

"If you'd come down fifteen minutes ago this wouldn't have happened."

Rix was thinking the same thing. Could he have saved Dessin if he'd come straight down? Possibly, though Rix was a bigger man; he could have been caught the same way.

"Get me out!"

He contemplated knocking Dessin unconscious and dragging him out bodily. It would be quicker. But before he could move the ground shuddered violently, the crevasse contracted again and he heard an ominous *snap*. Dessin screamed.

Blood gushed from the stump of his left thigh. The pincer action of the closing ledges had sheared his left leg off and cut deep into the right thigh, though it was still held immovably. They were now confined in a space only ten inches wide and there was nothing Rix could do to save him—he could not tie on a tourniquet with his dead hand, nor could he turn to use his good hand. And if the crevasse closed by another two inches, they would die together.

Dessin took a deep, shuddering breath, then looked up at Rix and the anger was gone.

"I'm a dead man, aren't I?" He had dark blue eyes; extraordinarily blue. The same eyes as his son.

"Yes," said Rix, fighting his own panic. "You're bleeding to death and I can't stop it."

"Sorry for cursing you. The pain, it was unbearable. But it . . . it's gone now."

"I'm glad." Rix clasped the soldier by the shoulder.

"You're a brave man, Deadhand, risking your life coming down here for us. The bravest I've ever met—I truly . . . truly believe you can save Hightspall. Get out, while you still can."

"I'll not leave you to die alone," said Rix.

Dessin looked up. "I'll die happier knowing you're leading the army—and my three boys . . . and not him. Beware of him."

A number of soldiers were on the planks now, looking down. He could not make out their faces, but even in silhouette he could see the rage emanating from the sacked general.

"I will," said Rix.

He extended his hand and Dessin grasped it. There was no strength in his grip. Shortly his hand fell away and his head slumped.

"Take care of my boys, won't you?" he whispered. "They've got to support their little sisters now."

"I'll do my very best," said Rix. "Pull me up!" he yelled.

No one moved. Were they going to leave him here? He looked down. The blood flow from the soldier's severed thigh had slowed to a trickle and he was unconscious. Nothing could hurt him now.

"Up!" Rix bellowed.

The rope jerked him up, ten feet, twenty, thirty, forty and more, until he was next to Tonklin, who was still supporting his collarbone. The crack was wider here and Rix was able to turn sideways, though only just.

"What are you doing here?" said Rix. "They could have pulled you out fifteen minutes ago."

"Waiting for you."

"Then you're a damn fool."

"I'm looking at a bigger one, if you don't mind me saying so."

Rix had no reply to that. He fashioned a harness around Tonklin's chest and he was heaved away.

"All right," called Rix. "Pull me up."

The rope remained slack. All the watchers were gone except Libbens. He stood there, quite still, then stepped off the boards and out of sight.

The ground jerked up and down. Rix dropped sharply for fifteen feet, grazing his back painfully against the side of the crevasse, before stopping with a jerk that snapped his teeth together. What the hell was going on? Had the rope broken? No, it was still taut. Had they dropped him accidentally, or deliberately?

"Pull me up!" he yelled.

The rope did not move. Afraid to trust it now, he drew his knife, jammed it into the soil and levered himself upwards. After a couple of minutes of awkward, painful progress he had climbed a yard, but there were still six or seven to go.

Again the ground shuddered then, with a roar, part of the crevasse to his right collapsed. Rix climbed faster, the breath burning in his throat. Cracks were forming in the wall to his right; it was going to collapse any minute. He moved to the left, jammed the knife in as far as it would go, heaved up with all his weight, and the blade snapped.

The fall lost all the height he had gained, and more. He studied the rim of the crevasse above him, sweating. It had developed an ominous bulge. No way could he climb up there—he would bring the lot down on himself.

Libbens appeared on the planks again and spat in Rix's direction. "It's too dangerous," he said to the troops. "No man is worth risking the lives of a dozen." He waved an arm. "Leave him."

He leapt off the plank, out of sight. Rix had no choice but to try and climb the rope, though he was at the end of his strength and climbing it one-handed was a mighty ask.

By jamming his steel-gauntleted right fist against the side of the crevasse, digging his toes in and heaving himself up the rope with his left hand, he managed to gain another three yards. Four to go, and he was exhausted, bone-deep. Dirt rained down into his eyes. As he wiped them, a lump of earth the size of his head struck him on the top of the skull so hard that it dazed him; it was all he could do to hang on.

A grinding sound issued up from the depths, then a hissing as of steam suddenly released. The whole crevasse was shuddering. If a geyser didn't boil him alive, or tons of rock come down on his head, the crevasse would snap shut and squirt him out through the closing crack in a bloody fountain.

He was climbing desperately when the rope came tumbling down. The end had been neatly severed.

Libbens was making sure that he died here.

CHAPTER 3

R annilt was too afraid to scream. In Cython, screaming had identified you as a victim. *Prey!*

Waves broke across the land, hurling boulders into the air. Trees thundered to the ground behind her; cracks opened in the ground then closed again; the air was full of dust, leaves and bark, and powdered stone.

Rannilt hunched over, whimpering, her whole body trembling. She clapped her hands over her ears but could not block out the roaring, grinding and crashing, as if the land was tearing itself to pieces. She sank onto her side, drew her knees up to her chest, wrapped her arms around them and rocked back and forth, eyes screwed shut.

Another tree fell, not far away. She let out a shriek—she couldn't help herself. She had to get away. Rannilt scrambled up and bolted, having no idea where she was going. She ran until she could run no further but it did not stop. Was it the end of the world?

The ground went soft and sank beneath her feet. Water spurted from a red, split rock and a gust blew it into her face—*hot water*. A ragged crack opened up before her but, as she leapt it, the ground on the other side was thrust upwards and she slammed into the freshly made scarp. She fell and lay by the open crack, aching all over. It reminded her of the beatings she had suffered as a bullied slave girl in Cython, before she had met Tali, when no one in the world had cared if she lived or died.

Tali had saved Rannilt's life; she had looked after Rannilt and taken her with her when she escaped. And through Tali, Rannilt had met Tobry, the kindest and gentlest man she had ever known. She ached for him, but he was gone, squashed beneath the tree.

Rannilt got up, rubbing her throbbing knees. They were bleeding. She plodded on, desperate to escape the chaos and the nightmare of the coming battle. Why were all those men planning to kill one another on the Plain of Reffering? It didn't make any sense.

She was out in the grassland to the west, trudging along, when her scalp began to crawl. She whirled but there was nothing behind her. Rannilt went on, uneasily now, and soon felt the crawling sensation again. She knew not to ignore it; something dark, something foul was creeping through the long grass not far away.

She dared not run; she was afraid of making a noise that would attract it. Rannilt spied an ant hill fifty yards away and headed for it, crouched down. She crept around the far side, lay flat on the slope of the ant hill and carefully raised her head.

She saw him at once—an extremely tall, cadaverous man, dressed in black, about a hundred yards away. He was perfectly still, his head bent as if staring at the ground. He turned, scanning the grassland around him, and as his gaze swept across the ant hill Rannilt felt that crawling sensation again, as if the top of her head was covered in maggots. It took all her strength to keep still while he stared at her hiding place. Could he make her out through the tall grass from so far away? She hoped not.

He went on, moving stiff-jointedly, studying the ground ahead. Rannilt had never seen him before but she knew who he was, for she had seen the light glinting off his opal eyes and his hideous black-opal teeth. He was Rufuss, one of the terrible Five Heroes. The most terrible of them all, she had heard: he was a broken man who preyed on people like her—the small, the weak and the defenceless. And he was searching for someone. No, *hunting* someone.

Hunting *her*? Surely not. Why would one of the Five Heroes hunt her? Ants were swarming all over her now, biting her on the legs and arms, but Rannilt did not move. She watched Rufuss until he disappeared from sight in a dip in the ground, then rose silently, brushed the ants off and scurried the other way. If he wasn't hunting her, who was he after?

There was no way of knowing. She kept going in the opposite direction and, hours later, found herself at the ruins where she had camped last night with Rix, Glynnie, Tali and Holm. It was raining gently now, windy and very cold. She limped between the broken stone walls, hoping to find her friends, but the camp had been packed up. Nothing remained save the ash-filled fire pit and a broken chair Holm had fashioned from sticks bound together with wiry grass.

She was alone again.

Some of the masonry had been toppled by the quake but Rannilt spied a dry hole between the angle of two standing walls and the tumbled, mossy blocks of stone in front. She crept into the hole, into the darkest, tightest corner she could find, and wrapped her coat around her. It reminded her of hiding from the bully girls in Cython.

Having been hungry all her life as a slave, she pilfered food whenever she got the chance, and one of her coat pockets was full of stale bread and hard cheese. She ate a small portion of each, curled up and slept. That was another of her slave-girl skills. She could sleep anywhere.

Later on she heard distant shouting and the sound of thousands of people running like a herd, in panic. She did not look out. People did terrible things in war. If the enemy caught her, they might kill her like a rat, just for fun. Rannilt scrunched herself into an even smaller ball and did not make a sound.

Sometime after dark she was woken by a whimpering sound, though it was not the kind of whimper an injured dog made. This was a far bigger creature and it was badly hurt; it was dragging itself across the ground.

She dared not leave her hiding place, but she had to know what it was. She screwed her eyes shut, pressed her fingertips to the sides of her head and tried to sense the creature with her golden magery, that strange gift she had never understood. Her fingertips tingled and a momentary gleam illuminated her hidey hole, but she sensed nothing. Her gift had never worked properly since that terrible time in Lyf's caverns, when he had drawn power out of her and nearly killed her.

Then, suddenly, Rannilt saw the creature in her mind's eye: a shifter, but not a fierce one. It was crawling between a cluster of hovels, pulling itself along with one arm, with broken chains scraping and clanking behind it. Its other arm was bent at an odd angle, badly broken, and her heart went out to the poor, suffering creature.

She did not know where it was, though the nearest hovels had been at least a quarter of a mile away. The shifter looked around—a flash of yellow eyes—clawed at the ground and lurched through the rubble into a partly collapsed hovel. It was dark inside and she saw nothing save various still shapes on the floor, dead men and women.

The shifter *shifted* to a huge cat-like creature—a caitsthe, seven feet of deadly muscle. It crept to the nearest body and she heard a dreadful rending and gulping until a quarter of the body was gone. The shifter settled, closed its eyes. She must have slept as well, for when she next looked it was in man form again.

He sat up awkwardly, cradling his broken arm and wincing, which was odd—shifting usually healed injuries. There must be something badly wrong with him. The chains rattled and he looked around. She could just make out the shapes on the floor, two dead men and a dead woman, further off.

The shifter looked at the first man, who was partly eaten. He stiffened, let out a howl of uttermost torment, then came to his knees and threw up violently. He looked around, wild-eyed, and she saw that it was Tobry. He was alive! His chains must have broken as the tree fell.

Rannilt could read the self-disgust in his eyes, the horrified realisation that he, once a decent and honourable man, had sunk so low that he had been feeding on the dead. His hands closed around his throat as if trying to choke himself to death. He squeezed for at least a minute, then his hands relaxed and he toppled over and lay there, weeping.

"You poor thing!" she whispered. "Stay there. I'm comin'."

She crept out and stood up. She was sniffing the foggy air as if she could scent him out when Glynnie said, "*There* you are. I've been looking everywhere for you."

She reached out to take Rannilt's hand, and all Rannilt could see was another slave master ordering her around, trying to stop her from doing what she wanted more than anything in the world.

She sprang at Glynnie, slapping and scratching at her in a frenzy.

"What's the matter? Rannilt, it's me! You're safe now."

Rannilt clawed at Glynnie's face, shoved her over and ran blindly into the fog.

"I can heal you," she cried. "I can, *I can!*"

CHAPTER 4

"Where the hell is Rufuss?" said Axil Grandys, stalking back and forth dangerously close to the edge of the cliff. "He should have brought Tali hours ago. I need that damned pearl."

"You know how he hungers for blood and pain," said Lirriam. "He's probably battered her to death. I can't think why you sent him."

"He does what he's told. He won't dare touch her . . . " Grandys' voice faded.

"He's been obedient *so far*. But he's getting worse—even you must have noticed that. One day soon, perhaps even today, he'll snap."

They were on the northern rim of Red Mesa, several miles south of the Plain of Reffering. Lirriam was trying to provoke him, as usual, and he wasn't biting. Grandys looked down at the plain three hundred feet below, where his army was carrying out formation manoeuvres, ten thousand pureblood Herovians marching as one in the chilling Heroes' strut. It lifted his spirits.

He paced more vigorously, pieces of red stone crumbling off the rim underfoot. Grandys was a huge, fleshy man with an enormous bloated head, an arching nose like the prow of a ship and hands the size of pumpkin leaves. His skin was covered in armour of precious black opal, a legacy of the millennia the Five Heroes had spent petrified by Lyf's curse—though the opal had cracked off here and there, revealing a venous, tomato-coloured complexion. His arching prow of a nose was bare of armour, crooked and flattened at the end, as if it had been smashed with a heavy object.

Lirriam could not have been more different. She was not tall, but buxom in the extreme, with creamy skin, no armour save for her hypnotic voice, and shimmering opaline hair down to her shoulders.

"'Scope!" snapped Grandys, holding out his hand.

Behind him, a fresh-faced soldier searched frantically in the gear stacked against a low, rocky bluff. He lifted a pair of saddlebags, fumbled at the straps, felt inside and extracted a brass telescope case.

"'Scope!" roared Grandys.

With a shaking hand, the soldier jerked the telescope out of the case, dropped it, and there came the crash of breaking glass. The other soldiers froze. Even Lirriam stiffened.

The young soldier let out a muffled sob. His dark hair was standing up. He picked up the broken telescope and crept across to Grandys, holding it out but looking away, unable to meet Grandys' eyes.

"Put it down," said Grandys.

The soldier laid the telescope beside Grandys. Grandys reached out slowly, clenched his fist in the soldier's shirt and lifted him off his feet. Grandys swung around until his arm extended out over the precipice. His arm was steady; he held the soldier over the three hundred-foot drop effortlessly.

"I'm sorry," the soldier sobbed. "Please, Lord Grandys, don't . . . "

"Why am I punishing you?" Grandys said pleasantly.

"Because I was slow," the soldier gabbled. "And careless. Because I broke your telescope."

"Anyone can make a mistake," said Grandys. "I, myself, often make mistakes. For instance, when I took you into my army."

"I'm sorry, I'm sorry."

"I don't punish a man for making one or two mistakes. But what I can *never* tolerate is a Herovian who begs, or whines, or *weeps*! That's why I'm going to punish you, Private Greller."

The six guards on the other side of the rock platform were quite still, staring at Grandys.

"Let him be, Grandys," Lirriam said softly.

"The men have to know what I stand for. And what I can never tolerate."

"They know all too well."

"Greller doesn't. Clearly the lesson has to be reinforced."

"Please, please don't hurt me," wept Greller.

"See," said Grandys. "He still hasn't learned the lesson."

He opened his hand. Greller's cry trailed off as he fell out of sight then, after three or four seconds, it stopped abruptly.

Lirriam let out her breath in a hiss. "You're a fool, Grandys. You'll never lead us to the Promised Realm."

"Are you challenging *me*?" he said incredulously.

"Not at the moment."

He snorted. "You don't have what it takes."

Grandys drew his enchanted sword, Maloch, touched it to the telescope, and the fragments of broken glass drew together to re-form intact lenses. He extended the tubes, put his eye to the ocular and scanned the enemy formations to the north.

"What a miserable lot they are," he said. "Hardly worth killing."

"They outnumber us five to one," said Lirriam.

Grandys swept the 'scope over Lyf's horde, which made a dark shadow across the undulating ground between Lake Bunt and the vast Lake Fumerous. How he hungered for a bloody victory. "I'll defeat them the way I've defeated everyone else."

"Except Rixium."

The tomato colour ripened. "I'm going to pull him limb from limb with these bare hands." He brandished his meaty paws in her face.

Lirriam wrinkled her nose and stepped backwards. "We Five Heroes will beat him," she said with heavy emphasis. "Not you alone. Though I'll concede you have some skill on the battlefield."

"One day you'll provoke me too far," he growled. "With Maloch in my hand, I'm invincible. No weapon ever forged can beat it in combat; no steel can break its tempered titane blade."

She yawned. "But how good are you without it and its protective enchantment? How good are you in a *fair* fight?"

"I'm the greatest warrior that ever walked this land—"

"Not to mention the most bombastic. If you're so great, why do you need the master pearl?"

He restrained an angry retort. She knew the answer as well as he did but her baiting was more irritating than usual.

"Magery is dwindling, as everything in this miserable land crumbles and fails. The sooner we cast the Three Spells and clean out its pestilential peoples, the better."

A man and a woman appeared from the other side of the rocky bluff. "I was starting to think that all you cared about was war," said Yulia, the third of the Five Heroes. "That you'd lost sight of the reason we came to this land in the first place."

She was a handspan taller than Lirriam but slender, with black hair, golden skin and wide, anguished eyes. The only opaline parts of her were her nails. Behind her stood the fourth Hero, Syrten, a hulking, golem-like figure half a head shorter than Grandys but a full foot wider. His skin was so thickly encrusted with coarse opal armour that his massive thighs rasped like millstones as he moved.

"War *is* all Grandys cares about," said Lirriam, displaying her small white teeth. "He needs to prove himself over and again. What inadequacy is he trying to make up for, do you think?"

Grandys swung around, one fist clenched, though he did not raise it. "We can do nothing about the Promised Realm until we've beaten Lyf," he said to Yulia.

"We should send for the *Immortal Text*," said Yulia.

"It's safer where it is until we're ready to cast the Three Spells," said Grandys.

Lirriam, unaccountably for such a strong woman, shivered. "I'm having second thoughts about using such world-shaking magery. What if the spells go wrong? They might not transform Hightspall—*they could end it*."

"By the time I have the power to use the spells," said Grandys, "I'll know how to use them properly."

"We've waited so long." There was a plaintive note in Yulia's voice. "When will we have the power, Grandys?"

"After I've taken king-magery, and I can't do that until I've got the master pearl. It'll take all five ebony pearls to raise king-magery from its hiding place." He looked Yulia in the eye. "Once I have it, I'll create the Promised Realm we so richly deserve."

"When?" persisted Yulia. "Two thousand years ago we were entrusted with the sacred task and it's further away than ever."

"After I've crushed Rix and cut him to pieces."

"But the Promised Realm was supposed to be the beginning, not the end. *Our* new beginning."

"Life is glorious. We don't need—"

"All you think about is ruin, Grandys. I want to create life, not destroy it."

He gaped. "You want *children*?"

"What else is life for?"

"It's for *glory*!" cried Grandys, raising Maloch high. "And for grinding your enemies into the dust."

"Syrten and I think—"

"Tell us what your *devoted slave* thinks," Grandys sneered.

"Syrten is a brave and fearless warrior," Yulia said stiffly.

"Because he's too thick-skinned to feel pain, too dumb to know fear. Unlike you, Yulia. You hang back in battle like a craven, emotional *woman*."

Lirriam's smile vanished. "Long before we stepped ashore from the First Fleet, Grandys, we Five swore a pact on *Incarnate. Each for all, all for each—forever*. Are you breaking the pact?"

An involuntary shiver ran through him. He stroked Maloch's worn blade, then thrust it back in its sheath.

"Are you defending Yulia's frailty?" said Grandys. "The Five Heroes have never tolerated weakness."

"You were defeated by a dead-handed man," Lirriam said coldly. "Then a slip of a girl not half your size beat you up, smashed your ugly nose and rescued Rixium. Maybe I should crush you and lead the Five Heroes myself."

"But you're just a woman!" he said incredulously.

Lirriam's face set granite-hard, then went curiously, icily blank. As she turned away, Grandys' mocking laughter echoed off the red cliff behind her.

He tried to ignore the shock in Syrten's eyes, the fear in Yulia's. Yulia blinked and it was gone, then she said quietly, "That wasn't a good idea, Grandys."

"Why not?" He thrust his opal jaw at her.

"No man can even hold *Incarnate* in a bare hand ... but it's said the right woman can *wake* it from its long sleep."

"The stone has been dead for twelve thousand years. I'm not afraid of it waking."

"You should be—it's the most perilous device ever created. If *Incarnate* should wake, and fall into the wrong hands, nothing will ever be the same again."

CHAPTER 5

Fear was an everyday emotion in the life of a slave.

So it had been for Tali in Cython, and often since her escape. Fear of Overseer Banj, a decent but rigid Cythonian who had beheaded her friend, Mia. Fear of the vicious guard, Orlyk, who had pursued Tali relentlessly across the Seethings, and caught her twice. Fear of the chancellor, who had imprisoned her in Fortress Rutherin so he could have her milked of her healing blood. Fear of Lyf, and his foul shifter creation the facinore, and the decrepit sorcerer Deroe who had tried to cut the master pearl out of her, and of so many others along the path to now.

Yet nothing life had shown Tali so far had prepared her for the blood-freezing terror she felt when Rufuss grabbed her.

After separating from Rix she had followed Rannilt's tracks through the dry grass. The child had bolted west after the quake, though after a quarter of an hour Tali had lost her footmarks. A sudden pang struck her and she stopped. *Tobry! Gone!*

It had been the best possible end, far better than putting him down like a mad dog. But it hurt. It hurt desperately.

She had been walking in widening spirals for a good while,

casting around for Rannilt's tracks, when Rufuss stepped out from behind a tree stump, clamped an elongated hand around her skull and jerked her off her feet.

Tali screamed, "Rix?" Though only once.

Rufuss slammed his other hand across her face from ear to ear and squeezed so hard that she tasted blood. He was a very tall man with disproportionately long legs and extraordinarily narrow feet and hands. He pressed a fingertip to her forehead. She felt the sting of magery and caught a whiff of something foul—like a long-dead animal—and her gift retreated beyond her reach. All Five Heroes were masters of magery, while she was still a novice, and she had no idea how to get her gift back.

"Rix?" she screeched again when Rufuss moved his hand.

She saw a momentary unease in his eyes; he was afraid of Rix. She tried to bite Rufuss. His fingernails dug in, holding her jaw shut.

"He didn't hear," said Rufuss, bestowing a ghastly black-opal smile on her. "He's already gone over the hill."

Nonetheless, he dragged her behind the stump and pressed an iron-hard knee so firmly against her breastbone that Tali could scarcely draw breath. Rufuss kept low for several minutes, checking carefully around the side of the stump, then withdrew his knee.

He knocked her onto her back and put his boot in the middle of her chest. His black eyes raked her, settling everywhere but on her own eyes. He bound her hand and foot, heaved her over his shoulder and set off towards the south at a fast pace, keeping to the bottoms of valleys and following the paths of streams where there was the best cover. After half an hour, when he must have covered several miles, he pushed into the centre of a thicket, threw her down again and rested his foot on her throat.

In a voice that trembled with rage, he said, "You're the *prettiest* woman I've seen since I was turned back from stone to man." His emphasis made the word *prettiest* seem offensive.

She did not reply. She could barely breathe. What was he going to do to her?

He kicked her in the ribs, hard enough to hurt. "Where are your manners? I paid you a compliment."

· "No—" she wheezed, "no—compliment."

He kicked her again in the same place.

"You'd better be nice to me. If you're rude, I'll punish you."

She had no intention of being nice to him; it simply wasn't in her. Besides, she could tell he was a coward as well as a bully and her only hope was to take him on. "You're full of hate, Rufuss. You hate the whole world."

"Beauty is a lie." He eyed her with undisguised loathing. "It has to be stamped out. Ugliness is truth."

"You'd know!"

His hand slipped to the knife on his hip and Tali's heart gave a sickening leap. He was either mad or a killer. Probably both, and she felt sure he wanted to kill her because she was young and attractive. He pressed down on her throat again. She gasped for air and he smiled. Did he get off on having the power of life, then death, over his victims?

But Tali had sworn to gain justice for her mother and her three female ancestors, murdered for the ebony pearls inside them. They had all died, directly or indirectly, because of Lyf and she was going to bring him to justice. Nothing could be allowed to distract her from fulfilling her oath. The thought strengthened her.

He removed his foot. "Beg for your life."

He favoured her with a sickening smile and her scalp crawled. Rufuss was just another obstacle she had to overcome to continue her quest.

"You're a pathetic little man, Rufuss. A miserable loser, and one day *you'll* be begging me for *your* life."

He swayed backwards, arms flying out to the sides as if he'd momentarily lost balance.

"I'm not afraid of you," said Tali. She lied; she was terrified. "You're afraid of me. Afraid of the power I hold inside me."

"I've blocked it."

"It's not that easy to block a master pearl."

His eyes widened. She had made a bad mistake—Grandys mustn't have told him she bore the master pearl.

"You're not here on your own behalf," she guessed. "Grandys sent you to bring me back. *Unharmed*."

Rufuss kicked her in the ribs again. When she cried out, he laughed. "You *are* afraid. Soon you'll be begging for my mercy."

"No I won't. Grandys needs me unharmed."

"What can he do if I kill you?" said Rufuss. "I'm one of the Five."

"If you kill me, he can't win the war," said Tali.

His laughter was a hideous, clotted sound that made every hair on her body stand up, and she caught that charnel reek again.

"He just wants to use you, kill you and display your body," said Rufuss. "He can have it after I'm finished—one corpse is the same as another."

The situation was almost out of control. If she did not take it back, fast, she was going to die. If she kept him talking, maybe she could uncover his weakness.

"The Five Heroes were formed on the First Fleet two thousand years ago," said Tali, "but no one knows anything about you before that. Where did you all come from?"

"Thanneron. We came from Thanneron."

The Hightspallers' ancestral land on the far side of the world. Once a mighty nation, Thanneron had vanished beneath the world-enveloping ice that was creeping ever closer to Hightspall.

"To be allowed on the First Fleet you must have been important people," said Tali. "From high families."

"We were—not high-born. We had always been persecuted, oppressed . . ."

Clearly Rufuss did not like to be questioned, but he wanted to talk about himself. Perhaps he'd never had the opportunity before.

"You look—" Bad choice of words. "There's an air about the Five Heroes. It sets you apart from everyone else."

"Grandys doesn't allow us—" Rufuss bit the rest off.

It was her opening. "Surely the Five Heroes are equals? How can Grandys tell you what to say?"

"We were on the streets!" Rufuss burst out. "Filthy, dressed in rags, starving in that rich, cruel land. We fled on the fleet—we came here to find our Promised Realm."

"I too have known starvation," said Tali. "And random cruelty."

"It wasn't random!" he cried. "I had a master from the age of two and he beat me daily; he tortured me because I was powerless and he was rich, and he could do whatever he wanted—"

"Why?" Tali said softly. "Was there no justice in Thanneron?"

"There was justice, but not for us."

"Why not?"

"We were Herovian!"

"I don't understand."

"We belonged to no caste, not even the lowest. They considered us sub-human; nothing done to us was a crime. I'm glad Thanneron has been crushed by the ice."

"Why did you have no caste?" said Tali. "Why were Herovians different from everyone else?"

He shook his elongated, fleshless head.

"Why did Herovians have no rights? Surely, the law—?"

"Without a caste," his voice went hoarse, "your master can lock you in a box until you lose your voice from screaming. He can make you sleep on broken glass . . . abuse you day and night . . . torture you a different way every day of your life until you sweat blood waiting for him to come, dreading how much worse today's torture is going to be from yesterday's, or the day before that. He can go on and on until one day he relaxes his guard for a second and you take him by the throat and choke him until his eyes pop out of his head."

He was almost screaming; almost sobbing.

"Then you run! But there's nowhere to run to because you have no caste. You hide in the endless warrens with all the other runaways but *they* know you're there. The warrens are where they come for their slaves, their serfs, their whores. They round you up and take you back and do it to you *again and again and again*."

So you were a slave, Tali thought. Like me, save that you were treated far worse than I ever was. And you killed your master to escape, just as I did.

It explained why Grandys felt such contempt for slaves, and why Rufuss had become a cold killer. His only power came from tormenting the powerless. It was eating him alive, and it also explained his appearance—a once big-framed man whose flesh had withered away from self-denial—but he could not stop.

And it told her his innermost need.

"But you had a dream," said Tali. "Your Promised Realm."

"Our Promised Realm." His hollow chest heaved.

"Where did that dream come from?"

"From the time, an *aeon* before we boarded the First Fleet, when we *were* noble. We were nobler and greater than anyone from the highest caste in the provincial backwater that was Thanneron, and we've never forgotten it."

What time was he talking about? For thousands of years before its collapse, Thanneron had been the greatest civilisation in the world. What kind of people could possibly see it as a provincial backwater?

"Who were the Herovians, way back then?"

Rufuss shook his cadaverous head, as if emerging from a dream, and his thin lips set in a ruler straight line. "You're trying to turn me against the other Heroes—"

"I'm not," Tali said truthfully. "But if you kill me, after Grandys ordered you to bring me to him unharmed, it would be seen as a direct challenge to him. How could he allow it, in the middle of a war, when his army is outnumbered five to one? How could he let you get away with destroying the weapon I can give him?"

He stiffened. He hadn't thought of that. "I'm one of the Five. We swore a pact to each other."

"Grandys would have to act to maintain his authority, and his power."

Rufuss did not speak. He was staring into the distance, eyes glazed.

"He would have to do something about you," Tali added.

"What?" Rufuss said hoarsely.

"To make sure you never undermined him again, Grandys would have to turn you into a slave to his will . . . and you couldn't bear to go back to that, could you, Rufuss? It would be like going back to your old master. It would break you."

Rufuss jerked like a puppet, then turned those coal-black eyes on her. He was quivering with rage, and she knew why. She could read him now.

He couldn't bear it that anyone so small, so apparently helpless, so offensively *pretty*, should be thwarting him. He ached to maim, disfigure, brutalise and butcher her.

"You can't touch me," she said quietly.

"Not until Grandys is finished with you."

CHAPTER 6

Rix clawed his way up the quivering crevasse, inch by desperate inch, the severed rope trailing behind him. Each laboured breath burned in his throat, yet the urge for revenge burned hotter. His hands were bleeding, he had broken every fingernail and his arms were shaking with exhaustion, but he was going to get out. He wasn't leaving his army in Libbens' incompetent hands.

A blast of steam came searing up past him, stinging his ears and heightening the stench of sweat and horse blood. He looked up. Ten feet to go. Ten feet too far, but he was going to make one last effort before the crevasse closed and squeezed him into a bloody smear.

He heaved, trying to drag himself up by will alone, but did not gain an inch. Rix pressed his fists into the sides to stop himself from slipping back. It took all the strength he had.

The ground twitched; more steam whirled around him and the walls of the crevasse moved in, now pressing so tightly against his chest and back that he could only draw half a breath. He could not move; he was held fast.

No! Rix focused his hate on Libbens and used it to force himself up another couple of inches. Then another two inches. One inch. He pushed again but gained no more ground. It was over.

He closed his eyes. All over.

"There, *there*!"

He recognised the voice of the hard-faced bruiser, Sergeant Tonklin, who had turned out to be a better man than his appearance indicated. Rix looked up dazedly. Tonklin was standing at the edge, still supporting his broken collarbone.

"Hoy, Jackery?" yelled Tonklin. "Get over here with a rope, quick!" He looked down. "Never give up, Lord Deadhand. We'll have you out of there as fast as spit."

"If the crack gets any tighter," Rix wheezed, "you'll have to scrape me out."

A troop of soldiers came running. Rix felt their footsteps through the ground. He also felt a subterranean quivering, as if the earth was building up to one final quake. Would it win, or would they? They bridged the crevasse with planks and dropped a rope down. He wound it around his hands several times, held them up, and three men took hold of the rope and heaved.

His shirt tore to rags, the death grip of the earth eased and he was dragged up half a foot, the rough ground scoring bloody grooves up his chest and back. They heaved again and again, lifting him a little more each time then, with a last, enormous effort, pulled him out and dropped him onto the beautiful, solid ground.

The earth rumbled and, as though he had been the last wedge holding it open, the crevasse snapped shut. They stood him on his feet but Rix fell over and could not get up; every muscle in his body was in spasm. He tried to speak though only a croak emerged—his throat was as dry as lime.

Someone handed him a mug of hot soup. He sat up and drank it in a single swallow. Another man approached with a knife, to remove the rope harness.

"Leave it," said Rix, hanging onto the severed end. "It's evidence."

The soldier retreated, looking puzzled.

"Thanks, Tonklin," Rix rasped. "Go and get that collarbone fixed."

Tonklin saluted left-handed and turned away.

Rix thanked the troop of soldiers who had hauled him out. They were led by a tall, lean sergeant with dark hair, green eyes and, though he was freshly shaven, a black beard shadow. Unlike most of Rix's army, these men looked fit and disciplined.

"What's your name, Sergeant?"

"Jackery, Commander Deadhand." His eyes settled on Rix's right hand, then flicked away.

Rix rose, unsteadily. His knees were wobbly and he wanted to lie down, but one matter had to be settled right now.

"Am I the legitimate commander of this army, Jackery?"

"The chancellor appointed you, sir."

"Then you'll obey my orders without question—even against my senior officers?"

"Yes, sir." Jackery did not sound quite so convincing.

Rix held up the end of the rope. "General Libbens cut this when I was down the crevasse. He intended me to die."

Jackery's face hardened. "Your orders, sir?"

"Gather your men and follow me, at a distance. Look unobtrusive until I give you the signal—then be quick."

"Yes, sir."

Rix's belly was an aching hollow, his legs had no strength and the cold wind struck through his shredded shirt and pants, but he had to act now. He found Libbens in a camp chair by a roaring fire, drinking a steaming mug of tea and eating cake. Cake!

Rix came up behind and kicked the chair out from under him. Libbens landed on his back, clawing at his scalded belly. When he saw Rix his red face empurpled.

"I ordered you to put the camp to rights," said Rix, hand on his sword.

"You're not our commander," said Libbens, scrambling to his feet. "You're a condemned man."

Rix held up the severed rope. "And this condemns you."

"A bit of cut rope proves nothing."

Libbens gave a subtle finger-flick and Rix's arm was caught from behind. It was another former general, Grasbee, a wiry fellow with bad teeth and cavernous, upturned nostrils. His incompetence had resulted in a bitter defeat in the mountains a few weeks back, the reason the chancellor had sacked him.

"Your *shifter* friend Lagger cast a spell on the chancellor," said Grasbee. "He forced the chancellor to give you the command, then killed him."

"Laying a hand on your commanding officer is mutiny, Grasbee," Rix said coldly.

Grasbee's grip relaxed. Rix pulled free and surreptitiously gestured to Jackery. "The chancellor died of a poisoned wound dealt to him by Axil Grandys, with Maloch."

It was the wrong thing to say, on two counts.

"A sword you once owned and used," said a third man, a lanky, hairy fellow with a low forehead and little white eyes like flies drowned in milk—Colonel Krebb. He had been such an uninspiring leader that a third of his troops had deserted to Grandys in a few days. "Until it was taken from you by Grandys. Then you served under the brute for weeks, obeying his most depraved commands."

Libbens, Krebb and Grasbee surrounded Rix. They were big men, and if they were game to attack together they could overpower him in his present condition. He had to keep them talking until Jackery's squad was in position.

"I was compelled by an enchantment within Grandys' sword," Rix said.

"Are we expected to obey a man who could be compelled by Grandys again, *at any time?*" Libbens' pocked face was an ugly bruise, his angled teeth clenched so hard that they interlocked.

Krebb's hand dropped to the hilt of his sword. Rix caught the hand with his left hand and squeezed, crushingly.

"Draw it and I'll hang you," he said softly. "With my own hands."

Krebb wrenched free and lurched backwards. Libbens and Grasbee moved in, but Rix had had enough and Jackery was in place. He brought his knee up into Grasbee's groin, then put his sword to Libbens' throat.

"These officers are rebels, sergeant," said Rix. "Take them into custody."

Jackery's men surrounded Grasbee, Libbens and Krebb, disarmed them and bound their hands behind their backs. Rix tore off the insignias of their rank and tossed them in the fire.

"Strip them, enter them in the books as common soldiers and give them uniforms and boots," said Rix.

"But . . . they're officers," said Jackery.

"Would your men follow them?"

"We obey our orders, sir."

"Would you follow them willingly?"

After a long pause, Jackery said, "Not willingly, sir."

"I'll get you for this, you stinking *shifter lover*!" said Libbens.

"You're a brave man, Libbens," sneered Rix. "When the fighting starts, you and your friends will be in the front line. See you set an example to the other *common soldiers*." Rix turned to Jackery. "Send them down to the worst unit. I don't want them infecting anyone I have to rely on."

Jackery gave another order and the trio were marched away.

"What about me?" said Rix. "Will you follow *me* willingly?"

It was a foolish question, he realised; the mark of an insecure man. He *was* insecure, but he'd better not show it again.

"The chancellor made you commander, sir," said Jackery, giving nothing away.

"So he did. Send a man to the lookouts. I need to know what the enemy—"

"I've recently come in from doing the rounds. The Cythonian army is still camped out east, by Lake Bunt, and the Pale are two miles south-east, huddled in their tents."

"In day time?" said Rix, surprised.

"It'd be cruel out in this weather if you're badly dressed and used to living underground."

Rix frowned. Tali had gone out this morning without a coat and the weather had changed suddenly. "What about Grandys?"

"No sign of him."

"Ten thousand men can't disappear."

"He could be behind any of a dozen hills," said Jackery, "or in any number of valleys, and we wouldn't see him."

He followed his squad. A slender, red-headed girl appeared at Rix's side with a mug of tea. Glynnie, who had once saved his life with an act of courage greater than anything ever done by this miserable army.

"Thanks," he said, warming his hands around the mug.

"How did this morning go?" she said quietly.

He told her about the tree falling and crushing Tobry.

"I'm sorry," she said. "He was a great friend. Still—"

"Yes, it was quick," he said dully. "Is Tali back?"

"No. Where did she go?"

"After Rannilt; she panicked and ran during the quake . . . but that was hours ago."

"I'll see if I can find them," said Glynnie.

"Where's Holm?"

"Over there." She nodded towards the healers" tents. "A dozen men were scalded when that geyser burst up."

The main tent was full of injured men. Half a dozen healers and as many assistants were tending scalds and broken bones. Three dead men lay on the ground at the far end, one of them burned all over. Poor bastard!

Holm was applying yellow salve to a hungry-looking young soldier with enormous brown eyes and a deep, scarlet scald covering his right shoulder and chest. He was biting his lip, trying not to cry out, though he must have been in agony.

"Will I be able to fight?" he said.

"Not today," said Holm, meeting Rix's eyes.

"Sorry, Commander Deadhand," said the lad, trying to salute Rix. "I—"

"You didn't cause the geyser," said Rix, more roughly than he had intended. "What's your name?"

"Albey, sir."

"How old are you, Albey?"

"E-eighteen, sir."

"Sure? You look about fifteen to me."

"I'm old enough to fight for my country."

Rix rested a hand on Albey's unburnt shoulder. "I wish I had more men like you. But you've got to be fit, to fight."

He did the rounds of the injured, including Tonklin, Harin and the man with the broken pelvis. They were all improving. Gam, the soldier who had been kicked by the horse, had been laid out beside the tent, dead. Rix stood looking down at him for a moment. A foot either way when the great quake occurred and Gam would have been unharmed. It was all that separated life from death, for any of them.

He returned to Holm. "Can we have a quick word?"

Holm wiped his hands and they went out.

"I can't bear the thought of that boy being butchered by Grandys like a beast in an abattoir," said Rix.

"Nor I," said Holm, "but now isn't the time to tell him. What's up?"

"You're a good judge of a man. Come and advise me."

"What about?"

"My officers. I don't know any of them . . . Er, Holm, I don't suppose—?"

"No!" Holm said fiercely.

"You don't know what I was going to ask."

"You want me to be one of your captains—"

"I had in mind a higher rank."

"No and no."

"Why not?"

"After my . . . disgrace I vowed to save lives, not take them. I also vowed never to go to war, and I broke that vow to help Tali in the slaves' rebellion. I saw thousands killed that day, on both sides, and I killed a few myself. Never again!"

"But you *will* fight?" said Rix.

"If I have to. And I'll advise you if I must, but never again will I lead men to bloody war."

"All right. Come and advise me on my officers."

Four of Rix's senior captains were slouched outside the empty command tent, chatting as though they were at a party. They were an unprepossessing lot, three of them unkempt and unshaven, and the fourth a gross, slovenly looking oaf. Rix stopped ten yards away, watching them.

The fifth captain came out; he was tall, immaculate and very handsome, with a square jaw and a mass of swept-back, wavy blond hair. Captain Hork.

"What do you think?" Rix said to Holm.

"Those four are useless," said Holm, indicating the unkempt ones. "Sack them."

"What about Hork?"

"Over-polished."

"Meaning?"

"He's too good looking—he's almost *pretty*! And judging by the way he struts around the camp, he thinks very well of himself. It's bound to cause trouble."

"I've already got rid of Libbens, Grasbee and Krebb. I can't sack all my senior captains as well."

"Why not?"

"There isn't time to train the junior officers to take over."

"Is there time to do all your captains' jobs, in battle?"

"No, but the men have to be led by experienced officers. I can't be in ten places at once."

Glynnie reappeared, red-faced and gasping. "Tali was following Rannilt but she must have lost her; Tali's tracks started going around in circles. But then—" She took a deep breath. "It looked like Tali was captured . . . by someone tall and strong . . . and I didn't see her tracks again."

For a moment Rix could not breathe. "Was there—blood?"

Glynnie shook her head. "He must have carried her away . . . "

"Which way?"

"South. A man with a very long stride—"

"Grandys?"

She shook her head. "His footmarks were long but really narrow . . . "

"Rufuss!" said Rix.

Glynnie cried out. "He was my gaoler once," she said, shivering, "after Grandys took me prisoner that time. Rufuss is afraid of everyone stronger than him, and despises anyone weaker. And . . . "

"What?" Rix barely knew Rufuss, who had avoided him while he was in Grandys' army, but the look on Rufuss's face in battle had troubled Rix. Rufuss had loved the bloodshed even more than Grandys.

"I think he's a killer."

"I'll go after him." He glanced at the sky. "It's 10 a.m. The quake was three hours ago."

"He'll be miles away. You'll never catch him."

"If you go after Tali," said Holm, "who's going to lead the army?"

Rix felt the acid rising in his gut. He wiped his sweat-drenched palms on the rags of his shirt.

"Who's the best of my senior captains—Hork, Tremlit or Belibo?"

"None of them," said Holm.

"But surely . . . Hork doesn't look too bad?"

"He's the worst of the lot, Rix. He's got no idea how to manage men, plus an inflated idea of his own brilliance—he believes *he* should have been made commander. If you put him in charge you might as well tell your army to lie down and die."

"Then what am I supposed to do? Tali's my friend—and if Grandys cuts the master pearl out of her, we lose the war."

"I'll go after her."

"You can't take on Grandys," said Rix. "I know him; I've fought him; I'm the only man who can."

"He's sworn bloody revenge on you—and Glynnie—for humiliating him. If he catches you—"

"I know," said Rix, choking on his own helplessness. "But I've seen the way he treats prisoners. The thought of Tali being in his hands makes me want to vomit, and as for Rufuss . . ."

"A commander has to delegate, then trust the people he's chosen to do the job," said Holm. "I'm going. You can send a squad with me to back me up."

Rix had no choice. The lives of five thousand men depended on his leadership, and his officers were useless.

"All right," he said in a dead voice. "But you'll never get her away from Grandys."

It felt as though he was abandoning her.

CHAPTER 7

Rufuss did not speak another word in the hours it took to carry Tali south to Red Mesa, and she avoided provoking him further. He burned with such barely controlled rage that any small impulse could tip him over the edge.

And then she would be dead.

Red Mesa, a ragged cylinder of red- and orange-layered rock, rose three hundred feet sheer from the plain, though a steep, wooded gully on the southern side permitted it to be climbed unseen. A mile further south, Tali saw when they had climbed fifty feet, were the cream cliffs of Lake Yizl, and a smaller lake whose name she could not remember.

Rufuss took his petty revenge, prodding her in the back with a pointed stick every step of the climb, until she was a mass of bruises from shoulders to hips. It was cold and windy, with frequent, driving showers that ran down the back of her neck.

When she reached the top, Grandys was standing ten yards away, holding a telescope in one hand, though he was not looking through it. Rufuss gave Tali a final, brutal jab that broke the skin and sent her sprawling on the red stone.

Grandys met Rufuss's eyes and said coldly, "Unharmed, I said."

"The slave isn't damaged," snapped Rufuss.

Grandys frowned. He studied Rufuss, then Tali.

She struggled to her feet and said to Rufuss, with icy calm, "You're more a slave than I'll ever be. A slave to your curse and your masters—*past and present*."

Rufuss's bony hands flexed and he took a jerky step towards her. Using all the self-possession she could muster, and all the acting skills she had perfected in her slave years in Cython, Tali laughed in his face.

Rufuss's eyes bulged and he went for her throat. Grandys sprang forward, caught him by the shoulder and held him back easily.

"She's provoking you, Rufuss, trying to turn you against us. You've done well; go and have dinner, then get some sleep. Tomorrow we march to war."

"I couldn't eat if I tried," Rufuss said thickly.

"Force it down. Hero or not, a starving man is no use to me."

Rufuss stalked away, his bony shanks scissoring. Grandys lifted Tali's chin, tilting her head back to look into her eyes. He looked older than when she had first seen him, at the peace conference at Glimmering several months ago, and the opal armour had been broken away from his nose. His eyes were deep brown with a hint of purple—bottomless, unreadable eyes. She had to look away.

"A fine *performance*," he said, "but Rufuss is transparent, for all he tries to mask it. Don't try such tricks on me."

Tali did not plan to. She was going to find a different way to attack Grandys. "What do you want?"

"You know what I want."

The master pearl. "Are—?" She faltered, and cursed herself for it. She must not show weakness before Grandys. But with her gift blocked, she *was* weak. He could snap her backbone over his knee if he wanted to, or walk to the edge and toss her over. "Are you going to cut it out now? Before the battle?"

"I don't know," he said cheerfully. "I'm a man of impulse. If the urge takes me, I might saw your head open and scoop it out with a teaspoon. Alternatively, I might save up the pleasure." He strolled away.

The casual way he described the operation brought her peril home to her more clearly than any threat could have. Tali considered her options. The top of the mesa was some hundred and fifty yards across, the layered rock like broad, broken steps. The open area here was flat and some thirty yards across. Beyond it a bluff of red rock, gently curved, rose like the back of a chair for twenty feet, sheltering the area from the southerly wind. Four large tents had been erected against the bluff, three or four yards apart.

There was no way to escape. The only way down was blocked by a pair of guards, and several other guards stood around on watch. The other three Heroes were also here. Tali had not seen them before but there was no mistaking them.

The golem-like Syrten stood with his back to the bluff, gazing in adoration at slender, sad-eyed Yulia. She was seated in a canvas chair, writing in a green, leather-bound journal. Beautiful, buxom Lirriam stood at the far end of the lookout, looking towards Lake Fumerous and brushing her shining hair. She rotated on the balls of her small feet, scrutinised Tali and curled her full lip.

Grandys ushered Tali into the nearest tent, which was the size of a large hut. He carved slices of dark, pickled meat off a haunch, and two inch-thick pieces of yellow bread, and handed them to her on a wooden platter.

He indicated a cube of rock. "Sit down."

She sat. He perched on another rock several yards away, leaned back and closed his eyes as if trying to think through a difficult problem. Tali took a bite. The bread was tasteless, the meat rank and stringy. She wondered what animal it came from but decided she would rather not know.

She had two vital tasks, both related to keeping king-magery out of Grandys' hands. She had to protect her master pearl, and hide all knowledge of Lyf's lost circlet, a headband made of woven platina which allowed king-magery to be used.

The tent contained a food box, a pile of furs laid on the bare rock and, at the far end, a small iron chest thickly covered in ice. To its right stood a blackwood cabinet with a hinged door.

"What's the chest for?"

Grandys grinned, as if he'd known she would ask. He thumped the curved lid to crack the ice off, raised the lid and lifted out a rack made from yellow wood. It held a couple of dozen phials of frozen blood, and she saw two more racks in the chest. Most of the phials were full. He picked out one of the empty ones and held it out so she could see.

It bore a small label in a neat hand: *Thalalie vi Torgrist*.

"For my blood?" she whispered. "Why?"

"You'll find out ... when it's time."

He showed her another phial, full of blood this time: *General Rochlis*. Lyf's greatest general had been exiled to the north because his conscience had not allowed him to carry out Lyf's order to kill all captured Herovians. Grandys had taken Rochlis in the storming of Castle Rebroff and put him to death at the victory feast, for the entertainment of his troops.

He showed her another phial, also full: *Rixium Ricinus*. She let out an involuntary cry. "Where did you get that?"

He did not answer.

"What foul sorcery are you up to?"

"I'm going to break him."

"Because he beat you in a fair fight? Because he and Glynnie humiliated the great Axil Grandys?"

He grimaced, then put the rack back and closed the lid. The chest was so cold that ice began to form on it at once. He went out and Tali followed him.

"I'm Rix's greatest fear," said Grandys. "He sweats blood at the thought of me. When we finally stand face to face he'll piss his pants."

Tali could not allow him to further his advantage, in anything.

"You're not Rix's greatest fear," she said, hoping to wipe the arrogant smile off his face for a few minutes.

It was his turn to take the bait. "Really? What *does* make him sweat?"

Lirriam strolled across, looking amused. Grandys was more than a foot taller, and twice her weight, but Tali sensed an equal strength in Lirriam.

"Rix's nightmares are about the portrait he painted of his father," said Tali. "For the Honouring."

Grandys frowned. "What about it?"

"He painted his father killing a wyverin. But in Rix's *recent* nightmares the wyverin was just pretending to be dead, and he keeps seeing it rising up to slay its attacker—"

Grandys reared back, groping for his sword. He half drew it, his breath whistling between his teeth.

"What did I say?" said Tali, exulting inwardly.

Lirriam let out a throaty laugh. "The wyverin is Grandys' nemesis—indeed, it's the doom of his family line."

"But ... I heard that Herovians came from bonded serfs and slaves. How would you know what your line is?"

"Long ago, before we were slaves, we were a great people—and we will *never* forget it," said Grandys.

Rufuss had said something similar, Tali recalled. But what did it mean?

"The wyverin is the one thing *he* truly fears," said Lirriam.

"I'm afraid of nothing," Grandys snapped. "Tomorrow morning I'm going to smash Lyf's army. Then destroy Rixium's before afternoon tea."

But between the joins of his opal-armoured fingers, the skin of his knuckles was white. He drew Maloch and hugged the sword to his chest then, realising Tali was staring at him, quietly sheathed it.

"Maloch's protective enchantment didn't save its first owner, Urtiga, when her killer called," said Lirriam.

"I expect it abandoned her because she was a weak, useless woman," Grandys said savagely. "Like you."

Lirriam's smile turned savage. "It's said the stare of a wyverin is especially deadly to the *impotent*."

The blow came out of nowhere, so fast that Tali didn't see it. All she saw was Lirriam's head snap backwards as Grandys' fist crashed into her jaw and knocked her off her feet.

He stood over her for a couple of seconds, panting, staring down at her.

Syrten let out a rumbling bellow, "Grandys! The pact!" He ran across, *thump*, *thump*, and forced himself between Grandys and Lirriam.

"It's the Five Heroes against the world," cried Yulia. "*Never* against each other."

Grandys seemed to come to his senses. He reached down to help Lirriam up. "I'm sorry," he said thickly. "Lost control. It won't happen again."

Lirriam knocked his hand aside. She wiped blood off her mouth onto the back of her hand, climbed to her feet unaided and stood there, swaying. Her jaw hung lopsided, either dislocated or broken, and the lower part of her face was swelling visibly.

"I'm really sorry," he repeated.

When Lirriam met his eyes, the hate Tali saw in hers was blistering. Grandys looked away first.

"You've broken more than my jaw today, Grandys," she said in a thick, halting voice, as if every word hurt her. "You've broken *the pact*."

"*No, not the pact*," said Syrten. "It's all we have. Take it back, Lirriam."

"We only have each other," said Yulia.

"We're the past trapped in the present," said Grandys. "Only the Five. Always the Five."

Lirriam turned away, swaying on her feet, and staggered into the middle tent. Tali was thinking fast. Was there any way she could make use of this fracture between the Five Heroes? Why was Grandys so afraid of the wyverin? Why was it his family's nemesis? Why was he impotent—and did it matter?

There came a flash from inside the tent, then a crack as though a lock had been shattered. Lirriam emerged, carrying a small but clearly heavy black stone, irregularly shaped as if it had once been partly melted.

She pressed it to her heart. "Axil Grandys, I swear upon this uncanny stone that I will ensure you meet the doom of your line."

Grandys, between the cracks of his opal armour, was almost as pale as she was.

"*Incarnate* has been dead for twelve thousand years," he croaked.

"And I'm the woman who's destined to wake it."

CHAPTER 8

Lyf had an army of fifty thousand well-trained men and women, amply supplied with alchymical weaponry that no one knew how to combat, and an unbeatable five to one advantage. And yet he dreaded the coming battle.

"The Herovians are advancing," said General Hillish. "What's your plan, Lord King?"

Lyf stomped around the leaf-strewn forest clearing on his crutches, wincing with every step. Until the great quake, the clearing had been a natural cathedral and a sacred site to the Cythonian people, but many of the oldest and most magnificent trees had fallen, their wrenched-out roots creating humps and hollows in the soft earth. Others had snapped halfway up, revealing hollow trunks full of rotten wood.

Just like the land itself. Just like the nation. Just like him.

Long boots covered Lyf's shin stumps where Axil Grandys had hacked off his feet in that treacherous attack two thousand years ago. In all the long centuries after his death, when he had existed as a bodiless wrythen driven by an all-consuming urge for vengeance, Lyf had never been without pain.

But since he'd regained a body, the pain had been worse—it was a bone-deep throb that was there day and night, awake and asleep. An agony as much in the mind as the body, for the amputations had been done with Grandys' accursed sword, Maloch. The sword had been thought destroyed, as Lyf had thought Grandys dead, because his wrythen had hunted Grandys and the other four Heroes down, turned them to solid opal and cast them into the Abysm, forever.

Generals Hramm and Hillish watched in silence, waiting for Lyf to reply. His adjutant, Moley Gryle, held a pain-relieving posset in a platina mug. She had covered it with a metal lid to keep it hot, though a trickle of steam curled from the top. He eyed the mug longingly but held back. He needed all his wits right now.

Unfortunately, Grandys had not died. The protective enchantment within Maloch had preserved him, and the other Heroes, in the petrified state. Maloch had been carefully hidden and lovingly guarded down the aeons, only to turn up six months ago in the hands of Rixium Ricinus.

If only it had stayed there. But the great enchantment within Maloch was also designed to aid its master, and from the moment Rix took the sword in hand its secret purpose had been to find Grandys and raise him from stone. Finally it had, and now Grandys was back, stronger and more terrible than ever.

"The plan, Lord King?" said squat General Hramm, Lyf's supreme commander. He was a taciturn, acerbic, impatient man, weak on strategy but strong on tactics.

Lyf limped to the centre of the clearing and with sweeps of his right hand sketched the land of Togl in the dirt. The so-called Plain of Reffering was terminated on the south by the linked lakes of Yizl and Rizum, on the west by the towering Crowbung Range and on the east by the vastness of Lake Fumerous. The land lay open to the north though the fast-flowing Rinkl River, the boundary between Togl and Nyrdly, could only be crossed by the bridge at Restin.

"The playground is ten miles wide and eight miles long," said Hramm. "I'd prefer it was smaller."

Moley Gryle's black eyes were fixed on something to the south. Lyf focused on her lovely face—the unblemished skin, cream with a hint of blue-grey, the neat, regular features framed by twin arcs of hair the colour of polished anthracite—then shook his head.

Concentrate! He followed her gaze and, through a gap in the trees, saw the top of a small tabular peak, Red Mesa. He felt an instinctive urge to hide.

"So Grandys' army could be almost anywhere," said General Hillish.

"At need, ten thousand men can be hidden in a square a hundred yards on a side," said Hramm. "They could be lying behind any small hill, in any of dozens of patches of woodland, or any small stretch of a myriad of valleys. Though our scouts—"

"Have found no sign of them or their supply chain within two miles of here," said Lyf.

"Grandys moves quickly and his men travel light," said Moley Gryle. "They carry several days' rations with them and don't wait for the supply wagons. He can strike anywhere, without warning."

Grandys had appeared out of nowhere at Glimmering and shattered the peace conference in a few violent minutes. Lyf felt the blood rushing to his face, the rage rising at the contemptuous way Grandys had struck him with that cursed sword. Never again!

"Only a fool would attack an army of fifty thousand with ten thousand," said Hramm. "Grandys is reckless, but he's no fool. So what's he going to do?"

"No one can predict him," said Lyf. "That's the problem." He beckoned to Moley Gryle, who handed him the mug. He took a sip of the posset, just enough to warm his mouth. It had a floral taste, like violets, and left an aftertaste of bitter orange. "But I have a plan," he said as he handed back the mug.

Lyf moved across the clearing until Red Mesa could no longer be seen and lowered his voice.

"I'm sending out battalions east and west, north and south. A thousand men in each, to lure him out, always mindful of the best battleground for us to fight on. Sooner or later he'll take the bait—"

"How can you be sure?" said Hillish.

"He craves battle and bloodshed," said Moley Gryle. "It's an addiction."

"How do you know?" snapped Hramm.

"I've read all the stories and dispatches about Grandys," said

Moley Gryle, "and talked to every surviving witness we could find. He has to prove himself, over and over, but it's weeks since he took Bastion Cowly, and that fight didn't satisfy him because they'd already surrendered. And afterwards—"

"He fought Rixium of Garramide hand to hand," said Lyf. "And Rixium brought him down; he almost defeated Grandys."

"I heard Grandys was drunk," said Hramm.

"He's always drunk after a battle," said Moley Gryle. "It doesn't affect his ability to fight."

"Grandys tried to drown Rixium in a cistern," said Lyf, smiling now, "but the men of Cowly counterattacked and Rixium's maid-servant, Glynnie, a slip of a girl, battered Grandys to his knees with a baulk of timber, and rescued Rix."

"She made Grandys a laughing stock and he'll be aching to make up for it," said Moley Gryle.

"He'll take my bait," said Lyf. "When he does, we surround his army with our fifty thousand—"

"He's a ferocious fighter, hand to hand," said Hramm. "A man who can destroy an enemy's morale all by himself."

"I'm not planning on fighting him at close range. We're going to attack from a distance with the greatest barrage of bombasts and grenadoes, shriek-arrows and fire-flitters the land has ever seen. Not even the Five Heroes can withstand a bombast blast at close range. Not even Grandys.

"Only then, when his army has been reduced to pulp, will I send in our troops. We'll collect the bodies of the Five Heroes, burn them and sift the ashes to make sure not a bone survives, not a grain of opal armour, *nothing*!"

"Nor the sword," said Moley Gryle.

"I'll have Maloch melted with *thermitto* to destroy the enchantment, then the residue ground to dust. Every speck will be cast into a different part of the ocean so it can never be recovered by accident . . . or by design."

Lyf wobbled on his crutches. His splintered shin bones ached worse than ever. Moley Gryle handed him the posset and he drained it.

"Well?" said Lyf to his generals.

"It's a plan," said Hramm. "Simple, brutal, effective. Just the way I like them."

After he had gone, Moley Gryle said quietly, "I'm afraid, Lord King. Grandys is coming for *you*. I know he is."

"I have fifty thousand soldiers to protect me."

"He always targets the leader when he gets the chance. It'll be a contest between him and you, and the victory he craves is victory over *you*, not your army."

"But I'll be in the middle of my army, Moley!" Lyf said in exasperation. "He can't attack me unless he gets past them—and my King's Guard as well. And with his small force that's not possible."

"Even so," she persisted, "I'd be happier if you had a defence against a personal attack by Grandys himself."

"All right," said Lyf. "You're my *intuit*. What's his greatest weakness?"

"I don't have to be an *intuit* to know that he needs to prove himself over and again. Which means he's insecure in his own mind."

"He doesn't show it."

"He's a considerable actor," said Moley Gryle. "How can you attack this weakness, I wonder?"

Three messengers appeared, one after another. Lyf held up a hand and they stopped. "Not physically. He's a foot taller and much heavier—and he has two good legs, the swine! Besides, with Maloch protecting Grandys it's almost impossible to land a blow on him."

"All the more reason to have an extra defence. How did he come by the sword, Lord King? Why does Maloch protect him and only him?"

"I don't know," Lyf said thoughtfully. "Where did it come from, originally?"

She walked back and forth for a minute or two, thinking. "Old enemy records say it was made back in Thanneron, on the other side of the world, for Envoy Urtiga. To protect her and further her quest."

"Urtiga?" said Lyf. "I haven't heard that name before."

"She was originally in charge of the search for the Herovian Promised Realm—she carried Maloch and the *Immortal Text*. But she died suddenly on the First Fleet and Grandys took her place."

"I don't see how this helps me," said Lyf.

Moley Gryle sat down, cross-legged, rubbing her forehead. "It's said that Maloch's enchantment protects the 'true master of the sword'. But is Grandys the true master, if it wasn't made for him?"

A fourth messenger appeared behind the others.

"I've no idea," Lyf said impatiently. "Moley, I've a hundred things to do. If you do have an idea, make it quick."

"Maloch protects Grandys, *always*; it's why he's proved invincible in battle. So if you could make it abandon him—or *seem to*—it would undermine his confidence."

Lyf beckoned the first of the messengers. "Unfortunately, Maloch is impervious to all known forms of magery. Forget it, Moley. If Grandys does attack me, that idea's not going to help."

Lyf lay in a blue, silken hammock stretched between two poles of his tent, taking the weight off his legs, though it did little to ease the pain. Moley Gryle entered with a tray of delicacies. He waved her away.

"Not now, Moley."

"Is something troubling you, Lord King?"

"The great quake. I don't know what to do."

"It probably has to do with the Vomits erupting."

"I know it does, but the quakes are getting worse. As are the eruptions, the landslides, the tidal waves and the ice sheets that have covered every land except this one. But is the land rising up against our enemies, *or ourselves*?"

"I don't know, Lord King."

"The first duty of the king is to use king-magery to heal the land. To prevent the balance tipping towards the Engine's natural tendency: *destruction*. But the balance has tilted too far, and if the Engine passes the point of no return—" He covered his eyes with his fingers.

"Surely, now you've got your body back ..." Moley Gryle faltered. "At least, now you've got *a* body back, surely you can heal the land?"

"Without king-magery I'm a eunuch," said Lyf. "And to recover it I must have the master pearl. I need advice."

"Anything," she said fervently.

"Not from you! I must consult with the ancestors. Leave me, and make sure I'm not disturbed."

Moley Gryle was hurt, but did her best to disguise it. "Lord King." She bowed and withdrew.

Lyf conjured his ancestor gallery into being—his spirit versions of the one hundred and six most important kings and ruling queens of old Cythe. He had created them long ago to advise him on complex or contentious matters, though latterly they were more inclined to browbeat him and lecture him on morality—and his failures in that regard.

They weren't real spirits; raising even a handful of such ancient beings would have overtaxed his dwindling magery. And as his creations, they could know nothing that he did not know. Nonetheless, their advice had proven useful on occasion, so he told them his plans for war.

"Your obsession with vengeance created this mess in the first place," said the red-faced, red-throated shade of Bloody Herrie, a king who had been an expert on vengeance, and had died from it.

"What are you talking about?" cried Lyf. "Grandys started it when he hacked—"

"The Five Heroes were mortal men and women. Had not your wrythen, out of black, unforgiving hatred, petrified them and cast them into the Abysm they would have died of old age within fifty years of your death. *You* preserved them, Lyf. *You* provided the means for them to come back, stronger than ever, in this present time."

"Leaving that aside—" Lyf began coldly.

"He's right," said Errek First-King, the oldest and most faded of all the shades. "For months now you've been wallowing in your lust for vengeance. Indulging your baser side and neglecting your primary duty."

"Without king-magery I can't heal the land."

"Leave war to your generals. Get the master pearl, *then do your duty*."

Lyf dismissed the ancestors, all save Errek First-King.

"Yes?" said Errek.

"The great quake this morning was the worst we've seen in a thousand years. It tells me that the Engine is hanging on the brink."

"I daresay it is," said Errek. "What do you want to know?"

"Where it came from. How it got here. When it began to cause trouble."

"I can't tell you."

"The founding tales say that there was no Engine in earliest times, but that it formed around the time of your reign, ten thousand years ago."

"I believe that to be the case," said Errek. "But as a shade created by you, I know no more than you know, or can discover in your library."

"What if I raised your spirit?" said Lyf. "As a wrythen, say?"

Errek frowned. "You have the power to do this?"

"I believe so. At a cost."

"I do not wish it," said Errek. "I see nothing but pain and unpleasantness in being wrenched from my final rest after such an age."

"But you do not forbid it?"

"I'm your creation—I'm not allowed that luxury."

"What if you had it?"

"Are you planning to raise me now?"

"No. Though if I should need to—"

"I expect I would forbid you to raise me," said Errek. A wistful tone crept into his faded voice. "And yet . . . to have another chance at life . . . even the kind of life a wrythen has . . ."

CHAPTER 9

"Grandys is marching this way," said Glynnie to Rix. "Marching to war."

Holm and his squad had gone looking for Tali and Rannilt yesterday morning. They had not returned and Rix, who was standing on a small rise in the middle of his demoralised army, had never felt more alone.

He reminded himself of what was at stake—the very survival of his country. In the past months Hightspall had suffered defeat after defeat, first at Lyf's hands, then at Grandys'. Hightspall's armies had been crushed; its capital and heart, the great city of Caulderon, had been brutally occupied by the Cythonians for three months now. Its treasures had been ransacked and its greatest buildings toppled.

At the same time, Grandys had been rampaging through the countryside at the head of an army of fanatical Herovians, slaughtering innocent people in droves and vandalising their towns and manors. He would not be satisfied until he had burned every library, smashed every statue and torn down every thing of beauty Hightspall had created in two thousand glorious years.

Rix and his five thousand troops were all that stood between these two great enemies and the annihilation of the land he loved. If he could not save Hightspall, no one could. That was what he was fighting for.

It focused his resolve. He mounted his great black warhorse and moved in beside Glynnie. "How far away?"

"Two miles. He could be here in under an hour."

Rix had instructed his third-rate officers, relayed his orders and personally supervised the troops into battle formation. It was a simple one, since neither the men nor the officers had the skill or discipline to change formations in the middle of battle. Indeed, after half an hour with the signallers Rix realised that his troops would be on their own: even if his captains received his signals mid-battle, they were incapable of acting on them.

"What if I'm leading them into a massacre?" he said quietly to Glynnie. "If I make one mistake … no, it's not even a matter of mistakes. I have to match every move Grandys makes, with my very inferior force, and if I can't, we die."

"Have you done all you can?"

"Yes. I've checked everything twice."

"Then there's no point agonising about it."

"I can't stop agonising. I've fought with Grandys. I've seen what he does to his enemies. I'm afraid of him."

"So am I. I've been his prisoner, remember?" A shadow appeared in her eyes. She reached across and pressed her hand to his chest. "Your heart's racing as if you've run up a mountain."

"I'm sweating like a pig. Practically sliding out of my saddle."

He stood up in the stirrups, staring at the dark mass in the south, then raised the field glasses hanging around his neck.

"What's he doing?" said Glynnie.

"Coming straight at us. Not hurrying."

"At us? Not at Lyf's army?"

"He's hardly going to attack an army of fifty thousand with a fifth of that number. I'd say he means to roll over us first to boost his army's morale."

"And then?"

"I can't even guess."

"Can you see Grandys?"

"He's riding out in front as if he owns the world. I'll say this much for the bastard—he's no coward. He's always where the fighting is fiercest and most deadly."

"I don't see why the people who know no fear get the medals. True courage comes from those who are terrified, but still go on."

"I'm terrified."

"Anyway, it's not as if Grandys likes an equal fight. He's one of the biggest and brawniest men in the world. He's got all-over body armour and a magic sword whose sole purpose is to protect him. I'd be surprised if he did as well fighting someone his own size."

"He fights well enough," said Rix. "I've slugged it out with the swine, twice."

"And the first time he only won by cheating," she said hotly.

"Since I cheated the second time, I can hardly complain."

He took a last look through his glasses—no change to Grandys' inexorable movement north—and lowered them. "I'm doing the rounds one final time," he said. "You'd better get going."

Glynnie's head shot around. "Where?"

"I don't know. The ruins. Or Garramide . . . " He realised they'd never talked about what they would do next.

"You're expecting to die, aren't you?"

He couldn't say it; not directly. "It doesn't look good."

Her green eyes flashed. "Do you see me as a faithless friend? We promised to ride together, *forever*."

"I don't see the point of you dying as well."

"Then you're a stupid, stupid man!"

He smiled. Her loyalty warmed him. "I dare say you're right. Tobry was always saying that." On that thought, his smile faded. "I'd better do the rounds before Grandys gets here."

At each of his thirty-one companies Rix swung down, shook hands with the captain and several of the soldiers, and reminded them that they were fighting for the very survival of their country. Judging by the amazement on the men's faces no commander had ever spoken to them personally before. No wonder morale was so low.

When he reached the third-last company, he discovered that the captain was Libbens and his lieutenants were Krebb and Grasbee.

Rix froze, his hand outstretched. "You've risen swiftly in the ranks," he said to Libbens.

"Someone has to take over the leadership when you fail your men."

"You're certainly an expert in that."

Libbens' hand dropped to his sword, though he wasn't fool enough to draw it. But if he got a chance, he would not hesitate to stab Rix in the back, even in battle. Rix realised that he had done the wrong thing, sending them to the ranks. He should have dismissed them from the army at once. It was too late now.

"Under a mile," called Glynnie.

Rix mounted hastily and rode back to the mound. Grandys was so close that Rix could see his bloated face in the binoculars.

"He looks different. As though he's aged. And—angry ... "

"Perhaps it's his battle face," said Glynnie.

"When he goes into battle he's normally roaring with glee, as though he's drunk on power. Or blood. This is ... worrying."

"Why?"

"Grandys fights even more ferociously when he's in a bad mood."

Rix gave his final orders. His archers were to prepare to fire at his command. Once they had weakened Grandys' leading ranks, Rix's cavalry would try to break through the front lines and destroy their battle formation. Then the infantry would attack the breach. A simple plan, though he had little hope that it would work.

The signalmen worked their flags. He stood up in his stirrups again. "Five hundred yards."

Then, "Four hundred. Hold fire."

His palms were so wet he could barely hold the reins. "Three hundred yards. Not yet, not yet."

Rix had his right arm upraised, the mailed glove glinting on his dead hand. He was about to signal his archers to fire when Grandys' army veered off to the west, heading towards the foothills of the Crowbung Mountains.

"What's he doing?" said Jackery, whose squad was in the front lines, directly behind Rix.

"I have no idea."

Was Grandys planning to come at them from the flank or the rear, or split his force and attack from two points at once? Rix shadowed Grandys' army, which continued marching over the hill and out of sight.

Rix rode back and ordered the scouts out. "The march-past was just a boast," he said to Glynnie. "*I can take you any time I want*. He plans to break me before we even begin to fight."

"He won't break you that easily," she said loyally.

As it was late in the afternoon, and they had been on alert all day, Rix stood the men down and ordered rations distributed. Before they had finished, Holm's squad rode in. Holm dismissed his men and came across to Rix.

"Rannilt went back to the ruins," said Holm. "But I searched every bit of rubble, and every crevice big enough to hold a cat, and found no trace of her after that."

"She knows how to take care of herself," said Rix. "She'll come back; she's nowhere else to go. I'll ask Glynnie to take another look there this evening. What about Tali?"

"We tracked Rufuss for a mile and a half. He held her in a thicket for a while ... questioning her, I suppose. I hope it was just questioning ..."

Rix and Glynnie exchanged glances. "I know what his interrogations are like," said Glynnie quietly. "I hope—"

"Any signs of a struggle?" Rix said hastily, to avoid thinking about the unthinkable. "Any blood?"

Holm shook his grey head.

"His tracks continued south, in the direction of Red Mesa. We lost him after a while—the tracks simply vanished. We spent all yesterday afternoon looking for them, and hours more this morning. When we saw Grandys' army on the march it seemed prudent to come back."

"You did the right thing," said Rix. "I can't afford to lose you as well."

"What are we going to do?" said Glynnie.

"There's nothing we can do until I find out where he's holding Tali. And—"

"If we do find out," said Holm, "it'll be because Grandys wants you to know. It'll be the bait in his trap."

CHAPTER 10

They saw no more of Grandys that day, though Rix's scouts reported that he'd taken his army in a circle west then north, before heading south and making a slow turn between Rix's army and Lyf's, then disappearing into a forested valley.

"Bastard!" Rix pounded his mailed fist into his left hand. "He's thumbing his nose at us."

"Why doesn't he attack?" said Holm.

Rix ordered the camp to be set up, the troops stood down and the sentries doubled. By the time he'd done the rounds, had a few words with each of his captains except Libbens, and finished planning for the day ahead, it was midnight.

He went to his bedroll exhausted but slept fitfully, every sound startling him awake. It was past 3 a.m. when he finally dropped into a deep sleep, only to jerk upright an hour later, gasping from another nightmare.

"What's the use?" he muttered, and hauled on his boots.

There was a light in Holm's tent. Rix put his head in. Holm

was reading by the light of a hooded lantern. "You can't sleep either?"

"Not these past thirty-five years. Fancy a warming cup?"

They strolled across to the camp kitchen, where the cooks were baking bread and preparing breakfast for five thousand. Glynnie was helping, looking as hollow-eyed as he was. She served them bread and cheese, huge mugs of tea sweetened with honey, and took one for herself.

"What are you doing up at this time of day?" said Rix.

She was always up working when Rix rose. Her eyes were puffy and she had been irritable lately. But then, given their probable fate, why wouldn't she be?

"You woke me," she said. "Crying out in your sleep."

"You didn't come in to find out what was the matter."

She flushed a pretty shade of pink. "It would hardly be good for morale."

"What?"

"Me creeping into the commander's tent at four in the morning, when the camp followers were sent packing days ago."

Holm chuckled.

"I suppose not," said Rix, not without a hint of regret.

"What were you yelling about, anyway?"

He looked over his shoulder, then lowered his voice. "I had another nightmare about the wyverin."

Holm looked up from his bread and cheese. "What wyverin?"

"The one in the portrait I painted for Father's Honouring," said Rix. "You never saw it—"

"I've heard about it."

"In my dreams, it's always rising, preparing to attack."

"It seems to me," Holm said carefully, "that you've got plenty of *real* problems to worry about—"

"Before the war began I kept dreaming that I was being ordered to 'go down and cut it out'," Rix said irritably, "and it turned out that Lyf had put a secret compulsion on me to cut the master pearl out of Tali. And some of my other paintings *have* come true . . . "

"Like that mural you painted in the crypt below Palace Ricinus—" began Glynnie.

Rix cut her off with a hand slash. The mural had shown himself and Tali about to kill Tobry, and that was too raw to think about.

"So when I start having nightmares about one of my greatest paintings," said Rix, "I've got to take them seriously. Tobry said, 'I've a feeling the portrait will be found one day, and then it'll reveal its *true* divination.'"

"What *true divination*?" said Glynnie.

"I assume it has to do with the wyverin rising. Where do they live, Holm?"

"There's no *they*. Just *it*."

"What are you talking about? You mean there's only one wyverin left?"

"To the best of my knowledge there's only *ever* been one."

"How can there only be one? That's against the laws of nature."

Holm shrugged. "So are shifters."

"Where did it come from?" said Rix.

"No one knows. It's too long ago."

"Then how do you know it exists? It might just be a legend."

"To the enemy it's the most powerful alchymical symbol of all—a symbol of regeneration and rebirth. That's why Cython's alchymists used a wyverin as their sign."

"To Hightspall it's a sign of the end of the world. In my portrait, Father was symbolically slaying the enemies of House Ricinus. And Hightspall's enemies."

"It didn't work, though," said Glynnie.

"I always hated that portrait," said Rix. "The wyverin was supposed to be dead but no matter how often I repainted it, it always looked as if it was secretly laughing at us . . . " He paused. "And there's another thing bothering me."

"What's that?"

"My last painting—the mural on the observatory wall at Garramide—changed by itself. Several times."

"What are you saying?" said Holm.

"I'm wondering if the portrait has also changed."

"It was lost in Caulderon," Glynnie said in a frosty voice. "It was probably destroyed."

"Tobry said Salyk hid it—before she was executed."

"He also said Lyf ordered her to burn it. Forget it, Rix, we've got far more pressing things to worry about." She put her head in her hands.

"What's the matter?" said Holm, putting an arm around her.

Rix realised, belatedly, that something had been bothering her for days. "Glynnie?"

"I've also been having nightmares—*about Benn*."

Her ten-year-old brother, who had disappeared during Rix and Glynnie's escape from Caulderon three months ago. Rix assumed he was dead, but Glynnie could not give up hope.

"What kind of nightmares?" he said.

"Benn's always sick, or in pain," said Glynnie. "And before our mother died, I promised I'd look after him. It's my fault—"

"If it's anyone's fault Benn was lost, it's mine," said Rix. "I was in charge when we escaped."

She waved his words away. "The only thing that matters is what I'm going to do."

"I don't see there's anything you can do."

She knotted up her fists as if she was going to punch him in the nose. "That's been the excuse for doing nothing *for three months*."

"It's not an excuse, it's reality. Caulderon is a huge city—it'd take weeks to search it. But if we went back, as soon as we started asking questions we'd be arrested and put to death as spies."

"I know!" she yelled. "But Benn's a little boy and I promised to look after him. And *you* promised to help me."

"'When it's over,' I said," said Rix, uncomfortably. He often remembered the promise, and felt guilty that he'd done nothing about it, but the enemy occupation of Caulderon was a barrier he did not know how to overcome.

"You always put things off," cried Glynnie. "You never keep your promises."

"That's a bit harsh," said Holm in his most reasonable voice. "What can Rix do—?"

"I didn't ask your opinion," Glynnie snapped. She turned back to Rix. "Benn's a little boy, lost in an enemy city with no money and no friends. He's got no one to turn to, and I've got to help him." She looked at him expectantly.

"I'll help you as soon as I can," said Rix.

Surely she could see that he wasn't free to do anything right now except try to save his five thousand men?

"I thought we were a team," Glynnie snapped.

"So did I."

CHAPTER 11

Eight a.m. and a cold mist lay over the plain, reducing visibility to a couple of hundred yards. Grandys could be anywhere. His army could be creeping up on them right now.

"What are the scouts telling us?" Rix said to Jackery, whom he had brought in as his adjutant. Being only a sergeant, Jackery did not have the rank for it, but he was a far better soldier than any of Rix's officers.

"They haven't come back ... yet," said Jackery.

The infinitesimal pause was telling. "What, *none of them*? They went out hours ago, for a quick recon."

"Eight went out. Two to each point of the compass. None have come back."

Rix looked all around but the mist defeated him; he could barely see past the edge of the ranks. A cold breeze stirred his cropped hair, sending shivers down the back of his collar.

"Signallers!" he rapped. "Signal full alert."

The chief signaller waved to his trumpeter, who blew the warning signals. The signaller waved his flags. The troops moved into formation and the archers strung their bows.

"I'll bet he's killed my scouts," said Rix, pressing his knuckles into his throbbing belly. "He must be preparing to attack."

In this weather, the first sign of an attack would be when the enemy charged into view. And they would have only twenty seconds to prepare for it.

The mist was thickening; visibility was now down to a hundred yards.

"If he's going to attack, now's the time," said Rix.

Holm grunted. Visibility dropped to fifty yards, twenty, ten, then the mist began to thin again and, within minutes, it was gone. Rix and Jackery rode towards the highest point, a gentle mound only fifteen feet higher than the surrounding plain. A watery sun attempted to penetrate the rushing clouds, but failed. A flurry of rain struck his face. At the top of the mound Rix stared all around him.

The Pale army was still camped where it had been for the past three days. The Cythonians, six formations of some eight thousand each, were also in their original position. They had been in practising drills and manoeuvres for days. He scanned the land all around. The plain was empty. A thin plume rose from the top of Red Mesa.

"What the hell is that?" said Jackery, who was standing on his saddle to gain a few extra inches.

"Where?" said Rix.

Jackery pointed. "The ground south-east of Lake Bunt is all blotchy, yet I'd have sworn it was pancake-smooth yesterday."

"You've got good eyes, Sergeant." Rix focused his field glasses on the patch of land half a mile south of the Cythonian army, between it and the Pale force. "Looks like someone has spread thousands of brown blankets across the land. I don't—"

"It's a bloody army!" cried Jackery. "Grandys' army."

"Signaller, sound the battle horns," rapped Rix.

As the horns were sounded, Grandys' ten thousand men tossed their cloaks over their shoulders and rose into battle formation in one coordinated movement. They were only half a mile from Lyf's army.

"Surely Grandys wouldn't be so stupid as to attack Lyf," said Rix.

Holm came running up onto the mound, with Glynnie close behind. "What is it?" she panted. "Are they attacking?"

"Yes, but not us."

"They're charging the Cythonians," said Jackery in an awed voice. "From behind that small rise, and the Cythonians can't see them from where they're camped. Grandys must have killed their scouts as well."

Rix peered through his binoculars. "Grandys is out in front, *on foot*. He's running straight towards the enemy. Rufuss and Syrten are there too, out very wide on either side."

"Any sign of Lirriam and Yulia?" said Glynnie.

No one answered. Then two riders came galloping out of nowhere, one from the west and another from the east, careering down the narrowing gap between Grandys' concealed, charging force and the oblivious Cythonians. The rider from the west was a woman, standing up in her stirrups with a metal rod or staff raised above her in both hands. Her shining hair streamed out behind her and her heavy bosom bounced with every stride.

"That's Lirriam," said Glynnie. "No one else has hair like that."

"Or a bosom like that," Rix said absently.

Glynnie glared at him.

"It just makes her easy to identify at a distance," he said hastily, but compounded his error by glancing sideways at Glynnie's modest chest.

She made a noise like a kettle boiling over.

"The other rider's too far away to identify," said Holm, "but you'd have to assume it's Yulia. She's also holding up a staff—or maybe a sceptre."

"Grandys' men are coming over the rise. The Cythonians have seen them now," said Rix. "They're swinging round their bombast catapults—they've got at least thirty on this flank."

"One bombast can take out a hundred men," said Holm. "Thirty bombasts would kill half his army and maim the rest."

"Lyf's front lines must be armed with grenadoes too," said Jackery. "They're loading slings and hand catapults."

Grandys raced ahead. Syrten and Rufuss slowed until they were a hundred yards behind. Lirriam and Yulia rocketed towards one another, then propped and skidded their horses to a stop, the Five Heroes now forming the five points of a pentagon. They thrust their staffs, sceptres and swords high. Grandys shook Maloch in the air, roared a word in an alien tongue and a ray of black light impaled the apex of the sky, drawing slender black rays to the same point from each of the other four Heroes.

The Cythonians froze, then frantically loaded their slings and bombast catapults. The archers on either side drew back their bow-strings.

The black rays separated from their sources and formed a steep five-sided pyramid which Grandys directed, with waving motions, over the centre of his army. He whipped Maloch out sideways. The black pyramid settled in silence.

Then the Cythonians fired every alchymical projectile weapon at once: thirty barrel-sized bombasts, hundreds of grenadoes and massed volleys of shriek-arrows, fire-flitters and other missiles that Rix had not seen before.

Months ago he had been at the head of an attacking force when a bombast had gone off in the ranks behind him, blowing at least a hundred soldiers to bits. Thirty bombasts bursting at once, in the middle of an army, was too awful to think about.

"It's going to be a massacre."

CHAPTER 12

"Grandys has lost his mind," said General Hramm, rubbing his leathery fingers together with a noise like a wood rasp. "This is going to be your greatest victory of all, Lord King."

Lyf's officers were laughing and cheering, and already congratulating one another. Lyf was grinning and shaking their hands when he happened to glance across to Moley Gryle. She was leaning out the side of their timber lookout, biting her lip.

"What is it, Moley?" said Lyf.

"It's too easy. Something's wrong. Lord King, I think you should prepare to order a retreat."

"How dare you speak such defeatist talk!" he snapped. "In fifteen minutes it'll all be over."

"But Lord King—"

"Not another word. Get out of my sight!"

She stood her ground, trembling, then the words tumbled out of her. "Lord King, Grandys' army is about to be blasted to bits, yet he's taking no notice of our alchymical weapons. Something is very wrong."

Lyf looked south. Grandys, now mounted as were the other Heroes, thrust his sword high and the Five Heroes converged. His army charged Lyf's First Formation, the enchanted black pyramid moving at the same pace to stay above them.

"If that's supposed to be some kind of shield, it's not working," said Lyf. "Our bombasts are falling straight through it and they're going to go off any second. Grandys' colossal arrogance has undone him this time." He leaned forward, lips parted. "I've waited a long time for this day."

Bombasts and grenadoes plummeted down; shriek-arrows fell in a howling rain and fire-flitters sizzled through the air. Several of the enemy went down, crushed under falling bombasts, but the rest kept moving as though there was no threat at all. Lyf waited, his fists clenched involuntarily.

And waited.

"Our bombasts aren't exploding," yelled Hramm. "What's going on?"

"Neither are the grenadoes," Moley Gryle whispered. "And our fire-flitters are extinguished as soon as they touch the black pyramid. It's magery, Lyf—foul, stinking magery." In her distress, she did not realise that she had called her king by his proper name.

"Hramm, signal my First Formation!" rapped Lyf. "Order it to pull into its tightest phalanx. It has to hold."

What was he thinking? Of course it would hold. This army had never been beaten on the field of battle.

"Order the Third Formation in from the east," he added, "and the Fifth from the west. Surround Grandys' army and cut it to pieces."

The horns were sounded; the signallers signalled furiously. The Five Heroes were riding full bore at the front lines of Lyf's First Formation, leading a seemingly suicidal attack. He shivered.

"Our troops aren't moving into position fast enough," he said. "What's the matter with them?"

"I'll ride over and sort them out," growled Hramm. He leapt down from the platform and lumbered towards his horse.

"Our soldiers are used to chymical weapons doing the hard work for them," said Moley Gryle. "They've forgotten how to fight conventional warfare. Lord King, I beg you, order the retreat before it's too late."

"My army is the greatest fighting force in the land," said Lyf, "and it outnumbers Grandys' five to one. We're going to tear him apart . . ."

The First Formation was still hurling bombasts and grenadoes and, by the time they realised that their chymical weaponry was never going to work, the mounted, heavily armoured Heroes and their cavalry struck the front lines with shattering force.

Lyf heard the impact from half a mile away. His guts knotted; he could only imagine what it must be like over there—the smashed bones and pulverised flesh as his soldiers were ridden down; the shocking mutilations they must be suffering; the agony as they fell into the mud and knew that, alive or dead, it was all over, that no one would be able to do anything for them . . .

He tore his thoughts away, and focused. The rest of Grandys' army poured through the breach and shortly his whole force was fighting inside Lyf's hollowed-out First Formation.

"It's being annihilated," whispered Moley Gryle.

It was a high price, but Lyf was prepared to pay it because Grandys was trapped. He was now surrounded by Lyf's five other formations, each almost the size of Grandys' entire army.

Lyf let out his breath in a rush. "We've got him now." He gave the order to attack Grandys from all sides. "He's lost at least a thousand men, the rest of his troops must be exhausted and he's got nowhere to retreat."

"Grandys never retreats," Moley Gryle said absently.

His soldiers did not look exhausted, either. They kept driving forward, in sickening slaughter, shielded by the outer ranks of Lyf's First Formation, until they exploded out through the rear towards the Second Formation.

And all the while the black pyramid kept drifting to remain above Grandys' army. In vain Lyf's troops fired more bombasts, hurled more grenadoes and used every other alchymical weapon they had. None went off.

"He's destroyed our First Formation," whispered Moley Gryle. She made a series of marks on a paper clipped to a copper tablet and added them up. "Out of eight thousand soldiers, a bare two thousand are still standing—and they were our strongest and most experienced force. Lord King, if they couldn't hold him, how can the others?"

"Enough defeatist talk!" snapped Lyf. "They'll hold. They've got to . . ."

He gnawed a knuckle, then abruptly thrust his hand into a coat pocket. He must not show the smallest trace of doubt. But on the inside, a caitsthe was gnawing on his liver. The mongrel was doing it to him again.

Grandys' force formed a five-sided phalanx and drove through the Second Formation's front lines, then hollowed it out from within as he had done before. It should not have been possible but he made it look easy. The Five Heroes were fighting like demons and so were their troops—Lyf's soldiers, experienced though they were, had no answer to their ferocity or their tactics. They were fighting as though they were already defeated.

Grandys' army burst out the western side of the Second Formation, again leaving thousands of dead and injured, and without stopping for breath attacked Lyf's Fifth Formation.

"Our counterattack will stop him," said Lyf, forcing a confidence he now struggled to feel. "We've got the numbers, and numbers don't lie. Grandys must have lost two thousand dead, and many injured. He can't keep it up."

Moley Gryle had bitten her lower lip so badly that it was bleeding. She gave him a doubtful glance but said no more. Now his Third and Fourth Formations were moving to support the Fifth, attempting for the second time to surround Grandys.

"He doesn't realise we've set a trap," said Lyf. "He's just driving onwards, as before."

"He realises," said Moley Gryle, "but he doesn't care."

In an instant the battlefield changed again. Grandys' disciplined force burst out of the north side of the Fifth Formation, wheeled around and charged at the narrow gap between the Third and Fourth Formations, tearing through and leaving countless more of Lyf's finest troops dead and dying behind him.

Now Grandys' troops separated into two armies, one attacking the Third Formation and the other the Fourth. After five minutes of furious fighting the Third Formation broke and ran, with Grandys' first army in pursuit, cutting them down from the rear. Lyf's Fourth Formation fought on for another minute, then broke as well.

For the first time Lyf was forced to consider that Grandys might do the impossible ... and what would happen if he did defeat Lyf's entire army. As Moley had predicted, he would come for Lyf himself, to seize his two ebony pearls ... and if he succeeded Grandys would publicly execute Lyf as barbarically and spectacularly as possible.

Grandys called his two armies into one, wheeled it and drove towards the centre of Lyf's battered force, the Second and Sixth Formations, with undiminished fury. He was a machine, both tireless and irresistible.

"He knows you're here, Lord King," said Moley Gryle. "He's heading this way. He means to take you ... "

"And kill me," said Lyf quietly. "I know."

In ten bloody minutes against the Third and Fourth Formations Grandys had turned the tide of battle. He was still greatly outnumbered but the morale of the Cythonian troops was broken, and Lyf did not see how he could pull it together again in time to wrest victory from defeat.

"Dare I try?" he mused. "Or would it be better to retreat and fight another day?"

"If you try," said Moley, "and he breaks the Fifth and Sixth Formations the way he's broken the others, there won't be another day."

She was right. Lyf had to give the most painful order of his life.

"Sound the retreat! Order all our Formations to pull into one army and march south to Mulclast, between the three Vomits."

The trumpets sounded. The signallers waved their flags, then Lyf turned to Moley Gryle, whose face was as white as a boiled egg. "Moley, call the King's Guard around me and bring my mount. Order the treasury wagons south with us."

She sprang down, landed awkwardly, twisting an ankle, and hobbled off. Lyf remained on the platform for another minute, his shin stumps throbbing as he watched the carnage. If there had been a more bitter day since Grandys hacked his feet off and walled him up to die, Lyf could not remember it.

He shook his head, trying to wipe away the slaughterhouse images; the butchery done to countless thousands of Cythonian youths, the flower of the nation. There would be no honourable burial for today's casualties—the dead and the wounded would lie together on the battlefield until the cold finished them off and the scavengers reduced them to cracked, bleaching bones.

He turned away, feeling every day of his long, long life and every ounce of his own disastrous failure.

"Our uncanny devices used to do the hard work for us," he said to the nearest guard. "We became complacent. We forgot how to fight without them."

"Yes, Lord King," said the guard, uncomfortably.

"We've got to learn the art of war all over again, and we don't have long to master it. Let this be the day when the tide turns for us."

Moley Gryle raced up on her small white mare, leading Lyf's bay stallion.

"He's only minutes away, Lord King," she said hoarsely.

Lyf scrambled off the platform into the saddle. The King's Guard, two hundred of his toughest and most loyal troops, surrounded him and they headed south.

At once Grandys called the other four Heroes, and a detachment of his own troops, away from harrying Lyf's army. They galloped between the King's Guard and the rest of his army, isolating Lyf.

Grandys turned and rode straight at Lyf.

CHAPTER 13

"Grandys is breaking through the King's Guard!" cried Moley Gryle. "That cursed sword is protecting him from every blow. Lord King, you've got to run now."

"It's happening just as you said it would," said Lyf. He did not move, for he had been neatly cut off and there was nowhere to go.

The Five Heroes were driving, in an arrowhead formation with Grandys at the point and several hundred of his troops forming the shaft, through the ring of Lyf's two hundred King's Guard. Several score of the Guard were dead and the rest were fighting desperately, spending their lives in defence of their king.

But they were fighting in vain; the Five Heroes were almost through the ring. Once they broke the inner line they would come straight for Lyf, leaving Grandys' men to hold the surviving Guard back. If he reached Lyf, and Lyf's last defence failed, he did not see how anything could save him.

"Lord King, please," wept Moley Gryle.

"I listened to your advice the other day, Moley. I've prepared myself a defence—of sorts."

"But Maloch is impervious—"

"I'm not attacking Maloch—or Grandys."

Lyf touched his two master pearls to his brow, then to each of the barbed arrows in his belt—first the lighter arrow, followed by the heavy one. He put the pearls back in their case and picked up the bow, already strung, that he had hooked over his shoulder. He nocked the lighter arrow to the string, and waited.

Grandys was swinging Maloch in all directions, cutting down another of Lyf's King's Guard with almost every stroke. Lyf fought back tears as his loyal men died, one by one. They had served him faithfully for many months now and he knew every man almost as well as he knew Adjutant Gryle.

Grandys broke the inner circle, decapitating Captain Lipits with a furious slash, then plunging Maloch through the chest of the man next to him, Sergeant Boyl, and forcing through into the open. Syrten and Rufuss followed, then Yulia and Lirriam. The King's Guard tried to attack the Five Heroes from behind but a band of Grandys' troops formed a barrier between them.

"Lord King?" said Moley Gryle.

She was only armed with a knife, and Lyf knew Grandys would end her life without a second's thought. "Run, Moley," he said gently.

She raised her small, pointed chin. "If my king is to die, I will die beside him."

"He isn't going to die just yet. Get going, Adjutant Gryle. That's an order."

She choked back a sob and stumbled away.

The Five Heroes were in their arrowhead formation again: Grandys at the point, Rufuss to his right, then Lirriam, and Syrten and Yulia to Grandys' left. They weren't running now; they were walking steadily towards him, though Lyf knew the four would play no part in the confrontation, save as witnesses.

Grandys wanted this victory all to himself.

And you're not having it, Lyf thought. But which of the Heroes should he target?

Not Grandys—Maloch would protect him. Nor Syrten, whose thick opal armour would be impervious to any arrow Lyf could fire. Nor the despised Rufuss, he decided. The other Heroes would not rush to his aid, and Lyf needed them to do just that. For his plan to have any hope, he had to separate Grandys from the other Heroes.

He focused on Lirriam and Yulia. Lirriam was the more difficult target; from this angle she was partly concealed by Rufuss. It had to be Yulia, and with luck . . .

She was fifty yards away. Lyf wasn't the greatest shot, but from that distance he could hardly miss, especially with the aid he planned to use. He raised the bow and aimed.

The Heroes did not flinch. Thousands—no, hundreds of thousands of arrows had been fired at them over the years, and thousands of spears thrown. Occasionally a projectile had penetrated the shield of magery that surrounded the Five, though none of the Heroes had ever taken more than a flesh wound. Could Lyf do better?

They came on. *Now!* He drew back the arrow, which was surrounded by the faintest green glimmer of his shield-breaking enchantment. He could barely make it out; from head-on it would be invisible to the Heroes.

He aimed carefully at Yulia's middle, tightened his aim with the magery of both pearls, locked it on target, and fired. The arrow shot away.

"Look out!" roared Grandys and swung Maloch out to his left, as if to shelter Yulia.

How had he known the arrow was driven by magery? He was incredibly fast, but not fast enough. The arrow took Yulia in the belly, lower than Lyf had aimed. She gasped and doubled over, clutching at her middle, then toppled and lay on her side. Blood poured out.

"Yulia!" Syrten's cry was a deafening roar.

He sprang to her side and thudded down to his knees, looking about wildly. He rose, his massive fists clenched, took a step towards Lyf, then let out another howl and stumbled back to Yulia.

Grandys inspected the wound, clearly shocked that she had been struck such a dangerous blow. He turned to Lyf and every muscle was taut with outrage.

"Syrten," said Grandys, "carry Yulia to safety and stand by her. Lirriam, do everything in your power to heal her. Rufuss, guard them and kill anyone who comes within a hundred yards. I'll deal with Lyf. Go, *go!*"

Syrten picked up Yulia. She was tall for a woman, yet in his massive arms she looked like a small, broken doll, and her blood was dripping off his arms and running down his right leg. He carried her away through the broken ring of the King's Guard and Lyf lost sight of them.

He checked around him. More than half of his Guard were dead, and the rest were fighting desperately, trying to get to him. All were mighty warriors with years of training and they had inflicted massive casualties on Grandys' troops, but they could not break through to defend Lyf. Grandys' men, clearly, had been ordered to keep the Guard away from Lyf at any cost.

This battle was to be man to man, Grandys against Lyf, and no one would be allowed to interfere.

When Grandys was thirty yards away he sheathed Maloch. "You've just forfeited your right to an honourable death by sword, Lyf."

"Because I attacked a woman who's killed hundreds of my people? Or because I used magery to break through your magical defences and render it a fair fight?"

"Because I say so. I'm going to choke you to death with my bare hands." Grandys held up his massive hands.

Lyf nocked his second arrow, knowing that he would be lucky to succeed again, even with all the power of two ebony pearls to drive his arrow through Maloch's defences to the target. Grandys was fast, he was expecting the arrow, and Maloch was forewarned.

Lyf moved the arrowhead in a figure-eight that extended from Grandys' head to his groin, so he would not know where the arrow was aimed until it was fired—by which time it would be too late. The arrow would reach its target more quickly than any man, even Grandys, could move.

He made another figure-eight as Grandys slowly paced towards him, and began a third. Midway down the figure-eight, Lyf fired without warning.

The heavy, barbed arrow went directly where it was aimed, at the centre of Grandys' massive neck. It should have torn his throat open, but Maloch flicked across so fast that Lyf did not see the blade move. His arrow struck the titane blade full on and the hardened steel arrowhead shattered.

A jagged piece of steel shot upwards and embedded itself in the underside of Grandys' chin, but otherwise he was unharmed.

"You've shot your last enchanted arrow," he said, grinning wolfishly. Grandys pulled out the bloody fragment and held it up. "I'm going to shove this through your right eye, into the middle of your brain, and twist it round in one of your figure-eights."

Lyf cast the useless bow aside. He couldn't run on crutches, he no longer had the power to fly, and he could not fight effectively. Though he wore a sword and carried a knife, neither were any use against a master like Grandys. He checked on his King's Guard. The survivors were still fighting desperately to get to him, and gaining the advantage, but even if they broke through it would be too late.

He had to fight for time. Lyf opened the pearl case and touched the two pearls, drawing all the power he could from them, though how could it be enough? He'd fought Grandys face to face at the peace conference, when Lyf had possessed four pearls and Grandys had none, and Grandys had still won.

"Lord King!" cried Moley Gryle.

She came running towards him through the bloody battlefield, her black hair flying in the wind. Grandys stopped to watch her, a faint smile on his bloated face.

"Go away, Moley!" said Lyf.

"I've thought of something."

"Go, and that's an order."

She stopped. Despite that she had been running, her face was paler than usual. She took a long, choking breath, made a hand sign over her heart, then kept coming.

"Two dismembered corpses for the price of one," leered Grandys.

Since Moley Gryle had twice disobeyed Lyf's direct order, there was no point in repeating it, but his heart throbbed as if it was being torn open at the thought of her coming death. His most loyal servant, the closest person he had to a friend, was going to be hacked to pieces by Grandys, and it was unendurable.

She reached his side, her breast heaving, then said under her breath, "Use a reversal spell, Lord King."

"What for?"

"You can't use magery directly against the enchanted sword, but a reversal spell might turn Maloch's strength against itself."

"How would that help me?"

"Tell Grandys that your spell gives Maloch the option to choose its true master. Then, if it doesn't obey him, he'll think you've succeeded. His confidence will be undermined and it might just give the King's Guard time to get here."

Only eighteen of his Guard survived, battling a dozen of Grandys' men. The chances were that none of his Guard would reach him, but it was worth the risk. He touched his ebony pearls, created a deception spell so Grandys would not recognise what he was doing, then wrapped it around the strongest reversal spell he could make.

Lyf met Grandys' eyes. "I'm giving Maloch the option to choose its *true master*, and it won't be you." He cast the spell.

Grandys swung Maloch in a circle as if batting the spell aside, then pointed the sword at Lyf from thirty feet away. Lyf felt a massive blow to the chest, as if he'd been struck with a full barrel of ale.

He went flying backwards, lost his grip on his crutches and hit the ground hard.

Grandys sheathed Maloch, grinning. "I'm its true master all right."

He advanced, flexing those thick, stone-hard fingers. Moley Gryle ran backwards and threw herself onto Lyf, vainly trying to protect him with her own body.

"This cannot be," she wept.

Lyf could see the desperation in her eyes as Grandys closed in. She slid her hands in between Lyf's, closed them around the pearls and, to his utter astonishment, cast a perfect, disguised reversal spell.

There came a *crack-crack-crack* and Grandys staggered backwards as though struck a blow the equal of his own. He cursed and went for Maloch but the sword would not come free of its sheath. Though he was not aware of it, the disguised spell had reversed the normal impetus of the sword to propel itself up into Grandys' hand. The harder he tried to remove it, the more tightly Maloch's own power held it in place.

Lyf pushed Moley Gryle off, sat up and said, "The sword's going to abandon you, Grandys, for the true master it's been looking for all along."

Grandys gave another heave. "I'm—Maloch's—true—master," he said through bared teeth. The sword did not budge.

"I think not," said Lyf. "I think it's Rixium, and one day soon, when he challenges you for the sword, it'll betray you."

"You won't be around to see it," snarled Grandys. Taking hold of the hilt with both hands, he roared, "Obey your master!"

The sword remained in the sheath as if it had been riveted into it.

"Lord King!" a deep voice yelled. "Hold on. We're coming!"

Grandys looked around wildly. Lyf's guards had cut down the last of Grandys' men and now the King's Guard came storming in, nine of them, determined to protect their king at any cost. Grandys let out a cry of fury then, realising that he was defenceless without Maloch, backed away. Five guards leapt at him. He turned and bolted, the sheath slapping his thigh as he went.

The King's Guard surrounded Lyf and helped him to his feet.

"Surely that's the first time Grandys has run from a battlefield," Lyf said wearily. "It must be his bitterest moment."

"And your greatest," said Captain Rembloy, his finest warrior, a huge rectangle of muscle. "Whatever that spell was, it was a mighty one, Lord King."

"Yes, it was," said Lyf. "Would you step back please, guards?"

They retreated; he turned to his deathly white adjutant and lowered his voice. "I've no idea how you did that, Moley, but you saved my life." He paused. But it had to be said. "How long have you been secretly studying forbidden magery?"

"I don't know any magery," she whispered.

"Then how—?"

"You know I'm an *intuit*. That's how I came to be your adjutant at such a young age. I—I must have intuited how to do the spell . . ."

He stared at her. The situation was unprecedented. "What am I to do with you, Moley?"

She dropped to her knees and bent her slender neck.

"Mag-magery is forbidden to us, Lord King. The penalty is death and there are no exceptions. There's only one thing you can do."

CHAPTER 14

It only took the Heroes ten minutes to pass over the rise and out of sight of Lyf and his King's Guard, though by then Syrten was drenched in Yulia's blood and she was failing so rapidly that Lirriam began to fear that no healing magery could save her. The bloody arrow was still embedded in her belly, her chest hardly moved with each breath, and she was as pallid as a corpse. Even her opal fingernails had lost colour; they barely shimmered in the fleeting rays of sunlight.

"Don't leave me, Yulia," said Syrten. "You—mustn't—die. *Lirriam, do something*."

Lirriam took off her sweat-soaked cloak and laid it on the driest patch of ground she could find. It was still cold from last night's frost; she could feel it through the fabric. She shed her green coat, laid it on the cloak and stood there, shivering, the keen wind raising goose pimples on her back and arms.

"Rufuss, I need your cloak."

His face hardened as if the mere request was an outrage. Perhaps it was to him; almost everything angered Rufuss these days and he had only one remedy for it—blood. She met his eyes and refused to look away, and shortly he drew off his black cloak and threw it at her.

"Stand guard," said Lirriam.

"I have my orders. I don't need them repeated." He stalked off.

The cloak had the same charnel smell that Rufuss trailed after him, though Yulia was beyond sensing it. Nonetheless it had a virtue that Lirriam's coat did not—it was huge as well as thick. She folded it three times, laid it on top of her coat to make the best bed she could, and gestured to Syrten.

He set Yulia down on the cloak and knelt beside her, holding her slender hand in his golem hands and gazing at her with tragic, dog-like devotion. Lirriam had to get him out of the way.

"If I'm to save her, I'll need a fire and hot water, lots of it," said Lirriam. "Right away."

He rose without a word, and ran. No one was better than Syrten at following orders—he lived to be told what to do. She did not check on Rufuss. Grandys had ordered him to guard them, and Rufuss would obey. Momentarily she wondered how Grandys' confrontation with Lyf was going, then dismissed the thought to focus on the healing.

Lirriam tucked the cloak around Yulia's feet and legs to keep them warm, then cut away her coat and blouse to expose the entry wound, which was in the lower belly, midway between her navel and pubic bone. It was only an inch-long slit on the outside but her middle was swollen as if she had lost a lot of blood internally, and while the arrowhead remained inside her she would keep bleeding. Unfortunately enemy arrowheads were barbed to make them difficult to remove; pulling it out could cause more damage than its impact.

With less dangerous wounds it was often simpler, though agonisingly painful, to push the arrowhead through and out the other
side, but the arrowhead was in a dangerous place, packed with
organs—bladder, womb, bowel—and blood vessels, and Yulia's
spine was behind it. Pushing it through wasn't an option. Lirriam
tugged on the arrowhead, very carefully. It moved towards her. Not
embedded in bone, then, but dark blood ebbed from the wound and
Yulia let out a little gasp.

Syrten staggered up, carrying a small dead tree over his shoulder.
He dropped it six feet away and stood there, staring at Yulia's face
and swaying on his broad, square feet.

"No change," Lirriam said without looking around. "Get a fire
going, then fetch water."

Syrten smashed the tree's trunk to pieces with his iron-hard fists
and made a pile of kindling and larger pieces of wood. After crumbling a chunk of wood in his hands he rubbed it together so
furiously that it smoked and burst into flame. Ignoring the flames
licking around his opal-armoured fists, he thrust the burning material into the kindling. It blazed high. He turned and ran.

Lirriam considered the arrow. Had Grandys been here he might
have used brute-force magery to crush the barbs on the arrowhead
flat, then draw it out through the entry wound. Lirriam could not
do that kind of magery; hers relied on subtlety rather than strength.
She could probably shatter the arrowhead, though how could she be
certain of getting all the fragments out? If any piece remained in the
wound it was unlikely to heal, and sooner or later infection would
kill Yulia.

Lirriam checked the vital signs again. Yulia was fading; if Lirriam
did not act immediately it would be too late. There was only one
thing to do.

She took a firm hold of the arrow's shaft and pulled. It moved a
quarter of an inch before meeting resistance. She rotated the shaft
each way until the resistance lessened and drew it out further.
Resistance again. She was bound to be doing more damage to the
organs the arrow had passed through but there was no alternative.
Lirriam continued, rotating the shaft each time until she felt the
least pressure on it, and finally it came free in a gush of blood.

And Yulia's heart stopped.

Lirriam *sensed* it in a tiny part of herself that had been bonded to the other Heroes ever since they had sworn to each other on the First Fleet. She felt the emptiness of loss, too. Tossing the arrow aside, she put her bloody hands over Yulia's breastbone, created a mental image of her heart and directed a sharp pulse of power through it. Yulia's heart beat once, twice, and stopped. Lirriam sent another pulse. Yulia's heart beat four times before stopping.

Why? Presumably she was still bleeding internally and there was only one hope of stopping it—by sealing the wound from top to bottom. Lirriam put her hands around the arrow wound and pressed down firmly. Blood flowed from the slit, at least half a pint. She pressed again, expelling a little more blood, then opened the wound with two fingers and looked in. What she saw, even through all the blood and torn flesh, shocked her. With the index finger of her right hand, Lirriam directed a searing blast down through the wound as far as it extended.

Yulia jerked convulsively and smoke wisped out of the arrow slit. Lirriam put her hands over Yulia's heart and sent another pulse of power through it. After a second Yulia's heart started—and this time it kept going, faint but steady. Lirriam moved her hands to Yulia's belly and gently began the healing process.

Thud, thud, thud. Syrten reappeared with two metal buckets of water. He put them on the fire.

"She's a little better," said Lirriam before he could ask.

Syrten crouched to take Yulia's hand.

"Go and stand guard," said Lirriam.

"She needs me," Syrten said brokenly.

Lirriam could not concentrate with his massive presence close by, radiating dumb terror.

"Go *now*!"

He went. She heated one of the buckets of water by thrusting her fist in and directing power through it, then washed her hands carefully. She tossed in the rags torn from Yulia's blouse, heated the water to boiling, fished the rags out and cleaned the wound as best she could. As she finished, Grandys appeared from behind her. He stood at Yulia's head, looking down. His mouth opened and closed.

She saw a large squad of guards further out. He must have brought them with him.

"I think she's going to live," said Lirriam. She took the second bucket, which was boiling, out of the fire. "Though at some cost. I had to cauterise the wound—I don't know how much damage that's done . . . "

He did not speak. She looked up, sharply. His face, where the skin could be seen through his patchy opal armour, was a bilious yellow-green, a colour she had never seen on human flesh before—at least, not on *live* flesh. His eyes were staring, his breath ragged.

"Grandys? Are you injured?"

Icy sweat dripped off his chin. He jerked his head from side to side. "Lyf attacked Maloch. Said I wasn't its true master. Said its true master was Rixium."

"That's absurd," said Lirriam. She had heard the *true master* mentioned before. Where, though?

"Lyf cast some spell and—and—" It exploded out of Grandys: a cry of pain and rage and, to her astonishment, no little terror. "*Maloch refused me!*"

"How do you mean?"

"It held itself in its sheath so tightly that no force or order of mine could budge it."

Lirriam put her hands on Yulia's cold belly and directed a gentle, healing force through her. She was breathing steadily now; she would live.

"Did you kill Lyf?" she said.

"No," Grandys gasped.

"He escaped?"

"Not exactly." He swayed on his feet, then scrubbed at his face with both hands. Small pieces of armour crumbled off.

Lirriam had never seen Grandys so shaken. A part of her wanted to gloat that the bastard had finally been mastered; another part was shivering. What did it mean? Were the Five Heroes finished?

"What happened?"

"I was weaponless. And his King's Guard were racing in, nine of them. I—I had to retreat."

"You ran?" she said incredulously. Lirriam struggled to contain herself. Was this her reward for Grandys breaking her jaw? "The invincible Axil Grandys," she said mockingly, "the greatest warrior of all time, ran from the field of battle like a rank coward?"

"I retreated," he said stiffly, "the better to fight again."

He drew himself up to his full, intimidating height. The bilious colour was replaced by his customary tomato-red flush, and his eyes hardened. Clearly he regretted telling her, though there had been little choice—Lyf would spread the story soon enough. But she knew that, more than anything, Grandys regretted revealing his own deep-seated terror to her.

"What if the true master *is* Rixium?" Lirriam said thoughtfully. "He's only twenty and a brilliant warrior, strong and fast."

"I'm bigger and stronger," snapped Grandys.

"But you're forty-four," said Lirriam, "and you look older. You're past your prime, Grandys, while he's yet to reach his. What are you going to do?"

"I can't believe what Lyf said was true. He must have used some kind of deception . . ."

"You sound doubtful."

"I'll sort it out."

"Are you losing your nerve?"

He bridled, as she had known he would. "Once I've taken the power of king-magery I'll be able to *command* Maloch's loyalty, and no power in the land can break such a command. Even if Rixium should be the true master, which I very much doubt, he won't be able to do anything about it."

"If you don't take him on he'll know something is wrong, and so will everyone else. It'll strengthen him and weaken us."

"I never said I wouldn't take him on. I'm going to play cat and mouse with Rixium. He'll never know when I'm going to strike— or which of his supporters I'm striking at. You can break a man's spirit quickly that way, without ever coming face to face with him."

He walked around Yulia several times, looking down at her, then turned away. "Take her—and Tali—to Bastion Barr with a guard of a hundred men. Syrten and Rufuss will escort you. I'll join you there shortly."

"What are you up to?" said Lirriam.

"When you're knocked down, you get up at once and fight all the harder." He headed west towards his army, leaving the squad of guards behind.

Lirriam, taking pity on Syrten, called him across so he could see that Yulia was going to live. After allowing him a quarter of an hour with her, Lirriam sent him to bring the horses, dry clothing and clean bandages, and a horse-drawn litter for Yulia.

Lirriam had much to think about. What could "Maloch's true master" mean? Where had she heard it before? And *was* Grandys losing his nerve? There was much to be lost if he was—much to be gained, too, if she had the courage.

She put her hands over the wound again. Yulia was too cold. Lirriam rejuvenated her healing charm, then followed it with the strongest warming charm she could manage. Yulia soon grew warm under her hands and the pallor began to be replaced by pink. Her breathing strengthened.

Lirriam sat back on her heels. Her head spun and she had to support herself with her hands. It had been a long, wearying day—her part in the creation and maintenance of the black, protective pyramid this morning had drained her to the marrow of her bones. Then the long, bloody battle, plus the shield charm she'd had to hold in place all through it to protect herself from errant arrows, spears and sword thrusts. And now this utterly exhausting healing. It had all come from within her and the day wasn't finished yet.

"Lirriam?" Yulia said in a faint voice. "Do you have—water?"

Lirriam rose wearily and tested the water in the second bucket. It was still hot, though not too hot to drink. She held a half mug to Yulia's lips and supported her head while she drank.

"Was I . . . dead?" said Yulia.

"Very close. Your heart stopped a few times."

"But you saved me." Yulia raised a hand as if to reach out to Lirriam, but lacked the strength to complete the gesture. Her hand flopped down.

"Yes." Lirriam looked around. Rufuss was still standing guard fifty yards away. There was no sign of Syrten or anyone else. "Yulia, do you remember when we were on the First Fleet, coming here from Thanneron?"

"I was just—sixteen. It was the adventure—of my life. Of course I remember."

"Do you remember how Grandys ended up with Maloch?"

"Why does it . . . matter?" said Yulia. Her voice was fading.

"It matters. I'm sorry; I need to know right away."

"It came to him after . . . after Envoy Urtiga was murdered . . . month out of Thanneron. She left a . . . a signed deed—"

"What did it say?"

"If she died before completing . . . quest," said Yulia, "Grandys . . . take over . . . aided by Maloch. That was when he bound us . . . in Five Heroes. You must remember."

"I remember. Was anything said about Maloch's 'true master'?"

"Heard it mentioned . . . " Yulia's voice went hoarse. Lirriam gave her some more water and she spoke more strongly. "Master has to be Grandys . . . can't be any of us. Couldn't bear to touch Maloch—could you?"

"Not willingly," said Lirriam. She lowered her voice. "Who do you think killed Urtiga? Could it have been Grandys?"

"Always thought . . . Rufuss."

"So have I—even then he had the air of a killer. I've never understood why Grandys protected him, or why he made Rufuss one of the Five . . . "

"Don't want to think about him." Yulia reached down towards her belly.

Lirriam moved her hand away. "Don't touch the wound; I'm worried about it getting infected."

Yulia caught Lirriam's hand instead, holding her in a surprisingly firm grip. "How—how bad is it?"

Lirriam had never thought of herself as being particularly compassionate but she could not bear to say the words. She did not want to cause Yulia, the closest person she had to a sister, so much pain, or to rob her of the thing she most wanted. No, Lirriam thought, I've already done that.

"You were dying," said Lirriam, looking away. "I did what I had to do to save you."

"Tell me the truth. I've got to know."

"The arrow missed your bladder and bowel, luckily, and it didn't touch the spine . . ."

"But?"

"It tore through your womb, and you were bleeding so badly—"

Yulia's hand clenched painfully around Lirriam's. "Tell me!" she gasped.

"There was no time. I had to seal the wound at once, to stop the bleeding. I'm sorry. It did a lot more damage. I—I don't think you'll ever be able to have children."

Yulia held her hand for a few more seconds, her eyes searching Lirriam's face as if hoping, desperately, that it was not true. Then her hand fell away.

"Then what's it all been for?" she said in a dead voice.

Lirriam did not reply.

"I was sixteen when I became one of the Five," said Yulia. "Now I'm twenty-eight."

"I know," said Lirriam. "I was eighteen and now I'm thirty-two."

"Thirty-two?"

"I lived another two years after you were turned to opal . . . before Lyf did the same to me."

"Oh!" Yulia continued, speaking in gasped phrases separated by long pauses. "I've spent almost half my life pursuing . . . sacred quest for the Promised Realm . . . and all that time I've made excuses for the bloodshed . . . the destruction, the barbarism. It's for our quest, I told myself . . . and once we found our Promised Realm . . . we'd make up for all the ruin by creating a beautiful new world . . . I told myself I'd make amends . . . for all the terrible things I've collaborated in . . . all the things I've turned a blind eye to . . . by little creations of my own."

"You've wanted children as long as I've known you," said Lirriam, aching for her.

"I kept thinking, just another year . . . and just another year. Now it's too late . . . I was a party to all the destruction . . . and there's nothing I can do to balance it. How empty our lives have been . . . how wasted . . ."

"Yes," said Lirriam. Not being the contemplative type, she had never thought about the meaning or the value of their lives. Now she did, and did not like what she saw.

Yulia clutched Lirriam's hand again, with both hands this time, twisting it back and forth in her agitation. "Promise me you'll do better. You're the only one of us who has a chance."

"Because I've got *Incarnate*?"

Yulia tried to sit up, moaned and fell back. "No, don't use it," she said in a ragged voice. "It allows perilous choices. *Forbidden* choices. Get rid of it!"

"Then why do you say I have a chance?"

"You're the only one . . . who never really believed in the quest . . . the only one of us who isn't irredeemably corrupt . . . You can change, Lirriam; there's still time. Promise me, when the war is over . . . you'll live a better life—a life of creation rather than destruction."

"There's only one way to do that," said Lirriam. "By going where no one has ever heard of the Five Heroes."

"That's not what I meant!" cried Yulia. "We're . . . only family you have. How could you bear to abandon us . . . for some land where you know no one . . . where everything is strange?"

"You can't imagine how I long for such a land, where no one knows anything about me. It's the only escape I have."

And there was only one way to find such a place. Lirriam had to wake *Incarnate*, whatever it cost.

CHAPTER 15

Rix lost sight of Grandys in the chaos of the great battle with Lyf, though it was clear he'd had a great victory. Lyf's army was retreating south, almost in a rout. Ominously, Grandys' force, which had been harrying them, had halted on the plain as if awaiting orders. Orders to attack Rix?

Several hundred yards north, a large squad of Grandys' troops stood guard over a group of people on a gentle rise. Two of them were kneeling and two standing, further away. Could it be a Herovian prayer ceremony? Rix focused his field glasses. No, it was the Five Heroes—and one of them was lying on the ground.

"Let it be Grandys," he said to himself.

"Sorry?" said Glynnie.

Her eyes were wide, her breathing ragged. She had seen fighting before, but not the hideous violence of a large-scale battle. Neither had Rix, for that matter, and though he had trained as a warrior and an officer since he was a boy, he never wanted to see it again.

"One of the Heroes is down," said Rix, "and I can see the blood from here."

"I don't suppose it's our mutual enemy?"

"No, the bastard is stalking back and forth, as mean as ever." He moved the glasses a fraction. "I can see Rufuss, and Syrten with his back to us. He's hunched over, that's why I didn't recognise him. It's one of the women—Yulia, and Lirriam is attending her. It looks like she's doing a healing."

"How bad is Yulia hurt?"

"I can't tell—but for all the others to be standing around, it must be serious."

As he spoke, Grandys turned his way and, as if he knew Rix was spying on him, shook both fists above his head. Rix choked, realised Holm was watching him and hastily turned it into a cough.

"He's saying, '*You'll keep*'," said Holm, who was squinting through a small black telescope.

Grandys mounted and rode across to his army, and Rix lost sight of him.

"What will he do now?" said Glynnie.

"After every victory he puts on a great feast for his troops. Then everyone gets roaring drunk and Grandys kills some of the prisoners for the general entertainment."

"Does that mean we're safe . . . for today?"

"I wouldn't bet he's finished fighting," said Rix. "He's got the taste for blood, and Yulia to avenge, and there's still hours of daylight left." He had just turned away when Jackery said sharply, "He's not finished."

A battalion of a thousand men had broken away from Grandys' main force, led by Grandys himself, and was streaming south-east.

"What's he doing now?" said Rix.

"Going after the Pale," said Holm. "A thousand against five thousand. The same proportions as he used against Lyf."

"Surely he can't hope to do it again," said Glynnie.

"He's luring me out," said Rix. "He knows I've got to go to their defence."

"Why, if he's only attacking the Pale with a thousand?" said Holm.

"They're our only ally. And I'm not sure how solid their allegiance is, so I'm not taking any chances."

"The moment you go to their aid," said Holm, "Grandys will attack with the rest of his force. It's the reason he's gone after them."

Rix did not reply. This was the trap.

"Let him attack," said Jackery. "Together our two armies number ten thousand. We'll show him that good Hightspallers aren't as easily beaten as the cowardly Cythonians."

Fine words, Rix thought, but he only had to look at his white-faced men to see what a battering their morale had taken.

"If we don't help the Pale we'll look like cowards. That'll be even worse for morale." He turned to the signaller. "We march."

Rix rode to the front. Holm and Jackery went with him. Then Rix had a sudden thought.

"Holm, you've got something of an alchymical bent. Take a few wagons over to where the black pyramid formed and see what you can find."

"Pick up some of their bombasts and grenadoes, you mean," said Holm.

"Collect some of every sort of alchymical weapon they have. Bring them back and see how they work ... if you can without blowing yourself to bits."

"I think I can manage that. Any particular reason why?"

"You never know when they could come in handy," Rix said vaguely.

Holm turned back. Rix looked the other way.

"The Pale are two miles east," he said, indicating their position with a sweep of his arm. "Grandys is a mile north of them; his battalion will get there first. We'll march directly towards the Pale, following that slight rise. Grandys will move to intercept us from the north before we reach the Pale. We'll stand and fight at the top of the rise, so he'll be attacking uphill. We'll have a bit of an advantage, his men being so battle-weary . . ."

It sounded like a good strategy when he said it aloud, though Rix knew it would not work out that way. Grandys never took the predictable approach. The only thing he could be relied on to do was attack with unmitigated savagery when and where it was least expected.

And he did. Rix's force was still a mile away when Grandys' battalion tore through the Pale army more quickly than Lyf's army had been defeated. Within minutes the survivors were stampeding south, abandoning their dead and injured on the field of battle. Grandys' battalion followed for a few minutes, cutting down the stragglers, then stopped, evidently awaiting orders.

Rix cursed. Unless he could bring the Pale back, it was now seven thousand against five thousand, odds he did not like at all.

"Halt!" he roared. "Close ranks. Wait here—I'll try and rally them."

He spurred off after the Pale and caught them within minutes. They were a miserable lot—a small people, poorly dressed in Cythonian clothing that hung off their slender frames.

He rode alongside, looking for a single face and praying she had not been killed. The Pale, having been slaves for a thousand years, were a cowed people, used to obeying orders without question. Most lacked initiative and it was no use Rix, an outsider, trying to sway them. Only one person could: their true leader in Cython and ever since—Radl.

It did not take long to find her; Radl was one of the few Pale who had never been cowed. Tall, olive skinned and black-haired, she was one of the least typical Pale he had ever met. She wore many bandages, both old and fresh, and he remembered Tali saying that she was a bold, even reckless warrior, always leading from the front.

"Radl!" he yelled, cantering up to her.

"No!" she said without turning around.

He rode ahead ten yards, dismounted and stood in her path. She stopped. She was a striking woman, though war and exhaustion had erased the best of her looks—her eyes were hollow and her face haggard.

"My little army is all that stands between Grandys and victory," said Rix. "And victory for Grandys means enslavement or death for everyone else."

"After we threw the enemy out of Cython," said Radl, biting each word off and spitting it in Rix's face, "we were flushed with victory, fools that we were. We came out to help you, despite that Hightspall had abandoned our ancestors, child hostages, to unending slavery. Abandoned them, then blamed us for our own enslavement and called us traitors for serving the enemy."

"It wasn't my doing," said Rix, "and we have to deal with the now."

"The present comes from the sins of the past," said Radl. "This sickening war is nothing like fighting for our freedom. Grandys fights for the joy of killing, and we'll have no further part in it."

"We need you," said Rix. "Without your aid, Hightspall must fall."

"I'm sorry, Rix," Radl said, and he knew she spoke the truth. "They say you're a decent man. But if Hightspall *is* doomed to fall, not you nor I can stop it."

"If it falls, all must fall."

"That remains to be seen. Cython is strong, and we know it well, all its pits and traps. Grandys won't find it easy to take. And perhaps, if all fails, your survivors will come to our doors."

"Please stay, we really need your help. We can't do it alone."

"No," said Radl. "Even slavery was better than the kind of war Grandys wages." She extended her hand. "Good luck."

Rix shook it. He could not blame her. She turned south and called her people on. He mounted and rode north, back to his personal Armageddon. He rejoined his men and the two armies faced each other across half a mile, waiting. But Grandys did not move all afternoon.

Or evening.

Or that night.

They could see the enemy campfires and hear the Herovians' battle songs. "It sounds as though the bastards are drunk," said Holm incredulously. He had sworn never to touch drink again after a tragedy in his own life, many years ago.

"They've got a great victory to celebrate," said Rix. "The Herovians are prodigious drinkers; I've known them to go into battle half rotten. The casualties were horrific, though that's never bothered Grandys. He cares no more about the lives of his own troops than he does about the enemies'."

He walked away, then, on a sudden thought, came back.

"How did you get on with the alchymical stuff?"

"We collected three wagon loads of devices that hadn't gone off. Bombasts, grenadoes, fire-flitters and so forth."

"Have you worked out what stopped them from going off?"

"Are you asking if I can find a way to make them work?" said Holm, one hand in his pocket.

"I guess I am," said Rix.

"From what I've seen so far, there's nothing wrong with them. In other words, they failed to work because they were under that black shield of magery."

"So if we needed to use them, and there was no such shield, they'd work."

"I expect so. I'll test one of each kind to make sure, when I get the chance."

"That's what I was hoping to hear."

"I also found these," said Holm. He opened his hand to reveal two small, stubby orange crystals, no longer than his little finger-nail and only half as wide.

"What are they?"

"I don't know . . . I took them from two dead Cythonian officers. Each man was holding a crystal up in front of his face."

He handed one to Rix. "Are they like some kind of poison pill?" said Rix. "In case of capture?"

"No, I rather think they might be some kind of speaking device, though I'm blessed if I know how they work."

Rix handed the crystal back.

"Keep it," said Holm. "You never know . . ."

At midnight Rix sent his troops to their bedrolls, still dressed for battle. He remained at the top of the rise, which was only lit by a couple of lanterns, scanning the darkness beyond his camp. Everyone was on edge and his sergeants had broken up dozens of fights. One man was dead, six others were too badly injured to fight and many more had been put on charges.

"I reckon some of the men wanted to be injured," said Jackery, who had returned from doing the rounds of the watch, "to get out of the real fighting."

"If they knew what Grandys does to prisoners they might change their minds," said Rix.

"What's he waiting for?"

"He's drawing it out to torment us," said Rix. "Me, particularly."

"The men are saying you should attack and get it over with. Why don't you, sir?"

"The one small advantage we have is this elevated position. If we attack, we have to go down onto his territory, and that gives him the advantage."

"Rumours are running around the camp," said Holm.

"I heard them too," said Jackery.

"What are they saying?" Rix had a fair idea.

"That you won't attack because you're afraid."

"I am afraid. Only a fool wouldn't be. But I'm more afraid of being led into a foolish attack and losing precious lives. If Grandys gets the chance to make an example of us, do you think he'll stop while anyone remains alive?"

"You have to do something," said Holm. "You're giving him the initiative."

"Let me guess where the muttering is coming from," said Rix. "Libbens and his cronies."

Jackery nodded, then headed off to his tent. Holm opened his mouth but closed it without speaking.

"I know," said Rix. "I should have got rid of them the moment I escaped from the crevasse." He smiled wearily. "You'd think I'd have learned my lesson by now."

"If you take on the role of commander you have to be prepared to be ruthless where necessary. It'll save you a lot of trouble in the end."

"I'll deal with them at first light."

Holm shrugged. "Good idea. I'm going to bed."

Rix yawned and rubbed his eyes. He stood there for a few minutes more, thinking, then turned towards his own tent. He took off his sword and scabbard, put it inside his tent, yawned and stretched. As he did, a rope was cast around him from behind and pulled so tight that he could not move his arms.

"Got you!" gloated Libbens, and punched Rix in the throat. "We're court martialling you for conspiring with the enemy. And the minute you're convicted—see this pole—"

Grasbee hefted a heavy, eight-foot standard, swung it around sideways and slammed it into Rix's ribs. He felt them crack and the impact knocked him to the ground.

"Your head is going right up top," said Libbens.

CHAPTER 16

Rannilt lifted her head, trying to pinpoint the psychic howl ringing through her mind.

The night was still but not dark. A long way behind her, blazing pyres dotted the landscape. The air reeked of charred flesh, dead soldiers being burned by the thousands. She closed her eyes, blocked her nose, shut down all her physical senses and stood, statue-still, trying to pick out one man from the thousands who had been injured that day.

Aaaarrrrgghh!

There it was again—Tobry. Broadcasting his agony, his grief and his shifter torment.

Rannilt did not stop to wonder how he could have survived the falling tree—her only urge was to get to him as quickly as possible.

She did not know the land and had no idea where his cries were leading her. If she had ever seen a map of Central Hightspall, she had forgotten it months ago. She only knew that her dear friend was injured, in terrible pain, and *desperate*. She had to help him. And get away from the killing.

She tracked him north for many miles, then east, travelling by night and hiding by day. The night was her friend. It reminded her of being a slave girl in Cython, when she had often roamed and hidden in the unlit tunnels far from the core of the underground city.

Days went by. Rannilt did not count them. She lived only for the moment, not long now, when she would find Tobry.

When her life's work would begin.

She was close now. So close that she could smell the distinctive, rank stench of the shifter he now was. It did not offend her; it was simply a part of him. But she had to be very careful. She had no fear of Tobry the man, even in his shifter madness, for he had been part father and part kindly uncle to her.

But if he shifted from man to caitsthe it would be a different matter. Caitsthes were the most savage predators in the land, shifters Lyf had specifically created to be uncontrollable and unpredictable; creatures designed to terrorise. She had to prevent Tobry from shifting, which he was liable to do if threatened.

They were in a flat land of a thousand lakes, large, small and tiny. It was called Lakeland although she did not know that. The ground was scattered with boulders that looked as though they had been melted. Here and there she encountered outcropping rock layers like petrified honeycomb.

Ah, there he was, crouched by a ragged pond with a halo of ice around the edge. He was filthy and clad in rags. A broken chain was locked around his left wrist. He cradled his right arm, which was swollen and hung at a strange angle. It was badly broken and he needed help. He needed her.

He was thin to the point of gauntness. Shifters needed twice as much food as normal people and by the look of him Tobry hadn't eaten in days—perhaps not since that terrible vision of him feeding on the dead. Rannilt thrust the image away; she didn't want to think about it. It wasn't Tobry, it was the shifter.

He broke off a section of ice and lowered his left hand into the water as if preparing to grab a fish. Rannilt salivated. Though she had been eking out her supplies for days, she had eaten the last of her bread and cheese yesterday.

Tobry lunged but the length of chain struck the water and whatever he had hoped to catch was gone. He let out a howl, quickly stifled. He rose, supporting his broken arm, sniffed the air and looked around.

Rannilt went still, her heart thumping in her bony little chest. Don't alarm him—if he shifts to a caitsthe, he'll eat you.

Tobry's head turned slowly. His hair was matted with mud and bits of twig. He had a few days' growth of downy red beard— caitsthe red—and his eyes were yellow. There was not a trace of the grey eyes he'd had before he'd been turned.

He sniffed again. Rannilt wasn't game to breathe. She edged backwards and a pebble rolled away behind her heel. A tiny sound, but Tobry's head shot around and his eyes focused on her.

They stared at each other for a stretched-out moment. His gaunt frame tensed, every muscle standing out. The fingers of his good hand hooked. His mouth gaped and a trace of slaver appeared on his lower lip.

"Tobry, it's me," she said softly, trying to temper her naturally shrill voice. "Rannilt. Your friend."

He stared at her, unblinking. She could not tell what he was thinking. Did Tobry still exist? Or had the shifter curse consumed every last good thing in him?

"It's Rannilt," she repeated. "I've come to help you."

His eyes widened as if he had recognised her, fleetingly. He made an inarticulate sound in his throat, "Rurrrh! Rurrrh!"

She took a tiny step towards him, reaching out carefully. "What are you tryin" to say, Tobry?"

He bared his teeth, which were worryingly fang-like, and then it burst out of him, a strangled cry. "Ru—ru—*run away*!"

Her heart crashed back and forth. She sensed that he was struggling, that the madness, or the beast, had far more power than the man. She wanted to run but knew it was the wrong thing to do. He needed her, and if she turned away from him now he would be lost.

"I ain't runnin' away, *Tobry*." She emphasised his name; it confirmed that he was a man, not a beast. "We're friends. You looked after me out in the Seethin's. And I helped save you from the facinore—"

He growled and slashed at the air with his good hand.

"You remember the facinore, don't you? And Lyf? And Tali—?"

Tobry wailed, thrashed involuntarily and cracked his broken arm on a boulder. His fists clenched; a cry of uttermost agony erupted out of him. His face had gone purple, engorged with blood, and from where she stood she could hear his heart thundering. She could also feel the shifter heat radiating from him, and for a dreadful second she thought he was going to shift. She should not have mentioned Tali.

She prepared to run, knowing that she could never outrun a caitsthe. It could catch her in a couple of bounds. And caitsthes liked to play with their food . . .

But there must have been more left of Tobry than it seemed, for he managed to contain the caitsthe and prevented it from emerging. The blood retreated from his face, leaving him waxen and corpse-like. The racing pulse slowed and faded, the rigid muscles relaxed until his flesh appeared to sag. His shoulders drooped; he looked as though he could barely stand up.

"Bein' a shifter burns you up," said Rannilt.

She had remembered Rix and Tobry talking about their first encounter with a caitsthe. Rix had finally killed the hungry beast by forcing it to keep shifting between caitsthe and man until its bodily processes consumed so much of its own flesh that its heart had failed.

"You're starvin', but with a broken arm you can't catch anythin' to eat. But I can." She met his eyes and drew his gaze sideways to the pond. "I could catch you a fish."

He frowned at her, then lurched over to a small boulder and squatted behind it. Rannilt could still see his head and shoulders, and half of his chest, but perhaps he felt it was safer putting that small barrier between her and the beast.

She edged towards the pond, maintaining eye contact and making no sudden movements. Rannilt took off the little canvas pack in which she hoarded all her possessions, plus every useful thing she came across that didn't specifically belong to one of her friends. She did not think of it as stealing; to an orphaned slave child, pilfering and hoarding were necessary for survival.

She extracted a coil of heavy, waxed thread attached to a small fishing hook. She had stolen it from one of the army cooks. Rannilt tied one end of the thread to a small stick, baited the hook with a yellow, squirming grub she picked out of a rotten log, paid out a length of line and tossed the hook into the water.

Tobry's eyes were on her hands and he was slavering again. She drew the line gently through the water and out. The bait had not been touched. She tossed it in again. And again, prepared to do it all day if she had to. A slave girl learned patience at her mother's breast.

On the fiftieth cast, or thereabouts, she felt a tugging resistance on the line and knew she had caught something. She worked it in, careful not to break the line. Her catch was a freshwater crayfish as long as her forearm, with heavy bluish claws and a rainbow of colours along each side.

As Rannilt drew it from the water Tobry's yellow eyes lit up and he began to quiver, then drool, behind his rock. She watched him with one eye while she studied the crayfish with the other. It had not taken the hook but was clinging to the grub and the line. She worked out how to catch it safely, by the back of the head behind its claws, and pulled it free.

Tobry rose slowly, eyes fixed on the crayfish, and she knew he was going to rush her and snatch it. If he did, the beast might emerge. She could not allow that.

As he was about to spring she held up her hand. "*No!*" she said sharply, commandingly.

He stopped, straining forward like a leashed dog, all his attention fixed on the food. His gaze travelled to her hand, then to her face. The fierce gaze of his yellow eyes softened and he made a yearning movement towards her, which she chose to interpret as *Please?*

Should she toss him the crayfish? No. She wasn't going to treat him like an animal. Rannilt took a step towards him, then another, holding up the crayfish. He tensed, clearly tempted to leap at her and snatch it. She held up her hand again, waited until some of the tension drained out of him, and took another step. And another, and so it went on, a minute for each step.

A small layer of the honeycomb rock outcropped a few feet ahead. Still holding his gaze, she set the crayfish down on top and stepped back. One, two, three steps. She lowered her hand. The crayfish scuttled for the edge. Tobry sprang eight feet, caught it in his good hand and tore into it with his teeth, cramming it into his mouth the way a starving beast would. He spat out pieces of leg and carapace, and took another huge bite.

Her heart sank. There seemed far more beast in him than man. Was it too late? People had said, over and over, that a full-blown shifter could *never* be brought back. But Rannilt could not allow herself to believe that. There had to be a way—there just had to, and she was going to find it.

She caught another two crayfish—first a monster, and then a small one, not much bigger than her hand. He bolted down the big one the same way as the first. The other he ate rather more delicately and she felt a trace of hope. It was just that he had been starving.

Her stomach rumbled. She made a small fire with the driest sticks she could find, then caught a fourth crayfish. Rannilt killed it with a quick stab behind the head and placed it carefully on the coals. After a couple of minutes she turned it over to cook the other side, levered it out of the fire and peeled off the shell.

The tail flesh was gloriously sweet and tender. She ate every skerrick, licked her grubby fingers and wiped them on her pants.

"That was the best dinner I've ever had," she said. "I'm glad we had dinner together, Tobry."

He was still staring at her, the man trapped inside the beast, with a desperate longing.

"I don't know how," she said with quiet self-assurance, "but I know I'm goin' to heal you."

CHAPTER 17

It would soon be dark, the most dangerous time to be alone in an empty wilderness with a mad shifter. Rannilt had no idea how she was going to manage the night. First she had to win his confidence.

She had made another fire in the most sheltered place she could find, in the lee of a small hill between a cluster of rocks. Tobry lay down a long way from her, faced the other way and closed his eyes. Even in sleep he cradled his broken arm.

"How did you break it?" said Rannilt, trying to make her voice soft and calming, speaking slowly and clearly in short sentences. "Was it when the tree fell?"

He jerked at the sound of her voice and his free hand clawed at the air.

"It hurts, doesn't it? The pain is terrible, but I can heal it."

Tobry went very still, slowly turned her way and made a yearning movement, akin to the ones he had made when she had caught the crayfish, though gentler and more poignant. Then he shook his head, and the firelight caught his eyes and made them blaze with yellow.

"You're afraid to come close," said Rannilt. "Afraid you'll hurt me or kill me."

The yellow eyes never left her face. He did not blink.

"I'm not afraid, Tobry. You're stronger than the beast. You would never hurt me. Come here."

He gave a swift, desperate shake of the head.

"Then I'm comin' to you."

Tobry's eyes went wide in alarm and he began to scramble to his feet. She held up her right hand, locked eyes with him and willed him to sit down. It took several minutes but, ever so slowly, he sat.

Rannilt took a step towards him, holding his stare. Another step, then another.

"I'm sittin' down right in front of you. You're gunna hold out yer arm."

Her mouth was dry, her breath rustling in her parched throat, and her knees were shaking. She slowly sat on the cold ground. The fingers of his good hand hooked into claws and he made a growling sound. Her heart fluttered, then raced.

"Stop that," she said hoarsely. "Hold out yer arm."

He went to move the broken arm, cried out in agony, then struck out wildly with the other hand. His knuckles caught her on the chin, hard enough to knock her backwards. She rolled onto her back, temporarily helpless, her eyes flooded with tears from the blow, and instantly the beast seemed to take over. Through the tears she saw him loom over her and reach down towards her unprotected belly.

"Tobry, *no!*" she said desperately.

He froze, mere inches from her. The beast receded and she saw the look in his eyes when he realised that he'd been about to tear her open. He let out a howl of anguish, whirled and, broken arm dangling, stumbled into the night.

"Come back!" she yelled, but he was gone.

Rannilt sat up, rubbing her aching jaw. Should she go after him? No, he was too distressed. Stupid little girl! She had tried to do too much, too soon. She drank some water and ate the tail of another crayfish she had cooked earlier. The fire had died down and she felt the need of its protection, its comfort. She built it up until it blazed three feet high, then wrapped her thin blanket around her and leaned back against a rock.

The stars wheeled. The hours passed. She was tired. Rannilt closed her eyes, telling herself that she must not go to sleep. It wasn't safe here, out in the open wild. She dozed, jerked awake, refuelled the fire and sat down again. And slept.

She came awake with a start, knowing she was not alone; not daring to move because she was in grave danger. The fire had died to a heap of ash-covered coals and it took some time to recall where she was. She was all alone, miles and miles from anywhere, and a big, threatening shape bulked out the darkness a few yards away. As she groped for her knife the shape made a familiar, yearning movement towards her.

Rannilt sat up slowly, thinking it through. Tobry had come back in the night and he had sat there, silently watching over her, making sure she came to no harm. Tears formed under her eyelids. She stirred the coals a little, looked into his shadowed eyes and in the reflected firelight she saw more grey than yellow. It was time. The first healing step had to be now.

She rose, making no sudden moves, went towards him and sank to her knees. He took a deep, shuddering breath.

"Hold out your arm, Tobry."

He extended his broken arm, supporting it at the elbow with his left hand. Rannilt took hold of his right hand. The hairs on his arm stood up; his eyes flashed red-gold and she felt his muscles tense.

"You're not the beast," she said softly. "You're my friend, Tobry, and I'm gunna heal you." She had to keep saying that, as much to convince herself as him.

She could see the injury clearly now. It was a dreadful break, the broken end of the large forearm bone protruding through the skin, and the flesh around it was swollen and inflamed. Rannilt did not start there—healing was a methodical art and before she began she had to know the full extent of his injury, major and minor. She began to trace the bones of the limb with her fingertips, beginning with his fingers and moving up his hand.

His sinews stood out and he growled. She paused for a second, then continued across his wrist and up the small bone of his arm, slowly and carefully. The flesh was hot and swollen; this bone must be broken as well. Yes, right here.

She moved his two forearms side by side, comparing the length. The broken forearm was a good inch shorter. Her stomach clenched.

She looked up into his eyes. "I've got to pull your arm straight so I can line up the broken bones. It's gunna hurt, Tobry. It's gunna hurt lots."

That much pain could make him shift involuntarily, his body choosing to take the best way out. When a caitsthe shifted from man to beast, the change normally healed most injuries, even major ones.

She wondered why it hadn't worked before; perhaps the bones had been too badly out of alignment, but next time—

"You *mustn't* shift ... Tobry." She had to remember to use his name every time, to reinforce her message. "You got to stay yourself, all right?"

The way he stared at her was making her uncomfortable. His hair was standing up and his muscles were as rigid as wood. She could not tell if she were getting through to him. Dare she go on? She had to.

"Tobry?" Her voice sounded higher than usual—squeaky-shrill. She told herself to calm down.

He lowered his eyes. Did that mean he agreed, or was he trying to hide his intentions? She had to take it as the former.

After taking hold of his right wrist with both hands, she closed her eyes and allowed her healing gift to sense out the muscles, bones, veins and sinews. Tobry was not a big man but he had always been strong and wiry, and the shifter curse had made him trebly strong. It would take all her strength to pull the bones back into position. More strength than a ten-year-old girl could employ sitting on the ground.

Rannilt kicked off her sandals and pressed her grubby little feet against his chest. He looked down at them in surprise. Taking a firm grip, she leaned back and pulled steadily.

He shrieked, backhanded her aside and convulsed. His eyes began to change shape; his fingernails were extending and turning into claws.

"No!" she shrieked. "Tobry, stop! Come back!"

Heedless of the danger she threw herself at him, wrapping her thin arms around his chest and holding him desperately. He let out a deep, rumbling growl; she could feel it vibrating through the wall of his chest. His jaw was oddly elongated already, the rigid muscles strong enough to bite through the back of her neck; the front teeth were like cat teeth. And he was hot, almost too hot to touch.

"Tobry, come back! It's me, Rannilt. Come back to me!"

She was losing hope that he could. Few people had fought the shifter curse for as long as he had, and no one had ever beaten it. She hugged him more tightly, shaking him.

"Tobry," she wailed. "Help me! *I need you.*"

She felt a shock pass through him, as if the shifting process had arrested. He removed her arms from around him, sat her down, tilted her chin up and peered into her eyes. His cat-like jaw worked as he struggled to shape the unfamiliar muscles for human speech.

"Need? *Me?*" he forced out.

"Mama died when I was three," said Rannilt in a little, aching voice. "A great lump grew in her belly and she died right beside me, of a wastin' disease. It ate her up, turned her to bone and skin."

Tobry made a pained noise, deep in his throat.

"She was in a fever, that last night," said Rannilt. "Mama was beggin' me to save her."

He let out a whimper.

"'Help me, Rannilt. Please, help me,'" Rannilt said in a frail, aching woman's voice.

"'I'll save you, Mama.'" Now she used a little girl's piping voice.

"I laid my hands on Mama and tried to heal her." Rannilt looked up at Tobry. "Lots of us Pale have the healin' gift, you know. I was sure if I tried hard enough, *if I wanted it enough*, I could save her. I tried so hard, so very, very hard, but she died anyway. I was just a little kid. I didn't know nothin' about healin'.

"I so wanted to heal, Tobry. I practised it every night after that, but it never worked. Never once, 'til the time Tali dropped that sunstone down the shaft at Cython and it smashed, and some great power burst out of it and knocked all the enemy unconscious. It knocked me out too, though not the other Pale."

He made a questioning sound.

"I don't know who my Papa was," said Rannilt. "But the burst of power unlocked my magery, and my healin' gift. You remember the golden light that used to flood from my fingers, don't you? I healed lots of things with it."

His jaw didn't look quite so cat-like now. He made a purring sound. Rannilt took it to mean that he remembered.

"When wicked old Lyf attacked us in his caverns, he tried to rob away my gift, but all he got was my magery. Tali kept sayin' that Lyf stole my healin' gift, but he couldn't get near it. It hurt him when he tried to touch it."

Rannilt smiled at the memory. Then the smile faded and she held out her bony, twisted hands. "So you see, I got to heal you, Tobry. I just got to. Give me your arm."

He extended his broken arm and she took hold of his wrist as before.

"It's gunna hurt," she said. "It's gunna hurt bad and the shifter is gunna try and get out, but you got to stop it."

Again that questioning note.

"The shifter can heal your arm, Tobry, but it won't heal the pain in your head. Shifter don't want to heal itself."

Tobry bared his teeth, closed his eyes for a moment, opened them and stared at her. The claw-like nails slowly reverted to human fingernails, the reddish fur on his arms thinned and turned pale brown. He was no longer radiating that scorching shifter heat. For the moment, the man was in control.

Her healer's gift sensed out the structure of his bones and tissues, the shape of the breaks, and what she needed to do to align the bones. She put her feet in the middle of his chest again and pulled steadily on his forearm.

He gasped and again began to shift.

"You're in charge," said Rannilt, deadly afraid but trying to sound calm and in control. "*You*, Tobry. Not the shifter."

The shifting stopped, though he was still resisting her. She kept pulling his forearm, overcoming the resistance of his contracted muscles. When she saw in her mind's eye that the broken bones no longer overlapped, she gave a couple of little twists that pulled the ragged ends into place. Rannilt wiggled his forearm back and forth until she knew that the breaks were in good alignment, then took his left hand and clamped it onto his right arm, over the break.

"Hold it. Don't let it move."

She bound two straight sticks to his forearm with strips of cloth to make a splint, then slid her fingers around the inflamed area above the broken bones.

"Anyone who cares can do what I just done," she said. "This is the hard bit—the healin' bit. The best bit."

She began to hum softly, tunelessly. A soothing golden light lined her fingers, growing and spreading until all her body was enveloped in it and rays burst out in all directions to light up the surrounding darkness. Rannilt could feel the warmth radiating from her fingers, passing through Tobry's inflamed muscles to the broken bones. Stimulating them to rejoin.

"It won't get better straight away," she said. "Only a master healer can do that. But the bones will heal in a few days, not a few weeks. And they'll be stronger than before."

As the minutes passed, it became harder and harder to sustain the golden light and the healing power that came with it. Her head drooped. She was exhausted. Her arms grew heavy and her fingers ached where the slave girls had broken them, years ago. But she was healing her friend, who really needed her help, and she wasn't giving up.

Rannilt felt the inflammation subsiding under her fingers. She sensed fibres stretching across the rejoined ends of bone, forming a structure on which new bone would grow. She felt the liquid rush and the warmth as the blood flow increased through a network of new blood vessels.

She swayed and almost fell over. It took all the strength she had left to remain sitting up, to finish the healing. Then, suddenly it was done. Her fingers slid away and the next thing she knew she was lying on the ground beside the fire, with Tobry looking down at her anxiously.

"Healin' hurts," said Rannilt. "But it's a good hurt." She smiled dreamily. "So hungry . . . "

Someone was shaking her, trying to wake her. Rannilt roused sluggishly. Tobry was kneeling beside her, holding out a small piece of crayfish flesh. She was too weak to sit up. He pressed the flesh to her lips. She ate it and felt a little better.

Rannilt beamed at him and sat up. He was looking at her expectantly.

"I've got to heal you three ways," she said. "The first way, the normal way, is healin' infections, wounds and broken bones. That's not so hard." She paused.

"But healin' the mind of a mad—" She corrected herself hastily, "Of a shifter . . . that's gunna be tricky. I don't even know how to start. But I'll work it out . . . "

He offered her another piece of crayfish. She took it absently.

"The last healin' is the hardest of all," said Rannilt. "Everyone says a full-blown shifter can never be turned back to a normal man or woman. They say the shifter curse can't be broken."

She looked up at Tobry. "But I'm gunna find a way."

Without any warning, Tobry picked up Rannilt, heaved her over his shoulder and bolted to the east, running tirelessly at a speed no normal, fully human man could have matched.

He kept running for hours, until they reached a landscape of jagged, black slate hills Rannilt had never seen before. He went back and forth until he found the triangular entrance to a cave, then carried her underground, as if into his shifter lair.

CHAPTER 18

As the survivors of Lyf's army retreated south, leaving sixteen thousand dead or dying on the battlefield, he sat in his command wagon, tearing a book to tiny shreds. His personal victory over Grandys, sweet though it had been, could never make up for his army's disastrous defeat.

"How did he do it?" Lyf raged. "It wasn't possible."

The blood was roaring through his veins and he felt a suicidal urge to turn back and charge the enemy with the men he had left, even at the risk of ending it all. Grandys would have done so. He would never have capitulated the way Lyf's troops had, and it burned him.

Moley Gryle sat at the other end of the wagon, her head bent as if baring her neck to the sword. Since the astonishing moment when she had saved him with that reversal spell, she had not spoken. Forbidden magery required the death penalty and not even the king was above the law. So why had he held back from enforcing it?

"That black pyramid was a magical shield—" said Errek's shade.

"I know!" Lyf snapped. "But how did Grandys make the shield work? How can magery neutralise our alchymical weapons? They're entirely different things."

"Herovian magery is designed for war," said Errek, "while our king-magery was entirely devoted to healing . . . at least, until you debauched it by creating shifters, and using it in other dire and destructive ways."

Errek never tired of pointing out Lyf's failings. "Even so—" said Lyf, "How—?"

"Powerful magery can stop a man's heart. Unlock a lock. Set wet wood alight. Why shouldn't it be able to stop a bombast from exploding?"

"One bombast, or two," conceded Lyf. "But magery must be focused precisely on the object it is to affect. How can it be used to blanket a battlefield—to smother every one of a hundred bombasts, a thousand grenadoes, ten thousand fire-flitters and countless more of our myriad weapons of war? *Not one of them* worked, Errek."

"I don't know. The Five Heroes linked their individual gifts, and that's never been done before. Never before have magians been able to join together without undermining the source of their power."

"I've got to strike back," said Lyf. "If I can't hurt Grandys, my people will lose faith in me." He turned to Moley Gryle, who was staring out at the dry grassland, though he did not think she was seeing it. "Moley?"

"I counsel caution," said Errek. "Grandys—"

"Moley?" snapped Lyf.

She started. "Yes, Lord King?"

"Advise me."

"His . . . his support is strongest in the north," she said in a whisper. "He's garrisoned half a dozen fortresses in Lakeland and Fennery, and Herovians are streaming out of the mountains to join his army."

"My spies tell me his garrisons are weak," said Lyf. "He brought most of his troops south, and he'll need to call more down to replace his casualties before he attacks again. He can't touch Caulderon with the numbers he has."

"That's what you said about your mighty army," said Errek.

"It's a different matter attacking a great, fortified city. I don't rely on chymical weapons to defend Caulderon—I've got twenty thousand men behind strong defences. Not even Grandys could take and hold the city with less than forty thousand."

"Why would he want to hold it," said Errek, "when you've purged Caulderon of his people? His Promised Realm will be pure of blood; the only outsiders in Herovia will be slaves."

"The—the best way to strike at him right now is by destroying his fortresses, Lord King," said Moley Gryle.

"I agree," said Lyf. "I'll send five thousand men west tonight, under cover of darkness, with orders to sweep north through the western forests, then attack his strongest fortresses and raze them. Then they'll return to safety down the eastern side of Lake Fumerous, to Caulderon."

"Grandys will strike back the moment he hears," said Errek.

"Let him try. I've a retreat prepared at Mulclast, between the three Vomits."

"Sounds like a dangerous place to hide," said Errek.

"But impregnable. It's a triangle of high ground in a volcanic wasteland, the only way in is via three narrow passes and there's no drinking water save at Mulclast itself. It's a perfect trap, and if Grandys is desperate enough to put his head in, I'll cut it off."

Lyf went out, gave the orders and returned. His army continued south towards the greatest and most unstable volcano in the land, the Red Vomit. That evening he sent his spies out to kill all Grandys' scouts, ostensibly as revenge for Grandys killing Lyf's scouts before the battle. Once it was done Lyf saw off his strike force and continued south.

"Happy now?" said Errek at dawn the following day. "Feel you've struck a great blow against the enemy?"

The Red Vomit towered above them, fourteen thousand feet high, erupting gentle billows of ash and steam. The pass to Mulclast lay a couple of miles to the east and there was no sign of pursuit.

Lyf scowled. "What would you have me do?"

"Leave war to your generals. Do your *primary* duty."

"If I give up the leadership now, I'll look like a failure."

"The only thing that matters is that the land be healed. Assuming you can," Errek said pointedly.

Lyf controlled his face with an effort. Did Errek know his secret fear, that he was an impotent king? He dismissed the shade, put the army under the command of General Hramm and sent it across the pass to Mulclast.

Once it was out of sight, Lyf, Moley Gryle and the nine surviving men of Lyf's King's Guard slipped into an ancient lava tunnel on the western side of the Red Vomit. They led the horses in and tethered them at a small, iron-stained spring shaped like a triangular bathtub.

"Wait here," said Lyf to his Guard, and headed down the steep lava tunnel.

Moley Gryle went after him. Once they were around a bend, out of sight and earshot, she said anxiously, "Lord King, you can't go down into the quaking depths alone."

"I'll have Errek with me."

"He's just a figment, Lord King, and you're on crutches. What if you fall on the steep slope and knock yourself out? He'll vanish."

"Errek?" said Lyf. "Come forth."

The faded shade appeared in a glowing oval above Lyf's head. He drew power, pointed at the shade and said, "Errek First-King, rise from the Abysm!"

The air crackled and Lyf fell onto his back, gasping. Sparks rained down, a distant wind howled, then the shade let out a fading wail and collapsed in on itself, consumed by the spell, leaving only a small, faintly glowing yellow oval where it had been.

Moley Gryle helped Lyf to sit up. Nothing happened for a minute or two, and he began to doubt the quality of his magery. Then the yellow oval expanded as though it was being stretched from the other side, and the wrythen of an ancient, hoary old king stepped through into the air. He was wispy, frail and scarcely more solid than he had been as a shade, though his faded blue eyes had a fierce glow Lyf had not seen before.

"Begone, child," Errek said to Moley Gryle. "This is no place for youth."

She stumbled up the tunnel, head down like a condemned criminal. Lyf levered himself down the uneven slope on his crutches. Errek drifted through the air beside him. The lower part of the

tunnel was deeply buried beneath the flank of the Red Vomit and
no one knew how far it went, or how deep. Warm air drifted up past
them, scented with salt and sulphur and hot rock.

"So," said Errek to Lyf, after several minutes.

"You know who I am?" said Lyf.

"I may have been dead ten millennia, but I've never passed
beyond the Lower Gate."

"Why not?"

"Niggling worries. And a need to keep watch over my land, powerless though I was to aid it."

"You must have had some bitter moments in that time."

"Watching you balls things up, you mean?"

Lyf flushed. "That's not what I meant."

"I also know why you've had the damned impertinence to drag
me from my eternal rest."

Errek, the wrythen of the first and greatest king of all, had been
renowned not only as a hero, a scholar and the incomparable magian
who had invented king-magery, but also as a good man and a just
ruler. Before his accomplishments, Lyf's greatest successes seemed
trivial, and his failings monumental.

"What are you going to do about your adjutant?" said Errek.

"Moley broke the prohibition and used forbidden magery. She has
to die."

"Then why is she still alive?"

"She . . . saved my life," said Lyf. "And dealt Grandys a blow he
won't soon recover from . . . and she's an *intuit*, the best I've ever
known."

"She's also a beautiful young woman and you like her very
much."

"Not the way you're thinking," Lyf said hastily. "She's a friend;
the best I can remember."

"In that case, why do you torment her so?"

"What?"

"Moley Gryle knows she must die, yet you haven't carried out the
sentence, or even said anything about your intentions. That's cruel,
Lyf. Either execute her, or pardon her."

"The prohibition is our First Law—"

"I know!" Lyf snapped. "I wrote the damned law . . . and I've often wished I hadn't."

"What would you do?"

"Am I king now?"

Lyf's fist clenched around a pile of gravel. "No, of course not."

"Then act like the king you are. Either change the law, or turn a blind eye to it. Now get to the reason you raised me."

"The balance has tilted too far," said Lyf. "I don't know how the land can be healed—or even *if* it can."

"What do you want to know?"

"What the Engine really is."

"Is that why you've brought me down here? To be close to the Engine?"

"It's miles away, deep below Mulclast."

"I know where it is," said Errek. "Or did you hope I might be able to tilt the balance, as I did back at the beginning?"

"I didn't even *hope* you could do that," said Lyf. "I know how constrained the powers of a wrythen are. Besides—"

"King-magery has passed on."

"Passed on down the ages from you, *until I lost it*," said Lyf. "And I don't know how to get it back."

"What do you want from me?"

"Why is the Engine causing such havoc? And how did it come to be?"

After a long pause, Errek said, "I can't tell you."

"Why not?"

"My death was so traumatic that my memories of the previous months were lost. Anything else?"

"To recover king-magery, I need the master pearl. But if I do get king-magery back, can I use it to heal the land?"

"You used it before Grandys killed you. Why wouldn't you be able to use it now?"

The question had an accusatory ring, as if Errek knew what was troubling Lyf. He did not reply at once, for this was his greatest worry and one he had, hitherto, kept to himself. But keeping it back from Errek would defeat the purpose of raising him.

"I've lost the ability to heal people," said Lyf.

"When did you lose it?"

"I first noticed it was gone after the peace conference at Glimmering—"

"When Grandys attacked you and you ran for your life?"

Lyf flushed like an errant schoolboy. "Could he have stolen my gift?"

"From what I know of him," said Errek, "it would be uncharacteristic. That all?"

"What if I can't heal the land either?" Lyf said softly, for he could scarcely bear to utter the words aloud. "Has my life's work been a failure? Are our present troubles all my fault—?"

"Because you spent two thousand years as a wrythen doing things that were doomed to fail?"

"How do you mean?"

"Instead of preparing for the future, you devoted your energy to two futile projects: trying to restore your people to a vanished past; and avenging your own betrayal."

"Was I wrong to want to restore my people?" said Lyf.

"The clock can't be turned back. You could have helped to build a new nation from the ashes. That would have been a worthy project."

"I didn't call you up from the dead to hector me about my mistakes," snapped Lyf.

"What an ill-mannered fellow you are," said Errek, crushingly. "I see no hope for you."

Again the blood rushed to Lyf's face, scalding his cheeks. He bent his head. "I'm sorry. I've been an utter fool. I can't—"

"Abasement has no more appeal than arrogance."

"I don't know what to do," said Lyf humbly. "Will you advise me?"

"Very well," said Errek. "Don't take Grandys on directly until you have king-magery. Once you do, strike with everything you have and finish him."

"And in the meantime?"

"Find ways to further undermine his confidence in Maloch, and in himself."

"I'll put Moley Gryle to work on it at once."

"Then you do plan to save her?"

"Yes; she's the best asset I have—apart from you."

"In time she'll prove more important than me. One more thing, and it's urgent."

"What's that?"

"Grandys has captured Thalalie vi Torgrist and sent her north to one of his fortresses. Once he cuts out the master pearl, Cython's fate will hang in the balance."

Lyf sat down abruptly and wiped his brow. "Which fortress?"

"You'll have to find out."

"And then? What should I do?"

"Take her back, of course."

"From Grandys' own fortress?"

"Yes. You must act swiftly, and with exquisite care. If you fail, or if Tali dies, Cython loses."

CHAPTER 19

Mad Wil screamed for ten hours, non-stop. By that time his throat was bleeding and his larynx was so swollen that he could make no sound save a rasping gasp. In his agony, he kept it up for another two hours before the Engine's luminous radiance shut down his overheated brain.

The ground continued to heave, for he had grossly interfered with the Engine at the heart of the world, and that had tilted the balance to the brink of disaster. Quakes had shaken the land from north to south, east to west. They had sent the whole side of a mountain thundering down into a valley far below, burying the town of Quivering a hundred feet deep and wiping twenty-nine villages, three manors and an abandoned Cythian temple off the map.

They had also cracked the solid lid of the great magma chamber, eleven miles below the surface, that fed the Red Vomit. With irresistible force, searing gases and scalding water began to lever the crack apart, seeking the fastest path to the surface.

Soon, soon.

Wil should have died long ago, for the infernal radiance from the Engine had blistered him like a roast chicken, but perhaps the alkoyl he had long been addicted to had counteracted the effects of the radiance on his flesh. Or perhaps he was being saved for a greater purpose.

Three days later he roused, tried to sit up, and screamed. His muscles had been baked to knotted strings and his skin was a thick layer of char beneath which the sinews stood out like cords.

He levered himself to the stubs of his feet. He was a blackened, twisted mess of scar tissue, barely human. Wil turned his empty eye sockets towards the Engine and he could *sense* the heat shimmering off it. The level of the water was lower now, because of what he had done, and the Engine was much hotter, but he could no longer feel it—he was quite refractory now.

He stretched this way and that until he could move more freely, then groped around him. The platina bucket lay on the tunnel floor where he had dropped it. The alkoyl it had held was gone; it had eaten a yellow-rimmed hole down through the solid stone, further than he could reach.

No, a dribble of alkoyl remained in the bucket. How he longed for it, and the bliss that sniffing always gave him. He put his head in the bucket and took a deep whiff. His muscles convulsed involuntarily, hurling him backwards, and a piercing pain sheared through his skull. His stomach heaved but it was empty.

Wil let out a howl of frustration, then picked himself up, crawled back to the bucket and took another careful sniff. Again his body hurled him backwards. His face was swelling and he felt spots erupting on his charred cheeks. He had become allergic to the one good thing in his life. He couldn't touch alkoyl, yet he couldn't bear to be without it.

He lay on the floor and screamed. Everything in his life had gone bad and now he was denied the one solace he had left.

"Not fair!" he shrieked, pounding the stone until pieces of charred skin flaked away. "All Wil ever wanted was to be special. *To matter*."

After he had been the first to read Lyf's iron book, *The Consolation of Vengeance*, Wil *had* been special. But later the Matriarchs had demanded he tell them about *the one*—the slave girl he had seen in that *shillilar*, or foreseeing, after he'd read the book. The golden-haired little slave girl called Tali who had to die to prevent her from changing the world.

Wil couldn't let them kill that little girl. He just couldn't. She was going to change the ending of the book and he had to know how the story ended. The *true* story. He loved stories more than anything.

So Wil had lied to the Matriarchs. He had told them that the girl he'd seen in his *shillilar* had black hair and olive skin, and that her mother had cleaned out the effluxor sumps. The Matriarchs had immediately rounded up all the little slave girls of the right age who fitted the description, and put them to death in front of Wil, to make sure they'd got the right one. *The one*.

But he had fooled the Matriarchs. Though the pain had been terrible, he hadn't given Tali away. He still had nightmares about that day.

"I didn't want to hurt anyone!" he screeched.

"Yes, you did," said the jeering, mocking part of himself. "You developed a taste for death when you witnessed those little girls being put down, didn't you, Wil?"

"Didn't, didn't!" wept Wil.

"Before each child was slain the Matriarchs asked you the same question: *Are you sure these are the right girls?* You had the choice to save each girl, or condemn her. And each time, *thirty-nine times*, you condemned an innocent little girl. You're the real murderer, Wil."

"It wasn't my fault! The Matriarchs did it, not me."

"You condemned those black-haired girls. You, who had always been powerless, loved having the power of life and death over children far more helpless than yourself. You're a killer, Wil, and you love it."

"Wil *doesn't*!" he cried. "Wil hates it."

Yet for months now, when there was no other way to relieve his pain, he would creep the miles along the Hellish Conduit and up into Cython, and there he would seek out one of the Pale, man or woman, it didn't matter, and strangle them.

He wanted to go to Cython now.

Someone had to pay.

CHAPTER 20

Glynnie was fifty yards away, coming back through the lines of sleeping men, when Libbens knocked Rix down and Krebb and Grasbee dragged him away to court martial him. But any court martial of theirs would be mere lip service. She had only minutes to save him.

She followed Libbens until she knew where they were taking Rix, then raced through the dimly lit camp to Holm's tent.

"Holm?" she hissed. "Holm, wake up!"

He was a still shape in the darkness. Had they killed him already? No, he was deeply asleep. She heaved him over onto his back.

"Holm!"

He woke abruptly. A hand clamped onto her wrist and twisted hard.

She yelped in pain. "It's me, Glynnie!"

He sat up. "What's the matter?"

"The generals have taken Rix. They're going to court martial him, then kill him."

Holm held his head between his hands, then shook it. "Where?"

"The senior officers' tent."

"Where's Jackery?"

"Asleep, I'd say."

"He's a good man. Find him and send him there. Go!"

Glynnie raced away. With the enemy so near, and the need for instant readiness, the soldiers were in their bedrolls on the ground, fully dressed. Jackery's squad was over on the east side, but so were another thousand men.

She reached the eastern edge of the camp, gasping for breath, and looked around.

"Jackery?" she said quietly.

No answer. "Jackery!"

"Piss off!" said a sleepy voice, not far away. "We're trying to sleep."

How long would they allow for the court martial? There might only be ten minutes before those gutless scum took Rix from her forever. She felt a scything pain in her chest.

"Where's Sergeant Jackery?" she yelled.

"Eastern corner. Go away!"

Glynnie ran along the rows, tripped over a man out of line, recovered, flailing wildly, then stepped on another man's belly in the dark. He sat up, roaring in pain and fright.

"Sorry," she panted.

She leapt over another man and ran on. What were they doing now? Beating Rix to a pulp? Or were they halfway through the "court martial"? They could not afford to take long. When the troops were woken, Rix had to be dead, executed as a traitor, so there would be no choice but to accept the authority of the rebels.

"Sergeant Jackery," she yelled. "Sergeant Jackery?"

"Who wants me?" said a deep voice only yards away.

She ran to him, clutched at him desperately, then leapt backwards, flushing in the dark. She barely knew the man.

"It's Glynnie! Libbens has taken Rix and they're going to kill him any minute."

"Where?" He was already out of his bedroll and pulling his boots on.

"Senior officers' tent. Holm—Holm said to go straight there."

"You armed?" said Jackery.

She felt her belt sheath. "Yes."

"Run and find out what's going on. Don't let them see you. We'll be two minutes." He turned away, rousing his men.

Glynnie bolted through the ranks towards the senior officers' tent, which stood apart from the other tents and wagons, then stopped. Libbens had guards around the tent, two at the front and two at the back. She fought down an attack of panic and tried to think. If Holm and Jackery planned to storm the tent, the sentries would warn the traitors inside and they would kill Rix.

The front and right side were well lit by lanterns. The shadows were deepest on the far left corner. She slipped across, went down on her belly and wormed her way to the corner of the tent. Could she collapse it on them? No, it was too big and she would never get to the pegs at the front without being seen. She eased up the corner of the tent and put her head in.

Grasbee, Krebb and Libbens were inside with their backs to her. Four guards were up near the entrance and another soldier stood to the right, leaning on the handle of an axe. The executioner. Where was Rix? Surely not dead already? Pain tightened to a fist in her chest; pain that paralysed her for a few seconds.

Libbens swung his right arm; she heard a thump, a groan. Libbens moved and she saw Rix, bound hand and foot to the central tent pole. His face was so bruised and swollen he was barely recognisable. They must have beaten him constantly since they took him. His shirt had been torn open and she saw bruises on his chest, too. Why did they hate him so much?

But perhaps it was lucky they wanted to make him suffer before he died, otherwise they could have executed him by now.

"How your parents used to lord it over us from your palace," spat Krebb. "Not so lordly now, are you, Ricinus? How does it feel?"

"You won't fight Grandys because you're in thrall to him, you cowardly swine," said Libbens, punching Rix in the kidneys. "You're just as treacherous as your mother, just as foul as your father."

Rix groaned and dribbled blood.

Grasbee heaved at the steel gauntlet Rix wore over his dead hand, wrenched it off and held up Rix's arm. His dead, grey hand pointed straight up.

"How can a man's severed hand be put back save by the foulest sorcery? It can only be the same sorcery that allowed Grandys and his cronies to come back from the dead."

"Haven't got a magical bone in my body," gasped Rix.

"You won't have an unbroken bone when we've finished with you, you stinking, treacherous mongrel."

They attacked him again, and every blow Rix took was a blow to

Glynnie's own heart. They wanted to batter him to pulp before they killed him, and there was nothing she could do to stop them. Where were Holm and Jackery? She put her head out but there was no sign nor sound of them.

What if they had been taken as well? What if it was all up to her? Glynnie drew her knife. One inexperienced girl against eight tough soldiers could only end one way, but if she was Rix's only hope she had to try.

Libbens slammed the steel gauntlet into the side of Rix's head, breaking the skin in three places and leaving knuckle marks on his cheek.

"You wore the cursed sword," said Libbens. "You carried it to the edge of the Abysm, where you attempted to raise Grandys from the dead. You would have succeeded had your friends not stopped you."

"But you kept on," said Krebb. "You worked a sorcerous painting of your master, Grandys, on the wall of your great-aunt's observatory at Fortress Garramide. The place where the foul sword had lain hidden for nearly two thousand years."

"The very fortress Grandys built for his only child," said Grasbee. "The daughter you're directly descended from, you stinking Herovian bastard."

"Not Herovian," Rix slurred. "Grandys—impotent. Daughter—adopted."

"Liar!" Grasbee struck him again, and again.

"You swore to Grandys publicly," said Libbens. "You served him and slaughtered our people for him."

Glynnie could not bear to witness any more. She pulled her head out, checked on the guards again and crept to the edge of the lighted area. There was still no sign of Holm or Jackery. What if he had decided it was too risky?

She was afraid to leave the area in case they killed Rix. She scanned the darkness. The camp was silent save for the sounds of repeated blows and an occasional groan from Rix. No, she caught a movement in the dark, down to her left. She slipped across. It was Holm, carrying a canvas bag, and with half a dozen troops close by. Jackery was behind him with another four men.

"Is that *all*?" Glynnie whispered.

"It's all we could get in haste." Holm checked the layout of the guards. Jackery disappeared in the darkness to her left.

"But Libbens, Grasbee and Krebb were all *sacked*," said Glynnie. "Rix is the rightful commander and they're rebelling on the battlefield. That's about the worst crime there is. The whole army should be up in arms about it."

"Libbens has spread a cunning lie—that Rix gained command by sorcery and murder. So if his command is illegitimate, leadership automatically reverts to the former generals. They've also spread another lie that he's still Grandys' man—that Rix is planning on leading our army into Grandys' trap so he can butcher every one of them."

Glynnie's fury rose until it was choking her. "The stinking, lousy mongrels. But who would believe that?"

"The men in the ranks have been fed a diet of propaganda for months, and they all know House Ricinus's foul reputation. Why wouldn't they tar Rix with the same brush? Enough talk." Jackery returned. "Jackery, you know what to do?"

"Burst in through the door and get Rix out," said Jackery.

"There's eight armed men inside," said Glynnie. "The moment you go through the entrance, they'll kill Rix."

"I picked up some unused Cythonian weapons from the battlefield," said Holm, hefting the bag.

"But they'll kill Rix—"

"They're not killing weapons; they just disable." He pulled a small helm out of his bag. It was an arrangement of overlapping strips of metal, with small pink crystals embedded at the intersections. He put it on Glynnie's head and buckled the chin strap. "This'll protect you from the worst of the effects . . . I hope."

"All right," she said as steadily as she could. "What's the plan?"

"First we have to take down the four outside guards, then I chuck these in—"

"How do we take down the guards?" said Glynnie.

"You and I have to kill the two sentries at the rear. The moment we do, we signal Jackery. He and his men will attack from the front, cut the guards down and storm the entrance. We'll cut our way in from the back."

"We have to kill the sentries?"

"Yes."

Glynnie studied her knife. "I can't fight a guard who's armed with a sword."

"We're not fighting—*just killing*."

"Killing!" she squeaked.

"Shh! The best way," said Holm with a grimace, for she knew how he hated violence, "at least the quietest way is to cut their throats from behind. But you're not tall enough to be sure of cutting a guard's throat, so you'll have to stab your man in the back."

Holm turned away and began whispering to Jackery, who gave his men quiet orders. They began taking small round objects out of the canvas bag.

"Go!" Holm said, pushing Glynnie away.

She crept through the dark towards the corner of the tent where she had been before, shuddering. How could she do it?

She had killed once before, several months ago. It had been in a desperate fight with Blathy, the terrible wife of the dead bandit Arkyz Leatherhead, during the mutiny at Garramide. But that had been self-defence. Blathy had been out to kill Glynnie and Rix, and she had partly caused her own death by running onto Rix's sword when Glynnie thrust it out.

Stabbing a man in the back was entirely different; it was a black act. No, it was murder, and a foul kind of murder at that. Could she do it? It was either the sentry's life or Rix's, and he was her man. He was also the only man with a hope of saving everyone from Axil Grandys.

She located her target—the man she had to murder. He was pacing in the shadows a few yards from the back corner of the tent. She could not see Holm's guard; he must be around the next corner.

Glynnie held out the knife in front of her. She had sharpened it this morning and could have shaved the skin off a ripe tomato with it. But could she murder a man she had never met?

In the long siege of Garramide she had tended dozens of injured and dying men and women. She knew how little effort it took to kill another human being, and precisely where to strike, but it wasn't easy thinking about thrusting the point in through the guard's back, between the ribs and into his heart. Killing was wrong, except in self-defence. And no matter how she tried to rationalise it, she could not convince herself that stabbing a man in the back to save Rix *was* self-defence.

She looked across and Holm was waving urgently at her, gesturing downwards with his thumb. He must have killed his guard; now everything waited on her. Including Rix's life.

It had to be done. She kept her position until the guard turned, then slipped in behind him and came up close.

Now, do it *now*!

Glynnie hesitated, then imagined Rix's bloody, battered face and the executioner waiting inside. She must not hesitate.

She took a quick step forward, selected her target and thrust hard. The knife struck a rib, glancingly. The guard jerked; she put her weight behind the knife and it went in all the way.

It must have gone straight through his heart because he made a small gurgling sound and toppled forward. The knife she was still holding slid out as he fell on his face.

He was dead. How could taking a man's life be that easy, that quick? That irreversible?

That's it, Glynnie thought. I'm a killer now.

CHAPTER 21

Glynnie did not see Holm signal to Jackery, nor Jackery wave back. She was standing as if paralysed, the bloody knife blade dripping on her boot, when there came a hollow thud from inside, followed by a hissing. The canvas walls bulged out like a blown-up balloon and she made out an angry cry, followed by Libbens' voice.

"Kill the bastard! Take his head clean from his shoulders!"

"I'm not the same as you," she said aloud. "*I'm not!*"

Something else went off with a bang inside the tent and pain speared through her head. She lost sight for a few seconds, swayed and thought she was going to fall, but the sick dizziness passed. There was still no sign of Holm—he must be in there, waiting for her.

Glynnie carved a curving slash down the wall of the tent and squeezed in. The air was full of a peculiar magenta fog, billowing from a stubby red canister on the floor—some kind of Cythonian grenado, she thought, though the fog was not dispersing. It hung in banners and tendrils that did not want to mix with the air.

A second, round yellow grenado on a table was gushing thick white smoke that must have been heavier than air, for it grew ever thicker below hip level and obscured the floor completely. Two of the guards had fallen and were only outlines through the smoke. A third was slumped across a second table, twitching, and the white-eyed Krebb was on his knees. She could not see the fourth guard; the other end of the tent was too thick with red mist and white smoke.

Rix was still bound to the tent pole, his face and chest covered in blood. He was slumped forward as if unconscious, his weight bowing the pole. The executioner was staggering towards him, or trying to, though he kept swinging around to the left as if that leg wasn't working properly. His foot caught on something on the floor—the other guard, Glynnie hoped—and he crashed down and began coughing and choking.

But Grasbee and Libbens were still on their feet. Libbens had tied a cloth around his nose and mouth and was making his way towards Rix from the left. Grasbee was lurching in from the right. They were planning to kill him now.

Where were Jackery and his men? She heard fighting from outside the front of the tent. Libbens' guards must be putting up unexpected resistance, and maybe some of the troops had come to their aid. Holm was supposed to cut his way into the tent from the far side but she couldn't see him either. Had he been caught? Or killed as easily as she had killed her guard?

Rix's life depended on her now—her alone.

A loop of the magenta fog, hanging in the middle air, drifted into her face and the insides of her nose and mouth began to sting, then burn. Her eyes flooded until she could barely see. She rubbed them but it only made the burning sensation worse, and now it was stinging its way down the back of her throat. She could feel her air passages swelling; each breath was harder to take than the previous one.

She had to be quick. Glynnie wiped her eyes on her sleeve and this time it helped. She checked on Libbens and Grasbee. Libbens was the ringleader, the man she ought to bring down first, but he was a huge fellow and he wore a mailed vest with a high collar, so she could neither stab him in the back nor cut his throat. But she couldn't take him on face to face when his sword was four times the length of her knife.

Her foot came down on something that rolled beneath her, turning her ankle. She slipped to one knee and the object came into focus through the smoke—the standard pole Grasbee had thumped Rix with earlier. Libbens had gloated about mounting Rix's head on it after the trial. She picked it up. It was heavy but unwieldy.

Grasbee was closer to her now. Glynnie stumbled after him. She wasn't game to throw the standard like a javelin. If she missed, it would be the end of Rix, and her as well. His broad knees made an inviting target, though. She speared the pointy end of the standard at the back of his right knee with all her strength. He screamed, his knee collapsed, he went down with a crash and she thumped him over the head.

He stayed down.

Libbens swung around, coughing, trying to see through the ever-thickening smoke. He tore off the sodden cloth that had been covering his nose and mouth and wiped his eyes with it. His meaty face was scarlet, tears were flooding from his eyes and both nostrils were running. Glynnie did not feel as bad as he looked—the helm Holm had given her must be doing some good.

He turned towards Rix, swaying from side to side; his sword was dangling from his right hand as if he barely knew it was there, and his body had a peculiar, twitching shudder—whatever the magenta fog was, he was badly affected by it. He looked back, saw Glynnie and she could see the cogs struggling to turn in his brain. What should he do first? Kill Rix and erase the humiliation of his own sacking, or defend himself against her?

He came at her, swinging the long blade with wobbly but deadly menace. Glynnie let out a squawk, thrust the standard at him and buried it an inch deep in his right thigh. He hacked at the shaft with his sword; Glynnie jerked the standard out and speared it at him again.

He duelled with it a couple of times, easily turning it aside, then caught it with his free hand and wrenched it from her grasp. He was immensely strong; bull-like. He tossed it aside and lurched towards her. Blood was running down his thigh, though the wound did not hinder him appreciably.

She could still hear fighting from outside, which meant that she could not rely on Jackery's aid. "Holm!" she screamed.

He did not answer.

She backpedalled, trod on Grasbee's face, overbalanced and crashed backwards into a long trestle table. Glynnie scuttled under it as Libbens swung the sword in a frenzy, left, right, left, his uncontrolled blows carving chunks out of the table top. She tried to shove the table at him but could not budge it.

As she was coming out the other side, she ran head-first into Krebb, who was also on hands and knees, coughing as if to bring up his lungs. He looked up at her blindly, his face covered in tears and his nose and mouth with mucus. Glynnie supposed she must look much the same.

He groped at her face; he couldn't see well enough to recognise her. Libbens came around the other side, still swinging the sword. He raised it above his head and hacked down at her, a mighty blow. She scurried back under the table as Krebb lurched forward and the blade caught him in the back of the neck. He sighed and settled on the ground, his left foot kicking.

Libbens stood looking down at the corpse of his friend, blinking and rubbing the flooding tears out of his eyes.

"Krebb?" he said incredulously. "Krebb?"

Glynnie reached the other end of the table but did not stand up. The white smoke was much thicker at floor level but at least Libbens could not see her. She crawled to Rix, drew her knife and was about to cut his bonds when she saw the executioner, not two yards away. How had she forgotten him?

He was bent over a canvas chair, hanging on to the frame with both hands while he threw up bloody, stringy mucus. He wiped his mouth, saw her, gave a wolfish grin and picked up his axe, which had a blade ten inches across. Heaving it up in one great knotted fist, he swung, not at her, but at Rix.

There wasn't time to think. She hurled her knife. He instinctively swayed backwards, losing hold of the axe, and her knife, which she had aimed at his chest, buried itself to the hilt in his left eye socket.

Glynnie couldn't bear to retrieve it, or to go near him. She grabbed the axe, ran around the tent pole and, carefully wielding the ten-inch blade, cut Rix's leg bonds, then the ropes on his wrists. He fell on his face.

She looked around, struggling to make anything out in the clouds of smoke. A bulky shadow moved a few yards away and she recognised Libbens by the curve of his mailed vest. He was leaning forward, propping himself up with the sword. His whole face was wet and every breath blew slimy bubbles out each nostril.

Glynnie stood over Rix, raised the executioner's axe and caught Libbens' eye.

"Try it," she gasped, for the magenta fog was burning her lungs now, "and I'll bury this axe in your head, all the way down to your kidneys."

Brave words—the axe was so heavy that it was taking all her remaining strength to hold it steady.

"You're just a maidservant," he sneered.

Her arms were aching. She could not hold it up much longer.

"The same maidservant who knocked Axil Grandys down and broke his nose," said Glynnie. "Come on—try me."

Libbens stared at her for a full minute, then evidently decided that it was too risky to take her on in his current state. He sheathed the sword, took the unconscious Grasbee under the arms and dragged him away. One step. Two steps and they disappeared in the fog.

Glynnie could not see the entrance and didn't know which way to go. She was trapped in a foggy circle only a few yards across, with no evidence that the world outside existed. But she had to keep going. She had to get Rix out—the downed soldiers could recover at any time.

She took him under the arms and heaved. He hardly moved; he was twice her weight and it was like trying to drag a carcass of beef. She bent over him and wiped his swollen face.

"Rix?"

He was alive, but did not answer. She checked and saw no sign of life behind her, though she could only see a few yards. If she turned her back, Libbens or one of the guards could kill her as easily as she had killed the sentry.

She slapped Rix's face. "Wake up. I can't get you out of here by myself."

He made a grunting sound. She rolled him onto his belly, then stood over him and heaved under his arms. "Crawl!"

He pulled himself a few inches. She heaved again, until her backbone felt as though it was cracking.

"Crawl!"

He crawled a foot further. A fit of coughing doubled her over. She wiped her streaming eyes, checked behind her and heaved again. Suddenly the skin crawled on the back of her neck. Glynnie whirled, her heart pounding. Was that shadow in the smoke to her left a man? She couldn't be sure. Libbens could be anywhere; he could be creeping up on her from any direction.

One of the guards lay two yards away, twitching. She drew the sword from his sheath, held it out before her in both hands and checked again. Nothing. She spied another prone guard, took his weapon and shoved it out under the side of the tent. She went another yard.

She turned around and could not see Rix. Glynnie ran three steps, stopped and felt along the floor. He was not there. She probed the choking fumes with her foot and kicked the executioner. Judging by the position of the body Rix should be a couple of yards further on. But he wasn't, nor anywhere nearby. Could Libbens have found him so quickly?

Her left foot came down on something hard—the mailed gauntlet Rix wore on his dead hand. She picked it up absently and turned around, wondering what to do. There was more shouting from outside the tent, then the sound of people running, and the tent slowly collapsed from the front. She panicked momentarily as it came down on her head—but after all, it was just one layer of cloth, and she still had the guard's sword. She shoved the point through the canvas, fell forward and she was out in the open, gasping at the fresh, cold air.

"There you are!" said Holm, taking her arm. "I've been trying to find you."

"I've been in the bloody tent," she snapped. "Where *you* were supposed to be. What the hell happened to you?"

"Later!"

"I've got to go back for Rix. I lost—"

"He's here. He crawled out."

"Is he all right?" She looked around frantically.

"More or less."

"Where is he?"

"Gone with Jackery and his men. The troops who remain loyal have to see his face." He tugged on her arm. "Come on."

She allowed him to lead her into the darkness. "What's the matter?"

"Libbens is rounding up a company of soldiers to search the camp. We've got about a minute to escape."

"You mean they've won!"

"Not if we get away with Rix."

He ran through the dark for a hundred yards. Glynnie stumbled after him. Rix was on his horse, tied into the saddle, surrounded by Jackery and a squad of twenty or so troops. She could see more horsemen beyond, mere shadows in the darkness, and hundreds of troops on their feet.

"How did all this happen?" said Glynnie.

"Jackery left half his men behind to rouse out all those loyal to Rix."

Back near the officers' tent, fire flared fifteen feet high, as if someone had lit a bonfire doused with oil. Holm heaved Glynnie into an empty saddle and mounted another horse.

"They're looking for Rix and you," said Jackery. He looked down at her; his white teeth flashed in a grim smile. "Well done. Come on."

He signalled with a partly shuttered lantern. She saw the signal repeated across that corner of the army, then everyone moved at once.

They were a hundred yards away before furious cries from the officers' tent indicated that their escape had been discovered.

"Go!" said Jackery.

They raced into the dark.

"We've only got the clothes on our backs and the gear in our packs," said Holm, "but at least we're alive."

CHAPTER 22

"Two hundred men?" said Rix when he had come around sufficiently to understand what was going on. "That's all I have left?"

"You've also got your life, thanks to Glynnie," said Holm.

"You saved me *again*?" said Rix. He turned to Glynnie, who was sitting quietly in the background, wrapped in a blanket. Her face was covered in mud, specks of blood and smoke stains, and her eyes were red. "How can I ever repay you?"

"I think you probably know that already," Holm said quietly.

Find Benn. If only he could.

Glynnie did not say a word. She seemed to be lost in some trouble of her own.

They had camped on Filby Rise, the highest hill in Reffering, some two miles south-west of Libbens' camp. Filby rose in a long, gentle mound to a flat, heart-shaped top covered in boulders, the largest of which afforded a view of the whole plain. It was the safest place they could find in an unsafe land.

Someone had wrapped Rix in a blanket and propped him against a rock. A couple of stony knobs were sticking into his back but it hurt to move, so he put up with it. Holm cleaned the blood off his face with a wet rag and smeared on a pink, foul-smelling balm. The swellings had gone down somewhat; he could see out of his left eye now.

"How the hell did you do it?" Rix mumbled through his swollen, split lips. His jaw ached and several of his teeth felt loose.

"Jackery tossed a gas grenado into the officers' tent," said Holm, "plus a couple of paralysis blastoes and a smoke cylinder. I was about to cut through the side when we were attacked by another dozen guards Libbens had hidden in the dark. We had the fight of our lives."

Holm turned to Glynnie. "I'd hoped everyone inside the tent would be knocked unconscious by the blastoes. I knew you were in there alone, but we couldn't break through—I was terrified one of the rebels would still be on his feet."

"Four of them were on their feet," said Glynnie. "Including Libbens and Grasbee."

Rix jerked. "Four! You faced four soldiers, all by yourself? How did you—?"

"I don't want to think about it." She took the balm from Holm and rubbed it into the bruises on Rix's shoulders and chest, then fastened his shirt and pulled the blanket around his shoulders. "He's cold. He needs a hot, sweet drink."

"It's coming," said Holm. "We'd cut most of the guards down when Rix came crawling out, blind from the smoke, right into the melee. That big bastard of a sergeant whooped for glee—he was about to split Rix's head open when young Harin spitted him, front to back. We finished them quickly after that, save for the last guard, who hacked the tent ropes down and ran. The rest you know."

"Save how you got anyone to follow a condemned man who had to be tied into his saddle," said Rix.

"A hundred men saw you risk your life for us in the crevasse the other day, Deadhand," said Tonklin, whose shoulder was bound and supported in a sling, "and everyone heard about it—Jackery and I made sure of that. We'll follow you anywhere."

"Thanks, Tonklin. You don't know how much that means to me."

"We propped you upright with sticks strapped to your front and back," said Holm, "lashed you on, we kept the lanterns away so no one could see more than shadows. Then Jackery revealed an unexpected gift for mimicry—he gave the orders as if it were you speaking. The sergeants accepted them and the men obeyed."

Rix glanced at Jackery, who nodded but did not add anything to the tale. A quiet man, but gold all the way through.

"Could have been awkward if I'd fallen off my horse," said Rix.

"We were going to say you'd taken more ale than was good for you," Holm said blandly. "What soldier would think worse of you for that?"

Rix managed a smile. "The only question is, what am I supposed to do now?"

"Depends what Libbens does," said Holm.

"I'm not sitting around waiting to see what a stinking mutineer is going to do. I'm taking my army back."

"I don't see how you can do that with only two hundred men, and no supplies save what they've got in their packs."

Commanding an army was a never-ending series of crises. "I'll find a way." Rix's eye fell on Glynnie, who was sitting cross-legged, slumped forward, staring at her hands. He raised her chin. "What is it?"

Her face was starkly white, and her red eyes were wet. "I'm a murderer."

"What are you talking about?"

"The guard out the back of the tent . . . I couldn't allow him to make a sound."

"You fought him and took him down. That was a brave—"

"It wasn't brave!" Glynnie said harshly. "He was too big; I couldn't take him on. I—I crept up and stabbed him in the back— I killed him in a moment, just like that."

Rix took her hand. "It's a terrible thing, taking a life. I see the faces in my bad dreams."

"I didn't see his face. *I wouldn't even recognise the man I murdered if I saw him.*"

Rix held her close. There were times when words were no use at all.

Rix slept for an hour then woke abruptly, his heart racing. *Do it now! Right away!* It took all his strength to pull himself upright. Every muscle ached, every bone.

"What are you doing?" Glynnie said sleepily from a few yards away. She was curled into a tight ball in her blankets.

"Let me think," Rix said sardonically. "Grandys wants me dead, as agonisingly as possible, and he's got seven thousand men to help him. Libbens, who's just stolen my army, has a standard earmarked for my severed head. And then there's Lyf, whose army, though recently defeated, still numbers more than thirty thousand. For some reason I can't fathom, he doesn't love me either."

She pulled a blanket over her head. "That beating sure put you in a bad mood!"

"I've got to take charge—right now!"

What was Libbens up to? Rix had to know. He took stale bread, hard cheese and mouldy sausage from his saddlebags, then hacked the bread into two chunks, put slices of cheese and sausage between them and charred the bread in a pan over the embers of the campfire. He took a small bite, trying to avoid disturbing his loose teeth, and hauled himself up to the top of the highest boulder, which stood ten feet above the level of the hill. By the time he reached it his injuries and bruises were throbbing, and every bite of his sandwich made his jaw ache.

"I can just see the lanterns of Libbens' army through the mist . . . But there's no sign of Grandys' force. I wonder where he's gone?"

Glynnie did not answer.

He clambered down and limped around the little camp until he found Jackery on the other side of the boulder pile.

"You're wasted as a sergeant," he said. "You saved more than my life last night."

"I like being a sergeant," said Jackery. "It's all I know."

"I want you for one of my captains."

"I'm not up to high command, Lord Deadhand."

"Neither am I, Sergeant. The chancellor said he knew damned well I wasn't ready to be the commander, but I was the best he had. You're the best I've got and if we're ever to get out of this alive you have to lead."

"Yes, sir."

"You served under Libbens for a good while, didn't you?"

"Couple of years," said Jackery.

"What do you think he'll do now?"

"Try to repair his ruined name."

"Pardon?"

"Libbens believes he's a brilliant general, and his reputation means everything to him, but the chancellor sacked him for incompetence. Libbens will try to prove himself."

"How?" mused Rix.

Jackery did not reply. Rix paced back and forth, aching in every muscle.

"Are you saying he'll attack Grandys?"

"Reckon so—and as soon as possible."

Rix dropped his breakfast. He picked it up, brushed the dirt off and took another bite. "Surely the bastard wouldn't be so stupid?"

"When Libbens gets an idea into his head he won't listen to anyone."

"But he led the army to defeat in Rutherin. I heard he lost his nerve and it was sheer luck the survivors escaped."

"But in Libbens' eyes it wasn't his fault. He blamed his second-in-command, Colonel Zavier, for not carrying out his orders, and had him broken to a common foot soldier."

"Did Zavier disobey Libbens' orders?"

"Yes," said Jackery. "That's what saved us."

"He still alive?"

Jackery shook his head. "Killed crossing the mountains when that imbecile Krebb was leading us."

"What's Libbens liable to do?"

"He hates Herovians and says they should all be put down. I'd reckon he'll attack Grandys head-on."

It was what Rix had been afraid of. "But Grandys has twice as many men."

"Grandys beat Lyf's army with a fifth as many men, and Libbens thinks he's a better general than Grandys. He'll take the first chance to prove it."

"Grandys won't take kindly to being attacked with an inferior force."

"What will he do?"

"He'll take it as a personal insult. He'll wipe Libbens' army out to the last man."

"I don't see what we can do about it," said Jackery.

"Nor do I, but I have to try something, right away."

"What, *now*? It's two o'clock in the morning and you've just been beaten within an inch of your life."

"If I wait until morning, I know in my aching bones it'll be too late."

CHAPTER 23

When Rix woke Glynnie and told her the plan, she hurled her bedroll aside and punched him in his bruised and battered mouth. *"No, no, no!"*

He stumbled backwards, wiping blood off his lip. "I've got to take my army back, and my only chance is to do it now—before they recover."

She went very cold. "I didn't risk my life back there so you could throw yours away. I didn't become a murderer for this!"

"Glynnie, what choice do I have?" He went towards her, holding his arms out.

"Don't touch me!" she hissed. "Don't come anywhere near me."

He felt a pang in his heart, but it didn't change anything. It couldn't.

"I've got a duty to my men. If there's a chance of saving them I've got to take it."

"What about your duty to us? To *me*?"

"When the chancellor appointed me commander, I swore a solemn oath to lead my army and serve my country."

"And after I rescued you from Grandys that time, *you and I* swore to each other."

"I haven't forgotten."

"Which oath matters more to you, Rix? Are you going to break your oath to the chancellor, who hated you—or to me, who l—, l—?" Evidently she could not say the word. Not now.

"I'm not breaking my oath to you," he said wearily. "But I am going to take Libbens down before dawn . . ."

"Or die trying, more likely. He might not be smart, but he's rat-cunning."

"So am I."

She let out a peal of hysterical laughter. "You don't have the cunning of a—a *butterfly*!"

"Be that as it may," he said stiffly, "the two of us—me and Jackery—are going to sneak past the guards into his camp."

She pressed her right hand to her heart. "Two against five thousand? You're insane."

"For every extra man I take, the risk of being discovered doubles."

"How can you ask Jackery to help you? It's suicide!"

"I didn't ask him. He volunteered before the request was out of my mouth."

"Then he's an even bigger fool than you are," Glynnie spat.

"I'm not enchanted with the plan either," said Rix. "But—"

"Rix, attack Libbens' army if you must," said Holm. "But don't do it this way. Gallop through his army with your whole force, all the way to the command post, and take Libbens prisoner."

"At a cost of hundreds of lives?"

"This is war," interjected Glynnie, "as you're constantly telling me whenever I mention Benn."

Not Benn again—Rix could not deal with one more thing right now. "The minute I ask my men to attack their former comrades, I'll lose them."

"I don't see why."

"If *you* had an ounce of rat cunning you'd know why."

She stiffened, as if he'd grossly insulted her, then folded her arms across her chest.

"This isn't a civil war, Glynnie," Rix said hastily. "All my troops have friends in Libbens' army, men they've served with for years. Many of them have brothers, fathers, uncles and cousins there, and I'm not fool enough to ask them to fight their own relatives. My plan is the only way."

"I'm with Glynnie," said Holm. "It's too risky. If you're wrong, you die, and we all lose."

"I can't think of any other way to stop Libbens," said Rix. "And he has to be stopped. If he attacks Grandys, Hightspall will lose the war. It's that simple; that stark."

"Are we the two biggest fools in all the world?" Rix whispered an hour later, as they wriggled across the ground, heading for the gap between the patrolling sentries.

"Dare say," said Jackery.

It was four in the morning and if anything Rix felt worse than he had after the rescue. Every muscle ached, every bruise throbbed and his belly churned with an awful, burning nausea.

They were dressed as common soldiers. Jackery had a signal rocket strapped to his back; once they took the generals he would set it off and Holm would race in at the head of Rix's two hundred men, who were waiting in the darkness a few hundred yards away in case back-up was needed.

Rix had dyed his face and hands dark brown, and rubbed his cheeks with burnt cork to simulate a black beard. It would not have passed inspection in daylight but he hoped it would be disguise enough, in the dimly lit camp, to get him to the tents of Libbens and Grasbee. Both men were injured, and both had been badly affected by Holm's gas grenadoes. If there was any justice in the world they would be asleep.

Rix planned to wake them, charge them with mutiny out in front of the soldiers and pass the customary sentence—death. A minute's quick work with his sword and rough army justice would be done. Assuming everything went perfectly . . .

The plan went well until they reached the tents where the officers slept. Rix and Jackery had bypassed the guards without being discovered, then strolled through the sleeping army, Rix hunched down to disguise his height. In a camp of five thousand there were always a few dozen people up, either heading to the jakes to relieve themselves or walking off their anxiety about the coming day, and he and Jackery attracted no attention.

They reached the officers' sleeping tents, which were in

darkness. Libbens' tent was identifiable because it was the size of a small cottage and had the commander's flag flying outside. A single guard stood outside the flap of the tent. There was no one else in sight.

Grasbee's smaller tent was twenty feet away, also guarded by a single soldier. Rix could hear ragged snoring from inside.

"First we take Libbens," he whispered. A trickle of cold sweat ran down his back. "Once we have Grasbee, send up your rocket, but I won't wait for Holm and his men. After the business is done I'll hold the mutineers' heads up and formally take back command. That's the most dangerous part. If the other officers rebel, and Holm can't get through in time . . ."

"Let's get it done," said Jackery roughly. It was the only sign of his anxiety.

They approached Libbens' tent from the rear. Rix cut through the canvas low down, careful to make no noise. They wriggled through and stood up. Rix kept still until his eyes began to adjust to the darkness. He could just make out a camp stretcher in the far corner of the tent.

"Now," he said softly.

He had taken two steps towards the stretcher when a smashing blow to the side of the head knocked him down. He saw Jackery whirl, his sword flashing, and heard a cry of pain, then Rix was struck again and the darkness returned.

He roused as a pair of soldiers dragged him out of the tent. Several more soldiers waited there, with lanterns. He made a desperate attempt to get free but someone thrust a bright lantern into his face, dazzling him for a few seconds, and he was whacked over the head again. His hands were bound and he could smell blood, his own. There was no sign of Jackery. He must be dead, which meant no signal and no rescue.

"You're so predictable," said Libbens exultantly. "I *knew* you'd come back."

His voice was hoarse, presumably from breathing the vapours from the gas grenadoes, and his normally red face was grey, but his eyes were alight as if he'd just won a great battle. In a way, he had. His rat cunning had beaten Rix and he was going to die.

The wake-up horns sounded; the sleeping troops groaned and stirred.

"It's the middle of the bloody night," a soldier said.

"Get up!" bellowed a sergeant. "Get up for the beheading of Lord Deadhand!"

That roused them. The guards dragged Rix down between the lines of bedrolls, punching him and prodding him with their spear butts. He eyed his troops as he went by and saw sympathy in many an eye, though they would not defy Libbens to help him. Common soldiers were trained to obey their officers' orders instantly, and if one officer was a prisoner and another was giving the orders, he would be obeyed.

Rix was hauled into a large open area illuminated by lanterns on long poles. It was surrounded on all sides by yawning soldiers and more were streaming in all the time. A log was dragged into the centre and a big man with a long sword marched across the arena and stood by the log, waiting to cut Rix's head off.

Ten feet away, on the other side of the log, Libbens could not contain his glee. Grasbee stood beside him, shivering, then went into a long coughing fit which ended in him spitting blood onto the grass. A guard stood by, supporting him. To either side were squads of armed men, thirty in each squad, Libbens' personal guard.

Sixty guards in all, to make sure no one interfered. Rix looked for sympathetic faces among the troops, hoping against all common sense that he could sway them to help. It wasn't going to happen—any soldier who came to his aid would die with him.

Rix's guards dragged him to the centre of the circle and threw him to the ground.

"Pick him up and hold him," said Libbens. "He didn't learn from my last lesson."

They held Rix's arms while Libbens gave him another beating, then let him fall. Rix marvelled that any man could have so much dumb hatred in him, such unfeeling brutality.

The guards heaved Rix into position with his neck across the log. He had one tiny hope left but he had to act now. The flickering lanterns made moving pools of light and shadow that would help to conceal small movements. He prayed that everyone was watching his head, not his hands.

With the thumb of his dead hand, Rix flicked open the signet ring on his left middle finger to expose the half-inch blade mounted inside. He twisted his wrists, worked the blade down to his ropes and rubbed it back and forth. The razor-sharp blade would have cut through the ropes in a single pass, had he been able to exert enough pressure, but in this awkward position he had to saw at them.

"This is what happens to traitors," Libbens announced, striding back and forth before the soldiers to Rix's left and waving his arms in the air like a showman at a fair. "Gather round! Gather round, one and all, and see the scoundrel's head come off."

He went around to the other side and made a similar announcement. The soldiers stared at him in silence. Rix sawed harder.

"Get it done," Libbens said to the executioner.

The ropes parted on the underside. Rix held them in place, awaiting his moment. He would only get one chance.

"Put your foot in the middle of his back," the executioner said to one of the guards. "Keep your head well out of the way, otherwise I might be tempted to whack it off, just for practice."

He sniggered. The guard's comrades guffawed. The watching soldiers were silent.

"You," the executioner said to the second man, "move out of the way or you're liable to get a drenching. The infamous Lord Deadhand looks like he'll pump a good few pints of blood."

The left-hand guard moved back to the others. The fellow on Rix's right put a boot in the middle of his back, though he was leaning so far away from the sword that there wasn't much weight on it.

"Do it with a flourish," said Libbens. "Then quarter the body, throw it to the dogs and hold his head up for everyone to see."

He gestured to a group of horn players. They blew a ragged fanfare.

Now! thought Rix. Or never.

He gauged the best spot he could reach, swung his arm backwards and slashed the little blade diagonally across the guard's thigh. The guard lurched away, blood pouring down his leg.

Rix rolled over a moment before the executioner's sword buried itself in the log. It only took him a second to free it but by that time Rix had taken the guard's sword. He swatted the guard across the head with it, rose and lunged and buried it in the executioner's belly.

The executioner's sword was longer and heavier, a better weapon by far. Rix caught it as it fell and swung it around over his head. He had to act fast; the guards were moving in.

"Kill him!" shouted Libbens, running backwards. He stumbled and fell, but scuttled away like a four-legged crab.

Several of the soldiers hooted and Rix took heart from it. The men did not like Libbens and few of them respected him. Could Rix sway enough of them to make a difference?

"I'm your commander, and I'm not alone," he shouted, walking back and forth, swinging the greatsword to cover first one group of Libbens' guards, then the other. "I have hundreds of loyal supporters here."

It was a colossal bluff, but for a few seconds, the guards froze. Everyone was staring at him, wondering what he was going to do next.

"My men are all through the camp," Rix added. "Anyone who raises a hand against me, or any of my troops, will die a mutineer's death."

Still no one moved and Rix knew what they were thinking. In a battle between rival commanders, common soldiers could only lose, and few would have the courage to move until they had a strong sign that they were on the winning side. It was a different matter for Libbens' sixty guards. If he fell, so would they, and they could end this in seconds. But they knew Rix's ferocious reputation—the first few men who attacked him would certainly die.

Rix kept moving, back and forth, swinging the sword. He met the eyes of those soldiers who had seemed sympathetic. He had to convince them to act.

"I'm your commanding officer," he repeated, so loudly that it hurt his jaw. "I was publicly appointed by the chancellor. Take the traitor generals and their guards, and hold them. That's an order!"

A small group of soldiers on the left stepped forward, then another group ahead. There were more than twenty . . . though not nearly enough to deal with sixty elite guards.

"Take Libbens and Grasbee!" he repeated, and ran at the nearest guards, swinging the executioner's sword.

But whenever he cut a man down, two more took his place and, at the moment it became clear he could not win, more of the waverers would turn to Libbens' side. Unless Rix could take him down first.

It wasn't to be. Rix and his nine surviving men were soon surrounded. He was preparing to be cut to pieces when a score of riders galloped into the arena, led by Holm and Tonklin and, to Rix's astonishment, Jackery. He must have got away after Rix had been knocked down.

"Kill him!" bellowed Libbens.

His guards surged forward. Defence was a hopeless strategy—Rix ran at them, swinging wildly, trying to dominate the guards with sheer size and ferocity, the way Grandys did in battle. And it worked; he cut three men down, several others scrambled out of the way, and he broke free.

"To me! To me!" Rix roared.

"Look out!" Holm yelled.

A flying wedge of Libbens' guards attacked from the left, hacking Rix's men out of the way and aiming for him.

"Close ranks!" Rix yelled. "Hold them out!"

But there was only one way to finish this. He looked over the heads of his troops, identified the coarse red face of his enemy and fought his way towards Libbens so furiously that the soldiers guarding him broke and ran. Libbens matched Rix stroke for stroke. Rix cut him, then again. Libbens took a step backwards, looking around for help, but most of his guards were dead and the rest had seen that it was over.

"Help me, you mongrel dogs," he gasped at the surrounding troops.

Not one man moved to his aid. He swung a wild blow at Rix, missed, then turned and fled. Rix sprang after him and dealt him a blow to the head with the flat of his sword. Libbens went down. There came a rousing cheer from the watching troops and Rix knew he had won. A few seconds later he saw that Jackery's men had taken Grasbee as well, and his eight surviving guards.

"Put them down, Deadhand," said Jackery. "They'll only stir up more trouble, otherwise."

"I'm trying them for mutiny. Quick justice is more than they deserve, but justice they will have nonetheless."

He called the troops in closer, his own men in a small semi-circle on the north, and the renegade army on the south side. Rix formed a jury of ten men, five from Libbens' army and five from his own men, and read out the charges. Grasbee did not speak. He was still coughing and spitting blood. Libbens blustered in self-defence but it did not avail him—the jury had already made up its mind.

"Ignominious death," said the foreman.

Grasbee was forced to his knees and his neck stretched over the log. Rix signed to Jackery.

"Only you can end this, Lord," said Jackery.

Rix grimaced. But then, he was commander. He hefted the executioner's sword, aimed carefully and brought it down, *thump*. When the blood had reduced to a dribble, he had Libbens brought to the log, two yards down.

"This man is the ringleader of the mutiny," Rix said to the deathly silent watchers. "When he dies, it ends."

There was a dark stain down Libbens' trouser front. "It wasn't me," he whined. "Grasbee and Krebb were behind it all."

Rix gestured to the log.

Libbens was forced down next to Grasbee's headless body, held in place and his thick neck pressed against the log. He looked right, at Grasbee's bloody stump, then down at his severed head. Grasbee's eyes seemed to be staring back at Libbens, accusing him.

"Any last words you wish conveyed to your family?" said Rix.

Libbens unleashed a torrent of abuse.

Rix listened to a minute of it, then raised the sword. Libbens broke off and tried to lift his head but he was securely held. A small green ant crawled across his cheek.

He was whimpering now. Time to put the swine out of his misery. Rix swung the sword down, *thunk*, all the way through skin, bone and gristle with surprisingly little resistance for such a heavy-set man, and two inches deep into the log. It was over.

He raised Libbens' head high, so everyone in the army could see it. His eyes had already gone blank.

"The mutiny is over," said Rix. He turned to the surviving men of Libbens' guard. "You knew that the chancellor had appointed me commander, yet you supported the mutineers. You too should die as mutineers . . .

"But I'm prepared to accept that you were obeying orders you believed to be legitimate. I will suspend the sentence as long as you swear to me and my officers. But if you should transgress again, in any small way—the sentence will be carried out."

They swore to him.

CHAPTER 24

Any minute now, Grandys was coming in to scan Tali's head. But what did that mean, and how was he going to do it? She felt sure it was going to hurt.

She paced around the wrecked great hall of Bastion Barr, the unlikely prison where she had been held since being brought north with Lirriam and the injured Yulia after the battle at Reffering. Grandys had arrived yesterday, in a cold and savage rage that no amount of bloodshed could assuage.

Tali's stomach muscles were clenched so tightly that they ached. She had to resist him and protect her secrets, though she was not sure how much longer she could hold out. Any defeat turned him into a brooding drunk, as liable to cut down an ally as an enemy, and she was his next target. He had told her so.

Though Grandys had broken Lirriam's jaw, she had emerged the stronger and it was eating him alive. Not even his crushing victory over Lyf's army, nor Grandys' routing of the Pale with a single battalion, could make up for his growing fear of the stone *Incarnate*, that only a woman could wake.

Something was bothering him about Maloch as well. Lirriam

kept making snide remarks about it, alluding to a confrontation where the sword had failed him and Lyf had emerged the victor, and questioning whether Grandys was still its *true master*. Every reference to that confrontation drove him into a fury.

Two days ago he had suffered another blow, one he took as a personal insult. Lyf had sacked and burned Grandys' two greatest bulwarks, Castle Rebroff and Bastion Cowly. The attacks had sent Grandys racing north to avenge the insult but the enemy's lead had been too great. They had fled down the far side of Lake Fumerous, to safety in Cauldron.

How Lirriam had laughed when Grandys brought the news. For the moment, he was stymied—he did not have the numbers to make an onslaught on Cauldron or attack Lyf's army in Mulclast, and for some reason connected to the sword's true master Grandys was saving Rix for "the endgame", whatever that was.

In the meantime Grandys drank, brooded and indulged himself in acts of unspeakable violence against the remaining prisoners, though not even that could bring him solace.

Only a win could do that, and Tali was his intended victim. Was scanning a way of mind-reading? Her gift was still blocked and she did not know how to protect her secrets.

Tali circled around a heap of smashed furniture, reached the end of the great hall and turned back. For reasons unknown she had been imprisoned in the largest room in the fortress, but only after his troops had smashed and despoiled every sculpture, painting, mural and tapestry there, and most of the furniture. She had spent days locked in this ruin, and it worked on her mind in ways that a dungeon's blank walls never could have. If Grandys won, this was a vision of the future.

A vision of hell.

And now he was coming. She could hear his heavy tread on the stairs two floors below. He moved with a deliberate, lumbering gait as if his lower limbs still remembered when they had been stone. One floor to go. Now he was thudding along the long hall. Let him not be drunk. No one could deal with Grandys in that state. Clever words only enraged him.

He approached the double doors. Tali stared at them, paralysed.

Any second now they would burst open and slam back against the wall. Grandys entered a room as though he wanted to tear it down.

But this time the latch lifted and fell, and the door was eased open. He came through silently, wearing an enigmatic smile. He pointed to the chair at the end of the big hall table, the only two pieces of unbroken furniture here.

Tali sat.

Slender, sad-eyed Yulia followed him in, moving slowly and painfully. She had been badly injured in the battle at Reffering, Tali knew, and though Lirriam had healed her, Yulia did not look well.

She carried a wide roll of heavy mapmaker's paper. Grandys gestured to the table and she unrolled it in front of Tali. The paper was blank. Was this part of the scanning process? How did it work? What would it show?

Grandys picked up the pieces of a broken chair, touched them with the flat of Maloch and they rejoined. He placed the chair in front of Tali. Yulia sat on it, facing her.

"What are you doing?" said Tali. Her voice had a tremor. She could not stop it.

Yulia opened her mouth to speak. Grandys scowled and she closed it again. She slipped a copper-coloured bracelet onto her left wrist and rotated it a couple of times. A line of glyphs ran around it. Tali could not read them.

"Don't move," Grandys said to Tali.

Yulia reached out with her left hand. Her hands were beautiful, the fingers long, slender and tapering, the nails jewel-perfect black opals that shimmered with her every movement.

She curved her hand around the left side of Tali's face, close but not touching. Now over the top of her head. Now down the right side of her face. Tali assumed Yulia was using some kind of magery and braced herself for pain or discomfort, but felt nothing.

Yulia rose from her chair, reached over and ran her hand down the back of Tali's head, so close that it stirred her hair. Yulia sat again and traced her fingers down the centre of Tali's face from hairline to chin.

Yulia was breathing heavily now, and the muscles that ran from her neck to her shoulders were taut. She turned to the table and set a handful of sharpened pencils beside the sheet of paper, their points aligned and sides parallel.

Taking a pencil from the middle, she inspected the point, put it back and took another. Now, again using her left hand and holding the paper steady with her right, she began to draw a huge skull, fully two feet long, in the top left corner of the paper.

Tali's skull.

Yulia worked quickly but with an engraver's skill, completing the front-on view of the skull in intricate detail in no more than ten minutes. She stood back, studying it from a distance, her lips pursed.

"Give it a face," said Grandys.

Yulia took a fresh pencil and sketched Tali's face and hair. The likeness was eerily good, almost life-like. Without looking at her, Yulia began a second drawing on the right. It showed the back of Tali's skull. A third drawing depicted the left side of her head and a fourth, the right side. By the time Yulia completed the last line and stood back, the best part of an hour had passed.

Her face was blanched; she swayed on her feet. Furrows had formed on her brow and to either side of her mouth. She pressed her hands against her lower belly as if in pain, and closed her eyes.

"Is it perfect?" said Grandys, leaning forward. His voice was hoarse. Whatever Yulia was doing, he wanted it badly.

"As perfect as I can make it," said Yulia.

"Get to the nub."

Yulia rotated her bracelet, four or five times. She ran her hands over Tali's skull and face as she had before, though this time her movements were slow and deliberate, and her fingers skimmed Tali's skin and hair. Yulia grimaced, as though she did not like to touch her, and the lines of her face deepened. By the end, her hands were shaking.

"Pull yourself together," Grandys said coldly.

Yulia clamped her right hand over the bracelet, took three long breaths and turned to the skull drawings. She quickly drew a small circle on each, beneath the top of Tali's skull, though not quite touching it.

The master pearl!

"You're sure the location is right?" said Grandys.

"Yes," said Yulia.

"Exactly?"

"Yes!" she snapped.

"Can you cut it out?"

"No!" she cried. "*No!*"

"Why the hell not?"

"Since I will never be able to *create* life, I will not willingly destroy another life."

He made as if to speak, restrained himself and said, "Finish the job."

Yulia scribed a circle around the pearl in the third drawing and swept a line from the circle down to a blank space at the bottom of the paper, where she drew a larger circle—a magnified view of the master pearl, Tali assumed. With swift, bold movements Yulia drew a thick, slightly curving line which Tali took to represent her skull then, using her sharpest pencil, a small circle: the master pearl. Yulia touched the pencil to the outside of the circle, making small irregularities all the way around.

"What's that supposed to mean?" said Grandys.

"The two pearls you took from Lyf have dozens of layers," said Yulia, "one atop another. It makes them strong—you could toss either pearl across this room and it would not be harmed. But Tali's master pearl has only one layer left, plus a few remnants of the layer that used to be above it."

She indicated the irregularities with the tip of her pencil.

"Why is there only one layer?" said Grandys.

"Have you used the pearl?" said Yulia to Tali.

She saw no reason not to answer; she had to know what was wrong. "Many times, though it's always painful. And it's worse each time."

"Ebony pearls aren't meant to be used within the host," said Yulia.

"Says who?" said Grandys.

"It's common knowledge. Tali has used her pearl often, and drawing all that power through it has ablated its outer layers."

"What the hell does *ablated* mean?"

"Eroded away."

"And?" said Grandys, his opal-clad jaw jutting.

"The master pearl is incredibly fragile now," said Yulia. "Any threat or trauma to Tali threatens it. If it bursts inside her she will die . . . and the master pearl will be destroyed."

"How do I get it out?"

"Even a master surgeon would struggle to perform such an operation—and keep her alive long enough to take it."

Tali stiffened. She could see where this was going.

"Do we have a master surgeon of that quality?" said Grandys.

"No," said Yulia, "though I believe there are several among the Cythonians . . . "

"No Cythonian could be trusted. What about the Hightspallers?"

"There were several in Caulderon before the war. But . . . "

"They'd be hard to find, even if they've survived Lyf's purges." He looked into Tali's eyes. "How long between her death and the pearl dying?"

"What are you saying?" said Yulia.

"All that matters is getting the pearl into a vessel of healing blood before Tali dies. Any butcher of a surgeon could do that."

Grandys leered at Tali. He was enjoying this.

"You'd trust the greatest prize in the land to a *butcher*?" said Yulia. "If the master pearl is broken, it can *never* be replaced. You'll never get king-magery . . . and we'll never create our Promised Realm."

Grandys stared at her but did not speak.

"It has to be a master surgeon," said Yulia. "The best there is. A healer who's committed to keeping her alive *and* protecting the master pearl."

"Tali reacted the first time I mentioned a surgeon," said Grandys. "She has one in mind."

Yulia thought for a moment. "The old man called Holm is her friend. It's said he was a great surgeon, long ago."

Yulia went out, hand pressed to her belly.

"He won't do it," said Tali. "He abandoned that career long ago."

"I have ways of compelling the most reluctant people," said Grandys. "If I can't torment you, I'll have to try twice as hard with Holm."

CHAPTER 25

Grandys was playing games with Tali and she had to find a way to strike back, but she could not use her gift. He had tightened the block on it in order to protect the master pearl.

She had been removed to a large, square room that he used as an office. He had created an invisible barrier across the far end to contain her. From time to time, retainers came in bearing magnificent works of art or scholarship: manuscripts, illuminated volumes, tapestries, paintings and engravings, old maps, musical scores. Grandys gave each work a cursory examination, after which the majority of these treasures were cast into the open fireplace, drenched with oil and burned to ashes.

Rarely, however, he would place the object in a small blackwood cabinet containing a number of other such treasures.

"Fifteen," he said on the first occasion, and on the second, "Sixteen. One to go."

"What are they for?" said Tali, unable to restrain her curiosity. "Why are you collecting them when you've burned every library you've come to, and destroyed every other thing of beauty you've found?"

"In time," said Grandys.

"You said 'one to go'. You're collecting seventeen items. Why seventeen?"

He did not answer.

Once or twice, empty phials from his ice chest were taken away then returned, filled with fresh crimson blood. "Seventy-nine," he said on the last such occasion. "Eighteen more."

"So you're collecting ninety-seven samples of blood," said Tali.

"Including yours, at the right time."

To reinforce the point he withdrew the phial labelled with her name and held it up so it caught the light. It twinkled off crystals of frost.

Tali felt as though it was forming on the back of her neck, then melting to chilly water running down her backbone. "Why ninety-seven samples? Why seventeen treasures?"

"That's what the Three Spells require."

For Grandys' endgame.

"Where did *Incarnate* come from?" said Tali as Lirriam entered, wearing the heavy stone on her breast. It had made a small bruise there and it must have been painful when she moved suddenly, though she gave no sign of it.

Although Yulia had healed Lirriam's broken jaw, it hung slightly left of centre. Tali thought Lirriam had ordered it healed that way, as a reminder of Grandys' unforgivable assault on one of the Five.

"From the moment the idea was conceived that stone gave our ancestors nothing but trouble," said Grandys, watching her warily.

"The term *conceived* is apt," said Lirriam. "The source may have been quickened by a male, but *Incarnate* grew from a female's tears, and only a woman can use it."

Incarnate! The very word gave Tali the shudders, with its hints of demonic possession, crimson blood and uncontrollable extremity. She reminded herself that it could also have an opposing meaning— the embodiment of some attribute of the Herovian race.

"It's dead!" Grandys said thickly. "The wretched stone was only used once, and it led our people astray and caused us ten thousand years of misery. It's cursed; useless!"

"Only to *males*," said Lirriam.

"Why are you bent on creating this division between our sexes? In all the time we Five have been together, we've always acted as one."

"That's because you were much older than us, and far stronger. Syrten, Yulia and I were still in our teens when you bent us to your foul will. You implicated us in your crimes and ensured we could never get free."

Tali came up to the barrier and pressed her hands against its invisible surface, testing it. It was as solid as ever. Even if she'd had full command of her gift she did not think she could have broken it.

"Together we changed the world," said Grandys to Lirriam. "Don't tell me you haven't enjoyed it."

"You corrupted me when I was an impressionable girl; you left me no way back. But to answer your question, *you* created the rift between our sexes by constantly putting Yulia down. *You* attacked me, though you're twice my size. You must have known I'd fight back."

"You fight with underhanded, *women's* weapons."

Lirriam sneered. "Is that the best insult you can come up with? Surely you didn't expect I'd match you stroke for stroke like one of your oafish comrades."

"It's always been the Heroes' way."

"No, it's always been *your* way." She rubbed her jaw, pointedly. "You taught us to fight the enemy on *our* battlefield, not his. With *our* weapons, not his."

"We're the *Five Heroes*! The rest of the world is our enemy, but we stand together."

"We used to. But you're past your prime, Grandys. Your strength is fading, and soon you'll fall the way you rose—in a bucket of blood."

He gaped at her. "*You* want to lead the Heroes."

"Do I?"

"Yes, you do."

"Who would you choose? Syrten, who hasn't had an independent thought in a thousand years? Rufuss, who's in thrall to his unslakeable need to torment the powerless? Or Yulia, sick with guilt at her forced complicity in the foul acts you forced the Heroes to commit?"

"I created the Five Heroes," said Grandys. "There can be no other leader while—"

She smiled coldly. "While you live."

Grandys shook in a passion, took a step towards her, then stopped.

"You want to hit me again," said Lirriam. "It's the only answer you have. You're such a hero."

"One day you'll push me too far," he choked.

"I intend to push you all the way . . . before Maloch deserts you for its true master."

"I *am* its true master. Envoy Urtiga left it to me in a signed deed."

"A signed deed means nothing. We all saw you use magery to forge Lyf's signature on the charter that began the Two Hundred and Fifty Years War. A time will come when the sword will betray you, Grandys."

Tali could see the fear in Grandys' eyes now, and his burning doubt in the sword. The balance was tilting. How could she increase the pressure in a way that would give her a chance?

"Why is the wyverin the Five Heroes' nemesis?" said Tali.

Lirriam shot her a sharp glance. "It's not *our* nemesis. Only Grandys'."

"Why? Where does it come from?"

"We don't talk about it," said Grandys.

Yulia entered silently, dressed in travelling clothes, followed by Syrten, who carried a heavy pack.

"Where are you off to?" said Grandys.

"To the Custodian, to get the *Immortal Text*," said Yulia. "Before we can use the Three Spells to cleanse our Promised Realm, we need the *Text* in hand."

Grandys grunted.

"You don't wish us to go?" said Yulia.

"Yes, *go!*" he said. "The time draws near."

"Are the Three Spells prepared?"

"What are the Three Spells, anyway?" said Tali.

"Stonespell. Writspell. Bloodspell," said Grandys, with a nasty smile. "They're *almost* ready to use." He waved Yulia away and she went out, followed, dog-like, by Syrten.

"And now," he said, turning back to Tali, "we come to the key."

That thud was her heart hitting the pit of her stomach. "What key?" she croaked.

"Surely you didn't think your pitiful attempts to distract me would work?"

Tali rubbed her cold arms but the goose pimples would not go away.

"You know what the key to king-magery is," said Grandys. "And you're going to tell me."

"I don't know what it is."

He walked through the barrier as though it did not exist, drew Maloch and held it above her head. "What's the key to king-magery?"

Her head throbbed. "I—don't—know."

"Maloch says you're lying."

As he laid the flat of the blade on top of her head, Tali felt a shrieking pain beneath her skull. She gasped and pressed her palms to the sides of her head. *Endure it! Don't tell him anything.*

"Careful," said Lirriam. "You don't know how much the pearl can take—or how little."

The pain grew until it was like having the sword thrust down through her skull; until she could not bear it. She fell to her knees, clutching at her head. Grandys followed her down with the sword.

"Stop it!" Lirriam yelled. "You'll burst the master pearl."

He scowled but rammed Maloch into its sheath. "They can endure so little pain, these Pale. They deserve to be enslaved."

"Violence isn't the answer. It rarely is."

"Maybe I can't torture Tali," said Grandys. "But I can torture her friends: Deadhand and the little maidservant, whatever her name is."

He knew Glynnie's name. Of course he knew.

"I'm making a beautiful trap and they're going to fall right in it." He grinned savagely at Tali.

She could not think of anything to say. She was helpless and he was back on top.

"And once I take them," said Grandys, "I'll also have Holm, the master surgeon. When I've got him, your life, and the fate of this land, will be measured in hours."

CHAPTER 26

"You look dreadful," said Glynnie. "If your eyes sink in any further they'll come out the back of your head."

"I don't feel too good." Rix rubbed the fading bruises on his face. They had not faded nearly as quickly as his triumph over Libbens and the mutineers. He sniffed himself. "And I stink."

"We all stink," said Glynnie. "You get used to it after a while."

"The bastard's playing his mind games again. Why won't he attack?"

"Grandys doesn't just want to win. He wants to break you . . . and ravage me, before he kills us."

She made a small, trapped sound in her throat, clutched at his arm and squelched on through the muck.

Grandys was not their only woe. Rix stood in the grey, dawn rain, surveying the mess. So much volcanic ash had fallen during the night that half the tents had collapsed, his command tent among them. The powdery ash had got into everything, even sealed containers of food, and the rain turned the eight-inch layer on the ground to a grey sludge. Marching through it was like walking in glue. It found its way between the wagon axles and their housings and set like mortar, locking them. And when the sun finally came out, the rutted ash would set as hard as stone.

There was no water for washing or anything else save drinking and cooking, because every stream was clogged with the muck. Even drinking water was at a premium, since the fine ash remained suspended in the water and every gallon had to be filtered through cloth. The tea, and everything cooked in water, had the same foul, mouth-puckering taste.

And there was still the matter of his officers. Rix had not sacked Hork and the other four captains yet, because he had no officers to replace them. Several of Rix's men showed promise, including the scar-faced Sergeant Waysman, and the innocent-looking Pomfree, and Jackery of course, though Rix knew none of them were ready for high command. But when the battle came he would have to throw them into the water and hope they could swim—or at least, dog paddle.

"It's getting worse," said Glynnie. "People are saying the Red Vomit is going to blow itself to pieces." She looked south to where the three Vomits were concealed by low cloud. "If it does, it'll put an end to all wars."

As if to underline her words, the ground quivered underfoot. Rix had tracked Grandys' army north-west through Togl. It had forded the Rinkl River in the foothills and gone to Bastion Barr, but Rix had not followed Grandys across the river. It felt like a trap and he did not know this country.

"If it's this bad twenty-five miles from the Vomits," she added, "what must it be like right next door? Or in Caulderon?"

Rix did not answer. He had other things on his mind, such as how to take on Grandys' vastly superior army; such as squeezing enough supplies out of this miserable, war-torn land to feed his 4400 men. He had begun with five thousand but the bad food and water had laid many hundreds low and he'd had to leave them behind.

"Grandys has seven thousand men," said Rix. "And he's bound to be recruiting more."

"You're recruiting too."

"I'm not finding many volunteers. For some reason they're reluctant to join an army led by a dead-handed man whose parents were executed for high treason—after he betrayed them." He let out a mirthless chuckle. "Can you credit it?"

"Let's focus on the positive," she said pointedly. "What are you going to do next?"

"Tali's the key. Since I allowed her to fall into Grandys' hands, I should be trying to rescue her."

"Which is what Grandys wants you to do."

"He's back," said Jackery the following morning.

"Who's back?" said Rix, who was supervising a battle drill

between his troops. They were fighting with wooden weapons so as to cause the minimum number of injuries.

"Grandys, on horseback. Watching everything you do."

"He was doing that yesterday."

"But today he's got a thousand men with him."

Rix's stomach knotted. He followed Jackery to the top of the hill, from where they could see across the braided streams of the Rinkl all the way to the spiked green towers of Bastion Barr, in the foothills of the northern Crowbung Range.

"Do you think he plans to attack?" Jackery added.

"Grandys is the master of improvisation. Sometimes he doesn't know what he's going to do until he's done it, so how can I possibly anticipate him?"

"He's changed lately. When he'd never lost, it made him reckless—there was no thrill in battle unless the challenge was enormous and the risk desperate."

"That's true," said Rix, rubbing his jaw, which still ached from time to time. "Something happened after he defeated Lyf's army, and he hasn't been the same man since. I wish I knew what it was . . ."

"He's lost two strong fortresses and he hasn't had a chance to retaliate. Grandys will be so hungry for a win that he won't take so many chances."

"He couldn't bear another defeat; he'll use everything he's got."

"In a shattering demonstration of his power," said Holm. "A warning, and a lesson to everyone in Hightspall who dares oppose him. *See what I did to Deadhand's army*, he'll be saying. *I'm going to do worse to you.*"

Rix glanced across at the twin white limestone cliffs that formed a rampart below Bastion Barr, half expecting to see an army streaming out between them, but the land was empty.

He dug his knuckles into his belly. It did nothing to ease the pain there, like embedded fish hooks.

"It won't be long," Rix said to Glynnie and Holm that evening. "He's not a patient man."

"I hope not," said Glynnie, who was plucking at her collar, over and over, "because once it's over and we've won, I'm holding you to your promise."

Rix stared at her, blank-faced. How could she blithely assume that it would end well despite all evidence that it would not? "What promise?"

Her eyes flashed. "How can you have forgotten? To help me look for Benn."

He groaned. "Not again, Glynnie. Not now."

"He's my little brother, you heartless bastard!" she snapped. "He's all I've got."

"Apart from me," said Rix, tearing at his hair. "Glynnie, I'm facing imminent battle with an enemy I can't hope to beat, one who'll gleefully slaughter everyone in this army if I lose. We can't drink the water, we're running low on food and all kinds of supplies and I have no idea how I'm going to get more. And Grandys could be cutting the master pearl out of Tali's head as we speak. So, as much as I care about Benn, right now I can't even think about doing anything for him . . . *if* he's still alive."

"You promised!"

"*After the war is over*, I said. I wouldn't dare go anywhere near Caulderon right now."

"Why not?" she said furiously.

"You know why. In an occupied city, anyone asking questions is liable to be taken as a spy, then tortured and executed. Everyone knows my face, I'm far too big to disguise myself and my dead hand would give me away instantly. Besides, I can't abandon my army with Grandys so close."

"You're obsessed with him! You've got a death wish."

"He's got a death wish on me, and my country. Am I supposed to run away and let him have it?"

"You don't care about Benn, or me, or anything except playing at your precious war," Glynnie hissed, and stormed out.

"What the hell am I supposed to do?" said Rix to Holm.

Holm sighed. "Isn't it obvious?"

"No."

"Show Glynnie you understand that Benn matters as much to her as anything you're doing here. More! You've still got a manor, wealth and an army—all she has in the world is Benn."

"And you. And me," said Rix.

"Don't persist in misunderstanding me," said Holm sharply.

"I'm not *persisting*. I don't understand her."

"You expect her to make allowances for all your problems. And she does. But you ignore her problems. She's in agony, Rix, and you're the only person who can help her."

"I'm not ignoring her problems. I just can't—"

"'Do anything about them at the moment,'" Holm chanted as though reciting an overworn excuse.

"That's right!" Rix said mulishly.

"All you have to do is sit down and talk to her. Show you care. Make her understand that you're determined to help her find Benn, the minute you can."

"I would, but I've got more things to do than I can get done in a twenty-four-hour day."

"It would only take fifteen minutes. You've just wasted twice that time denying Glynnie's right to be worried about Benn. You'd better sort this out, Rix, or you'll lose her."

If I can't sort Grandys out we'll all be dead, Rix thought, and I'll be blamed for it.

"I can't sleep!" he cried. "My bowels are running like tap water and on the rare occasions when I do doze off, I wake drenched in sweat, dreaming about the wyverin. And you know what that means."

"What does it mean?" said Holm, rather coolly.

"The same as it meant for my father—betrayal and an ignominious death."

"I don't—"

"It's a monstrous omen of our defeat, and the fall of Hightspall. I'm cracking, Holm. How much more am I expected to take?"

"Not much, by the look of you. But if you were *with* your friends rather than against us, you'd find the stress easier to bear."

"I'll talk to her in the morning," said Rix.

But before dawn he was woken to the news that Grandys' army was streaming out of Bastion Barr, heading for the ford. Rix mobilised his troops in a panic, issued his orders and made sure his formations were organised for defence, and in the tumult there was no time to talk to Glynnie.

Later that morning, when Grandys' troops were about to cross the ford, they turned as one, marched east along the Rinkl River and disappeared over a rise.

"What the hell is he doing?" said Rix.

"Taunting us," said Jackery.

"He's not going to fight you on your battlefield," said Holm. "Let him go."

"And be called a coward again?" said Rix. "A traitor secretly in Grandys' thrall?"

"He wants you to follow him."

"I know."

"You'll be walking into his trap."

"I know there's going to be a trap. I won't be walking into it."

"You're doing exactly—"

"Not exactly. He doesn't know what I'm going to do, and neither do you."

"I've got a pretty good idea," Holm muttered, "and I don't like it one bit."

CHAPTER 27

Rix doesn't care about me or Benn, thought Glynnie. All he cares about is war.

She was tossing in her sweat-damp bedroll, having been woken soon after she went to sleep by another skin-crawling premonition of doom about Benn. She couldn't bear to go back to sleep—she couldn't take any more.

After pulling on her boots, she went out into the still camp. It was silent and dark save for a handful of down-lanterns illuminating the benches at the cooks' wagons, where they were making stew and preparing the dough for tomorrow morning's bread. Rix required that his troops begin the day with a hot meal, the best available.

Glynnie avoided the activity at the kitchen wagons and walked south, out of the camp. She skirted a small lake, not much bigger than a pond, and headed down to the edge of a low crag, where she sat a safe distance from the edge and looked out across the lowlands. It was a clear night with no wind, the landscape lit slantingly by a waxing moon.

The false war, between the two armies several miles apart, had been going on for days now. Grandys had marched east along the north side of the Rinkl River, then crossed through Lakeland into the south of Fennery, a soggy lowland with a scattering of flat-topped hills standing out above large areas of marsh and mire. And Rix had continued to shadow Grandys . . .

Conveniently forgetting his promise. Glynnie's pulse rose at the thought. Damn him!

On the third day of the false war Grandys had captured the small manor of Flume, on the border between southern Fennery and Gordion. Rix had camped four miles north, on a long hill called Bolstir, where they were now. The little lake on its dish-shaped crest was blissfully free of the volcanic ash that had befouled every water supply further west, while low crags on the east, north and south sides made it easy to defend.

A few miles to Glynnie's right the moon reflected off a large tri-angular bay, several miles on one side, surrounded by the high, pale cliffs that formed most of the northern shore of Lake Fumerous. Further south, only ten miles away in a straight line, was the smoky smudge of the city of Caulderon.

Twice on the way here, bands of Grandys' raiders had attacked Rix's camp, shooting burning arrows into the tents then vanishing into the night. On another night Grandys' agents had silently killed all Rix's outer guards and outriders, and disappeared. No one had known of it until the guards' signals had not come in.

Holm had been right all along. Grandys was playing a mind game with Rix, baiting the trap, and Rix was too proud and stub-born to see it. Glynnie did not like the way war was hardening

Rix—he seemed to see his soldiers' deaths in these endless skirmishes and sorties as necessary, even *strategic*. But the war was out of his control. One day soon he would be killed in battle, or tortured to death by Grandys, and there was nothing she could do to protect him.

She couldn't bear it. And since there was nothing she could do for Rix, she had to look after the only person she could do anything for—Benn.

The moonlight was just good enough for her knife-throwing practice. Glynnie picked out a target, an inch-wide knot in the trunk of a small tree. If she was going it alone, she had to be ready to defend herself.

She had been practising with her knives for weeks now and could hit her target eight times out of ten, though it would be a different matter in real life. She had also trained with Holm, using a rapierlike blade, though her small size and light weight meant she would always be at a disadvantage in swordplay.

Her knife throwing would help to even the imbalance, though whenever she picked up a knife it reminded her of the sentry she had killed. Murdered! She shivered and dropped her knife. At the time she had thought it fortunate that she had never seen the sentry's face, though lately his faceless shadow had come to haunt her dreams almost as often as the wyverin did Rix's.

And her victim always had the killer's knife embedded in his back.

Her knife.

She tried to reason that she'd had no choice; that he had been a bad man and by killing him she had saved a good man's life, but it still felt as though she was a cowardly murderer. Well, if that's what she was, it could not be changed. And if she had to do it again to save Benn, she would! And pay the price afterwards.

Glynnie picked up the knife and hurled it true. *Thunk*, a few inches to the left of the knot. Good, but not good enough. She had to kill any attacker before he came within reach. If she could not, she would die and Benn would be lost.

Thunk, three inches right of the knot this time. Just as bad. Glynnie tried to aim but her throwing arm had developed a tremor.

She stood still, her arms hanging down, imagining some tall brute of a soldier advancing on her, flushed with battle rage and swinging back a broadsword the length of her body. Her only chance was to kill him first. She raised the knife but her arm shook violently and now there was a weakness in her elbow.

Pull yourself together, girl. This is your *life*.

The lecture didn't work. No matter how she envisaged the threat to her, or to Rix, she could not steady her arm. And she knew why. Rix had his true purpose in life—fighting and, if necessary, dying for his country; opposing Hightspall's enemies in every way he could. But it was not *her* true purpose. Her promise that she would look after Benn overrode everything else, even her love for Rix. Even her fear for him.

Glynnie's throwing arm was rock-steady now. She aimed with her heart, not her eyes, and threw her remaining knives, one, two, three: *thunk*, *thunk*, *thunk*. They embedded themselves side by side in the centre of the knot.

She retrieved the five knives, cleaned the sap off the blades and sheathed them. Glynnie turned and Holm was standing a few yards away. She started, guiltily.

"You look like a woman who's just come to the decision of her life," said Holm.

She headed back. He fell in beside her.

"I have," said Glynnie.

"Are you sure it's the right decision?"

"I dream about Benn every night. I can see his face as though he's standing right in front of me. Every night he's in greater danger and more pain."

Holm frowned. "You've dreamed about him every single night? For how long?"

She shrugged. "A week or so. What does it matter?"

"A dream repeated so regularly, so vividly, could have a dark origin."

She missed a step, stumbled. He caught her arm.

"You mean it's being *sent* to me?"

"Got any enemies, Glynnie?"

There was no need to answer. She moved on, her heart fluttering.

"I don't believe it," said Glynnie.

"You don't want to believe it."

"If Grandys had sent my dream, it'd be darker. It'd be tinged with rage, violence, blood and pain, because that's his signature."

"He might have had someone else send it. Someone kinder. Yulia, for instance."

"Do you think I don't know my own brother?"

Holm did not reply. They were approaching her tent now, a small outline in the darkness.

"In my dreams it doesn't feel like an *imitation* of Benn," said Glynnie. "It's just Benn, as only I know him."

Holm let out a heavy sigh. "And you have to go?"

"What would you do if it was your little brother or sister, or your own child?"

"I failed the test with my own child," he said quietly.

"You won't try to stop me, will you?"

"I should," said Holm. "You're only seventeen, not officially an adult . . . No, I'll worry about you, but I won't stop you . . . but—"

"What?" said Glynnie, when he did not continue.

"Are you going to say goodbye?"

"Goodbye, Holm."

"You're wilfully misunderstanding me. I meant goodbye to Rix."

"Why would I?" she said bitterly. "He doesn't care about me or Benn."

"You know that's not true."

"And you can't tell him I'm going!"

"I have to tell him. He's our commander; he's got to know."

"Not yet!" she cried. "After I've made my final choice."

"I thought you had."

"I'm still wavering," she lied.

"All right," he said reluctantly, "but the moment you choose, you've got to tell Rix. If you don't, I will."

"He doesn't care what I do," she muttered.

"Emotional blackmail won't work on me, Glynnie. Of course he cares—it's just that the oaf finds it hard to say so. Besides, Rix relies on you. He needs you, and if you leave he'll be devastated and undermined at a time when he has to focus everything on defeating Grandys. On saving this army and all of us."

It was painful for Glynnie to accept, though she had to concede Holm's point. If she left now, the chance of Rix beating Grandys must be lower than if she stayed. The chance of Rix's survival must be lower, too. If she left now, there was a good chance she would never see him again.

"You're trying to change my mind."

"No, I'm just making your choice clear."

"It is clear. I have to choose between Rix, the man I love, and Benn, my little brother."

"He's been lost for months," said Holm. "Surely a few more days don't matter?"

"I'm afraid that the next few days matter more than ever. Besides . . . if I stay here there's a good chance I'm going to die, and that would leave Benn all alone. If I go to Caulderon, how am I taking more of a risk? I'm just exchanging one danger for another."

"I wonder what Rix would do in this situation?"

"I already know," she said bitterly.

"And your choice?" Holm said wearily.

"Rix is a big, powerful man who has a whole army. Benn's a little, lost boy and he's got no one but me."

"Sleep on it, please. If you still feel the same way in the morning . . . "

"All right!"

CHAPTER 28

In all Glynnie's life, even in the dreadful days after she had been captured by Grandys and treated barbarously in his cells, she had never felt so alone as she did now.

She had given Holm the impression that she would sleep on her decision, though her mind had already been made up. She regretted lying to him but there was no choice. If she'd told him the truth he would have told Rix, and Rix would have prevented her from going.

She had lain in her bedroll for another sleepless hour, until the camp was quiet. Then she rose at midnight, made her way between the tents, bypassed the guards, and slipped away.

Now she was shivering in impenetrable blackness at the bottom of the hill, half a mile from the camp, heading for Caulderon. She had planned her route carefully last night, but the moon had since set and it was too dark to see any of the tracks through the mires. She had a lantern but dared not use it here—any light, however fleeting, would attract both enemies and allies.

The little hairs lifted on the back of her neck. Glynnie had an unnerving feeling that there was someone behind her. But how could there be? She could not see the tip of her nose.

She drew the knife on her hip, more for security than anything else, but as it came free of the sheath she took a hard, glancing blow to the top of the head. She struck out instinctively, slamming the knife backwards, and felt it pass through soft flesh before hitting bone. Liquid gurgled.

Her attacker let out a sharp cry, either pain or shock. Glynnie stumbled forward, caught her foot on a stone and fell. She struck her breastbone on another stone, knocking the wind out of her. The knife slipped from her hand. She groped around frantically for it before remembering that she had four more. She crawled a few yards, drew her second knife and rose to a crouch. Where was he? From the cry she could tell it was a man.

She could not hear anything save the faint sigh of wind across dry grass. Had she injured him? She could not tell. That gurgling sound might have been water flooding from a punctured leather water bottle.

Glynnie rubbed her skull and felt a long oval bruise there. The blow must have been intended to knock her unconscious, but perhaps he'd misjudged her height in the darkness. Though how could he see her at all when she could see nothing?

She took a careful step sideways, feeling that prickling sensation

on the back of her neck again. Did he know who she was? Had
Holm been right? Had Grandys sent the dreams about Benn to
entice her out?

Still there was no sound, though she had heard nothing before he
struck. He knew how to move silently in the dark and could be anywhere. He could be one step behind her—

Panic surged and she whirled, striking out wildly in all directions, though the knife touched only air. From several yards away
she made out a low, chuckling sound. Was he laughing at her panic
and her feeble attempts to protect herself?

There it was again. She turned slowly, straining into the blackness, trying to pinpoint the sound. It came from low down, as if he
was creeping towards her. Dare she use her lantern to check? She
didn't have a choice. Without light, her disadvantage was fatal.

With exquisite care she untied the lantern from the bottom of her
pack, slid the shutter across until it was almost closed, clicked the
striker and moved sideways in the same movement. It did not light.
She clicked again and moved again, sure he'd use the sound to
attack.

Nothing happened, though again she heard that faint chuckle.
On the fifth click the wick caught. Glynnie put her hand across the
top of the slit, tilted the lantern downwards so it could not be seen
from a distance and swept the narrow beam around her.

And froze. The lantern beam showed a lean, bald-headed gnome
of a man lying on the ground four yards away, head tilted back and
arms outspread. A red gash jagged across his lower belly, just above
the groin, to his left hipbone. Her instinctive backwards stab had
done terrible damage. Blood and dark fluids, pooled inside, were
ebbing out of the gash with faint chuckling sounds.

He wasn't dead, but Glynnie had treated enough war wounds to
know he had little time left. She went closer and bent over, watching his hands, though she did not think he posed any threat now.

"You're going to die," she said. "I'm sorry."

"Yes." He spoke faintly, as though it was a struggle to draw
enough breath. "Fair exchange . . . I suppose."

"Did Grandys send you?"

"Mmm . . ."

"For me?"

"Not . . . specifically."

"How did you find me?"

He tried to raise his left hand to his eye, but his fingers opened and a stubby crystal the size of her thumb slipped free, clacking against a pebble.

"What's that?" said Glynnie.

His arm struck the ground. He would never answer. He was dead.

She prodded the crystal with her knife. The ends were flat, as if the crystal had been cut and polished, and the cross-section was shaped like a hexagon. She picked it up gingerly and looked at it side-on, thinking that it might be cursed in some way. She waved it in front of her right eye and a round patch of the ground became visible, as if picked out by a dull grey light, though when she lowered the crystal all she saw was darkness.

She looked down at the corpse. How easily he had died; almost as easily as the sentry she had murdered. It reminded her that Benn was just a little, timid boy, alone in a violent city. How could he have survived all this time with no one to look after him?

She imagined his small body lying in some stinking alley, or thrown onto a heap with so many other dead. Abandoned to be eaten by vermin, as this unknown man would be—

Glynnie shuddered and extinguished the lantern. She had to crush all such thoughts or despair would freeze her and she would not be able to go on.

Holding the crystal to her eye, she hurried south-west through the marshes and mires towards the fishing village of Tinker's Cleft, on the cliffed bay she had seen last night. When the army had passed the bay yesterday there had been dozens of fishing boats on the water. Tinker's Cleft could not be more than five miles away.

Her plan was to steal a fishing skiff and sail to Caulderon while it was still dark. Though she had never sailed a boat, and could not swim more than twenty yards, it seemed a safer course than trying to make her way south through the war-scorched countryside. If she went that way she would have to pass Grandys' camp at Flume, and she wasn't going anywhere near him.

Sailing a skiff couldn't be that hard, could it? Back in the days when Glynnie had worked in the palace, she had sometimes sat on the lake wall on her half day off, watching Rix racing his little boat. It only had one sail and he had made it look easy ... though of course Rix had been sailing since he was a little boy.

It reminded her of that small, red-headed boy they had found floating face down in the lake on the terrible day of their escape; the day she had lost Benn. At first she'd thought the drowned boy had been Benn, and she had felt guilty about it afterwards. Guilty about feeling relieved that it had been another dead boy ...

She stopped in mid-step; she wasn't going to allow that line of thought either. Benn was alive! She conjured up the clearest image of him she could find, remembering the courage he had shown that morning as they fled down the tunnels. Benn was brave and clever. He would have survived, somehow ...

Glynnie reached Tinker's Cleft without incident. There was just enough light to make out the shapes of the nearest cottages of the village. She judged it to be a little after three in the morning. She put the crystal to her eye but it did not help—it was only useful for seeing objects within ten yards or so.

She skirted the village, afraid of dogs, and crept along a muddy shore towards the boats. Half a dozen fishing skiffs were drawn up along the shore and others were anchored in the shallow water. She heaved on the stern of the nearest skiff on the shore but could not budge it. She would have to take one of the craft in the water.

Glynnie picked out the smallest, hauled it in by its rope, climbed in and pushed it out with an oar, suppressing her guilt at stealing a poor family's livelihood. She sat in the darkness for a moment, expecting to be discovered, but all was still. No dogs barked, no light appeared in any cottage. There was no sound save the gentle lapping of ripples on the shore. Could it be this easy?

With an effort, she heaved the anchor out of the mud and stowed it at the bow. Now her hands were covered in smelly mud, and so were her clothes. She held a finger up to identify the wind direction—from the west—and used the crystal to study the layout of mast and sail. The sail was a simple, triangular piece of canvas tied to the mast and to a horizontal, swinging arm which she thought was called a boom. How hard could it be?

A wooden bucket under the bow was a quarter full of small, smelly fish. Bait, she assumed. A net was stowed neatly beside the bucket, and half a dozen hand lines, wound around short lengths of wood.

The bay, she knew, was shaped roughly like a triangle four or five miles on a side. The mouth, at Glimmering, was only a mile wide but if she headed for the distant glow of Caulderon she should find the mouth without too much trouble. Once outside, it was only a few miles across the lake to the city. There her real problems would begin.

She put that worry out of mind—first she had to learn how to sail. Glynnie unfastened the lashings, the skiff rocking beneath her, and pulled the sail out along the boom, but before she could tie it down the sail filled and the boom slammed into her chest, driving her against the side. The skiff rocked wildly and for a dreadful moment she thought she was going overboard, but the sail slid back along the boom and the pressure eased.

Glynnie drew the sail out again and tied it down as best she could in the darkness. She held the boom lightly, trying to sense the wind. It swung hard, the boat lurched, but this time she managed to hold it and the skiff began to move.

But the wind was driving her east, toward the cliff-bound shore, and it wasn't far away. She swung the boom and managed to turn the skiff a little more southerly, though not enough; she was still heading for the cliffs. To reach the mouth of the bay she would have to sail to the south-west though, with the wind coming from the west, how could she?

Glynnie had heard stories about ships tacking into the wind but had no idea how to do it. Could a skiff be tacked? She did not know, and no matter how she moved the sail the little boat kept heading east. Already she could hear waves breaking against the rocks, and if the skiff was driven against them it was bound to sink, and she would drown. She would have to row, though she had not done that before either.

She furled the sail and tied it to the mast, then got out the oars and inserted them in the rowlocks. Remembering the way Rix had rowed that dinghy on the night of their escape from Caulderon three months ago, Glynnie heaved on the oars. The blades skittered across the water but the craft did not move. She had to dig deeper, which meant holding the oar handles higher. This made it hard to exert enough force on them, especially with the mast in the way, but she dared not take it down. There wasn't time, and if she did she would probably never get it up again.

After several attempts with the oars she succeeded in moving the skiff a few feet, and looked over her shoulder. The cliffs were a dark mass looming above her, at least fifty feet high, and she could see the churning whiteness of waves breaking against the broken rocks at their base. She had to get away, now!

Glynnie dug deep with the left oar and to her joy the craft turned a little. She dug again and again, until she had turned the bow into the wind, then began to crab her way away from the rocks towards the centre of the bay.

Rowing was exhausting, and within minutes she had blisters on both hands. She had to ignore the pain, and the burning strain in her arms, back, neck and shoulders, and keep going … and going, as the sky cleared and the stars slowly wheeled, until a glow in the southern sky crept into view and she was looking out through the headlands of the bay. Was that Caulderon? No, it was too high up. It must be the top of one of the gently erupting Vomits.

She kept on for another ten minutes, clawing her way south-west, then the bay entrance opened up before her and she realised that the wind was behind her; she could use the sail at last. She looked south, then south-east and saw a thousand pinpoints of light on the hills of Caulderon, her destination. She shipped the oars, carefully unfurled the sail and tied it in place then, under a steady breeze, set sail for the city.

The greatest challenge lay ahead. Getting into Caulderon should not be that difficult, for its walls ran for five miles and much of that length had been broken in the war, or the great tsunami after the first eruption. The shattering earthquake a week and a half ago was bound to have brought more wall down, and Lyf's army could hardly guard it all.

After she got inside the city, Glynnie did not think she would attract much attention. Dressed in her drab, mud-covered clothes she would look like every other miserable citizen. As long as she kept her head down, why would anyone take notice of her?

The big danger would come as soon as she started to ask questions about Benn.

CHAPTER 29

Holm burst into the command tent. "Rix, she's gone!'

'Who's gone?" said Rix, without looking up. "Gone where?"

"Glynnie's gone to Caulderon. To look for Benn."

The acid in Rix's belly boiled. He dropped the map. "How do you know?"

"I happened upon her on the crag, last night. She was really upset and I got her to talk about things. Talk them through."

"And you didn't bother to tell me?" Rix said with soft menace. "Didn't think I'd want to know?"

"I told her that she had to tell you, otherwise I would. She promised she'd tell you when . . . *if* she came to a decision to leave."

"But she was lying."

"Evidently."

"When did she go?"

"Sometime after I went to bed, apparently. Around midnight, it appears. On foot."

"Six hours ago." Rix swore fluently. He looked around and realised that Jackery was staring at him. "Could you leave us for five minutes?"

Jackery nodded and went out.

"Grandys wants revenge on her, because she made him a laughing stock," said Rix. "He probably sent Glynnie's nightmares to lure her out of the camp."

"I told her as much," said Holm.

"But it didn't sway her."

"Would it have swayed you, if you were in her position?"

"Probably not," Rix said grudgingly. He knew damn well it would not have made any difference. "What am I supposed to do?"

"The key question is—is she safer here, or gone?"

"How can she be safe outside the camp, when Grandys is hunting her? Or in Caulderon, an enemy-held city?"

"I think—"

"I can't let her go," Rix burst out. "If you could have seen the way she took Grandys on that night at Bastion Cowly, great brute that he is. She was fearless, Holm. No, Glynnie was terrified, yet she took Grandys on, even though if he'd caught her he could have killed her with a single blow. She's the best woman there is, and I love her. She's everything to me."

"If you'd said all that to Glynnie last night, instead of me now, she might still be here."

"Well, I'm a bloody fool."

"That goes without saying," Holm said drily.

It was the kind of remark Tobry had often made. Rix felt his eyes prickle but he blinked the moisture away. There was no time for it.

"If Grandys gets her—If he's got her . . . "

"How would you find her, anyway? Besides, you've got—"

"Don't tell me—I've got this stinking army to command!"

Holm closed his mouth without speaking.

"Ten days ago I chose my army over Tali," Rix went on. "If I'd ridden after her straight away I might have got her back from Rufuss, but I didn't, and it's eating me alive; I can't do it again."

"You took on the command. You swore to put your country's army first."

"What the hell do you want me to do?"

"What matters most to you?"

"Don't do this to me, Holm. How can I be expected to choose between the fate of my country and the life of the woman I love?"

"You created the situation by ignoring her desperate need to find Benn. In a way, you forced her to act the way she has. Now you do have to choose."

"She went on foot," said Rix. "And it was a dark night; she might not have got far. On a fast horse, I might catch her in a couple of hours—assuming I can discover where she went."

"She was going to Caulderon."

"But which way?"

"The fastest, safest way, I'd imagine."

"She can't sail and she can barely swim. She'd have to go overland. Via Gordion it's only twenty miles."

"But that way she'd have to go past Grandys, at Flume . . . unless she swung way out to the east. Which would make the trip closer to thirty miles."

"I can't guess which way she'd go," said Rix. "I'll have to track her." He went to the door. "Jackery?"

He appeared at once.

"Call Captain Hork in," said Rix. "You and I are going riding. Get the horses ready, and a couple of days' supplies, just in case."

Jackery went out. Shortly Hork came through the flap of the tent, rubbing his eyes. Even half asleep he looked extraordinarily handsome, and Rix held it against him. As Holm had pointed out previously, Hork wasn't much of a leader, but he was the most experienced officer Rix had.

"I'm going scouting," said Rix. "I may be a few hours. In my absence, you're acting commander, but don't do anything foolish. Hold this position, and don't engage the enemy unless they attack up the hill. Got that?"

"Yes," said Hork.

"If you need advice, Holm will be close by."

Holm started to protest, saw the look on Rix's face and closed his mouth without speaking.

Rix went out. Holm and Jackery followed.

"Try to keep the lid on where I've gone," said Rix. "Though I dare say half the army knows that Glynnie has bolted by now."

"Probably not half," said Holm, "but everyone will know by breakfast."

Rix cursed. Jackery came up, leading two horses with bulging saddlebags. Rix nodded to Holm. He and Jackery mounted, rode through the camp and down the hill as the sun was rising.

"You know anything about tracking, soldier?" said Rix.

"She went that way," said Jackery, pointing south-west.

They followed Glynnie's light tracks through the dry grass, down off the ramp of the hill and south towards the mires. The knot in Rix's stomach was growing.

"She's just a girl," he said. "And a city girl at that. How can she hope to survive out here?"

"Something lying in the grass up ahead," said Jackery.

Rix raced past him and swung down, but it wasn't her. The dead man was on his back, eyes and mouth open, and the scavengers had already begun their work. In this hungry land, by tomorrow there would be nothing left of him save bones.

"How do you read it?" he said after a minute.

"The same way as you do, I expect. He jumped Glynnie and she managed to knife him . . . a lucky stroke, in the dark."

Fear tightened his windpipe. "Was he alone? Do you think they've got her?"

Jackery walked around in a widening spiral. "He was alone. And you can see her prints here, in the soft ground."

They remounted and followed. "She's moving faster now," said Jackery. "South-west."

"Why that way?"

"Looks like she's heading to Tinker's Cleft. A fishing village."

Rix considered that for a minute, his anxiety growing. "But Glynnie can't sail. Can't swim worth a damn, either. Not that it'd make a difference if she could. The water's too cold at this time of year."

"Maybe, after the attack, she figured it was a smaller risk than going by land."

"Let's ride."

They galloped across to the bay and down a track to the village, which was astir. The fishermen were gathered on the shore, children were carrying water up to the cottages and the chimneys were smoking.

Rix rode up to the men at the boats. "Has anyone lost a boat?"

They pointed to a skinny old fellow, white of hair and short on teeth.

"How long ago was it taken?" said Rix.

The oldster shrugged. "In the night."

Rix tossed him a small bag of coin, then scanned the water. Two skiffs were already out and he saw half a dozen sails in the distance, though they were too distant for him to make out their occupants.

"We'd get a better look from Cape Kimbo," said Jackery.

"Where's that?"

Jackery pointed to the headland that formed the eastern side of the bay's entrance.

"Come on," said Rix.

They galloped up the steep path and turned right along a track that ran south-west along the cliff-top of the bay towards the entrance, which was about five miles distant. At intervals Rix stopped, ran to the cliff edge and peered down, expecting to see a wrecked boat. He saw nothing.

At Cape Kimbo he dismounted and forced his way through a patch of wind-twisted pines to a bare rock platform, and looked south. Caulderon was only two miles away. There were plenty of fishing boats on the lake though none looked as though they had sailed south from this bay. He went back through the pines.

"No sign of her," he said to Jackery, who had been several hundred yards behind and was only now tying up his horse.

They returned to the lookout and Rix scanned the shoreline of Caulderon through his binoculars. A large number of boats were drawn up there, and more were anchored or moored offshore. He could see dozens of people on the shoreline, gleaning, he assumed. From this distance he could almost have identified Glynnie through the glasses, but he saw no one who looked familiar.

"She'd be in hiding long since," said Jackery. "If . . . "

If she got there. If she hadn't drowned. If she hadn't been caught.

"How could she be such a fool?" Rix said harshly. "Look at all the guards on the wall. How could she possibly think she could make it through?"

"I would never call Glynnie a fool," said Jackery cautiously. "But when you care that much about someone, you accept the risk . . . Because to do otherwise would be betraying the one you love . . . and if you did that you would die inside. "

Rix turned to Jackery in surprise, realising how little he knew about the man.

"Sounds as though you speak from personal experience."

"I had a wife. We lived in Tumulus Town, one of the first parts of Caulderon to be occupied when the war began. I was away with the army, down near Gullihoe ..."

"I saw what the enemy did to Gullihoe," Rix said quietly. What a night that had been.

"When we came back, Tumulus Town was enemy territory, swarming with soldiers, and they were making an example of the place to terrorise the rest of Caulderon. But my wife was there, and I loved her."

Rix felt his hackles rise.

Jackery's voice was flat, hard, dead. His eyes went bleak. "I had to get in. And I did get in."

Rix could imagine what it had been like. He'd seen all too much of it in the war, and for every atrocity he'd witnessed he'd heard stories of another dozen.

"But you were too late."

"They treated her the way women are treated in war. Then killed her."

"I'm sorry," said Rix.

"Hundreds of women in Tumulus Town suffered the same fate. I wish I'd never gone back; I'll never erase those images."

"If you could have saved her, you would have."

"Why couldn't it have been me?" said Jackery. "When I became a soldier, I half expected to die in combat—it's part of the job. Why her?"

"For every soldier who's died in this war, there have been three or four civilians."

"War is shit!" Jackery cried.

"And the sooner it's over, the better."

But Jackery wasn't listening. He was heading back through the forest, almost running. Rix did not go after him; no doubt he wanted to be alone.

Suddenly conscious that if he could see the enemy in Caulderon, they could see him, Rix went down on his belly. He swept his binoculars along the walls, making note of the defences. There must be a couple of thousand troops guarding the city walls, and many thousands more patrolling the streets, night and day. Caulderon might have been subdued but it was a great city with a population well over a hundred thousand, and controlling such a city would not be easy.

A wild thought popped into Rix's head. What if he attacked Caulderon, took part of it and roused the people to insurrection? If they rose to support him it would be a huge blow to Lyf and an enormous boost to Hightspall's crumbling morale. It would also go a long way to making up for his ignominious flight from Caulderon—a broken, dispossessed lord, universally condemned for helping to bring down his house and betraying his evil parents.

He shook his head, smiling at such foolishness. It would turn the city into a slaughterhouse and most of the dead would be innocent civilians like Jackery's wife. Besides, Lyf would not give up Caulderon easily, and his army at Mulclast was only a day's march away . . .

The more immediate problem was Grandys. Flume was five miles east of here, an afternoon stroll away—less than an hour's ride on a good path. Grandys would have scouts out, and if he were to discover Rix was here—

He withdrew into the trees. He had cursed Glynnie for her folly but it was nothing compared to his own; a handful of Grandys' men could trap him on this headland. And trying to find Glynnie was a monumental stupidity, so why was he contemplating it? Why wasn't he creeping back to his army by the safest route he could find?

Rix took bread and cheese from his saddlebags, ate it and washed it down with swigs of warm, flat beer from the skin tied to his saddlebags. He had just finished when Jackery returned. His eyes were a dark, bruised red, his face unnaturally pale. Rix did not remark upon it.

"I've been up on that little hill we saw half a mile back," said Jackery.

"Any movement from Grandys' direction?" said Rix. "Any sign of his scouts?"

"No. Are you going back, or on?"

"After Glynnie, you mean?"

"Yes."

"I don't know. I can't decide. What do you—?"

Jackery was shaking his head. "Don't ask me."

"Sorry," said Rix. "Indecision is one of my greater flaws."

"Whatever you do, and whatever its outcome, you'll regret you didn't make the other choice. The important thing is to do *something*."

"You're right—I'm going after Glynnie as soon as it's dark."

Jackery said nothing.

"Do you think that's the wrong decision?" Rix said, immediately regretting his rashness.

Jackery, wisely, did not reply. Rix sat there for another five minutes, twisting on the knife, then leapt up. "I can't bear it here, not knowing what's going on up north."

They rode back to the hill, which was pimple-shaped at its rocky top and, being mostly bare of trees, had a relatively uninterrupted view in all directions. After tethering the horses in thick forest along a rivulet they climbed the hill and wriggled onto the top.

Rix checked on Grandys' camp at Flume. There was no sign of movement, nor on Bolstir hill. He sighed, rubbed his eyes and yawned.

"I'll take the watch if you need a nap," said Jackery.

"I'm too wound up. But you should."

Rix sat with his back to a boulder, closed his eyes and tried to think, to plan, but his mind was too thick and sluggish.

"By the look of you, you need it more than me," said Jackery.

"All right." Rix glanced at the sun, a pale disc through the brown, ash-tinged clouds. It was after 10 a.m. "But just an hour, no more."

He closed his eyes, thinking about Glynnie only a few miles away. With the wind at his back he could sail there in under an hour, though how could he enter Caulderon without being recognised instantly . . .

Jackery was shaking him violently. "Deadhand, wake up!"

Rix's eyes shot open. "What's the matter?"

"Your army is moving south! And Grandys' men are marching north."

Rix scrambled to his feet, rubbed the sleep out of his eyes and stared north. Jackery thrust the binoculars into his hand. Rix peered through them.

"What's Hork up to? I gave him express orders to stay on Bolstir."

"Grandys must have lured him out."

"Surely Hork isn't that much of a fool?"

"He's hungry for glory. And he has a high opinion of himself—he doesn't like being told what to do."

"Then what the hell's he doing in the army?"

Jackery shrugged. "What are any of us?"

"How can he think to take on Grandys' army?" Rix stiffened. "Hork may want glory, but he's not suicidal . . ."

"What is it?"

"I think Grandys did lure Hork out—but not physically."

"I'm not sure what you're saying."

"Grandys once put a *command* on me with Maloch. The command was a form of magery and it forced me to obey him. I'll bet he's using it again—against Hork!"

"We'd better go," said Jackery, staring north.

Rix felt another gut spasm. He turned towards Caulderon. Glynnie, I'm sorry.

She would never forgive him for this abandonment, but he had little hope of getting into Caulderon without being caught, and no hope of finding her and getting her out. While only a few miles north his entire army was at risk, and leaderless.

"Come on," he said, running for the edge of the hill. "We're riding for Bolstir!"

CHAPTER 30

It must have been six in the morning when the skiff nosed in to a mud-covered beach. Only a hundred yards to go. It was still dark, though dawn was not far off, and Glynnie had to be well inside the city wall before the sun rose.

The line of the broken wall was illuminated here and there by flares, and through the lake mist she made out three watch posts, two on her left and the other to the right. Guards moved in and out of the light, never relaxing their vigilance.

She scanned the beach with the crystal, left and right as far as she could see. All she saw was mud and large blocks of stone, dumped there when the tsunami had broken the lake-front wall months ago.

She sat in the skiff for a minute or two, working on her cover story. She had to abandon the boat, since there was nowhere to hide it. It would not be here when she came back—*if* she did. She would have to find another way to escape the city.

If she were caught, Glynnie planned to say that she had been gleaning along the lake shore, trying to find food for herself and her little sister, who was ill. The story was plausible, though it was hard to imagine, in this ruined, half-starving city, that there was anything edible left to find. She stuffed a handful of bait fish into a side pocket of her pack. They stank, but no one in Caulderon could afford to be fastidious.

There was a gap of some hundred and fifty yards between the nearest guard post on the left and the one on the right. She made for the centre of the gap, keeping low, though in the darkness there was little risk of being seen. She moved carefully, testing each footstep. She could not afford to have a pebble clack underfoot; any sound would carry to the guards on this still night, and after Lyf's defeat by Grandys last week they would be on high alert.

Her heart was racing, her throat dry. She tried to calm herself as she crept forward. The broken wall was just ahead now, a jumble of shoulder-high stone blocks. She felt her way along them, looking for a gap, but did not find one.

She climbed up, feeling her way. The stone was damp, covered in moss, and slippery. She reached the top, felt a large gap ahead and hesitated, afraid of falling and making a noise, or breaking an ankle.

Glynnie found a way down to the left and reached solid ground. She was in the city! She swallowed a lump in her throat at the thought that Benn could be so close, then fished out the crystal to spy out the way forward.

As she put it to her eye, a strong arm locked around her neck from behind. She dropped the crystal and went for her knife but a hand caught her wrist in a grip she could not break.

"Lights," said a man's voice, a Cythonian accent. "Let's see who the spy is."

She lunged and kicked furiously but could not get free; the arm had tightened across her throat until she could not draw breath.

"Stop struggling or I'll choke you," the man said.

A bright lantern was unshuttered directly in Glynnie's eyes, dazzling her. Another man caught her free hand, searched her with meticulous thoroughness and took her knives.

Her wrists were bound behind her back. Her captor shoved her along a muddy path that wound uphill for forty or fifty yards to a beautifully built manse set on a small mound. Glynnie's eyes widened, for she recognised it. She was in the grounds of what had, until a few months ago, been Palace Ricinus. She had worked there as a maidservant all her life.

But Palace Ricinus was gone. A huge circle of yellow stone buildings, supported on rows of columns, had been erected where the centre of the palace had been. And she knew, with utter certainty, that she was about to be erased just as completely.

Her captor thrust her through the doorway of the manse into a long room with an ornate plasterwork ceiling and a series of windows along the left wall. There was a small square table in the middle with four chairs around it. Papers were neatly stacked on a longer table along the end wall.

"Sit," said the man who had caught her. He drew the nearest chair out.

She sat. He took the chair across the table from her. He was short and stocky, with pale grey skin, black eyes and wavy grey hair, cut short. He wore an officer's uniform and looked tired and harried. The other man, a burly fellow with close-cropped hair, stood by the door.

"I am Captain Ricips," the stocky man said. His voice was crisp, businesslike, with a slight rumble. "What is your name?"

"Halie," said Glynnie. She dared not give her own name, since it was bound to be on one of their lists. Halie had been the name of her little sister, three years younger than Glynnie. She had only lived for a year. Glynnie felt tears form as she spoke her sister's name. She had not thought about her in ages.

"Why were you sneaking through the city wall after curfew?" said Ricips.

"I wasn't sneaking," she said softly. "I—I'd been out trying to find food—"

"In the middle of the night?"

It was the weak point of her story, one she had not been able to find a good explanation for. "If something fresh washed up on the shore, I'd be the first to find it."

"In pitch darkness?"

"I'm so hungry, I'd smell it."

He gave her a disbelieving look, then opened his hand and rolled the hexagonal crystal across the table. It made a small rattling sound as each face turned.

Glynnie's throat closed over. She tried to pretend that she'd never seen the crystal before, but knew he would never believe her. She could feel the blood draining from her face.

"What's that?" she croaked.

"It's the Herovian night-shard you were looking through before you got out of your boat," he said with sudden, cold ferocity. "You tried to dispose of it as I caught you, because it's proof you're an enemy spy."

"It's not mine. I found it," she said weakly.

"What's your real name and who are you spying for? It'd better not be Axil Grandys!"

"I'm not a spy!" she cried, rising from her chair and looking him full in the eye. "I'm not! I'm just a poor maidservant. You've searched me. You know I've got no money, no food, *nothing*."

Ricips considered her for twenty or thirty seconds. She thought he was wavering but she could not think of anything to say that would improve her case. Better to say nothing than be caught in a lie. *Another* lie.

The burly guard started, came across and whispered in Ricips' ear. They both studied Glynnie.

"Are you sure?" said Ricips.

The burly guard's reply was indistinguishable. Ricips went to the end table, riffled through the papers and drew out several pages held together by a pin. Glynnie could not read what was written there, though it appeared to be a list of names.

"It was at the Glimmering peace conference," said the burly guard. "I'm sure of it. She cried out as Grandys took Rixium Ricinus away."

Ricips checked the list, looked down at Glynnie and read the list again.

"You are a maidservant, but your name isn't Halie. It's Glynnie. You were a maid at Palace Ricinus, and now you're Rixium's consort. His *lover*."

"No!" she cried.

"You deny that you are the maidservant Glynnie, formerly of Palace Ricinus?"

There was no point. "I'm Glynnie. But I'm not Rixium's lover, nor have I ever been."

"But he is your close friend?"

"Yes. At least, he *was* . . ."

"And Rixium served Grandys. He fought beside Grandys."

"Rixium was under Grandys' sorcerous command," she said desperately.

"And perhaps still is. Now you come spying for Rixium, or Grandys, carrying a Herovian night-shard. What were you looking for?"

Glynnie had to tell all or she was going to die. She was probably going to be put to death anyway.

"Rixium isn't serving Grandys!" she cried. "And neither am I. We're both on his death list—you must know that. We humiliated Grandys when we escaped from Bastion Cowly. I battered him to the ground with a length of timber."

"We've heard the *story*," said Ricips. "But it can't possibly be true. He would have torn you apart."

"He was so drunk he could barely stand up."

"Perhaps Grandys put the story about himself, to conceal his alliance with Rixium," said Ricips.

"That's just stupid!" she said hotly.

Ricips stiffened. His lips thinned.

"Grandys has an ego the size of a palace," she gabbled. "He would never spread a story about being humiliated by a little maidservant."

"Maybe not," he conceded, "but it doesn't explain how you got away with it."

"Grandys probably would have torn me apart, had not the men of Cowly counterattacked just then."

"Hunh!" said Ricips. "Why have you come back to Caulderon, Maidservant Glynnie?"

For the first time, she thought she might have a chance.

"To find my little brother, Benn," she said desperately. "He went missing when Rixium and I escaped three months ago, and I can't bear the thought of him being all alone and lost." Without thinking, she reached out across the table to Ricips. "Please help me. Benn is all I've got."

He leaned away from her, grimacing as if the plea was distasteful to him. He consulted the list, then frowned.

"Is he there?" said Glynnie. "Please?"

"How dare you question me? Who gave you the night-shard?"

"No one. I was attacked by a spy after I left our camp at Bolstir in the middle of the night. He hit me on the head." She bent her head so he could see the bruise and the blood in her red hair. "I stabbed out in the dark and killed him. I didn't mean to. He had the night-shard in his hand."

Ricips grunted.

"Please?" said Glynnie. "Are you a family man? Benn is all—"

To her surprise, he answered. "I am a family man, as it happens, and I accept that part of your story is true—the part about looking for your little brother. I would want to do the same, but—"

"Is he on the list?" she said softly. "Is he still alive?"

He looked down at his papers. "He *was* on the list, but nothing is known of him. I can tell you no more." He looked up to the burly guard. "Take her to the holding cells, Ferdo."

"Holding cells?" said Glynnie, looking from Ricips to Ferdo. She saw no hope in either man's eyes. "What for?"

"The executions are done as humanely as possible," said Ricips. "Once a week. You will die two days from this coming evening."

"But ... I told you, I'm just looking for Benn. I'm not a spy. Please, give me a chance to explain."

"You have explained," he said without looking up, "but I am tasked with the protection of my people, and it's a duty I care about passionately. You may be innocent, however the association with Rixium Ricinus, and with the monster Axil Grandys, is so grave that I cannot allow you to live."

"Then why don't you kill me now!" she screamed. "Go on, take out your sword and do it."

"It is not my business to execute. Only to try." Ricips gestured to Ferdo, who heaved Glynnie to her feet and led her out.

As she was taken to the holding cells, she reflected bitterly that Rix had been right. Only a fool would try to get into an occupied city in the middle of a no-holds-barred war. Guilt burned her. She had abandoned him, without saying goodbye, at the moment when he had most needed her support.

She was a fool, and now she was going to die, for nothing.

Worse than nothing. They had lost interest in Benn, but now she had drawn attention to him they would renew the search.

If he was still alive they would probably kill him too.

CHAPTER 31

We'll never get there in time, Rix thought. Grandys will be massacring my army by now.

He and Jackery galloped north for several miles, splashed through the stream that ran down to Tinker's Cleft, then rode up the slippery clay bank on the far side. Rix swung up a long, shallow slope, topped the rise, and the lowland called Lidden Field opened out before him. To the left was the expanse of the Lodden Mires: miles of trackless fens, fathomless lakes, and sticky bogs and marshes. He reined his horse to a stop, put the field glasses to his eyes and groaned.

"What is it?" said Jackery.

"They're already fighting. Whatever possessed Hork to attack at Lidden Field, with the Lodden Mire at his back? He's got no room to move, and if Grandys sends a detachment to the north to surround him—"

"As he's doing now—what are you going to do, Deadhand?"

"If we race west along the cliffs of the bay," Rix indicated the direction with a sweep of his left hand, "we'll be concealed by woodland, then the marshes. We'll swing north around Lodden Mire, turn east and head through that copse of pines up there. Then we'll burst out into the open only a couple of hundred yards away from the enemy's back line, there where it's thinnest. We'll hit them at full gallop and try to drive right through to our men."

"Two of us trying to fight through a hundred and fifty," said Jackery. "Sounds like suicide." He flashed Rix a savage grin. "Let's ride."

They rode west at three-quarter pace along the pale cliffs, where the land was bare save for a few windswept sudel bushes, leafless at this time of year, their deadly black berries still clinging to the tips of the twigs. Ahead the path wound slightly down and they could no longer see the battlefield.

As they crossed a path that ran down to another fishing village, Rix caught a snatch of the battlefield clamour—the distant, attenuated clang of sword on shield, the thunder of hooves—then lost it.

They turned north, racing around the northern side of the Lodden Mires, and east again. He estimated the distance—a mile and a half to go. The best part of ten minutes' ride in this country. Too long! Grandys could tear right through an army in ten minutes. Rix had seen him do it.

There was no sound now save their own horses' hooves and his thumping heart. They were low here and he would not see the battlefield again until they cleared the northern side of the marshes and emerged from the patch of pines beyond that.

"I'm worried," said Jackery.

Rix was too. He had laid out the battlefield in his mind and was calculating possibilities, though they all ended badly. Even if he could break through the enemy lines where they were at their thinnest and take command of his army, how could he beat a superior force from such a strategically poor position?

Which meant he was riding to his death.

"Be damned!" he said aloud, as they skirted the northen edge of Lodden Mire and entered the patch of pines.

"Sir?" said Jackery.

He could hear the clamour of battle again. They galloped to the edge of the trees, then stopped. His horse was blowing hard, though not exhausted. A couple of minutes' rest would do it good. Everything relied on the strength of the horses now.

He looked out and down into the bowl of Lidden Field. His army had been corralled into a tight space only a few hundred yards across, with any escape blocked to the west by the curve of Lodden Mire and to the south by a small lake. Grandys' forces enclosed them on the eastern side, with a crescent-shaped detachment on the northeast blocking their passage back to the camp at Bolstir. The crescent Rix had to break through.

Clearly, Grandys' plan was to annihilate Hork's army. Judging by the litter of bodies on the ground, the toll had already been horrific.

"We're going to win," Rix said fiercely. "We can't consider anything else."

"Yes, Deadhand."

"I mean it. We've got to save part of our army, at least. When we get to our men I'm going to take command and try to fight our way out. Are you with me?"

"I'm with you, sir . . . "

"What is it, Jackery?"

"What if this plan of yours is being influenced by enemy magery?"

Rix faltered. No, he thought. I'm not under their influence. *I'm not!*

"I don't see how anything I do can make things worse. Let's ride."

The enemy lines he was aiming for were only two hundred yards away, and ten ranks deep. He and Jackery backtracked through the woodland for fifty yards so the horses could get a good run-up. Rix drew his sword, made sure the mailed gauntlet was secure on his dead hand and spurred his horse. The great beast, eighteen hands high, accelerated smoothly; by the time they reached the edge of the forest it was going full gallop and already a few yards ahead of Jackery's smaller mount.

"Charge!" said Rix.

Horse and rider crossed the two hundred yards in ten seconds and slammed into the enemy ranks with bone-smashing force, the warhorse's chest armour battering the soldiers out of the way and driving in to the seventh rank before slowing. Rix hacked to left and right, taking a terrible toll on the foot soldiers, who had not realised he was coming until it was too late.

The lines of men before him panicked as the leviathan bored towards them; they went careering into the ranks to either side, knocking each other down. Rix ignored everyone save those enemy directly in front of him. The only thing that mattered was getting through to his army. He let out a great battle cry, spurred his horse on, took off a couple of heads and burst through.

Jackery had also made it through, though, being a smaller man on a lighter horse, he'd had rather more trouble and was bleeding from a wound in his right hip and a cut at the top of his shoulder. Not bad wounds, though.

Rix stood up in his stirrups so his men would be in no doubt as to his identity. They roared and surged towards him, though he could see no sign of Hork or any of his officers. Had they been killed in the first onslaught? It would be like Grandys to target them.

"We're fighting our way out," he shouted. He held up a hand. "Cavalry first, infantry to follow!" He raised his sword high. "Cavalry, to me!"

A hundred horsemen came around from the left flank. "Charge!" he bellowed, and turned back into the depleted enemy lines.

The cavalry went with him and, after a sickening minute or two of trampling and slaughter, they burst through the enemy crescent. Hundreds of the enemy lay dead and the rest of the detachment on the northern side were fleeing into the trees, though already a larger force was streaming up from the south to plug the gap.

Rix waved his sword over his head. Could he possibly get the rest of his troops out? *"Infantry, to me! To me!"*

A quarter of his surviving army, taking heart from the sudden reversal, streamed through before the enemy's reinforcements flooded in to close the gap. The rest of his troops pulled back into a defensive position.

Rix used his cavalry to shepherd his rescued troops away to a safe distance, then turned.

"It won't work twice," said Jackery, beside him.

"No." Rix was doing the numbers. "We got eighty riders out, and seven hundred men."

"Leaving another two thousand behind to die, and a thousand already dead."

"Thanks to that bloody fool, Hork," Rix said bitterly. "Did you see him?"

"Didn't see any of the officers."

"How am I going to save the rest?"

Jackery surveyed the enemy lines, which were now a phalanx of bristling spears twenty men deep. Ten ranks were facing him and the other ten had their backs turned. They were slowly moving towards the survivors of his once proud army, presumably intending to drive them into the marshes and the lake.

Rix did a quick count of the enemy numbers and felt a twinge of alarm. "Have you counted Grandys' men?"

"Haven't had a chance, yet." Jackery made an estimate. "That's odd. I only get four thousand."

"Me too. And maybe a thousand casualties. Where are the rest? Were they ever here?"

"I don't think so. And I'm not seeing Grandys either."

"Then who's commanding them?"

"No idea."

"If Grandys *was* here, he'd be out front, trying to take my head off," said Rix. "This must be the trap he's been planning for the past week and a half. He must be waiting somewhere nearby, to close the trap."

"What do we do?"

"We're not going to do anything useful here. Come on."

Rix signalled to his troops to follow, then rode south, heading over the low hills to the south of Lidden Field. It was one of the hardest things he had ever done.

"The rest of your army think we're abandoning them to die," said Jackery.

Rix did not reply.

CHAPTER 32

"Are we abandoning our men to die?" said Jackery as Rix, his eighty cavalry and seven hundred surviving men streamed south over the low hills beyond Lidden Field.

"I'm working on a plan," said Rix.

"If you can save them it'll be the most brilliant plan as ever was."

Rix kept a careful lookout but saw no sign of Grandys and the rest of his army. If there was a trap, it was well hidden. After a mile or two, when the armies behind him were out of sight, he turned west into a patch of scrub in the bottom of a valley and continued along it until it opened out into a broad, elbow-shaped swathe of marshland. He skirted it on the southern side and turned hard north.

"If I remember rightly," said Rix, "a narrow path runs north from here back towards Lidden Field, skirting the boggy eastern edge of the lake. Further north the path's hidden by the rise of that hill. The path is cramped down to a few feet wide and from the north, if you didn't know it was there, you wouldn't see it."

"Is it wide enough to get seven hundred men and eighty riders through in time?"

"It'd better be."

As they went north the track became ever narrower, squeezed between the rushy marshland on the left and the steep side of the small, curving hill to the right, until only two men could walk abreast and the riders had to go in single file.

"At least we can't be seen from the north," said Jackery.

"But if they send someone a mile south to the edge of the hill, and he looks down, he'll spot us. Then it'll be a simple matter to trap us here and kill the lot of us."

They continued forward until, after another mile, they could climb up and peer over the curve of the slope towards Lidden Field.

"They're cutting Hork's force to pieces," said Jackery, "and forcing them towards the lake. If we don't attack soon—"

"We can't burst out into the open from here," said Rix. "They'd have too much warning. We'll keep behind the rise until it peters out."

He drew on his steel gauntlet and manually clenched the fingers, one by one. The hill on their right had dwindled to a low, curving rise. The lake stood a quarter of a mile ahead and to the left, with good ground to the north but endless mire on its western side.

The enemy army extended in a menacing inverted comma from the south-east, where the great mass of the troops were, all the way to the northern side of the lake, enclosing Hork's army and allowing no way of escape.

"We follow the line of this rise around that way," said Rix, pointing north-east. "There's a narrow band of land between the rise and the edge of the marsh. It's a bit wider there and if we're careful, moving ten abreast, the rise and the rushes will give us cover until we're only a hundred yards away. Then we'll charge and try to tear a gap through the middle, isolating the southern mass of the enemy from the rest and trapping them against the lake. With a lot of luck we might get the survivors out."

"If we don't hurry up," said Jackery, "there won't be any survivors."

Rix had to ignore that possibility. As soon as they burst into the open it would be on, bloody slaughter, because the enemy never retreated. He mounted and led the way, making sure his head did not show above the rise.

"Stay back, Deadhand," said Jackery from behind him. "A lucky arrow could kill you, and where will we be then?"

"There's only one way to lead men to their deaths—from the front."

Ahead, the rise curved around to the east, not much higher than a mounted man. Now reeds and tall rushes rose on the left, seven feet high. In places reeds choked the way ahead and Rix had to push between them, the horse's hooves squelching and sucking. He could hear the battle now—the thud of sword on shield, the clang of blade on blade, the dreadful shrieking of men who had taken mortal wounds and now had to wait minutes, or hours, before death released them from their agony.

After a couple of hundred yards he stopped, unsure he was doing the right thing.

"Trouble?" said Jackery.

"Just gathering my thoughts," Rix lied. "Have the men stop for a one-minute breather."

Jackery held up a hand. Rix dismounted and cut across the edge of the marsh, trying to make no sound. The sounds of combat were louder here; he must be almost on them. He parted the reeds and peered through.

The southern edge of the battle was only a hundred yards away and it was as he had feared. The enemy force was driving Hork's battered army towards the eastern side of the lake. They were defending valiantly but the closest men were only ten yards from the edge and, as the enemy tightened their encirclement, Hork's troops would have to choose between being hacked to pieces or drowning.

Rix crept out, up the rise and peered over the top. The enemy had more than a thousand soldiers along this side and they had their backs to him. If he hit them hard with his seven hundred and eighty men and took them by surprise, he might just reverse the situation.

He went back and explained the battle plan to Jackery and his other captains.

"We'll charge, fanning out as we go. Then, follow my signals."

"What's to stop them breaking through the way we've just come?" said Waysman.

"Good point," said Rix. "We'll leave fifty men here to defend this path. Stay hidden until it's too late for them to turn back."

He took three deep breaths, shook his captains' hands and

turned away. He had trained for this moment all his life. He could do it.

Even against Grandys?

Yes, even against him.

He mounted again and went forward around the edge of the reeds. Ahead, the rise curved around from the right, sloping steadily down until it barely concealed him. The men were fanning out behind him. Rix squared his shoulders, putting on a confidence he did not feel. He raised his sword, swung it down and spurred his horse forward.

"Charge!"

The cavalry charged, his infantry followed, and the aches and pains from the previous battle vanished. All eighty riders went with him, racing north for the weakness in the enemy's lines.

Rix was aiming to tear through this flank, leaving them isolated and surrounded on three sides, with nowhere to go but into the lake. Hopefully Hork's force would show enough initiative to drive them the rest of the way. Waysman's fifty would guard the path along the edge of the marsh and Pomfree would lead another fifty onto the eastern hill to hold it as well.

Rix got to within fifty yards before the enemy realised they were under attack from the rear. Horns sounded; movement spread through the ranks like ripples from half a dozen points as the soldiers at the rear swung around.

But again, the warning had come too late for them to form a solid rank before Rix's charge struck them with terrible force. He cut three men down with successive blows, thumped another in the back of the head with his mailed fist, and skewered a fifth.

He took stock and moved on, doing his bloody job as efficiently as possible until he was covered with gore and the enemy's flank had been cut off. Most of them were just boys, younger than his twenty years. They had not known any kind of battle until Grandys recruited them a month or two ago, and they had never experienced defeat.

Hork's men, who had been facing death only a minute before, counterattacked ferociously from the other side as if to make up for their shame. Rix could see the dawning panic in the enemy's eyes.

But he could not afford to pity them; it was kill or die. He left his third company to finish the grim work and withdrew the first and second companies. They ran north for a couple of hundred yards then plunged into the enemy's lines again.

The enemy knew they were coming but they were under attack from the front and rear now and, being at slightly higher elevation here, they could see what had happened to their left flank. The nearshore waters of the lake were tinged with red.

As he fought, Rix could not help the feeling that he'd had it easy. The enemy weren't fighting the way Grandys fought—he definitely wasn't here. But where was he? When would the trap close? And how?

"The enemy have lost two thousand," said Jackery, who had blood on either shoulder, the left worse than the right.

"And Hork's lost almost as many of ours," said Rix.

He had known the cost would be high. Indeed, it could have been far higher.

"The big question," said Jackery, "is where Grandys is, and his other three thousand men."

"I questioned one of his dying lieutenants," said Pomfree. "Grandys went racing north with the rest of his army, not long before dawn."

Rix stared into the northern distances. "*North*? Why?"

"No one knows."

"He must have had important news. Let's hope it was bad news. Did the other Heroes go with him?"

"They weren't here in the first place, save for Rufuss."

"Then where the hell are they?"

"No one knows."

"That's bad," said Rix. "If Syrten, Lirriam and Yulia weren't here, what are they up to?"

The question was unanswerable.

"I know where Rufuss is," Pomfree said suddenly.

"Where?"

"Behind you."

Rix turned and five or six hundred enemy were charging. In the middle, a full head taller than everyone else, was Rufuss.

CHAPTER 33

Rufuss was brandishing a halberd with an immensely long shaft, urging his men on.

"Jackery?" yelled Rix.

"Here!"

Rix took off his commander's hat and tossed it across. "Put that on. Take a couple of hundred men and block Rufuss's path to the north, just in case. If he doesn't go that way, attack from his rear."

Jackery swallowed, then raised the hat high. "Company, this way!" he shouted, and spurred to the north.

After a second, the men followed him. They would not have known who it was; they were following the hat, not the man. Rix fixed Rufuss's location in his mind, spurred his weary, blood-spattered horse and fought his way through the enemy ranks towards him.

"That's Rixium!" he heard Rufuss shout in his distinctive hard, brittle voice. "Cut him down."

Half a dozen of the biggest bravos turned Rix's way, but many others moved aside, clearly unwilling to take him on. They would all know that Rix had twice fought Grandys to a standstill, and they had seen him in battle. He was a ferocious warrior, almost unbeatable with that enormous sword in his left hand and the mailed glove over his dead right fist.

They had also seen what had happened to their fellows on the northern flank earlier, and their morale must be faltering. Under Grandys' command they had become used to winning, but Grandys was not here, Rufuss could never be an inspiring leader, and the enemy were showing unexpected resistance.

Where had Rufuss gone? There, forty yards away, on horseback in a clear space. Rix raced towards him. Rufuss swung the halberd and Rix heard it sing as its tip passed through the air inches from his face. He felt the sting of magery, too—it was an enchanted blade.

But an unwieldy one. He rode forward and, as Rufuss swung the halberd back, hacked through the shaft. Magery burst all around him, burning his knuckles and singeing his eyebrows, then vanished.

Rufuss drew a sword, a black, double-edged blade inches longer than Rix's. He darted forward and thrust, not at Rix, but at his horse's chest. Rufuss found a gap in the armour, forced through and Rix's horse went down.

Rix leapt free, ducked a savage slash, parried another, then dived beneath Rufuss's mount and cut the saddle straps. He caught Rufuss's left boot, heaved and upended him as the saddle slid off.

Rufuss landed hard but bounced to his feet, his black eyes glittering. He cut at Rix, a surgical stroke that grazed his knuckles. He was a fine swordsman; Rix had seen his bloody handiwork in half a dozen battles. Rufuss might even be his superior, his only weakness being that he enjoyed the killing far more than was decent.

He did not speak, but Rix could see the bloodlust in the man's eyes, and the red tinge of his madness. Rufuss had always hated Rix, but unlike Grandys, Rufuss had never seen Rix's admirable side. Or if he had, he wanted to destroy it the way he longed to destroy all good things.

Rix fought within himself, deliberately holding back a little, and most times leaving a small area on his right side uncovered. Just a tiny, subtle window of opportunity for a maiming blow to his right arm and shoulder, a blow that would allow Rufuss the opportunity to kill with the next stroke.

Rix struck at Rufuss and cut him across the chest, a short, shallow wound of no consequence. Rufuss's eyes hardened and he directed a fusillade of blows against Rix, as though the wound was a personal insult.

Rix parried each stroke, again leaving that tiny gap in his defences, two strokes out of three. Would his opponent take the bait? Not yet. Rix leapt forward, pricked the tip of Rufuss's long nose—an insult that could not be ignored—and darted back.

Blood ran down Rufuss's mouth and chin. He dashed it away

with his left arm and took a wild swing, which missed. He struck again and again, measured strokes this time. Again Rix left that tiny gap in his defences and this time Rufuss went for it.

Rix acted in an instant. He slammed his mailed fist upwards, knocking the stroke aside, and brought his sword down with all his strength on Rufuss's extended right arm, just below the shoulder. The sword sheared through flesh and bone and the severed arm hit the ground with a dull thud.

Rufuss looked down at it in disbelief, momentarily ignoring the blood spurting from the arteries, then reached down for his arm. Rix, fearing that he would be able to reattach it with magery and fight on, shouldered him aside and kicked the arm away into the mud.

Rufuss lurched sideways, his face white—not even the Five Heroes were immune to shock and pain. He clamped his left hand over the stump, uttered a word of power and smoke rose between his fingers. His face was twisted in agony as the blistering spell cauterised the wound.

But he had lost a lot of blood and he was staggering now, struggling to stay on his feet. He looked around at his battered army, at his sword, at Rix, then lurched to the nearest horse and threw himself over the saddle, legs dangling on one side, head and shoulders on the other.

"Run!" he said shrilly, slapping it hard on the flank.

The horse bolted north through the ranks and Rix lost sight of it.

He picked up Rufuss's severed arm, holding it high and rotating it so the opaline fingers caught the light.

"Rufuss is defeated!" Rix shouted. "Rufuss of the Five Heroes has run like the cur he is. Hightspallers, the battle is ours to win. Drive the enemy into the mires. Show them no quarter until they surrender."

His army surged forward. The Herovians fought for a few more minutes then, as Rix continued to wave Rufuss's opal arm, and the word of his defeat and flight spread, the heart went out of them. But they were hemmed in to the north and east, and on the south-east.

They ran the only way they could, into the Lodden Mires, not realising that any step off the faint paths led to bottomless pools and sticky quick-mud which, once in, was impossible to get out of. Rix left Rufuss's arm where he could find it again and led his troops forward until, with the enemy floundering in the trackless morass and drowning by their hundreds, he called the battle off.

He lowered his sword and leaned on it, panting, then mounted a riderless horse and rode slowly around the bloody, corpse-littered battlefield, doing the sickening numbers.

One of the first men he recognised was the once handsome and dashing Hork. His body had been almost cut in two by a ferocious sword blow and he had died screaming in the mud. Hork's folly had caused this disaster but Rix could only feel pity for the man.

It was not yet 1 p.m. Halfway across the field he encountered Jackery, who was running the same count. He was drenched in blood and bore several bandaged wounds, but Rix saw a quiet confidence in the sergeant's eyes—he had been given a leadership role far beyond his experience, and it had transformed him.

The victory, Rix's first as commander, had changed him too, though the success was more bitter than sweet.

"When we left the camp this morning, I had 4400 men. Now I have 2100. It's a high price for leaving my army for six hours."

"You ordered Hork to stay put," said Jackery. "And you left him in a strong position; a position he could have defended if Grandys had attacked him there. The men are dead because Hork disobeyed his orders."

"I know. But if I hadn't gone haring after Glynnie, on a pursuit a moment's thought would have told me was hopeless, those 2300 men would all be alive."

Jackery said no more.

"And the enemy?" said Rix.

"Two thousand dead on the battlefield. At a rough count, another eight hundred drowned in the lake and the mires."

"And how many got away?"

"Around two thousand," said Jackery.

"That's what I thought. Which makes their original numbers only five thousand, as we thought. Grandys took the rest north, but where? And why?"

"No one I questioned knew."

"I'd better find out. Take charge of the men, see that the dying are dispatched as painlessly as possible and have everyone gather the surplus weapons and supplies—we'll need them—and head back to Bolstir."

Rix rode back and forth across the battlefield, searching for an enemy officer who was still alive, and found one not far from where he had fought Rufuss. He bent over the dying man, a thin fellow who had been speared through the middle and was slowly bleeding to death. Nothing could be done for him.

"Where did Grandys go?" said Rix.

The man looked at him weakly, struggling to focus. "North. Last night."

"Where to?"

"Don't know. But he'll be back to cut you to little pieces."

"How many men did he take with him?"

"Not saying—not saying any more."

Rix rose, thoughtfully. Grandys had a fortress, a few hours' ride north. The first fortress he had captured in Hightspall, in fact—Castle Swire. Perhaps he had gone there, but why?

It wouldn't take Rix's scouts long to find out. In this closely settled countryside the movement of an army could not be concealed once you knew where they had started from. He rode wearily back to where he had fought Rufuss, retrieved the severed arm and tied it onto his saddle.

"I didn't know you were a trophy-collecting man," said Jackery.

"I'm going to preserve it in salt and exhibit it in every town and village we come to. People might struggle to believe that we defeated one of the Five Heroes and sent his army running for their lives, but they can't argue with Rufuss's arm."

"A mighty victory," said Jackery, "and all down to you, sir."

"Every man who fought today contributed to it," said Rix, suddenly so exhausted that he could barely stay upright in the saddle.

"But you led us. You inspired us."

The nagging pain in his belly was gone. All things considered, he had done well. Better than he could have hoped. It was a small good feeling in a terrible, bloody day, and for the moment he did not even feel bad about Glynnie. He had done what he could. She had chosen her path and he had taken his.

In the middle of the afternoon they rode slowly north the few miles to Bolstir. The camp was still in place, along with most of the hundred men Hork had left behind to guard it. But Rix's heart lurched when he saw the single torn tent and the bodies, fifteen of them, lined up in the shade awaiting burial.

"What happened here?" he said to Sergeant Binner, who limped across to meet him. A thick bloodstained bandage was wound around his head.

"Enemy must've slipped into cover under the east cliff in the night, sir," said Binner. "Forty of them. Attacked not long after you left this morning. That's what drove Hork down off the hill, to retaliate."

A shiver inched down the back of Rix's neck. "They came for something."

"Holm, sir," said Binner. "They went straight for his tent, hacked it down and trapped him inside."

"Why Holm? Did—did they kill him?"

"No, sir. They went to great trouble to keep him alive, and unharmed."

"They kidnapped Holm?"

"Yes, sir. And left you a message."

Binner handed Rix a rectangular piece of parchment. On it, in Grandys' distinctive scrawl, were the following words: *Thank you for the use of Master Surgeon Holm.*

"He's taken Holm to cut the pearl out of Tali," said Rix.

CHAPTER 34

On their second night in Castle Swire, Lirriam came for Tali. She was woken by the door bolts being drawn back, then the lock clicking. As she sat up, pain spiked through the backs of her eyes, but faded. Lirriam entered, carrying a lantern and a yellow leather case. She locked the door behind her, set the lantern on the floor and turned to Tali, and the light caught her eyes so that they appeared to flame.

What was she doing here at this time of night? Was she taking advantage of Grandys' absence to make her long awaited move against him?

After days of marching east from Bastion Barr, dogged by Rix's army, Grandys had secretly taken Tali, escorted by three hundred troops, to Castle Swire in Lakeland. They had smuggled her inside in darkness, blindfolded, and locked her in the top room in the rear tower, where Grandys had sealed the door and window with an enchantment bound to Maloch, to prevent Tali from leaving the room or being carried out of it without his express orders. He had left the three hundred men here to guard her and headed south-east to rejoin his army at Flume, fifteen miles away.

Lirriam bent over Tali, *Incarnate* swinging on its chain before her eyes, mesmerising her ...

Tali tore her gaze away. "What do you want?"

"It's time."

Lirriam pressed her right forefinger to the midpoint between Tali's eyes and she felt the strength drain out of her, just as it had done when Rufuss touched her forehead. Her head flopped back on the pillow. Why did everyone do it to her the same way?

The answer was obvious—because of the master pearl.

"You're taking the pearl," Tali said dully.

"Boys' toys," Lirriam sniffed. "What would I want with it?"

"All five pearls were formed in the women of my family."

"A man's magery caused them to form there. And all the users thus far have also been men."

"Save me."

"What notable things have you done with your pearl?" Lirriam sneered.

"I killed my overseer, escaping from Cython, for starters," Tali said feebly.

"It's sickeningly easy to kill someone."

"You'd know."

Lirriam drew a razor from her leather case. Tali's heart began to hammer. She tried to roll off the bed but there was no strength in her limbs.

"What are you doing?" she cried, her voice going squeaky.

Lirriam took a handful of Tali's golden hair and cut it off. Then another, and another. When her hair was only the length of stubble, Lirriam heated Tali's jug of water by putting one finger in it and whispering a word of power.

She lathered a piece of soap, spread it across the stubble and shaved Tali's head bare, save for her eyebrows. Lirriam rinsed her down and stood back, a small smile playing on her full lips. The effect was chilling.

Tali managed to raise a hand. The skin was perfectly smooth, and her head felt naked and cold.

"If you haven't come for the pearl, then why—?"

"I never said I hadn't come for it," said Lirriam. "I said I'm not here to *take* it."

"I don't understand."

Lirriam slipped *Incarnate* over her head, holding it by its chain, then spoke another word of power. The air thickened and blurred, and at once Tali felt disconnected from everything around her, as if the room had been subtly separated in time and space from the rest of Castle Swire. The everyday sounds of the castle, which were normally distantly audible from here, faded away until the night was as quiet as death.

Lirriam went behind Tali, lowered the flattest surface of the black stone to the top of her shaved head and stroked it across caressingly, barely grazing the skin.

"*Incarnate, Incarnate,*" Lirriam said softly.

Before she finished the stroke, Tali threw up so violently that vomit struck the door ten feet away. Her heart was still hammering and her breath coming in shuddering gasps. Her legs kicked convulsively.

"Uurrgh!" she grunted. Her skin was covered in goose pimples. She felt hot and cold at the same time.

Lirriam set down *Incarnate*, frowning. "I didn't expect that."

She pressed her forefinger to each of Tali's arms and legs, and then to her belly, subvocalising a word of power each time. All feeling faded from Tali's extremities. A peculiar thudding crash penetrated the displacement Lirriam had cast over the room. It seemed to come from somewhere below them, in the lower levels of the castle.

She stopped, her head cocked to the left, then went to the door and, with an effort, opened it. Lirriam stood there for a minute, listening, shrugged, locked the door again and resumed her work.

Taking *Incarnate* by its chain, she chose another flat surface and stroked it across the top of Tali's head from her brow to the back of her skull.

"*Incarnate. Incarnate?*"

Tali felt the most hideous feeling in her middle—her body was trying to vomit but nothing came up save a small surge onto her chin. Her legs and arms wanted to thrash but they could not move.

Lirriam wiped Tali's chin with a handkerchief, tossed it aside and continued with *Incarnate*, using one side of the irregular stone, then another. She stroked it down the length of Tali's skull, across it at right angles, then across and across again on all the diagonals that passed across the master pearl.

"*Incarnate. Incarnate?*" She was beginning to sound anxious.

Tali felt a sharp, piercing pain in her head, but a different kind of pain from before. A pain she associated with her gift. Had *Incarnate* broken the block Grandys had put on Tali's gift? She could not tell, though the feeling was coming back to her limbs.

The cold was back as well, and the goose pimples, though not the feeling of fever. Tali felt cold all over now. Freezing. Her teeth began to chatter.

A red spark lit in *Incarnate*'s black core, swelled until the central quarter of the stone glowed like a searching eye, and slowly contracted to a red point, though it did not go out completely.

Lirriam swore softly. There came another muffled and curiously disconnected crash from downstairs, though this time she ignored it. All her attention was focused on *Incarnate*. She held it to her own forehead for a moment, then reached out to stroke it down Tali's skull again. Tali reacted instantly and violently, instinctively knowing that Lirriam must not touch her again.

"No!" she cried.

Her arm jerked up, her clenched fist stopping just short of Lirriam's chin, but a white balloon of force burst from Tali's knuckles, swelled enormously and snapped Lirriam's head backwards so hard that she landed onto her back. Her eyes were open, the pupils flicking wildly from side to side, though she did not seem able to move.

Tali had her gift back for the moment, although the relentless throbbing at the top of her skull reminded her how perilous it was to use. She searched Lirriam, pocketed a heavy purse and strapped on her knife. It took precious time adjusting the straps to Tali's more slender thigh. With an effort she rolled Lirriam over, stripped her coat off and turned, weak-kneed, to the door.

The effects of Lirriam's word of power had faded but Grandys' enchantment could still be felt on the door. Tali had to get out. She drew on her pearl—terrible, spiking pain—broke the hold on the door and heaved it open. Now she could hear a loud clamour below, plus swordplay in several places at once. Men were shouting to one another in Herovian and Cythonian accents.

The castle was under attack by Lyf's troops! They had surely come for her and if they got inside in numbers it would not take them long to find this room. She had to escape *now*. The fighting must have been going on for some time, judging by the crashes she had heard earlier, though Lirriam's spell had blocked most of the racket. Clearly, Grandys' three hundred guards had not been enough to defend Castle Swire.

Which way? Tali had been blindfolded when they'd brought her in and had seen nothing of the layout of the castle, though it wasn't a large one and it could not be too hard to find her way out. As she looked left and right, trying to work out which way to go, there came a boom that shook the floor—a bombast going off. The Cythonians were blasting their way in. How had they known she was here? Perhaps they had tracked the *call* of the pearl, which meant they could find her if she used it again.

Her head was still throbbing but she had to use magery again, whatever the risk. Tali drew power to *cloak* herself from human eyes, then blocked the *call* of her pearl the way Rannilt had taught her during their escape from Cython six months ago.

"Grandys?" The cry was Lirriam's, echoing hollowly inside Tali's head as if Lirriam were using magery to speak across a distance. "We're under attack by hundreds of Cythonians. We can't hold out. Grandys?"

Tali had no idea where Grandys was. He could have been outside in the castle yard for all she knew. Or ten miles away. She wasn't waiting to find out.

She edged down a sweeping set of stone stairs, reaching the bottom at the same time as a handful of Cythonian warriors burst in through the main doors at the far end of the hall. Her cloaking worked; they did not see her. None of the Herovian guards came after her. Did that mean all three hundred were dead?

Tali shrank into a crevice behind the stairs until the Cythonians went by, and the old familiar feelings came back, of being a helpless slave whose only defences were lying, hiding, and saying, *Yes, Master*. Would she ever get over that upbringing, that life?

She wasn't a slave any more. When all the Cythonians had passed by, Tali wrapped the cloaking spell more tightly around herself, tossed meat and bread from a dining table into a bag, lifted a skin of small ale onto her shoulder, stole a hat and scarf from the pegs by the entrance and slipped out into the dark.

And stepped onto a dying man.

As her eyes adjusted to the darkness she saw that the area outside the main doors, and the yard beyond, was littered with bodies. Hundreds of bodies from a horrific battle that must have raged for an hour before the Cythonians finally prevailed.

She took the first horse she came to, one of the enemy's lathered mounts. She dared not risk the time it would take to find and saddle a fresh horse. When Tali rode through the open gates and out into the night, momentarily the euphoria of liberation was so strong that she felt she could do anything and take on anyone.

Her gift was singing in her head. Reckless beyond caring, Tali headed south towards Caulderon. It was time to take on Lyf.

PART TWO

THE WYVERIN

CHAPTER 35

At a miserable village partway along the peninsula that led to Glimmering, Tali stood in the shadows, studying the small boats and canoes drawn up on the shore. Dare she take one? She had almost drowned once and, though she now knew how to swim, she did not want to go out on the water by herself. But crossing the lake would be far quicker and safer than trying to reach Caulderon via land.

She took the smallest canoe and set out. It was cold on the water; even with her hat pulled low and the scarf wrapped around her neck three times, the wind attacked her shaven head like an icy blade. The reckless fever of her escape was wearing off, she ached in every muscle and bone, and it was getting worse. In this condition she would never get to Caulderon—she was only minutes from collapse. She had to risk using her gift again.

She endured the pain until she was out of sight of land, which did not take long with the stiff nor'wester at her back. Tali hunched down in the canoe and released her gift for the few seconds necessary to cast a full-body healing on herself. Agony sheared through her head, the worst she had ever felt—it was as if the top of her skull was being lifted off. She slumped over, gasping, as the pain came and went in splintery throbs. Was the master pearl about to break apart?

Then burst, damn you! Burst and end it!

The pain was so bad that the end of everything could come only as a relief. She laid her head on her folded arms and tried to endure it . . .

The canoe swung sideways and water splashed over the bow onto her head and back, so shockingly cold that it roused her. It seemed to help with the pain as well. She sat up sluggishly, wiping her head with Lirriam's coat. There was something she needed to do right away but she was too dazed to think of it.

Taking up the paddle, Tali turned the drifting vessel south. Her healing would wear off before long and when it did the pain would return, perhaps worse than before. She had to reach Caulderon first, find a hiding place and plan her attack.

She had been paddling for an hour when she heard a single, sharp ringing sound in her head and froze in horror—she had not closed off her gift after the healing. Had it been sending out the *call* all this time? Could Lyf have located her? Or those soldiers who had attacked Swire with such desperate ferocity? They had been heading directly for her room, as if some track or trace had been leading them there. If they could locate her, going after Lyf was the worst thing to do. He would be forewarned.

Tali closed off her gift and tried to judge her position. Though it was misty on the lake, the glow of Caulderon was bright now. It could not be more than a mile away, and she judged that it was too late to turn around. If her enemies had tracked the *call* to the point where she had closed it off, there would be no escape if they found her on the lake, nor at the shoreline. The safest place was Caulderon, where she could disappear among a hundred thousand people.

She paddled harder, and after another quarter of an hour she made out land ahead. Where to enter? Tali judged that it was too risky to go to shore here—if the *call* had been heard, and tracked, they would know she was approaching Caulderon from the north. Trying, as far as possible, to keep to the banks of fog on the water, she navigated around the long peninsula on which the city had been built. On a map it rather resembled a crouching panther.

On the south side she paddled to shore in a rocky cove that stank of sewage. In the gloom she made out a trio of large stone pipes, discharging their foul waste into the water. Tali backed the canoe away a hundred yards, to a sloping shelf of rock, and crawled out over the bow. She considered the canoe for a moment, wanting to keep it for her escape, then shook her head and pushed it out. If she left it here, it would be a clear sign of where she had landed. It drifted away and disappeared in the fog.

She hunched down, released her gift for a second and wrapped her cloaking spell around her. Thus armoured, she turned Lirriam's coat inside out to disguise its quality. Her hat had blown off on the lake so she pulled the hood over her bare head and slipped through a gap in the broken city wall, into Caulderon.

From her concealed position on the repaired lake wall of the former Palace Ricinus, Tali saw that the palace was gone. The whole vast, incredibly ornate and staggeringly beautiful complex of buildings, that had struck such awe into her when she had seen them from Tobry's horse five months ago, had been razed to ground level. Only the wall surrounding the grounds, and the gate tower from which Lord and Lady Ricinus and their principal retainers had been hung and drawn, remained.

The gates were heavily guarded. Even concealed by her cloaking spell it had taken her hours to slip by the sentries and get onto a section of the wall, a presently unoccupied guard post, where she could see inside.

Her gift was clamped off tightly to block the *call* but Tali did not feel secure. Guards patrolled the wall ceaselessly, passing by her shadowy hiding place every few minutes, and she could not be sure that the grounds were not protected by other Cythonian devices— such as explosive mines or deadly pit traps—that she was all too aware of from her slave days.

The ruined grounds had been restored and now comprised a green, sloping lawn dotted with ancient trees. A circular cluster of yellow stone buildings, two hundred yards across, four storeys high and supported on rows of columns, had been erected in the centre, where the core of the palace had been. These structures were open at ground level, allowing a view through the columns to the centre of the circle, to the place that had been the heart of the capital of ancient Cythe.

The land had been cut away there to form, or rather to reveal, a long-buried circular amphitheatre dating back to ancient times, well before the arrival of the First Fleet that had turned Cythe upside-down. At the centre of the amphitheatre rose the oval domed roof of the king's personal temple. A sloping ramp led into the temple at the northern end of the oval.

In the peaceful past, she knew, any citizen of Cythe had been enti-tled to come to the amphitheatre to watch their king go about his duties or, on those days of the year so allocated, to petition him to resolve a grievance or perform a healing.

Now there were sentries everywhere. Six men and six women stood guard outside the temple door, while at least fifty more patrolled in interlocking circles in and under and around the circle of buildings. It told her one thing, though. Lyf must be in residence.

How to get to him? The iron resolve that had driven Tali in the early hours of her escape was wearing off. The healing was fading and her spearing headache had come back so strongly that it was a struggle to think clearly. The churning nausea she had felt after Lirriam touched her with *Incarnate* had also returned.

Guards patrolled the top of the wall, marching stiff-legged, in pairs, and the next pair were coming her way. Tali hunched further into the angle of the guard post. She was taking a huge risk just being here. Was it worth it? How could she get to Lyf now?

The guards were close. She tried to draw on that near magical ability she'd had as a child, to blend into the background so she would not be noticed. They came marching past, their blue caps fluttering in the breeze. A tall man and a short, stocky woman whose broad face reminded Tali of Orlyk, the vicious Cythonian guard who had taken such pleasure in tormenting her.

The woman stopped suddenly, three yards away.

"What is it?" said the tall guard in a rich, rolling burr.

The stocky woman turned, all the way around, then went to the wall, only feet from Tali, and stared over into the grounds of the palace.

"I thought I sensed something," she said. "Or *someone*, close by."

"An intruder?" His head, on a remarkably long neck for a man, rotated this way and that.

"I can't say."

She leaned over to look down at the base of the wall. The man joined her, his head bobbing up and down, tortoise-like. They spent a minute or two there before crossing to check the outside of the wall, bordering the lake. Tali tried not to breathe. Even if her cloaking charm held, they could walk into her.

The guards paced five yards, stopped and checked over the wall again, both sides.

"I can't see anything unusual," said the man. "Do you still sense it?"

"Yes, though not so strongly. Do you think we should report it? I don't want to alarm—"

"Our instructions are to report everything, no matter how trivial."

"It's just a feeling, no more."

"Feelings matter. Besides, Lyf's adjutant has ordered utmost vigilance."

"Oh?" said the woman.

"A spy was caught two days ago, after sailing across the lake."

"One of Grandys' spies?" said the woman.

"Possibly. A Hightspaller girl, once a maidservant in the palace that formerly stood here."

Tali started and almost gave herself away. It need not be Glynnie. It could be anyone—the palace had had dozens of maidservants, after all. Though how many of them would be sailing into an enemy-occupied city?

"Has she been executed yet?" said the woman.

"She's still being questioned. It's complicated."

"How so?"

"She carried a Herovian night-shard, but she's also the girl who helped Lord Deadhand escape from Grandys."

Definitely Glynnie!

"Splendid!" said the woman. "There will be much she can tell us about Grandys, and Deadhand, before she dies."

"The next batch of executions are set for sunset. She'll spill her guts before then."

"And after she's hanged, the executioners will spill them for real, for the entertainment of the gawking slum dwellers," said the woman. "I'll go and make my report."

Tali did not move until they had gone. This changed everything—the guards would be on even higher alert now, and it meant she had no chance of getting anywhere near Lyf, or his temple.

But she had to rescue Glynnie and she did not have much time to do it. Nor much of her cloaking spell left.

CHAPTER 36

Three o'clock passed, and Tali still had not found the cells where the condemned prisoners were held. Four p.m. Four-thirty. Her hope of rescuing Glynnie was fading as swiftly as Tali's own strength. At five o'clock she stopped looking.

There wasn't time to attempt a rescue, for the condemned prisoners would be surrounded by guards now. They were paraded through the streets to the place of execution, Murderers' Mound in Tumulus Town. The Cythonians made a public spectacle of their executions, and they made sure that the condemned could not be freed on the way.

Her cloaking spell had worn off and Tali was disguised as a grubby street boy. How could she rescue Glynnie now? Tali had seen far too much death in her eighteen and a half years and did not want to witness any more, especially not the hanging and drawing of a friend.

And yet she headed for Murderers' Mound. If she were there, an opportunity might come. It certainly would not if she took the coward's way out and stayed away.

Murderers' Mound was in the centre of the most desperate, overcrowded, reeking slum in all Hightspall—Tumulus Town. It had been the first part of Cauldron to be captured by the Cythonians, who had burst into the slum from deep tunnels they had secretly excavated years before.

Tumulus Town, which was home to ten thousand of the most miserable people in the city, had been brutally subdued, and a detachment of the Cythonian army was still garrisoned there to keep the embittered populace cowed. One way of doing that was the weekly executions, which were both a spectacle and a lesson.

Murderers' Mound turned out to be a steep-sided grey hill topped by a scaffold-henge where seven people could be executed at once.

It had been used for public executions since ancient times and, by tradition, the bodies were burned on an open hearth below the eastern side of the mound.

The ashes were then scattered across the mound, which had grown steeper over the aeons until it was forty feet across and rose twenty-six feet high. With its steep, crumbling sides and purple top it resembled an over-ripe boil that, for weeks after rain, oozed a thick, foul sludge like brown pus.

Half-burnt leg bones, jawbones, bits of skull and teeth were exposed in the eroding sides of the mound, which were bare of any vegetation. Not even the families of the victims dared to take their bones away, since doing so was widely believed to doom the whole family. The coarse, alkaline soil supported only a thatch of purplish, withered grass on the top.

Twenty feet from the south-western side of the mound, next to a rocky outcrop, Lyf had erected a tall stone gate facing Cython, to commemorate the place where his troops had emerged from the tunnels to occupy Tumulus Town. Since the Pale rebellion and the fall of Cython, however, the door that led into the tunnels had been securely locked.

Murderers' Mound was surrounded by a fifty-yard-wide annulus of bare land, the only open space in Tumulus Town. It might have been green once, but every blade of grass had been worn away centuries ago and now it was a dustbowl when dry, and a mud-filled doughnut after rain or snow. Beyond it reared a three-storey wall of rotting tenements, grubby little shops, tiny booths and labyrinthine alleys. Tumulus Town was a filthy, reeking firetrap so rickety that if one building collapsed it was common for a dozen others to follow.

But the grand height of the mound afforded the slum dwellers a fine view of the weekly executions, and several hundred grimy wretches had already gathered at the outside edge of the annulus, awaiting the show. A dozen guards patrolled the inner ring, making sure the wretched citizenry kept well back.

Tali had discarded Lirriam's coat which, even worn inside out, was too fine for her current disguise. She had hacked a ragged circle out of the back of the coat to use as a hat, which she held on with twisted threads looped under her chin. It attracted no attention; the slum dwellers wore as motley an assortment of rags and cast-offs as she had seen anywhere.

Tali had worked dirt into her pants and shirt until they were a dun colour, then rubbed her filthy hands over her face and shaven head. She looked like any of thousands of street lads and, as long as she spoke in the same kind of grunts, attracted no attention.

She ambled around Murderers' Mound several times, trying to think of a plan, but came up with nothing. The spectators kept well back from that dire place, so anyone approaching the mound would stand out. Besides, the crumbling ash cliffs were unclimbable. The only way up was via stone steps on the sloping eastern side, but she could not climb them without being seen by the guards. Her cloaking spell had worn off and she dared not draw on her fragile pearl to renew it—it could be one time too many.

Besides, even if she could rescue Glynnie in front of dozens of guards and a crowd of many hundreds, there was no hope of getting her to safety. None of the slum dwellers would help outsiders to escape. They wouldn't dare.

Therefore, Glynnie was going to die.

It was windy here, and Tali's crude hat provided no protection to the sides and back of her head. She casually moved in behind the protection of the memorial gate, a trilithon that stood ten feet high. The locked door within the gate, which led down to the Cythonian tunnels, was so small that even she would have had to stoop to pass through.

As she stood there, Tali caught a faint, familiar whiff of the earthy underground, a smell that raised conflicting emotions: her happy childhood before her mother's murder, the nightmare afterwards, her search for the cellar where it had taken place and her long hunt, still incomplete, to bring all the killers to justice—

A sudden thought occurred to her. If she *could* free Glynnie, they might, just possibly, escape underground. Assuming they could get past all the guards.

"They're comin'," a filthy, cross-eyed lad shouted. "They're comin' to be hanged, *yippee!*"

Everyone rushed to the far side of the mound to see the chained prisoners being driven up the zigzagging road. People began shouting curses, insults and death threats. In Tumulus Town, whether you were an enemy, an ally or even one of their own, to be accused was to be guilty, and the guilty deserved death. An execution was the best form of entertainment available in Tumulus Town, if not Caulderon itself.

If Tali was to do anything, she had to act now. The lock was a heavy affair that could only be opened by a particular triangular key. Tali had seen hundreds of similar locks in Cython, and Holm had once shown her how the mechanisms worked. With that knowledge, she ought to be able to open it with magery.

Dare she draw on the pearl again? Opening a lock would not take much from the pearl, but it could still be too much. She had to take the risk. Tali touched the lock, unsealed her gift for a second, only long enough to draw power and work the mechanism, and sealed it again.

And then the pain came, like a chisel being driven through the top of her skull. Her knees crumbled; she snatched at the lock to support herself and leaned against the door to conceal her weakness; her agony.

She counted to ten and felt a little better. Tali wiped her eyes, then checked over her shoulder. The slum dwellers were staring down the road, eagerly awaiting their first glimpse of the condemned, and the guards had their backs to her, watching the watchers. No one was looking at her.

She slipped through the door, closed it behind her and immediately felt back in her element. The smell of dust and mould, earth and damp and decay was hauntingly familiar, and so was the almost impenetrable gloom which heightened her other senses.

After prowling around for a minute or two she saw how the Cythonians had managed to mine up through hard rock without alerting anyone to their presence. There had been a passage here before. An ancient tunnel, judging by the look of the stone, that had opened at Murderers' Mound. It had been blocked an aeon ago, then forgotten, and the scaffold-henge had been built on top.

And rebuilt over and again as the death ash rose higher. When it had come time for the invasion, all the Cythonian miners had to do was blast out the last few feet of rock to open a hole beside the mound.

The roof rock under Murderers' Mound was cracked from the weight of all that wet ash, and an ash-coloured paste was slowly exuding through the largest crack. The clayey muck hung down for a foot until it broke off under its weight and formed gooey dollops on the floor.

At some stage the enemy miners had found it necessary to support the cracked roof with a pair of timber pit props, though they were slender and slightly bowed under the weight. Timber had always been precious underground, and Tali supposed there hadn't been time, at the end, to build a proper stone supporting wall. They had started one but it had never been finished, and after Caulderon fell it had no longer been needed.

As Tali eyed the bowed props, a mad idea surfaced, no more than a third of a plan. Was there time? She put her ear to the door but could hear nothing. She felt a spasm of panic. Surely the hangings could not be over already.

No, she had heard that the enemy made a great spectacle of the executions, and she had only been inside a few minutes. She eased the door ajar and heard the roar of the throng, the jeering and insults as the doomed prisoners were escorted up the hill. They would be here in minutes and she had to be outside beforehand—once they arrived she could not come through the door without hundreds of people noticing.

Tali ducked inside and made a tiny glimmer of light from her fingertips. It was trivial magery to her now, though even that small drawing made her head throb anew. She saw that the roof supported the whole weight of the scaffold-henge and Murderers' Mound and if either of the props gave, it was bound to collapse. But could she make it collapse at the right moment?

Tali made and discarded plans, one after another. Lacking timber or rope, she could not build a mechanism to yank either prop out, or topple the pile of rubble in the far corner against it. The first prop was wet from seeping water, which ruled out a fire. No, wait, the second prop was wet at the base but the dampness had only crept partway up it. The top was dry.

There was no more time; it would have to do. She drew more power—more pain, an axe splitting her skull bone in two—and directed fire against the pole, three-quarters of the way up, where one side was splintered. It took a long time to catch; she had to spray fire at it for the best part of a minute before it caught strongly. Her head was shrieking with pain by then and she could barely stand up. She had done too much.

Tali dashed cold water into her face from one of the puddles on the floor. It revived her a little but she would have to act quickly; she did not have much strength left, or much time. After noting the precise location of the fire, and the prop, she slipped through the door and closed it, and barely in time. As she stepped out from the shelter of the archway, trying not to be noticed, the seven prisoners were flogged up the hill past the jeering slum dwellers.

Their leg shackles were unfastened, though their hands were bound. The execution guards, one for each prisoner, were taking no chances. One by one, the prisoners were forced up the steep steps to the top of the mound. The first two prisoners were men so thin they might not have eaten in a month. They were followed by an oddity in Hightspall: an exceedingly fat old woman, her flesh jiggling with every step. Then two more men, dirty and wild-eyed, each with several weeks' growth of beard.

Glynnie came next, looking much younger than her seventeen years, her red hair rising and falling in the wind. She stopped halfway, looked around, and Tali saw her lips move, as if in a prayer. Or a desperate plea.

Benn, I'm sorry.

A Cythonian guard poked her in the back with a spear butt and she moved up, a blank look on her face now, as if she had resigned herself to passing beyond the material world.

The last prisoner was another woman, a toothless crone who muttered and snarled and swore vile oaths at the crowd, the guards and the other prisoners. She spat at the guards, taking no notice of their blows, then pulled her skirts up above her knees and, belying her age, thrust past Glynnie and capered up the steps all the way to the top.

There she raised her hands to the sky as if calling doom on her enemies, then leapt onto the first platform of the scaffold-henge and put the noose around her neck. The guards raced after her but she let out a mad cackle, kicked the lever and fell through the trapdoor.

The spectators began to mutter among themselves and wave their fists. Evidently they felt robbed; the hangings were supposed to be a proper spectacle. The Cythonian guards patrolling the annulus forced the watchers back with short spears. Up at the scaffold-henge, the execution guards waited until order had been restored.

Tali had to act now, though she had no idea how her plan would play out. Even if the prop burned through enough to snap, it was possible that the roof might hold for a minute, or even an hour. Alternatively the whole mound could collapse, crushing prisoners and guards alike under the stone henges and the weight of twenty-six feet of ash and rock. Being buried alive would be a far more unpleasant end for Glynnie than a quick death by hanging.

One of the execution guards read the seven names aloud, taking his time, then the guards began to put the nooses around the six prisoners' necks. Glynnie was forced at spear point onto the platform. There was no time for Tali to worry about being caught, the *call* being detected, or even dying should the pearl burst inside her head. She had to act *now*.

She opened the block, drew power from the pearl and directed everything at the burning patch on the prop below the mound. The bones of her skull creaked, though this time she felt no pain. She wondered why. Her jaw clicked; her ears popped.

There came a rush of air, a gush of smoke around the sides of the archway door, then a fluid surge of ashy sludge from the side of Murderers' Mound. Then another surge. The top of the mound quivered. One of the stone scaffold uprights tilted a few degrees. The fat woman cried out in terror.

The guards, each standing with a noose in hand, ready to slip it over a prisoner's head, stared at each other.

"What's going on?" said a hawk-nosed guard who wore a bright yellow bandanna around his wrinkled neck. "Is it another quake?"

"Murderers' Mound has survived a hundred quakes," said a moon-faced female guard, evidently their leader. "Get it done."

Tali could tell that the prop wasn't burning fast enough to

prevent the hangings. In one more minute the remaining prisoners would be dead. She looked down with her inner eye, fixed on the blazing prop and directed a mental blast of white fire at it. Blazing splinters flew everywhere, the prop shattered and the rock crazed above it.

Then the roof fell in.

CHAPTER 37

Rannilt kept sharing Tobry's recurring dream. Or was it a nightmare?

He was walking through the dark—through some cavernous underground space, judging by the way his footsteps echoed—where the air reeked of bat dung. He kept reaching out and up with both arms as if towards some monstrous, shadowy beast. Rannilt gained the impression that he was offering himself, but why?

Was it a longing for healing? Or for oblivion?

"Whatever it is out there, it can't heal you," said Rannilt. "No one can heal you but me."

He took no notice.

"Besides," she added, taking an enormous risk now, though it was one she had to take. "Tali needs you. Tali loves you and she's waitin' for you."

Tobry's howls shattered her nightmare. A hundred thousand bats took flight from their roosts on the walls and roof of the black slate cave where Tobry and Rannilt had sheltered for the night. The bats went wheeling through the air in a smoky cloud and out the entrance.

Tobry bolted out into the dark, still howling. Rannilt rubbed sleep out of her eyes, then sat cross-legged on a knob of rock, thinking things through.

"Well, that didn't work," she said laconically, and went after him.

It took hours to find him, even though his smell was now so rank and shifter-like that she could scent him downwind a quarter of a mile away. He was lying on a steeply-dipping shelf of slate only inches from the edge of a forty-foot drop. The jagged layers must have been digging into his flesh but he gave no sign that he was aware of the discomfort, or even of his surroundings.

She approached slowly, step by small step. There was blood around his mouth, stuck with bits of yellow fur. Rannilt stopped, shivering. He'd been feeding—and as a shifter, not a man. Dare she go closer? If the shifter was still in charge he might have no control over it.

But then, if the shifter was truly in charge, it could hunt her down no matter what she did or how cleverly she hid.

"Tobry?" she said softly, taking another step, and another, until she was only feet away. Her heart was a frantic bird trying to escape a cage.

He reached out over the drop with both arms, as he had in the bat cavern, but made no sound. She did not like the look in his eyes; it looked like desperation. He made a sound in his throat as if he were trying to speak, though no words came.

She met his eyes. "You're tryin' to tell me somethin'," said Rannilt. "But you can't speak. Is that because you turned shifter a while ago, to feed, and now the curse is takin' hold again?"

He slashed at her with his right hand. His nails were bloody and thickened, like a caitsthe's claws. The blow skimmed the knee of her pants.

"You're scared, aren't you? Scared you're gunna turn all the way and you won't be able to turn back. Scared you're gunna kill me. Scared you're gunna eat me."

He growled and slashed again, tearing her pants this time. She wanted to run for her life; it took all her will power to stay there and to hold his gaze. His eyes had a lot of caitsthe yellow in them again. Goose pimples rose on her arms. She tried to force them down again, to show she wasn't afraid, but the little bumps told otherwise.

"Don't do that," she said. "These pants are the only ones I've got."

He slashed again, though this time he missed by inches.

"Lie down," said Rannilt. "I'm gunna try and heal you again."

He snapped, snarled and crunched a piece of crumbly rock in one bloody fist.

"I'm not gunna hurt you," she said.

He did not move.

"Don't you trust me?" said Rannilt.

His eyes widened. In shock, or was it involuntary laughter? They stared into each other's eyes for a minute or two, then he lay back on the rough stone, shifter-still, save for the muscles of his splinted arm, which were trembling.

Rannilt moved towards him, very slowly, and put on her most calming voice.

"I'm not gunna make any sudden movements, and you're just gunna lie there. You're not a shifter, not a beast. You're *Tobry*. You're my dear friend, Tobry." She kept emphasising his name, hoping the message would take hold.

"And I'm gunna heal you," Rannilt added.

His howl rang out. A threat, or a challenge?

"Soft," she said. "Soft now."

Rannilt didn't know what she was going to say next. She was making it up as she went along. She did not think he believed her, but he was listening.

"Soft, Tobry. It ain't easy to heal a shifter. You know that. And caitsthes are the hardest shifters of all. I can't do it in one go. Maybe not in five goes, or ten. Or *fifty*! But you've gotta be patient. You're gunna get better, and you're gunna get worse. And better, and worse again. But after a while there'll be more better than worse . . . "

He whimpered, looking at her expectantly.

"That's as far as I've got," said Rannilt. "I'm not a grown-up who knows everythin'."

His unblinking eyes were fixed on her. His muscles were quivering again, his fingers clenching and unclenching.

"Layin' on hands," she went on. "That's a real important part of healin'. It's what I'm gunna do now."

She studied her grubby, twisted fingers, looked down at him and again saw a look in his eyes that could have been amusement. Or something more dangerous.

"First I'm gunna put my hands on your middle. That's where the caitsthe's twin livers are, and I reckon they're real important to the healin'."

He did not move, did not speak.

Rannilt reached out ever so carefully with her spread fingers, down towards his belly, which was exposed through his shredded shirt. Tobry bared his teeth and growled. She stopped, then slowly lowered her hands. He growled again.

"You're real scared," she said. "But you needn't be. You're not gunna hurt me." She paused. "And I'm not even a tiny bit scared of you. Look, my hands are steady as great big rocks."

His eyes flicked to her outstretched hands, which had a definite tremor. She tried to control it but did not succeed. She grimaced and lowered her hands further.

A louder growl this time. Rannilt flinched but kept on. Tobry let out a savage roar. She froze, gulped, swallowed, locked eyes with his and, deliberately, lowered her hands all the way to his midriff.

His belly muscles were iron-hard; he seemed to be straining away from her. As her hands touched him, he opened his mouth as if to roar, to rend, but managed to force it shut and some of the tension drained out of him. He let his breath out between his caitsthe teeth, *ssss*.

"That wasn't so bad, was it?" said Rannilt. "You're feelin' better already, I can see it."

She kept her hands in place for a minute or two, then lifted them. He made a sound somewhere between a whimper and a sigh.

"Now I'm gunna put my hands on your heart, 'cause the heart's the most important organ of all. You can't heal the beast without healin' the heart."

He growled, though Rannilt felt that his own heart wasn't in it this time, and he made no other effort to stop her. He jumped when her hands pressed down over his heart, and she could feel it thumping.

"Just healin'," she said softly. "That's all I'm doin'. Just healin' my dearest, bestest friend."

His heartbeat slowed, minute by minute, and when she finally lifted her hands away, ten minutes later, she could barely feel it. She rocked back onto her heels, rubbing her face with her sleeve, and closed her eyes for a bit.

He gave an interrogative howl.

"Healin' is exhaustin' work. Just give me a minute."

Rannilt closed her eyes again but almost fell asleep and shook herself awake. She was so tired that she could barely hold herself upright, and her belly felt as though she had not eaten for a week. What if he came to depend on her and she let him down?

She had to do it now; if she closed her eyes one more time she would not be able to open them again.

"The third layin' on of hands is the hardest," she said, forcing a smile. "Don't expect too much the first time. I hafta feel my way."

And besides, she didn't have the faintest idea what she was doing. She lowered her hands to his forehead, touched, then slowly slid them around to the sides of his head.

He lay still, staring up at her. She allowed her eyes to drift out of focus, trying to sense what was wrong in his head. No healer could heal without knowing exactly what was wrong, and *where* in the mind or body it had gone wrong.

She couldn't see anything now. All her faculties were focused on sensing. Golden light formed at her fingertips and spread until it bathed his head. She tried to reach into him, to discover what was wrong, and sensed something. A small dark core, deep down, was in terrible pain. She probed deeper, trying to turn it over, open it out and expose it to the light.

He let out a shriek, leapt up and his shoulder struck her in the mouth, knocking her backwards. Her eyes flooded, the back of her head cracked on a sharp edge of slate and when she could see again he was scrabbling up the steep slope of the ridge, howling in agony.

Rannilt sat there for several minutes, alternately rubbing her bruised mouth and the bloody back of her head, then picked herself up and went after him.

"You're gunna get better," she said, "then you're gunna get worse. And then you're gunna get better again."

CHAPTER 38

Tobry fled into the dark and wouldn't let Rannilt come near him again.

He could have outdistanced her easily; he could have run so far and fast that she would never have been able to find him, but he had not. He would run for a mile or two, stop until she had almost caught up, then run on again, first heading north, then east into the most rugged section of the Nandeloch Mountains.

That was all she knew; she had never seen a map of this part of Hightspall and had no idea where he was leading her, save that he was running as far from civilisation and humanity as possible.

For the moment Rannilt was content to follow, scavenging off the land, and allow time to do what it could for him. She had been alone most of her life and did not miss the company of other people. Indeed, they would have been a nuisance, telling her what to do and undermining her confidence. She knew what she had to do better than anyone else.

"You can't heal," Tali had often told her. "Lyf stole your healing gift in his caverns, remember? Besides, full-blown shifters can never be healed."

What would you know, you bossy cow? Rannilt had thought. Just because *you* couldn't heal Tobry, it doesn't mean no one can. It doesn't mean I can't. I know I can and I'm going to show you.

After following him for three or four days—or possibly five; she didn't keep count—Tobry led her into another bat-infested cave. This one was a broad hole, forty or fifty feet wide but only five feet high, at the base of a limestone mountain. It ran into the mountain in sinuous curves for miles, and judging by rounded pebbles on the bottom of the cave it had once held an underground river, though only a rivulet flowed there now, barely deep enough to bathe her sore feet.

"You ache for the dark, don't you?" she said to Tobry when she finally caught him. "You want to hide and never come out, to lie down and never get up. But it don't have to be like that."

He must have known she was coming by the golden light from her fingertips. This time he allowed her to get to within twenty feet before racing away, though he did not go far at all, not even out of sight. He was afraid of her touch, but he also wanted her.

He needed her. Perhaps he even believed that she could heal him. It made Rannilt feel warm inside.

"Your arm looks much better now. It's almost healed," said Rannilt when she was five feet away.

He just looked at her.

"First the body," she reminded him. "Then the mind. And last of all, the shifter curse."

Her stomach rumbled. She hadn't eaten in the past day and a half. In the pursuit there hadn't been time to hunt, and at this time of year there were no fruit, nuts or berries.

Tobry reached behind him, then held out a gruesome, bloody object, the head of a hare-like creature. Rannilt was not overly fastidious—slave girls could not afford to be—but the thought of eating it, raw or cooked, made her gag.

"No thanks," she said politely. "I'm going to catch a fish . . . after I've done the next healin'."

He stiffened, started to howl, but broke it off and savagely crunched up the morsel, spitting out the fur and bones. Rannilt allowed the light from her fingertips to die down so she wouldn't have to watch.

He finished in a minute or two but it didn't feel like the right time to try again. He was too tense; too afraid. The best thing she could do was talk, and see if it would put him at his ease.

"What are you lookin' for, Tobry? Why did you come into this black cave?"

He stared at her. He did that a lot.

"What are you thinkin'? Sometimes I think you want to be healed, and sometimes I think you just want to run into a dark hole and bury yourself. What are you really lookin' for?"

"Unh-unh!" he said.

"I don't know what that means. Can you say it again?"

"Unh-unh! Unh-unh!"

Rannilt wrinkled her forehead. "Perhaps if you mimed it."

He bent his arms, brought his fists to his shoulders, then flapped his arms up and down several times. His eyes were alive, yet he was trembling.

"You want to fly?" she guessed. "No, you're thinkin' about a bird. A big bird?"

He stared at her again, unblinking.

"All right, not a bird. But somethin' with wings. A bat? A *gauntlin'*?"

He was silent, quivering ever so slightly. He looked down at his shaking hand and tried to steady it, but could not.

"Maybe a gauntlin', and maybe not," said Rannilt. "You've got to find it, but you're scared of it, too. Why don't I call it the *winged terror* for now?"

He howled and bolted. She went after him, following his shifter reek in the dark. It wasn't hard. In this long, winding cave without any branches or side openings, the only way he could go was forward.

After an hour she was too tired to go any further, so she lay by the stream in the lowest part of the cave. The water was deeper here, hip-deep in places. By playing her golden light across the surface, Rannilt found she could attract small white fish, and after practice she learned to scoop them out of the water. She caught three, cleaned them and grilled them on a tiny fire she made from a piece of driftwood so white and smooth it must have been drifting down the underground stream for an aeon.

After she had picked the bones clean and returned them to the water, she lay down to rest, trying to work out why Tobry had come in here.

Why was he hunting the *winged terror*? What did he want from it? If it was a gauntling, she couldn't protect him. She was unarmed save for a blunt knife with a blade no longer than her middle finger. She rubbed it on the rock, trying to sharpen it, but the soft limestone had no effect on the steel.

He reappeared, silently.

"What do you want from the *winged terror*?" said Rannilt. "How can it help you?"

He was as still as a sphinx.

"How are you huntin' it, anyway?"

His eyes blinked, extinguishing the tinge of yellow and replacing it with the normal grey. Rannilt breathed out. Grey for the man, yellow for the deadly shifter cat.

"If it goes after you I can't help you," said Rannilt. "That golden magery I used to save you and Tali from the facinore, it don't work no more. Lyf robbed it away."

He bolted again. She followed wearily, for hour after hour, until her blistered feet were so sore she could walk no more. She lay on the bare rock, slept for a few hours and continued.

So it went on until she had no idea where she was, or if it was day or night outside, or even what week it was. She might have walked fifty miles under the mountains; she might have walked two hundred.

She came around a bend and his eyes reflected the glimmer from her fingertips. Rannilt stopped, uncertain now.

She couldn't think of anything to say; she did not want to raise the topic of the *winged terror* again. But she remembered how keenly he had listened the other day when she had talked about her dying mother, and her own desperate need to heal.

"In Cython, if you're an orphan everyone picks on you," said Rannilt. "Well, almost everyone. Tali was nice, but she was so sad when I met her. Her friend Mia had got her head chopped off and Tali just wanted me to go away ...

"I asked her if she would be my new mother," Rannilt added dreamily. "I used to ask all the nice slaves that. She said, 'Don't be silly.'"

Tobry's eyes had a peculiar shine. Rannilt could not read it but she felt he wanted to hear more about Tali.

"The other slave girls were the worst," she said, without rancour. "When I was a water carrier they were always trippin' me up and makin' me spill my water. They used to whack me round the legs with a wet rope, or make little holes in my buckets so all the water ran out and I had to fetch it again. I was always gettin' into trouble for bein' late with the water.

"And once they put alum in the bucket I was takin' to the overseer. It puckered his mouth up so bad he could hardly speak. Ooh, I got such a floggin' that day I couldn't sit down for a week."

Rannilt rubbed her meagre bottom, smiling faintly. "I got them, though."

He made a questioning noise in his throat.

"It wasn't revenge, exactly," said Rannilt. "Revenge is bad for you, everyone knows that. But you gotta defend yourself or they'll get you even worse next time. I put bath salts in the girls' dinner and they spent the next five days in the squattery, their bums flowin' like drains."

Tobry made a sound distinctly like laughter.

"'Course, they got even," she said in a matter-of-fact way. "Broke all my fingers." She studied her twisted fingers as if she had never seen them before, then rose. It was time to try again. "Don't move. I'm gunna have another go."

She eased towards him, holding her hands out, the fingers spread. He let out a muffled howl, quivered as if he was about to bolt, but managed to restrain himself. The faintest golden light limned her fingers and extended up her hands to her wrists.

"I went too far the first time," said Rannilt. "Looked too deep. I'm not gunna do that again, don't worry. I'm just layin' my healin' hands on your head, that's all. Not lookin' at all."

Nonetheless, as she knelt before him and put her hands around his head, he flinched. She lifted her fingers away then brought them down again. He stared into her eyes, unblinking.

As she held her hands there she could feel the tension draining out of him. His hands rose, as if of their own accord, and rested on hers. His eyelids drooped; his head sagged a little, and she felt that he had found a kind of release, perhaps for the first time in weeks.

After a while her muscles began to cramp. She moved her left hand as carefully as she could. His eyes flew open, he whipped his hands away and hurled himself backwards.

"It's all right, it's all right," said Rannilt, but he was gone, splashing up the underground river into the darkness.

Again, though this time she had done no physical healing, weariness overcame her. Her stomach was so empty that she could feel the sides rubbing together. There were blind fish in the stream but she did not have the strength to try and catch one. She lay on the stone floor, wrapped her coat around her, and slept.

He must have come back while she slept. Rannilt roused from an unpleasant dream about having her fingers broken by the water girls and realised that he was sitting close by, watching over her. Her mind heavy with sleep, she instinctively reached out to him for comfort.

Tobry stared at her, frozen, then took her in his arms and hugged her tightly. She clung to him for a few seconds, until the spell broke. He wrenched free and flung himself into the darkness again.

Rannilt lay down, smiling to herself, and slept the night away without dreaming at all.

CHAPTER 39

"Lord King?" Moley Gryle said urgently, from the door. "One of your commandoes survived the failed raid on Castle Swire and he's made it back."

Lyf was in the Hall of Representation. He often went there because the paintings, etchings and tapestries that covered the four walls of the hall depicted the whole vast sweep of Cythian history. They comforted him in a way that his ancestor gallery never did— the artworks revealed both the greatness and the brilliance of his nation, and his small place in its history. And they never criticised him.

"Send him in."

A wounded soldier was carried in on a stretcher, his head and chest swathed in bandages. His right hand was missing, the stump bandaged and bloodstained. The attendants set the stretcher down on the floor, next to a cluster of statues of Cythonian elders from the time of Bloody Herrie—the conspirators who had killed that unfortunate king.

"We failed, Lord King," the soldier said in a dry, rasping voice.

"I heard." Lyf knelt by his man. "But you did everything possible, and fought your way out to bring me the news in person. You will be honoured for your courage and determination, Captain Lanz."

"We had a bitter fight to get into Swire," said Lanz. His voice cracked. Lyf held a mug of water to his mouth. Lanz took a small sip, then continued. "Their numbers were higher than we were told. Three hundred." He took another sip, choked and began to cough.

Lyf wiped Lanz's mouth and held him upright until the fit passed.

"We lost half our force before we broke through the outer gate, and almost all of us before we blasted our way into the castle. It was very bloody." He held up his wrist. Blood was seeping through the bandage.

"I detected the *call* and followed its trace inside, but as I entered the *call* was blocked. It had come from a secure room upstairs, at the back, and Tali had been held there, but she had slipped away only minutes before. We never detected the *call* again."

"She knows how to block it," said Lyf. "And, evidently, how to cloak herself from sight as well."

"However we discovered a strange thing in that room," said Lanz. "Several strange things, in truth."

"Go on."

"There were traces of magery. Most enigmatic magery, and it had been used in the previous half hour."

"Magery to do with Maloch?" said Lyf.

"No, it was unlike anything we've ever encountered. It seemed . . . not of this world." Lanz began to shiver.

"Get him a blanket," said Lyf to Moley Gryle.

She fetched one and Lyf tucked it around the soldier. "Have you eaten, Captain Lanz?"

"I will complete my report first, Lord King. But if you have some small ale to hand . . . "

Moley Gryle brought a mug of ale. Lyf held it to Lanz's lips. He took a small swallow.

"You said that the magery you detected was *not of this world*," said Lyf. "What do you mean by that?"

"I didn't get the chance to look more deeply," said Lanz. "Though I did notice that it had a . . . a *feminine* character. It was nothing like Grandys' magery, or Maloch's—it wasn't destructive magery at all."

"How curious. And the other strange things?"

"There was gold-blonde hair on the floor—Tali's hair. And a razor. And fresh vomit, as though she had thrown up violently."

Lyf felt the blood draining from his cheeks. "Anything else?"

"After the *call* vanished, Lirriam burst out of that room, fighting like a red-eyed tiger. None of our weapons could touch her and the eight of us who had reached the room died there, save me. When I knew we had failed and Tali could not be found, I fought my way out to bring you the news."

"Did Tali escape, or did Lirriam recapture her?"

"I cannot say, Lord King."

"You did well," said Lyf. "You can rest now." Lyf shook Lanz's hand, called the attendants and they carried him out.

"You look worried, Lord King," said Moley Gryle when the door had been closed.

"Why would Lirriam shave Tali's head?"

"Perhaps she was planning to cut out the master pearl."

"I don't think Lirriam cares for the pearl. There must be some other reason . . . something to do with the enigmatic magery Lanz detected . . . "

"What is it, Lord King?"

"I have no idea; that's what's so worrying. If they have *another* kind of magery at their disposal, one they haven't even used yet . . . one they're trying to link to the master pearl in some way . . . "

He sat on a bench, deep in thought. There came a rapping on the door. Moley Gryle spoke to someone outside and came back. Lyf, though aware she was waiting for his attention, did not move. The news was too worrying.

After ten minutes, Moley Gryle cleared her throat.

"What?" he snapped.

"Grandys' spies are spreading a troubling piece of news."

"What news?"

"That he's captured Tali's friend, the former master surgeon, Holm."

Lyf reeled. "He's taunting us. Telling us he can take the master pearl any time he wants."

"Assuming he still has Tali."

"He must have."

"Or he wants you to think that. He's trying to force you into a rash act," said Moley Gryle.

"Tali knows the circlet is the key to using king-magery," said Lyf, "and so does Holm. Grandys will get the secret out of one of them, and once he knows *what* the key is, he'll know *where* to find it. If he takes the master pearl as well, he can command the other four ebony pearls, and king-magery will be his to control."

"What are you going to do?"

"Send out more spies—find out if Tali did escape, and if so, where she went. And Grandys must be watched day and night, no matter the cost. If he goes after the circlet, I've got to follow him there and take it first."

Lyf lay on the bench and closed his eyes. "I need to rest for an hour," he said when Moley Gryle did not move.

"Before you do, there's another urgent matter to be dealt with, Lord King."

"What?"

"The Resistance is growing again. Our intelligence says they're planning another uprising."

"We only purged them a month ago."

"Cut off one head and three grow back," said Moley Gryle.

"What does Hramm think?"

"He has a new idea, Lord King. A final idea."

Lyf sighed. Why couldn't she ever get to the point? "Which is?"

"Flushing their underground hideouts with stink-damp."

Lyf considered the idea for a minute or two. "Why not? We've got enough to deal with abroad without fighting rebels at home at the same time. Yes! If it'll solve the problem, tell him to do it right away."

CHAPTER 40

Grandys raced ahead of his troops, driving his mount to the limit of exhaustion. He reached Castle Swire two hours after dawn and stopped, staring. About a hundred dead Cythonian warriors were scattered across the road, and the gates had been blown to pieces. It looked as though Lyf's sappers had used a bombast on them.

He spurred his horse. It staggered through the gateway and collapsed under him. Grandys jumped free and stood in the middle of the yard, panting. There were bodies everywhere here as well, more than half of them men of his elite Herovian Guard. Tall, muscular, black-haired men for the most part; purebloods. The best.

Among them were more enemy dead, mostly men who were somewhat shorter than his Herovians, and more heavily built. There were some female warriors as well. Ugly brutes all. He kicked the nearest corpse.

"Grandys!"

Lirriam was standing on the front steps, at the spot where he had slain Bondy, the lord of Castle Swire, several months ago. It had been one of Grandys' happiest memories, the start of his victorious campaign, and now it was forever marred. How dare they attack his first bastion?

He hacked through the neck of an enemy corpse so violently that the head spun across the flagstones for twenty feet, then stalked towards Lirriam.

"Did they get her?" said Grandys.

"Tali's gone."

"That's not what I asked."

"I can't tell. Her path is cloaked."

"I blocked her gift before I left. She couldn't use it."

"Perhaps she unblocked it," said Lirriam.

"Not by herself!" He looked around the yard. "I left you in charge. What the hell were you doing?"

"They came too quickly," she said defensively. "And there were too many of them."

He knew she was lying. Lirriam hadn't been down here when the attack began, as she should have been, bolstering the defences with her subtle magecraft. What was she up to now?

"You had the numbers," said Grandys, reading the battlefield with an expert eye. "They can't have been more than two hundred to my three hundred, and my men were behind strong defences. It should have taken a thousand men to break them, so how did two hundred get so far, so fast?"

"I don't know."

"And how did they pass your defensive magery?"

"I—I was ill," she said.

"Some women's ailment?" he sneered.

"If you like."

"You're lying!" he rapped. "I can read it on you." He drew Maloch and pushed past her, heading for the stairs.

"What are you doing?" said Lirriam, hurrying after him.

She was unnaturally pale. Perhaps she *was* ill.

"I'm going to read the signs, starting with Tali's room."

"Where are your men? Or did you come alone?"

"A third of my troops are following; they'll be here within the hour. I left the rest under Rufuss's command, with orders to keep Rixium's rabble bottled up until I'm ready to take him."

"Why haven't you taken him already?"

He did not reply. Grandys crossed the hall, heading for the main stairs, but stopped. He moved Maloch carefully back and forth and shortly a faint aura appeared around the blade. He prowled around and under the staircase, and peered into the dark recess beneath it.

"What's the matter?" said Lirriam.

"She was here. Hiding!"

"Where did she go?"

He moved back and forth, holding Maloch out, but the aura

faded. "I can't tell." He sheathed the sword and turned to the stairs.

"Why do you keep toying with Rixium?" said Lirriam, running up ahead of him and standing in his way. "Why haven't you ground him into the dirt? Are you afraid he *is* Maloch's true master?"

He glared at her lopsided jaw, fighting the urge to knock it back into shape.

"As I keep telling you," he snarled, "Rix has to be there at the end because I need something from him as I cast the last spell. If I don't get it, Bloodspell may not work properly. Now get out of my way."

She didn't move. "I can't believe you let that puny maidservant beat you up when he escaped. You've lost it, Grandys."

He stared at her, eyes narrowed. "You're trying to distract me from something."

He swept her out of the way, slamming her against the side of the staircase, and stormed up to the room where Tali had been imprisoned. The door was closed. He kicked it open and studied the room, the bed, the blonde hair on the floor, the vomit. Maloch rattled in its sheath and when he lowered his hand towards the hilt the sword propelled itself up into his hand as if it could not wait to be there.

A crimson aura sprang up around the blade this time, bright and baleful. He rotated slowly, holding the sword out. A shadowy aura appeared on the floor not far from the bed, an aura unmistakably in the shape of a buxom, broad-hipped woman. As Grandys read the scene his eyes hardened.

"You were trying to take the master pearl," he said softly.

"I wasn't."

"And it was too strong for you," he went on relentlessly. "It knocked you down. You lay on the floor, helpless, for a long time. That's why you didn't realise Swire was under attack until it was too late. If you had, your magery could have kept them out. This disaster is of your making."

"I couldn't give a damn about the master pearl," said Lirriam.

"Then what the hell were you up to?"

"I was using *Incarnate*."

"Where is it?" he choked. "Don't tell me Tali stole it?"

Lirriam sneered. "She threw up at the merest touch of it." The lopsided jaw gave her smile an unnerving character.

"You *didn't* try to wake *Incarnate*!"

"I didn't *try*."

Her smile broadened. She looped a finger through the chain around her neck and drew the stone up from the depths of her cleavage; it made a moist, popping sound as it came free. The tiny red spark in *Incarnate*'s core matched the aura that had briefly limned Maloch.

Grandys took an involuntary step backwards. The sword's hilt felt slippery in his palm; he could barely hold it. He wiped his palms on his shirt.

"But you didn't succeed," said Grandys.

"Not completely. But I will." She stepped forward, *Incarnate* swinging in her hand like a pendulum, marking out the distance he had stepped back. "You're sweating like a pig, Grandys."

He tried to regain the initiative. "All right, it wasn't the master pearl that knocked you down. When you tried to wake *Incarnate*, you broke the block I'd put on Tali's gift and she attacked you. Your folly allowed her to free herself and paralyse you, and when my Herovian Guard most needed your aid, you failed them."

When she yawned, it drove him into a fury.

"Don't you even care that we've lost the master pearl?" he bellowed.

"I couldn't give a damn," said Lirriam. "You broke the pact. I want you to fail."

"But . . . what about our enemies?"

"*Your* enemies."

"And the Promised Realm?"

"It's your quest; it's never been mine." She went out.

Grandys wiped his dripping hands again, stumbled to his bedchamber and rested his head on the wall, trying to make sense of what she had said.

There was movement down below, hundreds of men riding in. His cavalry. He did not go down to greet them.

Grandys found a full flagon of wine, lay on his pallet and upended it into his mouth.

CHAPTER 41

Jets of wet grey ash and fragments of burnt bone squirted out of the sides of Murderers' Mound in all directions, splattering all over the watchers. The slum dwellers cried out in terror and fled into the alleys, evidently thinking the mound was going to collapse.

Tali choked—what had she done? The middle of the scaffold-henge began to tilt and the third of eight huge lintel stones toppled, crushing the moon-faced guard. The hawk-nosed guard and one of the emaciated prisoners disappeared under a falling upright. Another guard dived over the side of the mound, only to be enveloped by a mudslide of liquefied ash.

The eastern third of the scaffold-henge slid downwards into a hole that had not been there moments before, carrying three more guards and two prisoners with it. The whole top of the mound was falling in. A spray of grey water squirted up, followed by a perfect spiral of bluish smoke, spinning out of a tiny hole.

Where was Glynnie? Tali could not see her. The slum dwellers had vanished up the alleys of Tumulus Town and the guards placed there to keep them back had retreated down the road. The annulus of bare ground around Murderers' Mound was filling with sludge.

Tali ran for the steps to the top of the mound, taking them three at a time. They were already cracked and separating from each other—the whole mound was collapsing. Her hat fell off but she did not stop for it. She had to get Glynnie out now, because every step sent pain shooting through Tali's skull and she could not endure it much longer. When this was over, *if* she survived, she would pay dearly for all the power she had abused today.

Tali reached the quaking top. "Glynnie?"

She did not answer. One of the bearded prisoners was trying to strangle a guard with his bound hands. "Where's Glynnie?" she yelled.

He shrugged and kept strangling, even as the ground sank beneath him.

"You've got five seconds to get away before it falls in," said Tali.

He did not let go. Tali was risking her own life here; half the top of the mound had fallen in and the rest was about to go. She dodged around a toppling stone upright, along a rim of ground that looked solid but sank underfoot, and up to the other end of the broken scaffold-henge.

A flash of red hair: Glynnie was hip-deep in liquid ash and being drawn down. Tali would never be able to pull her out against the suction; if she tried she was liable to be sucked in as well. She caught hold of a swinging noose, yanked it down over Glynnie's head, shoulders and bound wrists, and slipped it up to tighten the noose under her arms.

"Keep your arms down!" said Tali.

The rope went taut as Glynnie was drawn further down. The scaffold that the rope was attached to was still standing, though it was wobbly. Tali threw her weight against it and it moved outwards, pulling Glynnie up a little. But this was a dangerous manoeuvre—once the lintel fell away down the slope, the rope would drag Glynnie sideways, under the sloppy ash.

Tali gave another heave. The rope twanged and pulled Glynnie up out of the muck. Tali hacked through the rope, caught the end and sprang aside as the lintel slammed into the edge of the mound, tearing it away, and rolled down the rear slope, creating a massive mudslide.

Glynnie was sliding down again. Tali heaved her up. There was no time to untie her. Tali took her by her wrists and they staggered down the crumbling steps and across to the door within the ceremonial gate. She wrenched it open, thrust Glynnie inside, banged the door behind her and mentally worked the lock. More magery; much more pain, an axe being buried in her skull. This had to be the very last time.

Tali staggered, fell to her knees and could not get up.

"Sorry," she gasped. "Magery . . . catching up."

"Cut my ropes," said Glynnie, holding out her wrists.

Tali barely had strength to hold her knife. She sawed at the ropes, which fell away. Glynnie hauled her along the tunnel past the half-built wall, which was all that was holding the ashy flood back. More of the roof below the mound fell in. The second pit prop snapped and the rest of the roof came down with a roar.

Glynnie dragged Tali into the darkness as a vast surge of sludge flooded down, carrying broken bodies with it and blocking the exit.

"We need light!" said Glynnie.

Tali managed a feeble glimmer, enough for Glynnie to heave them another hundred yards along the tunnel and down, then up again until they were beyond reach of the surge. She let go of Tali for a second, panting.

Tali fell down and could not move. She felt like throwing up; she wanted to lie there and die.

Glynnie lifted her under the arms, heaved her around a bend in the tunnel and sat her on a fallen lump of rock. Tali slumped and Glynnie had to steady her. She knelt before Tali, holding her upright. Glynnie's huge green eyes were filled with tears.

"Thank you," she said, throwing her arms around Tali and squeezing her until she could not draw breath. "I don't know why you risked your life for *me*. But thank you."

Tali could not speak. She leaned back against the cool rock and closed her eyes.

"Water," she managed to gasp after a few minutes.

Glynnie fetched a double handful from a seep and held it to her mouth.

"Over—head," said Tali, leaning forward.

Glynnie tipped it over Tali's bare head. It wasn't very cold, but it helped with the pain.

"More."

Glynnie carried another three double handfuls, then Tali croaked, "Enough."

Glynnie wiped her face. "What are you doing in Caulderon?"

"Escaped from Lirriam. Came to attack Lyf ... try to end it. You?"

"I came looking for Benn."

"Any news?"

"I'm so stupid!" Glynnie wailed. "Rix told me what would happen but I wouldn't listen."

"What *did* happen?"

"I was caught as soon as I came through the city wall," said Glynnie. "I didn't hear anything useful about Benn ... but I'm afraid ... I'm really afraid. It's been so long."

"Is Rix here too?" said Tali.

Glynnie's soft mouth set in a straight line. "No!"

"But he knows you're here?"

"I'm sure he does by now. Not that he cares about Benn," she flashed. "I've finished with Rix!"

Tali did not have the strength to argue for him. "What's going on—with the war, I mean? I've been Grandys' prisoner for a fortnight. I haven't heard any news save what he told me, and I don't know if any of that is true."

Glynnie filled her in on events up to the time of her leaving Rix's camp. Tali's head throbbed; she could hardly take it in. She lay on the floor and closed her eyes.

"Just ... need to rest."

"Take as long as you like," Glynnie said softly. "I'm not going anywhere."

Tali did not think she could possibly sleep, but she woke with her headache gone.

"Was I out for long?" she said, opening her eyes on pitch darkness.

"Hours," said Glynnie from some distance away.

Tali sat up abruptly and made a glimmer from a fingertip. "Any sound from back up the tunnel?"

"No. But in the morning ... "

"They'll dig out the mound and count the bodies," said Tali, "and they'll know you've escaped. Where can we go? I don't know Caulderon well."

"Where do you want to go?"

"To help you find Benn, of course."

Glynnie let out a shriek, threw her arms around Tali and sobbed as if her heart was breaking. "Thank you," she gasped, her eyes streaming.

Tali passed her a grubby bit of cloth. Glynnie wiped her nose, rubbed her eyes, then sat back on her haunches. "You would do that for us?"

"Benn's a lovely boy," said Tali, keeping firmly to the present tense. "And after the Honouring, when we were all trapped in Rix's chambers waiting for the end, it was us five against the world. Where should we begin?"

"I was going to look in Tumbrel Town, the shanty town closest to Palace Ricinus. It's the only place in Caulderon that Benn ... Benn *knows*," she said firmly. "We used to go to the markets there on our days off ... and a lot of the palace servants would have gone back there, after the chancellor cast them out. It's the only place I can hope to see a friendly face."

"Let's go," said Tali.

CHAPTER 42

"I'd better cut your hair off," said Tali. "It's too red, too recognisable."

"No!" Glynnie cried.

"Why not?" Tali had always worn her hair short and had not been particularly bothered by the loss of it.

Glynnie avoided her eyes. "It's the only pretty thing about me," she muttered.

"What rubbish!" said Tali, looking closely at her. "You have a lovely oval face ... a nice, slender figure ... beautiful hands."

Glynnie studied her hands. "They're callused; work-worn." She seemed determined to find fault with herself. "If you cut my hair off I'll look like some brat of a boy."

"That's the idea. As grubby boys, we can roam anywhere and no one will take any notice. But every guard on every street will be watching for the red-headed femme fatale who killed seven guards and escaped from Murderers' Mound."

"Femme fatale!" Glynnie burst out laughing.

"You're the legendary Glynnie who beat up Axil Grandys, then humiliated him."

"No one knows that."

"Everyone knows—before the execution they read out the names of the prisoners, remember?"

"I don't remember anything from the moment I climbed the mound," said Glynnie.

"Well, they did. And once they discover you've escaped, rumour will make you the most famous woman in Cauldron. There'll be a price on your head the size of a chancellor's ransom."

Glynnie shivered and wrapped her slender arms around herself.

"What's more," Tali went on, "a disaster at the execution of a notorious spy will arouse Lyf's suspicions—"

"I'm not a notorious spy—"

Tali sighed. "It's not what you *are* that matters, Glynnie. It's what you're made out to be, so if you hope—"

Glynnie's hands rose to her hair, involuntarily. "Rix loves my red hair. If it's gone he won't want—"

"That's a load of rubbish and you know it. Anyway, you said you'd finished with Rix."

"I was being a cranky bitch. You can't even imagine what he's been through in the past few weeks."

"If he turned away from you because you'd cut your hair off, it would prove what a fickle and unworthy man he was."

"He's a good man," Glynnie said stoutly. "It's just . . . sometimes he gets distracted by all his responsibilities."

"Anyway, that's not the issue."

"What *is* the issue?"

"Everyone knows you escaped, and there'll be a huge price on your head. So if you still hope to find Benn, you have to go in disguise."

Glynnie screwed up her eyes to hold back her tears. "*All right!* Cut my hair off, damn you."

*

"I feel like I've got a target painted on my back," said Tali as they emerged into the alleys of Tumbrel Town at sunrise.

She hadn't mentioned her other worry, but now it came down on her like a wagon load of turnips. She was bound to have been seen in the rescue and, despite the dirt, her unusually pale skin and fine complexion would have stood out. To say nothing of the unmistakable signs of magery she must have left on the lock. If Lyf had not identified her already, it would not take him long, and when he did, the hunt would double and redouble.

"I wonder you dared come to Caulderon, with Lyf after you," said Glynnie. "If it were me—"

"Yet you did come," said Tali.

"If the master pearl was in my head, I wouldn't have come anywhere near Lyf."

"Wherever I go," said Tali, "people want it. I'm sick of running and hiding."

She said it to bolster her own courage as much as Glynnie's. Tali's headache had gone but she was more exhausted than she had been before she lay down to sleep last night. She could not go through another day like yesterday. The pearl felt like an eggshell, one she was standing on, and any tiny thing could burst it.

"But if they get your pearl," said Glynnie, "it *will* be the end."

It took Tali a few seconds to recall what they had been talking about.

"I swore on my mother's body that I'd bring her killers to justice, and Lyf's the last one left." They turned the corner. She scanned the narrow street and they continued. "I can't do it in hiding."

"I swore to *my* mother I'd look after Benn," said Glynnie. "We're not so different after all."

Disguised as ragged, grubby boys, they tramped the narrow streets and reeking alleys of Tumbrel Town all morning, seeing dozens of guards but no one Glynnie recognised from Palace Ricinus. She dared not question strangers—it would attract attention and Lyf's informers would soon hear about it.

"I've got to find someone who knew me and Benn—and wasn't an enemy," said Gynnie.

"Did you have enemies in the palace?" said Tali, surprised.

"Did you have enemies among the slaves?" Glynnie retorted. "It's got to be someone who'll help me because we were servants together, in the good old days." She looked a little surprised at herself. "Well, compared to this, life in Palace Ricinus was the good old days," Glynnie said defiantly.

"And it has to be someone who won't betray you for a handful of coppers—much less a bucket of gold."

Glynnie missed a step and stood stock-still. "I hate this!" she said through her teeth.

"What?"

"Never knowing who to trust. Always thinking the worst of everyone. Always worrying that someone's going to betray me. I wish I was back—"

Tali took her arm. "Shh! You'll attract attention. You don't really wish that, do you?"

"That I was back in the palace, serving Lady Ricinus, and terrified I'd be beaten if I made any tiny mistake? Yes, I do. I had a warm bed there, and almost enough food. And my enemies only wanted to hit me; they didn't want me hanged and drawn on Murderers' Mound. And Benn . . . Benn was safe."

Glynnie's face crumpled; she was about to break down.

"Boys don't cry!" Tali hissed in her ear. "At least, not in public. You've got to focus on Benn. Finding Benn and getting him out of here."

"Even if we do find him," Glynnie sniffled, "how can we *ever* get out?"

Tali had no idea. With a whole city searching for them, maybe they couldn't get out.

They were continuing down the alley when Glynnie turned and pulled Tali in front of her.

"What is it?" said Tali. "Have we been spotted?"

"It's Cully and Hyaline."

Tali glanced back, casually. The rough-skinned, sandy-haired youth a year or two older than Glynnie must be Cully; Hyaline was a plump young woman with rosebud lips and a bosom the size of a pillow.

"Were they from the palace?"

"Cully groped me at the back of the stables once, when I was checking on Benn."

"What was Benn doing there?"

"He had to shovel muck in the stables for a month, for stealing a baked onion. A *small* baked onion."

"What did you do?"

"I punched Cully in the nose and made him bleed a gallon, the pig! He started to cry, and the other stable boys mocked him ever after. He hates me."

"Well done!" said Tali. "What about Hyaline?"

"*She* hates me because I caught her stealing Lady Ricinus's rouge and lip paint. Hyaline used to make other women up on her days off, you see, and charge them for the face paint she stole from Lady R."

"And you informed on her? Had her dismissed?"

"Of course not," Glynnie said indignantly. "What do you take me for?"

"Then why does she hate you?"

"She came to my room one night and asked what I wanted. That's how the system worked—I did her a favour, so she owed me. But stupidly I said I didn't want anything."

"Why did that cause a problem?"

"It meant she was still in my debt, and she hated it."

"Then surely she'll want to help you now?"

Glynnie rolled her eyes. "Palace Ricinus is gone, and so is the debt; the truth can't harm her any more. But she still hates me because I wouldn't let her repay her debt. It meant I wasn't truly one of them; that I couldn't be trusted."

"She doesn't need to trust you—just help you."

"You don't understand anything about being a servant in a great house, do you?" said Glynnie.

"Why would I? All I've ever been is a slave or a fugitive."

"Now Hyaline's free, she'd repay the favour by informing on me. It would clear her debt forever."

"I don't understand people," said Tali.

Glynnie managed a smile. Perhaps it helped to even the imbalance between them—the one that Glynnie imagined.

They were still trudging the alleys an hour later when she clutched Tali's arm. "Hang on. It's Treadgold!"

An elderly, stooped man was walking slowly along a group of market stalls, studying the goods on each stall but moving on without buying anything. He had scanty white hair, a red complexion and a jawline thinly covered in white stubble. His clothes were clean but worn, and hung off his thin frame. The stall holders weren't taking any notice of him; evidently they knew he was neither a buyer nor a thief.

"Treadgold was the assistant cellarer at the palace," Glynnie explained.

"Another of your enemies?" Tali was so exhausted that she found it hard to be civil.

"He's a lovely old fellow," said Glynnie. "He was always kind to us. Poor man, he looks like he hasn't had a good meal since he left the palace." She started towards him, then stopped, one foot in the air.

"Can he be trusted?" said Tali.

"He's an old gossip, but he wouldn't hurt anyone."

As Treadgold left the last stall Glynnie and Tali slouched across like indolent boys and came up beside him.

"Cellarer Treadgold," Glynnie said softly.

He turned so slowly and wearily that Tali could hear his joints creaking.

"Assistant Cellarer is all I ever was," he said, blinking at Glynnie. "But since the Master Cellarer was hanged with the lord and lady, I can't complain. What can I do for you, lad?"

"It's me. *Glynnie*," she said.

He stared at her face, blinking furiously, for a full twenty seconds, then beamed. "Why, so it is. What happened to your beautiful hair?"

"Shh! I'm in hiding. They're after me."

"I'm not surprised. There's a fabulous story about you rescuing young Rixium—"

"It's true, but that's not why I'm here."

"They seem to be after everyone," he said sadly. "Caulderon has been turned upside-down. Even the palace is gone—as if it never was. As if our lives of service never were."

Glynnie laid a hand on his frail arm. "Have you heard anything about Benn?"

"Benn?"

"My little brother. He was lost when we fled Caulderon, after the palace fell."

"Benn, with the red hair?" Treadgold frowned, then brightened. "Yes, he was taken to gain a hold over young Rixium, I heard. But Rixium escaped."

"What happened to Benn, do you know?"

Treadgold ruminated, seemingly for an hour as they walked along, before replying.

"Saw him in a work gang once, when they were knocking down the palace. They rounded up hundreds of kids for clean-up gangs."

"Where are they now?"

"The gangs were disbanded months ago ... but Benn ... there was something about Benn ..." He rubbed his eyes, which were watering badly. "What was it?"

"Not hurt," whispered Glynnie. She squeezed Tali's upper arm painfully hard, without realising it. "Not *killed*?"

"After we were cast out I tried to keep track of all my friends," said Treadgold. He sounded old, frail, forlorn. "So many are dead now, and so many lost." He rubbed his pouched eyes again, took hold of Glynnie's hand, glanced around and lowered his voice. "I remember now. Benn escaped in a storm."

"Where did he go? Did he come after us?"

"No," said Treadgold. "He joined the Resistance."

"What Resistance?"

"They live underground, in the darkest, foulest stews of all. It's said they're planning another revolt, but I don't think you'll find Benn now."

"Why not?" Glynnie said desperately.

"The Resistance has been crushed twice already, and the second time was only a month ago. The enemy executed everyone they caught, and there were a few boys and girls among them. I'm sorry, Glynnie. I don't see how Benn could still be alive."

CHAPTER 43

Lyf was woken at dawn by Moley Gryle with the shocking news that Tali wasn't in Grandys' hands. Or anyone else's.

"She's in Caulderon," said the anxious officer beside her. Lyf recognised him as Captain Ricips. "She arrived here two days ago."

"Two days!" Lyf cried. "Why am I only being told now?"

"I—I only realised she was here an hour ago, Lord King."

Ricips explained about catching the spy, Glynnie, and how, after interrogation, she had been sent to Murderers' Mound for execution.

Lyf swung his legs out of the bed. "Are you talking about the maidservant who escaped with Rixium Ricinus, and subsequently rescued him from Grandys?"

"Yes," said Ricips, wringing his muscular hands.

"Why wasn't I informed of her capture?"

"I'm dreadfully sorry, Lord King. I accept full responsibility—"

"Get on with it!" Lyf said coldly.

"The evening before yesterday, Murderers' Mound collapsed during the hangings. All but one of the seven scaffold guards were killed, and he's in a bad way."

"I heard about it yesterday."

"It was thought that all the prisoners died as well—but it appears one got away."

"Which one?" said Lyf, though he felt sure he knew. A woman brave and clever enough to rescue a prisoner from Grandys would have little trouble with a group of common scaffold guards.

"Glynnie's body wasn't found when the mound was dug out ... it was dangerous work and it took longer than expected. But two sets of tracks were found, heading down an ancient tunnel that led away from the mound. Small tracks. And there are reports, as yet unconfirmed, that a slender, pale-skinned boy helped Glynnie get away."

"A boy?" Lyf said sharply. "Or a small woman, disguised as a boy?"

"We don't know. The witnesses are still being questioned."

"But—a whole squad of guards attend the hangings to keep the throng back. Why haven't they been questioned, Captain Ricips?"

"They have . . . but they didn't see anything."

"Why not?" Lyf roared.

"They ran, thinking the whole hill was collapsing."

"Did they now?" said Lyf. "Get their names, Moley."

Moley Gryle made a note on a slate.

"There's no proof it was Tali . . . " said Lyf.

"Who else would risk her life to rescue an insignificant maid-servant?" said Moley Gryle.

"The surviving scaffold guard couldn't tell us much," said Ricips. "He was buried in ash and his lungs are full of it. Though he did see a boy run up the steps to the scaffold-henge. A boy with a shaved head."

"Lots of urchins in Caulderon have shaved heads. It keeps the lice away."

"They also have tanned heads. This lad had very pale skin—as pale as one of the Pale, in fact. The guard noted it because the boy's hat fell off. The description matches Tali . . . and the door into the tunnel below the mound had been unlocked and relocked with magery. I feel sure it's her, Lord King."

"So do I," said Lyf. He rose and pulled his boots on over his shin stumps. Ricips politely looked away.

"What's Tali doing in Caulderon?" said Moley Gryle.

"She swore to 'bring me to justice'. It's her weakness; it makes her predictable." Lyf turned back to Ricips. "Useful work, Captain, even at this late time. I'm putting you in charge of finding her. I want a report on progress every four hours, night and day."

"I believe I know where she's gone, Lord King," said Ricips. "As I was waiting outside for this audience, a message came from one of my most reliable informers."

"What message?"

"Two fugitives answering Tali's and Glynnie's descriptions were overheard late last night, trying to join the Resistance."

Lyf cried out, shot into the air, floated for a few seconds, then settled.

"Lord King?" said Moley Gryle.

"The tunnel flushing—with stink-damp. Has it been carried out?"

"Hours ago, Lord King. It was done exactly as you ordered."

Lyf groaned. "If she's dead ... if the master pearl is lost ... tell Hramm to get down there the instant it's safe. Check the bodies and report back to me."

CHAPTER 44

An hour before midnight, Rufuss staggered into the main hall of Castle Swire, his black opal teeth bared and the stump of his right arm dripping blood. Grandys was so shocked that he dropped his wine jar, which smashed on his right big toe. The Five Heroes often took minor wounds in battle but, apart from Yulia's arrow wound at Reffering, none of them had ever been seriously injured before. Could the day get any worse?

"What happened to you?" Grandys roared.

A movement on the stairs caught his eye. Lirriam was standing halfway up, holding a note. A message that had just come in by carrier bird, Grandys assumed. It could wait.

"Rixium—Ricinus," said Rufuss, and collapsed onto a chair, his left hand spasming around his stump. He was as grey as mud.

He choked out the tale: how he had lured Rix's army out with magery, knowing he would want to strike back for the abduction of Holm; how Rufuss had quickly encircled them and was cutting Rix's army to pieces when he realised that it was led by Captain Hork, and Rix was not there. Then—Rufuss struggled to get the words out—Rix's reckless counterattacks that had turned victory to utter defeat and taken his arm.

"Why did you attack in the first place?" Grandys said coldly.

Rufuss stared at him as if he did not understand the question. "They're the enemy!"

"I've told you, over and again, that Rixium is part of my endgame. He has to be there, *alive*, when I cast the Three Spells."

"He's alive and well," Rufuss said defensively.

"Only because of your incompetence and cowardice."

"I'm not a coward!" cried Rufuss.

"You ran from the battlefield!"

"As did you, from that fight you had with Lyf at Reffering."

"There's a big difference," Grandys said glacially. "I was alone and weaponless, so I had to retreat. You abandoned your entire army, knowing that without a leader they would be cut to pieces. Aaarrgh, get out of my sight!"

Rufuss stumbled from the hall.

"It gets worse, Grandys," Lirriam said with offensive good cheer. "News of your defeat has spread faster than a forest fire. Rixium rode across Fennery this afternoon, displaying Rufuss's severed arm in every town and village, and calling for the news to be spread by carrier bird to the four corners of the land. All Hightspall will know by tomorrow night."

"It's Rufuss's defeat, not mine," snapped Grandys.

"Rixium is broadcasting the defeat in *your* name. '*Grandys* lost. *Grandys'* army stampeded into the swamps and drowned. *Grandys* fled the scene leaving his men to die.' He's turned the tables on you, so you'd better do something to counter this defeat, right away."

Grandys stood up abruptly, shards of the wine jar crunching under his armoured feet. He kicked the pieces across the hall and stormed up to her, trying to dominate her physically.

"I won't be mocked by a woman who's just failed me disastrously."

Lirriam did not flinch. She looked up and met his eyes. "How many men have you got left? Five thousand, counting Rufuss's survivors down at Flume. You can't do anything with five miserable thousand."

"With five thousand good Herovian warriors," he said with reckless passion, "I could storm the strongest bastion in the land."

Lirriam's smile was as red as blood. "The strongest bastion in the land is Lyf's personal temple in Caulderon, the very heart and soul of his realm, and it's beyond you. You couldn't storm Caulderon if you had twenty thousand men."

He knew she was trying to provoke him, but after the triple blows he'd suffered in the past day he had to bite. "Couldn't I?"

"You wouldn't dare—not with Maloch's loyalty in question."

"It's *not* in question." He walked across to the fire. "It's 11.30 p.m.," Grandys said aloud. "Two and a half hours to feed and mobilise the men; we can be gone by 2 a.m.; a little earlier if I push them. Six hours to march to Flume. Two hours to discipline the troops who ran from the battlefield. Then the men can rest until 9 p.m. And then we'll march through the night, to strike Caulderon at the instant of dawn. Yes, it can be done."

He drew Maloch and slashed it through the air above her head. "I swear on the blade of this enchanted sword that I'll stand victorious on the altar of Lyf's personal temple by this time two days hence."

"Assuming you're still Maloch's true master."

He smiled. "I've always been its true master. Lyf used a deception last time and he won't get away with that again."

He strode to the doors, bellowing, "To arms, to arms! We ride to battle this very night."

Lirriam drew *Incarnate* from her bosom. As she brought it to her lips, her eyes caught the crimson gleam in the centre and reflected it back.

It said she hoped to win the sweetest victory of all.

CHAPTER 45

"Rufuss should have reached Swire by now," said Rix that evening. "Grandys will know about the defeat. How will he strike back?"

After discovering that Holm had been abducted, Rix and Jackery had spent the rest of the afternoon riding across Fennery, displaying Rufuss's severed arm at the nearby towns and villages and spreading the news, before rejoining his army on Bolstir hill.

Now the healers were attending to the last of the injured and his troops were lying about, resting or sleeping. Rix and Jackery perched on stones by the pond in the moonlight, drinking tea.

"If I were Grandys," said Jackery, "I'd attack us with everything I had, right away. He's got five thousand men, over half of them rested. You've got two thousand and they're battle-weary. How could the result be in doubt?"

"If we can predict it, he won't do it," said Rix. "Grandys takes pride in being perverse. But he will do something . . . " Rix tossed a pebble into the water and watched the ripples spread. "My best chance is to take him on before he's ready. Right away."

"You mean tonight?" said Jackery in alarm.

"Why not? Our troops are on a high, and they haven't had the chance to get drunk yet. Grandys and his men will be dead drunk by now—"

"How do you know?"

"They always are; victory or defeat, it's the Herovian way. We can march to Swire in three or four hours and attack in the middle of the night."

"Drunk or sober, his army greatly outnumbers ours."

"Ah, but does it?"

"I don't follow you."

"The survivors of Rufuss's army headed back towards Flume. Grandys can't have more than three thousand at Swire."

"They still outnumber us."

"And the longer I give him, the more new recruits he'll gain, and the more savage he'll be when he finally attacks."

"This is a bad idea, Deadhand," said Jackery. "It's reckless—too many things are unknown, and too much can go wrong."

Rix suppressed his own doubts. "He's got Holm, and if he also has Tali—or can find her—he can take the master pearl at any time. I can't risk it. I've got to attack now."

"All right," Jackery said unhappily.

"We ride north at ten o'clock. Make sure the men are well fed. They can have enough grog to make them happy, but not enough to get them drunk."

At 2 a.m. they stopped by the western shore of a large lake, half a mile south of Swire, and Rix addressed his officers.

"The plan is simple. We kill the guards, as silently as possible, open the gates and burst in. But we're not trying to *take* Swire—just to cause as much chaos as possible in the shortest possible time, then get out of there."

"Grandys will be ropeable," said Sergeant Tonklin.

"That's the idea," said Rix. "We'll be doing to him what he's always done to others; let's see how he likes it. Pomfree and Waysman, you'll lead the men to attack the Herovians in their tents. Then torch their supply wagons and set their horses free. Jackery, you and I will spearhead the attack on the castle and try to rescue Holm. And Tali, if Grandys has her."

"A quick attack," said Jackery.

"In and out in fifteen minutes, if we can manage it. That's all."

They moved in a silent mass. The night was still; a scattering of spring snow muffled their footsteps. No dogs barked, no night birds called.

"It's too quiet," said Jackery. "I don't like it, Deadhand. What if it's a trap?"

Rix was worried too, though he could not afford to say so.

"How could it be? We only made the plan a few hours ago. And we can rely on Grandys and his men being pissed."

Rix wondered, briefly, about the poor fellow who, after Grandys' first victory, had pleaded a bad liver. Grandys had forced half a gallon of wine down the soldier's throat. It had probably killed him.

They topped the rise. Rix scanned the land with his binoculars. Castle Swire was a quarter of a mile ahead. The front of the castle lay in the shadow of the setting moon and he could not make out its details, though he saw no lights and no indications of movement. Again his unease stirred. Grandys probably had scouts out.

He was bound to. Rix shivered. If Grandys was forewarned, he'd be rousing his men right now . . .

"Go!" said Rix. He scanned the walls and the gate one last time. "No, wait!"

"What is it?" said Jackery.

"The gates are broken."

"How?"

"It's too dark to tell."

"Who would have attacked Swire?"

"Only Lyf," Rix said grimly. "Presumably after Tali. That must be what brought Grandys back in such a desperate hurry. Go!"

The signal was relayed back. The army moved forward and, when they were a hundred yards from the gate, they charged. Rix scanned the walls as he ran but he could see no sentries, no lantern lights and no glow of braziers. It was eerie.

They reached the gate, which was loosely barricaded with heavy beams as though the guards had begun a temporary bulwark after Lyf's attack, only to abandon it. Rix and another dozen men took hold of the beams and heaved them aside, and they burst into the castle yard. The squad behind them lit their oil-soaked brands and held them high, casting a guttering light across the crowded yard.

Hundreds of bodies were stacked on a pyre—no, two pyres, ready for burning. Judging by the smell, they had been dead for more than a day.

"It must've been one hell of a fight," said Jackery.

Where the yard bellied out to the left, a forest of tents arose, a makeshift soldiers' barracks. A man staggered out of one tent and stood there swaying, blinking into the light of the brands. He did not seem to understand what was going on. Then he turned and ran between the tents, shouting.

"Get moving!" Rix bellowed.

Most of Rix's army stormed the tents; others ran to free the horses. Rix clamped his steel gauntlet around a blazing brand, raised his sword and ran for the front doors of Castle Swire. They weren't locked. He burst in, followed by Jackery and another fifty men.

A junior officer emerged from a door, cried out and turned to bolt. Jackery cut him down. Rix raced down the hall to his left, kicking doors open and waving the light inside. Most of the rooms were empty. A few contained sleeping, drunken officers. He killed any who tried to fight, disarmed three others and drove them out into the main hall to be taken prisoner.

"Where's Tali?" he bellowed.

No one spoke. Rix put his sword to the throat of the nearest officer. "Where—is—Tali?"

"Who?" the officer said, seeming genuinely puzzled.

"Into the hall, hands above your heads. Do anything suspicious and you die."

"Grandys can't be here," said Rix, stopping for a moment to catch his breath.

"Why not?" said a soldier whose name Rix did not know.

"He's like a roaring bull—at the first hint of fighting he'd be down here, tearing through us. So where the hell is he?"

Tonklin came running in. "Deadhand, most of the tents are empty. Grandys' army is gone."

Chills whirled across Rix's back. Could he have got wind of the plan? If he was in hiding outside, they would be trapped here.

"Set guards at the gates and lookouts up on the wall. Then find out where he's gone."

Tonklin saluted and ran out.

Rix went back to the three prisoners, the officers. "Where's Grandys?"

"Wouldn't you like to know," blustered a red-faced lieutenant who reeked of cheap grog. He swayed, still drunk.

Rix knocked him down and addressed the second man, but he refused to answer and so did the third, no matter how Rix threatened them. They were more afraid of Grandys' retribution than they were of dying at Rix's hand.

"Deadhand!"

It was Tonklin again, yelling from the doorway.

"Yes?" said Rix.

"Grandys left with his army at 1.30 a.m., heading for Flume."

"One-thirty? Then how did we miss him? We were outside at 2 a.m."

"We came up from the south. He was heading east to clear the lake, then south-west to Flume."

Jackery came back. "Nothing down there."

Rix ran up the stairs; he sent Jackery and his men to search the second floor, and continued up to the third. It did not take him long to find the room where Tali had been held prisoner, and the hair on the floor. He had never met anyone else with hair that particular golden-blonde colour. He picked up a clump and rubbed it between his fingers, remembering all the times, and all the dangers, they had shared. What had happened to her?

Jackery burst in, saw Rix standing there, and made to retreat. Rix gestured to him to stay. "Any trace of Holm?"

"No. Is that her hair?"

"Yes," said Rix.

"Do you think she's—?"

"I don't know," Rix said hastily, to prevent him from finishing the sentence.

Jackery went out and Rix searched the room carefully, looking for evidence that Grandys had taken the master pearl. Or rather, that he had forced Holm to cut it out.

He found no blood, no sign of any kind of operation or butchery. It gave him a little comfort, though Grandys could have had it done somewhere else. Or, more likely, taken Tali with him.

Jackery reappeared. "There's a locked door down the end. Nothing will open it."

Rix followed him down. "Not even a sledgehammer?"

"Nope."

It looked like every other door in Castle Swire, made from inch-thick planks reinforced with cross-braces, but the lock could not be picked, forced, broken or opened with the battle magians' most subtle spells.

"There's magery here, though," said Jackery.

"And I'll bet it's got to do with Maloch," said Rix. "The door must lead to Grandys' rooms, but we can't afford to spend any more time on it."

He had planned a quick raid, in and out, but they'd been here the best part of an hour already. And always, in the back of his mind, was the fear that it was a set-up to lure him in and trap his whole army here. Grandys might have pretended to head for Flume, then doubled back around the lake. He could be out there now, just waiting for the right moment.

The gate guards had nothing to report, so Rix continued the search. At the rear of the ground floor he caught a whiff of freshly baked bread—real bread such as they'd eaten at home, back in Palace Ricinus. A wave of longing overwhelmed him. He followed the smell, shouldered open a door and found himself in the castle kitchen. It was empty save for a red-faced cook, who turned from a vast brick oven, saw Rix and dived for a rack of knives.

"Touch one and you die," Rix yelled.

The cook froze.

"What's going on?" said Rix. "Where's Grandys?"

"Gone," said the cook.

"When?"

"One-thirty a.m."

"Where?"

"I can't say."

Rix pulled the steel gauntlet off his right hand. "Do you know who I am?"

The cook's eyes drifted to Rix's right hand, then flicked away. "You're Deadhand. Lord Rixium. Commander of Hightspall's army."

"What's left of it," said Rix. He put his sword to the cook's throat. "Speak or die."

"Word is, Grandys has gone to attack the enemy," said the cook.

"Which enemy? Me, or Lyf?"

"No one knows ... but they say Lirriam goaded him into it."

"Why would she do that?"

"They hate each other. Lirriam's been at his throat for weeks. She won't let up ... "

"And?"

The cook licked dry lips.

Rix menaced him with the sword. "If you won't tell me, I'll kill you and find someone who will."

The cook looked over his shoulder, licked his lips again and lowered his voice to a whisper. "It's said she's got some ancient magical artefact, long dead, and she's trying to wake it."

"What artefact?"

"No one knows. Speak about the Heroes' business and you get a sword through the guts."

"But something bad?"

The cook nodded stiffly. "Very bad. So they say."

"Where's Tali?" Rix said without changing expression.

"Who?"

"A small blonde woman. The escaped Pale who led the slaves' rebellion in Cython a few weeks ago. She was Grandys' prisoner."

"I know nothing about a female prisoner."

Rix prodded him in the belly with his sword. "You must have prepared meals for her."

"If she was here, it was a deadly secret . . . but the whole top floor of the tower was off limits. Locked. Only Grandys and Lirriam were allowed up there."

"Surely the servants were curious about that."

"Around Grandys, curiosity gets you a blade through the heart."

"What about Holm?"

"What's Holm?"

"A prisoner brought here yesterday. A man in his sixties. Grey, thinning hair."

"I saw him brought in," said the cook. "And taken out again. Grandys took him to Flume, and that's all I can tell you." He took off his apron and wiped his hands on it. "Are you going to kill me?"

"Why would I?"

"It's the way in this war. If you're not, I'm going."

"Where?"

"Running for my life. Grandys will know I've talked. He always knows."

"Are you a good cook?"

The cook tossed him a loaf of freshly baked bread. Rix tore off a piece, chewed it and swallowed. It was magnificent.

"Want to cook for Hightspall's army?" said Rix.

"Beats hiding in a ditch, waiting to die."

"I'll ignore that ringing endorsement. Put your apron on, gather your implements and your apprentices, and wait outside."

Rix met his lieutenants in the yard and they discussed what they had found. There was nothing to show what had happened to Tali.

"There's barely a hundred people in the whole place," said Jackery, who had done the numbers as usual. "And forty of them are servants. Most of the tents were empty; he only left a skeleton guard. We killed half of them and the others surrendered."

"He must've gone in one hell of a hurry," said Rix.

"Only two and a half hours from Rufuss's arrival to Grandys' army marching out the gate. He must be planning a lightning raid on our camp, since he took no supply wagons. The infantry had their packs and the mounted men only what they could carry in their saddlebags."

"It's a favourite ploy of his. He makes a high-speed night march, appears where no one imagines he could possibly be and attacks with such ferocity and determination that he carries all before him . . . "

Rix looked around the yard, taking a mental inventory. "We're low on supplies. Low on almost everything an army needs. Get his wagons loaded with all the food here, plus his spare weapons, blankets, tents and gear."

The army worked furiously, and in another hour the laden wagons were moving out the broken gates.

"What about them?" said Jackery, indicating the bodies.

"Light the funeral pyres. They were good men once."

"And the castle?"

"Burn it. Let's see how Maloch's magery stands up to that. Whether his secret room burns, or whether it doesn't, the loss of Swire and all his supplies will set him well back."

They torched the pyres and the castle, and followed the supply wagons east to Manor Assidy, in the foothills of the Nandeloch Mountains, to await Grandys' vengeance.

CHAPTER 46

"Give me one good reason why I shouldn't have you killed," said Asy Dillible, the leader of the Resistance.

She leaned back in her chair until the front legs lifted off the floor and the rungs groaned under the strain. She was a big, meaty woman with a furry moustache, hairy arms and scarred knuckles, and Tali and Glynnie were in her power.

"Please, I just want to find my little brother," said Glynnie.

Tali could tell that she was getting desperate. They had been interrogated for hours but Dillible, the Resistance leader, would not answer any questions about Benn. Tali kept silent; it was all she could do to stay on her feet. It was up to Glynnie now.

"Who gave you my name, girl?" said Dillible.

"I can't say," said Glynnie, her fingers clenching and unclenching.

"Why not?"

"I don't want to get anyone in trouble. Look, Benn's just a little boy, only ten. He's got red hair and he's skinny and small for his age."

"What use would he be to the Resistance, then?"

"He's quick and smart, and he looks innocent. He'd make a good messenger boy."

"So would five thousand other boys in Caulderon," said Dillible. "Besides, if he's been lost for months, and there's been no news of him, he's surely dead." She gestured to the pair of guards at the back of the room. "Take them to the lock-up until I work out what to do to them."

Glynnie looked as though she was going to scream. There was only one avenue left, though Tali took it most reluctantly.

She stepped around Glynnie and pulled off her baggy hat. "My name is Tali. I'm the escaped Pale who went back into Cython and incited the slaves to rebellion."

Dillible heaved herself to her feet, grunting with the effort, and held up a hand to the guards. She studied Tali carefully, including the short golden stubble on her head.

"Strip!"

As a slave, Tali had spent the first eighteen years of her life wearing only a loincloth, and the order did not bother her unduly. She took her clothes off and stood there, shivering. Glynnie, however, flushed a brilliant red as she began to unfasten her shirt.

"Not *you*," said Dillible.

She walked around Tali, studying her from all angles and paying particular attention to the slave mark on her shoulder and her various small scars.

"How did you get that?" She was pointing to the inch-long scar halfway down Tali's right thigh.

"An arrow when I was fleeing across the Seethings, months ago."

"And that?" A small, elongated scar low on her belly.

"Cythonian chuck-lash."

Dillible nodded. "You're Tali. What do you want?"

Tali dressed. "If you help Glynnie find Benn, I'll help you."

"Indeed you will." Dillible gestured over Tali's head.

The guards took them from behind and bound their hands.

"Do you want them dead, like all the others?" said the guard holding Tali. He was only a few inches taller than her, but twice as wide.

"No!" Asy Dillible snapped. "Treat them well, but don't let them escape."

"If you *are* planning a rebellion—" began Tali.

"You'd like that, wouldn't you?" sneered Dillible. "The famous Thalalie vi Torgrist, hero of the Cythonian rebellion, comes swanning in after we've done all the work and tells us how to run our Resistance."

"All I want is to find Benn and get out of here."

"You're a walking catastrophe. House Ricinus was toppled because of you, and you left Cython drenched in blood. You're not having anything to do with our insurrection . . . " She pressed the points of her fingers to her mouth, thinking. "Though you might serve as a figurehead, to inspire the rank and file." She gestured to the guards. "Take them away."

Before they could move, the ground shuddered and a pot fell off a shelf and smashed. From some distance away, Tali heard shouts and screams.

"Find out what that is," rapped Dillible.

A girl burst in, about fourteen years old, large-bodied and red in the face. She bore a distinct resemblance to Dillible.

"It's an attack, Ma," she panted. "They're flooding the tunnels with stink-damp."

Dillible cursed, then swept sheaves of paper off the table into a canvas bag. "Which way's it coming?"

"From the west," said the girl. "And the south."

"Which means the northern way out will be guarded. We'll have to go east. Spread the word—everyone is to take the old Charnel passage; we can seal its doors."

"What about all the people in Dimly Passages, Ma? How will they get out?"

"They won't." Dillible swung the heavy-looking bag over her shoulder.

The girl clutched at her mother's arm. "But all my friends are in hiding there. Sal and Lili. *And Jel!*" The girl let out a shriek. "Jel went over to Dimly this morning. I've got to warn him, Ma."

"There isn't time!" Dillible grabbed the girl's wrist as she prepared to break away. "You'll have to make new friends." She pushed her daughter out a small door, then looked back at the guards. "Bring the prisoners, you fools, it's *stink-damp*! Make sure every door is double-sealed behind us."

Glynnie sagged. "What if Benn's in there?"

There was no answer.

The guards shoved Tali and Glynnie down a dark passage. Ahead, she could hear the girl pleading desperately with her mother. The girl began to scream, but it grew ever fainter as Dillible dragged her away. A door slammed and her screams were cut off.

Glynnie and Tali were taken down a long way. It became warmer and damper, and so humid that they were sweating. They plunged down a steep ramp, but halfway down the leading guard skidded to a halt, sniffing.

"There's stink-damp down there," said Tali, whose keen nose had picked up the distinctive smell, like rotten eggs. "And it'll be thicker at the bottom. If you go down there, you'll die."

He scrambled up, caught Tali by her bound wrists and took another turning, hauling her through the gloom until she was gasping for breath. They passed through a heavy stone door, which the second guard closed behind them and bolted.

A bucket of putty stood in the corridor. He hastily filled the gaps around the door with the putty. The first guard ran to a door at the other end of the long corridor, opened it and took a careful sniff. The second guard prodded Tali and Glynnie along and into a large room with small breeze holes high on the walls to the left and right. The room was empty save for a round wooden table and four rickety chairs. The guards went out and bolted the door.

"You have no idea how sick I am of being locked up," said Tali.

"We lost forty-one rebels," said Dillible later that day. Her face was flushed with rage, her lips white, her tight shoulder muscles standing out like armour plate. "They were gassed or killed in stink-damp explosions. We've got to finish Lyf and take our city back. Tali, we want your help."

Glynnie made as if to speak but Tali got in first. "In exchange for Benn, if he's alive . . . or if not, the truth about what happened to him."

Dillible cracked her knuckles. Tali tensed, thinking that the rebel leader was going to punch her in the mouth.

"Don't you care about your own people?" said Dillible.

"You imprisoned me—don't try to make me feel guilty. If you'd given a damn about those rebels you'd have made an effort to warn them, instead of running for your own miserable life."

"Considering your puny size, you've got an awfully big mouth."

"Considering what a great muscly lump you are, you show a remarkable lack of courage."

Dillible struck Tali in the belly, winding her.

"As a slave, I learned how to cope with brutality," wheezed Tali. "The answer is still the same."

Dillible appeared to consider hitting her again, then thought better of it. "All right."

She swung the door open and stood aside. A guard was waiting at the other end of the corridor. He gestured behind him and a small boy came limping out. The man held up his hand and the boy froze. His eyes were huge, his hair red.

A shiver ran up Tali's spine.

"Benn!" Glynnie shrieked. "Benn!"

She ran for the door. Dillible blocked her way. Glynnie flew at her in a fury, kicking and biting. Her nails tore three bloody stripes down Dillible's right cheek. Dillible knocked Glynnie down and sat on her, driving all the air from her lungs.

"Sis!" the boy cried.

He tried to get to Glynnie but the guard lifted him off his feet. His arms and legs thrashed uselessly. It was definitely Benn—Tali recognised his voice—though he was so thin that he was barely recognisable. His left arm was in a filthy, cracked splint, his eyes were huge and hollow, and there were bruises on his arms and legs.

"Take him away," said Dillible. "Hold him safe."

The guard carried Benn off. Dillible rose, kicked the door closed and put her back to it. Glynnie scrunched herself into a ball and lay there, sobbing.

"You have a strange way of getting people to cooperate," Tali said coldly. "No wonder your pathetic rebellions keep failing."

Dillible knotted a fist and started towards her.

Tali had taken more abuse than she could endure. She extended her hand, the fingers spread and pointing at Dillible's face. "With my gift for magery, I once sheared a man's head right off his neck," she said conversationally.

Dillible froze. Her mouth opened and closed.

"Benn looked like he's got a fever," moaned Glynnie. "I've got to take care of him."

Dillible perched on a woodworm-eaten chair, which gave off little puffs of wood dust under her weight. "How did you start the rebellion in Cython?" she said to Tali.

"I called everyone together in the assembly area and told them Lyf had given orders for all the slaves to be put down. I told them their only hope of survival was rebellion."

Dillible sniffed. "And that did it?"

"Of course not. They wouldn't listen to me."

"Why not?"

"Because I'd escaped—I wasn't one of them any more. But I managed to convince one of the Pale leaders, Radl, and she talked a few thousand slaves into rebelling."

"That's *all*?"

"It's not even the beginning. We led them into the bloodiest and most terrible battle of my life. We were lucky to win, and I'm still not sure it was worth it."

Glynnie looked up. "Holm said the Pale won because you were absolutely brilliant."

Dillible looked sour. "You won't be leading us into battle, puffing yourself up and taking all the credit." She went out.

"She just wants to use you," said Glynnie.

"Of course she does. She's hungry for power and she sees me as a threat." Tali laughed mirthlessly. "If only she knew. I don't want to see another rebellion as long as I live."

She sat beside Glynnie and put an arm across her shoulders. "Feeling better now?"

"No," said Glynnie. "Yes, of course I am. *He's alive!*" Her eyes filled with tears. "But did you *see* him? Poor Benn. How he must have been treated."

"He looked strong, though." Tali was determined to be positive. "He'd been beaten, but he wasn't *beaten*. He's a tough little chap, your Benn."

Glynnie wiped her eyes and managed a smile. "He used to comfort me when I was really down. I can't bear to be stuck here, knowing he needs me and I can't do anything for him." She looked up. "Can't you get us out of here with magery?"

"It's not like a tap I can turn on and off whenever I want."

"What is it like?" Glynnie said eagerly. "In Palace Ricinus, people talked about magery all the time. It was so exciting, especially when Tobry was talking about it ..." She looked mortified. "Sorry, I didn't mean—"

"I like it when people talk about him," said Tali. "It reminds me of the *real* Tobry, before the shifter curse took him ..."

The grief never went away. She tried not to think about him but it only took a word to bring the memories flooding back.

What to do? Tali did not want Glynnie to think she was unwilling to use her magery to save a little boy, but even the smallest magery was a risk to her life now. She moved away from the air vents, in case Dillible was listening, lowered her voice and told Glynnie about the dire state of the master pearl.

"It's excruciating to use," Tali concluded, "and if I keep using it, it could burst at any time . . . and kill me."

"But you used it to save me at Murderers' Mound," said Glynnie.

"You were about to be hanged," said Tali.

"I meant, you didn't *have* to use the pearl, yet you risked your life *just for me*. And you suffered terribly afterwards."

"It's more painful each time I use it."

"Then it's up to me to get us out," said Glynnie. "I'm the one who promised to look after Benn, yet ever since you got here, you've been looking after me."

The door crashed open. "Grandys is here!" cried Dillible, her broad face alight.

Tali, who was asleep slumped at the table, woke with such a start that her rickety chair collapsed under her. She came to her feet, groping for her knife, then remembered that the guards had taken it.

"What, down *here*?" she said.

"Why would he come down here?" sneered Dillible. "He's attacking Caulderon right now, heading for Lyf's temple. I hope he smashes it to pieces."

Had Grandys tracked her to Caulderon? He must have done— why else would he make a seemingly suicidal attack on Lyf's greatest stronghold?

"We're planning to strike a deal with him, for his support," said Dillible. She gave Tali a meaningful look. "We're bringing the rebellion forward. We rise within the hour."

"But you don't have the numbers," said Tali.

"Lyf's so desperate to stop Grandys that he's pulled most of the guards out of the streets. The moment we start the uprising it'll spread like fire in the shanty towns. We'll pin Lyf's army between Tumbrel Town and the old palace, and hack it to bloody shreds."

"But . . . rebellions have to be *organised*. Every leader on the street has to know what to do, and when to do it. If you rise now, there'll be the most sickening massacre—"

"There'll be a massacre all right," said Dillible, and went out.

Tali's heart was going a hundred and fifty beats a minute. She slumped onto the nearest chair. "I know what Dillible's deal is going to be—*she's going to offer me to Grandys*."

Glynnie paced up and down, waving her arms. "All right. This is what we'll do. The next time someone comes to the door, I'll attack them."

"What with?"

Glynnie picked up the largest piece of the collapsed chair, a length of carved timber two feet long.

"This," she said, testing it over her knee. "The timber's solid in this chair. It just came to pieces." She swished it through the air. "I'll knock them down. You disarm them. We lock them in and run . . . run for Benn."

"We don't know where he is."

"We'll thrash our prisoner until he, or she, tells us," Glynnie said fiercely. "We've got to do whatever it takes, Tali. And the moment we get Benn, we run for it."

The plan had more holes in it than Cython, but Tali could not think of a better one. They sat down to wait.

Minutes passed, and hours. The corridor outside, which had been bustling earlier in the day, was silent.

"The rebellion must have failed," said Glynnie after five or six hours had passed. Her fingers were knotted around her piece of chair. "Lyf's troops will come down any minute, to round up everyone who stayed behind."

"If Grandys doesn't beat him to us," said Tali. "I don't know which fate to hope for."

CHAPTER 47

Grandys reached Flume in the early hours and ordered his troops to rest until dawn. When it came he entered the fortress and called out the survivors of Rufuss's army, some 2300 exhausted, hollow-eyed men, many of them carrying badly tended or infected wounds. They looked desperate; they knew his retribution was going to be dire but such was his power over them that not a man thought of disobeying.

"Line up around the inside wall of the fortress," said Grandys in a voice devoid of emotion. His own troops stood to attention behind him, though they were not needed to reinforce his orders.

The soldiers of Rufuss's defeated army lined up, sick with terror mostly, though some looked defiant and a few were resigned to their doom.

"Every tenth man will step forward," said Grandys. "Beginning with you." He pointed to a short, burly man with a bandaged head, chest and shoulder.

"I fought bravely, Lord Grandys," said the man, desperately. "Anyone will tell you so. See how many wounds I took—and every one of them from the front."

"I know you're a brave man, Gudgin," said Grandys in a voice that would have carried throughout the fortress. "And yet you're here, which proves that you shamed yourself, and your fellow men, *and me*, by running from the enemy. Step forward!"

Gudgin stepped forward, shuddering and leaning as far away from Grandys as he could. Grandys did not move for twenty seconds, then he calmly drew Maloch and thrust it through Gudgin's chest to the right of his heart.

He fell, though it took some time for him to die. Grandys studied the blood on his sword blade and walked to the next tenth man, a lean, rat-faced, prematurely bald fellow.

"You shamed yourself, Fendur, and your fellow men, *and me*, by running from the enemy. Step forward!"

"I heard you shamed us all by running like a dog from Legless Lyf," sneered Fendur.

With one furious blow, Grandys cut Fendur's head off, then hacked the body to pieces. He stared at the bloody chunks that had been a man, breathing heavily, looked round almost furtively, then stormed to the next tenth man.

Grandys killed him the same way as he had the first, and the tenth man after that, repeating the condemnation each time so that no one in his army could be in any doubt as to why it was being decimated.

When all two hundred and thirty men were dead, the bodies had been hauled to a pyre for burning and the blood was being scrubbed away, he said, "Justice has been done and every surviving man is forgiven. See that the lesson is learned. Rest now. Tonight we go on a forced march to war, to restore our glorious name."

And so commanding was his presence, and so powerful his rhetoric, that despite the decimation, the forced march, the exhaustion and the lack of a supply train, they would have followed him into the jaws of hell. They may have been terrified of him, but they were as much in his thrall as Rix had been when Grandys had laid that unbreakable command on him.

Rufuss came up to him, his long face fissured with pain lines. "What about me?"

"You're one of the Five," said Grandys.

Rufuss's bony fingers clutched at the stump of his arm. "What are you saying?"

"You ran first; you deserve decimation more than any of them. Unfortunately, because of the pact I can't touch you."

"Then what are you going to do?"

Grandys took a wine skin and squirted the red fluid into his mouth. Should he order Rufuss into the fray, despite his severed arm? No—as a proven loser, he would cost more in morale than his cold battle ferocity added.

"I'm leaving you with a hundred men to mind the house, and the surgeon, Holm. I hope you can be trusted to do that much."

Rufuss's face turned grey; he whirled and stalked off.

"Was it wise to insult him?" said Lirriam. "He's close to snapping as it is."

"He let me down," said Grandys. He turned to her. "As did you."

She met his eyes. "I've never run from a battle in my life."

Was it a challenge? He decided to ignore it for now.

That night they crept up on Caulderon in a lake fog that lay heavily over the city, reducing visibility to less than twenty feet. Lirriam and Grandys put aside their differences for the moment to create a joint attack with magery. Using her most subtle spells and his brute power, they sought out and killed all Lyf's scouts and outriders—but so cleverly and so late that none had time to give warning or set off an alert.

The army of five thousand wormed its way to within two hundred yards of the walls of Caulderon, and waited. Lirriam paced, her red cloak flapping, unable to disguise her anxiety. The troops took no notice; Grandys was leading them, not her.

Those who could sleep dozed on the ground. Grandys was one of them. He lay in the middle of his men on the damp ground, pillowed his head on his hands and put on a good show of sleeping.

When the hour was up, he rose and his men rose with him. He walked along the lines, speaking words of encouragement. In the case of one of the new recruits, though, a skinny young fellow who could not contain his terror, Grandys drew Maloch and, without word or warning, thrust it through the soldier's heart.

"He was no good to anyone," said Grandys. "Including himself. He's better off dead."

From the looks on their faces, his men agreed with him.

"When the top of the rising sun tips the horizon," he said quietly, "we hit the wall."

He looked east. The light was growing, though it would be some minutes yet. He laid his hand on Maloch's hilt and his doubts resurfaced. What if he wasn't its true master? What if the sword would not come to his hand when he needed it? Last time its failure had been due to Lyf's reversal spell, and Grandys had since crafted defences against all other kinds of spells. There was no way Lyf could get to Maloch again. Surely not . . .

He dismissed the worry and raised his hand. They waited. It looked as though every man in the army was holding his breath. Then Grandys slashed his arm down, turned towards the city wall and ran. And they went with him.

Ah, the joy of war! He could not get enough of it. They burst through the broken wall into the city before the sentries realised they were there. Killing squads on either flank stayed behind to deal with the wall guards and make sure no one sent out an alarm. The main force, led by Grandys and Lirriam, pounded through the back streets where there were few people at this time of day, and even fewer of Lyf's troops. They cut down everyone they came to, to be sure.

Grandys' vanguard was half a mile into Caulderon before the great clangours sounded, but not even Lyf's highly trained troops could dress and run from their barracks to the point of conflict, armed and armoured and ready to fight, in less than fifteen minutes. By then Grandys and his advance guard were a mile further on, driving inexorably towards the prize: Lyf's personal temple in what had once been the grounds of Palace Ricinus.

The temple guard had been reinforced with detachments from a dozen places, but the walls of the former palace were a mile long and they were designed to keep out thieves and malcontents, not armies. Grandys' men came storming through the myriad alleys of Tumbrel Town, re-formed outside the gates and cut down all the guards in a single minute. It took another minute for Grandys' magery to smash the locks; then they forced the gates and poured through into the palace grounds.

Down across the lawn they raced, joining another battalion that had come over the wall from the lake side, and pelted towards the circle of column-mounted buildings enclosing Lyf's amphitheatre-like private temple. Hundreds of guards stood in tight ranks around it, determined to protect the temple, and Lyf, no matter what it took.

They fought desperately, and even more strongly than Grandys' Herovians. The Temple Guard had trained for years to defend their king and their highest honour was to spend their lives in his service. Grandys knew they would never give way. The only way through was to kill every man and every woman.

The bloodshed was so horrific, and the casualties so high, that progress stopped. Grandys' front line faltered and for a moment it looked as though his men were going to break and run, abandoning him to stay and die ... or run, as he had when Maloch had failed him on the Field of Reffering—

No! What was he thinking?

"Our line does not break," bellowed Grandys. "Herovians never yield. Forward!"

Without waiting to see if anyone was following, he hurled himself into the most desperate mêlée, the strongest concentration of resistance, directly in front of the temple entrance.

"Forward! Follow my example!"

After several more minutes of desperate battle, Grandys, through sheer strength, with Maloch's aid and by iron force of will, gained a yard, then another. He struck the temple guardsmen down to left and right, and advanced another yard, and another. His men came with him, driving the enemy ever backwards.

The guards retreated inch by inch, tightening the ring around the temple and spending their lives gladly in defence of their king, but hundreds could not hope to stand long against thousands. Their line thinned, the last guards in front of Grandys fell, the ring broke and in a minute they were overwhelmed.

He let out a roar of sheer euphoria, "Herovia, Herovia forever!"

Life was wonderful, the day almost perfect.

Almost—it could still get better.

It would be perfect once he brought Lyf down, and the only thing stopping him was a layer of brass and wood. He ran for the brazen doors. Lirriam matched his pace even though his stride was a foot longer than hers. Though he hated her, he had to admire her courage; she had fought beside him all the way. They were both exhausted, covered in blood, and gasping as though they could not find enough sustenance in the cold air, but on they went to the glorious finale.

Yet Grandys could *never* allow a rival to beat him. He let out a roar and raced ahead, leaping into the air and driving an armoured shoulder at the doors with all his weight behind it, as if to burst them from their hinges.

When he was in mid-air Lirriam pointed to the door and muttered a command, "*Hold firm!*" The hinges froze; Grandys slammed into the door with an almighty thump that rattled his teeth and audibly snapped a rib. His shoulder armour cracked and fell off. He hit the ground, cursing her.

"You always have to win," said Lirriam softly, so the men coming up behind them would not hear. "We Heroes never get the victory; it's always *Grandys* and his Heroes."

"I'm the one who brought us all this way!"

"Because *I* manipulated you into it."

She extended a small hand as if to help him up. He knocked it aside. She laughed. Grandys rose, wincing, rubbed his shoulder, probed the broken rib with a fingertip, then thrust Maloch at the lock. It shattered. He kicked the doors open, turned and held up a hand to his men.

"Hold this temple, no matter what. Allow no one in or out."

Grandys strode in and turned to close the doors, but before he could do so Lirriam was inside. He considered throwing her out, decided that would not be wise, and sealed the doors with magery. She was the most minor of irritants in a glorious day, an unprecedented victory.

"This is a personal battle, just me and Lyf," he growled. "Don't interfere."

She bowed and said ironically, "As you command, *master of the sword.*"

He clenched a fist, but released it. He would deal with her in the endgame. Let it not be long in coming.

Lyf was at the altar with a black-haired, remarkably pretty young woman in an adjutant's uniform, and a scar-faced, burly general. Hramm, Grandys assumed.

He stalked up the open centre of the temple, past the scarred and time-worn redwood table where the Five Herovians, as they had been known at that time, had sat that fateful evening two thousand years ago. When Lyf, in naïve friendship, had invited them into his personal sanctum.

Fool! Grandys thought. He deserved everything we did to him.

Lyf turned, smiling, and Grandys faltered. Lyf's eyes were on Maloch and his two ebony pearls were in his open right hand. What if he *could* attack the sword? What if he *could* make it abandon Grandys? No, that was absurd. Maloch had come to him; it had served him faithfully all this time. He *was* its true master ...

"Go, Moley," Lyf said to his adjutant when Grandys was twenty yards away.

"I won't leave you, Lord King," said Moley Gryle.

"If you stay, you will die."

"I will gladly give my life to defend my king," she said faintly.

"I reject your sacrifice. Get going! That is my order."

She did not move. Lyf sighed.

"Carry her with you, Hramm. Take charge of my armies. Defend our city and our land."

"Yes, Lord King," Hramm said reluctantly. He swept Moley Gryle up in his arms and carried her out the secret way.

Lyf turned to Grandys and Lirriam, and held up a hand. They stopped, Grandys several yards ahead. "Like curs, you return to the scene of your foulest betrayal," said Lyf.

"You pathetic fool," said Grandys, "words mean nothing. Only one law matters, and I hold it in my hand." He raised Maloch.

"Until it finds its *true master*," said Lyf.

"I broke your deception days ago. I know you used a reversal spell at Reffering, but it won't work this time. I've protected Maloch against the workings of all spells."

Lyf seemed to sag a little. Clearly he hadn't expected Grandys to break his deception spell.

"All *known* spells," said Lyf.

Grandys, detecting a note of bluster, smiled grimly. "There's no spell in the world that can touch Maloch now. This is where it ends, Lyf."

CHAPTER 48

"I saved your lives two thousand years ago," said Lyf. "Saved all five of you from your folly. I befriended the Five Heroes when the rest of the First Fleeters turned the shoulder to you. I helped you. Advised you."

"In lofty condescension," said Grandys.

"Liar! With my own hands I served you meat and bread at that table," said Lyf, nodding towards it. "And in return, you magicked my signature onto a parchment purporting to give you the best half of Cythe. Then your brave *Heroes* held me down while you hacked my feet off and walled me up to die, alone and unshriven, in the catacombs. All to get king-magery for yourself."

Grandys bared his teeth in a savage grin. "It was a good plan. It should have worked."

"It could never have worked. You misunderstood the very nature of king-magery. It's not like any other kind of magery—it's solely a healing force."

"That restriction can be broken."

"Only by breaking the very thing that makes king-magery what it is—and only a fool would do that."

"Magery is just another form of power. It does what the magian commands."

"I swore eternal vengeance on the Five Heroes, Grandys, and I will have it."

Grandys yawned. "Yet here we are. With less than five thousand men I've invaded your city and taken your sacred temple, and all you can do is make empty threats."

"Do you truly think I didn't anticipate your return to the scene of your greatest infamy—and prepare for it?"

Grandys' throat constricted, though only for a second. "In under twenty minutes I broke the best defences you could create in months."

"Not all of them," said Lyf, smiling.

Behind Grandys, Lirriam drew in a sharp breath and he heard her moving backwards. He felt the faintest shiver of unease, but dismissed it.

"I've beaten you in every encounter," Grandys sneered.

"Except when you ran like a whining mongrel dog from the Field of Reffering," said Lyf.

Lirriam snorted, and it burned Grandys. Oh, how he was going to make her pay!

"I didn't run," Grandys said coldly. "I made a strategic retreat so I could return today—"

"To bitter defeat," said Lyf.

"Even if you've got a hundred men waiting in the wings—even if you have a thousand—I'll lead my men to victory."

"I don't have anyone waiting in the wings," said Lyf, still smiling.

"Magery then. Whatever spell you've prepared, I can best it."

"I have no spells prepared."

"I thought as much," said Grandys. "You're all bluff and bluster, Lyf, and behind it there's only craven emptiness." He drew Maloch.

Belying his previous words, Lyf closed his fist on the ebony pearls, then pointed it at Maloch and subvocalised the words of a spell. The fool must be trying to use his reversal charm again. Grandys grinned savagely and surged forward.

Lyf thrust his fist at Grandys again, and again. Grandys stopped, one boot in the air. Could Lyf have developed a spell he knew nothing about? But nothing happened, and now he saw a hint of panic in his enemy's eyes.

Grandys took another step, and another. The floor quivered a little beneath his feet but he took no notice. This close to the Vomits, the ground was always shaking.

"I have the simplest of all defences," said Lyf, "but it's enough to deal with you."

He tapped the foot of his right crutch on a black tile and a twelve-foot-wide section of the floor beneath Grandys swung down. As he fell he made a desperate grab for the edge, but it was too far away.

"Maloch, hold me up!" he cried.

But Maloch did nothing to save him and he plunged into a deep stone pit whose base and sides were armoured with dozens of conical, foot-long spikes, so thickly clustered he would be hard pressed to avoid them.

"Maloch, get me out!"

The sword was dead in his hand; what had Lyf done to it this time? Grandys twisted in mid-air, contorting his body as best he could, and landed hard between the spikes. The breath was driven out of him and Maloch was jarred out of his hand. The hinged floor swung up again, leaving him in darkness, then retracted under the floor to his left to reveal Lyf's head and shoulders beyond the far edge of the pit. He was watching, arms folded and expression unreadable.

As Grandys took hold of the nearest spike to heave himself to his feet, it snapped off at the base. Red-brown fumes gushed out and within seconds the battle wounds and grazes on his legs were sting-ing. He leapt backwards, flailing with his arms to prevent himself from overbalancing, but broke off several more spikes, which also spurted fumes.

They rose around him. Within seconds the myriad of small wounds he had taken in the battle were stinging and the skin exposed through his broken armour was beginning to blister, crack and weep. A wisp of the corrosive vapour went up his nose; he dou-bled over, gasping and choking and crashing about, breaking off more spikes, and more.

Grandys gasped down clean air, held his breath and groped beneath the heavy, floor-hugging fumes for Maloch. His hand closed around the hilt and he sought desperately to identify the enchantment Lyf had used. When he found none, fear coiled around his throat—a deeper fear than when Maloch had been frozen in its scabbard at Reffering. What if he could not get out of the pit? What if Lyf closed the hinged floor and left him here to choke to death?

It was not the first pit he'd been trapped in, though with Maloch's protective enchantment every other pit had been easy to escape from. He'd simply held tightly to the hilt and the sword had flung him out.

But not this time; it made no attempt to save him.

"Lyf's pearls must be blocking you, Maloch," he forced out. "Attack the damned pearls."

Maloch lay dead in his hand. The alchymical fumes were thick-ening around his lower limbs until he could no longer see anything below the knee. The fumes pooled inside his boots and his feet and calves began to burn so cruelly that even Grandys, who was inured to most forms of physical pain, could not keep still.

Lyf was now drifting in the air, twenty feet above the floor, look-ing down at him in his torment. Grandys could not read Lyf's expression, though surely the bastard was gloating. Instinctively, Grandys pointed Maloch at Lyf to blast him down with magery, then let his arm fall. The sword's enchantment wasn't working; it was empty, useless.

His feet burned and blistered; they were now dancing of their own accord like a sailor doing the hornpipe, faster and more frenzied every second, yet nothing he could do could mitigate the agony and, no matter how desperately he willed his feet to be still, they would not answer him. He went staggering from one side of the pit to the other, snapping off more and more spikes and setting off ever more jets of the corrosive fumes until he had to face the agonising truth.

Lyf had beaten him.

Lacking either the ability or the magery to fly, there was nothing Grandys could do to save himself. The pit was far too deep to leap out of and its sides were also lined with spikes, sharp enough to impale him yet so fragile that the smallest sideways pressure snapped them. If he could not get out, he was going to die. There was only one thing to do, and he did it with uttermost, galling reluctance.

"Lirriam!" he bawled.

She came to the edge of the pit and looked down. "Yes?" she said sweetly.

He went crashing from one side to the other. His boots felt as though they were filled with acid. "Get me out."

She folded her arms across her bosom. "You told me not to interfere."

"And now I need your help."

"Are you begging?"

He almost choked on his own bile. "Yes, I'm begging."

"What a sweet sound that is. But it's not enough."

"What do you want?"

"The truth about Urtiga's death."

Grandys' throat narrowed until he could hardly breathe. Above the other side of the pit, Lyf watched them, unmoving. It did not look as though he planned to interfere.

"Urtiga?" Grandys said hoarsely.

"Yes."

"What about her death?" said Grandys.

"She was the greatest, the noblest, and the most farseeing of all Herovians—it's why she was made Envoy. I don't believe either Rufuss or Syrten killed her, Grandys, and I know damn well Yulia didn't. That only leaves you. I think *you* killed Urtiga—to get Maloch."

His throbbing feet carried him back and forth, crushing more spikes, and back and forth. His skin was being eaten away, the flesh beneath it starting to dissolve. "What does it matter?" he choked. "She died two thousand years ago."

"To the world it's been two thousand years," said Lirriam, "but time stopped for us Heroes the moment Lyf turned each of us to opal. To me Urtiga's murder was only fourteen years ago, and justice must be done to her. *Did you—or didn't you?*"

Only the truth would serve; Lirriam would detect a lie instantly, and then she might well leave him here to die.

"Yes, I killed her, dammit! But Maloch came willingly to *me* afterwards. It's served me, and me alone, ever since."

Lirriam's eyes went hard. She was barely breathing. "It also served Rixium."

By sheer force of will Grandys forced his feet to stop moving. "Only until I returned from opal, when it abandoned him at once ... for me! Now *get—me—out*!"

She stared at him for so long that he began to fear for his life. Then she held up *Incarnate* and pointed it at Lyf, who flew backwards out of the way. Lirriam pulled a thin coil of rope from her pack, knotted one end around her waist, tossed the rest of the coil over the edge of the pit to Grandys and walked backwards out of sight.

Shortly the rope went tight. He climbed it like a sailor, threw himself over the edge onto the floor of the temple, rolled over and over until he was well away from the pit, then dragged desperately at his boots.

They were full of broken pieces of corroded opal armour that had already lost its colour and gone the dull grey of ash. He wrenched his wet, stinking socks off, and the skin of his feet and ankles came off with them, exposing red-raw, weeping flesh extending halfway to his knees. He lurched to his feet, staggered to a water-filled font and plunged his feet and calves in.

"Aaarrgh!" he cried, and had to scrub at his eyes to conceal the shameful tears of agony—the first he had ever shed publicly.

"How does it feel, Grandys?" Lyf said quietly.

Grandys looked up. "At least I still have *my* feet."

"But you'll never be free of the pain, until the day you die. For every spasm of agony I've felt where you amputated my feet, you'll feel three spasms in yours. There will come a day when you'll want to cut off your own feet—to do to yourself what you did to me—just to escape the torment."

"I doubt it," gritted Grandys. "When you turned me to opal I became inured to pain."

"And yet you weep. My alchymical fumes eat opal away and bring pain redoubled and redoubled."

"You're in no position to make threats. You're all alone, and I've got thousands of men outside."

"You may force me from my temple, yet I do believe I've won," said Lyf. "And will return to win again."

"You may have topped me in this battle," Grandys spat. "But know this, Lyf! Though you run, you can never run fast enough to outrun me. Within days I'll have the master pearl and the key to king-magery. And once I do I'll put you down like the mangy, leg-less dog you are."

"Unless I get it first!" said Lyf, and vanished.

Grandys glanced towards Lirriam, wondering what she really wanted. She did not say a word, which bothered him even more. He stumbled to the temple doors, leaving bloody footprints on the tiles, unsealed the doors and thrust them open.

"This is what we came for!" he bellowed. "Tear this place apart. Destroy it utterly."

He stood aside to let his troops through. A thousand men flooded in and began smashing and hacking. Smoke belched up as the foul Cythonian treasures were burned.

Grandys watched the destruction, scowling. It should have been the perfect ending to an astonishing victory, yet no matter how much desecration they did he took no pleasure in it. Lyf had robbed him of the triumph that was rightfully his, and having to beg Lirriam to save him was so galling that his insides burned more painfully than his raw feet.

"First you allow Rixium to live, and now Lyf," said Lirriam. "I begin to doubt your courage, Grandys."

"Lyf attacked Maloch."

She raised an eyebrow. "But you said there was no way. You said the sword was perfectly defended."

Grandys tasted bile; he wanted to spit it in her face. He ground his teeth and resisted the urge. "He must have used a new kind of spell to block it."

Her voice was soft, gentle and oh-so-reasonable. "No, he didn't. Surely you realised that Lyf's show of the ebony pearls, the subvocalised spell words, the hand gestures, the look on his face when they failed, were all an act designed to disguise his true defence. He did nothing save open the pit and let you fall in."

Ice formed on his intestines. "What are you saying?"

"I was watching Lyf carefully. There was no spell ... which can only mean the sword *is* looking for a new master."

How she was loving this. He wanted to take her head clean off her shoulders, but that would mean the end of the Five Heroes—perhaps the end of everything. With a supreme effort he restrained himself. "No, it's not."

"Then what are you going to do? How can you recover from this humiliation?"

"I have a plan for the endgame, and they're both in it."

He limped away, his knees unaccustomedly weak. What if she were right? What if Maloch *was* preparing to leave him for a new master—Rixium perhaps? Grandys tried to think things through and come up with a plan, but every thought led into a tangle he could not undo. He *was* the greatest warrior of all time, and the most successful general. Why had it suddenly gone wrong?

"Lord Grandys?" said a young lieutenant from outside. He was a fresh-faced giant, a pureblood Herovian.

Grandys limped to the door. If anything, the pain was getting worse. He had to get out of here.

"What the hell do you want, Urfis?" he snarled.

Urfis flinched. "Three of the townsfolk beg an urgent audience."

"Why?"

"They lead a rebel alliance, Lord Grandys. They plan an uprising and seek our aid to help take Caulderon back."

His right foot gave an unbearable throb. His toenails were turning black and lifting off. "No," snapped Grandys.

Lirriam spun around, staring at him in disbelief.

Urfis was sweating. "Could you clarify your instructions, Lord Grandys?"

"I won't give them an audience. I won't help them."

The sweat was flooding down Urfis's boyish face now.

"May I ask why, Lord Grandys? So I can explain—"

The agony in his feet and legs was so unbearable that he did not have the strength to talk. He could think of nothing save fighting their way out of Caulderon while they still could, and that was not going to be easy.

"My spies have told me all about the rebels, Lieutenant Urfis. They've failed twice. They're a power-seeking rabble with not a single pureblood Herovian among them. They have no hope of succeeding and I won't help them."

"Lord Grandys? I don't understand."

"This attack was merely a demonstration, Lieutenant. A strike at the heart of Lyf's empire and a shattering blow to Cythonian morale. But not even I can hold Caulderon with the men I have left. Not when Lyf has twenty thousand in the city, and a greater army only a day's march away at Mulclast."

Urfis saluted and withdrew.

Grandys looked inside. The temple was in ruins. "Enough!" he roared. "Withdraw."

When they were assembled outside, he said. "We've done what we came to do, and now we have to fight our way out. We have a greater task ahead."

"Really?" drawled Lirriam. "What now?"

"Rixium Ricinus. I'm going to take him and publicly dismember him, alive."

"So you keep saying, but when?"

"In the endgame, which is not far off."

He headed back towards Swire, more afraid than ever. Lirriam was right; Lyf had used no spell. Maloch had simply refused to protect Grandys. What if it *was* preparing to abandon him—for Rixium?

CHAPTER 49

"I may have had another small victory over Grandys, but my people paid for it," said Lyf, leaning closer to the fire and rubbing his blue fingers. No heat could warm them. "How many troops did we lose this time?"

"General Hramm's latest dispatch says 5600," said Moley Gryle. "And the fighting isn't finished yet."

They were in the front sitting room of the former chancellor's palace, a red and black, debauched monstrosity of a building next door to the temple grounds. Lyf had originally ordered it demolished along with Palace Ricinus but had subsequently countermanded the order, for reasons he did not fully understand himself. It was one of the few great buildings from the Hightspall era still standing, and almost completely intact.

"How did you do it?" said Moley Gryle. "Did you use some new spell on Maloch?"

"No," said Lyf.

"Then how—forgive me, Lord King. I have no right to your secrets."

"You have every right. When the pit was being made, I secretly lined its floor, sides and lid with sheets of platina, the only known substance that can form a barrier against magery."

"I didn't know it could."

"Few people do, thankfully. Then, once Grandys was in the pit, Maloch was powerless ..."

"Are you saying that after Lirriam got him out, Maloch would have aided him again?"

"Yes—had he thought to try it. But Grandys was too troubled, and in too much pain, and my little trick worked. Let's hope it keeps on worrying him until the end."

"Let's hope so."

"Leave me now, Moley," said Lyf. "See I'm not disturbed."

She bowed and went to the door, then came back. "If I might advise you, Lord King . . ."

"Yes?" he said tersely.

"You've kept secret your encounter with Grandys at Reffering. No one knows save your King's Guard and me."

"What of it?"

"I think you should spread the news about that victory, and your win in the temple. Let everyone know that Grandys can no longer rely on Maloch. It'll gladden our people's hearts, and undermine him."

"Good idea," said Lyf.

When she had gone he summoned the wrythen of Errek First-King. "You know what's happened?"

"I haven't returned to my tomb," said Errek, sardonically. "I just haven't been visible."

Without thinking, Lyf gestured him to the other chair by the fire, and indicated a flask and a goblet.

Errek chuckled. "I've no weight to take off my aged feet. I would certainly enjoy a glass of that liqueur, had I only the capacity to taste it. Ah, to feel its fire surging through my ethereal veins!"

"My small victories over Grandys only throw his vast wins into sharper relief," Lyf burst out. "What must I do to defeat him, Errek?"

"I've said it before. Leave the war to your commanders."

"They haven't done well either. But Grandys has burned men getting to this point, and he's not recruiting them as quickly as he used to. His allure is fading and even if he fights his way out of Caulderon—"

"As he will," said Errek. "If he does, he'll be lucky to have three thousand men left. You've got fifty thousand. Even Hramm should be able to do something with those odds. Have you found Tali?"

"No, but a spy tells me the rebels contacted him to make a deal."

"And Grandys agreed?"

"My spy didn't know."

"What deal?"

"It wasn't specified, though I'm afraid . . ."

"They offered him Tali," guessed Errek.

"And he's got Holm the surgeon, so he'll soon have the pearl—"

"Then it's time to go on the road," said Errek.

"What for?"

"To find out about the circlet. Who knows about it?"

"Holm and Tali—but I'm not going into Grandys' camp looking for them. That's exactly what he wants me to do."

"Anyone else?"

"I dare say Tali told Rix about it."

"Rix has an army to protect him; he's also out of your reach," said Errek. "What about Tobry?"

"The mad shifter?" cried Lyf. "He's dead."

"How do you know?"

"My spies said Rix and Tali were going to put him down weeks ago. Just before the great quake."

"Did any of your spies see the body?"

"No, but even supposing Tobry *is* still alive. And supposing we *can* find him, and subdue him, how do we get any sense out of a mad shifter?"

"If he's the only other one who knows, you'd better think of a way. Grandys' endgame is fast approaching."

Half an hour later, Lyf took his seat on Grolik, the greatest of his gauntlings. He detested the beasts but Lyf no longer had sufficient magery to fly and there was no other way of getting there in time. Errek was mounted behind him, for wrythens were bound to the vicinity of their place of death. They could only roam further afield in the shelter of someone else's magery.

"To Reffering, Grolik," said Lyf.

Grolik turned her long, leathery neck back on itself and aimed a gob of slimy saliva at Lyf's eye. He raised his hand.

"If you *ever* try that again, I'll burn your eyes out," Lyf said coldly.

Grolik's stinking gob hissed past Lyf's ear. She snorted, propelled herself ten feet in the air and flapped off, west-north-west.

"Disgusting creatures," Lyf muttered.

"You created them," Errek said cheerfully, leaning back so the air ruffled the few threads of white hair remaining to him.

*

"Are you sure this is the place?" he said several hours later.

They were standing in what was left of the clearing by the stream.

"Yes," said Lyf. "My spy said Tobry was chained to a great tree here, but it toppled in the quake. This must be the tree—see the chains running around it."

"And here's the remains of a packet of powdered lead," said Errek, drifting weightlessly across the leaf-littered ground.

"Whether they put Tobry down or not, he could not have survived that tree falling on him."

"I'm old-fashioned. I always like to see the body."

Lyf conjured a saw and set it to work on the trunk above the chains. The trunk was two yards through; it took a long time. He then had it saw through below the chains and when that was complete, with considerable effort he rolled the sawn disc of wood out of the way.

Errek hovered overhead. "Broken chains, with a length missing, and no body. Tobry got away."

"Even so, once a shifter goes into its final madness, it rarely lives long."

"Ah, but this shifter was treated with Tali's healing blood only hours after being *turned*. It may have given Tobry a longer life—or made him a different kind of shifter entirely. You can't assume anything. Besides, he's the only chance you've got."

"How to find him, though?" said Lyf. "He could be anywhere."

"You must have faced this problem before," said Errek. "Mad shifters have been a menace ever since our people emerged from Cython."

"Normally they were hunted down with specially trained dogs."

"Gauntlings have a keen sense of smell, don't they?"

Lyf grimaced. "Very keen. Though I was hoping to minimise contact with the vile beast."

"Think of this as your penance for creating them," grinned Errek. "And while Grolik's sniffing Tobry out, start working on a shifter-hunting spell to take its place. Tobry is liable to be hiding somewhere a gauntling can't go."

CHAPTER 50

Lirriam, who had refrained from provoking Grandys further since rescuing him from the pit in Lyf's temple, came galloping back to his battered, exhausted army. "Oh, this is ripe. *Grandys?*"

"What?" he said.

After collecting Rufuss, Holm and the hundred men left at Flume they had plodded north to Castle Swire, which was now only a mile away. Despite his personal defeat by Lyf and the agony in his feet, Grandys was marching at the head of his men, singing their victory song in his rich bass voice. It had been a brilliant victory, he had to keep reminding himself. One of the greatest military victories of all time—and he had led them to it.

"Mount up and you'll see," said Lirriam.

He mounted, rode to the crest of a small rise and looked around him. Rufuss followed, looking more bitter than Grandys had ever seen him. A broad plume of smoke was rising from due north.

"That must be close to Castle Swire," said Grandys.

Rufuss sniffed the air. "Bodies are burning," he grated. "You didn't light the pyres, did you?"

Grandys resisted the urge to spur his weary horse and gallop the rest of the way, though not out of consideration for the horse. He did not want to look desperate in front of his men. His triumph had already been badly tarnished.

He dismounted and walked the rest of the way at the head of his army. His guts were knotted, his feet throbbed and rancid sweat oozed out from between the cracks in his opal armour. Then, as they topped the final rise, the dreadful truth became evident.

Castle Swire had been burned to a shell and most of the internal walls had collapsed. Only one small section remained; the part of the tower at the rear where his chambers had been. He'd left his ice chest and script cabinet there, protected by Maloch's strongest enchantment. But had it been enough?

Worse was to come. Attached by a bloody dagger to one of the broken gate beams was a piece of parchment, and on it was scrawled a brief note.

Thanks for the supplies.

Deadhand.

Fury gave way to fear. Was the tide turning against him, as Lirriam kept saying? No, he was Axil Grandys, the greatest of the Five Heroes, the greatest warrior Hightspall had ever seen, the most brilliant strategist and the most creative tactician. He had a destiny, and he was never going to give in.

He forced his way inside. All his supply wagons were gone, and so were his supplies, spare weapons and provisions. He had a hungry army to feed but nothing to feed them with—and even worse, not a drop of drink for the long-promised victory feast. Worst of all, after the forced march, the furious battle and the long trip home, the men were desperate for sleep, yet he had no beds, spare blankets or tents, and the yard reeked of burnt bodies. He could not camp them here.

Throb, throb, throb went his scarified feet, and the more his fury grew, the more they hurt. Curse Lyf to the grave and beyond, and curse Rixium too!

With an effort, Grandys held his temper. He gave orders for the men to be looked after with what little food and drink could be found, then scrambled up onto the rubble, which was still hot. He climbed up to the top of the precariously leaning tower and peered into what was left of his rooms.

Part of the wooden floor had survived. There was still frost on the ice chest and the cabinet and crate were unscorched. He wiped his brow. All was not lost.

Not yet.

He carried the chest down and set it by the gate, under guard. Two men assisted him with the script cabinet and the immensely heavy crate. He made a padded litter so the chest, cabinet and crate could be dragged behind his horse. Grandys needed the work; it was the only way he could distract himself.

"Scour the land for food and supplies," he said to his lieutenants.

"Now?"

"Immediately! Take food from the mouths of babes if you have to. We ride after Deadhand in two days."

He was walking inside when an unobtrusive, balding little man called Yurd galloped in. Grandys' most accomplished spy had been at work in Caulderon for weeks, and he had sent much useful intelligence. What was he doing here?

Yurd stopped at the broken gates, waiting for the guards to allow him through. Lirriam went to his stirrup, spoke to him briefly, and pointed. Yurd nodded and turned his horse down the side of the yard, towards the stables.

Lirriam came in, spied Grandys and turned his way, smiling.

"Good news?" said Grandys, hopefully.

"Not for you."

Throb, throb, throb. "Spill it, then."

"Guess who was in Caulderon when you attacked?"

"Deadhand?" That would have been the last straw.

"No," said Lirriam. Her fingers slipped to the chain linked to *Incarnate*, but withdrew without taking it from her cleavage.

"Then how the hell would I know?" snarled Grandys.

"Tali was there!" Lirriam said gleefully. "She was in the tunnels under Tumbrel Town when we fought our way to the temple. She was only half a mile away."

He restrained his fury—something he'd done more than enough of lately. Lirriam was enjoying this too much, and judging by her expression it was only the beginning.

"Tali was held prisoner by the Resistance," said Lirriam. "And if you hadn't driven their deputation away unheard, if you had agreed to hear and help them, they would have given you Tali and Glynnie in exchange."

"Tali and Glynnie," he whispered. The two women he hated most . . . apart from Lirriam. "Together?"

"Tali rescued the maid from Lyf's gallows. This is your biggest error of judgement yet, Grandys. It's the beginning of the end."

He pulled out a dagger and twisted it in his armoured fists until the hilt snapped off. "I'll go back. I'll get her if it's the last thing I do."

"If you try to return to Caulderon with three thousand hungry, exhausted men it'll be the last thing you do. You can only push them so far—but cross that line and they'll turn on you. Besides, Hramm has already put the Resistance down, so Tali will either be dead or in Lyf's hands."

He hurled the shards away. "Where's Holm?"

"Rufuss has him under guard."

"Then he's probably escaped by now," he said sourly. "Rufuss!" he bawled. "Bring Holm."

Rufuss appeared a minute later, thrusting Holm before him. The old man looked grey and ill; no doubt Rufuss had been up to his sadistic tricks. Normally Grandys would have left Rufuss to it, but he was in too foul a mood.

"What the hell have you done to him?"

"Did you expect me to coddle the swine?" said Rufuss.

"You know what I want him for."

"What do you want me for?" said Holm.

"After I get Tali back, you're going to cut the master pearl out of her head."

"I don't think I am."

"I'm in no mood to be defied. The pain you've suffered in Rufuss's hands is nothing to what I'll put you through."

"If you want me to remove the master pearl, you'd better look after me. Only a fit and healthy surgeon could hope to succeed."

"You're a master surgeon; you'll manage."

"I haven't done that kind of operation for more than thirty-five years."

"I've plenty of injured men you can practise on. But first, you've a little secret I'd dearly love to have."

"What's that?"

"The key to king-magery."

"Didn't know there was one," said Holm.

"I know you know," said Grandys. "Either you tell me, or I make you suffer the most excruciating pain any man can experience. Magery pain—the kind that leaves no trace and does no lasting damage. The kind of pain Lyf has been suffering for two thousand years."

"Do your worst," said Holm.

Grandys drew Maloch. "I've had a bad day, Holm. A very, very bad day. I'd prefer this was quick, but I can take it slowly . . . "

Holm's eyes were fixed on the blade, which had a faint greenish shimmer, and Grandys could read the fear there, no matter how hard the old man tried to conceal it.

"Maloch is especially good at pain," Grandys said.

"I doubt if you can put me through more pain than I've put myself through over the years."

"Oh, I think I can."

And he did. After only twenty minutes of Maloch's excruciations, Holm gasped, "The key is Lyf's platina circlet."

"You're saying that Lyf's circlet—his kingly crown—is the key to using king-magery? That the circlet *allows* king-magery to work?"

"So I've been told," said Holm.

"And I know where it is," Grandys said to himself. "It's in the treasure hoard I hid long ago."

He turned to Lirriam. "Would you be so kind as to lock Holm up, somewhere where he'll be safe from Rufuss?"

Lirriam took Holm away to one of the unburnt outhouses.

Grandys called his lieutenants. "How long until we can go after Rixium?"

"I won't know until the men come back with supplies, Lord Grandys. They're doing their best."

"Tell them to redouble their efforts. We must ride in two days."

After Lirriam had gone out and locked the door, Holm poked his little finger into his left ear, picked away a covering of earwax, and carefully eased out the small orange crystal he had secreted there during his abduction from Bolstir. It was one of the two crystals he had found on the Reffering battlefield weeks before. Holm had never stopped thinking about all the Cythonian devices he had collected that day, and how this one might work.

He cleaned off the wax. He was sure that the crystal was some kind of battlefield communicator, though he still wasn't positive how it worked. But he had to take the chance.

Holding the crystal by both ends, he pressed its middle against a sharp window edge, bent over it, and thrust hard. The crystal snapped with a small cracking sound. A tiny orange bubble formed at the break and swelled to the size of a lemon.

Holm pressed his mouth against the bubble. "Rix, go home. Grandys knows!"

The bubble collapsed with a little, reverberating pop. Had it worked?

There was no way of telling.

CHAPTER 51

Rix was working in his tiny stone room at the back of Manor Assidy when he felt a sharp stinging sensation on his right thigh, and a hollow voice echoed through the room. Holm's voice. He sounded as though he were in considerable pain.

Rix, go home. Grandys knows!

Rix felt in his pocket and brought out the small orange crystal Holm had given him weeks ago. It was broken neatly in two and the orange colour had faded. He walked in circles around the central table, trying to suppress the panic.

"*Go home*. That's got to mean Garramide. It's the only home I've got left. But what does *Grandys knows* mean? If it means the circlet, then he must have tortured the secret out of Holm, and I've got to assume Grandys knows everything Holm knows."

"Unless it's a trick," said Jackery, who was sitting quietly in a corner.

"I can't afford to think so. We've got to get moving."

"What are your options?"

"I haven't got any. Grandys has been after king-magery ever since he came to Hightspall. He'll go after the circlet right away."

"Then the real war is about to begin. How many ways are there to get to Garramide?"

"Not many." Rix unrolled a map on the table. It hung over all four sides. "The shortest way through the Nandeloch Mountains is from the north-west. But the mountains are higher there and the last two passes are usually closed for months in winter ... and spring."

"Why closed in spring?" said Jackery.

"Avalanches. You can also get to Garramide from the east coast—assuming you're already on the east coast. But from here that route would take weeks."

"The main way in is this way?" asked Jackery, tracing the route marked from Caulderon north-east to the plateau of Garramide.

"Yes. I don't know it well, though I have travelled it in each direction. That's the way Grandys will go, so we've got to stop him getting there first. We have to make time."

"For what?"

"For us to find the circlet and hide it—and Grandys' ancient hoard won't be easy to find. We have to delay him as long as possible, which means defending the three passes on route."

"That shouldn't be too difficult, as long as we can get into good positions," said Jackery.

"Leaving out the sick and wounded, I've got 1800 men. Grandys, I'd guess, has three thousand." Rix knew about the attack on Caulderon.

"It costs a lot more men to take a defended position than it does to hold one."

"Grandys has never been afraid to lose men. If he's prepared to lose three men for every two of mine, and he will be, he'll win." Rix rolled the map up, packed spare clothes into his pack and gathered his bedroll. "And his magery is an added advantage. We've got to be on the road within the hour."

Jackery stood up. "Why the hurry? Our spies say his army is still at Swire, desperately scouring the land for supplies. We're ten miles closer to Garramide than he is."

"That's true," said Rix, the panic easing.

At this time of year supplies would be hard to come by. It had been a long, hard winter and several armies had already ransacked the land. Most of the common folk would be on the edge of starvation—or over the edge—and not even Grandys could glean food where there was none to be had.

"Of course, he could have ridden ahead by himself," said Jackery.

The panic was back, worse than before. "Grandys doesn't need an army to search Garramide—he knows exactly where he hid his treasures. Come on!"

They raced downstairs and Rix gave the order to move out. Though all was in readiness, it would still take an hour or two. He packed his saddlebags, mounted and walked around his troops, making the automatic checks he did every time they decamped, and cursing every delay. How long ago had Holm sent the message? This morning? Yesterday?

"I can't wait any longer," he said after fifteen frustrating minutes. "Take charge, Jackery. I'm riding for Tuling Pass."

"You can't defend it by yourself."

"I've got to know if Grandys is ahead. If he is, I'll try and stop him."

"Assuming you can catch him. You might have to ride all the way to Garramide, and even on a fast horse that's probably at least five days in good weather. Got enough supplies?"

"Yes."

"What about horse feed? You won't find much good grass in the mountains at this time of year."

"I'll take a spare horse, just in case. It can carry a couple of bags of oats."

"What do you want me to do?" said Jackery.

Rix thought for a moment. "If I don't come back, you'll know Grandys is ahead and I'm after him."

"Or he's killed you."

After a long pause, Rix said, "Yes—there's a good possibility he will, especially if he discovers I'm behind him and sets up an ambush. But if I don't come back it doesn't change much—his army will be following as fast as they can march. Grandys' hoard will be well hidden and it could take me days to find it. I can't do that with an army besieging Garramide—it can't hold out for more than a day or two."

"Then you need me to defend the three passes," said Jackery, "and delay the enemy as long as possible."

"It'll be a bloody business," said Rix. "No, it's too much. I can't ask it."

"Ask what?" Jackery responded coolly.

"Ask my men to die in their hundreds to make time for me, while I ride away. You'll have to go."

"What, to Garramide?"

"Yes. I'll give you a note to the castellan—whoever that is now ..."

Rix's old castellan, Swelt, had been killed by the mutineers months ago, after which Rix had left for the peace conference at Glimmering. He had not been back, though the chancellor had taken refuge at Garramide for several weeks after the fiasco at Glimmering. Rix had no idea what changes he had made, or who was in charge now.

"No," said Jackery.

"Are you disobeying a direct order?"

"I guess I am. What's the point in sending me to Garramide when I don't know the place? Why would your people listen to me, even if I have your note? And if Grandys is ahead, he'll kill me a lot easier than he will you."

"Good men are going to die defending the three passes," said Rix. "I don't feel that I can order them to sacrifice their lives when I'm not there to lead them. Especially not you."

"The passes have to be defended," said Jackery stiffly. "And you've got to get to Garramide first. No one else can do it."

"But still—"

"You're not ordering me, anyway. I'm volunteering." Jackery's eyes flashed fire. "And frankly, Deadhand, I'm insulted that you're trying to shield me from doing my duty. I'm staying and you're going, so get on your bloody horse and piss off before I'm tempted to punch my commanding officer in the mouth."

They faced each other, fists clenched.

"I mean it," said Jackery.

Rix let out his breath in a rush. "You're a good man, Jackery."

"Damn right I am. And you're running late, so bugger off."

"The longer you can hold Grandys up the better," said Rix. "But don't fight to the bitter end at each pass. Don't waste lives if it's only going to gain me a few minutes."

"Don't tell me how to do my job," said Jackery.

Rix said goodbye to his other officers and his men, collected a second horse from the stables and roped on the bags of oats. He wheeled his mounts and galloped off. Behind him, Jackery began shouting orders.

Rix did not look back.

He raced along the eastern road, heading for the track to Garramide at the fastest pace his mount could maintain. He was a heavy burden for a horse, riding uphill and, even with a spare, he could not afford to injure it.

"On the other hand," he said aloud, "Grandys has got to be three stone heavier than me. That's a huge weight for any nag to carry."

His horse lifted its ears as if it agreed.

He rode for several hours without seeing any hoofmarks. The path was stony here and had been washed clean by a recent rain shower, probably yesterday, so any more recent tracks would show.

There were none, and he felt sure that Grandys was not ahead of him, but he recalled that several other paths joined this one before it became a single route up into the mountains. Rix kept going. He had to make sure.

Half an hour later, a path joined his from the left. It was unmarked. Twenty minutes later another path entered from the left, also unmarked. Was it the last? Rix could not remember. He had only taken this road twice and the last time had been months ago.

He continued for another hour, climbing steeply now but still seeing no tracks. He was about to turn back when he noted a track winding up from his right, to join his path a couple of hundred yards ahead. He cantered up to it.

The road was wet from seepage and the ground was softer. Soft enough to show deep, widely-spaced hoofmarks. A heavy rider on a big horse.

It had to be Grandys.

CHAPTER 52

There came a thumping sound, followed by a *smash-crash* as if stone had been broken and fallen onto a hard floor. Tali could not tell where it had come from—sound travelled oddly underground.

"That must be Lyf's troops breaking in," said Glynnie.

"We can't wait any longer. I'll have to risk my gift."

Though the way things had gone lately, even if Tali did succeed, she would be lucky to stay on her feet afterwards.

"It could kill you," said Glynnie.

"It'd be better than falling into Grandys' hands."

Tali was reaching within herself, trying to find the gentlest way to draw the magery she needed, when there was a rustling sound outside the door and the bolt was drawn back. She thrust out her hand, prepared to kill.

"No!" cried Glynnie, knocking her arm aside, then hurled herself at the small figure standing there. "Benn!"

He held onto her for a few seconds, tears streaming down his face. "Sis!" he whispered. "Sis, after you went down that drain I thought I'd never see you again."

"I was sure ... sure ... They were after us, Benn. They were everywhere. Rix and I, we couldn't get back."

He pulled free. His eyes were huge, his skin pale and clammy. "Quick! They're coming."

He took Glynnie's hand, hauled her out the door and ran, stumbling a little. Tali followed. At the end of the corridor he turned left into a small room whose door was open. He closed it and darted to the far side, where he worked a hidden mechanism. A hatch in the floor popped open.

"Go down!" said Benn.

Glynnie hesitated and Tali did too. It was utterly dark down there.

"Jump in, quick!" said Benn, his voice thick with fear. "It's only six feet."

Glynnie jumped—a hollow thud. Tali gave her a few seconds to move out of the way and followed. As she fell in the dark, it seemed like a lot more than six feet. She scrambled aside and her hand landed on something small, furry and pulpy, with a disgusting smell. A rotting rat corpse? She choked back a yelp.

The light was blocked as Benn fell through, pulling the hatch shut behind him. It became absolutely dark. Tali could smell sweat, fear and lots of putrid rats.

"Take my hand, Sis," he said, his voice even higher than normal. "T-Tali, hold onto Glynnie. Come on, come on."

Tali groped for Glynnie's hand. Blurred noises reverberated down through the rock. It might have been Lyf's commandoes storming up the corridor. Fear speared through her. They were lost in the dark with only a small boy to help them. How could they get away when their hunters were so close?

"Are you sure you know the way?" said Glynnie.

"Spent months down here," Benn said scornfully.

Glynnie jerked on Tali's hand. She stumbled forward. It was so dark that not even her Cython-bred senses could help her. She reached out with her free hand. There was rough rock to either side, less than a foot away, and more rough rock only a few inches above her head. This passage had been made for small folk.

They stopped. Judging by the faint scraping sound, Benn was opening a door. They went through and Tali cracked her forehead on the roof. It was even lower here; she had to walk with her head bent. Benn closed the door.

"Oh, Benn, thank heavens I've found you," said Glynnie, her voice trembling with emotion.

"Not now, Sis!" he hissed. "Don't make a sound."

Tali heard Glynnie's sharp intake of breath. They followed a convoluted path, often dropping into narrow holes or crawling down passages only two feet high. The air grew increasingly hot and stale. There was not a breath of circulation. And without circulation there were liable to be pools of heavy air which would suffocate them without their ever realising it. They would grow sleepy, lie down and never wake . . .

Tali fought to dismiss the thought. Benn wasn't any ordinary small boy—he had survived in Cauldron for months, and she had to trust that he knew what he was doing.

The muffled sounds continued behind them, sometimes loud, sometimes faint. Sometimes they would die away for a while, but they always returned. Lyf's troops would never give up.

Benn stopped so suddenly that Glynnie and Tali ran into him.

"They're still behind us," he said. "They must be tracking us, somehow. I don't understand how they're doing it."

Tali went cold inside. She had been about to use magery when Benn appeared, and she hadn't closed her gift off. She did so. It hurt.

"I'm sorry, it's me. They've been tracking the *call* of the master pearl. I've closed it off now."

Benn said a word no ten-year-old boy should have known. "How could you be so stupid?"

"Hush, Benn!" said Glynnie. "Tali risked her life to save me. They were just about to hang me on Murderers' Mound, and when she used her magery to save me, it hurt her bad."

"*Hang you?*" he cried, and suddenly he was a little boy again, lost and desperate for comfort.

Clothes rustled, as if he was hugging his sister. They hurried on and, after another ten or fifteen minutes, emerged from a drain into a stinking alley. It was late in the afternoon. The air reeked of smoke and the light had a yellow-brown tinge.

"We're in Tumbrel Town," said Benn. "Keep your head down, Tali."

"I'd be better off with a hat."

He darted up the alley, shortly returning with two pilfered, baggy hats. Tali put hers on and pulled it down to her eyebrows. It smelled like a drain. They pushed into the crowd. They were so dirty and dusty now that they looked like all the other slum dwellers. Everyone was talking about Grandys' ferocious attack on the temple, and the Resistance's revolt. Tali could hear the distant sounds of warfare.

"Who's that fighting? Is it Grandys?" Benn said to a passer-by, an aged veteran with only half a nose.

"Don't know, don't care," he whined. "I hope they all kill each other." He slouched away.

"If the revolt fails," said Tali, "Lyf's troops will take bloody revenge on the rebel-held areas."

"And come looking for you," said Glynnie.

"For *us*. You and Benn are in almost as much danger. We've got to get out of Caulderon right away."

They made their way diagonally across the great city. Buildings were burning all over the place and several times, as they crossed a broader thoroughfare, they saw dead soldiers, Herovian and Cythonian, lying where they had fallen.

As they reached a corner, Tali heard an angry muttering which rose and fell. It was almost dark now. A series of bright torches appeared out of the smoky gloom and a group of people came stumbling by, laden with chains and driven by Cythonians with whips and chuck-lashes.

Tali drew Glynnie and Benn back. "Turn away. Don't let them see your faces," she said quietly.

They turned away.

"Who are they?" said Glynnie.

"I saw Dillible and several others I recognised," said Tali. "I'd say the rebellion has failed and they're taking the rebels they've caught for execution."

Tali pulled her hat down another half inch, making sure none of the rebels could get a good look at her and betray her out of spite. The death march passed by. The light faded and suddenly it was night.

"How are we going to get out?" said Glynnie.

"The way we entered," said Tali. "Via the lake."

As they approached the northern lakeshore, klaxons sounded all across the city.

"What's that?" Glynnie whispered.

"Curfew in fifteen minutes," said Benn. "Anyone caught on the streets after curfew will be killed on the spot." He shivered. "Seen it done."

Hundreds of fishing boats were drawn up along the muddy shore and fishermen were gathered nearby, watching their property and mending their nets. Tali plodded along until she found a suitable boat, and a fisherman who looked hungry for coin. She palmed gold out of the little bag she had stolen from Lirriam.

"We need a ride across to Reffering," she said to the fisherman, though that was not her real destination.

"Not even for a silver *lorm*," he said.

She opened her hand. A large disc of gold gleamed there, enough to buy half a dozen boats like his. "How about this?"

He took the gold, tested it with his teeth, and said, "Get in. I'll grab my gear."

"I'll come with you," said Tali.

"It's not necessary."

"Neither is your death, but I'm prepared to make an exception if you're thinking of betraying us."

He stared at her, weighing her up.

Tali raised her hand and pointed it at his throat. "I know how to kill with magery, and I also know how to sail. I don't need you."

His eyes darted back and forth. She could see him weighing the risk—whether to betray her and keep her gold, or to do what she said.

"You won't be the first to die at my hands," said Tali.

It was taking all her strength to hold her hand steady, and if he went for her she wasn't sure she would be able to defend herself in time. She tried to project an air of overwhelming confidence.

"You're the Pale who escaped from Cython!"

"Yes, I am," said Tali. "So you know I mean what I say."

He shivered and gestured her towards the boat.

"After you," said Tali.

Glynnie and Benn were sitting side by side, their arms around each other. They had handed over responsibility to Tali and were totally absorbed in one another.

When the boat was half a mile out, heading west and invisible in the nightly lake mist, Tali said, "I've changed my mind. Take us east to Grume."

"That'll be an extra fee."

"It's only a third of the distance."

"If you'd said Grume in the first place I'd have charged more."

"As I mentioned, I know how to sail. It'll only take me thirty seconds to kill you and heave you over the side."

He tried to stare her down, but failed, and with a muttered curse he turned east.

He gave them no more trouble and, half an hour later, landed them on the jetty at the small town of Grume. It was dark and there was no one about. When he had gone they went into Grume, where Tali bought the only horse available for sale, again paying far more than it was worth, and all the supplies that were to be had. It was a miserable amount of food for three people, but she thought it would do.

The horse was a big, ugly brute, but it looked strong and that was all she cared about. Glynnie climbed into the saddle. Tali helped Benn up in front and mounted behind Glynnie. Benn clung to the saddle horn, looking more afraid than he had at any time in Caulderon, and they rode out.

"Where are we going?" said Glynnie. "Are—are we going to find Rix?"

"I don't know where he is and I can't afford to go looking for him," said Tali. "Not with Grandys and Lyf both hunting me. Besides, Grandys has Holm, so it'll only be a matter of time before he knows about the circlet. And once he does, he'll go after it. I've got to beat him to it."

"Does that mean—?"

"We're riding for Garramide, as fast as we possibly can." She tapped Benn on the shoulder. "How did you come to be lost when Rix and Glynnie escaped?"

Benn let out a little squawk of dismay.

"What's the matter?" said Tali.

"I'll get into trouble."

"I think we're way past that," said Glynnie, hugging him so tightly that he let out a little grunt.

"I disobeyed orders," said Benn. "When Sis and Rix swam down the drain and Rix didn't come straight back, I was really scared. I walked up the drain to the corner but two of the enemy saw me and

I had to run for it. I ran the other way, so I wouldn't lead them to Rix."

"Stupid boy," said Glynnie, without rancour.

"I was sure they were going to kill me, but they took me hostage. They wanted to use me to trap Rix. Why didn't you come back, Sis?"

"Rix did come back, but you weren't there and they must have wiped away your tracks—he couldn't tell what had happened to you. Not long afterwards we were attacked on the lake, and nearly killed, and then the enemy were everywhere. We couldn't get back to look for you. Oh, Benn," she said, hugging him again. "I've been sick with guilt for leaving you."

He wriggled free. Tali smiled to herself. Had the light been good enough, she felt sure Benn would have been blushing.

"What happened to you after that, Benn?" said Tali.

"They took me ..." He gulped. "They took me to Lyf himself. That was *really* scary."

"What did he want?"

"He asked lots of questions about Rix. And about you, too. I tried ... I really tried not to tell him anything, but Lyf always knew when I was telling a lie. He got real angry."

"He's a mighty king," said Tali. "Powerful adults can't resist him, so how could you be expected to? What happened then?"

"He let me go."

"He let you go?"

"He said I was just a stupid kid ..." He gulped.

"You're not!" Glynnie said indignantly.

"What is it, Benn?" said Tali, reining in.

"I found out later, when it was too late, that he'd put some kind of magic link on me," Benn said in a whisper. "Before he let me go."

"What for?"

"So he could have me followed."

The bottom fell out of Tali's stomach. "Is it still there?"

"I don't think so. My head stopped hurting a long time ago ... though when Lyf is close by, I know it. When he moves it leaves shadows in my mind."

"I'd better check." She put her hands around his head and

opened her gift momentarily. It hurt so much that she could not speak for several minutes. "I don't sense anything, not that it matters. Lyf will soon know where we're going. Why did he want to follow you?"

"He must have been hoping I'd lead him to Rix, but I didn't know where Rix was . . . " Benn's voice died away. He drew in a desperate breath.

"But?" said Tali. "What happened?"

"I joined the Resistance. Just cleaning, running errands, taking messages . . . "

"And the link led Lyf's soldiers to the Resistance."

"Yes. They killed dozens of Resistance fighters, and it was all my fault."

"No, it wasn't!" Tali said sharply. "How could the link be your fault when you didn't know about it?"

"It was me who led them there."

"It was *Lyf's link* that led them there. You're just a little boy, Benn. It's Lyf's responsibility, not yours."

"I might be little," Benn said soberly, "but I've seen more bad things than most grown-ups see in their lives. I'm not a boy any more."

CHAPTER 53

Tobry had not come near Rannilt since that brief hug last night, nor would he allow her to approach him, and she ached with the loss—and the rejection. Did he not want to be healed?

"What are you so scared of, Tobry? Are you scared I'll fail, and your shifter side will break out and kill me?"

She was preparing another fish dinner on a rock ledge above the stream, miles further underground. There was no driftwood here to fuel a fire and she would have to eat her catch raw, but she did not mind—hungry slave girls could eat almost anything. Rannilt filleted the little fish and sliced the fillets into slivers, so they would last longer.

"Or are you scared I'll succeed?"

He crouched on a higher ledge thirty feet away, arms hanging over his knees, watching her every movement. He was salivating, but did not move.

"You're lookin' scrawny," said Rannilt. "I don't reckon you've eaten nothin' since that horrid hare's head."

She picked up the filleted fish, her dinner, and the head and bones, his meal, carried them a few yards towards him, set everything down on a rock and backed away. Tobry stared at the food. Rannilt watched him from the corner of an eye. Her empty stomach was grumbling but she swallowed her saliva and waited, praying that he would not gobble the lot. It had taken her hours to catch three small fish.

After a few minutes he sprang off the ledge, crossed the distance in a few bounds, bolted the fish heads and bones, and disappeared up the tunnel. Rannilt ate the fillets, extinguished the light and lay down to sleep.

Later that night he returned to the ledge. Rannilt did not move, nor make any finger light. She lay perfectly still, trying to sense out his mood.

At last she said, very softly. "Tali's waitin' for you."

He made no sound but she knew he was listening. Shifters had cat-keen hearing.

"She's achin' for you, just as much as you're achin' for her." Rannilt did not know if this were true; Tali was a strange one and she had never truly understood her. But every iota of Rannilt's romantic little soul hoped it was true. "You're the love of her life, and she's yours. You were born to be together and if you don't come back, somethin' will die in Tali. I know it will."

He let out a sudden, single howl of grief, startlingly loud in the empty cavern. It echoed back and forth, sounding like her name, *Tali*, *Taaaalllii*. Cat claws scraped on the soft limestone and he was gone again.

Rannilt sighed. It was all so hard! She was afraid she had failed this time, but she wasn't giving up.

The days passed, each like the one before, as they went deeper under the mountains. The rock changed from limestone to green slate and then to a shiny mica schist, and later to other kinds of rocks she did not recognise because they had not occurred in Cython.

The linked caves and tunnels weren't natural any more. They had all been excavated out of the native rock, though Rannilt could not imagine why people would have gone to such enormous labour. There was no sign that anyone had passed this way since the passages were constructed.

Tobry still watched over her at night from a distance, but she seldom saw him during the day. He was always well ahead, leading her who knew where. Whenever she stopped to rest, he soon appeared out of darkness at the furthest reach of her finger light. He would stand there, facing away from her and spreading his arms as if to embrace the *winged terror*, whatever it was. As if to embrace his doom.

Rannilt's euphoria at her first steps in healing had faded long ago. What was she doing wrong? She redoubled her efforts, and kept talking about her own feelings and trying to articulate his, but it wasn't working. The shifter curse was fighting her all the way and she had no idea how to combat it.

Could anyone?

No one has ever healed a full-blown shifter.

"Well, I'm goin' to!" she shrieked, spraying needles of golden light in all directions. They reflected back at her from a million crystal facets in the walls and roof of the cave. "You're not stoppin' me."

She looked up and he was standing on a fallen slab of rock, not twenty feet away, watching her. His eyes were mostly yellow now, which was a bad sign. He turned away and she did not try to stop him. Rannilt never did. She was his defender and his healer—she did not want to be his master.

In this awkward and frustrating way they continued, day after day, deeper under the mountains until they came to an area where the tunnel branched, again and again, and she realised that Tobry was no longer sure which way to go. He kept stopping at junctions, looking frustrated, and sometimes he backtracked for miles before he found a way that seemed, or smelled, right to him.

The next morning—Rannilt insisted on calling it morning when she woke, and night when she lay down to sleep—she roused in a high-ceilinged cavern to see him standing at a three-way intersection. He sniffed the first tunnel, and the next, then the third before going back to the first.

Rannilt picked up her sandals and went soft-footed towards him. She did not creep—that was likely to alarm him. This time he allowed her to approach within a few feet before leaping aside. She sniffed the three openings.

"Limestone all the way," she said of the first.

Having grown up in Cython, she knew many rocks and minerals. All the slaves did but Rannilt had another unique gift: she could tell them apart by licking the rock and tasting it, and she could distinguish many kinds of rocks solely by smell. It had been handy when she had run away from the bully girls into the unlit tunnels of Cython. It enabled her to know where she was, and to find her way back.

"And lots of water," she added. "Flooded, maybe."

He took a deep breath and let it out slowly.

"Lime shale," Rannilt said of the second opening. "Also greywacke, marble and layers of schist in the knotted heart of the mountain. But dry. No fish in there."

Tobry was utterly still, and she sensed that he was waiting for something. Waiting for her to test the third passage?

She sniffed, frowned, sniffed again.

"It's warm," she said after a minute or two. "Warm and humid. There's water . . . lots of water, but it smells funny. It reminds me of the chymical level in Cython . . . " That gave Rannilt pause. She did not want to go anywhere near such a place. "And I can smell a great jumble of rocks all twisted and ground together: serpentinite! Marl! A funny kind of basalt! Quartzite!"

Her eyes widened. She took another sniff. "There's precious ores, too. Rich ores: I can smell cinnabar, realgar, native silver, native bismuth, sulphur—lots and lots of sulphur! Galena—that's where lead comes from . . . " Rannilt paused. She probably shouldn't mention lead to a caitsthe. "Even pitchblende, and that's the strangest of all—when it's really rich ore it glows in the dark."

Rannilt took a final, questioning sniff, because all those scents were overlain on another, one she did not recognise, though it made the hairs on her arms rise up. No, she could not place it.

She glanced at Tobry, whose eyes had turned grey again. He let his breath out with a whistling sound and turned to stare at her. There seemed to be a question in his eyes, almost as if he were asking her opinion.

She did not want to give it. She did not like the smell of the third passage—it raised her hackles—though the others felt like dead ends to her.

"If this is the way you want to go," she said, pointing down the third tunnel, "then you should go."

He shot past her into the dark. Rannilt headed after him, tasting the air every time she thought of it. It smelled just as worrying.

The path was rough. She stubbed her toe and sat down to put her sandals on. The more she sniffed, the less she liked the place. She felt that it had a toxic air. Was that why he had sought it out?

On she trudged, limping now, every so often raising her hand to light the way immediately ahead. Her golden light wasn't as bright as before, probably because she was half starved. She hadn't found any fish yesterday and there would be none today, now they had left the underground stream.

After a mile or so she smelled cleaner air. Rannilt thrust out her hand and her finger beams lit up two tall stone statues, at least twenty feet high—stern old women who looked like the Matriarchs of Cython. Rannilt had seen the Matriarchs once, when she was four, and had never forgotten them. Cranky old witches, she had thought.

The statues looked ancient; they were covered in dust and brown stains where seeps had dripped on them for aeons. The women had been carved with their arms extended in front and their hands upraised as if to say, *You cannot enter*.

Magery! Rannilt couldn't do it any more, but she could always sense it. There had been powerful magery here once, to prevent people going past, and these stone women were there to warn them off. Warn *her* off.

Tobry emerged from the darkness beside the left-hand figure, walked past the front of the right-hand one, then stood between them. He took a deep sniff, reached forward with his right arm and felt the air ahead of him, as if sensing for traps.

There had been traps here, Rannilt knew instinctively, but they must have failed long ago.

He took a step, his left arm now extended. Another step and another and another. Then suddenly he was through. He looked back at her, his teeth flashed white, as if in triumph, then he ran.

She allowed her finger light to die down to a glimmer that only lit the floor one step ahead, and went after him. But she had only gone a few yards when the strangest thing happened—she sensed an opening in the wall on her left, though to her eyes it was solid rock.

Rannilt felt the stone, back and forth, and up as high as she could reach. It was solid everywhere, though when she closed her eyes she *saw* a great opening there, intricately carved around the sides in the ancient Cythian manner, like an enormous gate. She moved back and forth. What was the gate for? Where did it lead?

She could sense nothing beyond the gate but miles of solid rock, so why was it there? Was it just a decoration? She did not think so. There was something secret about it. Something *hidden*.

She opened her eyes suddenly. Nothing! She closed them and turned around three times, so fast that it made her dizzy, followed by a fourth time, slowly. For a fraction of a second she saw through the gate, not solid rock but all the way to a ruined stone temple she had never seen before, set in a park with fallen stones in the background. Then the image was gone and nothing could bring it back.

Rannilt shrugged and went after Tobry.

After several hours the passage began to wind down and down, as if they were inside a spiral that grew wider the deeper it went. It was warmer, too. Ever warmer, and the worrying smell she had detected hours ago had thickened. Every time she caught a whiff of it, she shivered.

The passage began to open out. The floor sloped down before her and the roof rose up to form a vast open cavern, her faint finger light twinkling off millions of facets—no, more like droplets—up there. She extinguished her finger. She could not see the cavern now, but she could sense lots about it.

It was humid, sticky, sweltering. A vast, gloomy chamber hundreds of yards across and half as high. The dripping roof was festooned with crystals. The floor was covered in sluggish pools, one of them silvery, others tar-black, and heaps of broken rock. And in the centre—

Rannilt's heart stopped.

Now, *now* she understood.

This was it. Life and death and dissolution.

The *winged terror* Tobry had been looking for all this time.

CHAPTER 54

I t wasn't a gauntling though, nor any kind of flying beast Rannilt had ever seen. It was a wyverin, and it was enormous.

Rannilt knew that Rix had painted Lord Ricinus standing by the fallen beast, his sword thrust into its heart. But this wyverin was so vast a sword could never have reached its massive heart. No warrior's weapon could have killed it; no steel could have pierced its adamantine armour. It was a hundred and fifty feet long, maybe more, and twenty-five feet high. It seemed too big for the world.

As the wyverin moved in its sleep, rock cracked beneath it. Its breath was a rush of wind one way, stirring the hair on the back of her head, then a heavy gush in her face, hot and metallic.

And if it woke, it could gobble her and Tobry down in a single gulp.

He was standing a few yards ahead, quite still, leaning forward as if yearning towards the creature. Yearning for what? Rannilt had to see more, but she was afraid to wake it or disturb it in any way. She wrapped the fingers of her left hand around the middle finger of her right, made a glimmer of golden light from her fingertip and stopped the enclosing fingers down until only a tiny ray emerged from the hole.

It revealed the parts of the cavern floor ahead of her, though not the wyverin itself. Just ahead was a thick, oily pool, skinned on top, as black as the inside of a mountain. It reeked of tar. Further on were puddles like pools of silver metal, mirror shiny.

Yellow clouds hung around the wyverin's nostrils, moving in and out as it breathed. Its eyes, which were only open a crack, were inflamed; tears drip-dripped continually from them. They must have been watering for ages, because twin stalagmites three feet high had formed where the tears fell.

She crept to Tobry's side, reached up and took his hard hand. To her surprise he did not resist her. She tugged on his hand but he did not budge.

"Come away," whispered Rannilt, pulling harder.

She might as well have been pulling on a rock.

"How did the wyverin get here?" she said quietly. "Where did it come from?"

He made no sound, though she knew he was listening.

"The wicked Cythonians call it the Sacred Beast," she added. "The One That Heals All."

His fingers clenched around hers, then relaxed.

"They say it eats up the old world and makes it new again. They say it burns all foulness away, turns everythin' to its elements."

From the stories that had been rife in Cython, Rannilt remembered another alarming fact.

"And when it wakes from its enchanted sleep . . . they say it has to restore its magery by eatin' a magian's flesh, and drinkin' his blood."

And Tobry had been a magian . . .

Could it restore its magery by eating him? Was that why he had sought it out? To end the agony of being a shifter the only way he could?

Suddenly its vast head moved and lifted. Rannilt bit down on a scream. Tobry thrust her behind him, shielding her with his body, holding her tightly.

She peeped around his middle, her mouth open, gazing at the awesome sight. The wyverin's heavy-lidded eyes did not open as its head rose in the air, thirty feet on its long neck, and swung around to the left, towards the side wall. The rock or slag that was its bed cracked and crumbled. Its nostrils glowed the colour of fire, illuminating a thick vein of scarlet ore.

The great mouth opened and crunched through the solid rock, biting out half a wagon load of ore. The neck swung back, the head settled. The jaws moved, crushing the rock. The wyverin swallowed. The crushed rock settled audibly in its innards and she heard liquid flowing over it, and a distant churning and hissing and rumbling. The wyverin lowered its head and went as still as it had been when they'd arrived.

"Now that's weird," whispered Rannilt. "Of all the things I ever imagined, I never thought of a beast that ate rock. Cinnabar, that red ore is—quicksilver ore. There were veins of it in Cython, beyond the heatstone mine, and if you or I ate a bit of it, we'd go mad and die."

The beast began to breathe heavily, then its nostrils gushed a scalding yellow vapour that ignited in the air, producing thick white fumes. Burning sulphur! Every slave in Cython knew what sulphur was, and the ways it could be used. It was one of the most important elements in Cythonian alchymie. For instance, she remembered, if you dissolved those acrid fumes in water you got the corrosive oil of vitriol, which had all manner of useful, though dangerous, purposes.

The wyverin's hindquarters heaved. It urinated a heavy stream of silvery metal that settled in the silver puddles on the floor.

"It's piddlin' quicksilver!" whispered Rannilt. "And quicksilver is deadly poison—even just its fumes."

Tobry's hand went over her nose and in a single movement he turned, lifted her off her feet and carried her away up the spiralling tunnel. It was half a mile before he put her down, in an embayment off the tunnel that had ventilation holes to either side.

Rannilt looked up at Tobry, expecting him to bolt from the physical contact, as he had so often done over the past days, but he did not move. She sat on the floor, legs crossed, trying to ignore the empty feeling in her belly and the bitter taste of failure in her mouth.

"That's why you came all this way, isn't it?" she said dully. "You came to find the wyverin."

He did not move or speak. His whole body had gone rigid.

"Do you think it can undo the shifter curse? Or do you . . . just want to be . . . *eaten*?" She could scarcely bear to think it, much less say it aloud. "To put an end to the pain."

Rannilt reached out and laid a hand on his arm. He did not flinch or draw back.

"Tali's waitin'," she reminded him. "She'll be there when we get back."

When he did not react in any way, fear touched her more deeply than it ever had on this interminable journey. She laid her hands on his head, closed her eyes and reached out to him as she had done the first time. He did not try to block her; nor did he howl or show pain.

"You're letting me try," said Rannilt, "but it's not workin'; I can't reach you. You can't think of anythin' but the wyverin, can you?" She caught an upwelling sob, tried to choke it back, but it burst forth. "You're goin' to give yourself to the beast. You're goin' to leave me all alone, a failed healer."

Tobry took her in his arms, as if for the last time, and rocked her back and forth. A day ago she would have been overjoyed; she would have felt that she had made the breakthrough she had been working towards all this time.

She knew better now. He wasn't afraid to be near her any more because he had conquered his fear of the shifter beast inside him. He and the shifter were both in pain, and they were going to go gladly down to the wyverin.

And dissolution.

CHAPTER 55

R ix stopped and looked back the way he had come. His army would be fighting to hold the second pass by now, or at worst, the third, and his men would be dying by the score to give him a chance to find the circlet.

Though he had ridden his two horses to the point of exhaustion, he had not come close to catching the rider he'd been tracking all this time. How could Grandys, a much heavier man, outdistance him when he had no remount? Not even magery could drive a horse beyond its strength—it would simply fall down dead.

But if the tracks weren't Grandys', why were they heading straight for Garramide? Rix was at the bottom of the escarpment now and the hoofprints continued up the track to the plateau, four thousand feet above.

He had only gone fifty yards, though, when he noticed footprints in the mud beside the hoof marks—*three* sets of small footprints. All this time he had been following children, or a small woman with two children. But at least he was here first, and with luck he would have a few days to look for the circlet. Anything could happen in that time.

Rix rubbed the back of his neck where the wet coat had chafed it and led his horses up the track. The higher he went, the heavier the rain became. After a four-hour climb he reached the top and had to sit down in the pouring rain. He was bone-weary but could not relax; if things had gone badly Grandys could have taken the third pass and might be close behind.

"I'm worn to rags," he said to the horses. "And I dare say you're looking forward to a big bag of oats and a rubdown in a nice dry barn. Come on, then."

The rain had grown ever colder as he'd climbed the escarpment; it was icy at this altitude and he was soaked through. He hauled himself to his feet, wincing, and climbed into the cold saddle. There was no sign of spring up here. He turned onto the road to Garramide.

The plateau was a steep, fertile oval four miles by two, bounded by cliffs or escarpments on the east and south and by rearing mountains to the north and west. It looked as though it had not stopped raining in a month and every low point was a lake, every rivulet a torrent.

He rocked in the saddle as his horse splashed along the winding road to Fortress Garramide. In the distance, behind the thirty-foot-high outer wall, he could see the golden walls of the great stepped castle, with its four corner towers each topped with a copper-clad dome tarnished to green, and the larger central tower whose massive dome rose high above everything else. It was topped with a circular platform that overlooked the whole of the plateau.

There were other towers further back, large and small, massive and pencil thin, and dozens of other smaller buildings, though he could not see most of them from here.

Within the hour he reached the front gates which, Rix was pleased to see, were in good repair. There were guards on the walls, but were they *his* guards? Months had passed since he'd left with Tali, Tobry and Glynnie for the peace conference at Glimmering, and anything could have happened in that time. The place could have been taken over by bandits again.

"Hello?" he said as he approached the gate, enveloped in cloak and hood.

"Name?" said a familiar voice from the high war platform behind the gates. "And yer business?"

"Sergeant Nuddell!" said Rix, pushing back his hood.

"Deadhand!" said Nuddell. He barked, "Open the gates. Lord Deadhand has come home at last."

Rix rode through, swung down, gave his horses a weary pat, then turned to Nuddell and put out his left hand.

"Welcome home," said Nuddell. "We were worried. Especially after Tali and Glynnie turned up and told us all the tales of the war."

"Tali's here? And *Glynnie*?"

"And a young lad, Benn. Skinny little runt. They got in yesterday morning."

The breath rushed out of him, as if he had been holding it for the weeks since Glynnie had left. "That's the best news I've heard all year. Are they in their old rooms? Quick, man!"

"Wouldn't know where they're sleeping, Deadhand. But Tali's not here."

"Why not?"

"She went out this morning, searching for something. Don't know what."

"I think I can guess. Thanks, Nuddell. Come up for a mug of ale this evening and you can fill me in." Rix turned away, his knees shaky. He had to see Glynnie *now*.

"Yes, Lord Deadhand. Er . . . "

Rix swung back, suppressing his impatience. "What?"

"What's happened to your army? You're not . . . It's not . . .?"

"It's coming. They stayed behind to hold the passes and give me time for . . . for the search."

"Ah," Nuddell said wisely.

"They'll be here in a day or two." Rix crossed his fingers behind his back.

"What about Grandys?"

"He's coming too, with a bigger army than mine. But not soon, I pray."

"We all hope that, Deadhand."

Rix shook hands with the guards at the gate, greeting each of them by name. He took off his saddlebags, led his two horses to the stables and handed them over to the chief ostler, then headed across the yard towards the front door of the great castle.

The place was in good order, he noted, and the work he had ordered months ago, to strengthen the gate and several weak points in the outer wall, had been completed. There was some new damage, though. One side of a small tower had collapsed and several walls had cracks in them. He assumed the damage was due to the great quake.

There was always more to do. He went in and up the eastern stairs into the main tower, to the chambers he had occupied previously. Everything looked freshly dusted and the fire had been set, ready to light. He sighed. Oh to be warm and dry, to sit beside a blazing fire with a goblet of wine and nothing to do or worry about—

That wasn't even a dream right now. Rix dumped his saddlebags on the floor and sat down to heave off his sodden boots. The walls and ceiling seemed to close in on him for a moment—he had not slept inside a building in over a week.

He shook his head and the feeling was gone. He heaved off his boots, stood them on the hearth, stripped off his filthy socks and washed his face and hands and feet in the water basin. Rix trudged to his bedchamber, leaving wet footprints on the carpet, trying to remember when he had last slept here.

He stopped in mid-stride. He had not gone to bed the night of the mutiny and that had saved them—that and Tali's folly in trying to heal Tobry with her healing blood.

How much blood had flowed under the bridge since then.

He looked down at a small stain on the carpet. Blathy had struck him down here, temporarily paralysing him, and she had been about to cut his throat when Glynnie had sprung to his defence—

"Ahh!" came a cry from the doorway.

He spun around. Glynnie was standing there, staring at him. She had flint and tinder in her hand; a green scarf was wrapped tightly around her head and pinned on the left side. She must have heard the news and come in to light the fire, not realising he was already up here.

Rix swallowed and a flush spread up his face as if he were an errant schoolboy. Her own face was drawn; she looked as if she hadn't slept all night. Her fingers plucked at her ragged sleeve, rose to the scarf then plucked at her sleeve again. His heart was racing. She must be furious with him, and rightly so, and he had to make it right. He sank to his knees before her.

"I'm desperately sorry," he said. "I don't deserve your forgiveness, but if you can find it in your heart—"

Two red spots appeared on her cheeks. She was breathing heavily. "What are you talking about?" she said harshly. "Get up! Get up this minute."

He rose awkwardly, for his overworked muscles had stiffened. He swayed and clutched at the end of the bed for support.

"You told me a dozen times," she said bitterly. "Over and over you told me that it was the wrong time to go looking for Benn, and that I'd get caught as soon as I started asking questions."

"And I was a fool. A selfish, bloody fool."

"Will you shut up!"

Rix shut up.

"I wouldn't listen," said Glynnie. "You were carrying the fate of thousands of people on your shoulders, all alone—the fate of Hightspall itself. But did I help you?"

Rix made a movement towards her, as if to interrupt.

"Sit down," she said softly. "Keep your gob shut!"

He sat.

"No, I didn't," she went on.

"You saved my life when Libbens had me court martialled——"

"If you interrupt again," said Glynnie icily, "you're going to be really, *really* sorry. I kept pestering you about Benn when you couldn't do anything to help him; I undermined you when you were already close to breaking point. And then . . . and then I walked out in the middle of the night without having the courage to tell you I was going . . . though I knew in my deepest heart you'd be frantic when you discovered I was gone. And . . . I got caught the second I went through the wall into Caulderon—just as you'd said I would."

"You were caught?" Rix's heart lurched.

"Caught, interrogated, condemned . . . and sent for execution."

"Execution?" His head was spinning. He jumped up and reached out to her but she sprang backwards, holding up her hands to block him. "But . . . I heard Benn was here. You found him."

"No, I didn't!" she cried. "Tali rescued me, at the very moment when they were putting the noose around my neck."

"Noose?" he croaked. It was all he could do to get the word out. A sentence was beyond him.

"Another minute and I would have been dead. Tali saved me at great risk to herself; and great pain, too; and when we were taken by the Resistance, it was her bargain that found Benn."

"But Benn's here—you saved him in the end."

She shook her head violently, dislodging one end of the green scarf. She hastily tucked it back in place. "Benn saved us—he got us out only moments ahead of Lyf's troops, after the rebellion failed. I didn't do *anything*. I'm useless. I don't deserve——"

"If you hadn't gone to Caulderon would Benn be free now?"

"That's beside the point," she said feebly. Her shoulders slumped; she looked like a prisoner awaiting her fate.

"Actually, it's the whole point," he said softly. "You held to your promise to look after your little brother, and because you did, you've got him back."

"But it wasn't——"

"I think you've been talking long enough," said Rix.

"I haven't——"

"Don't interrupt. I did go after you, as it happens."

"You—*what?*" said Glynnie.

"Holm told me you'd gone, and Jackery and I went after you. We found the spy you killed, but—"

"It was an accident. He whacked me and I struck back at him, instinctively."

"We found his body but you were long gone. To Caulderon, I assumed, after discovering that you'd stolen a skiff and . . . not seeing it floating upside-down anywhere."

"I'm sorry," she whispered. "That must have been terrible."

"It was certainly reckless, since you can barely swim and you've never sailed before."

She did not reply.

He went on. "I was preparing to sail after you—"

"And you call *me* reckless!" she flashed. "Anyone in Caulderon would have recognised you on sight."

"I made you a promise," said Rix. "And I didn't keep it."

He told her about Holm's abduction while he, Rix, was looking for her. And Hork's strike on Rufuss's army that would have ended in disaster had he not counterattacked at the last second.

"I had to choose between you—the woman I loved—and our army," said Rix.

Glynnie jerked at *the woman I loved*.

"And I chose the army," said Rix. "That's the kind of man I am. I'm sorry—it was unforgivable."

"Unforgivable to hold to your sworn word?" said Glynnie in a cracked voice.

"You know what I mean. I promised to help you, and I didn't."

"'When it's over,' you said. 'When you were free.' I can't criticise you for that. Anyway, I have to go now—"

"How's Benn?" said Rix.

"Got work to do, Lord," she mumbled, curtsied and fled for the door.

"Stop!" he bellowed.

She turned and stood there, head downcast, trembling. "Yes, Lord Rixium?"

It was like a knife in the belly. "Don't call me that! We were friends—no, far more than friends. After you rescued me from Grandys that time, we swore to each other, *forever*. Do you think I'm the kind of man who swears such an oath lightly?" Now his voice cracked.

"I deserted you when you needed me most. And I know what the penalty is for ... for desertion in the face of the enemy."

Finally, finally Rix understood what this was all about. And he'd thought *he'd* let *her* down.

"How's Benn?" he said. "And don't tell me I'm not allowed to ask. I've been worried about him."

"He's ... all right."

"For months now, I've blamed myself for losing him. I want to see him, right away."

She went out. Rix slumped on a chair. Though he was only twenty, he was too old for this life.

After a quarter of an hour he heard rustling outside. Benn was in the doorway, staring at his feet. Glynnie hovered a few yards back.

"I'm sorry, Lord Rixium," said Benn.

He had been scrubbed until his skin was pink and was dressed in worn but freshly pressed clothes. The battered splint on his left arm looked as though it had been made from the rungs of a black chair. His eyes had a shine and his cheeks a flush that suggested a touch of fever, and he was exceedingly thin. But he was alive and safe and that was all that mattered.

"What for?" said Rix.

"When you and Glynnie and me were trying to escape that time, I disobeyed orders. I didn't wait at the bottom of the drain like you told me to. I went back up and got caught by the enemy."

Rix frowned. "I thought you must have. I came back to get you and you were gone. Glynnie was frantic."

"I'm really, really sorry."

"Say it to your sister, not to me."

Benn turned to Glynnie. "Sorry, Sis."

"So you should be," she said furiously. "Just look at all the trouble you caused."

"Is that the only bad thing you've done lately?" said Rix.

"Yes," said Benn, though his face went as red as a boil.

"But you freed Glynnie and Tali, and saved them from the enemy."

"Yes, but . . . "

"Who's in charge around here, Benn?"

"You are, Lord Rixium."

"And what I say goes. No argument, right."

"Yes, Lord Rixium."

Rix held out his left hand. "You're one of my bravest young soldiers, so we'll say no more about it."

"But—"

"Are you questioning my orders, soldier?"

"No, Lord Rixium."

"I didn't think so." They shook hands. "Stand over there for a while. I need to talk to Glynnie."

"She's really sad. See you talk nicely—"

"Benn!" cried Glynnie. "If you say another word I'll wallop you good."

"Go on, lad," said Rix. "Spit it out."

Benn looked from Rix to Glynnie as if uncertain who was liable to give him the more dire punishment, then moved closer to Rix.

"Sis was awake all last night, sobbing her heart out for you. She thinks you won't want her with her hair gone."

"*Benn!*" Glynnie shrieked, her face crimson.

"Gotta go," said Benn, and bolted.

"What happened to your hair?" Rix said carefully.

Glynnie tore off the green scarf and hurled it across the room. Her scalp was covered in red fuzz an eighth of an inch long. "Tali shaved it off so we could disguise ourselves as boys—and it's horrible!"

She glared at him, a mixture of defiance and despair.

"It didn't work," said Rix.

"What are you talking about?"

"You don't look anything like a boy."

She shook her head. Clearly she hadn't got the message.

"You're the most beautiful woman I've ever seen," said Rix. He opened his arms.

Glynnie threw herself into them so hard that she knocked him off his feet.

CHAPTER 56

Midnight, and Rix was still up, checking the ledgers. The lists of livestock, food, grain and hay, supplies and weapons were endless, but the stocks were short. When his army arrived, Rix did not see how he was going to feed it or its mounts.

The door opened behind him. "Is that you, Glynnie?"

"No, it's me," said Tali.

He sprang up, scattering the papers and ledgers, and embraced her, and even through her heavy coat he could feel how thin she was. She took off her coat, and the blue, knitted hat enveloping her small head, and dropped them on a chair. Her golden stubble was longer than Glynnie's hair but it did not suit Tali. It made her face seem gaunt.

"You've lost weight," said Rix.

"I was fed better as a slave than as a prisoner."

"Oh, I'm glad you're here. It feels as though the world is swinging back on its axis at last."

"If we get the circlet it might," said Tali.

"Any luck with the search?"

She shook her head, settled in a chair by the fire and, to his surprise, for she seldom drank, accepted a goblet of wine.

"I've scoured the whole of Garramide," she said, "and the land for a mile around, using all the old maps and plans—and my gift, too, when I had the strength for it. If Grandys did hide his treasure hoard here, it's surpassingly well hidden."

"I suppose it's under a charm of concealment."

"It's a mighty spell that still works after two thousand years."

"Maloch was hidden here most of that time. Maybe it's protecting the hoard."

"Maybe," she said wearily. "I don't know what more I can do."

"Then we'll have to try the next plan."

"Which is?"

"Watch what Grandys does when he gets here, and if it looks like he's going after the circlet, try to get it first."

"How close is he?"

"I'll know when my army arrives, which should be tomorrow."

Tali leaned back in the chair and closed her eyes. They were sunken, ringed by dark circles, and he could see the tiny blue veins in her eyelids.

"You look worn to the quick," said Rix.

"My gift is going to kill me one day, but I keep ending up in situations where I have to use it, or fail. I can't go on, Rix." She paused, then added, "I suppose Glynnie filled you in on everything?"

"Everything she knew. Does your gift still hurt?"

Tali twisted the goblet in her fingers. "It hurts more each time I use it. My head aches day and night and it's wearing me away, as I'm wearing the layers of the pearl away. I was strong when you met me—whenever that was—but I feel weaker every day."

"We met six months ago."

"Is that all?" said Tali. "It feels like ten years."

"I think the end is close now."

"I'm *afraid* it is, but not a good end. Lyf's tightening his grip on Hightspall, all save the north, and Grandys holds the north. What do we have?"

"Only Garramide," said Rix.

"When he attacks we'll be lucky to hold out a week. The end's certain now—either Lyf wins, or Grandys does. We can't."

"If we find the circlet—"

"What can we do with it?" said Tali. "Save try to destroy it."

"We could raise king-magery for ourselves—"

"That can't be done without the master pearl, but it's so fragile now it's liable to break the moment someone tries to take it. And even if it didn't, and even if we had the circlet and could raise king-magery, who would use it?"

"Surely—?"

"Only a truly great magian can command king-magery. Do you know any *great* magians?"

"Not any more," Rix said soberly. "The Cythonians have executed every magian they've been able to catch." He paused, staring at the fire. "I rather imagined—"

"That *I* would use it?"

"Bringing Lyf to justice has been your quest as long as I've known you."

Tali sighed and closed her eyes again. "But surely you've realised it by now."

"Realised what?"

"If anyone gets the master pearl, I'll be dead."

"Oh!" Rix stared into the fire for a good while. "What about Grandys?"

"I don't know what he's up to."

"There are some curious rumours going round."

"Like what?"

"That Lyf and Grandys fought each other at Reffering, and again in his temple recently, and both times Lyf blocked Grandys from using Maloch. Apparently Lyf said it was going to desert Grandys for its true master—and he was really shaken."

Tali sat up, rubbing her stubble. "When I was held at Bastion Barr, Lirriam kept making snide remarks about the sword's true master, trying to provoke him. I wondered if the true master could be you."

"I doubt it," said Rix. "Grandys took Maloch far too easily at the peace conference."

"They're coming!" yelled Thom, the little wood boy. He was perched on the wall of the main guard post, looking out. "Lord Deadhand, we're saved!"

Rix went across to the wall, plucked the lad from his precarious perch and swung him onto his shoulders. He watched his army move up onto the plateau, trying to estimate their numbers. Less than a thousand—half as many as he had left with Jackery.

"Want to ride out to meet them, Thom?" Rix had befriended the boy when he first became master of Garramide, and whenever Thom had no work to do he was at Rix's side.

"Can I really?" cried Thom. "Thank you, Mister Deadhand!"

Rix smiled to himself. They went to the stables, he mounted his warhorse and lifted Thom up in front.

"Wow!" said Thom. "This is—wow!"

"Haven't you been on a horse before."

"I'm just a wood boy."

"Not *just* a wood boy—it's an important job."

As they cantered down the road, the knot in Rix's belly tightened. How bad would it be?

Thom gazed about himself excitedly. "It's huge!" he said as they approached.

"The army?"

"Yes."

To Rix it looked small and battered, and many of the men looked wounded and worn. He galloped the last hundred yards, searching the ranks for familiar faces, though he only saw one—the man he had rescued from the crevasse, Sergeant Tonklin. Rix swung down, leaving Thom in the saddle.

"Well met, Tonklin." Rix shook his hand. "Looks like you've had a hard time of it?"

"Aye, but Grandys had a worse one. We held him back two full days, and he lost fifteen hundred men—half his army. He's a day or two behind."

"I'd say you've lost more than half—"

"No, it's not that bad. We had an outbreak of dysentery early on and Jackery sent five hundred men off on that track that wends due south after the second pass. They were too sick to fight, but they should be over it by now. Our casualties were relatively light ... until the third pass."

"What happened there? Where's Jackery? I don't see any of my officers." Rix was getting a very bad feeling.

After a pause, Tonklin said, "Grandys was more frustrated after each pass. And angry; by the third pass he was a berserker. He used some almighty magery there to set off an avalanche and sweep us away ... but it didn't go as he expected. I'm sorry, Deadhand. It took Jackery ... and your other officers, and Sergeant Waysman, plus a couple of hundred of the troops. And twice as many of Grandys' men—it just swept everyone away, broke them and buried most of them." Tonklin shook his head. "Grandys was coming and we couldn't do anything for them, so we came on."

It was the bitterest of blows, especially the loss of Jackery. In the few weeks since they had met, Rix had grown closer to him than to any other man, save Tobry. It wasn't right, and it wasn't fair, but there was nothing to be done except carry on.

"I'm sure you did your best," he said. "Thank you, Tonklin. We'll talk further tonight."

"There is one thing though," said Tonklin. "We ran into an old ally of yours on the way."

He turned, raising his arm, and shortly the front line separated to admit a tall, striking, olive-skinned woman.

"Radl!" said Rix. "This is a surprise; a very welcome one."

"We ran from the battle at Reffering," said Radl, who was at the head of some fifty Pale. "It's troubled us ever since and we had to make amends. We've come back to help you, any way we can."

Rix, Radl and Glynnie were in his chambers that evening, talking strategy, when Tali entered. She froze, staring at Radl, then her face hardened. Rix recalled Tali saying that they had been enemies since childhood.

"What are you doing here?" Tali said coldly.

"We came to help," said Radl.

"I heard you ran like a coward from the battle at Reffering. I don't see that your help is worth much."

"Tali!" Rix said sharply. "What's the matter with you tonight?"

"We ran, and that was bad," said Radl mildly. "Now we've come back to remedy our mistake."

"It's a bit late for that," said Tali.

Clearly, Tali was in a very bad mood. Rix supposed her headaches were worse than usual.

"I don't know that *you* qualify as a reliable friend either," said Radl.

"What do you mean by that?" Tali cried.

"I mean the trail of bodies you've left behind. Like your friend Mia, who lost her head because she tried to save you from your reckless stupidity. And Lifka—"

"I didn't hurt Lifka—well, not badly ..."

"You forced a Purple Pixie toadstool into her mouth to make her too sick to go to work, then you stole her clothes and her identity so you could escape."

"Yes, but—"

"What do you think happened to Lifka after you got away?" said Radl.

"I don't know," said Tali. "I didn't think ..."

"The guards blamed her for helping you. They tortured her to death."

Tali's knees buckled. She grabbed the edge of the table. "I didn't know," she whispered, shivering.

"I wonder how many more people you've used and cast aside since you got out," Radl said relentlessly.

"I—I only did what I had to do—"

"And how many more lives will you ruin in your sad obsession with 'justice' at any cost. Your obsession isn't justice at all; it's *vengeance*!"

Tali was shaking her head, over and over. She tried to speak, but nothing came out save a strangled cry—"No, no!" Then she turned and bolted.

CHAPTER 57

"I need to paint," Rix said to himself two days later, after waking from his latest wyverin nightmare. "I need it more than ever now."

In the past, drawing and painting had been his only solace in difficult times. In Palace Ricinus, where everything else had been bought for a price he was never allowed to forget, painting had been the one thing that was truly his, the one thing Lady Ricinus could not put a price on.

And for the moment nothing required his immediate attention.

He had inspected the fortress, spoken to every one of the three hundred-odd people who dwelt here, personally thanked his little army and Radl's people, reorganised the guard, and given orders for the defences. And just in time. Grandys was only a day's march from the base of the plateau.

For the first time in months an idle hour or two stretched before him, and Rix ached for the release his art could give him; to simply lose himself in the joy of creation.

He went to the cupboard where, months ago, he had kept his paints and brushes, the sketching charcoal and palette. Everything was as he had left it. A wide drawer was stacked with drawing paper, and at the back stood a small canvas he had stretched and primed but never used.

He set the canvas up on a chair in the salon, by the window. The primed surface, a light buff colour, called to him. He squatted in front of it, imagining the first painful strokes, the inner struggle it took to create something out of nothing, the carping self-criticism every time he looked at the work in progress, and finally the bliss when hand and eye took over and the outside world vanished.

"Rix?" said Glynnie. "Are you—ah?"

He rose. "You've no idea how much I long to paint."

"Then paint. What's stopping you?"

"Fear, mostly."

"Fear?" she echoed.

"Of what I might see."

Her eyes took on a vacant look. "Your art is a great gift. Everyone says so."

"Even the chancellor said it," he added drily. "And not long afterwards he ordered my painting hand struck from my body."

He studied his dead hand. It matched the left, save that it was a steel grey colour.

"Sometimes my art feels like a curse forcing me to act out a role laid down for me long ago. That's why I hesitate. There are times when I wonder if I should strike it off permanently, to rid myself of the curse."

"You did divinatory paintings before your hand was severed and . . . reattached," said Glynnie. "Long before, I heard."

"Perhaps the curse isn't in my hand," said Rix. "Perhaps it's in me."

"Don't say that."

"Look at my last four paintings."

"I'd rather not."

"Take the one I did for Father's Honouring—the portrait of him killing the wyverin. That turned out well, wouldn't you say?"

"Everyone said it was a brilliant masterpiece," Glynnie said stoutly.

"Did you like it?"

She shivered. "I don't know anything about art."

"*I hated it!*" said Rix. "The whole time I was working on the portrait I knew there was something wrong with it, and by the end I knew it was the opposite of what I'd tried to paint. The wyverin wasn't dead, it was just pretending: it was laughing at Father for being such a fool. He thought he was symbolically slaying his enemies, when in reality he was bringing about the downfall of our house . . . and his own death."

Glynnie rose abruptly and sat in an armchair by the fire. "How can a painting say all that?"

"If I could see it now I'm afraid it would be saying a lot more than that. Next there was my painting of the murder cellar. Cheerful little piece, wasn't it?"

She did not answer. He could just see the side of her head; she was staring at the flames.

"Third," he went on, "the terrible mural I sketched on the wall of the crypt below Palace Ricinus, using bone charcoal and my own blood. It told the future too—it showed Tali and me putting Tobry down."

"That didn't happen!"

"Only because the quake did our job for us. Finally, most inglorious of all was my painting of the tormented Grandys on the wall of the observatory, up top. It showed him twisting in agony in the Abysm. *Then waking!*"

"That wasn't your fault."

"The image kept changing, and do you know why?"

She avoided his eye.

"Because Grandys—or Maloch—was working on me through the painting," said Rix. "Twisting my mind; trying to influence me to go to the Abysm and raise him from petrifaction. And if Tali hadn't stopped me on the very brink, I would have."

"There's no saying it was through the painting," Glynnie muttered. "I heard that the evil enchantment in Maloch raised Grandys."

"But Maloch directed *me* here to Garramide. And it certainly worked on my mind when I was painting. So, no matter how desperately I ache to paint, I'm afraid to. Afraid Grandys will use any painting I do to get to me."

"It's Grandys who's afraid now—*of you*. Besides, you broke his command over you months ago, and Maloch isn't here to influence you any more. You should paint whatever you want, and damn him."

Rix went across to the fire and sat in an armchair facing hers. "He'll soon be here. Do you remember the siege of Garramide three months ago? It almost fell. It was so very close."

"Of course I remember. But it'll be different this time. We've got far more men to defend the walls, for starters."

"Grandys has far more men to attack them. Plus powerful magery. And better weather."

"Not much better." Glynnie glanced out at the incessant rain. "Besides, Tali could still find the circlet."

"I pray she does, though it won't help us win the war."

"Having it would help keep us from *losing* the war. Where is Tali, anyway? I haven't seen her since the argument with Radl."

"Hiding, I expect. Licking her wounds."

"I've got things to do," she said, rising. "If you don't, then paint for your heart's ease, if nothing else."

She went out.

Rix did not feel up to painting, but he took out some sheets of paper, laid them on the table and began to sketch left-handed. He did not plan to try his right hand, which had twice come alive when he'd taken a brush in those dead fingers. His right hand had been amputated with Maloch, and he had also been holding Maloch when Glynnie had rejoined his severed hand using the last of Tali's healing blood. He did not plan to tempt fate.

He had no particular subject in mind, though there was nothing unusual about that—he preferred to let his hand and eye, or perhaps his subconscious mind, create whatever they wished.

He unfocused his eyes, drew for a few minutes with great sweeps of charcoal across the paper, then tossed the charcoal down without looking at what he had drawn and sat by the fire. His whole body was tingling; the blood seemed to be racing through his veins. At last!

He rose, stretched and went to the table. He had drawn a wyverin waking, raising its head on that long, questing neck. No surprise there—over the past weeks he had often dreamed about the wyverin rising.

How gigantic it was, almost unnaturally so. Not bad, he thought grudgingly, though it would have been better in the days when he could use his right hand.

He pushed the sketch aside and began another, though this time Rix felt uneasy as soon as he began it. He sketched furiously, completing it in a minute, tossed his stub of charcoal at the fire, and focused.

The sketch showed a wyverin falling on a great city whose skyline resembled that of Caulderon, consuming it in fire and poisonous fumes.

"Enough damned wyverin!"

Rix threw the sketch on top of the first and began on a third, using a fresh stick of charcoal. This time he kept his eyes focused; he was going to control the sketch from beginning to end. He tried to draw life, hope and rebirth.

His drawing depicted a grey, smoky land where hundreds of wyverin flocked, devouring the world and scattering their befouling, elemental wastes across it.

Was that all? No, he had one more sketch in him, though it turned out to be the worst of all—a bleak, empty land stubbled by dead forests. A land never touched by cleansing sunlight, but lit only by a cold, silver moon. A land scoured of humanity, perhaps *erased*.

Rix cursed it, grabbed the blank sheets, the paints and charcoal and everything else, and stuffed them back into the cupboard. He went to the window and looked out across the sodden plateau.

It had all begun with his father's portrait. What had Tobry said about it, the night he'd miraculously reappeared at the height of the siege of Garramide?

"I've a feeling the portrait will be found one day," Tobry had said, "and then it'll reveal its *true* divination."

What could that mean? Lord Ricinus's fate had been sealed a month before that night, so the divination must be about the wyverin itself.

When the wyverin wakes, the world ends. So Cythonian legend said. But that was just a legend. It wasn't real.

CHAPTER 58

Grandys dragged off his boots and stood knee-deep in the icy stream, though not even that could numb the bone-deep pain of his feet. After several painful healings the sloughed-off skin had grown back like scar tissue, thick and red and ropy, but the flesh beneath it burned constantly, as though his feet had been bathed in oil of vitriol. There were times when he considered hacking them off, as Lyf had suggested. It seemed the only way he would ever escape from the pain.

"Curse Lyf for all eternity," he raged. "And Rixium too."

"He's getting to you," said Lirriam, making no effort to conceal her glee. "He's defended the three passes brilliantly and it's shaken your confidence, Grandys. You're on the slide—and you'll never get off."

She touched *Incarnate* and, momentarily, her eyes took on the red-purple glow he had seen in the stone previously—the glow she had woken by bringing it close to Tali's master pearl. *Incarnate* had since gone out, though for how long? Lirriam was as stubborn as he was; she *never* gave up.

He wanted to smash her down and trample her into the muck, but he dared not raise a finger against her. Not even Rufuss, sick sadist though he was, would tolerate another attack on one of the Heroes.

Each for all, all for each—forever.

Who was Rixium anyway, Grandys mused, still standing in the stream. Who could this young man be who, at only twenty, had turned Grandys' lessons back on him and troubled him more than any other commander ever had?

Was it because Rixium had once worn Maloch, and had used the sword brilliantly? Had some of its enchantment rubbed off on him? Or, chilling thought, did Maloch see Rixium as its true master, now that Grandys was past his best?

Lirriam must have read his thought, for she walked across to the edge of the stream and held a steel mirror up to his face. Grandys was shocked to see how badly he had aged since he'd come out of the Abysm a few months ago.

His skin, where the opal armour had broken away to expose it, had once been ruddy but it was now a bilious greenish-brown, splotchy and wrinkled. His hair was falling out, his jowls were sagging and his broken nose had a distinct droop at the end. Even the black opal armour, once so perfect and jewel-like, was losing its colour and turning milky.

And his guts were in turmoil, his bowels in constant flux. He was starting to think that he was disintegrating on the inside as well.

I won't have it! Grandys almost screamed. He barely caught himself in time.

He caught Lirriam's hateful eyes on him, saw the amusement there and turned away. He was not going to allow her another advantage. Once he had the master pearl and the circlet he would turn the ageing back, and he would be the old Axil Grandys again: proud, indomitable, fearless, undefeated.

"You've fallen into a funk," said Lirriam. "After the hidings Rixium gave you, you're terrified of him. No wonder you've held back every step of this journey."

"If you don't let up, I swear I'll kill you."

"You'd better, Grandys, because I never forgive and I never forget. But you won't lay a finger on me—the Heroes would cast you out, and that would destroy you."

"I made the four of you Heroes," he blustered. "I can make others."

"No, you can't."

"Why ever not?"

"We Five have shared pasts, shared agonies and shared persecution back in Thanneron, yet we rose above those lives to remake ourselves when we stepped onto this land. Our past is two thousand years dead, Grandys—we Five are living fossils, the last of our kind."

"I have thousands of pureblood Herovians."

"But they're not *our* people; they don't share our past and they've not been persecuted and forged in our cruel fires. Your brave Herovians concealed their race for the past fifteen hundred years, so as to live easy lives in Hightspall. Where's the honour in that, Grandys? Where's the nobility? And I doubt if many of them are purebreds, either. They're a bastard race, no more like we Five Heroes than the Hightspallers are. You can't replace us with any of them, no matter how hard you try."

In his heart he knew she was right, though he wasn't going to admit it.

"All you have is us, Grandys," Lirriam went on. "That's why you look so desperately to us for approval after each of your little victories—*because we're all you've got*. And *you're* all we've got, which is why we allow your brutality, and Rufuss his sickening sadism. Without the other Heroes none of us are anything—we'd be lonely aliens in a world that's changed beyond our understanding."

Grandys did not reply. They were bound together, right or wrong, for good or ill, for as long as they survived. All the more reason to make sure they did survive.

"When I'm ready, I'll act," said Grandys. "Only a fool tries to predict how I think, or what I'll do next."

"That fool is you," said Lirriam, and went to her tent with a spring in her step.

He stood outside her tent most of that night, watching her magelight flare and flicker. It heightened his unease. Lirriam was a brilliant sorcerer whose full potential had, hitherto, not been tapped. Now he gained the impression that she had been waiting for something—perhaps the chance that *Incarnate* offered—all her adult life.

That she had been content to wait, saving her strength and never exerting herself fully, knowing her chance would eventually come.

Grandys wasn't going to let her win. He was the most formidable man this land had ever seen, and he wasn't done yet. The ultimate prize still lay ahead of him. The thought lifted his spirits.

It was time to start looking for the circlet.

CHAPTER 59

Even riding on gauntling-back the hunt for Tobry was taking too long, and Lyf was frantic. He'd had no news from Caulderon or his army in five days; no news about Grandys or Rixium either. All communication between Lyf and the outside world had been severed.

"The world could have ended for all I'd know," he fretted as he clambered onto the vile beast his disability required him to use, and prodded it with the end of one of his crutches.

Grolik lashed her barbed tail at Lyf. He used precious magery to block it as painfully as possible. She screeched, hurled herself into the air and twisted into a series of vicious aerobatics, trying to dislodge him and drop him on his head from a hundred feet. He curbed her with a fireball that seared off half of her crinkly right ear. Grolik flew on, hissing and spitting and curling her tail up like a scorpion.

They went through the same rigmarole every morning, until she finally submitted. One day, if he wasn't careful, Grolik would catch him unawares and then he would die like any normal man, his work undone.

"The world looks as solid as ever to me," Errek said. "But if you can't trust your officers to do their jobs, there are spells that will allow you to speak to your people in Caulderon, and in the field."

"I know the spells," Lyf snapped. "I can't afford the power it would take to use them."

"And you can't let go." Errek settled back, arms folded behind his head, to enjoy the journey.

Nothing seemed to faze him. Indeed, being *raised* as a wrythen had made him blossom—he even seemed to have more hair than before. It irked Lyf since he was rapidly losing his own.

They had wasted days doubling back and forth between the ten thousand lakes of Lakeland, trying to make sense of a trail that meandered like a drunken ant and was often buried by spring snow or washed out by rain.

It had taken the best part of a week before they traced Tobry into a limestone cave that led deep into the Nandeloch Mountains, but the gauntling had baulked last night and would not approach the entrance. Lyf hoped it would be less recalcitrant in daylight.

"Go in!" he commanded.

The gauntling flew straight past, ten feet up. Lyf forced it to turn and fly back. It headed towards the entrance then shot away at the last second. Errek snorted.

"Giving you a body was a mistake," Lyf muttered, as the gauntling streaked around in a mile-wide circle.

"Why so?" Errek said innocently. "Not that I'd call this barely tangible wrythen form a body."

"You used to be so stern and kingly. Raising you has made you frivolous, scatty and just plain silly."

Errek bowed ironically. "I was a stern and kingly shade because, like everyone in your ancestor gallery, you *created* me that way. I was a mere figment of your imagining; one you put together from scraps of history and a mouldy old portrait in the Hall of the Kings and Queens of Cythe."

Lyf tried to force the gauntling to go in. She spiralled upwards.

"I preferred the stern and kingly you," Lyf muttered. "It was easier to deal with."

"This wrythen, feeble though it is, is the *real* me. I may be a great king in legend, but in real life I also had a sense of humour. Do you have a sense of humour, Lyf? I don't think I've ever seen you laugh." Errek grinned. "And certainly not at the funniest thing I've ever seen—yourself."

"Life is no laughing matter. It's deadly earnest."

"On the contrary, life is an eternal joke. A man who can't laugh at his own frailties and follies is a man who has no capacity to learn from his mistakes."

"I don't have time for this," Lyf snapped.

"More's the pity."

"If you've got so much spare time, why not put it to good use and find your lost memories?"

"They'll come, in time," said Errek. "Or not. They can't be forced."

"I need them now."

Errek shrugged.

"That was a remarkably fluid shoulder movement for such an aged wrythen," Lyf said sourly.

"I was only forty-two when I died."

"You look at least a hundred."

"You reshaped my wrythen when you raised me, to fit your mental image of me."

"Do you want me to change it to the real you?"

"I could do that myself, if I wanted to."

Lyf stared at him. "You can do magery?"

"Some."

"Then why don't you change your shape to the real one?"

"It amuses me to be a middle-aged spirit in an ancient form. It also humbles me, and that's no bad thing, because I was once over-proud. A common failing in kings, I believe. It's one of the hazards of the job."

Lyf did not reply. The gauntling was approaching the cavern mouth again. He prepared a command.

Go in!

The gauntling turned at an impossible angle, skidded sideways across the air, turned upside-down, dumped Lyf in the cave mouth then shot away. Lyf landed hard on his backside, rolled over and came to a stop with his stumps in the air. Errek's wrythen was floating fifty feet up, laughing at him.

"I fail to see the humorous side," snapped Lyf.

"The beast told you twice that it was afraid to go in. Why wasn't that good enough for you?"

Lyf picked up his crutches and stumped inside without answering.

"The Defenders!" Errek gazed at the matriarchal stone figures standing with their hands upraised, one on either side of the passage. "I'd forgotten I'd put them here."

"What are they defending?" said Lyf.

"No idea."

"But you created them."

"Yes, and the defences and traps beyond . . ."

"You must have some idea what they're for."

"It was ten thousand years ago," said Errek. "And I died after considerable trauma. I don't remember anything . . . *except the fear*."

"The fear?" cried Lyf.

"I sealed this place for a very good reason, with the best traps and the most long-lived spells I could muster, to make sure that no one would ever find a way past."

"But Tobry—or the shifter, whichever he is—*has* found a way past."

"We kings try to control the future but we can't even manage the present. Nothing endures forever, neither devices nor spells, nor even rock itself. In the end, all fails."

"Then whatever your Defenders are defending against may also have failed."

"I hope so," said Errek.

They continued, but a few yards past the Defenders Lyf stopped again, staring at the wall.

"What is this structure?" he asked, peering through the gateway that was there one moment and solid stone the next.

"It used to be called the Sacred Gate."

"What's it called now?"

"Nothing. I'd say it was forgotten thousands of long years ago."

"Why does it lead to a ruin in Caulderon?"

"*One* way leads to the ruin, though it wasn't a ruin in the olden days."

"One way? You mean there are two?" Lyf glanced behind him but saw only stone, and no gate, ephemeral or otherwise.

"There are two ways through the gate. The Sacred Gate leads directly to Caulderon. The other path—you have to enter the gate to see it—goes to Turgur Thross."

"The sacred ruins on the northern edge of Garramide plateau?"

"Precisely, and only a mile or two from the peak called Touchstone—where the craft of alchymie was invented, ten thousand years ago. By my humble self, as it happens."

"A lot seems to happen in that area."

"The original capital of Cythe was at Turgur Thross, in my time. I wonder why it was moved?"

"The population outgrew the plateau," said Lyf. "And it was too cold, wet and remote."

"Too uncomfortable for my luxury-loving successors, you mean?" Errek sniffed the air, and again, then wrinkled his brow.

"Can you smell?" said Lyf. "In all the time I was a wrythen, I smelled nothing."

"Faintly. And I don't like it."

"What can you smell?"

"I can't remember, but the smell is familiar. Alarming!"

"Why did the shifter come here?" said Lyf.

"He's a dying beast, looking for a hole to hide in."

"But why all this way, with such relentless purpose? He's bypassed a thousand holes and hollows suitable for dying in."

"I don't know . . ."

"What is it now?" said Lyf.

"Memory echoes," said Errek. "Echoes of echoes of the distant past, of the dark time before I invented king-magery . . . and the reason why I invented it."

"That's not helping," said Lyf.

"We should not be here." Errek looked down the dark passage. "We should turn around right now."

"The shifter went down there and I have to find him."

Lyf went on, not without a shiver, and Errek followed.

"The shifter has a child with it," said Lyf, staring at the small, damp footprint.

"Why a child?" said Errek.

"Perhaps the shifter brought it along to eat. We're getting close. I can smell the stench of the creature."

They continued down a passage that became an expanding spiral, to a place where it broadened out and the roof rose, though the stone chamber was too gloomy for Lyf to make out any further details.

There's the child, said Errek into Lyf's mind. *On the right. She's sleeping. Don't make a sound.*

Can you see the shifter?

No.

Errek drifted by. Lyf crept past on his crutches, trying to move as silently as possible. He could see her now. The child murmured in her sleep, turned over and settled again. They continued down the widening spiral.

We're close, said Errek. *I don't like that smell at all.*

Shifters' stink, said Lyf.

Not the shifter smell. Nor the tang of burnt sulphur. The other *smell. In the cavern.*

What other *smell? What cavern?*

Just ahead.

They entered the vast cavern. The mixture of smells was much stronger here, and it was hotter—very much hotter. Lyf could sense the vastness opening up ahead and below him, though the cavern was in a darkness his eyes could not penetrate.

Suddenly a hand gripped his shoulder, surprisingly strong for a wrythen. *Stop!*

Lyf looked back and Errek's spectral hair was standing on end. "What is it now?"

A fragment of memory. An ancient horror, never to be woken.

The shifter's down there. I can smell him.

As Lyf moved down the slope a faint red glow appeared, as if around a pair of gigantic nostrils. Light grew in the chamber and he knew what it was.

That's no horror. The wyverin is our Sacred Beast—it's the living symbol of the enemy's destruction and Cythe's rebirth.

That's what our people have always been told, said Errek.

What are you talking about?

I can't remember, but I know it's not the Sacred Beast—it's not even of this world! It's the Chymical Beast, *and it's more deadly than anything you have ever encountered.*

Chymical as in alchymie?

That's where I got the idea to invent alchymie in the first place—from the beast. And there's something else. Something really *troubling.*

What?

There's a connection between the Chymical Beast and the Engine.

Lyf jumped. *Why? How?*

I don't know.

You said the wyverin isn't of this world. What's that supposed to mean?

Errek did not answer.

Where did it come from?

I—don't—know.

Seems to me you don't know much at all, said Lyf. *I can't think why I brought you.*

You didn't. I brought myself, to keep you out of trouble.

I'm going down, said Lyf.

You know what a wyverin has to do once it's roused? said Errek.

Consume a magian to replenish its own magery. Don't worry, I'll be careful.

I'm not worried about you, said Errek with a faint chuckle. *I'm worried it might consume* me, *for* my *magery.*

I didn't know you had any worth having.

There're a lot of things you don't know.

Lyf crept down. Errek followed. Far below, but only a few yards from the wyverin, Lyf saw the man-shape, its arms extended towards the beast.

Shh! said Lyf. *There he is—the shifter. What the blazes is he doing?*

He's communing with the beast, said Errek in wonder. *It's almost as if they're sharing each other's pain.*

What are you talking about! The wyverin isn't in pain.

It's in great pain—see the tears flooding from its eyes, even in its enchanted sleep? And the twin stalagmites where the tears have been falling for aeons? Tobry's own pain must be disguising his gift for magery, otherwise it would simply eat him, waking or sleeping.

They eased closer. Now Tobry was scratching enigmatic signs on the rocky floor before him. He reached up again. "Khar—, Khar!"

"What's he trying to do?" Lyf said aloud.

A child's scream rang out from behind them. "Tobry, no!"

Then the wyverin stirred, a vast, terrible creature rising out of the darkness, and Lyf realised what Tobry was up to.

He was trying to wake the beast.

CHAPTER 60

"Sacrilege!" Lyf said aloud. "The Sacred Beast must not be disturbed in any way."

"It's the Chymical Beast," Errek reminded him, "and I'd be more worried about it consuming Tobry before he tells you where the circlet is. Stop him."

"How?"

"By any means possible."

"You mean magery? Is it safe to use it here?"

"No, it's desperately unsafe, but you've run out of options."

Lyf slid two fingers into the pouch that contained the ebony pearls, each kept secure in a crushproof, magery-proof platina box. He flipped the lids up, touched the pearls and cast a sleep spell at Tobry. The wyverin snapped in Lyf's direction. He stumbled backwards on his crutches but the snap was just a reflex; the beast was still deep in its enchanted sleep.

Rannilt came running down. She shouldered Lyf aside and tried to catch Tobry as he fell but he collapsed on her, knocking her to the floor. She struggled out from under him.

With a sweep of his hand Lyf raised Tobry, who was deeply asleep, and began to drift him back up the tunnel, through the air.

Rannilt flew at Lyf. "Leave him alone!" she hissed. "You're not doin' your evil magery on Tobry."

Lyf raised his hand to blast her out of the way but Errek, with a strength Lyf had never imagined a wrythen could have, jerked him around.

"She's a child!" Errek thundered. "And that is not the action of a Cythian king!"

Lyf rubbed his shoulder, which had been badly wrenched. "I don't know what possessed me," he said meekly.

"Besides . . . " said Errek, looking thoughtfully at Rannilt.

"What?"

"Nothing. Come away."

They went up the spiral to the place where Rannilt had been asleep. She followed, scowling. Lyf set Tobry down, bound him with spells strong enough to contain a caitsthe, and woke him.

Tobry howled, tried to lunge at Lyf and fell over.

Lyf, with a gesture, stood him upright. "Where is the circlet, shifter?"

Tobry stared at him the way a dumb animal would.

"Speak, beast!"

Lyf directed a stinging blast at Tobry, knocking him backwards. He bared his teeth in pain, then wrapped his arms around himself and stood there, shivering.

"Stop it!" cried Rannilt. "Leave him alone, you pig!"

"I know you know where it is, *beast*," said Lyf, ignoring her. "And I'm not going to stop until you give me the answer."

He stung Tobry again. Tobry doubled over, gasping, then began to claw furiously at himself as if stinging insects were burrowing into his flesh.

"Stop it, stop it!" shrieked Rannilt. "You're hurtin' him."

"All he has to do is speak," said Lyf irritably.

"What are you gunna do then?" Rannilt said furiously, pushing between Lyf and Tobry. "Kill him, I'll bet."

"What's the difference?" said Lyf. "He's a mad shifter, and it's obvious he wants to die."

"He doesn't! Not really! Besides, I'm gunna heal him."

"Get out of my way, you absurd child," said Lyf.

"I'm not movin'," said Rannilt. "And you can't make me."

"You dare defy me?" cried Lyf. "I could blast you to pieces with a twitch of my fingers."

"That's 'cause you're a *nasty*, *evil*, *little* man," said Rannilt, trembling with fear but breathing fire in every syllable. "That's why everyone hates you, even your own people. You don't care about nothin' good because there's nothin' good left in you. You're rotten all the way through; rotten as Axil Grandys."

"You go too far, child!" Lyf thundered. He raised his hand.

Errek ostentatiously cleared his throat. Instead, Lyf pointed at Tobry over Rannilt's shoulder.

"Speak, you verminous beast." Red flashed from his fingers.

Tobry shrieked, dropped to the floor and curled up into a whimpering ball.

"Stop it!" shouted Rannilt. "You're undoin' all my healin'."

She kicked one of Lyf's crutches out from under him, whacked him over the head and shoulders with it, then ran to Tobry and sank to her knees beside him, laying her hands on his forehead.

"He was gettin' better!" she screeched. "Now you've driven him mad again, you stupid, stupid man."

"I don't take this kind of abuse from anyone," said Lyf. "Get out of my way."

Rannilt tried to cover Tobry with her own body. "You'll have to kill me! I bet you'd enjoy killin' a little girl, you—you *monster*."

Lyf balled up his fists helplessly, then turned to Errek and snapped, "Don't just float there, laughing. Help me."

Errek drifted towards Rannilt. "Do you know who I am, child?"

"You're a rotten old wrythen," she muttered. "Just like him, only old as bones."

"Indeed I am old. Older than bones, in most cases. My name is Errek and they call me First-King, because I was the very first king of Cythe, ten thousand years ago."

She shrugged, unimpressed. "I can only count to a hundred."

"If you counted to a hundred not once, but *a hundred times*, that's how long ago I was king."

Now Rannilt did look impressed. "What do you want?" she said grudgingly.

"We don't want to hurt your friend, Tobry—"

"Lyf does! He's a pig!"

"Sometimes Lyf gets carried away," said Errek, waving Lyf's outrage aside. "But all he wants is the secret that Tobry knows."

"Tobry can't hardly speak," said Rannilt.

"He nearly spoke in the wyverin's cavern. I think he can manage a word or two."

"I don't see why—"

"We need that secret, child, and I'll tell you why. If Grandys gets it—"

"I know!" cried Rannilt. "I've heard it a thousand times. He'll get king-magery and destroy the world. But you're no better."

"Lyf *is* better. Do you know what the highest duty of a Cythonian king is, child?"

"Don't know, don't care."

"It's to protect his people, *and heal the land*."

She went still, staring at him.

"Yes, child, what Lyf wants most of all is to heal his troubled land. Just as you want, most of all, to heal your friend Tobry. You're not so different after all, you and Lyf."

"Except he's mean and horrible!"

"I concede he has some unfortunate character traits," said Errek. "But if the land isn't healed soon, the Vomits will blow it to bits and everyone will die."

"How soon?"

"Not even I know that. Maybe weeks; maybe years. But soon, and no one can heal it save the king—"

"Why is it always the king?" said Rannilt. "Why can't a queen heal the land?"

"There have been ruling queens, and some of them have been great healers," said Errek. "But Lyf is the king now, and he needs king-magery to heal the land. Yet without the key—"

"I *know*!" she said rudely. "He needs your circlet to make king-magery work."

Lyf gasped. Errek raised an eyebrow. "You know about our most closely guarded secret?"

"I hear things," said Rannilt. She glanced at Tobry, who was still clenched into a ball. "All right! If you promise to leave him alone, I'll tell you where the stupid thing is."

"You know where it is?" said Lyf, his voice rising.

"You've got to promise."

"I promise," said Errek. "On my solemn word, as the first king of Cythe that ever was." He looked pointedly at Lyf.

"I promise, upon my kingly oath," Lyf said sourly. "Well, child?"

"It's at Garramide," said Rannilt. "In the hoard with all the filthy old treasures Grandys hid there thousands of years ago."

"Where at Garramide?"

"If anyone knew, his treasures wouldn't be there any more, would they? Now go away. I've got healin' to do."

"It can't be that easy," said Lyf.

"She's telling the truth as she knows it," said Errek.

"But is her truth the *real* truth?"

"The only way to find out is to go and see."

"Garramide isn't far away, via Turgur Thross," said Lyf. "But first I've got to make a quick trip through the Sacred Gate and back. There's something I need to do in Caulderon."

He set off up the tunnel as fast as his crutches could carry him. Errek floated along on his back as though he were taking an afternoon nap on a sofa.

When Lyf looked back, Rannilt had her thin arms around the beast and was speaking healing words to him.

"We're goin' to go back to the beginnin'," said Rannilt briskly. "But this time the healin' is going to work. Isn't it?"

Tobry let out a plaintive sound that could have been affirmation, or denial.

"And then we're goin' home," Rannilt added.

CHAPTER 61

"How many dead this time?" Rix said quietly. "Benn, close your ears."

It was late morning, and Glynnie had just come up onto the watchtower to give her report from the healery—how many injured men had died in the night, and how many her team had been able to save. The first number was usually larger than the second.

He did not want to alarm Benn, who spent all his free time on the wall, carrying food and water, cleaning up and generally helping out the guards. Though as it happened, Benn seemed less troubled by the carnage than Rix, and that was terribly wrong. What dreadful atrocities had he seen in Caulderon that the nightly bloodshed on the wall had so little impact on him?

Grandys' army had been camped at the foot of the escarpment, half a day's march away, for five eternal days. He seemed in no hurry to bring his army up the mountain; apparently he planned to soften Garramide up first with nightly terror raids.

Another of his raiding parties had attacked late last night, taking advantage of fog to creep in close and pick off patrolling guards with arrows, then shoot fusillades of fire arrows over the walls and into the yard. The roof of the temporary barracks had caught alight and half of it had burned before the fire was extinguished.

"Twelve guards," said Glynnie in a grim voice. "Plus a stable boy who was carrying water for the fire-fighters. He was burned to death when the roof collapsed on him. Poor lad; his was the worst death."

Her eyes were hollow and her cheeks concave. Glynnie had always taken her work to heart, but her anguish about killing the tent guard to save Rix after the mutiny, plus her own narrow escape from death at the scaffold-henge, had heightened her concern for all those who came under her care. She often sank into depression after the night's work. She could do so little to ease their suffering, or save their limbs or lives.

"Are you going after the raiders?" she added, dully.

"I'd like to," said Rix, glancing at Benn, who was soaking it all up, wide-eyed. "But Grandys is trying to lure me out and I'm not going to be tempted. If he wants the circlet, he's got to attack Garramide where it's strongest. Then we'll see how he likes it."

Hollow boast, he thought. Grandys likes it very well.

Glynnie turned away, plodding towards the steps down to the yard, but turned back at Benn's excited cry. "Sis! I saw someone moving out there."

"Where?"

Glynnie trudged to the wall and looked over. "That way," said Benn, pointing to the north.

"Good sentry work, lad," said Rix. "It's not a raiding party, though. It's just an adult and a kid. From one of the northern steadings, I expect." He turned away. The plateau was home to several thousand people and they came and went all the time. "Go to bed, Glynnie. You're swaying on your feet."

She rubbed a hand over her eyes. "I thought the whole world was wobbling back and forth." She rested her head on the wall for a minute, then looked out again. "Rix?"

"Yes?"

"Can I have your binoculars?"

He handed them to her. She focused on the two people, lowered the binoculars and raised them again.

"It's Rannilt!" she cried. "And—*and Tobry*."

"Tobry's dead," Rix said flatly.

"I dare say he'll argue the point when he gets here. Take a look." She held out the binoculars.

Rix waved them away. "He's already come back from the dead once," he muttered. "It beggars belief that he could do it twice."

She left the binoculars teetering on the wall and ran down the stairs. Rix stared at the distant shapes but could not make out the faces. He glanced at the binoculars, looked away, then snatched them up and focused . . . and shivers ran up the back of his neck and over his head.

His heart began to race. It could not be true; not twice! He rechecked, and there was no doubt at all. Rannilt was sauntering across the plateau as if she owned it, leading a bearded, shaggy, but unmistakable Tobry by the hand.

Rix's heart was pounding now, and tears were flooding from his eyes. He set the binoculars down and ran down the steps, taking them six at a time in dire risk of breaking an ankle, if not his neck. He passed Glynnie at the bottom, raced for the gates, forced them open with both hands and exploded out.

He ran through the puddles and slush for a hundred yards, then stopped, feasting his eyes on them. Rannilt looked much the same as ever, only grubbier and more ragged. And thinner. She could hardly have had a decent meal in the month—had it been a month?—since he had last seen her.

Tobry was as dirty as a pig in a wallow. He looked more animal-like, too. His shoulders, once so broad and square, sloped more like a big cat's, and there was a lot of yellow in his eyes.

Yet there was still something distinctly Tobry about him—an indefinable quality in the way he held his head, and the way he walked, that made him instantly recognisable.

Rix ran towards him. Tobry reared back and Rix stopped four yards away, his eyes flicking from Rannilt to Tobry. Glynnie panted up beside him.

"Stay back," Rannilt said softly.

"Ah . . .?" said Rix.

"He's still a shifter, but he ain't dangerous now . . . hardly ever. Are you, Tobry?"

Tobry made an incoherent sound in his throat.

"What . . . How did you . . . ?" said Rix.

Rannilt seemed to have grown inwardly. There was something stronger and more confident about her. Under the grime, she was glowing.

"The chains broke when the tree toppled, and Tobry got away before it hit the ground. I followed him, to heal him." Tobry let out a yearning cry. "That's what we've been doin' all this time. Healin'; me and Tobry."

"You always said you could heal," said Rix, "and people never believed you."

"You mean *Tali*," said Rannilt. "Tali never believed me. But you do."

"Yes, I do."

"I haven't finished yet. Tobry don't have those mad shifter rages any more, but he can't hardly talk either. There's a long way to go, but we're gunna get there, aren't we?"

She turned to Tobry, her eyes shining. Again he gave that little yearning cry.

"He wasn't ready to come back, but I've been talkin' to him about Tali, and how she's waitin' for him. Tali's here, ain't she?" Rannilt said anxiously, and she looked like a little girl again, fretting about whether she had done the right thing.

Rix felt a sudden, indefinable unease. Tali had also been here last time Tobry had come back from the dead. Why was history repeating itself?

"Yes, she's here," said Glynnie. "She's out looking for . . . something at the moment, but I expect she'll be back tonight."

A shadow passed across Rannilt's face but Rix paid no notice. He was too overcome.

"Come in to the warm," he said. "You need feeding up, both of you."

There was some muttering among the servants when they learned that the shifter was back, though it died away when they saw how well Rannilt worked with Tobry, and how different he was. Besides, the rabblerousers who had so feared him before were dead—either killed in the mutiny at Garramide months ago, or executed for their part in it.

Late in the afternoon, after they had bathed, fed and rested, Rannilt brought Tobry up to Rix's salon. Tobry would not sit by the fire with the others, but prowled back and forth.

"He don't like bein' inside," said Rannilt. She smirked. "Or bein' bathed."

After some minutes she cajoled him into sitting in an armchair well back from the fire in the unlit shadows, and she perched beside him. Rix and Glynnie took chairs on the other side of the fire and Rannilt went on with her tale, telling it backwards.

"I told Lyf about the circlet," she confessed. She leaned away from Rix, afraid of his reaction.

"I wasn't aware you knew about it," said Rix.

"I hear things . . . Aren't you angry?"

"After all you've done for Tobry? What did Lyf do?"

"I followed him and Errek, watchin' and listenin'. They took a gate—the Sacred Gate, they called it—to Caulderon. But they came back an hour later and went the other way. He was headin' to a place he called Tur-Turgur Thross."

"Old Cythian ruins," said Rix. "About four miles north of here."

"And then he was plannin' to hang around Garramide and watch for Grandys to go after the circlet—so he could get to it first."

"Was he now? That's very interesting."

Rannilt told them how badly Tobry had relapsed after Lyf's interrogation, and how much healing she'd had to do in the following days to get him to the docile state he was in now.

"I'm glad you're here," said Rix. "The whole world seems to be gathering outside our walls. It won't be long now until . . . the end."

"Is that what the wyverin means?" said Rannilt, wide-eyed. "The end of the world?"

She glanced at Tobry, who let out a muted howl, although very loud in the small space.

"What do you know about the wyverin?" said Rix, glancing towards the table by the window.

"The *winged terror*," said Rannilt. "We went underground for ages—maybe a week—and Tobry sniffed it out in its lair." Her voice dropped to a whisper. "You shoulda seen it. It's *gigantic*!"

Rix went to the table, then returned with his first sketch, which he held up so the firelight fell on it. "Like this?"

Rannilt started. Tobry let out a wild cry and sprang to his feet, reaching out with both arms to the image.

"It's just a picture, Tobry," Rannilt said. She snatched the sketch, folded it over so only the blank surface on the other side of the paper showed, then unfolded it again. "Just a picture. It ain't real."

The tension slowly drained out of him. He gave a great shudder, drooped, and she dropped the sketch and helped him back to his chair.

"It looks exactly like that." Rannilt sat, laid her head on the arm of the chair and closed her eyes. "So tired."

"How did you do it?" said Glynnie.

Rannilt blinked at her. "Do what?"

"Heal Tobry when everyone said it couldn't be done. I've been helping in the healery for ages, trying to save wounded men and women, and I do everything I possibly can, yet still they die before my eyes, day after day. How do you manage it?"

Rannilt shrugged. "I've wanted to heal since I was a little girl."

Rix smiled. "Some might say you're still a little girl."

Rannilt bristled. "I'm nearly *eleven*! I drove off the evil facinore. And fought wicked old Lyf."

"*Some* might say it," Rix said hastily. "But I wouldn't be one of them. Thank you for bringing Tobry back, Rannilt. Thank you from the depths of my heart."

She stared at him.

"And for finding a way to do what no one else in the world could have," he added.

"He ain't healed yet," she said quietly. "There's miles to go. I haven't even touched the hardest bit—the shifter curse." She bit her lip, and suddenly she *was* a little girl again, struggling to do something beyond her comprehension. "I don't know how I'm goin' to heal him of that . . . "

She frowned up at Rix. "Don't you dare tell me I can't," she said fiercely. "Tali was always sayin' that. I can heal Tobry. *I can!*"

"I believe you," said Rix. "No one wants Tobry healed more than I do."

She snorted, then turned and took Tobry by the hand. "Time for us to do some more work."

When the door had closed behind them, Rix took up the wyverin sketch and went to throw it into the fire.

"I don't think that would be a good idea," said Glynnie.

"Why not?"

"You drew it, and then the wyverin turned up."

"If we believe Rannilt's story, and I see no reason not to, it was the other way around. Tobry found the wyverin—and sometime after that, I drew it. Besides, judging by those statues Rannilt described, it's been there thousands of years."

"Why do you say that?"

"The statues—those elderly, female Defenders—must be Cythian, which means they date back before the time of the First Fleet."

"What kind of a beast eats rock, breathes out sulphur and pees quicksilver, anyway?"

"And what else does it breathe and pee?" said Rix.

"I don't understand."

"Rannilt said the wyverin was eating a bright red ore called cinnabar. I know about cinnabar, as it happens, because House Ricinus used to own a cinnabar mine."

"What's cinnabar?"

"Quicksilver ore, and it's easy to get the quicksilver out. We just heated the ore on an iron plate until it gave off sulphur and left behind globules of quicksilver. Very quick. And very deadly. Hardly any of our miners or smelter workers lived to old age, and most of those who did went mad. They used to call it madman's ore."

He fetched the other sketches he had made and spread them on the floor—the wyverin rising; the wyverin falling on a great city, consuming it fire and fume; the land where wyverin flocked, devouring all. Finally that bleak, empty land lit by a gelid moon. As the firelight played on the sketches, he imagined that the beasts were rising, flying, feeding.

"Why am I painting the *end*?" said Rix. "The end's no use to me. I need the beginning."

"Your divinatory gift has been wrong before," said Glynnie. "Why do you let it bother you so?"

"It's also been *right* before, and you have no idea how much I hate it!" He rose abruptly, trampling the sketches and kicking them aside. "I don't want to know anything about the future."

"Good, because every time you talk about getting your father's portrait back—"

"Father's portrait!" said Rix. "That's it! What if it's changed, as my mural of Grandys did?"

"Why do you think the portrait would change?"

"When I was painting it, every time I looked at it I saw something different."

"That was a desperate time," said Glynnie. "The war had just started, Caulderon was besieged and the chancellor was threatening to bring down House Ricinus. It wasn't the portrait that was different—it was you. You were changing, so you kept seeing new things in it."

"How would you know?" said Rix. "You weren't there."

"As it happens, I was."

"What are you talking about?"

"Around the time you started the portrait, I wangled a shift in my roster. I was one of the housemaids who cleaned your chambers when you and Tobry were out, or asleep. I saw the portrait every time I was there."

"And I never knew," sighed Rix.

"Lords who live in palaces never notice the servants," she said acidly.

"Why did you wangle a shift in your roster? Why were you so interested in Father's portrait?"

"I didn't give a damn about the portrait. I was interested in you."

"But you—" Rix bit the rest off. He wasn't that stupid. Not quite.

"Were just a maidservant?"

"I didn't say that."

"I wasn't thinking about *getting* you," she said hastily. "That wasn't even a dream. But I liked you, and you'd always treated me and Benn kindly. I—I just wanted to be near you."

He reached out to her. "And now we are with each other."

She squeezed into the armchair next to him and he put his arms around her.

"You're not going to go after it, are you?" said Glynnie.

"The portrait?" He knew she was talking about it. He just wasn't ready to answer.

"Yes, the damned portrait."

"I might have to."

She stiffened in his arms, then propelled herself violently out of the chair.

"You couldn't come to Caulderon to help me find Benn," she said with icy fury, "but you'll neglect your responsibilities to us and your army and Garramide, and risk your life, to get back a painting you loathe?"

"What happens if the wyverin—this otherworldly beast that feeds on the earth itself—does wake? Does it signify the end of everything? We have to know, Glynnie."

"If we can't hold Grandys out when he brings his army up the mountain tomorrow, or the next day, the wyverin won't matter."

CHAPTER 62

Tali crept into Rix's rooms late that night as if she had been trying to avoid meeting anyone. She probably had—all Garramide knew about her argument with Radl, who had only been here a week but was already far more popular than Tali.

"Any luck with the circlet?" said Rix.

She shook her head. "Tell me something that's not about Lyf or Grandys. Anything at all."

Should he tell her that Tobry and Rannilt were here? How would Tali react to the news that Tobry was alive? If she tried to take over his healing—and Tali might well feel it was her right—there would be big trouble, and Rix did not have the energy to deal with any more trouble right now.

He decided to introduce the matter obliquely. "The wyverin has been seen."

"*The* wyverin?" she said with odd emphasis. "Like the one in your father's portrait."

"More or less—though it's ten times as big, apparently. Almost too big for the world, I've heard. It's not a good omen."

"It certainly isn't for Grandys," said Tali. She sat up, bright-eyed.

"How do you mean?" said Rix.

"He's got a superstitious fear of it."

"Why?"

"It's some kind of Herovian nemesis, for his family."

"Really?" said Rix. "How do you know that?"

"When they held me prisoner on Red Mesa, I happened to mention it to him—"

"How come you didn't tell me this before?"

"I've had a lot on my mind lately."

"No doubt," he said drily.

"Anyway, on Red Mesa, Grandys was boasting that he was your

greatest fear, and that he was going to destroy you. I had to wipe the smirk off his face somehow, so I said *he* wasn't your greatest fear— the wyverin was. Or at least, your nightmares about it rising up. I'm sorry. I shouldn't have—"

"It doesn't matter," Rix said roughly. "What did he say?"

"As soon as I mentioned the wyverin rising, Grandys reared up. He was shaken, Rix, absolutely shaken. I asked why and Lirriam said it was the doom of his family's line—the one thing he truly feared. She kept taunting him about it until he knocked her down and broke her jaw."

Rix whistled. "When thieves fall out . . . "

"The other Heroes were shocked to the core, and Lirriam swore she would get revenge. After that she began wearing *Incarnate* openly."

"What's *Incarnate?*"

"Haven't I told you?"

"No."

"It's an ancient stone. It was powerful once but it's been dead an awfully long time. Lirriam is trying to wake it and that really bothers Grandys, though I'm not sure why. But getting back to the wyverin—"

"My nightmares about it always involve Father's portrait," Rix said thoughtfully. "But it's different each time. And the wyverin is definitely rising."

"If you still had the portrait, it'd be interesting to see if it's changed. It was destroyed, wasn't it?"

"Lyf ordered it destroyed, but the Cythonian soldier who found it thought it was a masterpiece, and hid it. So Tobry said."

At the mention of Tobry's name a spasm crossed her face and she clenched her hands in her lap. Then she rose. "I'm so tired. I'll see you tomorrow."

"Wait a moment," said Rix. "I've got something to show you."

He went to the door and sent a servant to bring Rannilt and Tobry up. Rix sat down.

"What is it?" Tali said dully.

"Just something you might be interested in," Rix said vaguely.

She stared into the fire, hunched up in the chair. Shortly the door opened and closed, and he heard them come in.

"Tali?" said Rannilt in that small, high voice.

Tali sprang up and embraced her. "How did you get here? Where have you been? I was so worried when I met Glynnie and heard you were still lost. I was sure that you . . . you know."

"I've been off," said Rannilt. "Wanderin'. Healin'."

Tali smiled, but did not say anything. "You look good. Though too thin."

"I am good." Rannilt was beaming. She looked back around the corner, then gestured.

Tali frowned, evidently wondering what was going on. Tobry came around the corner and stopped, staring at her, and there was such desperate yearning in his eyes that it sent shivers up Rix's spine. He glanced from Tobry to Tali, and saw the blood drain from her face.

"T—T—Tali," Tobry whispered. "Tali." He reached out to her with both arms.

"No!" she gasped.

"Tali, it's *Tobry*," said Rannilt, her smile fading.

"I can't do this," Tali said in a cracked, breathless voice.

"But it's *Tobry*," said Rannilt, unable to comprehend what the matter was. "I've been healin' him with the thought of you, the love of you . . ."

"I've seen him go to his death, twice." Tali's voice rose, becoming shrill.

"Tali," said Rix, "calm down."

But, clearly, Tali could not calm down. She was shaking, gasping, on the edge of hysteria.

"I've ached for Tobry; I've wept for him," she wailed. "I've grieved for him *twice*, and I can't do it again. I can't look into those caitsthe eyes and try to find one tiny speck of the man I loved. *It just— hurts—too—much.*"

Tobry's arms dropped to his sides. Something died in his eyes. He let out a howl of anguish, then relapsed into gibbering madness.

"You're a mean, nasty woman." Rannilt ran at Tali and slapped her about the face five or six times, knocking her head from side to side, then shoved her so hard in the chest that she fell over backwards.

"I hate you, I hate you, *I hate you*!" Rannilt shrieked. "You've ruined everythin'."

Sobbing desperately, Rannilt dragged Tobry, now shambling and dribbling, from the room.

CHAPTER 63

Rix prowled the long outside wall of the fortress, checking for chinks in the defences. He did not need to—everything had been checked and rechecked days ago, but he needed to get away. The atmosphere in Garramide, formerly so good, was poisonous, and he did not see how he could fix it.

He thrust the point of his sword into the gap between two stones. It was as solid as everywhere else, fortunately. He eased it out and looked out of the plateau, trying to find a solution for the insoluble.

Glynnie was angry with him because he wanted to leave the fortress at such a dangerous time, to recover the portrait. Everyone was furious with Tali for her betrayal of Tobry and Rannilt. And down in the lowest level of Garramide, in the Black Hole where he had slept the last time he was here and had now returned to, Tobry howled like the tormented beast he was.

"Damn you, Tali!" Rix bellowed, hacking through the green turf again and again. "What's the matter with you?"

For most of the war she had been a tower of solidity and determination, seemingly able to overcome any obstacle, including inciting the Pale to that miraculous rebellion in Cython. She had escaped from Grandys and—he could never repay her for this—saved Glynnie from the noose and brought her safely home, along with Benn. Tali had done the job Rix had been unable to do; she had been his rock for so long that he could not come to terms with her sudden collapse. It was as if her adamantine shell had finally been breached to reveal that she was empty inside—as empty as the thin-walled pearl inside her.

She had locked herself in her room and rarely came out. Whenever Rix saw her she looked smaller than ever, thinner and frailer, and the food left outside her door was taken away untouched. He began to think she was dying of guilt, but he did not know how to bring her out of it.

Grandys was still camped at the base of the escarpment, rapidly rebuilding his army with new recruits and sending up deadly raiding parties every night. Rix's spies said that he had nearly three thousand men now, more than enough to overwhelm the walls, and surely he must attack any day. When it came, though Rix had strengthened the defences in every way he could, he did not see how he could keep the enemy out for as much as a day.

Putting his back to the wall, he looked down the potholed approach road, weighing the most probable routes of attack. The ground outside the walls was sodden by rain and would be difficult for the enemy to fight in—they would soon churn it to sticky, knee-deep mud. Grandys' army would probably come down the road, then fan out.

After Lyf's defeat by Grandys at Reffering, Holm had collected dozens of bombasts and grenadoes, plus wagon loads of other alchymical weapons, from the battlefield. He had tested them and found that they still worked—it appeared that their failure at Reffering had been solely due to the magery of that black pyramid.

Soon after arriving at Garramide, Rix had mined the ground outside the walls across the most likely attack front—the approach to the gates—by burying the bombasts there, then covering each one with green turf. When the attack came he planned to set them off, though it was a once-only defence which might or might not work. If Grandys even guessed they were there, presumably the Five Heroes could render them useless by creating another pyramid shield.

A frigid wind buffeted him in the face. He shivered, headed inside and up to the main guard post behind the gates. He was pleased to see Benn there, scooping mugs of steaming honeyed tea out of a large bucket and handing them to the waiting guards. Rix waited his turn, then took a mug for himself.

"How's Glynnie?" he asked. "I haven't seen her today."

"Still cranky about the portrait. Why do you need it so bad, Rix?"

"Well, the wyverin is Grandys' weakness—"

"Because of the legend?"

"No, because he's so afraid of it that it's changing the way he thinks and acts. If I had the portrait to look at, I might get an idea about how to beat him."

"Then go and get it," said Benn, who believed Rix capable of all things.

Rix smiled down at the lad. If only things were that simple. "Problem is, only Tobry knows where Salyk hid it. How can I ask him in . . . his current state?"

"You can't. But Rannilt could."

"Rannilt isn't very pleased with me at the moment."

"She'd be happy to go away with Tobry. She hates it here. I'll ask her if you like."

"Best if I ask her myself. I wouldn't want to seem more of a coward than I already am."

"You're the bravest man I know," said Benn.

"And yet I dread to raise the topic with Glynnie." Rix studied Benn thoughtfully, a faint smile playing on his lips. "Wait, I've got an idea. *You* could explain to Glynnie why I have to go to Caulderon. That way I wouldn't get into even more trouble."

"See you later," said Benn, and raced down the steps, swinging the empty bucket.

"Going to Caulderon is a stupid idea," said Glynnie.

"Are you forbidding me to go?"

"You're the lord of Garramide," she said stiffly. "I can't forbid you anything."

"As my dear friend you can."

"It's desperately dangerous, even if you use Lyf's Sacred Gate . . . no, *especially* if you use it."

"But dare I use it, based on the word of a child?"

"Rannilt is no ordinary child."

"It doesn't mean she can't get things wrong. What if the gate's a trap?"

"Surely you're not asking me to talk you into it?" Glynnie said wryly.

"Sorry—I don't think I've ever been more confused."

"You've been worrying about the damned portrait for a month. Having nightmares about the wyverin rising . . . doing sketches of it devastating the land."

"Yes, but—"

"Don't *yes but* me!" she snapped. "We've got to take it seriously. Hightspallers think the wyverin's appearance spells the end of the world. Errek, the very first Cythian king, put those stone Defenders, and great protective magery, in the entrance tunnel to keep intruders away—"

"Or to stop it from getting out."

"And now Tobry wants to give himself to it."

"But what does it all *mean*?" cried Rix. "That's the real problem."

"Everything circles around the wyverin—and if getting the portrait gives us an advantage over Grandys, we have to take the risk."

Rix took that as her permission to go. "Thank you," he said, and kissed her on the brow.

"I don't think you will thank me when it comes time to go," she said softly.

When Rix entered the Black Hole, Tobry was squeezed into a corner, holding his hands up before his face. Rannilt was talking softly to him but he kept putting his hands over his ears.

"Rannilt?" said Rix. "Can I talk to you for a minute?"

She turned away reluctantly. Rix had never seen a child looking so haggard. Tobry slumped to the floor and covered his head with his hands again. His nails, Rix noted grimly, looked more claw-like than ever. Rannilt's previous healing had been almost completely undone and he did not see how she could ever reverse it. Tobry seemed too far gone.

He cursed Tali, inwardly. Why couldn't she have restrained herself? She had been so strong for so long. Why did she have to crack and reject Tobry at the worst possible moment?

Rix sat on the foot of the bed, which creaked and sagged. It was the same bed under which Holm had hidden Tobry, deeply asleep from a double dose of sleep draught, on the night of the mutiny. The night Tali had made that disastrous attempt to heal him with her healing blood. Rix wondered if Tobry remembered anything of that night; if the present and the past had any resonance because of what he and Tali had experienced here.

Rannilt perched at the other end, her thin legs crossed, glaring at him. It was a look she reserved just for Rix, because when they'd first met it had taken her a long time to trust him. Or to look at it another way, he thought wryly, it had taken him a long time to prove himself. But their worlds had changed out of recognition since that time, and so had they.

"I need your help," said Rix.

"I can't do nothin'," she said desperately. "It's takin' every minute I've got and he's still gettin' worse, because of *her*." Rannilt spat the word out. "I shouldn't have brought him back. But Tobry—"

She reached out and grabbed Rix's hands without thinking. Rannilt looked down, startled, when she realised she was holding his dead hand, but did not let go.

"If you could only have seen the look in his eyes whenever I mentioned Tali's name," she said softly. "He loves her so, Rix. She was the only thing stoppin' him from givin'' himself to the wyverin . . . and now she's rejected him. I'm really afraid. What if he doesn't want to be saved?"

Look at the poor, miserable bastard, Rix thought. We should have put him down when we had the chance. But he and Tali had delayed and delayed, and the quake had given Tobry the chance to get away, and now he was in an even greater agony than he had been then. He was utterly, hopelessly ruined.

And yet . . . Rannilt had worked miracles with him before. He had to give her the chance to do it again, for both their sakes. If she was robbed of the chance, Rix wasn't sure she would get over it.

"If anyone can save Tobry," he said with all his heart, "you can."

"Do you mean that?" said Rannilt, her eyes glowing. "Do you *really* mean it?"

"Yes I do. You've done so much for him. When I saw you coming across the plateau with him the other day it was like a miracle."

"I can't heal him here," she muttered. "Not with *her* around."

"That's why I've come," said Rix. "I need to go through the Sacred Gate and I was wondering—"

"Yes!" she cried, throwing herself at him and hugging him around the neck. "Yes, yes, yes!"

She pulled away at once, flushing. Tobry looked up, startled, but covered his head with his hands again.

"I haven't asked you yet," said Rix.

"Can we go now? This minute?"

She jumped down and began to stuff clean clothes into a little pack she'd pilfered from somewhere. Not that she needed to; Rix would gladly have given her the best clothing and gear Garramide had to offer.

"I need your help, *and* Tobry's," said Rix.

"Tobry's?" she squeaked. She lowered her voice. "How can he help you?"

"Do you remember the portrait I painted of my father? For the Honouring?"

"I never saw it."

"Of course you didn't. You were held prisoner by the chancellor, and after that you were really ill. But you know about it?"

"Nasty Tali said it was horrible," Rannilt said spitefully, "so I'm sure it was beautiful."

"No, it *was* horrible. It showed my father, Lord Ricinus, killing a wyverin. But I always thought the wyverin was secretly laughing at Father, and preparing to rise up and eat him. And on the night of the Honouring Father was condemned—so the omen came true."

Rannilt's eyes never left his face but she did not speak.

"The portrait's hidden in Caulderon," he went on after a pause. "And I need to see it again in case it's changed, because Grandys is really afraid of the wyverin. But only Tobry knows where it is, and," he glanced at the cowering wreck in the corner, "I don't see how he can ever tell me."

"Get us out of here," said Rannilt, "and I'll find a way."

The door eased open and Glynnie stood there, dressed in travelling clothes and wearing a pack. She looked anxious but determined.

"There's a slight change to the plan," she said quietly.

"You're not coming with us," said Rix, jumping up.

"Not with *us*, no." Glynnie took a deep breath. "You're not going, Rix. You can't possibly leave Garramide with Grandys half a day's march away."

"It's a risk, but if we use Lyf's gate it's a quick trip—I can go to Caulderon, get the portrait and be back here in under a day . . . "

"Assuming everything goes well," said Glynnie sarcastically, "which it never does. Besides, how do you think your people will react when they hear you've deserted them on the eve of battle?"

"I'm not deserting them."

"That's how they'll see it. And you're the one who's always blathering on about morale."

Rix saw the trap and avoided it. "What else can I do?"

"Delegate! I'd have thought you'd have learned that lesson by now."

"It's my responsibility—" he began.

"To lead the defence of Garramide. No one else can do that. And what if you went after the portrait and couldn't get back? Or you were delayed by a week or two? Or were captured . . . or *killed*? Without you, Garramide will—*must*—fall within days."

He did not reply. He knew it was true.

"When Garramide falls, Grandys will put all of us to the sword. Me, Benn, Thom, Tali—everyone! It's that simple, Rix."

"You're right," he said wearily. "I'd be derelict in my duty if I left at a time like this. But who can I send?"

"You don't have to send anyone. I'm going, and *nothing* you can do or say is going to stop me."

"Why you?"

"Think of it as a way for me to atone for the guard I killed to save you from Libbens."

She met Rix's eyes and he saw utter, uncompromising determination there. And fear. She didn't want to go—she was terrified, but felt she had no choice. He slumped back on the bed. There was no point arguing.

"I'll live in terror every minute you're away."

"Then you'll know exactly how I would have felt had you gone," she said stiffly.

He groaned.

Glynnie softened. She kissed him on the lips and turned away. "We'll be back before you know it. Coming, Rannilt?"

Rannilt picked up her pack, put on her coat, took Tobry's hand and they followed Glynnie out of the room.

CHAPTER 64

"There's a great carved openin" here somewhere," said Rannilt. "The Sacred Gate, Lyf called it. But I can't find it."

She was by the paired stone matriarchs that stood guard over the passage down to the wyverin's lair. Tobry had scrunched himself into the narrow space between the left-hand stone Defender and the wall, and he was staring down the passage.

"Sacred Gate?" Glynnie said wearily. It sounded ominous; sacrilegious.

They had spent hours riding across the plateau through deep, sticky mud to reach the overgrown ruins of Turgur Thross, and another hour finding the way down via narrow tunnels to this point. She was cold and wet and afraid, and bitterly regretted her decision to go after the portrait. How, after barely escaping the noose, could she have been such a fool as to put her head back in?

Even worse—far worse—was the unknown peril only a short walk along the tunnel . . . so close that she could smell its peculiar chymical reek . . . could feel the heat emanating in waves from it . . . and the faint breeze that stirred her hair, as if the air was moving in and out with each breath the gigantic beast took.

Even the Sacred Gate was better than the wyverin. She touched the rock, half hoping Rannilt wouldn't be able to find it and they could go home again. Home to wait for Grandys—unless he was attacking Garramide right now.

If he was, there might not be anything to come home to.

No Rix. No Benn.

Her heart hurt.

"I couldn't feel nothin'," said Rannilt. "I only saw it a couple of times—a great gate of carved stone—and the first time it was closed. Solid rock was behind it for miles."

"What about the other time?" said Glynnie.

"I saw all the way to a ruined stone temple in a little park . . . just for a second, then it was gone. There's somethin' secret about the gate, Glynnie. Somethin' *hidden*. You better stand real close. You too, Tobry."

Tobry did not move. Did he understand what she had said? Glynnie was trusting her life to a little girl and a witless shifter, which made her almost as mad as he was.

"A ruined temple in a park?" said Glynnie. "That's all?"

"All I saw," said Rannilt.

"How do you know it was in Caulderon, then?"

"Wicked old Lyf told Errek he was going there."

"But it doesn't mean *this* gate leads there." Glynnie's voice rose. "He might have changed the gate—or, or *anything*."

"It doesn't change. It only goes to the ruined temple."

"How do you know?"

"I just do. Come close."

Glynnie needed to get back to Garramide. If it was under attack, if it was all going to end, her place was with Rix and Benn.

"Quick!" said Rannilt.

Glynnie, uneasily, moved close to her. Tobry let out a small howl.

"None of that," said Rannilt sternly. "Come here!"

He went to her like a chastised child, his head so bowed that he seemed to have no neck. He was in a bad way. Apathetic and almost unresponsive.

Rannilt moved back and forth for several minutes. Glynnie stood close but sensed nothing. Even if Rannilt did find the gate, where was the ruined temple? Glynnie did not know of one in Caulderon. What would the enemy do if they saw them coming out of a sacred Cythian gate? It didn't bear thinking about. And how were they supposed to get from the temple to the portrait, when only a mad shifter knew where it was—and he couldn't talk?

Rannilt closed her eyes and turned around three times, quickly.

After a pause she turned a fourth time, slowly. Then again, inching around . . .

"There!" she cried.

"Where?" All Glynnie could see was the layered brown rock of the tunnel walls.

Rannilt grabbed Tobry with one hand, Glynnie with the other and drove herself backwards, pulling them off balance against the wall—no, into the gate Glynnie could not see.

And the gate took them.

Her stomach felt as though it had been twisted into a helix, then spun like a rotor. Her breakfast rose up her throat, retreated as she was tipped upside-down and advanced again as she spun in a horizontal arc.

Bubbles of amber light burst inside her head; she clung desperately to Tobry's shirt; Rannilt was crushing her hand. A flare of light whited everything out before fading to black. Tobry and Rannilt were torn away and Glynnie fell three or four feet onto her hands and knees on a rough surface, in darkness.

Her stomach gurgled as it resumed its former position. She groped around her. She was on a floor that had once been covered in small glazed tiles, triangular in shape, though most of them had come off, exposing the rough mortar beneath. She heard heavy breathing, caught the pungent reek of a shifter and nausea surged through her.

"This way," said Rannilt, taking her by the hand.

"How do you know?" said Glynnie.

"It's lighter over there."

As Glynnie's eyes adjusted, the shadows of stone columns appeared around them, some tall, some mere stubs, others broken into segments where they had fallen. They emerged into the open on the crest of a round hill, a small park somewhere in the great city. The lights of Caulderon, surrounded by haloes from a thin lake mist, extended as far as she could see. She guessed that it was hours after midnight.

Rannilt's eyes were wide, the pupils enormous since coming through the gate, and her hair was sticking out in all directions. Tobry looked anxious and confused. Panic stabbed Glynnie in the chest.

"They'll be really jumpy after Grandys' attack, and the rebellion," she said in a rush. "People out after curfew are killed on sight. I should never have asked you to come. I'm just as bad as Tali, using people—"

"You think too much," said Rannilt.

"I murdered an enemy guard to save Rix—I stabbed him in the back! Now I'm using a little kid."

"I'd do the same to save my friends," Rannilt sniffed. "And I wouldn't moan about it afterwards."

Glynnie rubbed her belly, which still felt *displaced*; she thought she might heave at any moment.

"Where did Salyk hide the portrait?" Rannilt said to Tobry.

He stared at her, mutely.

"The portrait Rix painted of his father," she added, "where he was killin' the wyverin."

On the last word, Tobry reached out with both arms as if he longed to embrace the beast, and made a yearning sound. Shivers radiated out from the back of Glynnie's neck and along her arms. Something was terribly wrong with him.

"Lyf ordered Salyk to destroy the portrait, but she didn't," said Rannilt patiently. "She hid it, and you know where."

He reached out again, as if *wyverin* was the only word he had understood.

"You should've sorted this out before we left," said Glynnie. "If we've come all this way for nothing—"

Rannilt quelled her with a cold stare and turned back to Tobry. "Rix needs this portrait to beat evil old Axil Grandys. Where is it?"

He remained mute.

"This is hopeless," said Glynnie.

"Shut up!" snapped Rannilt. "Tobry, Salyk saved your life after the chancellor had you chucked off Rix's tower."

Tobry showed no reaction.

"I know you remember her," said Rannilt, a tremor creeping into her voice. "She looked after you while you got better ... but the enemy put her to death because she betrayed—"

His quivering moan rent the night silence. He crouched, hands covering his eyes as if trying to hide from what they had done to her. Dry sobs wracked his gaunt frame.

Rannilt put her arms around him. "Sorry, sorry."

Glynnie clutched her knife and stared around her, sure the guards would come to investigate the noise.

After several minutes Rannilt tried again. "Where did Salyk hide the portrait, Tobry?"

He sprang to his feet, knocking her over, and darted down the hill. Rannilt and Glynnie had to sprint to catch him. At the edge of the park he headed down the middle of the street, in plain sight of any guard within a hundred yards.

Rannilt tried to drag him onto the footpath where there were deep shadows. "You can't walk down the road," she hissed. "You'll be seen."

He resisted her and continued. Glynnie followed, feeling dreadfully conspicuous. If they were seen, the city guards would shoot them without warning.

After several hundred yards Tobry turned left along a broad road, empty at this time of night, and continued for another couple of minutes towards a large, square building built of grey stone. As they approached, Glynnie saw carved words over the entrance in the ornate Cythian script—Hall of Representation. She had not heard the name before. The doors were closed. A lantern glowed in a small guard booth on the left-hand side.

Tobry turned right and headed down a shadowed alley towards the rear of the hall.

"How are we going to get in?" said Glynnie, trotting behind him.

"Shh!" said Rannilt.

Though she gave the impression of having faith in Tobry, Rannilt's breathing was quick and agitated. Tobry pressed against the wall; in the darkness, Glynnie could not tell what he was doing. What was going on in his shifter-addled brain?

A door opened inwards with a faint grating noise. They followed him down a pitch-dark corridor and around several corners. He slid a door sideways and they entered a vast, high-ceilinged hall lit by foot-long cylinders of yellow glowstone mounted on brass wall brackets.

The main doors at the far end of the hall were painted dark green. The open centre of the hall contained about thirty huge statues and sculptures of men and women carved from cream stone, and arranged in small groups as if they were in conversation, or arguing in one case. There were also half a dozen huge sculptures of mythic beasts, each standing in isolation. The beasts were shaped from pieces of yellow or red timber, some as much as six feet across and three times as high, each cut from a single tree trunk.

The side and end walls were hung with a series of paintings, drawings and tapestries ranging in size from a handspan to many yards high and wide. They appeared to represent important scenes from Cythian history.

Tobry went to a large painting depicting a group of robed men and women in an open-air forum—actors or debaters. He pulled the painting away from the wall, looked behind and released it. He continued past several small engravings on copper plates, then a three-foot-square portrait of a nobleman, to a large tapestry and again checked the back.

"Did Salyk hide the portrait stuck to the back of a painting?" said Glynnie.

"I suppose she must have . . ." Rannilt checked behind a small charcoal sketch, then a head-and-shoulders drawing of a long-faced child with two front teeth missing.

"It won't be behind those."

"Why not?"

"The portrait was six or seven feet long . . . and nearly as tall as me. It must have been five feet high. We'd better be quick. If the guard comes inside to check—"

Glynnie ran from one large artwork to the next, lifting each away from the wall to check behind it. Rannilt crouched, rested a scrap of paper on her knee and laboriously wrote something on it.

The anxious minutes passed. Glynnie was halfway around the hall, Tobry approaching from the other direction, and she was beginning to think the portrait wasn't here. After all, Salyk had hidden it months ago and if the paintings were ever taken down it would have been discovered at once.

She looked up at the next painting, a serene landscape threatened by black storm clouds, with the ominous red sails of an approaching fleet in the background. It told the story of the First Fleet, bringing the Five Heroes who would soon destroy the eight-thousand-year-old kingdom of Cythe.

She eased the frame away from the wall. A shaft of light from a nearby glowstone slanted along the back of the painting—and touched the wyverin's vast, searing eye.

"Got it!" she said softly.

Rannilt came running. Tobry ambled away. The landscape painting, which was set in a broad frame of etched grey metal, was very heavy. Glynnie heaved it upwards with both hands to free it from its hooks, then began to lower it to the floor to cut the portrait free.

Clang, clang, clang. The sound was shockingly loud in the empty hall.

Within seconds a guard appeared from a concealed doorway ten yards away, a lantern in his left hand and a heavy, red-leather-covered nightstick in his right. He was a big, muscular fellow with a battle-scarred face, a milky left eye and an embittered cast to his mouth. A former soldier, Glynnie thought. He raised the lantern and its light shone full on her and Rannilt.

"Intruders!" he bawled.

He stared at Glynnie, his lips moving, as if trying to identify her. She dropped the painting and went for the knife on her hip, but the heavy frame landed hard on her left instep and the knife went skidding across the floor. Her four new throwing knives were in her little pack, out of easy reach.

"You're the filthy spy who got away from Murderers' Mound." The guard's jaw muscles hardened as he studied Rannilt. "And you're a stinking Pale."

He shone his lantern around the hall but it did not reveal Tobry. Glynnie prayed that he hadn't wandered away, thinking his job done.

"Intruders!" the guard bellowed. "Inside the hall!"

When there was no response he ran at Glynnie, swinging the nightstick, and struck her an agonising blow to the right shoulder that knocked her off-balance. He whaled out at her left knee, *crack*. She fell hard; it felt as though he had broken her kneecap.

She was trying to get up when he clouted Rannilt viciously over the forehead, knocking her off her feet. She lay where she had fallen, blood flooding down her face from a long cut below the hairline. The guard struck her again and turned back to Glynnie, his teeth bared. He was enjoying this.

She began to hop towards her knife, knowing he wanted to beat her unconscious, or kill her. She supposed he would get a medal for disposing of two intruders by himself.

He swung at her. Glynnie ducked under the nightstick and made a desperate, one-legged dive for the knife, trying to protect her injured knee as she landed, but it struck the hard floor and such a piercing pain shot through her knee that she screamed. The guard's nightstick swished as he raised it for a bone-breaking blow she could not avoid. She covered her head with her arms.

Whack, across the small of her back. *Whack, whack* into her ribcage as she tried to crawl away. The blows flattened her to the floor and she felt a rib crack.

With a roar so ferocious that it rippled the tapestries, Tobry hurtled out from behind a blocky statue of a mountain kobold, *shifting* to a caitsthe as he came. The guard squealed in terror and swung the nightstick at him but it was useless against the most deadly shifter of all. The caitsthe swatted the guard's arm aside, breaking it, then struck him a blow to the throat that almost took his head off. He fell, blood gushing from his neck, and lay there kicking one foot, choking on his own blood.

Glynnie crawled to her knife, then forced herself to her feet. The caitsthe had picked up Rannilt and was cradling her in its red-and-black-furred arms, looking down at her and crooning.

"The other guards will be here any second," said Glynnie.

The caitsthe made no response, and neither did Rannilt, who was slumped in his arms, her eyes closed. Her forehead and half her face were covered in blood. An awful lot of blood . . .

Glynnie was looking for the exit when she recalled the portrait. She turned the painting over and poked her knife under the canvas glued to the back, facing inwards. She paused—now why was that odd? She shrugged and continued. It was only glued around the edges; she pushed the knife all the way around, breaking the glue, and rolled the portrait. There wasn't time to look closely at it.

The caitsthe wiped the blood off Rannilt's forehead, then bolted with her towards the main doors. Glynnie sheathed her knife and hopped after them, praying that the caitsthe was going back to the gate. Praying that the shifter reversion wasn't permanent. Praying that it wouldn't decide to eat Rannilt—

It hit the green doors with a massive shoulder, bursting them open, and stormed outside. As she hobbled after it, using the tightly rolled canvas as a walking stick, she heard shouting, then hoarse cries. She reached the doors in time to see the caitsthe batter a quartet of lantern-waving guards aside, cradling Rannilt in one arm and flailing at them with the other. One guard fell, bleeding from chest and shoulder; his lantern rolled across the ground, leaving a burning trail of oil behind it, then going out. The other guards scattered.

In the darkness, she caught another enigmatic flash of the wyverin's eye. Glynnie lost sight of the caitsthe. She hoped that it would soon revert to Tobry; that the gate would still be open, and it would work in reverse. If it only went *to* the temple they were lost.

A noise behind her rendered all such fears irrelevant. The guards, emboldened by the caitsthe's disappearance, were after her.

"Tobry?" she yelled uselessly. "Rannilt?"

No response. Glynnie drew her knife and tried to go faster, employing an awkward hopping limp, but the few hundred yards up the hill to the ruined temple might as well have been miles; there was no way she was going to make it.

She would have to fight.

The leading guard was not far behind; she could hear his heavy breathing. She spun on her good leg, aimed and threw her knife in a single fluent movement. It struck him between the ribs on the left side, carving a deep gash there before falling out. It wasn't a serious injury but he looked down at the blood flooding from his side and evidently thought he'd been dealt a mortal wound. He moaned, fell to his knees and frantically tried to staunch the bleeding with both hands.

Glynnie fished another knife from her pack and held it up so the other two guards could see it. She backed away, propping herself up with the rolled portrait.

"I've got three more knives," she said loudly. "And I can hit an eyeball from thirty feet away."

The lie helped. They kept coming, though more slowly and warily. But then she heard a discordant clanging from the direction of the hall, as if a cracked bell was being thumped with a hammer. The alarm had been raised, and in a few minutes the hilltop would be swarming with guards.

She ran, alternately limping and hopping and trying vainly to ignore the agony in her knee, up to the park surrounding the temple. The caitsthe was at the Sacred Gate, thirty yards away, still carrying Rannilt.

"Wait!" Glynnie screamed.

Rannilt raised her head, looked up at the caitsthe and blanched visibly. "Glynnie?" she said shrilly. "Wait for Glynnie."

The caitsthe growled.

"Stop that!" said Rannilt.

It took several loping steps towards Glynnie, carrying Rannilt so lightly that she might have been weightless. The guards froze, then began to back away. The caitsthe reached Glynnie and stopped, staring down at her as if it did not know what it was doing there, then loped back to the gate.

Ignoring Rannilt's cry of "Stop!" and her flailing fists, it leapt in, transformed into Tobry as it passed through the gate, and vanished.

Glynnie staggered on, cursing him. It felt as though there was broken glass under her kneecap, cutting deeper into flesh and bone with every step. The guards whooped and ran after her, closing the distance rapidly now.

She hurled two of her knives, one after another. The first missed. The second struck a guard in the shoulder, a superficial wound. He plucked it out and flung it at her. She ducked, lurched on and reached the gate only yards ahead. He dived at her, swinging his sword while he was still in mid-air. She wove aside, forced her throbbing knee to one last effort and fell into the gate.

If either guard followed her, she would die. She thought they were going to come through but at the last second they baulked.

The gate twisted her stomach into a figure-eight and carried her away.

Only then did she realise what had been so odd about those glimpses of the wyverin's eye. The first time, the portrait had been facing inwards, and the second time it was rolled up, so how could she have seen the eye, or anything else?

Unless the portrait wanted to be found ...

Suddenly, taking it home to Garramide did not seem like such a good idea.

CHAPTER 65

Tali spent an agonising day and a sleepless night sick with guilt, trying to work out how to repair the damage she had done, and how to find the courage to act on it. Radl had been right, except for one small detail—Tali was worse than the worst things Radl had said about her. The way she had treated Tobry proved it.

She was creeping down to the Black Hole, trying to avoid being seen, when she ran into Rix and discovered that Rannilt and Tobry were gone.

"They went to Caulderon?" she cried. "Through some mysterious enemy gate?"

"Yes. With Glynnie."

She caught his arm with both hands. "What if they're caught and killed? What if the gate's a trap? Or it takes them to the wrong place? Or it's booby trapped? How could you let them go?"

Rix prised her hands free, irritably. "It had to be done," he snapped. "And with Grandys so close I can't leave the fortress." It was clear that he was worried sick about Glynnie; about the three of them. "Why did you have to treat Tobry so cruelly? Don't you have an ounce of empathy in your body?"

"I used it all up rescuing Glynnie for you," Tali snapped, and bolted back to her hide.

The minutes inched by; the hours did not seem to move at all. She endured most of a second sleepless night waiting for them to come back. Finally, unable to bear the agony any longer, she went up onto the wall, doubly wrapped in one of Rix's spare oilskin coats against the driving rain.

Tali spent the rest of the night pacing around the wall, staring into the darkness in the direction of the ruins at Turgur Thross. She avoided Rix and the other guards and vainly tried to divert herself from her endlessly cycling guilt. It did not work.

Few of the guards spoke to her, save Nuddell, and that suited her. She did not want to talk to anyone. She just wanted to wear the night away and, in the morning, see Tobry, Rannilt and Glynnie coming across the plateau.

They did not come in the morning, nor the middle of the day. It wasn't until late that afternoon that Glynnie's grey horse appeared. Its small rider, presumably Glynnie, was almost completely hidden by a huge oilskin-wrapped rectangle which Tali assumed to be the portrait.

A second horse followed, but its saddle was empty. Where were they? The ten minutes Tali waited, as the rider rode to the gates, were the longest she had ever experienced.

If Rannilt and Tobry were dead, she would bear the guilt all her days. She knew why Rannilt had gone—the whole of Garramide knew. The child couldn't wait to take Tobry away from that "mean, nasty woman".

"Where's Tobry?" Tali gasped as the rider, definitely Glynnie, rode through the gates. "Where's Rannilt? They're not—?" She could not utter the words.

"They're safe," Glynnie said wearily.

She passed the wrapped rectangle down to a guard. "Careful," she said. "Don't bang it on anything."

"Why did you leave them behind?" said Tali. "I don't understand why you'd do that."

"They're coming ... later on. Rannilt wanted some time alone with Tobry." Glynnie looked directly at Tali. "To repair the damage."

Tali flushed. "She's a ten-year-old girl. How could you leave her in charge?"

"She needs time to heal him."

"She can't heal! Lyf stole her gift."

"Tobry was doing pretty well until you came along," Glynnie said coldly.

Glynnie swung down, slipped and had to cling to the saddle for a moment. She straightened up, took the wrapped rectangle and trudged across the muddy yard, limping a little.

"You got the portrait," said Tali, trotting after her.

"Yes."

"From Caulderon?"

"Yes."

"That must have been dangerous." The moment she said it, it sounded stupid.

"The city's still under martial law and civilians can't move at night. Fortunately we didn't have to go far. Salyk hid the portrait almost in plain view, stuck to the back of a Cythonian painting."

"It's a wonder you got it away at all, lugging all that."

"It was rolled up, but the paint was cracking so I stretched it out."

"Lucky you had all the gear."

"That was Rix's idea; I took it with me and left it with the horses."

"Did ... did Rannilt say how long she would be?" said Tali hoarsely.

"No."

"How long do you think?"

"How would I know?" Glynnie snapped. "As long as it takes."

She carried the package up to Rix's chambers and into the salon, very quietly. Tali followed, though she knew she wasn't welcome. The fire was blazing and Rix was sitting with his back to it, working through a stack of ledgers. He did not notice Glynnie enter. She poked him in the back with a corner of the painting.

He turned irritably, then shot to his feet. Glynnie dropped the portrait and ran to him, and they wrapped their arms around each other.

"You're safe!" said Rix, crushing her against his chest. "Oh, you're safe."

Tali stood in the salon doorway, aching for the kind of passion they shared. Her stupidity had destroyed all possibility of it.

After what seemed like an hour, Glynnie noticed Tali standing there. She gave her a hard stare, pulled free then took off her heavy coat and hung it over the back of a chair. Rix picked up the portrait, unwrapped it and propped it on two chairs where it would catch the light from the window.

Tali had seen it a hundred times when Rix had been painting it, but it looked different now. Starker. Bleaker and less ambiguous.

"It's changed," she said.

"The wyverin is definitely alive now," said Glynnie. "Its eye is open."

"Its leg muscles are taut, as if it's about to stand up. And it's grown. It's *huge*."

Rix's eyes slipped to the pile of sketches on the table. He picked up his sketch of the wyverin waking, frowned, carried it across and held it out next to the portrait.

"The size and shape are almost the same," he said. "It's as if—"

He let the sketch fall and absently scratched the back of his dead hand with his left hand. Tali saw that the skin was darker there, and raised, as if he'd been scratching it with his fingernails for ages. Scoring it.

"It's as though my sketch changed the portrait," said Rix. "At least, changed the wyverin in the portrait."

"To Hightspallers," said Glynnie, "its appearance symbolises the end of the world."

"There's a terrible irony here," said Rix. "Mother chose the subject of the portrait and told me exactly what to paint. Maybe that's why I hated it."

"Why did she choose this particular subject?" said Glynnie.

"Father's slaying of the wyverin was meant to symbolise him slaying time and change, and the enemies of our house and our country. But I now know the sleeping wyverin is the secret symbol of Cython—it's their Sacred Beast."

"The sword has changed, too," Tali said quietly.

Rix glanced at it and she saw the shock on his face. "It's become Maloch!"

"You didn't paint your father with Maloch?" asked Glynnie.

"Definitely not," said Rix. "I never liked that sword; its enchantment always made me uneasy. I painted Father with his favourite sword and it looked nothing like Maloch. It wasn't enchanted, either . . . " He studied Lord Ricinus's face, and started. "But . . . he's changing too."

His father's face seemed to be dissolving before their eyes. The purple, venous drunkard's nose that had given Rix so much trouble was gone, replaced by a vast horn of a nose. He looked younger, stronger, more coarse-featured and more unpleasant. But he no longer had that triumphant air. He looked uneasy . . . almost afraid.

Abruptly, Rix turned the portrait to the wall. He was breathing heavily. "I can't tell you how much I hate it. I should break the damned thing up and throw it on the fire."

"But you're not going to," said Tali.

"It's still trying to tell us something. And . . . "

"And maybe it isn't finished changing," said Glynnie when Rix did not go on. "I'm worn out, Rix—I'm going to see Benn, and to the bathing room, then I'm having a long sleep."

"Wait," said Rix.

"What?" she said wearily.

"Thank you for going after the portrait . . . and thank you for coming back." He hugged her again.

She stood on tiptoes, rested her chin on his shoulder for a moment, and went out.

Rix rubbed his hands through his short hair, making it stand up. He looked around distractedly and noticed Tali still standing there. They stared at one another. She felt he was judging her and finding her wanting.

He went across to the fire, stood there for a moment, warming his hands, then picked up Glynnie's coat to put it away. He checked the pockets out of habit, frowned and pulled out a ragged scrap of paper. Something was written on it in an untidy, furious scrawl, as if the writer had been screaming. Tali leaned in close, trying to make out the words.

Tobry can't bear to see that mean, horrible woman ever again.
We're never comin' back.

Tali reeled backwards, tears flooding from her eyes.

That mean, horrible woman.

An enormous ball of guilt and pain and nausea was churning inside her, heaving, swelling, rising up irresistibly. She tried to fight it down, tried with everything she had, but the guilt kept rising and choking her.

Never comin' back.

She threw back her head and pressed her hands to her belly, but nothing could stop the nausea, or the agony, and as she screamed, the contents of her stomach burst out of her. She fell to her knees, heaving and heaving until there was nothing to bring up save bile streaked with blood.

But she could not rid herself of the guilt that easily. Tobry had loved her. He had clung to the memory of her love as a lifeline in his weeks of madness and torment, and at the moment he had most needed her she had rejected him.

Tali wiped the bloody bile off her mouth and tried to stand up.

"I'm going—" she croaked. "I'm going after them."

Before Rix could speak, Benn ran in. He skidded across the carpet, stood staring down at Tali, on her knees with a puddle of vomit in front of her, then turned to Rix.

"Grandys' army is coming across the plateau. Nuddell says it'll be here within the hour."

PART THREE

THE LOWER GATE

CHAPTER 66

Wil could not bear the loneliness any longer. Nor the guilt. He had to unburden himself and the only place he could do so was Cython. All his people were gone but he was going there anyway. He had injured the Pale; he had to make it up to them.

"It'll be different this time," he kept telling himself. "This time they'll care."

It took him the best part of a day to crab his way along the twisted, steaming passages of the Hellish Conduit and back into the familiar tunnels of the empty lower levels of Cython—the levels the Pale still did not know were there. One day, after he saved his people, they would return and build an even greater city here.

Up he went, through the ruined chymical level. Something bad was leaking; the fumes stung his ruined nose and tingled in his empty eye sockets. This level had been blocked off after the great battle during the Pale's rebellion, but Wil knew a way through.

As he went, he rehearsed his story. He had to tell the Pale about all those little slave girls put to death by the Matriarchs; he had to explain why it had happened, and pay for it.

He reached the main level of Cython and turned a corner. Wil could read his location by running his fingertips along the Cythonian wall carvings, which were ever different. He went fifty yards then stopped abruptly.

"Gone!" he wailed.

He stumbled on, whimpering. The magnificent, carved and painted stone diorama, which had depicted an unspoiled mountain meadow, had lifted his spirits every time he passed by, but it was gone. The filthy Pale had smashed it to pieces and chiselled it off, leaving only bare, crude stone.

"How dare they!"

Wil's scarred hands clasped and unclasped, involuntarily. To

Cythonians, their art was their life, and even the lowliest of them, like himself, could tell the difference between good art and bad. But even bad art, even the worst, was better than this desolation. Why would they smash such a beautiful diorama? What kind of monsters were these Pale who, for a thousand years, had been slaves in Cython? The coarse, uncultured brutes! They deserved to be slaves.

He turned a corner, sweeping his fingers up and down the wall in arcs. The vandalism continued. When he'd lived here he had known every carving in Cython and he could still tell where he was—within a few feet—by feel alone, because every carving was different and the images and patterns were never repeated. Now he could have been in any wasteland, anywhere.

"Who—who are you?" someone cried out. "What are you doing here?"

A youthful voice. A girl. Wil turned his blind eyes in her direction.

"I'm Wil," said Wil, remembering why he had come here. "Don't be afraid."

"What are you doing? You don't belong here."

He could hear the fear in her voice, and it hurt him. "Wil does belong! He used to live here. They used to call him Wil the Sump because he cleaned out the effluxor sumps. It's a filthy job but Wil did it gladly."

"Why are you so scarred and twisted?" she said, curious now.

"Wil delved too deep. He went too close to the Engine and it burned him. What's your name?"

"Susi," she said quietly.

"How old are you, Susi?"

"Nearly thirteen," she quavered.

"Too old," Wil said to himself. The girls he must apologise to had been much younger. "What colour is your hair?"

"Black."

"And your eyes?"

"Brown."

"And your skin? Is it pale, or olive?"

"Why are you asking all these questions?" The tremor was back in her voice.

"Don't be afraid," said Wil. "The Matriarchs did a great wrong many years ago, and Wil has to make it right. Wil has to apologise. Is your skin pale or olive?"

"Olive. But I've got to go now."

"No, wait," said Wil. "It'll only take a minute."

He rubbed his empty eyes. Susi's hair was right, as were her eyes and skin. Did it really matter that she was a bit too old? No, it didn't.

"Why do you have to apologise?" she said.

"It started a long time ago, when Wil still had his eyes. Matriarch Ady let him go into the Chamber of the Solaces to check on the Great Books, and Wil saw a new book—*The Consolation of Vengeance*. It was Lyf's most important book, and Wil was the first to see it, to read it."

"It doesn't sound like a very nice book," said Susi.

"It burned Wil's eyes out, but it also gave him a *shillilar*—that's a foreseeing—about *the one*."

"Who's *the one*?"

"A slave girl of the Pale. A little girl then, much younger than you. She had blond hair and blue eyes, and pale, pale skin."

"I don't understand why you're telling me this," said Susi.

She was fidgeting, getting bored. Stupid girl! How could she be bored by *this* story?

"Nearly finished," said Wil hastily. "*The one* was going to change the story, you see. She was going to rewrite the ending of *The Consolation of Vengeance*, so the Matriarchs ordered that she be found and killed."

"Killed?" Her breath made a hiss as she exhaled.

"But Wil couldn't let that innocent girl be killed. She was *the one*!"

He could hear Susi's teeth chattering. She was scared, but she wanted to know how the story ended. Just as Wil had saved Tali to find out how *she* would change the ending of the greatest story of all.

"But then ... but then ... " It was hard to confess what he had done; very hard.

"What did you do?" said Susi.

"Wil had to let them die ... the innocents," he whispered.

"*What—did—you—do?*"

"The Matriarchs made Wil watch."

"Watch what?"

"Wil had to watch while those thirty-nine black-haired, olive-skinned girls were put to death, one by one." His confession was raw with passion, quivering with self-hatred. "It wasn't Wil's fault."

"It *was* your fault, you stinking murderer," screamed Susi, her voice ripe with loathing. "One of those girls was my big sister, Asi. You could have saved her. *You killed her.*"

"What was Wil to do? If he'd said it was the blonde girl, the Matriarchs would have had her killed. They would have ruined the ending of the story."

She advanced on him, screeching. "You killed my sister!"

"Not Wil, not Wil," he wailed, stumbling backwards. "It was the Matriarchs."

Susi threw herself at him, screaming and slapping him about the face, and Wil could not bear the dreadful sound. It brought back the memories he had been trying to suppress for more than ten years. But the only way he could stop her screaming was to close his hands around her throat.

When Susi died, when history repeated itself, Wil knew he was cursed beyond redemption.

CHAPTER 67

"It's a perfect day for war," said Grandys.

The miserable weather that had plagued him for a week had cleared overnight. When he rose at dawn and mounted his warhorse the overcast skies had cleared and the breeze was a mild northerly. It was time to end the false siege—time for the real battle to begin.

Lirriam was already in the saddle, talking to the men, studying the battle arena and checking all was in readiness. In the other Heroes it would have been duty done; in her it always felt like a challenge.

"It's going to be a beautiful sunny day," he said, savouring the fresh mountain air.

He rode slowly by Fortress Garramide at a distance of three hundred yards. Close enough to taunt them; far enough away that only the luckiest of shots could hit.

"I'm sure Rixium thinks so," said Lirriam, her yellow mare matching his black stallion stride for stride, "since there's no rain or fog to hinder his archers. They'll shoot your men down in their hundreds before they get to the wall."

"I've got 2800 men and I'm happy to lose a thousand to wear him down. He can't take that number of casualties. He can't win."

"You're back to your bombastic worst, Grandys."

"Besides, attacking Garramide is just a diversion. I don't care if I take it or not."

"Rubbish! You're a spoiled little boy who *always* has to win."

He reined in and looked her in the eye. "How little you know me. I'm after the big prize, and it's so very close. Tali's inside, and so is the circlet."

"How are you going to get to them without taking Garramide?"

"You'll see."

"They could have found the circlet already," said Lirriam. "And cut out the pearl. They could be luring *you* into a trap."

The stallion reared; he curbed it savagely. "My treasures are protected by a great, ancient spell. If they'd found my hoard, Maloch would have alerted me."

"Everything fails in the end, Grandys—even great spells. Yours could have died long ago."

"Ah," he said, "but all the omens have turned my way. Including *that* one."

Grandys gestured towards the escarpment track. Two people had just reached the top and one was unmistakable, even at this distance: massive; golem-like.

"Syrten and Yulia are back," said Lirriam.

"The Five Heroes will stand together for the final onslaught. The final triumph."

"It's your final *outing*, Grandys, though I don't think it will end in triumph."

"I notice you haven't been wearing your precious *Incarnate* lately," he sneered. "Having trouble bringing it to life?"

She forced a smile. "You have no idea how patient I can be."

"I've often wondered if it was patience—or lack of nerve."

She did not reply and Grandys felt sure he had struck his target. He kicked his horse into a canter, heading directly across the sodden fields towards Yulia and Syrten. Lirriam wheeled and raced along the meandering road across the plateau.

"Be damned!" he said to himself.

He spurred his mount cruelly, driving it at reckless speed across the boggy land to get there first, and arrived a few seconds ahead, coated in mud to the top of his head. The stallion was lathered in sweat and so exhausted that it was trembling.

Lirriam reined in, smirking. "It's so easy to manipulate you. You just can't help yourself."

"You're the one who came second."

Grandys beckoned to Syrten and Yulia. Syrten raised an arm thicker than most men's thighs. When Yulia did not acknowledge the gesture, or even look up, Grandys felt a stab of unease.

"You brought back the *Immortal Text*?" said Lirriam.

Syrten nodded stiffly. "Custodian didn't want to give it up. Yulia insisted."

Yulia continued to stare at her hands, which were knotted around the reins. Her face was as blanched as the day she had been struck by Lyf's arrow.

"What's the matter with you?" Grandys said roughly.

"There's something wrong with it!" Yulia burst out.

"What?"

"I don't know."

"How can there be something wrong with the *Immortal Text*? It's been locked away for two thousand years."

"The moment I touched it, my magery told me that there was something false or deceitful in it."

"Then it can't be the genuine *Text*."

"It passed the Seven Tests. There's no question it's the one. And yet—"

Grandys extended a meaty hand. Yulia took a cylindrical brass case from her saddlebags, unscrewed the end and slid a smaller leather case from that. Opening it, she carefully drew out the contents, a coiled sheet, which she passed to Grandys.

"Careful. It's fragile," Yulia said anxiously.

He wiped his muddy hands, unrolled the sheet, held it out in his right hand and gripped the hilt of Maloch with his left. He scanned both sides of the sheet, his lips moving.

"I sense no wrongness here . . . " He frowned. "What's *that*?" He scanned it again. "No, it's eluded me."

"Yulia's magery is the subtlest," said Lirriam. "And the most suited to this purpose. If she says there's some wrongness in the *Immortal Text*, I believe her."

"Can it have been tampered with?"

Lirriam held out her hand. Grandys gave her the text. She passed her left hand over it, back and forth, up and down; she subvocalised a charm. After several minutes she said, "It's not been touched in this land. Any fault or failure or falsity in it—if such exists—has been in the *Text* since Envoy Urtiga carried it onto the flagship of the First Fleet."

She handed it back. Grandys gave it to Yulia, who replaced it in its cases.

"I'll need stronger magery to probe it fully," said Yulia.

Grandys handed her an ebony pearl, the smallest one. "I'll have this back when you're finished with it."

"I'll look in the morning, when my mind is fresh."

He nodded and wheeled his horse away.

"Still think the omens are good?" said Lirriam as they rode back, shoulder to shoulder.

He grimaced, drove his stallion to the lead and raced along the perimeter of the fortress wall, only two hundred yards away this time. He was within range now, though even for Rix's best archers it would be a difficult shot. He stopped, faced the wall and spread his arms wide, taunting his enemies. Yulia's doubts about the *Text* nagged at him and only risk taking could quiet the inner voices.

Arrows fell around him though none struck. Rix appeared on the wall. Grandys stood up in his stirrups, swept his hat off and bowed ironically. Rix plucked a longbow from the nearest archer, aimed and fired in one furiously controlled movement. The arrow plucked the hat out of Grandys' hand and drove it into the mud ten yards behind him. He flinched, instinctively, then cursed himself.

The guards on the wall let out a collective roar and banged their swords on their shields. Behind Grandys, Lirriam laughed.

"It was a bad shot," Grandys said sourly. "He was aiming for my head."

"But he gets the credit," said Lirriam. "Round One to Rixium."

Rix ran to the topmost tower and took up a speaking funnel.

"The *great man* Axil Grandys claims to have built Garramide for his daughter," he boomed, speaking to his own troops as well as Grandys', "but he's always kept secret that she was adopted. Grandys had no children, and do you know why?"

He paused for half a minute, making sure he had their attention.

"He's *impotent*," Rix bellowed. "Grandys is a failure as a man—that's why he always has to win. It's a desperate attempt to prove he's a *real* man."

The Herovian army stared at Rix in silence, then turned as one to Grandys. He let out a roar of laughter, though to his own ears it sounded forced.

"It's true that Mythilda was my adopted daughter," he yelled. "It is also true I have fathered no children. If that makes me less of a man, then I'm one among many. Neither will Rixium Ricinus ever father children—*because I'm going to kill him*."

As he rode back and forth before them, Grandys could see his men looking at their neighbours and wondering about him. That could not be allowed, though to take back the initiative he would have to put on a show no one would ever forget.

"I have nothing to hide," said Grandys.

He climbed onto his saddle, stood tall, then stripped off his clothes item by item and dropped them. Finally, balanced on one foot, then the other, he removed his boots and socks and let them fall into the mud. His huge feet and thick ankles were still red and inflamed, but he was used to putting that pain out of his mind. Proudly naked, his patchy opal armour glinting in the sun, he urged his horse forward, directing it by moving his weight, and rode back and forth before his army.

He raised his fists skywards. "This is the man I am," he roared. "What you see is what I am, without concealment, falsity or artifice. Am I enough for you?"

It was the kind of gesture only Grandys could have pulled off, and he grinned when he saw Rix scowling at him from the wall.

"Yes, Lord Grandys!" several of his soldiers said.

A flight of arrows came his way and he remembered, too late, that he'd dropped Maloch in its sheath, along with his trouser belt. It was now a hundred yards away—too far for its protection to keep arrows at bay. He ducked, but too slowly, and a low arrow embedded itself in his left shoulder. As wounds went it was more painful than most but he forced himself to show no pain, no fear, and rode on.

"That's a taste of what it'll be like when Maloch deserts you for its true master," said Rix.

Grandys stood up straight and tall again, raised his fists high once more and boomed over the top of Rix's voice. "Am I your man?"

"Yes!" they roared.

"Cut the bastard down!" shouted Rix.

Grandys calmly turned and rode down past the front lines again. Dozens of arrows were fired from the walls of Garramide, and some came close. He did not flinch. When he passed his sword, he reached down and it flew up into his hand.

"*I—am—your—man!*" Grandys roared. He thrust Maloch heavenwards and a jagged spear of red fire roared up from its tip.

"Yes, yes, yes!" they shouted, beating their swords on their shields.

"Does Rixium Deadhand have the courage to bare himself?" said Grandys, turning towards the gates of Garramide and throwing down the challenge. "Will Deadhand show us what *he's* made of?"

"No, no, no!" chanted his men.

"Whether he does, or whether he doesn't," said Grandys quietly, "I win."

Rix did not move. Grandys had not expected that he would.

"Rixium talks loudly," yelled Grandys, addressing his own troops and the people of Garramide, "but he doesn't have the spine to back his words with action—it's as dead as his right hand. Garramide *will* fall."

He saluted his army, rode back to his clothes and pulled his trousers on, knowing he had turned a small defeat into a morale-boosting win. The other Heroes clapped, even Lirriam, though she did so with ill grace.

"How much of that display was Maloch, and how much was you?" said Lirriam.

"I don't need Maloch to prove I'm a man—the way you need *Incarnate* to prove you're a woman."

"There was a time when you didn't need to make such extravagant gestures—*old man*."

"I make extravagant gestures because that's the kind of man I am."

Grandys' smile faded as he turned to Yulia and, for the first time, revealed how much pain he was in.

"Get the damned arrow out," he gasped. "It's grating on bone; pinching a nerve."

Yulia worked the arrowhead out, then pressed a bloody hand against his shoulder and cast a healing charm that slowed the blood flow to a trickle. She bandaged the wound.

"That the best you can do?" he said roughly.

"At the moment, yes. I'm worn to the marrow, Grandys."

"I need to use the arm."

"When?"

"Tomorrow morning, at the latest."

"Why then?"

Grandys lowered his voice. "Tomorrow we break into Garramide."

"How can you be sure you can?" said Lirriam.

"There's more than one way to crack a nut, and a fortress. I built this place, remember? I know all its secrets."

"You built it near two thousand years ago. There must have been hundreds of changes since then—buildings torn down or rebuilt, passages unpicked, resealed, blocked, collapsed—"

"Do you imagine I haven't checked already?" said Grandys.

"How?"

"What do you think I do on my nightly walks? There's a secret way in, known only to me." He turned back to Yulia. "I've got to be fit to fight. I'll soon be taking on Rixium hand to hand, and he's the toughest opponent I've faced since we came out of the Abysm."

"I'll work on your shoulder again tonight," said Yulia. "Rest the arm as much as possible. And don't rely on it too much tomorrow."

CHAPTER 68

"Grandys has broken through!'

The cry rang through the fortress, and was followed by a cacophony of trumpets and warning horns.

"Grandys is inside the walls. Reinforcements to North Tower at once!"

It was the moment Tali had been dreading. She scrambled up to the open-air observatory, the one place from which most of the fortress could be seen. As she passed the deeply chiselled wall where Rix had once painted his twisted Grandys mural, she noted that the outline was still visible. She stopped, staring at the stone. It had been a powerful, prophetic work. It still was, even in outline.

It reminded her of Rix's portrait. That thought led to the wyverin, to Tobry and Rannilt, and to Rannilt's note about never coming back because of that *horrible woman*. It was so painful that even the bloody battle going on outside was a welcome distraction. She went to the surrounding wall and looked down.

Grandys' army had attacked the gates at dawn, and shortly afterwards the whole eastern wall of the fortress. The attack had been going on for hours now and dead men littered the sodden ground outside the wall. The defences were holding, though only just. But everyone knew Grandys was toying with them—he had held a thousand men back in reserve.

Rix had no reserves. Every healthy man in Garramide was on the half-mile-long wall, either firing arrows, crossbow bolts or catapults, dropping rocks on the enemy outside, or using long hooks to tear away their scaling ladders. Boys and girls and old men were hauling up baskets of arrows and stones, dragging their comrades' bodies off the walls and walkways so the defenders would not trip over them, and washing away the blood. Even shrivelled little Gummy Ned, the oldest person in Garramide, was up there doing his bit, and he would not have had it otherwise.

Healers were sorting the injured into three groups: those who were liable to die, those who would probably live even if treatment was delayed, and those who, with immediate attention, might be saved. Teams of stretcher bearers carried the wounded down, either to the healery, the resting rooms or the screaming hell of the dying chamber.

Tali was the only person in all Garramide with nothing to do, and since the inhabitants of the fortress all avoided her, no one was likely to ask her to do anything. She felt like a ghost who did not belong anywhere, but could not escape.

No, she did have one job—to find the circlet. But where could she look where she had not already searched several times? She trudged around to the other side of the observatory, where she could see the surroundings of North Tower.

"How did Grandys get in?" she muttered. "If I knew that—"

"He came up through a secret tunnel," said a small voice behind her.

Tali whirled. It was Benn, now recovered from his fever, though he had not put on any weight. "What are you doing up here, Benn?"

"Keeping watch."

"All by yourself?"

"There were three guards, but they were called down to fight. And the other messenger boys haven't come back."

"Did you see where the enemy got in?"

"Yes, I gave the alarm," he said proudly. "The Five Heroes came up out of a secret shaft, down there." He scrambled up onto the wall and pointed.

"Careful," said Tali. "It's a hundred-foot drop. Where was the shaft, exactly?"

He leaned right out, hanging on with his left hand, his right arm waving wildly as he tried to point to the place. Tali leaned out as far as she dared but wasn't tall enough to see it.

Rix came pounding up the steps. "They're saying Grandys has broken in. Tell me it's not true."

"I saw him," said Benn. "See that black square, across the yard by North Tower?" He leaned out again, too far. Rix caught him and held him. "They must have had a tunnel, because they lifted the flagstone from underneath and—"

"How many?"

"The Five Heroes—"

"What, *all of them?*"

"Yes," said Benn. "Is that bad?"

"Hop down off the wall, lad, and don't ever lean out like that again."

"Sorry," said Benn.

"If *all* the Heroes have sneaked into Garramide, and he's left the fighting to his troops, that's worrying," said Rix. "It means he's close to what he really wants."

Benn's face fell. "But you'll beat them . . . won't you?"

"Who else was with them?" said Rix, flexing his fingers. He had the steel gauntlet on his left hand again.

"Ten big, tough soldiers. They burst into North Tower and closed the door. That's all I saw."

Rix looked across to the top of the tower, but it was empty. "I don't like this," he said to Tali. "Why break into North Tower, of all places?"

"It's got its own defences, hasn't it?" said Tali.

"Yes, it was the first tower built here, in ancient times. The walls are ten feet thick and solid stone all the way through—but even so, five people, or even fifty couldn't hold it against us for more than a few hours."

"He's after the circlet."

Rix punched his steel-encased fist into his cupped left hand, *smack*, and looked down. "My attack squad's on its way. I'm going to winkle the bastard out."

"Be careful."

Rix raced down the steps.

"Why are you frowning, Tali?" said Benn.

"I'm trying to work out what Grandys will do," said Tali. "The

Five Heroes are taking a huge risk, coming inside so early in the siege."

"Maybe they don't need to hold North Tower for long."

"Good thinking. There must be a secret passage running underground from North Tower, to where Grandys' hoard is hidden. But how to find it . . . " She turned, frowning. "Wait a minute. Did you hear Rannilt's story?"

"Bits of it," said Benn.

"Apparently she said that Lyf was going to hide close by . . . waiting for Grandys to go after his hoard, so Lyf could snatch the circlet from under his nose."

"But *we* don't know where Grandys is going."

"There's a way we might find Lyf," said Tali. "And if he leads us to the circlet, *we* might grab it first."

It was a mad, desperate plan, but then, they *were* desperate. If Grandys or Lyf got the circlet, they lost.

As Tali looked down at the small, scrawny boy, she saw Mia's dead face overlain on Benn's, then Lifka's, and then Radl saying that Tali would use anyone to get what she wanted. "No, forget I mentioned it."

"You're talking about the link Lyf put on me," said Benn. "Aren't you?"

She did not answer.

"When Lyf's near me, he leaves shadows in my mind," Benn said excitedly. "Shadows that'd let me track him."

"I couldn't take a child on such a dangerous mission."

"You let Rannilt go through the gate to Caulderon."

"I had no say in it—Rix asked her. Besides, she was with Glynnie."

"And a mad shifter."

"How dare you!" she cried. "He's Tobry. Always Tobry."

Tali could see the judgement in Benn's eyes, not that she needed to. Whenever she thought about what she had done to Tobry, she felt like throwing up. Radl had been right about her.

There came a tremendous crash, down in the yard.

"Again!" Rix yelled.

Some twenty men were moving backwards from the door of

North Tower, carrying a pole the size of a small tree trunk. Armoured squads stood to either side of the great door, their weapons drawn, ready to rush in.

"It's a battering ram," Benn said excitedly. "They're going to smash the door down."

"North Tower is strong. They won't break in easily."

The ram struck the door three times but it did not give. And somewhere below North Tower, Tali knew that Grandys was going after his hoard. The moment he recovered the circlet he would come for her master pearl. Pain spiked down through her skull.

"Please, Tali," said Benn. "I need to do this."

"Why?"

"Because Lyf used *me*! He followed the link he put on me to the Resistance, and killed dozens of them ..."

"And you feel guilty," said Tali. "But you're not responsible for their deaths; you did nothing wrong."

"I knew Lyf was after something," he said quietly. "Why else would he spend so much time on a kid like me? But I went back to the Resistance because I had nowhere else to go. I led Lyf to them, and he killed them, and I've got to make up for it."

"Only if Glynnie says you can."

"She'll never let me." Benn clutched Tali's hand. "And if you wait to ask, we'll be too late."

She bit her lip. Tali looked over her shoulder at the observatory steps, expecting to see a cold, knowing Radl there, or a furious Glynnie. Tali could imagine how *she* would react. She paced, stopped and turned to Benn. It couldn't hurt to ask, could it?

"Is Lyf making any shadows in your mind now?"

"Haven't looked," said Benn. "Since he killed the Resistance fighters I've tried to keep him blocked out. Those shadows, they're scary ... but if you need me to look, I will."

His eyes were alive. For his own peace of mind he needed to help.

"Just quickly," said Tali, massaging her conscience. "We need to know what Lyf is doing—if he's following Grandys ..."

Benn sat and rested his chin on his hands. "It takes a while." He closed his eyes, then let out a yelp.

Tali jumped. "What is it?"

"Lyf's really close. He's *here*!"

"What, in this tower?"

"No, but he's somewhere in Garramide—or under it."

"Where?" said Tali. "Can you tell?"

He stood up, keeping his eyes closed, then linked the fingers of both hands and held his arms out in front of him. He turned slowly, his arms rising and falling.

"There!" said Benn. His clenched hands were pointing down at a steep angle. "Underground."

Tali traced the direction he was pointing onto her mental map of Garramide. It was a particular skill she had, honed from a lifetime living underground.

"Beneath the stables," she said.

"He's moving; he must be following Grandys. Come on, before I lose him."

Tali wrestled with her conscience. If she took Benn with her and Glynnie found out, as she must, Glynnie would crucify her. Involving Benn in something so dangerous was grossly irresponsible. But then, the survival of Garramide was at stake. If Grandys won, he would put everyone to the sword, including Benn. Tali had to take the risk.

"All right, but you have to do *exactly* what I say."

"Yes, Tali."

"I mean it. No matter what my orders, you have to follow them instantly."

"Yes, Tali."

"All right, lead the way. And try not to look conspicuous."

"What's that mean?"

"We don't want anyone to notice what you're doing."

Benn headed down the steps. Tali stopped for a few seconds, knowing that she would pay dearly when Glynnie found out. If anything happened to Benn, Glynnie would kill her—and she would deserve it.

At the back of the stables he followed the steps down to a mouldy basement filled with straw and bins of oats. He squeezed between two bins, pulled aside a heap of mouldy straw and exposed a half-rotten door. Tali dragged it open. They went down more steps into a sub-basement granary that had not been used in centuries, judging by the festooned cobwebs and mounds of rat droppings.

At the far end, a rusty wheel opened a creaking hatch. It led into tunnels that were even older and more disused.

"He's down there," said Benn, pointing along the dark tunnel to his left.

"How far?" Tali whispered.

"I can't tell."

She dared not create light. She took Benn's hand and they crept along. Shortly she heard someone talking, a wispy old voice that she recognised as Errek's.

"I forged the circlet when I was at the height of my powers, and I've always had a communion with it. I can *almost* sense it."

"How can you *almost* sense something?" Lyf muttered. "Either you can or you can't."

"Shows how much *you* know," said Errek. "In the wrythen state—at least in mine—you *can* almost sense something."

"I wish I could. For a minute there, I thought I heard the *call* of the master pearl."

"Hardly surprising, since Tali's in Garramide."

"And now I'm sensing the link I made to that errand boy—the maidservant Glynnie's little brother."

"I thought you broke it after you'd finished using him?"

"I did."

"He's in Garramide too," said Errek. "Focus on Grandys. What's he doing?"

"I can't detect him—only the hateful emanations from Maloch."

"Where Maloch goes, there goes he. Is the sword still in North Tower?"

"No, it's moving down! Maloch is moving down."

"Is Grandys alone?"

"I can't tell."

"Where is he now?"

"In the lowest basement of North Tower. He's opening a secret door, I'd say—Maloch just flared bright for a second. Now he's moving away."

"Can you track him?"

"I think I can get to him from here."

The voices faded. Lyf and Errek were moving away.

"This is it," Tali whispered into Benn's ear. "It's the most dangerous thing you've ever done, so keep well behind me. And remember your promise."

"I remember," said Benn. His hand was trembling.

Tali gathered her strength. If she was caught or cornered, she had to be ready to use her gift, whatever it cost her.

And if she failed, neither she nor Benn would survive.

CHAPTER 69

The pain in Lyf's severed shinbones spiked, a pain forever linking him to the enchanted sword that had done the damage. It was only slightly mollified by the perpetual pain Lyf had inflicted on Grandys in the pit in his temple.

"He's moving!" said Lyf. "It's on."

He kept still. He was breathing noisily and his eyes were unfocused.

"Lyf?" said Errek.

Lyf let out his breath, took a couple of steps, then stopped. "I'm afraid of that sword, Errek. Even after two thousand years the pain hasn't gone away. What kind of a blade can do that?"

"It's not the blade, it's the enchantment on it."

"But who created the enchantment, and to what purpose? Who cast it on the blade?"

"Maloch was the way it is when Axil Grandys stepped ashore from the First Fleet," said Errek.

"Moley Gryle said it was made in Thanneron for Envoy Urtiga—to protect her and further her quest . . . "

"From what I know about Urtiga, she was honest, decent and noble."

"And yet she carried this foul blade."

"What if it wasn't foul then?" said Errek.

"I don't follow you."

"If Urtiga hadn't used Maloch to spill blood, the character of the enchantment may still have been plastic—some Thanneronian magery is like that."

"How do you mean, plastic?"

"Unformed. Only taking shape when the blade was first used."

"Um?" said Lyf.

"If Grandys was the first person to use Maloch, the character of the enchantment may have been fixed by the way he first used the sword—for some foul purpose, we can be sure."

"How does this help me?"

"If it's true, there'll be a conflict in the blade—between the noble purpose it was created for and the black way it's always been used. You may be able to use that conflict to undermine Grandys' faith in it."

"You grow more like Moley Gryle every day," sniffed Lyf.

"I'll take that as a compliment," said Errek.

Lyf moved on, following Maloch's trail by the pain it caused him. Reliving the moment when Grandys had hurled him to the floor of his temple that long-ago night and—it was still shocking, still incomprehensible—hacking his feet off with the cursed sword. The world and the future changing in a bloody instant.

His heart was fluttering one minute, thumping painfully the next, but for king-magery he would endure any amount of pain.

"You're crashing about like a drunken burglar," said Errek several minutes later. "Calm down or you'll give yourself away."

Lyf slipped on his crutches and nearly fell.

"You should take on a less physical form," said Errek.

Lyf squirmed. "Every minute of the centuries I spent in wry-then form, I ached to have a body again. And never thought I would."

"Ah, but to hold the circlet in your hand," said Errek, "you'd endure almost anything."

"I'm not sure I have the power to go back."

"Or, perhaps, the courage."

Errek reached out, touched Lyf on the chin and a little pink

flower formed there. Lyf felt a blow to the jaw, an extraordinary contraction, followed by a *vanishing*. His body crumpled and he barely
had the strength to squeeze himself and his crutches into a dark
recess before the wrythen separated completely from the man.

"What if Grandys finds my body?" said Lyf the wrythen.

"That would be awkward," Errek said with a wry laugh.

"Should I cast a concealment on it?"

"Maloch would detect it instantly."

They followed the trail along dusty tunnels, down a ramp and
through a series of concealed doors that had recently been opened,
leaving streaks and swirls in the dust. A single set of huge, broad
footmarks ran down the centre of the passage. Only one man had
come this way in centuries.

"Grandys is alone. Good!"

"He doesn't want to share his triumph," said Errek. "And he
doesn't trust the other Heroes."

"Would you?"

Lyf grunted. "Yulia, perhaps."

"She may be an unwilling member of the Five, but she's
collaborated in most of the foul things they've done. How's the pain
now?"

"If I still had a body, it'd be getting worse." Lyf floated a few
inches into the air. "It's good to be weightless again."

Errek grinned. Lyf managed a rueful smile. Something rattled,
not far away, and his smile faded.

"What *is* that sound?" said Errek.

"Maloch, rattling in its scabbard. I think it's sensed me."

The two wrythen eased backwards into the wall. Ah, the safety
of stone. Grandys could not see Lyf here, or touch him in any way.
He extended his spectral eyes, and waited.

Grandys turned the corner, limping badly, and edged forward,
Maloch in hand. The blade was surrounded by the faintest blue
glow. He swung it from side to side as if searching for something
and Lyf, momentarily forgetting that he was a wrythen, tensed.

The glow brightened fractionally. Lyf retreated back into the wall
and lost sight of Grandys, though, this close to Maloch, the ache in
his phantom shins was a constant throb.

Shortly it died away as Grandys returned the way he had come. The two wrythen went after him, keeping further back. After several minutes, Grandys stopped midway along a solid stone wall.

He stroked the tip of Maloch across the stone, down, up and across, screeching a little on the hard surface, and a door appeared there. Grandys pressed his palms against it, feeling the stone . . . or working some mechanism inside it. The door quivered but did not open.

What's the matter? said Lyf, mind to mind.

It's hard enough to open a door locked for a hundred years, much less two thousand, said Errek. *The hinge oil dries up or, thickened with dust, sets hard as stone. Metal corrodes and fails. Everything fails in the end . . .*

So you keep saying, Lyf said acidly. *Is this the door to his hoard?*

I don't know.

I think it is. I'm sensing the circlet strongly now. It's close. Should I show myself?

To what purpose? said Errek.

To rattle him.

If it will help. Not if it's just for petty revenge.

Surely I'm entitled to a little revenge. Yes, I'm going to do it.

Lyf eased out of the wall fifteen feet behind Grandys, who was performing the same mechanical operation over and over, then heaving. The door did not budge. He cursed.

Maloch gave a tiny rattle. Grandys stilled it with a hand. It rattled again, more loudly, and Lyf saw the thick, boar-like bristles rise on the back of Grandys' armoured neck. He stopped, head tilted to the left, and slowly turned.

Though Lyf was a bodiless spectre, he felt his heartbeat rise, his confidence falter.

Steady, said Errek. *He can't hurt a wrythen.*

Rix hurt me when he carried that sword. And Grandys is its true master. He can do me a lot of damage.

Grandys' eyes widened as he saw Lyf's wrythen. He was shocked, and perhaps a little afraid. Lyf allowed himself the pleasure of gloating, just for a second.

"How are your feet, Grandys? Still excruciating?"

"They're still attached to my legs! Unlike yours!"

"Ah, but I can pass through the wall quicker than you can open that door," said Lyf.

Grandys sprang ten feet from a standing position, whipping Maloch out. Lyf had been expecting the attack and slid sideways into the wall. He got halfway, but stuck as if he was partly solid. What was the matter? Was he turning back to a man? He panicked as the sword whistled towards him.

Errek caught Lyf's arm and jerked him inside. The blade screeched across the stone, then the pain in his shins spiked as Grandys ran back to the stone door and furiously tried to open it.

You're a fool, said Errek.

I know. But it felt so good.

Lyf edged around in the wall, which was solid basalt and difficult even for a wrythen to move through. Or was Grandys' hoard protected by additional magery? Lyf's head emerged and he was in a cube-shaped room walled in polished black basalt, twenty feet on a side—he was inside Grandys' long-lost treasure store.

At last! At last!

A wrythen did not need to breathe, yet in his joy Lyf experienced the symptoms of being unable to draw breath: the constricted windpipe, the heaving lungs, the desperate feeling that he was suffocating.

Errek thumped him in the chest. *How the hell did king-magery come to select* you *as king?*

Lyf scowled at him, created light and scanned the hoard. The walls were lined with shelves and compartments all the way to the ceiling, and they were stacked with items of fabulous value: crowns and gemstones and bars of precious metal, jewelled cups and enamelled weapons of every description, necklaces, torcs, bracelets and diadems too many to count. But there were also more mundane items, perhaps kept for personal or sentimental reasons—a single child's glove, a rudely carved bat, a battered brooch in brass and worn enamel, a scratched knife.

None of them were the least bit interesting to him. But it was here somewhere.

"I can sense it," said Lyf aloud, turning around and around.

"There!" Errek was pointing to a small silvery object at the back of a low shelf, halfway up the far corner.

Lyf could feel his strength growing, and his wrythen form filling out, even before he lifted the circlet from the shelf. And when he touched it, and when he held it in both spectral hands, it was like coming home to Cythe as the newly crowned king.

He wiped phantom tears out of his arid eyes. The circlet was a simple headband made from woven wires of platina. It had been made by Errek himself in the time of his reign, but platina was a very hard metal and it showed no sign of wear.

Lyf tapped it on the wall to shake off the worst of the dust, put it on, and it fitted snugly across his forehead. Power surged in him. Nothing like king-magery, of course, but nonetheless a strength he had not felt since his death. It reminded him of the last time he had worn it—for a healing he'd done the day before the red sails of the First Fleet loomed over the horizon.

A terrible thought struck him. "The circlet is solid metal, Errek. How do I get it out through solid stone?"

"When you wear the circlet, it takes on your form," said Errek. "When you take it off, it reverts to its own form."

"How does it do that?" said Lyf.

"I made it that way."

"Why?"

"I thought it might come in handy," Errek said airily.

"Why do I keep getting the feeling that you're not telling me everything you know?"

"Your head isn't big enough to hold everything I know."

Crash! Crash! Grandys was attacking the door with Maloch. He had given up trying to release the time-frozen mechanism and was trying to cut his way in.

"Can Maloch's enchantment cut through three feet of solid basalt?" said Lyf.

"Not easily, nor without great cost in magery and pain. But yes, I think it probably can. Come on."

"I have to see his face," said Lyf.

"One day your obsession with vengeance will be your downfall."

"It's not that, Errek. At least, not wholly. It's just that—he's beaten me far more often than I've beaten him . . . and, now that the victory is mine, I have to see what it does to him. For my own confidence."

"You froze back there. That's why you couldn't get through the wall."

"All the more reason to do this," said Lyf.

"All right, but I'll take the circlet. We haven't come this far to lose it for some petty indulgence."

Lyf handed it to him, reluctantly. Errek slipped it onto his brow and let out a deliberately provocative sigh. He looked ten years younger. Lyf scowled.

Chips and chunks of basalt flew out of the wall as Grandys hacked his way in. The tip of Maloch broke through, glowing a livid, luminous purple. It was withdrawn, and Lyf heard Grandys gasping and grunting, then with a furious thrust he forced it through the stone for three feet. He was holding the sword two-handed, as if unsure of it. He drew back, groaned, thrust again and again, and shoved the rubble out. His head appeared.

Grandys' eyes were staring and sweat poured off him. Though Lyf had no sense of smell when in the wrythen form, he could taste the acrid stench of Grandys' fear on the back of his tongue.

Grandys turned and saw Lyf, and Errek behind him, wearing the circlet. A curious expression crossed Grandys' bloated face, a mixture of rage and terror. Lyf laughed.

"It's fighting you," said Lyf. "That's why you can't cut through."

"What are you talking about?" said Grandys.

"There's a conflict in the blade—between the noble purpose it was created for, and the foul way you've always used it. That's why it's holding back. It's saving itself for its true, *noble* master."

Grandys hacked and battered his way through the hole, enlarging it so he could force his own way through.

"Enough!" said Errek.

He dragged Lyf backwards into the wall. Grandys burst out, hopped up and down as though his feet were tormenting him, then attacked the wall Lyf had slipped into with unmitigated savagery. But he had spent all Maloch had—or all it was prepared to give him. It clanged off the rock and the sword's glimmer went out.

"He's drained its enchantment," said Errek. "Temporarily at least."

Grandys cast Maloch to the floor and let out a howl of frustration. Blood began to dribble out through the lace holes of his boots.

"He's lost," said Lyf, snatching back the circlet.

"Not yet. He'll go after Tali," said Errek, "and the master pearl that can give him victory. And since he knows we can travel up through stone, he won't waste any time."

When they checked again, Grandys was gone.

"We can't leave my empty body lying in that recess," said Lyf, tapping more dust off the circlet. "A wrythen can't raise king-magery. Only a real human can do that."

He put the circlet on, turned around and froze, looking back the way he had come.

"I can *see* the master pearl," he whispered.

"What's it doing down here?"

"And the link to that boy, Benn. I'll be damned!"

"What?"

"When I broke my link to the boy, months ago, it didn't completely break. He's used it to track me—for Tali."

"What sort of a woman would use a child so recklessly?" said Errek.

"A desperate one. She must have followed us, hoping to get the circlet first."

"Where is she now?"

"Not twenty yards to our left."

"Had Grandys gone that way, instead of back the way he came, he would have run into her."

"And this story would have had a very different ending."

"It hasn't ended yet," Errek cautioned.

"But it's going to." With the circlet on his head and the power flowing in his ethereal veins, Lyf knew he was going to take Tali. "Go through the stone around to the right and block their escape. I'll come at her from this direction."

For once, it went as planned. Errek emerged behind Benn and said softly, "Stop right there."

Benn yelled, "Tali, look out!"

Before she could move, Lyf emerged from the wall beside her.

"Run, Benn!" Tali screamed.

He did not move.

"You promised, Benn. Get going!"

Lyf pressed a finger to the side of Tali's head and said, "Sleep!"

"Benn, find Rix—"

Tali slumped to the floor. Benn dived through Errek, let out a shuddery yelp and fled.

CHAPTER 70

Glynnie was exhausted but there was no possibility of the briefest of naps. Not with the enemy attacking the walls, the Five Heroes barricaded in North Tower and Rix risking his life to break in. He always led from the front and sooner or later his luck was going to run out.

Probably today. Glynnie was beginning to think that Garramide's luck was about to run out, for the first time since it had been built almost two thousand years ago.

She went looking for Benn but could not find him. Glynnie plodded down to the healery, where she found all the patients well attended to—for the moment there was nothing for her to do. Her muscles were as tight as clock springs and, needing something to occupy her hands, she headed up to tidy Rix's rooms, but one of the maids had already been through it and all was in order.

She sat by the ashes in the fireplace, trying to calm herself. Her eye settled on the portrait, which was propped against the side of a chair. Why was Rix so obsessed with it? She went to her knees, staring at the wyverin. It was so big, so *alien*.

Rannilt had said it ate rock and ore, breathed sulphur, peed quicksilver and crapped out slaggy chunks of spent rock. How could such a creature exist? Was it another kind of shifter?

Lyf had made the first shifters with the art of *germine*—a vile corruption of his healing magery—as a terror weapon against the people of Hightspall. But the wyverin was far older than Lyf. Errek

First-King had built the stone Defenders in that entrance tunnel, and he had died ten thousand years ago.

Therefore the wyverin must have been here before that. So where had it come from?

Her eye was drawn to the man in the portrait, Lord Ricinus, who had been a disgusting drunkard. As a maidservant in Palace Ricinus, Glynnie had encountered him thousands of times; she had known his face better than she did her own. Rix had been praised for his rendering of Lord Ricinus in the completed portrait; even the chancellor had said it was a masterpiece. So why did Lord Ricinus's face now look so wrong?

Everything about him was wrong. The man was bigger, fitter, stronger, and his aggressive posture oozed a determination that Lord Ricinus, even in his finest moments, had never had. A determination that Rix, obsessed with painting truth, would never have portrayed in the portrait.

The face was different, too—it was much fleshier; almost bloated. The eyes were smaller, the nose a great horn. Glynnie trembled; it could almost be Grandys. The image was closer to him than to Lord Ricinus, *and it had changed recently*. When she'd first glimpsed the portrait in the Hall of Representation it had definitely looked like Lord Ricinus.

The germ of an idea came to her, but before it fully crystallised, Benn burst in.

"Sis, Sis! Quick!"

"Where have you been?" she said sharply. "I've been looking for you for hours."

He went bright red but did not answer. "Where's Rix?"

"Outside North Tower, but you can't—"

Benn turned to run out. She caught him by the arm. "He's attacking the tower. Don't go anywhere near the fighting. Why do you want him?"

His mouth opened and closed. He looked as though he was going to explode, then it burst out of him. "Lyf's got Tali."

She rose so suddenly that she felt faint; she had to cling to the chair until her head steadied. "Where?"

"Taken her to the old ballroom," he mumbled.

"How do you know?"

He did not answer.

"Benn?" she said sharply.

"Followed them . . . after they caught her," he muttered.

She pressed a hand to her thumping heart. "Lyf's here? You—you *followed*—Lyf?"

"Not closely. Just with that old link he tried to break. Tali needed—" He broke off and looked away, flushing.

Glynnie's fists knotted and a red rage washed over her. She opened her mouth but no words came out. She tried to calm herself, then caught Benn by the shoulders, gripping him so tightly that her fingernails dug in.

"Please tell me Tali didn't put you up to following Lyf?"

"It's not her fault," he gabbled. "It was my idea. She knew Lyf would follow Grandys and she needed to track Lyf, to get the circlet first. I offered to help . . ."

Glynnie clutched at her heart. "*And she let you?*"

"Not at first. But . . . you don't understand. I betrayed the Resistance, Glynnie. I had to make up for it."

She shook him, slapped him and shook him again.

"Firstly," she said in icy rage, "you didn't betray the Resistance. Lyf used you; *it's not your fault*." She slapped him again. "Secondly, you've got nothing to make up for." Benn squirmed and tried to escape but she held him tightly and would not let him go. "Thirdly, when I find Tali, if Lyf hasn't already killed her, *I will!*"

"She saved your life," gasped Benn.

"And by using a little boy," Glynnie said savagely, "by taking a little boy into deadly danger, she's cancelled the debt."

"I'm not a little boy—I spent months looking after myself."

"You're brave, determined and clever. And only ten."

"Sis, Lyf's got her. He's going to cut the master pearl out, I bet."

"Good! I hope it hurts."

"You don't mean that!" he cried.

"I suppose not," she said wearily. "But I don't know what to do about it. Rix is attacking North Tower and trying to defend the walls of Garramide at the same time. He can't do anything else."

"Then you've got to do something."

But what? Every man who could stand up was on the wall, trying to hold the enemy out, and every able-bodied woman and child was working night and day to support them. Who could help her?

"The kitchen women!" she said. "They're experts in knife work."

She ran for the door. Benn followed. She turned on him.

"Not on your life!" Glynnie said ferociously. "Go and help in the healery."

He started to protest, took one look at her face and trotted off.

"I'll be checking on you," she yelled after him. "If you put a fingernail outside the healery door without my permission I'll give you such a walloping that you won't be able to sit down for a year."

There were at least twenty women in the castle kitchens, all working furiously. With Rix's army added to the normal complement of the fortress they had twelve hundred people to feed, three times a day.

Glynnie burst in. "Lyf's got Tali in the old ballroom and we've got to get her out. Bring your biggest, sharpest knives."

She held her breath. After the way Tali had treated Rannilt and Tobry, she was cordially disliked. Would they risk their lives to save her?

After a long pause, Catlin, the chief cook, pointed to ten women, one after another. "Arm yourselves. Let's get the bastard."

They picked up knives, meat skewers, and a cleaver or two, and streamed after Glynnie.

As she ran for the old ballroom, Glynnie could not help wondering whether Catlin had been referring to Lyf as "the bastard", or Tali.

CHAPTER 71

Rix was fighting two battles at once and losing both of them. "At all costs we've got to hold the wall," he said to Nuddell, who had come running across to the base of North Tower with the latest grim report. "If the enemy come over it in numbers they'll take Garramide within the hour."

Nuddell studied the battered door of North Tower, which had resisted all attempts to break it. "It'll take more than a ram to get through that."

"Grandys has been in there for over an hour," said Rix. "If he gets the circlet, and takes Tali, not just the battle is lost—the war is!"

"We need you on the wall, Deadhand—at least for a few minutes. It'll give the men confidence. They don't like being led by a mere sergeant."

"I've got confidence in you."

"It ain't enough, if you'll pardon me saying so."

"Radl is up there too."

"She's a fearless fighter, but she ain't one of us."

Rix sighed, but took his point. He instructed the battering-ram team to keep trying, told the men who were to storm the door to stand by, then ran with Nuddell back to the wall. When he reached the top of the main guard post he saw that the situation was dire. The Herovians had thrown two thousand troops into the latest attack, keeping only a few hundred in reserve. The remainder of the enemy littered the boggy ground before the walls, either dead or dying.

"They're running in everywhere with scaling ladders," said Nuddell. "Raising them quicker than we can push them away. If they get a couple of squads up on the wall and clear out a section of our guards, they'll soon put up a hundred ladders."

He paused, spat over the side, then added, "And that'll be it."

Half a dozen arrows sighed through the spot where his head had been moments before. "Whoops," said Nuddell.

"You're right," said Rix. "It's time to use our emergency weapon. Get the crystal."

Nuddell grimaced, went into the guard's hut and came out carrying an object swathed in a blue velvet cloth, and a large hammer. He put the object down halfway between the inner and outer walls, took away the cloth and stepped back, wringing it in his hands.

"Can't say as I like such uncanny things," he said, wiping his leathery neck with the cloth.

"Me either," said Rix.

A fist-sized white crystal was revealed. It was round like a ball, with many facets reflecting the light dazzlingly, and gave off a faint acrid smell. Rix's belly muscles clenched.

"How does it work?" said Nuddell.

"I wouldn't have a clue. Holm came up with the idea after he picked up all those enemy bombasts at Reffering, weeks ago. He worked out a way to set them off from a distance."

"Pity he's not here now."

There had been no news of Holm since the crystal-borne warning Rix had received at Manor Assidy. He prayed that Holm was safe in Grandys' camp. No, he prayed he had escaped and was a hundred miles away.

"You can set the mines off if you like, Sergeant."

"You wear the commander's hat, Deadhand." Nuddell managed a small smile; it was a reversal of something Rix had once said to him.

Rix used a polished steel mirror on a pole to check over the wall, and to the left and right. Further down, at Basalt Crag, the enemy had a dozen ladders up, though he did not think they would prevail. It had once been the weakest point on the wall, though since then he had greatly reinforced it against this kind of attack.

The assault on the gate was a different matter. Eight hundred men were attacking it and they were bringing up dozens of scaling ladders. A squad of archers were a hundred yards back, directing such devastating arrow fire at the guard posts and wall walkways that the life of any exposed guard was measured in seconds. It had to be now.

Rix took up the heavy hammer. "Stand well back, Sergeant, and cover your eyes. This isn't the recommended method of setting off a bombast ... "

He swung the hammer up, aimed carefully at the centre of the crystal and struck, turning his head away as he did. The crystal shattered into a flat patch of white powder.

"That all?" said Nuddell. "Expected something a lot flashier."

The white powder burned with a small yellow flare, though no smoke or flame. Rix dropped the hammer and raised his pole mirror above the wall. An arrow struck it, spinning the pole in his hand. He steadied the mirror and raised it again.

"Didn't work," said Nuddell. "Got another crystal?"

Rix turned the mirror from side to side to cover the area outside the gates, and for a hundred yards to right and left. "Afraid not—"

Then suddenly the ground erupted in dozens of places at once, flinging grass, mud, rocks and bodies a hundred feet into the air. Thousands of huge mud clots spattered the walls, the tower and the walkways, and the massive stone wall shook so violently that every man in Rix's line of sight was tossed off his feet. Two men went over the side.

Then it rained blood. And pieces of men.

Rix picked himself up, wiped blood out of his eyes and went, wobbly kneed, to the battlements, stepping carefully around the ghastly fragments. He edged his head around a battlement and peered over.

His caution was unwarranted. The men who had been attacking the gate were gone, and so were the archers further out, apart from a handful who were dragging themselves away as fast as their broken limbs would allow them. The knots of enemy troops further along the wall stood frozen in horror, then backed away.

"Hold fast!" an enemy officer shouted. "Hold, hold!"

They did not break and run, as they might well have done, but they did not hold either. They retreated in a relatively orderly fashion for a few hundred yards, then stopped.

"They're afraid you've got more of them ... what did you call them?"

"Mines," said Rix. "What the Cythonians call bombasts. I wish I had."

"Isn't there one in—?"

Rix gestured him to silence. "I've kept it for an emergency, but there's no reason the enemy shouldn't think we've mined the rest of the ground. You can taunt them to that effect."

Nuddell grinned and picked up a speaking trumpet. "Pleasure."

"I've got to get back to North Tower. Keep the gate area well guarded; they know they can attack there safely now."

"If they have the guts."

Rix headed for the steps. "Get the blood and bodies cleared off the walkways—and make sure the men keep low. I don't want any more casualties."

He ran down to the store, collected the last bombast and carried it over his shoulder to the door of North Tower. The battering-ram crew were hauling the ram back for another attempt, but they were so weary now they could barely hold it up. There was no point continuing; someone would be badly injured and he needed every man.

He waved them away. They dropped the ram and sat on it.

"Further away," said Rix.

They rolled the ram across the yard. Rix put the bombast at the base of the door, inserted the fuse and packed pieces of stone around the sides.

"How are you going to set it off?" said Ellem, the captain of the ram crew, a stringy man with a shock of yellow hair and pale, watering eyes.

"Drop something on the fuse," said Rix.

He began to stack heavy pieces of stone one on another, up the right side of the door.

"If that topples while you're stacking—" said Ellem, blinking furiously.

"It'll kill us both. *Move away*."

He kept stacking stone until it was higher than his head, then tied a rope around a large block of stone and perched it precariously on top. He backed away with the rope as far as it would go, only thirty yards. Rix frowned and indicated to his troops to shelter around the corner of North Tower. He yanked the rope and ran, but he did not reach the corner in time.

The blast drove him to his hands and knees and fragments spiked into his back in half a dozen places. He rocked there for a moment, decided he was not badly wounded, and stood up.

His men peered around the corner. Rix felt his back. He was stuck all over with shards of shattered rock and splinters of wood, though only the longest ones had penetrated through to the skin. He picked them out; it hurt more than they had going in.

The door was broken. Rix gestured to his men and they charged.

"Search the place," he rapped. "If you find Grandys or any of the other Heroes, sing out and retreat. Don't take them on by yourself."

He checked inside. Two men—Grandys' door guards—lay dead, killed by flying splinters from the door. There was no sign of the Five Heroes and no way to tell where they had gone, though Rix assumed that Grandys would be searching under the tower. He ran to the top of North Tower, scanning every level on the way.

He stood on the flat tower roof for a moment, looking around him. The golden bulk of the castle was to his right. He was at the same level as the domes of its four corner towers, though the massive central tower rose another hundred feet above this level, and the platform at the top of its enormous copper-clad dome stood another seventy feet above that.

There was no sign that any of the Heroes had been up here. Surely Grandys would have gone down, not up. Nonetheless, as Rix headed down, he checked each room. On the second level below the top he made out a heavy rasping coming from behind a closed door, as though someone was struggling to draw breath. He eased the door wide. The sound came from by a window, though it was so covered in dust and cobwebs he could not tell who was there. He checked behind him in case it was a trap, then moved across, his sword out.

A faint movement caught the light, a distinctive shimmer of black and red, then blue and red, like polished opal. It surely came from one of the Heroes. He tensed and edged across, ready to strike. A slender figure lay on a window seat, the reflections coming from her opaline fingernails.

Yulia!

Though she was the least aggressive of the Heroes, Yulia was a powerful magian, and very dangerous. What was she up to? Her head was slumped to the side and her breath came in agonisingly slow rasps, half a minute apart.

He took another step. The room was otherwise empty and there was nowhere for anyone to hide. It did not seem like a trap. She must have seen him coming yet she did not move. Was she ill? Did the Heroes get ill? He checked the door again, then warily bent over her.

Yulia's eyes were glazed, her lips blue, and he saw a faint trace of white powder clinging there. Beneath the white specks her lips were blistered. A tiny copper box lay on the floor, its lid open, and more white powder had spilled out. Was she an addict?

He licked a finger, placed it in the powder and was about to taste it when his fingertip began to sting and blister. He wiped the powder off, very carefully, then wiped it off her upper lip as well, bursting several of the blisters. It must have been painful but she did not react.

She took another faint breath. Her chest barely moved. Had it been anyone else Rix would have said they were dying, but the Five Heroes had always seemed immortal.

"Yulia?" said Rix. "What happened?"

"All ... for ... nothing," she rasped. Her right hand opened and a rolled parchment slipped free. It looked very old. "Dishonour ... can't ... be endured."

Surely she hadn't taken poison? But why would she try to kill herself when the Five Heroes were on the verge of completing their two-thousand-year-old quest? Of all the Heroes, Yulia was the most honourable ... perhaps the only one with a conscience. What could the dishonour be?

She tried to take another breath but the rasping note was not completed. Her head sagged sideways; she was dead. He glanced at the parchment, which was a familiar rant about the racial superiority of the Herovians. He put it in her hand and closed her fingers around it.

He had spent too long here. Conscious that he had been present at a fateful moment, Rix closed Yulia's staring eyes and went out, but he had only gone a few yards along the corridor when he heard Grandys shouting, far below.

"It wasn't there?" said Lirriam. Her voice was silky, smug.

"Lyf turned up," Grandys snarled. "He changed to a wrythen and snatched it from right in front of me."

"How did that feel?" she said, as if she cared. "You must be wondering if you can do anything right these days, Grandys."

He must have drawn Maloch and hacked at the wall, judging by the racket that followed. Rix imagined that Grandys would sooner have hacked at Lirriam's neck.

"How did Lyf find me?" said Grandys.

"Maloch," said Lirriam.

"What about it?"

"It's always been a double-edged sword, if you'll excuse the pun. When you chopped Lyf's feet off the enchantment put a perpetual curse of pain on him . . . and now he can use the pain to locate you. Ironic, isn't it?"

"What was that crash a few minutes back?"

"I don't know; I've been in the lower basement. Though it sounded like the door."

They would discover the tower door broken down, Grandys' guards dead and Rix's men in their place. Rix prayed that his men would hear them coming and retreat. There was no point in dying for North Tower now.

He heard the sounds of a short, sharp battle. The moment it was over the Heroes would come looking for Yulia. He had to get away before they found her body, but the tower only had one stair and Grandys was on it. Rix squeezed out the first window he came to and caught hold of a rusty cast-iron drainpipe that funnelled roof water into one of the cisterns, hoping the drainpipe would not fall to pieces under his weight.

They came up the stairs: Grandys' heavy, wincing tread, the lumbering, rock-like thud of Syrten, and Rufuss's jerky, lopsided gait. If Lirriam was with them, she made no sound.

"Yulia?" said Syrten in anxious tones. Then, more loudly, "Yulia!"

Rix heard him run to the window seat and fall to his armoured knees with a crash. He let out a howl of anguish. "*Yulia!*"

"What's the matter with him now?" said Grandys.

The other Heroes came running. Rix took advantage of the clamour to climb down the drainpipe another twenty feet. There was a moment's silence, after which the Heroes all began talking at once.

Grandys' voice broke through. "No, I can't accept it. Yulia would never kill herself."

"The evidence seems plain to me," said Lirriam. "She took a fatal dose of undiluted *gloxime*."

"Where did she get it?"

"I gave it to her."

"Why?" Grandys snapped.

"She's been in constant pain from the arrow wound she took at Reffering. Nothing but *gloxime* could relieve the pain."

"I still don't believe it," said Grandys. "Her body is still warm, and Maloch tells me there was an intruder—Rixium! Rixium murdered her, and he can't have gone far. Find him!"

Rix scrambled down the drainpipe. The noise no longer mattered, nor the risk of falling.

"How could she do this to me?" said Syrten in a bewildered voice. "It's the end, Grandys. The *end*!"

"We've never been closer to victory," said Grandys.

Syrten howled in anguish.

As Rix reached the ground, Grandys came to the window above him and looked down. Rix ducked around the corner out of range.

"There he is! Heroes, the hour has come," roared Grandys. "Storm Garramide. Find Tali, and get Rixium!"

CHAPTER 72

"You can't cut the pearl out here," said Errek. "It's too dangerous. Carry her to Turgur Thross."

Tali wasn't paralysed; she could move her fingers and toes, and everything felt normal—she simply could not move her limbs. Lyf floated a yard above the floor, carrying her in his arms. He wore the circlet on his brow and it gave him a regal air she had not seen in him before. Clearly, it also greatly increased his power.

"Flying burns magery," said Lyf. "Even wearing the circlet I couldn't fly her that far."

"You've got people at Turgur Thross now, and you can call more through the Sacred Gate."

"It's miles away and they've no way of getting here. I've got to take the pearl *now*."

Lyf carried Tali up several levels into a long, cavernous ballroom which, Tali knew, had been closed off for decades. It was dusty, cob-webbed and smelled of damp and wood-rot. There was a stage at the front end and a large pair of outside doors across the ballroom, twenty yards to her right. A gallery level, high above, extended around the four sides of the ballroom. In the gloom at the rear she saw narrow stairs leading up and down, and beside them a long, cur-tained alcove.

Errek drifted beside Lyf, a tenuous, frowning figure, thin and wispy. Yet despite his appearance he exuded strength and self-con-fidence, and she had no idea how to deal with him, even assuming that she could get away from Lyf.

Lyf bound her to a hard wooden chair, so tightly that she could feel her hands and feet going numb.

"Where's your gear?" said Errek.

"Below, where we slept last night," said Lyf.

"Better hurry."

Lyf barricaded the doors and clattered down the stairs.

"The master pearl is eggshell-thin," said Tali. "It'll burst as soon as he tries to cut it out."

"Who said anything about cutting it out?" Errek said mildly.

"That's how the other pearls were taken. I saw one hacked out of my mother's head."

"Do I look like such a brute?"

"No . . . but Lyf does!"

"I've given him instruction in the necessary magery. You'll barely feel it as he takes the pearl . . . at least, I hope not."

"It's part of my life—a very painful part. Even if you could remove it without breaking the skin, *I'd feel it*."

Lyf flew up the stairs, lugging a wooden case. As he snapped open the latches, Catlin, the chief cook, appeared behind the rail of the gallery level, then headed quietly for the shadowed stairs. A group of kitchen women followed, and last of all Glynnie, who looked fero-cious—Benn must have told her how Tali had used him. Tali's innards clamped painfully. Though, given the circumstances, it seemed unlikely she would have to face Glynnie's fury.

Lyf was facing the other way and did not notice as the women crept down the dark stairs to the alcove. Tali assumed Glynnie and the kitchen women were planning to burst out and take Lyf by surprise. It wasn't much of a plan. His magery would be a match for a score of warriors; the kitchen militia could not hope to take him on.

Without warning there came a heavy thump on the main double doors, as if someone had driven an armoured shoulder against them. The doors did not yield.

"Grandys!" said Errek.

Heavy, thudding footsteps were followed by a colossal crash. The doors moved an inch or two.

"That's Syrten and the doors can't hold him," said Errek.

Lyf· extended an arm towards the doors. *Fzzt!* Blue light surrounded them. The blows continued, though now his binding spell held the doors firm.

Errek went ten yards along the wall and put his head through it. "Lirriam and Rufuss are with them. How long will it take you to get the master pearl?"

"At least ten minutes."

"That's way too long! Call the gauntling to the lookout on the top of the dome, then put every binding spell you know on the door and carry Tali up."

Lyf summoned Grolik and began to bind the doors, drawing such vast amounts of power through the circlet that it left him shaking. While his attention was on the doors, Glynnie came creeping down the shadowed stair.

The doors were struck from the outside with a blast of magery that made the handles and hinges glow red. It faded, then they were struck again by such a massive impact that it could only have been Syrten running at them full bore. The doors splintered, but held.

"They can't take another blow like that," said Errek.

"And I haven't got anything left," said Lyf. He drew a knife to cut Tali's bonds.

Glynnie was only ten yards away, behind the dusty curtain. The kitchen women had gathered in the darkness behind the stair, awaiting her signal.

Glynnie waved an arm. *Now!*

They raced at Lyf, brandishing knives, pokers, skewers and cleavers. He whirled, his right hand flashed red at them and several women fell, unconscious, though the others were unaffected. He was weak, Tali realised. Lyf had used too much power, too quickly.

Catlin swiped at Lyf with a meaty fist and caught him on the side of the head, sending him flying. Glynnie slipped behind the chair that Tali was bound to.

"Radl was right about you," Glynnie hissed in Tali's ear. "If we do get away with this, *you're dead*!"

She hacked through Tali's bonds. Tali tried to get up but the ropes had cut off the circulation. She stumbled and fell, dragging Glynnie down with her. She caught Tali under the arms and heaved her towards the stairs.

"Retreat, everyone!" Glynnie yelled as Errek flew at her.

She dropped Tali and swiped at the wrythen with her knife. It passed straight through him. The kitchen women retreated to the stairs, and up.

Lyf recovered and flew after Tali but the moment he took his eye off the door the blue light surrounding it went out—the Heroes had broken his binding spell. Syrten's next charge tore the left-side door off its hinges. Lyf managed to create a shield where the door had been, an oval of seemingly solid air. For a full minute he held the Heroes, and even forced them back a couple of feet, but the effort was draining him visibly. His right arm began to droop.

Tali's circulation was returning. She hobbled, supported by Glynnie, for the stairs.

"I'm all right now," said Tali. "Go!"

Glynnie ran up to the first landing and stopped. Tali was halfway up when Grandys burst through Lyf's shield and charged. Lyf was slow to react; Grandys was within a foot of snatching the circlet from his head when Lyf shot in the air, out of reach. Grandys cursed, skidded for several yards before he regained his balance, turned on one foot and sprang after Tali.

She had not considered that such a big man could be so agile. She scrambled up, missed the next step, fell and landed hard. Before she could get to her feet, Grandys leapt ten feet forward and eight feet high, smashed straight through the banisters and landed on the steps in front of her.

He picked her up in one giant hand, sprang down and turned

towards Glynnie. She hurled her knife at him. He batted it aside with an armoured forearm. Glynnie hesitated for a second, then raced up and out of sight.

"You'll keep," said Grandys, glaring after her.

He tossed Tali fifteen feet to Rufuss, who caught her and held her in an unbreakable, one-armed grip. Lirriam was duelling Lyf with red spikes of magery. He did not seem to have the magery to float up out of reach.

Grandys came at Lyf from the other side and managed to prick him in the shoulder with the tip of Maloch, in the same place where he had wounded him at Glimmering months ago. Though it was a minor wound, in seconds it had swelled to the size of a half-lemon.

"The only conflict in Maloch is with *you*," said Grandys. "It aches to drink your blood."

Lyf went backwards, the circlet teetered on his head and Grandys made a wild swipe at it, but again missed. Lyf sprayed a burst of orange fire at Grandys' feet, setting his boots ablaze.

Grandys howled and tore his boots off but the bale-fire clung to his inflamed feet. He snatched out Maloch, touched the fire with the tip and spoke a word of command. The flames roared up to his knees. He staggered through the door and plunged himself waist-deep into a water-filled barrel across the courtyard.

"Up!" cried Errek. "Now!"

Lyf propelled himself through the air, up over the gallery rail and disappeared from sight.

Rufuss's arm was hard across Tali's throat, as if he wanted to throttle her. "I haven't forgotten the way you mocked me at Red Mesa," he hissed in her ear.

She could not reply; she could not draw breath.

Grandys limped in, dripping. "What the hell do you think you're doing?" he bellowed. "You're choking her."

He tore Tali out of Rufuss's grip, crushed her to his massive chest and headed down several flights steps to an empty basement. Using the tip of Maloch he opened a concealed passage in the right-hand corner of the basement.

"Rufuss, get my boots. Syrten, run to the camp; fetch Holm and the box of surgeon's instruments underground to North Tower.

Bring everything Holm requires—he's cutting out the master pearl, *right now*. Tell my army to attack the walls with everything they have. And send through a full company of my doughtiest defenders; nothing is stopping me this time."

Grandys did not give Lirriam any orders. Perhaps he no longer dared.

Syrten plodded off, his footsteps shaking the floor. He looked as though his heart had been cut out.

Grandys carried Tali through pitch-dark underground passageways to North Tower and re-barricaded the broken doors. He set her on her feet and prodded her up to the open top of the tower. Lirriam followed, then Rufuss, carrying Grandys' charred boots, his nose upturned as if he could not bear the stench.

The sky was heavily overcast, the light as dim as a midwinter day. The air was still and a fine, misty rain drifted down. Grandys' surviving guards lugged up chairs, a trestle table, a telescope, and a gigantic rectangular object covered in canvas. Finally they staggered up bearing two ominous marble slabs, each eight feet by four, which they set down on the trestles.

Syrten reappeared with Holm and a hundred heavily armed Herovians. The weeks of imprisonment and bad treatment had aged Holm. He looked thin and old, and Tali's heart went out to him.

"I'm sorry about this," he said quietly.

"There's nothing to be sorry about. We do what we must."

"You," said Grandys, indicating most of his soldiers with a sweep of his right hand, "go down and guard the main doors, and every window and opening into North Tower. Syrten, bring Yulia's body up. I'll have the Five Heroes together for one last time."

Ninety of the soldiers went down. The other ten stationed themselves around the roof wall, on watch. Syrten plodded down the steps, each thudding footstep a beat of a death roll.

Lirriam sat in one of the chairs and peered into *Incarnate*. What did she hope to find? Grandys scowled but said nothing. Rufuss slumped in an angle of the five-sided tower, nursing the stump of his arm. He looked paler than usual and was, clearly, in great pain.

"Not in as much pain as *you'll* be in, in a minute," said Grandys, evidently reading Tali's thought.

She began to regret resisting Lyf earlier. If her pearl had to be taken, having it magicked painlessly out of her head was preferable to anything Holm would be able to do, even at his gentlest, with scalpel and bone auger.

Grandys pulled his boots onto his raw, scarred feet. It must have been agonising but he allowed himself no more than a wince. This was it—the moment she had dreaded ever since her mother's murder. Lyf was beaten, and Rix had no way in. Nothing could save her from her mother's fate.

"Holm hasn't operated in decades," said Tali.

"Actually, he's been working as my healer for weeks," said Grandys. "And Rixium's healer before that."

"He's never done this kind of operation before. He can't do it safely."

"He doesn't have to do it safely. He only has to keep you alive until the pearl is removed."

"Holm could break it deliberately," said Tali, avoiding Holm's outraged eye.

"He's your dear friend," said Grandys. "Would he rob you of the chance to achieve your sworn quest for justice? Would he risk my vengeance on everyone you hold dear? I think not."

Syrten reappeared, bearing Yulia's body as tenderly as a newborn infant. Grandys indicated the right-hand marble slab. Syrten laid Yulia there, arranging her head and limbs so she seemed to be sleeping. Tali expected Grandys to mock him for it, but he did not. Grandys stood staring down at Yulia's body, his face grave.

"She was the youngest of us," said Grandys, putting an arm around Syrten's shoulders. "And the best of us. I will miss her all my days."

Syrten choked back a gravelly sob.

Grandys went to the east side, where he seemed to be assessing the state of the siege. He peered over the south side, above the main door of North Tower, and when he came back to Tali he was smiling.

"Rixium is staggering back and forth between the tower door and the fortress walls. He's trying to fight two battles at the same time and he can't win either. He's a beaten man."

"This is your last gasp," said Tali dully. She did not believe her own words but she had to keep fighting. "You're on the edge of the precipice, and once you go over there's no way back."

Grandys laughed in her face. Lirriam, who had been talking to Syrten, looked up sharply, then strolled across.

"You've had a setback at the wall, Grandys."

"What are you talking about?"

"Syrten would have told you, had you asked."

"Syrten?" Grandys said commandingly.

Syrten turned his red eyes on Grandys, then lumbered across.

"What's the state of the siege?" said Grandys.

"Rixium—mined ground outside—gates," said Syrten. "Many bombasts. Boom!" He swept his hands up and out, miming a huge explosion. "Eight hundred dead."

"Eight hundred!" choked Grandys. "But the siege continues?"

"Withdrawn. Troops afraid—go near wall."

Grandys took several deep breaths. "We still outnumber them, *just*." He looked around. "Rufuss, no one can encourage men the way you can. Run underground to the camp and urge them to do their duty in the strongest terms."

"Can I decimate them?" Rufuss said eagerly.

Grandys' fists closed and opened. "Don't be a bigger fool than you look," he said coldly. "I need every man now."

Rufuss's cold face hardened; he stalked down the stairs.

"What if they won't do their duty?" said Lirriam.

"The demonstration I've got planned will soon have their morale on the rise."

"What kind of a demonstration?" Lirriam said curiously.

Grandys did not reply. "Prepare your surgical instruments, Holm. Once you have, you'll find these sketches helpful." Grandys handed him the rolled sheet of drawings that Yulia had made in Bastion Barr weeks ago.

Holm studied the drawings. "Are they accurate?"

"Does it matter?"

"Tali's life depends on it."

"Since Yulia made them, they will be precise to the hundredth part of an inch."

Grandys picked Tali up and laid her on the empty slab. Her head was only three feet away from Yulia's. Lirriam touched Tali on the forehead and the strength drained from her limbs yet again.

"You can't move," said Grandys, "but you'll still be able to feel pain—a good deal of it, I dare say. That's regrettable for you, but the pearl must be cut from a conscious host."

Beside Tali, Yulia's dead face radiated despair. "W-what happened to her?" said Tali.

Grandys did not answer. Tali noted the blistered, bluish lips and the trace of powder clinging in one corner of her mouth.

"Why did she kill herself?"

Syrten let out a cry of uttermost anguish and hunched over Yulia, a massive, uncomprehending figure, utterly bereft. "*Didn't* kill herself. Yulia—never leave me. Alone. *Alone!*"

"Pull yourself together, rock-man," said Lirriam. "You'll always have us."

"End of Five Heroes."

"It's not," Grandys said gruffly. "Take him over there, Lirriam. Look after him."

It looked like suicide to Tali. What could have made Yulia do it, after going all that way for the *Immortal Text*? After finally coming so close to the quest that was everything to her?

"Surgeon Holm," said Grandys, "begin!"

"I've never done this kind of operation," said Holm.

Grandys snatched up a razor-edged chisel and brandished it in his face.

"If you don't, I'll hack it out myself."

"That could kill her," said Holm.

"I'll take my chances," said Grandys, grinning savagely.

"I'll need hot water, lots of it."

Grandys drew Maloch and plunged it into a water barrel, which boiled in seconds.

"And freshly laundered towels," Holm added.

"The covered basket by the wall is full of them."

Holm lifted the lid, then closed it again. "The operation needs to be done indoors, in a scrubbed room. Up here, dirt and dust in the air—"

"You're doing it here," said Grandys. "Now!" He handed Holm a large wooden instrument case with brass corners.

"These aren't my instruments," said Holm.

"They're new," said Grandys. "Never been used. There's ten times as many instruments as you had—everything you could possibly need. Get started."

Holm scowled and opened the case.

"It's the only way, Holm," said Tali. "And . . . you have no idea how much I want to be rid of the master pearl."

He bent over the instruments for a minute, stood up straight and held out his right arm. It had a slight tremor.

"I've operated with worse," he said. Then Holm added wryly, "Though not successfully."

Grandys pulled the canvas off the rectangular object to reveal a large wooden box, closed on all sides, on four metal legs. There was a tiny hole in the middle of the end facing Tali. In other respects the box seemed to be just a box.

He unscrewed a cap from the right-hand side of the box. In the gloom, a thin beam of light could be seen issuing from inside.

"It's a camera obscura," said Grandys, with a flourish.

"What the blazes is that?" said Holm.

"A device of my own invention, to show my army that I hold the master pearl. It'll give them heart, while Rixium's exhausted people will see it and despair." He rubbed his hands together.

"I'm not seeing anything," said Tali.

"You will when I amplify the light beam, thus!"

Grandys touched the box with the tip of Maloch. At once the beam blazed out so brightly that the slab, and Tali lying on it, was projected onto the wall of the castle immediately below the great copper dome, in an image at least fifty feet long and forty feet high. It would have been visible for miles.

She stared at herself lying there. She could see every detail of her face, yet it seemed remote; it was her, yet not her.

Grandys bent over his little, ice-covered chest. The ice chest—she had not realised he had brought it here. He unlocked it, took out the empty phial and held it up. She could see her name on the label.

Thalalie vi Torgrist.

"What do you want it for?" said Tali. "Is it for my healing blood?"

But if it was, why only take one phial? Why not take all of it?

"Let the bloodshed begin," said Grandys.

CHAPTER 73

Rix, back in the yard with his battering-ram crew, watched the projected image on the wall as Tali's head was shaved—once again—washed and dried. After an interminable wait, Holm raised his scalpel and prepared to make the first cut.

Rix reached out blindly and took Glynnie's cold hand in his own sweating hand. High above, Holm looked around, wild-eyed, as if he had never wanted a drink more. His hand shook. He put the scalpel down and his lips moved.

"What did he say?" said Rix. "Can you read his lips?"

"He said, 'I can't do it'," said Glynnie. "And Grandys said, 'Cut! Or I'll cut for you.'"

"Holm's afraid he'll botch it and kill her."

"She'll probably die even if he doesn't botch it. The master pearl is like the thinnest, most brittle eggshell now, and if it breaks before Holm gets it out, Tali dies."

"You said *you* were going to kill her," said a small voice behind her. Benn.

"I didn't mean it," said Glynnie. "Not really. I wouldn't wish that operation on anyone. Off you go, Benn. You don't need to see this."

"I have to see everything!" cried Benn. "I have to know what the enemy are doing to us."

When Holm made the first cut, Tali screamed so loudly that she could have been heard on the other side of the fortress.

"You've got to save her, Rix," Benn said desperately.

"I know," said Rix. "But I can't get in, lad."

"Can't you blast the door again?"

"I don't have any more bombasts."

Tali let out another scream, more terrible than the first.

Benn jumped. "You've got to do something."

The battering-ram crew were almost ready, though Rix had no more hope that they would succeed this time. Grandys' men had blocked the doorway with stone which Lirriam had reinforced with magery.

Holm made another cut. Tali let out a third scream. It was fainter now; weaker, and that was not a good sign. She had been incredibly strong and resilient when Rix first met her; she had been able to endure almost any physical and mental torment. But both the strength and the resilience were long gone and he did not think she could take any more. She might simply slip from this world, as Yulia had done.

Rix ran to the ram, took hold of it and urged his men on. They went forward at a fast walk, gathering to a trot as they climbed the sloping ramp they had laid over the steps, and the ram hit the stone.

The shock jarred him all the way to the top of his skull. It must have jarred everyone, for he felt the ram falling at the rear. Rix tried to hold the weight by himself, realised that was folly and let go. The ram hit the ground and he heard the sickening crack of breaking bones, followed by a shriek.

One of the men at the back, a tall, slender fellow, had held on too long, slipped and the ram had fallen across his thighs. Both legs were broken.

"Get it off him," Rix yelled, running that way.

They heaved the ram off. Someone fetched a wide plank and they worked it under the injured man. Rix strapped him down and sent him to the healery. Glynnie followed, looking back over her shoulder at the scene projected on the wall.

Blood covered the end of Tali's marble slab—an enormous amount of blood. Holm's hands were covered in it and so was the top of Tali's head. Her eyes were huge and staring, her mouth wide, though she had stopped screaming. Rix turned away—he could not bear to see what was being done to her. She had done so much for him; and given so much for his country.

A lad came running. It was young Thom, the wood boy.

"Lord Deadhand?" Thom's gaze fixed on the image from the camera obscura and he froze.

"Yes, Thom?" said Rix. "What's the news from the wall?"

"Nuddell says the Herovians are attacking with everything they have, led by Rufuss. Nuddell ain't sure he can hold them."

"I'd better go," said Rix.

"You can't leave Tali," cried Benn.

"I'm sure she wouldn't want us to witness her agony," said Rix. "Why don't you come with me?"

"But Tali came to my rescue. I can't abandon her, not while there's any hope."

"All right; I need a watchman here anyway. If the Heroes break out of North Tower I've got to know instantly."

"Yes, Rix," said Benn.

"Or if anything happens with ... with Tali."

"Yes, Rix."

"Stay with the battering-ram crew. Don't go wandering off."

"No, Rix."

Rix headed to the defensive wall with Thom.

"Things are bad, Lord Deadhand, aren't they?" Thom said soberly.

Previously, Thom had shown an unshakeable belief that they would beat the enemy, because they had right on their side.

"They're very bad, Thom, but we're not beaten yet."

"Are we going to lose? Is Axil Grandys going to kill us all?"

Rix considered the question. If ... *when* Grandys got Tali's master pearl, he would be able to command the other pearls and draw on the power of all five. None of their lives would matter any more and he would either kill everyone out of hand or, if he were in a particularly cruel and vengeful mood, hold certain people prisoner so he could torment them before killing them. Rix, Glynnie and Holm certainly fell into that category.

"Lord Deadhand?" Thom said anxiously.

"We're going to fight to the end," said Rix. "We're never giving in, no matter what ... "

"But?" said Thom, taking his hand and moving closer to him.

Rix put an arm across the boy's shoulders. "I won't lie to you, Thom. I don't see how we can win."

CHAPTER 74

In the healery, Glynnie made sure the man with the broken legs was being attended to, and ran back to North Tower. The battering-ram crew stood guard on the doors and Benn was out in the middle of the yard, watching the images from the camera obscura flickering on the wall.

"What's happening?" panted Glynnie.

"It's awful," said Benn, without looking around.

It looked the same as before. Blood all over Tali's head; blood on Holm's hands and forearms, his scalpel and bone augers; Grandys in the background, arms folded, watching and waiting for the prize.

"It's been going on for half an hour," she said. "Surely Holm must be close to the pearl."

"I think he is," Benn said absently, totally focused on what was happening up above.

"Has there been any news from Rix?"

"No."

"Run and tell him what's going on."

"He can see the operation as well as we can," said Benn.

"Well, go and ask him how the siege is going," she snapped.

"Do I have to?" said Benn.

"Right away!" Glynnie said sharply. "We're fighting a war." And losing it.

Benn ran. Glynnie knotted her fingers together. Watching the operation, seeing the battle being lost with every stroke of Holm's bloody instruments and being able to do nothing about it, was unbearable.

Which was why Grandys was showing them the operation. He

was a vengeful brute who liked to torment his victims to the cracking point before he finally crushed them.

There had to be a way to turn the tables; to use his strengths, or his fears, against him. He had two weaknesses that Glynnie was aware of—his superstitious terror of the wyverin, and his rivalry with and fear of Lirriam and *Incarnate*.

Tali had tried to turn Lirriam against Grandys; she had told Glynnie so when they were held by the Resistance. But it had not worked. The Five Heroes could be bitter rivals, but at any threat to one the others always closed ranks.

That left the wyverin. If Glynnie could have woken it she would have, because even the slightest hope was worth the risk, but its lair was too far away.

How then?

She walked around the yard, looking up at the sky and wondering what Lyf was up to. He had been planning to take Tali to the top of the dome; she had heard him call the gauntling there, though it was a huge, ominous beast and, if it had been seen, Glynnie would have heard about it by now.

It must still be on its way and presumably Lyf was waiting up top for it, and renewing his strength. But he must attack soon—probably at the moment Grandys took the master pearl. Lyf would not go far from it, now that he had the circlet.

Benn came racing back. "What news from the wall?" said Glynnie.

"It's holding," he gasped. "But only just. Rix says they might keep the enemy out for another hour, but that's all."

"Then we need a miracle."

Benn looked up at the camera obscura image. Glynnie did too. Holm was slumped over the end of the slab. He took several deep breaths, washed his red hands and moved back to Tali.

"What's he doing now?" said Benn.

"Looks like he's cleaning her up."

Tali's eyes were closed and she lay still. Glynnie could not tell if she were dead or alive. Grandys bent over her head, concealing her for a moment, then turned and slowly raised his right arm as high as he could reach. He was holding something in his fingertips—a small, bloody object: shiny, black. His coarse, bloated face glowed with triumph.

"He's got it!" said Glynnie.

A collective groan ran through the battering-ram crew.

"Benn, run and find Rix, quick! Tell him Grandys has the master pearl."

Benn ran off.

Holm appeared to be stitching Tali's head, though thankfully Glynnie could not see it clearly. Even inured as she was to the butchery she'd often watched and carried out on wounded men in the healery, she had seen enough.

"I have the pearl," said Grandys, holding a speaking trumpet to his mouth. "Now let my enemies tremble."

His voice boomed out. He was using magery to amplify his words, to make sure everyone in the fortress, as well as his own troops outside, knew he had prevailed.

"But can you command the other four pearls?" said Lirriam. "And can you call upon their power to raise king-magery?"

"Yes, and yes!" said Grandys.

Benn came running back. He must have only gone halfway before Grandys had made his announcement.

"Pray that the master pearl bursts and blasts him to bits in his moment of triumph," said Glynnie.

"Do you think it could?" said Benn in a hopeful voice.

"Anything *could* happen."

Though she did not think it would. The tide had turned and it was running the Heroes' way. With the power of all five pearls, Grandys might be able to wrest the circlet from Lyf as well.

She heard a roar from the far side of the fortress. Had the besiegers taken heart and gained a foothold on the wall? After a war that had lasted six months, was Hightspall's last bastion going to crumble in a few bloody minutes?

"I command the pearls!" roared Grandys. "The power is mine. King-magery, come forth."

The sky went black. The ground shook, deep and low, though this tremor was unlike any of the quakes Glynnie had experienced in the past months. The ground seemed to be rolling up and down, lifting her to her tiptoes then falling away beneath her—she felt a sickening lurch in the pit of her stomach each time it dropped. Five times the ground moved up and down, each wave stronger than the time before.

A whirling, tumbling nebula of force blasted dust into her face and grit into her eyes. The yard cracked in an irregular curve from one side to the other, only feet from where Glynnie and Benn stood, and dust and steam spiralled out. She saw down several feet into what appeared to be an old graveyard, or perhaps a mass grave, judging by the number of bones.

A host of spirits wisped into visibility, rising, fluttering. Not full spirits—most were little more than faces, or heads and shoulders—but all were shouting angrily at being disturbed. As they rose into the grey light they faded and disappeared, and their cries died away. The ground shifted and the crack closed.

Now a vortex appeared on the golden stone of the castle wall below the dome, projected through the camera obscura. It was whirling around the rooftop of North Tower, spinning smaller and tighter and faster all the time. It was so dense that nothing could be seen through it; so compact that objects seen near its edges were distorted as though the very light was bent as it passed by.

Grandys was directing it with the master pearl, moving it in the air like a conductor waving his baton. Every movement tightened the vortex, thickened it and spun it faster, until it had contracted from yards across and twice as high to a tiny, shrieking cyclone only a foot tall.

"Syrten, the platina canister!" said Grandys, his magnified voice booming and echoing off the walls and towers. "The one substance that can contain king-magery."

Syrten carried a large conical canister to the end of the second slab, near Yulia's feet, and set it down. It stood as high as his knees.

"Cap!"

Syrten took the cap off and stepped back.

Grandys, his jaw knotted with the effort, directed the vortex over the opening of the canister, then brought the hand holding the master pearl down sharply. The vortex dropped into the canister.

Yulia's body heaved, her legs rising a foot into the air. Syrten put the cap on smartly and Grandys held the canister up.

"King-magery is mine," he exulted, kissing the canister. His voice was thick and slurred, as if he were intoxicated by the moment.

"*Ours*," said Lirriam.

"What?" he said, shaking his head as if he did not understand.

"The pact, Grandys. *Each for all, all for each—forever*. King-magery doesn't belong to you—it belongs to the Five Heroes, as we were."

"Whatever you say!" said Grandys. "I won't let anything mar this magical moment."

He turned his back to her and walked forward until he stood squarely in front of the camera obscura. After taking a deep breath, he lifted the canister high in the air and amplified his voice until it rattled the slates on the surrounding roofs.

"I, Axil Grandys, hold king-magery in my hand. Men and women of Garramide, you have fought bravely, but nothing can prevail against me now. Lay down your arms."

CHAPTER 75

"Do you believe him?" whispered Benn.

"Yes," said Glynnie. "But I'll never trust him."

Two figures appeared on the platform above the great dome, the highest point of Garramide. The big man was Rix and the boy could have been Thom. Clearly, wherever Lyf and Errek had gone it wasn't to the dome, so what were *they* up to?

"Men and women of Garramide," Rix bellowed through his speaking trumpet, "Axil Grandys is a cheat and a liar, and the Five Heroes can never be trusted. We fight on!"

"How dare you defy the man who holds king-magery in his hand?" said Grandys.

"I do because I must. We will *never* submit."

"Then die!"

Grandys attempted to blast Rix off the top of the platform. It missed him, though Glynnie saw Thom go tumbling backwards. Rix dropped the speaking trumpet, ran after Thom and disappeared from view.

"Thom!" whispered Benn.

"He'll be all right," Glynnie said unconvincingly. "Rix won't let any harm come to him ... "

Lirriam was speaking to Grandys, and the amplifying charm picked up her words as well. "You may have *taken* king-magery," she said, "but you can't *use* it without the circlet."

"Lyf won't have gone far. I'll have the circlet this very hour."

Grandys looked down at the master pearl, and the two other pearls in his hand, then held his hand out to Lirriam.

"Why are they no longer black?"

The camera obscura showed the three pearls clearly. Most of their black, pearly lustre was gone, changed to a cloudy grey.

"They did the work they were created to do when you raised king-magery with them," said Lirriam. "*You'll* get no more from them."

Grandys drew his arm back as if to hurl them against the wall.

"Wait!" she said. "They may still have a part to play ... when you cast the Three Spells."

Grandys handed them to her, indifferently.

"It's time to tidy up," he said. "And I don't need these two any more."

He drew Maloch and advanced towards Holm and Tali, who lay as still as before. Was she unconscious? Dying? Holm did not look up when Grandys approached him, raising the sword.

"Stop!" said Lirriam.

"What now?" said Grandys.

"You'll need Tali for the endgame," said Lirriam "and she's in a bad way. Holm has to keep her alive."

"I suppose so, dammit!"

Grandys picked Tali up and disappeared from the eye of the camera obscura, which continued to project the scene onto the castle wall after Syrten gently raised Yulia's body and everyone left the rooftop.

"They're coming down," said Benn. "Do we have to fight them?"

"He's got a hundred guards," said Glynnie. "Fighting would be suicide. Run and tell Rix that Grandys is on his way up. Don't take any risks."

Benn raced away. Glynnie called the battering-ram crew away into hiding, then crouched in the shadows as the door of North Tower was unblocked and Grandys led the Heroes towards the long stairs leading to the platform above the dome. He did not look back. He had the air of a man who saw victory within his reach.

"Stinking mongrel bastard!" Glynnie said under her breath. "How I'd love to bring you down."

And then, as Syrten headed up with Yulia's body, Glynnie recovered the thought she had lost hours ago. The portrait! She raced up to Rix's chambers, went to the window and checked on the fortress wall. It was still in friendly hands, though that could change in minutes. She had to act fast. She picked up the portrait and began to lug it down.

The fortress was eerily empty, unnervingly silent. No doubt everyone who did not have urgent duties was in hiding, guarding the children and the elderly, and waiting in terror for an enemy they could not hope to stop. An enemy whose brutality was legendary.

She took the darkest and most obscure passages, knowing she wasn't safe anywhere, but encountered no one. The portrait was awkwardly large and troublesome to manoeuvre around the corners of the stairs. Glynnie reached the lower side door, stopped and checked outside. There was no one in sight.

She scurried across to the broken entrance to North Tower and began to heave the portrait up the stone steps. She was nearing the top when she heard someone coming down, a heavy tread.

There was no chance of avoiding detection. She grounded the portrait and was feeling for her knife when she remembered that she had lost it during the fight in the old ballroom. In all the drama since, she had forgotten to replace it. Glynnie was turning to run when Rix came around the corner.

"What are you doing here?" they said at the same time.

"What's that for?" said Rix.

Glynnie would have thought it was obvious. "Give me a hand. And pray that the device still works. How's Thom?"

"Not good. Grandys' blast drove him against the wall—he's got two badly broken legs."

"Oh!" said Glynnie. "But he'll be all right? He'll be able to walk?"

"That'll depend on the healers. Poor lad; I should've been more careful."

He took one end of the portrait, she lifted the other and they carried it up to the top of the tower. She studied the area in front of the camera obscura, picked the best spot and dragged the portrait into position.

"It's changed again!" said Glynnie.

Rix glanced at the wall beneath the dome, where the gigantic image was projected in brilliant detail. The warrior now lay on the ground with the wyverin tearing at his belly, disembowelling him.

And the warrior's face had completed the change—from Lord Ricinus to Axil Grandys.

Rix gaped. "I never saw the likeness before. Glynnie, you're amazing!"

"It's taken you long enough to realise it," she said, grinning.

He picked her up under the arms, whirled her around in a circle, kissed her on the mouth and put her down again. He looked around, frowned and cleared his throat. Glynnie spotted a speaking trumpet lying on the ground and tossed it to him.

"Tell the whole world to look at the wall. Tell Grandys."

Rix raised the trumpet to his mouth. "People of Garramide! Herovians! Heroes! You know the legend of Axil Grandys. Look to the wall! Look and see his doom for yourselves."

Silence fell. Even the sounds of battle from the distant wall ceased.

Glynnie took Rix's hand. "It might be an idea if we get out of sight. Out of danger."

They took shelter in one of the corners, where they could see the image on the wall without being in the line of fire from the platform at the top of the dome. There came a roar from the outer wall, and the sounds of cheering. But there was no reaction from Grandys. Why not?

"His army can see the image," said Glynnie, "but he can't—not from the top of the dome. He'd have to come down."

"They can signal him," said Rix.

"Whatever the trouble is, he'll want to see it for himself. He's that kind of man."

"And then he'll want someone to pay."

There came an echoing, fearful cry from high above. Grandys had seen the image of himself being disembowelled by the wyverin.

Rix dived and grabbed the portrait. Grandys blasted the camera obscura to bits and the image vanished.

CHAPTER 76

When Grandys successfully summoned king-magery, Lyf's heart stopped for ten beats.

"He's done it," said Errek, who was sitting on the side wall of a small tower to the left of the main dome. "I never thought he would. You've got to hand it to the brute—"

"Don't!" choked Lyf.

Errek raised a wispy eyebrow. "Don't what?"

"How dare you praise him? How dare you admire him?"

"To beat your enemy, you first have to know him. Grandys is a violent, treacherous swine, but there's also much that's admirable about him. In ingenuity, strength and sheer, dogged determination, he's certainly *your* master."

"Stop it!"

Errek pretended to weigh Lyf up, head to one side. "You too are admirable, in your own way, but self-indulgence makes you less of a king than you could be."

"What self-indulgence?" Lyf said coldly.

"The petty despairs you wallow in after every setback. You lack determination, Lyf; you fail in persistence."

"For almost two thousand years as a wrythen I fought the long fight, always cleaving to my plan, never giving up."

"You gave up several times, I believe. Besides, it's an easy life being a wrythen, if I may be excused the joke." Errek chuckled. "We can't die, we barely feel pain and we don't require clothing, shelter or sustenance. In short, a human's basic needs are irrelevant to us."

"He commands all the pearls," said Lyf. "He's on his way here, after my circlet."

"All the more reason for you to strike first."

"With what?"

Errek's reply was cut off as the gaustling, which Lyf had called an hour ago, came swooping down.

"Where the hell have you been?" snarled Lyf.

The gaustling twisted her head around and spat a slimy gob at him. Lyf ducked, hauled himself onto her back and rode in circles around Garramide, trying to come up with a plan.

"Well?" said Errek after the beast had made several circuits.

"Nothing."

Errek sighed. "The solution is staring you in the face."

"What solution?"

"Look at the wall beneath the great dome."

Lyf turned that way. "I don't see anything."

"You will on the next circuit."

The gaustling circled and finally the image came into view. Lyf studied it incredulously, suspecting a trick.

"It's the portrait Rixium painted for his father's Honouring," he said at last.

"The portrait you ordered destroyed, though you didn't check to make sure it was. Just as well, in the circumstances."

"It's changed," said Lyf, staring at it until his eyes watered. Then he laughed. "I know what to do."

"Have you fully thought it through?"

"There isn't time. I'm going to wake the Sacred Beast."

"It's the Chymical Beast, and it's liable to eat the magian who wakes it," said Errek.

"It's worth the risk." Lyf felt the blood burning through his veins at the thought. "Grandys is terrified of it."

"It's also an enigmatic omen for our land, which is why I created king-magery in the first place."

"Why did you create king-magery?"

"I still can't remember; those memories were lost when I died. But beware—"

"Of what?"

"When the wyverin last roamed the land, nothing but disaster befell Cythe."

"Your memories are clear enough when you want to hector me," Lyf snapped.

"Wake it and you could bring calamity down on us. Calamity that could tip the Engine over the edge."

"Where did the wyverin come from, anyway?"

"It came *through*," Errek said cryptically.

"What's that supposed to mean?"

"Another memory I can't recover."

"Try harder!" Lyf tilted his head to one side and pursed his lips, mimicking Errek's actions a few minutes previously. "When I analyse your character—"

"I'm sure you identify all manner of faults," Errek said with an ironic little bow. "And all true, but beside the point. If you are going to commit this disastrously reckless act, do it now, before Grandys makes all our actions redundant."

"How do I command so great and unfathomable a creature?" whispered Lyf as he prepared to cast the final stage of the waking spell Errek had given him. It was the reverse of the spell Errek had used to put the wyverin to sleep before his own death, and a most difficult and perilous spell it was.

"You don't command the wyverin," said Errek. "You entice it."

"How?"

"It's a magical creature, but after such a long sleep its gift will be sorely drained, and soon after rousing it must be replenished—"

"With the body and blood of a great magian. I know."

"If you're not careful, the magian will be you."

"I have a plan," said Lyf, and cast the final stage of the spell.

The wyverin's nearest eye opened; the gravel and slag of its bed cracked and formed little landslides to either side as it moved. It raised its head, swung it towards the nearest wall and bit through several cubic yards of rock, out of habit. Then it began to lever itself to its feet.

With a gesture, Lyf created an image on the end wall. A picture very like Rix's original portrait, save that the man triumphantly killing the insultingly small and feeble-looking wyverin—the brutish oaf gloating over its downfall and trumpeting the superiority of man over beast—was Axil Grandys.

The wyverin eyed the image as if it were having difficulty bringing it into focus—or, perhaps, taking time to recognise what the image signified—a colossal insult to the greatest and noblest beast of all.

It roused like an earthquake and thundered into the air, lashing the walls of the cavern with its tail, shattering the rock and flailing fusillades of gravel in every direction. It bit wagon-sized chunks from the wall, chewed them and coughed up a spray of acid-drenched slurry powerful enough to have eaten through inch-thick plate armour.

The wyverin raced around the cavern three times, gathering speed, then tucked its wings back and shot towards the spiralling tunnel that ran up to the ruins at Turgur Thross, leaving a landslide of crumbling and tumbling rock behind it.

Lyf drew on the circlet and flew after it, with Errek close behind. They followed it around four of the spirals, but the wyverin was rapidly leaving them behind.

"That way!" cried Errek, pointing up a small, vertical chimney barely wide enough for a human. "If we don't get out first, the chance will be wasted. And call the gauntling, *now*."

Lyf called Grolik back to Turgur Thross, though not without a deep foreboding for what he had unleashed.

"Why first?" said Lyf.

"We must reach Grandys at the same time as the wyverin does— otherwise it may eat him *and* the canister of king-magery. That would be unimaginably bad."

Lyf did not ask why. He did not want to know about any possibilities worse than the current ones. They scrambled up the narrow chimney. Distantly he could hear rock being smashed to pieces as the wyverin fought to get out the long way; he could feel the shuddering transmitted through the solid earth.

"Faster!" said Errek.

Lyf squeezed out the top of the chimney into the open, into the holy, lichen-covered ruins of Turgur Thross.

"Where's that blasted gauntling?" said Errek.

Lyf could not see it anywhere. He called Grolik again. The wyverin was close to the surface now and the noise, as it battered its way out, was eardrum-shattering. Lyf drifted higher, turned and saw the gauntling plummeting at him in a vertical dive.

He flinched. The creatures were prone to madness and generally untrustworthy. He raised a threatening fist as if he still had magery to burn. The gauntling adjusted the angle of its dive to come down behind him. It flattened out and, as it passed beneath, he dropped onto its back.

It shot past Errek and Lyf plucked him out of the air. It was no easy feat to catch an almost bodiless wrythen but he'd had plenty of practice by now. The gauntling jagged away as the wyverin forced its head out of a small entrance a few hundred yards from Turgur Thross. Its claws were scrabbling against the solid rock, tearing it apart and sending chunks of broken rock the size of boulders flying in all directions.

Lyf conjured the image of Grandys killing the wyverin again and projected it onto the air a hundred yards ahead of the beast, in the direction of Garramide. The wyverin's vast eyes turned towards the image. Lyf vanished it and the wyverin's eyes focused on the scene that had been concealed behind it: the platform at the top of the great dome, where Grandys stood with two fists raised in the air, broadcasting his dominance.

The wyverin exploded out, opened its wings and shook itself in mid-air, scattering rocks like missiles. The gauntling swept around behind it. Lyf and Errek slid off onto the wyverin's back, unnoticed, and it took off.

Lyf stood up, holding the circlet high and shaking it in the direction of Garramide. "This is both the means and the hour of your doom, Grandys."

Lyf settled the circlet on his brow and rode the Chymical Beast to Garramide like an avenging fury.

CHAPTER 77

"Is this what Grandys called 'the endgame'?" said Glynnie. Rix scrambled onto the circular walkway that ran around the inside of the dome, thirty feet below the top. She followed him up. Now he could see the platform through one of the small skylights at the top of the dome. Grandys and the other Heroes were moving about on the platform though Rix could not tell what they were doing.

"If it isn't, it can't be far away."

"What's our plan?"

"Lyf has to go after the king-magery right away, and the moment he attacks—"

Glynnie sucked her breath in through her teeth. "You can't fight king-magery with a sword, Rix."

"I'm not planning to. When Lyf attacks I'm going to try to snatch the canister and the circlet, then rescue Tali—if she's still alive—and Holm." He smiled wryly. "Not aiming too high, am I?"

She clutched at his wrist. "They'll kill you."

"They'll certainly try."

"You can't possibly take both. Go for the platina canister—it's really heavy—and I'll try for the circlet."

He opened his mouth to say no.

"Don't insult me by trying to protect me," said Glynnie. "We're a team and if you're risking your life, I'm entitled to risk mine."

"That doubles the chance of . . . a bad outcome."

"You mean one of us being killed? I know, but it also doubles our chances of a *good* outcome."

He put his arms around her. "We'll live or die together. Probably—"

"Don't say that either." She tightened her arms around his chest until he could hardly breathe. "What's happening on the wall?"

Rix was so focused on Grandys that he had not thought to look. He pulled free and peered out and down. "Looks like the Herovians have drawn back. Your brilliant work with the portrait must have unnerved them."

"They'll attack again."

"First they'll have to gain back all the ground they've given up. It doesn't give us a big advantage, but . . ."

"We'll take what we can get," said Glynnie.

They crept around the walkway and checked through the next skylight, which offered a better view. Grandys was swinging Maloch in complex patterns, though each ended with the blade pointing in the same direction—towards Turgur Thross.

"What's he doing?" said Glynnie.

"Scrying for Lyf, I'd guess. Even in the days when *I* carried Maloch it always seemed to know where Lyf was."

Ahead, a copper-clad door opened through the side of the dome onto a second, narrower walkway that ran around the outside. Rix opened the door and went through. Glynnie stepped out beside him. Away to the right, a dozen steps ran up towards the platform, though the people on it could not be seen from this angle.

They crept around until he could see up to the platform. Glynnie looked north and her eyes widened.

"Is that—?" She pointed. "Is that—?"

The wyverin—for it could be nothing else—was howling towards them. Rix gazed at it in awe. He had imagined it hundreds of times since he'd begun the portrait. At that time he had drawn dozens of sketches, and he'd done many more since his return to Garramide, yet none did it justice. Rannilt had been right—it was too big for the world.

"Look out!" hissed Glynnie.

She pulled him down as the wyverin struck the side of the copper dome like a thunderbolt, ripping it open and scattering crumpled lengths of copper sheeting like shredded paper. The screech of metal being torn in two stung his ears. Lyf, wearing the circlet on his brow, flew through the air towards the platform and landed on the other side, twenty yards away from Grandys. Errek drifted through the air high above.

"Now!" said Rix. "Slowly."

He crept up the steps and stopped with only his eyes above the edge of the circular platform, which was some twenty-five yards across. Glynnie squeezed up beside him. Grandys was a few yards away and had his back to them, holding the canister in his left hand and Maloch in his right. Lirriam was beyond on the left, along with Holm and the still figure of Tali. Syrten, further on, was gazing at Yulia, oblivious to everything around him.

The wyverin tore another half dozen sheets of copper off the dome, let them fall and raced around it, sweeping its fifty-foot tail from side to side. Its first blow knocked the steepled roof and top floor off the pencil-shaped tower to the right of the castle, scattering stone and roof timbers across the fortress yard and onto the top of North Tower.

The next sweep of its tail smashed through the top of the observatory tower, demolishing the wall onto which that tormented figure of Grandys had been etched. Rix hoped the symbol mirrored the reality to come.

It looked like a beast out of control, though Rix gained the impression that it was putting on a display—and that the destruction was coolly calculated. It settled on the supporting metal frame of the ruined dome, swaying back and forth and shaking the castle to its foundations. Its great head was moving from side to side but its inflamed, weeping eyes, each a yard across, swivelled to keep Grandys in view the whole time. Then, to Rix's astonishment, it let out a *huff-huff-huff* that was, unmistakably, laughter.

"What's it laughing at?" asked Glynnie, pressing closer to Rix.

"Us, I'd say," said Rix. "I think it finds people ridiculous."

"Too ridiculous to gobble us down, I hope."

"They say it needs to eat a magian or two soon after it wakes."

"Let's hope it can tell the difference between them and us."

The wyverin extended its long neck towards Syrten and Yulia, then snorted and swung towards Lirriam, sniffing her and staring at her chest. She gave a little shiver, then drew out *Incarnate* and held it up, like an offering. The wyverin opened its maw as if to take the stone, and her arm as well, but closed it again and nudged *Incarnate* away with the tip of its snout.

It lifted off the ruined dome, inflated its belly to twice its normal size and floated up into the air beside the platform, drifting around Rufuss and eyeing the stump of his arm. He clutched his sword and swallowed audibly. The wyverin's left leg flashed out and an extended claw raked down his front, tearing Rufuss's clothes off to expose a fleshless frame whose fish-belly pallor contrasted unattractively with the sparse clumps of coarse black hair on his chest and back.

The wyverin let out a series of rolling chuckles which rumbled through it from one end to the other. Two claws closed around Rufuss's middle, lifted him onto a broken column like a naked statue on a pedestal, and left him there, crouched low, shaking with mortified rage. A thunder of laughter shook stones out of the side of the observatory tower and sent them crashing to the ground.

It cocked its head to one side. Silence fell and Rix heard crying from the ruins. The wyverin rotated in the air, dived and plucked twisted iron and crumpled copper sheeting out of the way, then hooked out a boy and raised him to its eye.

"Benn!" whispered Glynnie. "Benn, no . . . "

"He must have followed us. Stay back!" Rix drew his sword and prepared to hurl himself at the wyverin, useless though the gesture must be.

"It's going to eat him," Glynnie moaned.

But the wyverin made a crooning sound, touched Benn's forehead with the back of a talon and set him down at the edge of the platform. He scuttled across to the steps, unnoticed, and down into Glynnie's arms.

"Take him down and stay with him," said Rix.

"I don't want to leave you . . . " said Glynnie, clearly torn.

"He's not safe here. Go!"

She went.

As the wyverin turned to Grandys, the line of spines down the back of its neck stood up. It lunged at his face, stopped a yard away and stared at him, eye to eye. Its eyes were watering.

Hmn, hmn, it went. Could it be mocking him?

Grandys let out a hoarse cry and attacked with a flurry of strokes, faster than the eye could see, still holding the canister of king-magery in his left hand and Maloch in his right. The wyverin did not move—it simply took the blows, which cut into its inch-thick scales, though not even Maloch could penetrate to the flesh and bone beneath. Then it snorted, as if in derision—*is that the best you can do?*

It lifted sharply on its wings, the down-draught driving Grandys backwards into the iron railing around the platform. It pinned him there and struck at him with its smallest talon, tearing a shallow gash from his left shoulder to mid-chest. Blood flowed freely. Grandys bared his teeth but did not cry out.

"You'll have to do better than that, my nemesis," he said.

He blasted at it with brute-force magery, attempting to drive it backwards, and fire licked across the scales around its nostrils, though it soon went out.

Pouches on either side of the wyverin's neck inflated and it breathed out a stream of some pungent elemental fluid, red-brown in colour, which caught fire in the air and gave off orange fumes that bleached Grandys' clothing, and his ruddy, exposed skin, white. The fumes etched the iron rails and the metal platform wherever they touched, and puddles of fire formed and flickered there.

But Grandys was no coward. He leapt forward, smashing the wyverin on the end of its snout with the sealed canister, then striking a series of sword blows in quick succession. Again, none did any damage. The wyverin gave him an identical gash, though to his right shoulder.

"It's playing with him," said Rix, forgetting Glynnie had gone.

Grandys attacked in a frenzy and an almighty blow hacked off the last joint of the wyverin's small toe, complete with a talon the length of a sword blade. The wyverin reared up, its second toe striking Grandys under the chin and knocking him over. The tip of its flailing tail slammed into Syrten, who was holding Yulia's body in his arms as if to shield it. The corpse was torn from his grip, went over the rails and bounced off the side of the dome several times before disappearing from view.

Lyf flew into the air and dived away.

Syrten cried, "Yulia!" and ran.

Rix was about to be discovered and there was nothing he could do—he could not get out of the way in time. But Syrten leapt over him, landed on the walkway and thrust through the copper door.

The wyverin shook its injured limb, drops of its dark blood flying through the air and spattering on the platform in plate-sized red-black gouts. It bit a chunk out of the side, propelled itself into the air and raced away, streaming blood. Grandys fell to his knees, dazed. Rufuss dropped onto the platform and dragged on his shredded clothes, looking around furtively as he did.

Rix stared after the beast. It flew low across the fortress, jinked around the main watchtower, then let out an eerie shriek and dived towards the Herovian camp, half a mile outside the gates of Garramide.

"What's it doing?" whispered Glynnie, slipping back into place beside Rix.

"I told you to stay below."

"We've already had that argument."

There was no point persisting. "I'd say it's hoping to feed on a couple of Grandys' battle magians. After such a long sleep its own magery must be exhausted; no wonder it's been so quiet."

"You call *that* quiet?"

"Compared to what it could do, yes."

"Why didn't it eat Lyf or Lirriam or Grandys?"

"No idea. But it'll rest for an hour or two after it feeds—the digestive torpor, it's called."

"How do you know?" said Glynnie.

Rix had to think for a minute. "I read all about wyverin before I started painting Father's portrait. But once it's replenished its magery, Grandys had better look out."

"So should we. I dare say it eats ordinary folk as well."

"I dare say," said Rix. "Now's our chance, while Grandys is down and Lyf isn't here."

CHAPTER 78

Rix leapt onto the platform and went for Grandys, who was still on his knees. Before he could get Maloch into position, Rix's blow knocked the platina canister from his hand and sent it rolling across the floor.

Rix dived for it but Lyf shot out from under the platform with the circlet on his brow and *called* the canister to his hand.

"King-magery, at last!" he exulted.

Rix swore and backed away, into Glynnie. He pulled her down onto the steps.

"What are you doing?" she hissed.

"We can't fight king-magery."

"I already told you that. So what *do* we do?"

"We wait for another chance."

Lyf flew into the air. Grandys attempted to impale him with Maloch but could not reach high enough. Lyf blasted at Grandys and Lirriam, driving them towards the steps. He did not bother with Holm or Tali—perhaps they were irrelevant now.

"Come away!" said Glynnie.

They darted down the steps and around the outside walkway, out of sight, then peered back around the curve of the dome.

Grandys, Lirriam and Rufuss retreated into the dome. Lyf used binding magery on the copper door and stood on the platform, gazing around him and breathing heavily. Errek floated cross-legged in mid-air to his left.

"Lyf's won," said Glynnie. "What's he going to do now?"

"Who knows? I don't think he expected it to be so easy."

Lyf raised the circlet above his head and blasted white flares at the sky in a display that must have been visible for fifty miles.

"It must be a victory message to his people," said Rix.

"Enough play-acting!" said Errek from above. "Do your kingly duty!"

Lyf carefully removed the cap on the canister and put his hand over the top, as if to prevent king-magery from escaping. He nodded to himself and removed his hand, which was outlined with pale green. He paced to the north, south, east and west sides of the platform, each time pointing the circlet out over the land and intoning a five-word phrase in a language Rix did not recognise.

"He's trying to heal the land," said Glynnie.

Three times Lyf repeated his healing, and the words of power. Three times he drew on king-magery, and three times nothing happened. His shoulders slumped; he twisted the cap onto the canister and set it down.

"It's as I've long feared," said Errek.

Lyf stood with head downcast, breathing raggedly, then staggered to the closest railing and slumped over it with his arms hanging down. Great magery takes a great toll, Rix remembered Tobry saying, and sometimes the toll is worse if the magery fails.

"My healing gift is gone," said Lyf.

"Why do you think that might be?" said Errek, the way a master might speak to an errant pupil.

"I broke the kings' commandments."

"And?"

"I debauched my healing gift into the evil art of *germine*, in order to create shifters and poxes that had never been seen before."

"And?"

"I twisted the perfection that was alchymie into a foul art devoted solely to weapons of war."

"And?"

"Isn't that enough?" Lyf cried.

"It's far more than enough," said Errek, "but is it all you have to confess?"

"I used my sacred art to create magical ebony pearls inside the heads of innocent Pale girls, and when the pearls were mature I tasked my agents to hack the pearls out so I could get king-magery back."

"And?"

"I even corrupted my own people after I sent them underground—"

Lyf conjured his crutches from wherever he had left them and stumped around the platform, swerving to avoid a puddle of wyverin blood. He stood looking down at it, his fingers clenching and unclenching.

"You began well," said Errek. "You gave your people the Books of the Solaces—survival manuals written out of love and compassion. Books to show them how to rise again, after they'd lost the Two Hundred and Fifty Years War and the enemy's work camps had turned them into debased and despicable *degradoes*."

"Don't try to comfort me—I don't deserve it. Even as I began the first book of the Solaces I had the last in mind—the iron book. *The Consolation of Vengeance*."

"It's gone, Lyf. Mad Wil melted it down. It's as if it never was."

"But not its consequences. The book created Mad Wil," Lyf said bitterly, "and sent him on his murderous quest all the way down to the Engine. And there he interfered with the Engine, which is now desperately out of balance and getting worse all the time—*and I can't heal it*."

Lyf sat on a crumpled piece of copper sheeting and took off the circlet. "This crown seems a lot heavier than it used to."

"Platina is a heavy metal. One of the heaviest."

"I didn't mean heavy in that sense."

Lyf set it on the platform beside him and rubbed his eyes.

"A king who's lost his healing gift is no king at all, and now I've roused the wyverin for nothing. Have I brought about the doom of my land, *and* my people?"

Errek looked in the direction the wyverin had flown. "I . . . don't . . . know."

"Perhaps it's time for *me* to be unmade."

Lightning sizzled through the open side of the dome and struck the rail beside Lyf, sending him tumbling, his crutches going in one direction and the circlet in another. Grandys burst through the copper door and exploded up the steps. Lyf came to his knees and tried to strike back, but without the circlet he could not command king-magery, and without king-magery he could not defend himself.

Errek soared after the circlet. Grandys snatched it from his feeble grip and threw himself onto the canister of king-magery, landing so hard that it drove the breath from his lungs. He lay on it for a few seconds, winded, then rose with both the canister and the circlet in his left hand. He raised Maloch and advanced on Lyf, who was still on his knees.

Lyf did not move. He looked as though he wanted to die and put an end to the nightmare.

Errek rose ten feet in the air and let out a high-pitched call of "Grolik?" then extended an arm down and heaved Lyf off his feet.

Air whistled over leathery wings as the gauntling raced across the rooftops and banked around the side of the dome. As Grandys prepared to blast Lyf down, Grolik caught Lyf in her teeth and carried him away, swinging back and forth like a ragdoll, towards Turgur Thross.

Lirriam slipped out through the copper door. Rix edged backwards out of sight.

"This is worse than Lyf getting it," he said. "Unimaginably worse."

"And only you and I to stop Grandys," said Glynnie. "Shh! Someone else's coming."

The lead-footed tread was unmistakable. Syrten came lumbering after Lirriam, carrying Yulia's cloth-shrouded form in his arms. Judging by her shape, the fall had broken her. He sat on the crumpled copper sheet Lyf had perched on earlier, then uncovered Yulia's face and gazed longingly, desperately at her.

Grandys, despite his triumph, was surveying the sky anxiously. The clouds had thickened; now it began to rain.

"The wyverin is feeding on your battle magians," said Lirriam, "but once it's replenished its gift it'll come back, and the last of the line of Herox will be consumed by his bastardised creation, just as it ate the first—Herox himself."

"The ancients were always spouting dire prophecies," said Grandys. "Most of them never came true."

"No one believes this one more strongly than you do." Her white teeth flashed in the gloom. "You know it's your doom, Grandys."

"Bah!" He turned to Syrten. "Guard the stairs. I'll watch the sky."

The rain grew heavier, fat drops splashing on Yulia's face until it looked as though she was weeping. Syrten laid her body down carefully, covered her face and rose, wincing. His right hand went to his ribs, the thick fingers probing along them. The ribs moved in and out.

"That blow from the wyverin's tail must have broken a rib or two," Rix said quietly.

"Good!" said Glynnie. "Syrten acts docile, but he's as bad as any of them."

"Their injuries don't weaken them nearly as much as king-magery strengthens them."

"And Lirriam is unharmed."

"Yes, Lirriam," said Rix, staring at her.

"Keep your eyes off her. You're mine!"

Rix grinned. "I'm trying to work her out. What's she up to?"

Glynnie did not reply. She was looking at Holm, who had swathed Tali in a blanket. Her eyes were closed and she was shivering fitfully. Holm bent over her.

"Tali's alive!" said Glynnie.

"But she doesn't look well," said Rix.

Grandys, still wearing the circlet and swinging the canister, was walking around the platform, looking down.

"What's he after?" said Rix.

Grandys bent, probed with the tip of his sword and heaved something out from behind a stone bench—the wyverin's severed little toe, complete with talon. He picked it up, sat on the bench and peeled the leathery skin off. After scraping the inside of the skin he laid it aside, rested the three-foot-long talon across his knee and began to carve it into a curved blade with Maloch.

"He's making a sword," said Glynnie.

"Why?" Rix said absently. "He's already got the best sword there is."

"Maybe it's a way to assert his power over the wyverin."

"Or to convince himself that he can."

Grandys completed his work, wiped the talon blade down and shook it at the empty sky. "Come on, beast! Do your worst!"

"You weren't so bold when its face was in yours," said Lirriam.

"I admit it," said Grandys, uncharacteristically. "My dread of the creature almost overwhelmed me."

"When it returns, so will your naked, shivering terror."

"Fear can be useful. I'm using it to strengthen myself for the endgame."

"What, *here?*"

"Of course not—I've had the perfect location in mind for months."

"Where?" she said curiously.

"We're going underground to our camp so I can collect the *seven* items, the *seventeen*, and the *ninety-seven*."

"And?"

"Then we're going to Touchstone Peak."

"But that's a sacred Cythian site," said Lirriam.

"Yes it is."

"Why there?"

"It's where the circlet was first worn, ten thousand years ago, when king-magery was cast for the very first time. To the enemy, it's the most holy place in all the land."

"And you're planning to profane it with the Three Spells."

Grandys smiled.

CHAPTER 79

After a furious ride across the plateau in heavy rain, held in Holm's arms, Tali's head was a mass of pain and she could feel cold blood running down behind her ear. The stitching must have torn, but she was too ill to care.

She felt strangely empty. Though she had come to hate the master pearl, and though she had often cursed it and longed for it to be gone, she felt lost without it. Grandys had robbed her of the very thing to which she owed her identity.

The four Heroes and their twenty guards bypassed Turgur Thross, continued through thick forest for a mile or more beyond the plateau in increasingly rugged country, then rode across a patch of grassland to the top of a rocky hill. Directly ahead, set in a field of standing stones, stood Touchstone Peak, a rain-drenched blade of hard black chert that rose almost sheer for four hundred feet to a trio of narrow, hand-cut platforms, and the bowl-shaped tip above them. Beyond, untouched rainforest stretched over the hills to the east until it blurred into the distance.

The lower platform was on the south side of Touchstone, the middle platform on the west and the highest platform faced east. Steep steps, carved into the resistant rock long ago, wound up to the platforms, though they were covered in moss, lichen and ferns and would be treacherous to negotiate.

Grandys set out his guards among the standing stones and ordered them to defend the way up. "But not too vigorously," he added.

"I don't understand, Lord Grandys," said the captain of his guards.

"All ends on Touchstone," said Grandys. "But for it to end the right way, captain, the main players must reach the top, because I need something from each of them. When Rixium comes, defend vigorously so he won't become suspicious—*then let him fight his way through*."

Syrten laid the wrapped bundle that was Yulia's body down against the base of Touchstone, where there was a modicum of shelter from wind and rain, and slumped beside it, desolation in his eyes. Lirriam took Tali from Holm's arms and laid her beside the body. Holm dismounted stiffly and Lirriam bound his wrists.

"What is this place?" said Tali.

"The earliest alchymical works in Cythe were on Touchstone," said Holm. He managed the ghost of a smile. "Errek First-King built them. How are you feeling?"

"Lost," said Tali dismally.

"Because your pearl is gone?"

"Yes."

"It was surprisingly small," said Holm. "Not much bigger than a pea."

"I should be glad to be rid of it. From the moment it woke, on my eighteenth birthday, it gave me terrible headaches. And lately it's felt like a grenado inside my head, one that could burst and kill me at any time. I've wanted to get rid of it for months, yet now it's gone I feel empty; robbed."

"It stands to reason, after such trauma—"

"No, I feel ... *reduced*. As though I've lost a vital part of myself; my very core. I don't know how I'm going to get by without it."

"How are you otherwise?"

"So weak I doubt I could sit up. Did you have to cut such a huge crater in my skull?"

"It's less than an inch across, and I fixed the bone back in place before I stitched you up."

"An inch is a hell of a lot bigger than a pea."

"Would you have sooner I went too close, and broke the master pearl?" he said mildly.

"The way my head feels, death seems like an attractive alternative." She rubbed her face, limply. Her fingers were as weak as rubber. "Sorry to be so crabby."

He put his bound hands on her shoulder. "If you were cheerful after that operation I'd be really worried."

"What does he want from us? I assumed, after Grandys got the pearl ... "

"That he'd have us killed? So did I, but he needs you for something—and me to keep you alive."

From the pack horses, Grandys lifted down a small, ice-covered chest, a large and immensely heavy crate, and the cabinet Tali had seen when he'd held her prisoner weeks ago.

"Take the chest and crate up to the lowest platform," he said to Syrten and Rufuss.

Syrten stared at Grandys blankly, then hefted the crate as though it were a matchbox and headed up. Grandys took the cabinet and Rufuss the ice chest, one-handed.

"What—what's Grandys going to do up there?" Tali said to Lirriam.

Lirriam took out *Incarnate* and polished it, but did not reply. She climbed a few dozen steps up Touchstone and stood there for a few minutes, looking back the way they had come, before strolling down again.

"Rix will come after us," said Tali.

"That's Grandys' intention," said Lirriam. "Everything ends at Touchstone."

"It might not be the ending you expect," Tali said feebly.

"You have no idea what I expect."

Tali lacked the strength for any further verbal jousting. She closed her eyes and endured the throbbing pain as best she could. Time went blank; she was barely aware of Grandys and Syrten returning, or of Syrten picking her up, though she felt each step of the climb as a spike through the top of her skull, *thud, thud, thud* . . .

"She's fading," said Grandys.

Tali tried to open her eyes but they were too heavy. The air was colder here, and it was windy. She felt that they were high up on Touchstone.

"People die all the time," said Lirriam.

"To bait the trap, I may yet need her. Do a partial healing, just in case."

"It's harder to do a partial healing than a full healing."

"I don't want her fully healed—she's caused me too much trouble already."

"The strain of a partial healing could kill her."

"So could doing nothing!" Grandys snapped. "I need her alive until I've finished the Three Spells. Then you can heave her over the side for all I care."

"I'll leave that to you. It's more your style."

Tali's bandages were removed. She felt the cold wind on her freshly shaven head, and a flurry of raindrops. Lirriam's fingertips touched her all around the circular wound. She did not touch the wound itself, though the slight pressure was enough to cause Tali more splintery pain. She would have given almost anything to be free of it. Dying began to seem like a good way out—

No! It came from her subconscious, fiercely. Her oath had not been fulfilled. Justice had not been done. Lyf had not paid.

"A remarkable job," came Lirriam's voice, as if from a long way away. "You have a fine hand for an old man. And a good eye."

"I once thought being a surgeon was the most vital job of all," said Holm. "Until I made my fatal mistake."

The chilly fingertips worked outwards from the wound and the pain eased a little. Tali felt a sudden urge to throw up. A bowl was held to her lips. She heaved into it. Her mouth was wiped with a wet rag and Lirriam's fingers resumed their gentle probing.

"Only one?" Lirriam said to Holm. "No matter how good the surgeon is, a proportion of his patients will die."

"My mistake was too grave," said Holm. "I could not risk another."

"How many died because of that decision?"

"I don't follow you," Holm grated.

Tali felt another bout of nausea, not as strong this time. She managed to hold it down.

"How many people, condemned to second-rate surgeons because you refused to use your great gift, died from their butchery?" said Lirriam.

"The question is immaterial," said Holm.

"On the contrary, it cuts to the very meaning of life. You shaped your own life to avoid a risk which, had you learned from your mistake, is unlikely to have recurred. In doing so, you probably cost hundreds of people their lives."

"One could use that argument to justify almost anything."

"Everything comes at a cost, surgeon. Choosing to follow a course, or choosing not to. Offering people in need the benefit of your great skills, *or denying them*."

Tali heard Holm rise and move away, his footsteps agitated. She felt a little stronger and managed to open her eyes.

"Can you sit up?" said Lirriam.

Tali could not bear to think about moving. "No."

Lirriam sat her upright. Tali's head spun. The pain jagged through her head, though not unbearably, and to her surprise she found that she could remain in the sitting position.

"Thank you," she whispered.

Lirriam gave her an enigmatic smile. "Grandys isn't keeping you alive for your health."

"And you? What about you?"

"Place no reliance on my good offices. In my own way, I'm almost as corrupt as he is. *Almost*."

Lirriam seemed to consider that thought, her full lips pursed, then walked across to the edge of the platform and stood there, looking down. Tali studied her lush figure for a moment, so different from her own petite, reed-slender frame.

Grandys was down the other end of the platform, bent over the crate. Tali could not see Rufuss or Syrten.

"Where are we?" she said to Holm.

"On the third-highest platform of Touchstone."

It was shaped like a wedge, about twenty yards by six, straight at the back and cliff-bounded, slightly curved along the sheer outer edge. Water streamed down the cliff from the constant rain and trickled across the platform in a dozen places, before tumbling over.

Two-thirds of the way along, where the wedge was widest, a circle of rock two yards across was raised the height of a step. Tali saw faint black traces on top, as if it had been used for burning. Behind it stood a white stone arch, ten feet high and covered in moss up to a height of three feet.

"It's said," said Holm, "though no one knows if it's true, that this open hearth was used by Errek when he first cast king-magery to heal the land. It was certainly used by the Cythian kings and queens for thousands of years. And now Grandys is planning to debauch it."

Grandys, limping badly, lugged the crate up and put it down beside the hearth. He unpacked seven pieces of cut stone, each a different type of rock, and each with mortar clinging to them. He began to stack the pieces on the open hearth, naming them as he did so.

"This piece of basalt comes from the altar in Lyf's temple. This slab of granite once formed part of the threshold of the Great Library at Lammum, which I personally burned at the beginning of the Two Hundred and Fifty Years War. This marble moulding was taken from the Lady's bathroom in the palace latterly known as Palace Ricinus ... "

Tali tuned him out. "The Three Spells are meant to tear Hightspall apart," she said to Holm, "so the Heroes can recreate it as their Promised Realm. But what does that actually mean? Will the spells tear the very land down—mountains and valleys, rivers and lakes—and rebuild it?"

"I wouldn't think any spell, or set of spells, could do that."

"Then what?"

"I believe the Three Spells are intended to tear down the *civilisation* of Hightspall. To erase everything our people, and the Cythonians, have done here. To create a *tabula rasa*, if you will, on which the Heroes can build the homeland they so yearn for."

"Is there any way to stop him?" she said quietly.

Holm mutely held up his bound hands. Tali had seen him trying to free himself, though thus far his bonds had resisted all efforts.

"Rix is following," said Holm, "with a company of mounted men."

Tali looked south, but mist shrouded the distance and from where she was sitting she could not make out Turgur Thross, much less Garramide. "How did he get past Grandys' army?"

"It scattered when the wyverin went hunting Grandys' battle magians, and his troops are afraid to come back together."

"So the siege is over."

"Unless Grandys succeeds with his spells."

"Where is the wyverin, then?"

Holm shrugged. "I dare say it'll return once it's digested its prey—and bolstered its own magery enough to resume the attack."

"And Lyf?"

"This is the battle he's been preparing for all his life. He'll be back."

"What can he do? He's lost king-magery, and the pearls are dying."

"His greatest weapon is still loose, and it's Grandys' nemesis. I'll bet you Lyf turns up the moment the wyverin goes for Grandys. It'll be his chance to take back king-magery—to literally snatch victory from the jaws of Grandys' defeat . . ."

"Now he has the power of king-magery, Grandys might be able to defeat the wyverin as well."

"He very well might," Holm said heavily.

Grandys looked up at Holm. "There's no *might* about it."

He completed his stack at the hearth, walked to the edge where he had the best view of the sky, and looked up. His left hand slipped to the talon blade, which he carried in a crude sheath of wyverin skin. Tali assumed he must have made it on the ride to Touchstone.

The rain grew heavier. Syrten was sitting with his back to the cliff, holding Yulia's shrouded body and crooning to her. Water ran down his back and puddled all around him but he was oblivious. Tali wondered if he had lost his wits with grief.

Rufuss stood at the narrow end of the platform with his black cloak wrapped around his shredded clothes, staring into the rain-pregnant clouds. He was so still that he might have been carved from the same chert as Touchstone itself. Every so often he glanced Tali's way and she saw that his utter hatred of her had not abated. He had wanted to kill her when he took her prisoner after the great quake, and subsequently she had humiliated him. Now he ached for her life; he burned to take it. She shivered and looked away.

Lirriam sat on a lump of rock, beneath a ledge that sheltered her from the rain, surreptitiously stroking *Incarnate* with the master pearl Grandys had discarded, gliding the pearl just above the surface of the black stone.

"Wake," she whispered. "Wake properly."

"It's been dead for twelve millennia," said Grandys. "You'll never wake it."

But every so often Tali caught a faint red radiance within *Incarnate*, the same radiance she had seen there before her escape from Castle Swire. She shuddered; it seemed even darker and more dire than it had then. What would it be like if it did wake properly?

The red radiance caught and grew, and momentarily *Incarnate* was alight with crimson. Lirriam studied it from all sides, smiling that chilling smile. Then, evidently satisfied that, if not fully woken, at least it was on the way, she touched the stone with a fingertip and the crimson retreated until it was no more than a spark at the centre.

The last patches of ebony lustre faded; the master pearl was now a creamy white.

"Dead!" she said. She tossed it into the nearest puddle and returned to her study of *Incarnate*.

Tali stared at the tiny pearl, hating it; longing for it. Holm picked it up, rolled it around in the palm of his hand and handed it to her.

"It may not be quite dead to its rightful owner," he said out of the corner of his mouth.

Tali held it up to the light, marvelling that something so small could have changed the world, and caused her so much grief and pain. She had not seen it before—she had fallen unconscious the moment Holm removed it from her head. The surface was lustrous, the colour rich cream now but with the faintest hint of blue.

Could Holm be right? She sensed something lingering within it; a tiny wisp of magery. But even if she could draw on it, how could it be of any use against the vast power Axil Grandys commanded?

Tali tried to imagine how she might draw on it, but at the thought pain speared through her head, as if someone had shoved a jagged piece of metal down through the hole in her skull. She would have fallen on her face had Holm not caught her.

"You must have a death wish," said Lirriam, stroking *Incarnate* with her fingertips.

"We begin!" Grandys announced.

"The hour starts now, Grandys," said Lirriam, putting *Incarnate* away and rising. "One hour for all three spells, and not a minute more."

Syrten set Yulia's body down in the shelter of the overhang and went to the hearth. Rufuss stood beside him and Lirriam on the other side. Grandys was at the edge of the precipice again, looking down.

"Rixium and his guards have reached the base of Touchstone," he said conversationally. "But take no comfort from that, Tali; I've lured him here. He'll fight his way up just in time to go blindly to the fate prepared for him."

"Rix isn't a fool," Tali said hotly. "He knows you've set a trap."

"But he's so hungry to beat me, he believes every little victory comes from his own cleverness."

"Why take the risk?" she wondered. "With king-magery you could wipe him away from here."

"The whole point of fighting is to pit yourself against your

enemies, face to face and hand to hand," said Grandys. "To blast your
enemy down from a distance, to kill without giving him the chance
to kill you, is the action of a cowardly cur, and I'll have no part of it."

He straightened the circlet on his head, made sure the canister of
king-magery was close by, then cracked the seals on the first of three
short tubes he held in his hand. It appeared to have been hollowed
out of pale stone. The second tube was either leather or thick parchment, while the third was made from a red metal much darker than
copper.

"These spells," Grandys said in an elevated tone, "were created by
Eluciman, the second greatest Heroxian magian of all—"

"Second in infamy only to Herox himself," murmured Lirriam.
"The very same Herox who was the wyverin's first victim—as you
will be its last."

"By Eluciman," Grandys repeated irritably, "in impossibly
ancient times, in order to cleanse the tainted land so we can remake
it into our Promised Realm, as stated in this, our *Immortal Text*."

He held the parchment up, its edges fluttering in the wind. A
flurry of raindrops darkened it. He held it out of the rain and strode
to the open hearth.

"King-magery is a healing force," said Holm. "Using it for
destructive purposes must tip the balance beyond the point of
return. If you do this, the land can't ever be healed."

Grandys knocked him down with a casual backhander. He
twisted the cap off the stone tube and shook it in the air. Nothing
fell out, though scintillating glyphs appeared in the air below. Tali
could not read them.

"Stonespell," said Grandys.

Drawing on the full force of king-magery, he spoke the incomprehensible glyphs in a deep, booming voice. After several seconds,
a creeping yellow stain formed on the edges of the mortar holding
the stones on the hearth together. It ate the mortar away, the stack
collapsed, and the slender white arch behind the hearth cracked and
toppled.

"As on this hearth, so too throughout the land of Hightspall,"
said Grandys. "Every mortared stone laid by our enemies will
tumble . . . until all their works have fallen."

Tali caught a whiff of something unidentifiable but pungent, and felt a series of distant shudders, transmitted through the rock to Touchstone. Had every building in Hightspall come down? Had Garramide? And this was only the first spell.

Grandys' arm was shaking but he kept it extended, holding the spell for several minutes, before staggering sideways and falling to one knee. His head drooped. He remained that way for another half minute before slowly raising his head.

Lirriam let out a harsh caw of laughter. "Well done, *old man*!"

In the few minutes Grandys had held Stonespell, it had aged him. Half his remaining opal armour had lost colour and flaked off, revealing saggy, sallow skin beneath. Tali could not believe it was the same man who had stood proudly naked before his troops only yesterday.

"Why has it aged him so?" she asked Holm.

"Mighty spells take a mighty toll. And he powered Stonespell by corrupting king-magery—by using healing magery for a destructive purpose."

"Are you sure your lifetime is long enough to cast the Three Spells, Grandys?" said Lirriam.

She wore *Incarnate* openly now. The crimson flame inside it was flaring and fading in a steady rhythm that suggested it matched her own heartbeat. Her eyes reflected the colour, almost as if she had taken its power within her.

"I—can—do—it," said Grandys, with an all-out effort.

"Then lead on!" she said ringingly.

CHAPTER 80

Tali felt strong enough to stand unaided now, though Grandys was taking no chances. He ordered Syrten to carry her up to the next platform, the second highest on Touchstone.

The mist had thickened and she could no longer see all the way down. Considering the steepness of the wet, mossy steps and her own fear of heights, this was a blessing. By the time they reached the second platform it was raining heavily and a keen easterly wind was driving it into their faces.

Syrten put Tali down under an overhang shaped to keep out the worst of the rain. He turned and plodded down again, for Yulia's body, Tali presumed. Holm came up, panting, and crouched beside her.

Grandys set down the cabinet and put the *Immortal Text* and his spell tubes in a dry, half-domed niche behind a rusty cast-iron furnace. It was five feet high, with a side door and a sinuous chimney with a cap at the top to keep out the rain.

From the cabinet he took seventeen written artefacts, one after another. Tali had seen many of them before, when she had been held in Bastion Barr. There were scrolls, books, an etching or engraving, the blueprint of a complicated device that might have been a pump, two musical scores, a map showing the depths of Lake Fumerous, an illuminated manuscript, and other items on paper, parchment and wooden panels.

Grandys barely glanced at each item before casting it into the fire box. He did not name the items, though Tali felt sure they were treasures that could never be replaced.

"You're too slow, old man," said Lirriam. "The Three Spells must *all* be cast within the hour."

He scowled, took a backwards step when he saw that she was openly fingering *Incarnate*, and cast in the last items.

From below, Tali could hear the clash of weapons. She exchanged glances with Holm. Rix could not hope to defeat a man who had king-magery at his fingertips. Unless she did something to help him, he would fall into Grandys' trap.

Her questing gaze fell on Yulia's long face, forever fixed in despair.

"Why did she kill herself?" Tali said quietly.

"Lirriam and Grandys were talking about it on the ride here," said Holm. "Yulia used an ebony pearl to read something concealed in the *Immortal Text*, then took poison and died with the *Text* beside her."

"What did it say?"

"I don't know."

Yulia had been the noblest and most decent of the Heroes. For her to take her own life, when the Heroes were on the brink of achieving their two-thousand-year-old goal, what she had read must have been shattering.

But was it worth risking the tiny hope Tali had left? Yes, she thought. It's too late to hold back now. If Yulia's secret could possibly help Rix, she had to go after it.

Grandys was occupied at the furnace, Syrten oblivious in his grief. Rufuss stood on the brink again and Lirriam was peering into *Incarnate*, her face lit eerily by its pulsing light.

Tali touched the master pearl in her pocket and tried to draw on the tiny wisp of power remaining in it. Pain spiked, again and again—cruel, savage pain. She forced herself to endure it, took a wisp of power from the master pearl and drew the coiled *Immortal Text* to her, just above the ground so it would not be noticed. The pain grew worse. She clenched her teeth, caught the coil of parchment and unrolled it in her lap, and read.

The *Immortal Text* was a xenophobic rant about the superiority of Herovians in all things. It exhorted them to cleanse the land of its foul taint, with the Three Spells, so they could recreate it as their Promised Realm.

All this she had long known. She skimmed to the end and turned the parchment over. The other side was blank. She turned it back and forth. There had to be more. She touched the master pearl to the parchment and writing appeared on the back.

I, Neverio Bunce, forged this parchment at Hierarch Virch's behest, to send you Herovian pigs on a wild-goose chase to the far side of the world. You're gullible fools all, desperate to believe you're a chosen race . . . when in fact you spring from hereditary serfs.

The physical qualities that epitomise your Herovian race, of which you're so inordinately proud, came from our selective breeding of your serf ancestors—like prize pigs.

Don't come back, swine!

Tali let out a snort of laughter. Grandys spun around; the Heroes' eyes were all on her, and the parchment in her hand.

"It's a forgery," said Tali. "That's why Yulia killed herself."

Syrten howled and drove his armoured fist six inches into the black, obdurate chert. Grandys sprang forward and snatched the *Immortal Text* from her hand.

"How dare you impugn the sacred text!" He raised his own fist as if to punch her head from her shoulders.

"Stop!" cried Lirriam. Grandys stopped. "Explain yourself, Tali," Lirriam said coldly.

"The scroll is signed on the back in secret writing," said Tali, "but it can be read with an ebony pearl. The parchment was forged on behalf of Hierarch Virch. Who was he?"

"*She*," said Lirriam. "Layla Virch was our greatest foe, back in Thanneron."

The three Heroes advanced on Grandys. Lirriam handed him one of the ebony pearls he had previously discarded. They each touched the pearl and Grandys held the back of the parchment up so they could read it.

"Well?" he said when Syrten's opal encrusted lips had stopped moving. "Are we agreed?"

Lirriam jerked her head at the furnace. Grandys tore the *Immortal Text* into shreds and cast it in.

"I *will not* accept that my life's work was based on a lie," he said in a low voice that belied his monumental fury. "How our enemies must have sneered as we left Thanneron on the First Fleet—but they were wrong. Their foul lie only reinforces a deeper truth. *We are noble!*" he thundered. "Far nobler than the highest and greatest nobles of Thanneron."

"How can you say that when your ancestors were serfs?" said Tali.

Grandys took a deep breath, as if to reveal something that had never been said before. Perhaps he felt a need to convince her of his truth.

"Before we were enslaved, we Herovians—originally Heroxians—came to this world from another place. A place beyond a thousand stars."

Tali gaped.

"And I'm a direct descendant of the incomparable Herox, the leader of Clan Herox," said Grandys, "before whom the greatest nobles of Thanneron stand as base-born scum."

He drew Maloch and brandished it at the sky. "We came from another world, searching, even then, for our Promised Realm. But we did not find it; we ended up in vile Thanneron, naked and defenceless. We were taken into bondage there and ever after persecuted . . . yet we never forgot where we came from, nor what we were looking for. We *will* have our Promised Realm."

"We *are* chosen," said Lirriam, standing with him for once. "And this is the proof." She held up *Incarnate*. "The stone died when our ancestors went astray on the way to this world. Now I've begun to bring *Incarnate* back to life, we can find our true path."

Tali's revelation had backfired. It had only made them all the more determined.

"The *Text* may be a fake," said Lirriam, "but the Three Spells are not. You have the power, Grandys. Use it! Time is running out."

Grandys turned to the furnace, jerked the cap off the parchment tube and shook it in the air. A different set of glyphs appeared, black outlined in red, like paper charring without ever catching alight.

"Writspell!" he intoned. "To burn every written work of Cythe, Cython and Hightspall to ashes, and erase all evidence of their decadent civilisations."

As he prepared to read the spell, Rix burst up onto the platform, followed by Glynnie, who was carrying a rolled canvas. Grandys blasted at Rix but missed, perhaps deliberately. Glynnie held onto one end of the canvas and threw the rest forward so it unrolled across the black rock. Every eye turned to the canvas, which had changed again.

Grandys let out a gasp.

No one moved for a few seconds. The fallen warrior was the image of Axil Grandys now, even to the places where his opal armour had broken away, and the wounds the wyverin had inflicted on each shoulder.

The painted Grandys was looking up in terror as the wyverin lunged at his middle and tore out glistening loops of intestine. The real Grandys looked down at his image, his mouth hanging open. Several biscuit-sized chunks of opal flaked off him.

He stooped and, with a furious wrench, tore the canvas across. He stuffed it through the side door of the furnace, kicked it shut and stood there, his chest heaving. Glynnie and Rix were creeping back towards the steps. Grandys blasted at Glynnie; Rix took the blast on the flat of his sword, which glowed yellow, then dragged Glynnie down the steps out of sight.

"You're dead," Grandys roared, running after them.

Lirriam caught him by the arm. She must have been far stronger than she looked, for she held him. He whirled, raising his fist.

"You also need Rix for the endgame," said Lirriam. "Besides, there's no time!"

"What?" he said, shaking his head dazedly.

"The Three Spells must be cast within the hour or Bloodspell fails."

"Yes," he said. "Yes, of course."

Reaching skywards, he read the glyphs of Writspell that were still hanging in the air, and cast the spell to burn all written evidence of the greatness of Cythe, Hightspall and Cython away.

The contents of the furnace ignited in a great conflagration. The cast-iron walls cracked and it fell into three pieces. A howling wind scattered the ashes, revealing a white outline burned deep into the black rock—the wyverin devouring Grandys.

He cried out and blasted away the top foot of rock. The outline was still visible.

"Up!" he roared. "To the topmost platform. The Third Spell will prove all."

"Bloodspell!" said Lirriam.

CHAPTER 81

In the middle of the highest platform stood a basalt crucible the size of a cauldron, coated in moss inside and out. Syrten dumped Tali beside the crucible and ran down again. His devotion to Yulia's corpse was beginning to make her uneasy.

This platform was an egg-shaped cut-out facing east that took the full force of the wind and rain. Behind it the peak was reduced to a thin crescent, up the crest of which the steps ran for another twenty feet to the bowl-shaped tip of Touchstone. It was barely visible through the wind-churned mist that kept opening to reveal the forested hills, only to close them off again.

Every surface up here was covered in emerald moss, as deep as a carpet, interspersed with waving strands of feathery grey lichen as long as Tali's hand. A single small, wind-twisted tree grew from a crack in the rocks near the brink.

The wind sighed, whispered, howled, screeched. The rain was torrential and blown almost horizontal. She was soaked through, miserably cold and feeling worse all the time. Lirriam's partial healing was already failing, probably because Tali had used the master pearl.

What was the basalt crucible for? And why had Grandys brought her here for the endgame? Was she to be a blood sacrifice?

Holm, noticing that she was shivering, took off his coat.

"You need it just as much as I do," said Tali.

"Because I'm old?"

"You've lost weight in captivity. You were never thin before."

"I've often been thin before. I also spent years on my boat, working out at sea in all kinds of miserable weather, but *I've* never been stuck out in driving rain after some old fool cut a hole in my head." He wrapped his woollen coat around her and put his cap on her head. "Wool keeps you warm even when it's wet."

"Thank you." She pulled the coat around her. "That's much better."

Grandys scanned the sky again. He was doing it all the time now, not that he would have seen his nemesis in this weather if it had been ten yards away. He set down the ice chest, which was inches thick in ice. The rain slicked the surface and froze into another layer, and another.

After tipping the water out of the crucible, he blasted fire into it, burning the moss to ash which he scrubbed out with his thick fingers.

"Stand there," he said to Syrten, indicating a point two feet east of the crucible.

Syrten did so, his massive body shielding it from the rain.

Grandys thumped the top of the ice chest with a fist, cracking the ice. He picked it off and opened the chest. Frigid mist drifted out. He lifted out the racks containing the phials of frozen blood, stood them on the mossy ground and bathed them in a warming yellow radiance created via king-magery.

He counted them. "Ninety-seven."

"Get on with it," said Lirriam. She seemed more anxious than he was.

"The Third Spell must be cast within the hour," said Grandys, "but it must be cast right. The blood must be thawed gently—too much heat would cook it and the spell would fail."

He picked up a phial, inspected it, and snapped his fingers. The yellow radiance went out.

"One—the chancellor," he said, reading the label, and poured the blood into the crucible. It was thin and watery.

"Two—General Libbens," he said as he emptied the second phial.

He kept on, naming each involuntary donor, most of them the great people of Hightspall and Cython. General Rochlis, Lyf's most brilliant and Castle Rebroff, was followed by a list of names she did not know.

"Ninety-four, Surgeon Holm. Ninety-five, Rixium Ricinus, known as Deadhand. Ninety-six, Glynnie, a doughty maidservant."

Grandys poured the contents of the three phials in together and scanned the sky again. Tali wondered how he had obtained Rix's and Glynnie's blood. He must have taken it when Rix had been under his thrall and he had held Glynnie captive, months ago.

Tali's heart was beating erratically; her head wound throbbed mercilessly. Her blood was next. Lirriam was on her feet beside Syrten, watching Grandys' every movement. Rufuss stood behind Lirriam and Syrten, tall enough to look over their heads. He was staring blackly at Tali's throat as though he longed to close his bony fingers around it and squeeze the life out of her. And she knew he did.

"If Rix is going to attack, he's got to do it now," Tali said softly to Holm. "If he waits any longer he'll be too late."

"He can't take on king-magery with just a sword. He'll be waiting for the wyverin to attack."

"I wish it would hurry up."

"I'm not sure I do," Holm said darkly.

"Why not?"

"It's more than twice the length of this rock platform. If it attacks Grandys here it's liable to crush us all to jelly."

"Ninety-seven," said Grandys. "Thalalie vi Torgrist, known as Tali." He met her eyes and smiled thinly. "Her blood is special and magical because it's been bathing the master pearl all this time."

He poured it in, a long, crimson stream, as rich as the light that glowed inside *Incarnate*. The bottom of the great crucible was now inch-deep in blood.

"It's up to us. We've got to stop him casting the third spell," Tali said quietly.

"At any cost?"

"Yes."

Seeing that the Heroes were intent on the crucible, Holm held out his bound hands. Tali touched the master pearl with the hand in her pocket and poked the ropes with a fingertip. They loosened. He moved away, casually.

The rain increased to a deluge. The mist had gone but the sky was a uniform grey. Grandys checked for the wyverin, then set the talon blade on a mossy pedestal as if to warn off his nemesis. After adjusting the circlet he wiped away the water streaming down his face, put the canister down next to the crucible and reached up with both hands.

"Since the *Immortal Text* no longer plays a part in the spell," he said to Tali, "I'm drawing on the power of king-magery to call a mighty fire bolt all the way from the storm clouds above the Vomits."

Holm was edging closer to the cliff behind the crucible. Closer to Grandys. Tali had to keep him talking.

"Why are you telling me this?" she said acidly.

"Just a whim," said Grandys. "The fire bolt will sear the ninety-seven samples of blood to vapour, symbolically and actually erasing all Hightspallers and Cythonians from the land."

Despite Holm's jacket, the cold became icy. Genocide was what she had long feared, though in the beginning she had feared it from Lyf.

"But not Herovians," said Lirriam. "Our blood is different."

"Pure!" said Rufuss.

"Dead!" Syrten said dolefully, gazing at Yulia's face.

It was uncovered and rainwater had puddled in her open eyes. They appeared to be staring up from the bottom of a lake. He reached down and tenderly closed her eyes.

"The Engine is on the brink," said Tali. "If you use king-magery to cast this spell, you could tip it over into catastrophe. It could destroy the land."

Grandys went still, his hands upraised. "There is no Engine at the heart of the land! It's a lie fostered by Lyf to control his sheep-like people."

He looked to Rufuss but evidently saw nothing worthwhile in his mad eyes. Nor in Syrten's downcast eyes. But Lirriam's eyes were shining.

"Risk all to gain all, Grandys," she said passionately. "And if by some mischance it does lead to apocalypse, *let it be a glorious one.*"

Tali had to stop him. She climbed to her feet, slowly and wearily. She swayed there, then reached out to Grandys, trying to hold him back with the scrap of power remaining in the master pearl.

"Get away!" Grandys cried. "Don't come near me."

He kicked her legs from under her, the way a brute might kick a dog, and she fell hard. Grandys shook a set of crimson glyphs from the tube and spoke the words of the spell, carefully enunciating each word.

As he completed the spell and reached up to call the fire bolt down, Holm cast aside his bonds, sprang in behind Grandys and wrenched Maloch from its scabbard. Holm had chosen his moment well. Grandys could not stop him, for he had no option but to complete the spell.

Holm swerved around Grandys and brought the enchanted blade down with all his strength across the stone crucible, cleaving away the right-hand side. The larger part of the crucible tilted to the left, carrying the blood with it. The cut-away section fell down and the fire bolt thundered into the base, shattering it to gravel and grit.

Bloodspell, devoid of blood, failed, and the consequences were brutal.

Grandys shrieked and doubled over. Lirriam clutched at *Incarnate*. Blood spurted from the healed stump of Rufuss's arm. Yulia's eyes sprang open. Syrten let out a glad cry and ran to her, only to wail in desolation when he realised that nothing had changed. She was still dead.

Pain speared through Tali from the top of her skull to the soles of her feet. Holm stood slumped to one side, still holding Maloch, panting. Then Maloch reacted violently, hurling him backwards against the jagged rock face. He screamed, doubled up, but, oddly, did not fall. He hung on the rock, four feet above the ground, and the sword fell from his fingers.

Blood slowly began to seep through the front of his shirt, dripping off something dark protruding halfway down the right side. He had been impaled on a spike of rock.

"Maloch suffers no hand save my own," said Grandys, wheezing a little. He took the sword back.

"I knew that before I took it," said Holm.

"Then you're a brave man and I salute you."

Tali crawled across to Holm.

"Lucky I gave you my coat," he said wryly. "If I'd still been wearing it, it would have been ruined."

Her eyes flooded. "How can you joke?"

"How can I do otherwise?"

She struggled to her knees, her head still pounding mercilessly, and reached up. "I'll try to get you down."

"The spike is the only thing stopping me bleeding to death," said Holm. "If you pull me off it I won't last another minute."

"Then I'll heal you," she said desperately. "There's still some power left in the master pearl."

He laid a weathered hand on her shoulder. "You made your choice in the Pale's rebellion, Tali, and you chose destruction. You can't take it back."

"Then I'll give you my healing blood, as much as it takes."

"Don't waste it. This wound is beyond any healing," said Holm.

"You can't die! Please, tell me what to do."

"There's nothing you can do. Besides," he smiled down at her, sadly and a trifle remotely, "would you deny me the solace I've craved these past thirty-eight years, since my folly cost me my wife and unborn child?"

CHAPTER 82

R ix gestured behind him. Careful now. We're nearly there.

Grandys' guards at the base of Touchstone had fought hard, though not as hard as Rix had expected. It had strengthened his belief that Grandys wanted him to fight his way up to the highest platform of Touchstone—that he needed Rix for the endgame. When Grandys had blasted at them on the second platform, and missed both times, it had confirmed Rix's suspicion.

"What does Grandys need you for?" said Glynnie.

"I don't know. I've been wracking my brain about it for hours."

Rix's plan was much the same as it had been back at the dome: wait for Lyf or the wyverin to come, and hope he could take advantage of the ensuing chaos to bring Grandys down, and save Tali and Holm. And he only had three men left. Plus Glynnie, who had refused to stay behind, and Radl, who had insisted on riding with them to Touchstone.

He peered around the mossy rocks, squinting through the rain. The mist opened to reveal the people at the other end of the topmost platform, then closed again, reducing them to wraith-like shadows.

Rix looked left, and reeled. Holm, who had done so much to support him over the past months, in fearless action and through wise counsel, hung on the stone wall, impaled. His torso was drenched in blood which the rain was washing down his legs in red rivers. He was still alive, though one glance told Rix that nothing could be done to save him.

Tali was on her knees before Holm, her tiny frame swathed in his coat, her shaven head covered by his woolly hat. There was blood on her neck from her head wound. And she looked almost as bad as Holm; deathly bad.

Was this the end for all of them? It seemed probable. The final battle would surely be won with magery, not might, and neither he nor Glynnie had any magery. Nor did Tali, by the look of her.

Rix took Syrten and Rufuss in at a glance. Both were very dangerous, despite their injuries and their fragile mental states. Lirriam sat under the ledge, toying with *Incarnate* as if she were waiting for something. She was more dangerous than either of them, though she had always been enigmatic and Rix could not guess how she would act.

Finally, he assessed his enemy. Grandys was haggard, his opal armour was flaking off, and he appeared to have aged twenty years in the last few hours. Rix could hear every ragged, whistling breath. He felt a tiny surge of hope, but dismissed it. Nothing Grandys said or did, *or appeared to be*, could be trusted. Everything, including his current appearance, could be part of the endgame he had been planning for at least a month.

Grandys swayed, spread his feet to better support himself and peered into the left section of the cloven crucible. "Blood—still there. Can—Bloodspell—be recast?"

"As long as it's within the hour," said Lirriam. "You've got sixteen minutes left."

Tali forced herself to her feet. Rufuss turned on her.

"Can I kill her now, Grandys?"

Lirriam glanced across at the steps. "Rix is here."

Rix ducked down.

Grandys was so exhausted he could not draw enough breath. "That's how—I planned it. Don't kill him—I need him. Just—hold him off—until—"

"But *you* command king-magery," she said.

"Three Spells—more draining than—expected. Must save strength—repeat Bloodspell."

"Syrten!" said Lirriam. "Guard the entrance. Let no one through."

Syrten rose like an automaton, took his sword in his right hand, hefted a war hammer in his left and moved towards the steps.

"Can I kill her?" Rufuss repeated.

"No!" snapped Grandys.

When Rix saw Rufuss turn those black eyes on Tali, the madness was visible from ten yards away. He was cracking, and it looked as though he planned to disobey Grandys and kill Tali anyway. Rix could wait no longer. He had to attack, despite king-magery.

"Now!" he hissed.

He exploded up onto the platform. His three men followed him, then Radl, and Glynnie last.

"Hold them back, Lirriam!" cried Grandys.

"Fourteen minutes!" She continued to stare into the flickering stone.

"Stop them, Syrten!" shouted Grandys. "I can't move until the spell is cast." He raised his arms to the sky again.

Rix had to get to Tali before Rufuss did, but Syrten was blocking the way. Rix ducked a blow from the war hammer that would have smashed his head right off his neck. Syrten must have forgotten Grandys' first order—to not kill Rix—and was obeying his command to stop them, any way he could.

On the other side of the platform, Grandys was slowly intoning the words of Bloodspell, and it was taking all he had. His upraised arms were shaking as if he were holding up a boulder.

Rix parried Syrten's sword thrust and drove the point of his own blade into Syrten's chest. The thick opal armour cracked but absorbed the blow. Syrten blinked and struck again. Rix dived past him, caught Syrten's upraised arm from behind and tried to wrench the hammer from his hand. It did not budge. Though Rix was immensely strong, Syrten was far stronger and his flesh was as hard as stone.

"Out of the way!" Rix cried. If he could not get past, Rufuss was going to kill Tali.

Rix hacked at the side of Syrten's massive neck and this time felt the armour crack. Syrten's head was knocked sideways; a line of blood ebbed out along the crack. He rubbed his neck, more in irritation than pain, and slowly turned.

Rix kicked him in the groin and yelped. It felt as though he had broken his big toe. He retreated. Syrten followed, *thud*, *thud*. Rix's guards attacked Syrten from the sides, though their blows had even less effect than Rix's. He attacked with a flurry of blows but could not get past, and Rufuss was moving ever closer to Tali.

His face was an icy, dripping mask and blood was oozing from his stump. Rufuss slowly raised the five-foot-long blade. Rix fought desperately but knew he could not get there in time.

"Break the master pearl," Holm croaked to Tali.

She was staring at Rufuss's sword as if mesmerised. "What will happen then?"

"Don't know."

Syrten was fast when he got going, Rix realised, but slow to move from a standstill, and he was not agile. The key to beating him was speed and dexterity. Rix ducked left, spun on one foot and dived under Syrten's upraised arm, but too late. Rufuss was beginning his downswing.

Tali raised the master pearl and pointed it at his chest.

"Then let it be destruction," she choked.

Only now did Rufuss realise what she was doing. "No!" he screeched. "Please, not that!"

"I once told you that you'd beg," said Tali.

As he swung the sword at her, she extended her arm towards him, squeezed hard, and the master pearl crumbled like an eggshell. Fire flared all around her hand and fingers, then leapt towards Rufuss. His sword splintered into thousands of tiny, red-hot shards that peppered his face and chest but were concentrated on his middle.

He stood there, open-mouthed, as his middle was enveloped, then concealed, by a cloud of steam. Behind him Grandys, the platform and Yulia's swathed corpse turned red. The steam thinned and there was a hole in Rufuss's middle that Tali could have dived through. He looked down in bewilderment, tried to get to her and even took a step forward, but toppled, smashed his head on the cliff and landed beside her, dead.

Tali crawled out of the way. Her hand was crimson and blistered. She plunged it deep into the wet moss.

Grandys was still struggling to complete Bloodspell, the words coming slowly and hesitantly. Rix turned back to Syrten.

Two Heroes down. Three to go. And Syrten was the toughest.

He had dropped the war hammer and was staring at Yulia's body.

Her white shroud was drenched in the middle with Rufuss's blood and there was blood all over her face. He turned away from Rix, ran and crouched beside her.

"Yulia was everything to him," Lirriam said absently. "They stowed away on the First Fleet together when they were boy and girl, and they've seldom been parted since, even in the eternity of the Abysm. The pain is unbearable and there's only one way to stop it."

She bent over Syrten, put a hand on his head and spoke a word of command. He jerked, looked around and picked up his war hammer. His first blow killed Rix's leading guard. His second sent the next guard tumbling over the side, his third killed the third guard and his fourth grazed Radl's head hard enough to knock her unconscious. He turned towards Rix, a dumb, grief-stricken killing machine.

Was that what Lirriam had meant—that only blood could relieve Syrten's grief. No, it didn't fit what Rix knew of her, or Syrten.

Rix cut him on the shoulder, between the cracks of his armour, and blood flowed freely. Aha, Rix thought. He struck again in the same place and thrust the point in as far as it would go.

Syrten went to raise the war hammer but it fell from his fingers. Rix's thrust must have cut a tendon. He attacked the other shoulder, parrying Syrten's sword blows and aiming his own precisely at the joins in the opal armour. He caught Syrten on the right hip, a driving blow that pierced the join and struck bone.

Syrten stumbled, his guard dropped, and Rix attacked the most vulnerable part of all. He drove his sword in through Syrten's open mouth, all the way to the spine.

Syrten's teeth snapped closed on the blade, which broke off, but it had done its work. He was dead before he hit the ground. But then, he had lost the will to live hours ago. Before Yulia's death he would not have been so easily beaten.

Grandys let out a roar and leapt at Rix, swinging Maloch. Had Bloodspell been cast? The crucible wasn't smoking—he must have abandoned it before the spell was complete. Rix hurled his sword hilt, missed and backpedalled, looking for a weapon. The war hammer was only yards away but only a golem like Syrten could have wielded it.

Grandys backed Rix into a corner and raised Maloch.

"You've fought bravely," he said. "No man has given me as much trouble as you, and I salute you for it. But your fate was sealed the moment you took the bait."

"I knew you needed me here for the endgame," said Rix. "But the matter of my fate is yet to be settled."

"It's about to be."

In the background, Tali was on the verge of collapse. She had done all she could.

"Just you and me now," said Grandys. "It's the way it was meant to be."

"And me," said Glynnie, darting around the mossy rocks, carrying a handful of her throwing knives.

"Stay back!" Rix yelled.

Lirriam raised a hand towards Glynnie, smiling as if she could not take any maidservant seriously, but Glynnie was quicker. Her knife went straight through the muscle of Lirriam's upper right arm, to the hilt, beside the bone. Lirriam gasped and lowered her arm.

Glynnie hurled a second knife at Grandys, followed by a third. Maloch knocked them both aside. Rix dived for Syrten's sword and rose with it in his hand. It was heavier than he was used to but he struck three furious blows at Grandys, one after another.

He almost pierced Grandys' guard with the third blow. Grandys turned at the last second and Syrten's blade snapped against Maloch. Grandys turned on him and Rix knew he was going to die.

"Remember this, Grandys?" shrieked Glynnie. "Remember how I beat you up and made a laughing stock of you?"

She was holding up the nose-shaped piece of opal armour she had broken off Grandys' face months back, when he had been about to drown Rix in the cistern. She put it up to her own small nose, mocking him. It covered half her face.

He let out a bellow of rage. She hurled another knife at him. It missed. Then another, which he caught in his left hand. Glynnie threw her last knife hard and low. It struck him in the left thigh at a spot where the armour had broken off, and went in to the hilt.

He grunted, faltered, then raised the knife he had previously caught. She backpedalled, overbalanced and fell backwards against the small tree on the brink. Rix heard its roots creak and one of them pulled out of the crack. Grandys laughed, then hurled his knife. It buried itself in her right shoulder, pinning her to the trunk.

"Don't move!" cried Rix. "Don't move or you'll go over."

Another root snapped. The tree began to tilt backwards. Rix ran towards her.

Grandys pulled the knife out of his thigh and hurled it into Rix's back.

CHAPTER 83

Rix staggered and fell. He reached around and, with an effort, yanked the knife out from between his lower left ribs. It had gone in more than an inch but had it done serious damage? He could not tell. It was so sharp that he had barely felt it, though the wound was throbbing now and warm blood was ebbing down his back.

He looked from Grandys to Glynnie, weighing the danger. The tree she was pinned to had stopped moving—it wasn't going to topple over the edge right away. Grandys' thigh was bleeding freely though he did not appear to be badly injured. He still had Maloch and he still had king-magery, and if Rix tried to save Glynnie, Grandys was liable to send them both over the side.

Rix couldn't duel Maloch with a knife. He thrust it into his belt and was moving backwards in an arc, trying to reach one of the dead men's swords, when his right hand struck a rocky pedestal and he felt a curved blade that was oddly warm. It was the talon blade, and he had actually felt it! It must have roused his dead hand—the hand with which he had originally painted the wyverin.

Considering how often he had painted and sketched the creature, and how many times he'd dreamed about it, the talon blade had to be an omen, and on balance it was a better omen for him than for Grandys. And Rix had been a far better fighter with his right hand than he was with the left . . .

As he lifted the weapon by its toe-bone handle, he felt a surge of strength and confidence that almost made up for the slowly ebbing wound in his back. Almost.

"Don't move," he said to Glynnie. "Try not to breathe until I've finished Grandys."

"You're a treat, Rixium," said Grandys. "How you make me laugh. I'm going to miss you."

The grin froze on his face when he saw the talon-blade in Rix's right hand. Grandys swallowed, licked his lips and took hold of Maloch with both hands, as if uncertain of its loyalty . . . or, perhaps, his own strength. Rix glanced at Lirriam, who was sheltering from the rain under a triangular ledge. She was bandaging her upper arm, her eyes fixed on Grandys, and Rix did not think she would intervene, though you could never be sure with the Heroes.

He could not reach Glynnie without exposing his back to Grandys. Rix turned on one foot, grit squealing beneath his boot, and lunged—and the talon-blade moved with glorious, fluid perfection, as if it were a natural extension to his arm. Grandys parried the blow with Maloch, watchful now. He had never seen Rix fight with the right hand and would want to gauge his strength before mounting a full-scale attack.

Rix was very good with his right hand—at the time it had been amputated he had never been beaten. He thrust. Again Grandys parried, though more slowly than before; he barely turned Rix's point in time. His wounds must be taking their toll, and perhaps the Three Spells had aged him on the inside as well as the outside.

"Maloch isn't serving you as well as it used to," said Rix.

"Is this the challenge Urtiga foretold?" said Grandys, evidently trying to unsettle him with bluster. "It can't be—*you're* not the true master."

"I never said I was," said Rix. There was no point pretending now. "Well, not seriously. When I had Maloch, it always felt alien to me."

"Then—who—is?" Grandys ground out.

"Lyf, of course," Rix lied. He had no idea about the sword's true master.

"He's not! I've cut Lyf many times with Maloch, and each time it drank his blood eagerly."

As it had when Rix had wielded it against Lyf's wrythen in his caverns, he recalled, at the very beginning of this adventure. No, definitely not Lyf. Then who?

They fought across the platform and back, across and back again. Rix struck Grandys three times, and Grandys wounded him once, a painful cut across the upper chest, though not one that slowed Rix measurably. Not as much as the knife wound in his back, which was still oozing blood and sending piercing stabs of pain through him with every movement.

Grandys was also tiring. He wasn't moving his feet nearly as much as before; his legs were weakening, which would hinder his ability to evade Rix's blows, and strike his own.

Yet the longer they fought, the more certain Rix became that Maloch's protective magery gave Grandys an unbeatable edge. Rix had penetrated his guard a dozen times with blows that would have killed any lesser man, and each time Maloch had turned Rix's blade; he either missed or only caused a flesh wound.

His knees were beginning to wobble now. He was stumbling with weariness, starting to give Grandys chances, and the brute only needed one. If he ever got through Rix's defences, Maloch's attacking magery would drive the point deep, and the trap he had been trying to avoid for the past month would close on him forever.

As he had that thought, Lirriam stepped forward, *Incarnate* throbbing on her bosom. She wore an enigmatic smile, but who was it directed at? She held up her right hand to Rix. He stopped reluctantly, for he wasn't sure he would be able to get going again. He leaned a shoulder against the black cliff, panting.

"He's mine to kill," Grandys gasped. "Don't interfere."

"You broke the pact." Lirriam rubbed her lopsided jaw. "I told you that you'd pay for it."

Grandys was so shocked that his arm fell. Maloch's tip hit the ground with a clang and a shower of sparks, and slipped from his hand.

He snatched it up as if unsure of its loyalty. *"Each for all,"* Grandys said desperately. *"All for each—forever!"*

"That applied when we were the *Five* Heroes, but there's only you and me left, Grandys, and soon there'll only be one."

"Why are you doing this?"

"You attacked one of your own. You broke my jaw."

"It was a moment of madness—you provoked me unbearably. And I apologised."

"Never in the history of the Five Heroes had one of us laid a violent hand on another," said Lirriam. "It was always we Five against the world."

"It—still—is."

"There is no Five—only me and you."

"We can rebuild."

"No."

"Why—not?"

"Because in our age-long opal dreaming, something broke in you, Grandys. It wasn't about us Five any more, it was about *you*, and we were only there to support whatever you wanted. It showed the true character you'd been hiding all this time—and it forced me to question the very meaning of my life." She paused. "And I wondered . . ."

"What?" said Grandys, unsteadily.

"I wondered what other crimes you might have committed . . . in the past."

He stopped dead. "Urtiga? That's what this is about?"

"Yes, Urtiga. For the past month you've been agonising about Rix being the sword's true master—which was patently absurd, since he's not even part-Herovian—yet you never asked yourself if it could be *me*."

"You?" His voice was thick with derision. "How could the sword's true master be a woman?"

Lirriam's face lit up, as if she had been waiting for this moment for a long time. "It first belonged to Urtiga, and Urtiga's death . . ."

"What about it?" Grandys said roughly.

Rix looked from Lirriam to Grandys, back to Lirriam. What was she so happy about? And why did Grandys suddenly seem mortally afraid?

"Urtiga's death," Lirriam repeated, "left me as the last of our line."

Grandys let out a gasp; he could not suppress it in time. "You— *a blood relative?*"

"We were second cousins . . ."

He went the colour of chalk. He knew what this meant, and so did Rix. Under Herovian law, once Lirriam identified the killer she had to avenge her cousin's murder.

"And all these years—you never let on?" Grandys whispered.

"When she died I was just a girl of eighteen. Had I admitted I was her kin, I would have been dead within the hour. Besides, I nurse my grievances, Grandys. Until the moment suits me—and the price is right."

"You're planning to take Maloch and kill *me*?" He laughed. "Then begin!"

Lirriam took another step. "Remember Urtiga's last words, Grandys? 'While you dominate Maloch, the enchantment will take on your foul character, and even advance your fell purpose . . . but one day the sword's true master will challenge you, and you will make your fatal mistake.'"

As if attempting an experiment she did not expect to work, Lirriam reached out towards Maloch, her fingers spread, and strained until the sinews in her neck stood out. Maloch rose a few inches, rattling in its sheath and making a low-pitched hum.

Grandys forced it down and held it in place, though it was still clattering about; *it was fighting him!*

Lirriam favoured him with a chilling smile. He stared at her, open-mouthed, and Rix saw the moment when he could no longer evade the truth.

She reached out again, pushing harder this time. "Maloch?" she whispered. "Rise!"

Again Grandys thrust Maloch down, his arm muscles knotting under the strain.

As she reached towards the sword a third time, the hum rose in pitch and Maloch jerked so powerfully that it forced Grandys' whole arm up; with all his strength he could not hold it in place. Red light pulsed from the blade.

He gestured towards the canister to draw on king-magery. "Maloch, return to your sheath."

A trace of yellow fire flared out from the hilt and tip of the sword. The metal let out a deep thrumming sound and the blade dropped until it touched the slot of the sheath, though it did not go in.

"Why isn't it working?" he said.

"*Up*," Lirriam said in a husky whisper.

Thrumming and radiating crimson light, the sword rose until it was above Grandys' head. He threw all his weight behind it, attempting to swing it at Lirriam's face. The sword did not budge and his hand was bent back almost to his wrist. He let out a gasp and clamped his other hand around the hilt.

"*Down!*" Lirriam said.

Maloch flared red and shot towards its sheath. Grandys could not hold it and it plunged in to the hilt, cutting off the light. The hum rose to a shrill pitch.

Lirriam allowed herself a weary smile. "Getting the hang of this, Grandys."

His face went the colour of a blood bucket. "Maloch," he said, desperately trying to draw on king-magery again, "I *command* you to ignore Lirriam. Rise to my hand."

Maloch rose a foot in the air. "Down!" said Lirriam, her teeth bared.

The sword dipped, then dropped in a series of jerks, each accompanied by a pulse of crimson light and a whining note, back into its sheath.

Grandys cast a desperate glance at the canister of king-magery. "What's wrong with it?"

"You haven't taken the cap off," said Lirriam sweetly. "No magery can pass through platina, Grandys."

He looked at her suspiciously, then wrenched the cap off.

"Maloch, using all the power of king-magery I *command* you," Grandys said for a third time. "You will obey me, and me alone."

The sword shuddered, then jerked forward and back in the sheath so violently that the straps tore away and the sheath fell to the rocky platform. Maloch slid out. Lirriam held up *Incarnate* and spoke a mighty word. Rix's right hand burned; blood beaded the scar around his wrist but was reabsorbed.

A crimson beam lanced from the stone and struck Maloch, mid-blade. The worn inscription etched down the blade, that notorious quote from the *Immortal Text—Heroes must fight to preserve the race—* shone out brightly, then faded.

"What have you done?" Grandys croaked.

He picked the sword up. Maloch twisted in his grip until it was pointing at Lirriam's heart. No, at *Incarnate*. It jerked so hard that Grandys was dragged several steps. The sword was trying to get at *Incarnate*.

Lirriam called another crimson bolt from the stone, and a third. They struck the blade in the same place as the first. The titane blade shrilled as if something was trying to get out.

Grandys drew on king-magery again. "I *command* you to obey only me!" he screamed.

The sound rose to a whine, a howl, then the enchantment broke with a banshee shriek and a burst of brilliant, searing light. Grandys staggered around, his face and arms covered in blisters, staring at Maloch. His face crumpled; clearly he knew, as Rix did, that with the enchantment gone Maloch was a sword like any other.

"You didn't get it either, bitch!" he spat.

"I didn't want it," said Lirriam calmly, though she was breathing hard. "The enchantment was forever tainted by the way you took Maloch from its true master—just as Hightspall became the Tainted Realm by the base way you betrayed Lyf and stole his people's land."

"The Five Heroes betrayed Lyf," said Grandys. "And you were there—you were one of us."

"I was under age, and so was Yulia—we were both under your thrall. Nonetheless, it's to my shame that I didn't try to stop you; that I was complicit in the sordid business."

"If you don't want Maloch, what do you want? What's the point of all this?"

"To make you break the enchantment—your *fatal mistake*."

"But . . . you broke it . . . with *Incarnate*."

"*Incarnate* has never had that kind of power. I merely made it look as though those blasts were coming from the stone."

"I don't understand," said Grandys.

"I couldn't take the enchantment from you," said Lirriam, sagging. "I don't have the strength. I tricked you into forcing it beyond its breaking point."

"But . . . why?"

"To rob you of the unbeatable protection you've enjoyed ever since you killed Urtiga for Maloch."

"Why would you want to do that?"

"All this time you've been obsessed by winning, because you're desperate to prove to yourself that you're the man you never were— the greatest warrior of all. Yet all this time you've been hiding behind Maloch's protection spell, *like a cowardly boy hiding behind his mother's skirts*. Now it's gone, you have the chance to truly prove yourself . . . in a fair fight."

He picked Maloch up. "You think you can kill *me* in a fair fight? Then do your worst."

"I'm not going to rob Rixium of his triumph after he's come so far."

Grandys glanced at Rix. "He can barely stand up; he's as weak as a baby."

"And you're as feeble as an old man. Rixium is going to crush you so utterly that people will laugh when your name is mentioned. And when he's finished, your nemesis is going to eat you. The only memorial you'll leave behind will be a stinking wyverin turd."

"I'll win," he blustered. "I'm the greatest warrior this land has ever seen."

"You were," conceded Lirriam, "when you were young and Maloch protected you from all harm. Let's see you fight as a man— *if* you still are a man without the enchantment."

Grandys hurled himself at Rix in a blinding attack he had not expected from a man so wounded and worn—Maloch was moving so fast that it blurred. Rix reacted instinctively, not planning his moves but allowing hand and arm and eye to take over, as he had done back in the days before he had lost his hand.

Grandys leapt forward, striking a furious triple blow and penetrating Rix's defences with the last thrust, to pink him in the chest under his right arm. Despite his age, Grandys was brilliant; he had a longer reach and he was fighting with the strength of desperation.

He drove Rix backwards, almost to the edge.

Glynnie shrieked, "Rix!"

Rix sidestepped, leapt out of the way and came at Grandys from the side, trying to force him over. Grandys was too strong; again he drove Rix backwards, this time until he came up against the scarp. Rix ducked a blow that would have taken his head off and Maloch struck the rock, causing a shower of sparks. Grandys went off balance momentarily, jarred to the shoulder by the impact, and Rix struck him on the left collarbone.

Grandys knocked the talon blade aside with a sweep of his arm and advanced again, but now, despite the ferocity of his attack, or perhaps because of it, Rix began to feel that he was gaining. He struck again, and again.

Yes, Grandys was tiring! Rix definitely had his measure, now that he wasn't fighting the enchantment as well. Grandys was bleeding from a dozen cuts, while Rix had taken but three. He feinted, feinted again, and when Grandys failed to pick the second feint Rix swung a mighty blow against Maloch and snapped it at the hilt.

There came a metallic screech, perhaps the last remnants of the enchantment jetting from the broken end of the blade. The blade shot vertically, turned over, plunged down and embedded itself an inch deep in Grandys' breastbone, as if it had aimed itself there.

An inch was nothing in Grandys' massive chest, but he reeled backwards, his arms flailing. The circlet fell off, ringing as it struck the rocky platform. He tried to heave the blade out but his bloody fingers could not maintain a grip; the blade was wedged in and would not come free.

"Not the greatest warrior after all," said Lirriam.

Grandys stood there, bloody-handed, gasping.

"Say it," said Lirriam.

"I—can't," said Grandys.

Rix could see that defeat was agony to him. It hurt more than any physical wound could have, for it struck at his very identity.

"It doesn't matter to me whether he says it or not," said Rix.

"Justice demands you say it," said Lirriam to Grandys. "Justice to Urtiga."

He extended his red hands towards her. "Help me."

She folded her arms across her breast. "Say it!"

"All right!" he screeched. "Rixium beat me in a fair fight. I'm not the best. Lirriam, please, there's just you and me now. I'll give you anything."

"There's just me," said Lirriam. "And you have nothing I want."

She turned, casually surveying the sky, and smiled.

"Now look," she said, gesturing skywards. "The doom of Herox's line approaches."

CHAPTER 84

Glynnie was tugging on the dagger that pinned her shoulder to the tree, trying to extract it without putting any more strain on the roots. Blood flowed freely down her arm and she was unusually pale. In shock, Rix thought, and shock was not conducive to clear thinking.

Suddenly, his injuries and his own blood loss took their toll. He slipped on a puddle of blood, fell down and could not get up.

The wyverin came sweeping in, Lyf riding on its back. Grandys lurched around, the broken blade still embedded in his breastbone. He was covered in blood from many wounds and, momentarily, naked terror showed on his face. Poetic justice, Rix thought. Hundreds—no, thousands—of Grandys' victims must have felt an equal terror before he brutally ended their lives.

Grandys tried to blast the wyverin down with king-magery, but it failed. He tried again. Nothing! He looked around wildly. Lirriam was wearing the circlet and holding the canister.

He reached out to her, imploringly. "Take out the blade, Lirriam. That's all I ask."

"But it's always protected you," she said.

"Please. For all the good times we shared together."

"I remember good times, though none I've shared with you recently. Besides, the cursed blade is half the attraction to the wyverin. If I took it out, the beast might go for me."

The wyverin shot past, lashing its fifty-foot-long tail. The tip cracked like a whip only feet above Grandys' head, so loudly that it stung Rix's ears. The shockwave shook the little tree and pulled another of its roots out.

Rix's heart went into spasm. He forced himself to his feet and lurched towards Glynnie. Lyf leapt off the wyverin and soared through the air, directly for Lirriam and the circlet. She held up a hand and he was frozen in mid-air.

The wyverin snapped at Grandys. He tried to fight it with the hilt and stub of Maloch, a pitiful weapon against such a beast. The wyverin hovered, darted its head, neatly nipped the stub from Grandys' fingers and swallowed it.

It darted again, caught him by the shins, swung him upside-down and bit his feet off.

"Justice is poetry!" cried Lyf. "And again, wyverin!"

Grandys fell on his head. It caught him by the knees and swung him again. Grandys reached up and caught hold of one of the scales surrounding its nostrils and tried to tear it away, but he did not have the strength.

It laughed, *huff-huff-huff*, tossed him high and bit through him at the knees. It swallowed and let Grandys fall. He flailed around on the ground, caught hold of a long knife lying there and, as the wyverin went at him again, struck at its scaly snout. The knife skidded off the inch-thick plates. He struck again and again, but could not penetrate its armour.

He tried to stab it in the eye but could not reach high enough. It tossed him down, tore open his belly and ripped the entrails out, just as it had in the final version of Rix's portrait.

Grandys screamed and made another desperate attempt to kill it. It bit through him at the hips, and then at the chest, driving the blade that had once been Maloch right through him. Grandys died as he had lived, cursing it all the way, and then it swallowed the rest of him.

He was gone. Gone forever. Rix found it hard to come to terms with.

Of the Five Heroes, only Lirriam survived.

The wyverin's wings battered the air; it lumbered higher, as though weighed down by Axil Grandys, then settled on the rocky tip of Touchstone, twenty feet above them, eyeing them balefully. Its stomach was churning visibly, and Rix could hear liquids gurgling and swishing.

"It looks as though Grandys is proving difficult to digest," he muttered.

"But once it does digest him, it'll be stronger than ever," said Lirriam.

Radl, who had earlier been knocked unconscious, roused, rolled over and tried to get to her feet.

"It looks stronger already," Glynnie said weakly. She looked as though she was about to faint.

"They replenish their gift by feeding on magians," said Lyf, still in mid-air. "And the more powerful the better."

"You're not dining on me," said Lirriam. "Stop!" she said to Rix. He stopped, only six feet from Glynnie, watching *Incarnate* warily.

"Did Bloodspell work?" said Rix.

"It was never completed—" Lirriam rubbed her face with her hands. "And that's bad."

"Are you going to complete it?"

"There may well be a Promised Realm, but it doesn't lie here. Even so, such a deadly spell can't be left hanging ... Thirty seconds left," said Lirriam to herself. "Can it be undone in time?"

She raised *Incarnate*, walked to the half crucible and spoke the Bloodspell anew, though with a different ending. It drained her, though not as badly as it had Grandys. The rock began to shake violently.

A fire bolt streaked down towards the blood-filled half crucible.

The blood from ninety-seven people boiled, burned, and the half crucible shattered. Rix went skidding towards the edge, stinging all over from the blast. The wyverin leapt into the air, shaking the top of Touchstone, but settled again.

"No, Rix!" Glynnie said despairingly.

With a convulsive jerk she wrenched the dagger out, pushed against the tree with her feet and threw herself into his path. They collided; his momentum carried them towards the edge; Rix grabbed at several cracks but could not get a grip on the slippery moss. Glynnie, who was still holding the dagger, slammed it down into a crevice.

Rix expected it to snap. He expected them to both go over, but the blade held, and they swung around and came to rest, locked together, only inches from the edge. They rose together, their arms around one another, holding each other up.

Lirriam was studying them with an unfathomable smile. "It would have been just like Grandys," she said, "at the moment you thought you'd won, to tip you over. He would have taken great pleasure in dashing your hopes."

She walked to the edge, only feet away. Rix tensed, though if she chose to hurl him and Glynnie off he was too weak to stop her.

She pursed her lips. "I've done much evil in my life. I dare say I *am* evil."

Rix's heart was thudding. She could kill them all with the least amount of power, deliver them to any fate she wished.

"But I was coerced into being one of the Five," said Lirriam, "and now I long to escape my past, not repeat it; to create rather than destroy. I wish you well—whatever you plan to do next."

Rix and Glynnie edged away from the precipice, and from her. Just in case.

"Why aren't we all dead?" said Tali. "Why did the Bloodspell fail?"

Errek First-King appeared above Lyf. "Lirriam reversed it. But it would never have worked anyway."

"Why not?"

"Grandys should never have used Tali's blood in the Bloodspell. It's *healing* blood, and it would have nullified the destructive aspect

of the Bloodspell. It would never have set up their Promised
Realm."

"We were looking in the wrong place, anyway," said Lirriam.
"Maybe the wrong *world*."

"Then go after it," said Errek.

She directed a casual blast at him, sending him tumbling
through the air, but a spirit could come to no harm from magery, as
she must have known.

"Thank you," said Errek once he'd righted himself.

Lirriam moved along the edge of the precipice. "What for?"

"Your blast helped to rouse the memories lost at the time of my
death. And one particular memory . . ."

"What?"

"Layla Virch was right. "

Her eyes narrowed but she did not speak.

"Your Heroxian ancestors weren't nobles exiled to our world,"
said Errek. "They were criminals, banished to die in the void for an
unforgivable crime."

"Grandys claimed to be of noble stock, not I," said Lirriam. "And
I fail to see why I should be blamed for the crimes of ancestors
twelve thousand years ago. I plan to begin my new life, right now."

She tossed the circlet up to Lyf. "I wish you every success with
your healing."

Lirriam took *Incarnate* in both hands, frowning as if trying to
solve a tricky problem. She stepped backwards onto a smooth patch
of rock slick with blood. Her feet went from under her and, with a
little cry, she fell backwards over the edge.

Rix went carefully to the brink and looked over, but she had disappeared into the mist. He turned, shaking his head.

"So ends the last of the Five Heroes. And I can't say I'm sorry,
even if she did redeem herself at the end."

No one spoke for a minute or two, then there came a long, gassy
rumble from above. Everyone looked up.

"It sounds as if the wyverin has nearly digested Grandys," said
Errek. "I'd recommend you deal with it sooner rather than later."

"You're the expert on dealing with the beasts," said Lyf. "What
should I do?"

"Put it to sleep before it decides to feast on the only magian left—*you*."

"I don't know the sleep spell."

"It's the reverse of the waking spell I taught you before."

"*Exactly* the reverse?"

"Well, not exactly." Errek grinned.

"Just tell me the damned spell," said Lyf. "Tiny errors in great spells can have bad consequences."

Errek told him the sequence and Lyf rehearsed the spell under his breath. It took a long time, and Rix was uncomfortably aware that the wyverin was rousing quickly from its digestive torpor. When fully roused it would be faster, and twice as ferocious. Not that it needed to be—it could squash everyone here, simply by settling on the platform.

"Better hurry," said Errek.

Lyf was going through the spell for the second time.

"It's moving; it's lifting. Quick!" yelled Glynnie.

The wyverin was already thirty feet in the air, its vast wings beating slowly, its head turning to look down on them. Its slit-pupilled eyes blinked; it let out an exploratory belch of flame, thirty feet long.

"Now!" said Errek.

Lyf pointed up at the wyverin, drew on the strongest power he could bear, spoke the words of the spell and said, "Sleep!"

The pouches on either side of its neck inflated and it snorted another blast of that noxious red-brown fluid at him. It caught fire in the air and burned orange as it jetted towards them.

"Block it!" cried Errek, and for the first time there was a note of panic in his voice.

Lyf blocked the jet of burning fluid, only feet away from his face. The orange fire flared out all around him, sending Errek tumbling, and instantly bleaching the moss on every surface to a bony white. Lyf was driven backwards several feet.

"You pronounced the last word wrong," said Errek. "*Say the spell properly*."

Lyf tried again, but halfway through the spell the wyverin whirled in the air and lashed out with its tail, smashing the end of the platform to pieces. He ducked chunks of flying rock and began again.

The wyverin soared high, rolled over and plunged down towards him in a vertical dive, faster and faster. It looked as though it was planning to slam right into the platform and smash him, and everyone else, to paste.

"Slow and careful," said Errek. "Last chance, Lyf."

He cast the spell again, carefully enunciating each word, and this time the wyverin's streaming eyes drifted closed. But it was still diving in the same direction; right at them.

"Look out!" roared Rix, sweeping Glynnie up into his arms.

The wyverin's wings completed their last flap, moving it off course a little; it screeched past Touchstone only inches away, diving steeply, and disappeared. Shortly there came an impact that shook the peak to its roots.

"What were you planning to do, exactly?" said Glynnie. "Dive over the side with me?"

Rix smiled and put her on her feet. "I've no idea."

"Do you think it's dead?"

"It will be a mighty beast indeed if it can survive that impact," said Lyf.

"It is a mighty beast," said Errek, "and not of this world, though I don't see how any kind of flesh and blood could withstand such a fall."

Touchstone gave one final shudder and Holm slid off the spike he had been impaled on. Rix and Glynnie ran across. The fist-sized hole in his back, which had been staunched by the spike, was filling with blood. Tali was on her knees, tearing up clumps of moss and packing it into the wound.

"It's no use," Rix said gently.

"I tried to tell her that," Holm wheezed. "But she wouldn't listen. She never does." He put an arm around her, fondly.

"I've got to do something," wept Tali. "Why did I make the wrong choice back in Cython? Even at the time I knew I'd regret choosing destruction."

"If you hadn't, neither of us would be here now. You have to accept the past for what it is and move on. As I have done."

Tali tore the bottom off her shirt, wrapped it around his chest and back, and tied it tightly. The blood seeped through it in seconds.

Rix turned to Lyf, his hand resting on the hilt of the talon blade, and tried to look stronger than he was.

"Well?" he said.

"Enough," said Errek.

Lyf went to the edge of the precipice, wearing the circlet.

"The Five Heroes are dead," he said in a booming voice that could have been heard right across the plateau. "The war is over. Lay down your arms."

CHAPTER 85

It was pouring again, washing down the blood-drenched platform, cleaning the wounds of the living and the dead, and leaching the corpses of all colour. Even the opal armouring on the dead Heroes was fading now, save for Rufuss's black-opal teeth, which still grinned insanely up at them from his bleached face.

Holm was fading too. He reached out to Tali.

"I'd hate for my bones to get mixed up with the bones of the so-called Heroes," he wheezed. "There's an eyrie at the very top of Touchstone. Would you lay me there, where the pure east rain can bathe my tattered soul and the sun bleach its last stains away?"

She held his scarred hand, remembering the first time she had met him, back in Fortress Rutherin on the far side of Hightspall. He had been old Kroni then, the clock attendant, and she had been held prisoner by the chancellor-in-exile so she could be milked of her healing blood.

Lyf and Errek had gone down the steps, out of sight. Rix carried Holm up. Radl, who had roused some time ago, stooped and hefted Tali in her arms.

"What are you doing?" cried Tali. "Put me down!"

They had been enemies since childhood, and even after the

successful rebellion in Cython she had never felt that Radl liked her. Her bitter accusations back in Garramide had made it clear that nothing had changed, and it was no comfort at all that Radl's assessment of Tali's character had been proven right.

"The Five Heroes were forever rivals," said Radl, "yet the bond between them, arising out of all they endured and shared and fought for, bound them together down the centuries."

"Uh . . .?" said Tali.

What was Radl on about? She and Mia had been friends; was Radl planning to avenge her? If she was, there was nothing Tali could do about it. She wasn't even sure she wanted to.

"And so it is with you and I," Radl continued. "I don't like you, Tali—I never have and I never will. But we're the only Pale to have led our people in defeat and victory, the only Pale to have made our own way in a foreign land. We're tied together, you and I, in ways no one else can ever understand."

"Are you . . . planning on killing me?"

Radl laughed. "Haven't you listened to a word I've said, today or back at Garramide?"

"I thought, perhaps . . . revenge for Mia?"

"If I was the vengeful type, my best revenge would be to save your life, not take it."

"You're a strange woman," said Tali.

"Not as strange as you."

Radl carried her up, and Tali was glad to get away from the bodies and the once-sacred platforms, now forever defiled. It did not take long to reach the top—there were only twenty-eight steps to the bowl-shaped eyrie where the wyverin had perched.

The bowl was thirty feet across and eight feet deep and, long ago, slots had been cut in the sides to allow rainwater to flow out, though they were now choked with a thick carpet of brilliantly green moss. Rix set Holm down on the broad rim and poked through the slots with the talon blade. The water half filling the bowl began to drain away.

"This will do me nicely," said Holm. "Prop me up so I can see."

"Which way?" said Tali.

Touchstone quivered, then quivered again. "Quake," said Rix. "Big one!"

"Don't face me east," said Holm, "or I'll always have the rain driving into my face. Nor south—the stinging sleet comes that way." He chuckled. "North's no good either—sun gets in the eyes— so it'll have to be west. On a clear day I'd be able to see across the mountains all the way to Caulderon."

Rix lay Holm on the upper slope of the mossy bowl, facing west. It was still sodden but he was soaked through—everyone was. Tali wiped the rain off his face and the tears from her eyes.

Rix sat down wearily on the far rim of the bowl, his shoulders slumped.

"Turn around," said Glynnie.

He did so. She pulled up his shirt, cleaned the small knife slit in his back and bandaged it. He did the same for her shoulder.

"What else can we do for you?" Tali said to Holm.

"Half a cup of water would be nice."

She caught some clean rainwater in her cupped hands and held them to his lips. He drank a couple of mouthfuls.

"Better not take any more in case it comes pouring out the hole in my back." Holm managed a grin. "Funny, isn't it?"

"No," said Tali.

"We all have to go sometime."

"You're too young."

"It's nice to have been appreciated."

Touchstone shook violently and small stones rattled down the steps.

"The Three Spells have tipped the balance," said Holm, "and the quakes are going to get a lot worse. You need to find shelter, quick as you can—"

He looked up as Errek and Lyf appeared overhead. Now that Lyf had king-magery at his command he had taken to flying again.

"If this is another attempt at healing the land," said Holm, "you'd better make it quick."

Lyf hovered, scowling. "You speak over-boldly for a humble clock attendant."

"And you sound more like a harassed clerk than an almighty king."

Errek chuckled and extended a wispy hand to Holm. "I've a feeling we would have got on, had we met in more cheerful circumstances."

"I think so too," said Holm, shaking the wrythen's hand as if it were a real, solid hand. "Can he do it?"

Errek glanced up at Lyf, who was preparing himself as he had done back at the great dome of Garramide. "I'm not going to jinx him by answering that."

"Sit by me a moment. I could do with some advice."

Errek settled into the bowl beside Holm. "You look troubled," said Errek.

"I'm burdened by a youthful folly I've never been able to atone for."

"I'm aware of the life you've lived. And by living that good life you atoned long ago."

"Then why can I never find peace?" said Holm.

"You don't need atonement—what you need is absolution." Errek raised his hand and rested it on Holm's head. "And with my kingly perspective of ten thousand years, I give it to you."

Holm sighed and leaned back, and the deep lines on his face smoothed out. They sat together in an amiable silence.

Tali settled on Holm's left side. Lyf hovered above the centre of the bowl and cast his great healing spell over the land, three times. And three times he failed.

Errek rose a few feet, looking grave. "Only one hope remains to us now. It won't heal the land, but it might postpone the catastrophe."

"The one caused by my failure to do my kingly duty?" said Lyf bitterly.

"The greatest failure of all is to give up. This is what you have to do: create a full body shield for yourself—"

"Why?"

"Because you won't survive where you're going without it. Then make a gate to the Engine, go through and I'll tell you what to do next."

"The art of making gates was lost long before I became king," said Lyf. "I've only ever used gates made by the ancients."

"Then divert the Sacred Gate—it's not far from here," Errek said testily. "You can do that, can't you?"

"I dare say I can, if you tell me how."

Errek floated up to him and they conferred.

"You don't look any better than I do," Holm said to Tali.

She tried to emulate his light-hearted mood. "I don't normally go on a life-or-death adventure with a big hole in my head."

"Sorry. You've no idea how hard—"

She stroked his scarred hand. "I do, actually. Thank you."

"What for?"

"For getting rid of the damned pearl."

"You don't miss it?"

"There's a loss—a terrible loss. But every time I used my gift it was like having an axe slammed into my skull. And as long as the master pearl was there, half the scum in Hightspall wanted to hack it out. I just want to live a normal life again."

"Have you ever lived a normal life?"

"Slavery seemed normal when I was little. When my parents were alive."

Tali stared into space, reliving that long-ago time when she remembered being truly happy.

Zzoouun!

A round gate, six feet across and rimmed in shimmering grey, had opened above the far rim of the bowl. She sat up and looked through it, along a whirling tunnel that led all the way to the Engine at the heart of the world, the enigmatic Engine that had caused all the natural disasters that so troubled Hightspall.

"Can you see?" She propped Holm a little higher.

"There's a cavern, glowing a luminous bluish-green. And a pool of water on the floor; clear, steaming water. I can't see far through the steam."

"Keep talking. You can be my eyes."

Tali closed her own eyes, just wanting to hear Holm's rich, comforting voice one last time. It took her back to happier days in his beautiful little boat. To the difficult time they had spent together

in the cave in the iceberg. To their weeks on the tortuous road to
Tirnan Twil, now destroyed, and on to Garramide ... and to Tobry,
back from the dead for the first time—She closed that thought right
down.

Holm's voice strengthened. "The steam's clearing a little ... I can
see a stack of rectangular metal plates rising up into the fog. The
air's shimmering above them; they must be really hot ...

"The stack's enormous, like a pillar ten feet across. And it's made
of silvery-grey plates, each the shape and size of a large book ...
they're just like the wyverin's scales, Tali, save that they're made of
metal ... "

"Maybe they're its cast-off scales," said Tali.

"I think they must be ... but who put them there, and who
arranged them so perfectly?"

She did not answer, and shortly he continued, "There's a breeze
blowing through the gate. It's clearing the steam—"

When he did not go on, Tali opened her eyes and looked up.
Holm's mouth hung open and his eyes were wide with awe.

"I can see more stacks—dozens of stacks of metal plates, rising
high out of the water." Holm's voice rose. "They're in a vast oval
cavern ... it must be hundreds of yards across and a hundred yards
high. The roof's like a dome but the rock's all glassy—as if it's been
melted ...

"There are hundreds of stacks ... No, *thousands*, Tali, stretching
right across the floor of the cavern ... and there must be thousands
of metal plates in each stack. And ... and the stacks are joined at
their tops by soaring arches and domes and spirals, all made of perfectly stacked plates ... arranged in extraordinary patterns. It's ...
it's the most beautiful thing I've ever seen."

"But who would build such a thing?" said Tali. "And why?"

"I can't imagine," said Holm. "It would have taken decades ...
perhaps *centuries*. And there are piles of oval stones in the water,
stones the size of watermelons, one pile beneath each arch and dome.
They must be very old—they're covered in brown watermarks." He
paused for another breath. "The water looks hot. The steam's rising
again."

"The stacks are supposed to be flooded," said Errek, "but the cavern's nearly empty. That's why the Engine's overheating, and why the balance has tilted so far. Lyf, the water channels must be clogged up—you'll have to go in and clear them out."

"Where are they?" said Lyf.

"See those square outlets around the wall? There's eight of them and water should be flowing in to keep the Engine cool. Go through, unblock the outlets and flood the cavern."

"They're ten feet across," said Lyf. "It'll take days to clear the muck out of all eight of them."

"Do what you can. Go, *go*!"

Tali opened her eyes as Lyf flew across to the gate, only to bounce off with a dull thud and tumble to the bottom of the bowl. He tried twice more with a similar result.

Rix clambered up to the gate and poked his arm through. "There's nothing here."

"Well, it won't let me through," snapped Lyf.

"There's someone in the cavern," said Holm.

Tali stared at the silhouette. She knew that skinny, capering figure. "It's Mad Wil. What's he doing there?"

"No good, I'd imagine," said Holm.

"He was there when the Engine first ran out of control," said Lyf. "Wait! The outlets haven't clogged up—*they've been walled off*. And only Mad Wil could have done that."

"The power Grandys drew for the Three Spells has overheated the Engine," said Errek, "and there's no water to cool it down. This is bad." He called out to Lyf, who was hovering at the top of the gate. "What's he saying?"

Lyf made a movement with his fingers and Wil's voice shrilled out through the gate.

"All Wil's fault," he wailed. "Wil could have saved those little girls, but he let them die. Wil has to pay. Wil has to give himself to the Engine."

"Wil?" Lyf bellowed through the gate. "Unblock the outlets. Flood the Engine to the rooftop."

Wil turned his empty eye sockets one way and another, evidently trying to work out where the voice came from. The radiance in the Engine chamber changed from blue-green to yellow.

"Wil, this is your king speaking. Unblock the outlets *now*."

"Yes, yes," said Wil. "Wil is the true hero." He gazed around him, beaming idiotically. "Lyf's iron book was wrong. This the way the great story was supposed to end all along—Wil gives up his life to save the world."

He waded into the water and picked up a steaming metal plate in his charred hands.

"It's not even burning him," Lyf marvelled. "Unblock the channels!" he yelled. "Hurry!"

"Which one first?" said Wil.

"The nearest one, you imbecile!"

Wil put the plate back and waded across to the closest outlet, which had been neatly walled off with pieces of rock. He took several rocks from the top, then put them back and headed along to the next opening. He hefted another rock and stood on one foot, staring at it.

"Just do it!" screamed Lyf.

Wil put down the stone and went back to the first outlet, but again resolve eluded him.

"Useless fool," hissed Radl from behind Tali. She ran around the rim towards the gate.

"No!" cried Errek. "No normal human can survive in there, unprotected."

"I know," said Radl, "but someone has to go."

She dived through the gate, disappeared and landed in the pool several seconds later, raising a great splash. She stormed across to Wil and thumped him so hard under the jaw that he turned a backwards somersault and disappeared beneath the water.

She ran through the steaming water to the nearest outlet and began heaving out the rocks and hurling them in all directions. Water trickled out. She sprang high and kicked the top of the wall with both feet, knocking down a layer of rock. The flow increased.

"She's doing it," said Tali.

"The water isn't coming in nearly fast enough," said Errek. "The level is still dropping."

Wil bobbed up to the surface, floating spreadeagled on his back and choking up spurts of water. The radiance in the chambers suddenly shifted from yellow to orange. Radl kicked at the rock wall again and again, though her kicks were weaker now.

"She can do it," said Lyf.

"No, she can't," said Errek. "That infernal radiance will kill her."

"It's taking too long," said Rix. He stood up. "I've got to help her."

Tali felt an awful premonition. "Rix, wait!"

Glynnie, who had been sitting silently in the background, let out a howl of anguish. "You can't go!"

"It has to be done," said Rix, "or Hightspall will die, and everyone in it."

The radiant glow changed from orange to an ominous red-brown. He moved backwards around the rim of the bowl as far as he could go, to get a small run-up, then tensed. Glynnie tried to hold him back but he pulled free. He ran around the rim and was in the air, diving for the gate, when Errek turned it solid.

Rix bounced off and landed hard in the bottom of the mossy bowl. "What the hell did you do that for?" he snarled.

"It's too late," said Errek.

The radiance in the cavern shifted to a brilliant crimson, a lurid purple, then a coruscating blue-white glare that hurt the eyes. The luminescence increased a thousand fold. Radl's olive skin blistered, her hair smoked, then the great Engine went wild, boiling the remaining water and, in a few dreadful seconds, burning her and Wil to writhing columns of smoke.

"If you'd gone through—" Glynnie whispered, clinging to Rix. "If you'd gone through—"

He got up and they stared into the fatal cavern, but nothing could be seen except smoky steam, lit from behind by the blue-white luminosity. Tali rose and bent her head, acknowledging her honourable enemy.

"Radl was the best of us, and the bravest," said Tali. "She knew no fear."

"She was a true hero," said Holm. "Though one might argue . . . no, never mind."

"The hour I've always feared has come," said Errek. "The Engine is out of control. Use the gate, Lyf. Get as many of your people out of Caulderon as you can."

Lyf swung the gate away, sending one end to Caulderon and the other to Turgur Thross. Moley Gryle appeared at the Caulderon end and he spoke urgently to her for a minute or two. She turned away and began shouting orders.

The gate disappeared. Lyf stood up wearily and let out a booming call. The gauntling raced in and he leapt on its back.

"Get to shelter while you can," said Lyf.

Then he and Errek were gone, taking the circlet and the canister of king-magery with them.

CHAPTER 86

Touchstone shook three times, each more strongly than the last. The clouds closed in.

"Get going," said Holm.

Rix and Glynnie crouched beside him. Rix held out his hand and Holm took it.

"I'm not leaving you here to die all alone," said Tali.

"I've only a minute or two left," said Holm. "Clear out or you'll be spending eternity with me."

The colour was gone from his face and the tone from his flesh, leaving him grey and haggard.

"Don't go," she said. "I need you."

"You did once, but you don't any more." He smiled at her. "It . . . it's been good, Tali. You've helped to heal me, more than you know."

"I couldn't do the most important healing."

"You did that months ago." He closed his eyes then said, as if from far away. "Go, go!"

"Holm, wait," said Tali, tears streaming down her face.

"He's gone," said Rix. "He was a good man, one of the best, and he gave everything for us."

They bent their heads in farewell. Rix picked Tali up and began to carry her down. Glynnie followed, wincing as each step jarred the knife wound in her shoulder.

"I should have given you my healing blood," said Tali, mortified. "I didn't even think."

"It's all right," said Glynnie. "Rix bandaged it up."

The shaking grew wilder. When they were halfway down, the sky cleared like a window rubbed free of dew and Tali saw, way beyond the mountains, a vast area of land between Lake Yizl and the Red Vomit collapse and fall in.

A great chasm formed there. The land cracked on the other side, between the chasm and Lake Caulderon, and lake water flooded down into the chasm. Explosive jets of superheated steam burst up for thousands of feet. The ground and the lakes disappeared behind the clouds of steam. Within seconds she could only see the tops of the three Vomits.

Lightning flashed, then black ash erupted and the northern side of the Red Vomit blew out in a monumental eruption. A black cloud of steam and ash boiled up; boiling lava blasted out in all directions, obscuring all the land.

And racing their way.

Rix began to run. Tali was sure he was going to slip on the mossy steps and carry them both over the side.

"Careful," cried Glynnie.

"If we're not in shelter when that cloud gets here," said Rix, "we're dead." He ran faster.

As they reached the bottom of Touchstone, the land seemed to bounce like rubber. Peculiar patterns appeared in the sky, and colours Tali had never seen before. Rix ran towards the standing stones, some of which had toppled, then stopped. Errek was drifting back and forth there, scanning the ground.

"Looking for something?" said Rix.

"*Incarnate*. It should be close to where Lirriam fell—around here somewhere."

Rix could see no sign of a body among the rocks, but there wasn't time to look for one. And no point.

"If you survive what's coming," said Errek, "find *Incarnate*—and destroy it."

"Why?" said Rix.

"There isn't time to explain." He looked between the standing stones. "What's *that* still doing here?"

A few hundred yards further on, a shadowy portal was slowly whirling above a steaming crater, sixty feet across and half filled with rubble, evidently where the wyverin had fallen.

"Did Lyf make that for us, do you think?" said Glynnie. "Should we go through?"

Rix hesitated in front of the eerie portal. The hair stood up on his bare forearms.

Errek materialised in front of them. "Keep well away from it. There are worse worlds than this one. Terrible worlds."

"How do you know?" said Tali faintly. The pain in her head was worse than ever. Unbearable pain.

"My memories are coming back. Fly, fly to Garramide." He vanished.

"Should we make sure the wyverin's dead?" said Glynnie.

"How could any creature survive such an impact, against solid rock?" said Rix, his fist tightening on the hilt of the talon blade. "And if by some chance, or magery, it isn't dead, I'm not going any-where near it."

He ran, carrying Tali, to the point where they had tethered the horses. The horses left by Grandys' party were close by. Glynnie mounted. Rix passed Tali up to her, climbed into his own saddle and they raced back to Garramide with their riderless horses, and the Herovians', galloping behind.

Tali hardly had the strength to open her eyes. When she did, the boiling black cloud already covered half the sky and the light was a lurid greenish-yellow.

"Is this the end of the world?" she said.

No one replied. When they were halfway across the plateau she saw the scattered remnants of Grandys' army stampeding down the escarpment. Rix and Glynnie pounded on, in rain which was turning grey, for it was now three parts water and one part ash.

They reached the front gates of Garramide. Nuddell, who had seen them coming, ordered the gates opened. They rode in, Rix saw the horses safely delivered to the stables, then staggered inside, carrying Tali.

He took her down to the lowest level of the castle, where everyone was gathering. All the doors and windows were shuttered, and the emergency supplies of food and water were in place. They closed the stone doors and settled down to await their fate.

CHAPTER 87

"**A**m I losin' my gift?" said Rannilt as she trudged across the steep slope.

Tobry remained as mute as ever.

She had taken heart after he, shifted to a caitsthe, had rescued her from the Hall of Representation. After returning through the gate Rannilt had healed Glynnie's injured knee. She had said goodbye, and Rannilt and Tobry had left the plateau.

Rannilt had begun her healing afresh, but she had made no progress. Tobry seemed content to be with her yet he met every attempt at healing with blank indifference. It was crushing her belief in herself.

"Got to sit down for a bit," said Rannilt. "Sorry! Bad headache."

She perched on a crumbling, fern-covered log that was rapidly rotting away, and rubbed her head. She still had headaches from the blow she'd taken in the Hall of Representation and was starting to worry that it had robbed her of her gift.

Tobry crouched in front of her, touched her forehead with a dirty finger, then crossed his arms and made a rocking motion. *Heal yourself.*

"Can't afford to waste my gift . . . besides, a healer ain't supposed to heal herself."

Tobry let out a piercing screech, sprang up onto a fallen tree and raced along the slippery trunk, thirty feet in the air where it crossed a ravine. He was increasingly reckless these days.

She rose and was walking up towards the ridge crest, hoping to see out of the confining forest, when the ground shuddered so violently that the tall trees swayed and groaned. Further along the ridge a loose boulder went crashing down the steep slope, bouncing higher and higher and smashing trees to bits.

Each quake was worse than the one before, just as they had been before the great trembler that had broken Tobry's chains a month ago. They were building up to something bad. Did it mean that Grandys had beaten Lyf? There was no way of finding out. They had been lost for days, Rannilt had no idea how to get to Garramide from here, and if Tobry knew he wasn't saying.

The trees here were two hundred feet tall, their interlocking crowns blocking out the sky. Nonetheless, she could tell that it was clouding over; an overwhelming blackness was creeping out of the west, obliterating the sun and turning the light a peculiar olive green.

Then it began—a distant roar like storm waves crashing against a cliff face, save that it grew ever louder and more high-pitched until it became a wind-shriek so unnerving that she had to block her ears.

She reached the top of the ridge. The trees were further apart here; she could see due west along the crest to a monstrous, billowing blackness shot with coils of red fire and illuminated by gigantic lightning flashes. It seemed to be racing directly at her. The ground was shaking wildly now, the trees creaking as they swayed back and forth and smashed their crowns together. A foot-thick branch crashed to the ground not ten feet away; Rannilt let out a screech and looked up. The air was full of leaves, twigs and falling branches.

"Tobry?" she yelled. Her voice was drowned out by the roaring wind and the groan of tormented trees.

There was no sign of him, and even if he had been within sight he would not have heard her. The storm front was only minutes from here and she had to find shelter before it hit. This exposed ridge was the worse place she could be.

She went skidding down the steep southern slope. The soft ground was thick with fallen leaves; her boots cut through to the damp soil and left twin brown streaks behind her. Soon her knees were trembling but she had to keep going; she was only down fifty yards. If she made it all the way to the bottom she might find shelter between the buttress roots of a forest giant, or in a hole—assuming it wasn't already occupied by some other cowering creature.

Her head was throbbing worse than ever and her breath came in tearing gasps. She ducked under a fallen tree whose crown was caught in the branches of its neighbour, then stopped and considered the cave-like space between its roots. No—if it slipped any further she would be squashed to jam.

The storm struck like a hurricane, with a shrieking roar and a savage wind that tore the tops off the trees that rose above the ridge crest, reducing them to shattered, quivering stumps. Pieces of smashed wood were falling all around her. She ran back and forth; where could she go?

Twenty yards away through the greenish gloom she spied a small, rocky bluff with a niche at the base. It wasn't a cave; it was no more than a foot-deep space below the overhang, but it had to be safer than being out in the open. She covered her head with her arms and ran for it.

As she reached the niche, a savage storm cell corkscrewed its way along the ridge, tearing trees out by the roots and letting them fall. A length of tree trunk crashed to the ground a few yards in front of her, shaking the ground and sifting grit down into her hair, before rolling down the slope, smashing the saplings in its path. Rannilt squeezed herself into the niche as tightly as she could. Another tree fell, then half a dozen at once, followed by a hail of shattered branches. Splinters of wood, some longer than she was, flew in all directions. If one hit her she would die, just like that.

"Tobry?" she whimpered. "Where are you?"

The storm grew wilder; trees were torn up by the hundred, snapped to pieces and flung down until the slope below her was a tangle of shattered trunks and branches. Further down, one of the largest trees began to bow under the weight of the wreckage caught in its crown. The stressed trunk groaned, groaned, groaned, then snapped, firing shards of wood in all directions. A branch came whirling through the air at her; she ducked sideways and managed to get her body out of the way but could not draw her right leg up in time. The end of the branch struck her ankle an agonising blow and she felt it break.

And a broken ankle down here was probably a death sentence. She shoved the branch away and took her right boot and sock off. Her skinny ankle was already swelling, and throbbing worse than her head. She locked her fingers around it and drew upon her gift to sense out the break, the way she had sensed the broken bones in Tobry's arm a few weeks ago.

Healers weren't supposed to heal themselves but she had no choice. She reached deep for her healing gift to make the broken bone grow together but nothing came, no matter how many times she tried. It surely meant that she had lost her gift. No wonder Tobry wouldn't let her try to heal him.

Rannilt screwed her eyes shut to hold back the scalding tears. Healing was the best thing in her life, the one thing she had all to herself. It was her hope, her joy and her future. How could it be gone, just like that?

The windstorm passed but the gloom thickened until it was almost as dark as night. Warm grey rain began to fall, so thick with ash that it looked like mud. Reeking of sulphur and hot, broken rock as it did, it reminded her of the Seethings and the smoking Vomits next to them. She guessed that one of the Vomits had blown itself to bits, as the Cythonians had long forecast.

Mud ran down the face of the bluff above her, along the roof of her niche and dripped onto her head. She wiped it off and moved aside but it began to drip there as well; there was no escaping it. She could not heal Tobry and she could not heal herself, and now she was going to die, all alone in a ruined wilderness.

Rannilt closed her eyes, gave herself up to her misery and, finally, slept.

*

A presence woke her, raising her hackles and sending shivers racing up the back of her neck. She could hear it breathing a foot away. She was afraid to move; afraid to open her eyes.

Rannilt squared her scrawny shoulders and gave herself a stern lecture. She might be small and skinny, but if she was going to die she would face death bravely—not like some scaredy-cat. She opened her eyes and all she could see were golden yellow eyes; caitsthe eyes. Was it Tobry? In the dim light she couldn't tell. There were bound to be other caitsthes in these mountains ... and they liked to play with their food.

She tried to say his name but her mouth was too dry for speech. She licked her lips.

"Tobry?" she said hoarsely.

The eyes blinked and she saw a hint of grey in the corners—*it was him*. Though that did not mean she was out of danger. The caitsthe generally controlled the man, not the other way round.

Rannilt decided to act as though he were a man, not a shifter. A normal, reliable man. Her friend.

"Thanks for comin' back," she said softly. "Stupid branch broke my ankle."

His eyes flicked down to her ankle, then back up. If the caitsthe was in charge, she had just told it she was helpless.

"Give us a hand," she said.

His right arm twitched, an instinctive blow stifled at the last minute. Tobry was barely in charge of the caitsthe, and any sudden stress could tip it over into full control, but she had to trust the man inside the beast. She reached up as though nothing was wrong, and after an agonising pause he took her hand in his hot, shifter hand. It *was* a hand, not a paw, and as she clasped it she felt it changing in her grasp, becoming more hand-like.

More like Tobry.

He lifted her out of her muddy nest, pointed to her right ankle and made a noise in his throat—'Ur-uh!" *Heal it.*

"Healer can't heal herself," said Rannilt. "I'll have to make a splint ... and you got to help."

She told him what to do and he fetched several lengths of green wood from a freshly broken sapling. She carved notches to go around either side of her ankle, and smaller notches to tie the splints to her calves and boots, the ends extending an inch below her heels to take her weight. Tobry tied the splints on with strips of canvas cut from the top of her pack. Finally she carved a knobbly length of wood into shape for a walking stick.

"I'm really thirsty," she said, "but the rain's full of ash, and I suppose the streams are too. Look for a seep comin' out of the ground."

He helped her up. She gingerly lowered her right foot until the splints touched the ground. Pain shrieked through her ankle; she gasped and had to grab his arm.

Tobry howled. He could not bear to see her in pain.

"It's all right," she said. "I'm all right—the ties just need adjustin'."

She sat, her leg extended, retied the canvas strips and tried again. "Ahh!" she cried.

Tobry let out another howl.

"It's not that bad," she lied, readjusting the canvas straps. "Gettin' used to it."

She still could not walk without wincing, though the pain was bearable this time. At least, until her splints skidded on a rock, jarring her ankle so painfully that she screamed.

At once, Tobry swept her into his arms and carried her down to the bottom of the hill, ignoring her orders to put her down. Remembering his previous reckless behaviour, she wondered if the need to look after her was the only thing keeping him going.

Every rivulet and puddle was choked with foul grey ash and sludge that tainted the water and made it undrinkable. They came to a rock pool and found dozens of yellow-tailed fish floating on the water, evidently killed by the ash though still good to eat. They feasted on half of them and Rannilt cooked the rest to eat later.

Tobry climbed the next ridge but found no untainted water. He carried her down the far side and up three more ridges, each higher than the one before. He was exhausted but would not put her down.

The eruption storm had smashed the exposed trees along each ridge top for as far as she could see. She had no idea where he was going and was in too much pain to care—right now, one place was as good as another. The day had been cold and was getting colder as the afternoon waned. It was still raining watery mud.

"It's gettin' late," said Rannilt when they were halfway up another ridge, which was much higher than the previous ones. Dirty snow covered the ground here. "We've got to find shelter for the night. Put me down; I'm all right now."

He kept climbing through the mucky mixture of snow and ash, as if she had not spoken. They reached the crest and the land opened out before them to reveal a series of towering, snow-clad peaks. The snowfields were partly covered in grey ash, with white streaks here and there marking places where the saturated ash had slid away.

"I can see a road," said Rannilt, looking down.

Below them a broad track wound its way towards a pass, only to disappear beneath an avalanche of snow and broken ice that had long, dark shapes scattered through it. Many long shapes . . .

"What's that in the snow?" said Rannilt.

Tobry covered her eyes and walked the other way.

She yanked his hand aside. "Put—me—down!"

He kept walking. With a furious squirm she slipped free, landing on her good foot and the foot of the walking stick. She let out a yelp and hopped down towards the track, every jarring step sending stabs of pain through her ankle. How dare he treat her like a little kid!

By the time she was halfway she could smell the dead, and not long after that she was close enough to see what—or who—they had been before the scavengers came. Soldiers wearing the uniforms of Rix's army and Grandys' Herovian force. At least fifty of the former and hundreds of the latter. And more buried under the snow, she thought.

"Rix's men fought at three passes, one after another," said Rannilt. "This must be the third pass."

Tobry howled.

"Those poor men shouldn't be left here like this," she added hoarsely, for her mouth was as dry as paper. "It ain't right."

But there was nothing she could do—she couldn't bury hundreds of men with her bare hands. She licked her dry, cracked lips. She was scanning the slopes of the pass, looking for a spring or seep where she could find good water, when she made out a dark mark a third of the way up the slope on the other side of the pass.

"That's a cave," said Rannilt.

They crossed the track and headed up. The ground was wet here; a few minutes' excavation with a flat stone created a hole which slowly filled with clear water. She drank as much as her belly could hold, washed her face and hands and continued towards the cave.

"We'll need a fire. Can you find some dry wood?"

She collected kindling and sticks from sheltered spots beneath ledges and boulders, and dumped it in the cave entrance. It was broad and low, with an overhang at the front. Rannilt lowered herself to the ground, sighing as the weight came off her throbbing ankle. She made a nest with the kindling, wove a network of smaller sticks over it and had just struck sparks into the kindling with her flint and steel when someone groaned behind her.

Her hair stood up. She dragged herself around on hands and knees.

"Who's there?"

CHAPTER 88

There came another deep groan; a man's groan. Behind Rannilt the tinder caught and a little blaze flared up through the nest of sticks. She peered into the back of the cave, which was too dark to make him out. Whoever he was, he sounded ill. How could he be a danger to her . . . unless he was one of Axil Grandys' cruel followers.

Tobry was nowhere in sight, and as a healer she had no choice—if the man was injured she had to help him. She made a bundle of half a dozen sticks, poked the ends into the fire until they caught and held them up.

The flickering light revealed a pair of bloodshot green eyes, a lean, tanned face and a strong chin covered in a week's growth of dark stubble. His clothes were dark with dirt and she could not tell what uniform he was wearing—wait, there was a sergeant's insignia on his left shoulder.

"You're one of Rix's men, aren't you?"

"I am." His voice was weak; he sounded in great pain.

"Where are you hurt?" Rannilt said warily.

"Thigh bone—smashed." He tried to sit up, gasped, and slumped sideways, breathing shallowly. "Avalanche."

She took several steps up the sloping floor. His pants were blood-stained above the left knee and the whole limb was swollen—no, *bloated*. She caught a bad smell, one that sent a shudder down her spine.

"Tobry!" she yelled over her shoulder. "Come here!"

She wasn't afraid of the soldier now. She crawled to him, since the back of the cave wasn't high enough to stand in. The smell was really bad here.

"Seen—you before," said the man. "You're Pale, aren't you?"

"I'm Rannilt," she said absently. "I'm a healer."

"Won't be—healing me. It's gangrene! I'll be dead tomorrow."

She cut his pants leg away, inspected the mess and gagged. A piece of broken bone just above the knee was sticking out for a full inch through the swollen, livid flesh. How had he crawled all the way up from the avalanche with such a terrible injury? It must have been agony. And how long had he lain here, waiting to die? Ages—the battle for the third pass had been more than a week ago.

"What's your name?" said Rannilt.

"Jackery."

She looked up in surprise. "I heard about you in Garramide. You saved Rix's life."

"He's—good man," said Jackery. "Is he—?"

"He'll beat that lousy Axil Grandys, you'll see," she said stoutly.

Jackery lay back and closed his eyes, as if the brief conversation had exhausted him.

Rannilt could hear Tobry coming. She returned to the blaze and pushed the burning sticks together. He climbed the slope and dumped his load by the fire with a crash.

"One of Rix's men is here, and he's hurt bad," she said in a rush. "His leg's got gan-gangrene."

He sniffed and made a questioning sound.

"His name's Jackery and he saved Rix twice. I've got to do some-thin'."

Tobry went to the rear of the cave, squatted beside the soldier then came back, shaking his head. He piled wood on the fire until the blaze lit the whole cave and reflected off Jackery's feverish eyes.

"You can't heal gangrene," said Rannilt. "What if I . . . cut his leg off?" That was the darker side of healing, and terrible to contem-plate, though if it had to be done she would try her best.

Tobry made another enigmatic sound. It might have meant, *Maybe.*

"I'll need hot water. And more firewood. And bandages."

"No job for—eight-year-old girl," said Jackery.

"I think I might have turned eleven," Rannilt said vaguely, as if that made it all right.

Jackery held out a metal canteen. Tobry took it down the slope, filled it with water and put it in the fire, then hurried off. Was he running away, as he had run so many times before?

She sat by Jackery, sharpening her knife on a stone. While she worked she studied the wound in the firelight. Could she cut a man's leg off? It would be a terrible, agonising operation.

"I'd have to cut well above the bad flesh," she said aloud. "But the shock could kill you . . . or you could bleed to death."

"Dead man—anyway," said Jackery. "You're a brave girl."

"I'm a healer," said Rannilt with a touch of pride. "It's what I got to do."

But could she still heal? She'd failed with Tobry, and her own broken ankle. She had to try. Without her help Jackery would die.

Tobry came running, carrying an army healer's pack covered in icicles. He'd been all the way down to the avalanche. He opened it to reveal packets of bandages and jars of lotions and balms. She washed her hands, set her knife and various balms out on a piece of rag, and knelt beside Jackery's broken leg.

"Come here," she said to Tobry.

She wasn't sure he would come, but he knelt beside her and

looked down expectantly. Rannilt felt a tiny grain of hope for him as well.

"This is good," she said. "You and me, workin' together like friends."

He began to smile, glanced at Jackery's strained face and the smile faded.

"Not so good for him," Rannilt agreed. "Now, first we got to tie off the leg, else he'll bleed to death. We'll need rope or somethin'."

"My belt," said Jackery.

Tobry removed Jackery's belt and handed it to her. Rannilt poked several more holes in it with the point of her knife, ran it around Jackery's thigh above the injury and moved it back and forth until she felt the position was right. She pulled it as tight as she could and sat back, frowning.

Tobry took hold of the strap and pulled it two notches tighter, then looked meaningfully at the knife. Rannilt swallowed. It's just like cutting meat, she told herself. No, Jackery wasn't a piece of meat—he was a brave man who had done great things for Rix and for his country, and she had to do everything in her power to save him. Yet she was just a kid, pitifully small and weak and ignorant about healing ...

"I'm sorry," she said to Jackery. "This is really gunna hurt."

"Yes, it will," he said.

Some healers talked all the time but she did not know what else to say. She raised her knife, put it down and, with a piece of charcoal, drew a line around his thigh. Taking up the knife again, she studied it in her small hand.

"Your hand's nice and steady," said Jackery. He slipped a twisted rag between his teeth, bit down on it, and nodded.

She took a swift, gasping breath. Panic surged; she fought it down. Don't think about it—just do it! She pressed the blade against his skin and began the cut, as straight and steady as she could. Blood flooded out.

"Tighter, Tobry!" she cried, panicking. She hadn't thought healing would be this hard and she'd only just begun.

Tobry tightened the belt another notch. Rannilt continued the cut until she had gone all the way around, taking care to make the line straight and neat. Jackery's fists were knotted, his arms shaking, his eyes bulging as he bit down on the rag with all his strength. There was nothing she could do about his pain save to finish the job as quickly as she could. She cut deeper, and deeper.

"I can't see where to cut. Wipe the blood off."

Tobry mopped it up with a clean bandage, which he tossed onto the fire.

After several minutes the first part of the gruesome business was done—she had reached the bone. Rannilt swallowed. Now came the really hard bit—cutting cleanly through his thigh bone. She drew Jackery's heavy sword, raised it as high as the low roof would allow and aimed at the point where she had to cut. Her arm shook; she lowered the sword.

After taking three deep breaths she raised the sword, but again let it down.

"Sorry. I'm really scared."

Jackery took out the sodden rag and wiped his face with his sleeve. His skin was sallow, sweat-beaded, and his lips colourless. "Afraid you'll miss—and do more damage?"

She nodded. "Never used a sword in my life."

"Just do your best." He took up the rag and bit down on it again.

As Rannilt picked up the sword, her arm shook so badly that its tip hit the floor, *clang*. "I can't," she wailed. "I'm useless!"

Tobry plucked the sword from her hand, took aim and with a single sharp blow sheared through Jackery's thigh bone. He shrieked and the twisted rag shot from his mouth. His severed leg slid six inches down the sloping floor, as if to emphasise that it was no longer part of him.

Tobry thrust the sword into the coals and helped Rannilt up. She threw her arms around him. "Thank you. I knew we could do it, *together*."

She eyed the severed leg. Jackery was staring at it too, perhaps wondering what use he would be without it. Rannilt turned away. The worst was yet to come, and it was going to be really bad. The stump had to be cauterised, otherwise he would bleed to death as soon as the belt was undone.

"Fire's ruining my sword," said Jackery. He added wryly, "But then, I won't be using it again."

Rannilt shuddered as she inspected the bloody stump. Being a healer was harder than she had ever imagined. How could she press the red-hot blade against his raw flesh until it charred, again and again? How could she bear the screams of the bravest man she had ever met?

"If you've got the courage," said Jackery, "I might survive. If you can't do it, I will die."

"I don't think I can bear to do it," she whispered.

"Healing is the hardest profession of all, but I believe in you."

It wasn't enough. "Tobry, do you think—?"

He let out an echoing howl and bolted. She had pushed him too far.

"For pity's sake, be quick!" said Jackery. "Or if you want to see the depths a man can be reduced to, draw it out . . ."

If I can't do it, Rannilt thought, it means I don't have the courage to be a healer.

Her knees shook as she rose and, supporting herself on her stick, went to the fire. She wrapped several layers of rag around the hilt of the sword and drew it out. The blade was a dull red—she could feel its heat on her face.

She limped to Jackery, head bent. When she was close he spat out the twisted rag and sat up, the stump of his leg extended.

"It'll take a few goes to do the whole stump," she said.

"Yes," said Jackery.

She wanted to toss the hot blade aside and run, but his quiet courage gave her strength. Rannilt lined up the flat of the blade with the end of his stump and pressed the red-hot metal hard against the bloody flesh. He screamed, and every muscle in his body was at full strain, yet he did not pull his stump away. As the smoke belched up, sympathetic agony speared through her own thigh.

Her arm shook. She steadied it, lined up a different part of the blade with the underside of the stump and jammed it against the flesh again. Again he screamed, and again when she cauterised the left side, then the right, and finally the little triangles of raw flesh she had missed.

The sword fell from her hand. She was shaking all over and so weak that she could barely sit up. She fought it as she had fought everything else today, drawing on the last of her strength. A healer could not stop until the job was done.

Jackery lay on his back, as still as death. Pain speared through her heart; had the shock killed him? No, his chest was rising and falling. Mercifully, he was unconscious. She inspected the charred stump carefully, then slowly released the tension on the belt tourniquet, one hole at a time.

Beads of blood appeared on the stump here and there, though it did not flow freely. She smeared the stump with the strongest balm she had and bandaged it carefully. Yet even now her healer's job was not done. He had been weak before she began and the stump might become infected; he might get a fever. It would not take much for him to slip away.

After an hour or so he shuddered and opened his eyes. "You can't know how much I loved her."

"Your wife?" Rannilt took his icy hand.

"The enemy treated her terribly ... before they killed her. I couldn't get home in time. I should've been there to save her—or die with her ..."

"It wasn't your fault."

"*I wasn't there!*" he wailed. "I should be with her now."

"Would she want you to die?" said Rannilt. "Or live?"

Tears formed in his eyes. He turned away and drifted into a restless sleep. Rannilt felt that, despite his words, he did want to live. But did he want it enough?

Tobry did not come back. She sat beside Jackery all the hours of that night, wiping his brow, giving him sips of water and making sure he was neither too cool nor too hot, and only leaving his side to put more wood on the fire. But despite her efforts, he was fading.

There was only one thing left to do. Any good surgeon or nurse could cut a leg off the way she had done, but only someone with the true healer's gift could heal an injury by laying on their hands and drawing on the power within them. It was how she had healed Tobry's broken arm so quickly, weeks ago. She was afraid to test her gift in case it was truly gone, but there was no choice now.

She laid her hands on Jackery: on his brow, over his heart, and on his thigh above the stump, trying to draw on her unfathomable gift and pour her golden glow into him. But the golden glow, which used to flood from her fingertips when she was healing, would not come. Not a glimmer.

Rannilt's mouth tasted as if she had been drinking the bitter, tainted water. Her gift *was* gone! Her eyes prickled with tears. She went to rub her eyes but Jackery stirred restlessly and she lowered her hands again; she sensed that the human contact was helping him.

Finally, after an hour that felt like a day, his eyes flicked open. "Water, please."

She gave him a drink and several small pieces of the cooked fish.

"What's the matter?" said Jackery, as he ate.

"I've lost my healing gift." She told him about being struck down in the Hall of Representation.

"Don't see why that would rob a healer of her gift," said Jackery. "It comes from the heart, not the head."

"How would you know?"

"My wife was a healer."

"I healed Tobry before, but it doesn't work now. He won't even let me try. I think he's given up and just wants to die ... "

Jackery stared out into the darkness behind her, then closed his eyes and lay quietly for so long that she thought he must have gone to sleep again.

"I felt the same way after she died," he said at last. "I thought that way for months ... until a ten-year-old girl taught me the true meaning of courage."

"I didn't do—"

"You saved me when I wanted to die, and should have died. You're a great healer. You can heal Tobry, I know you can."

"No one's ever healed a full-blown shifter," she cried. "Never, *ever*!"

"Then you'll be the first," said Jackery. "And you'd better start right away ... at least, as soon as you've healed your ankle."

"No healer wastes her gift on herself," she muttered.

"Why would Tobry trust you to heal him when you won't heal

yourself? Besides, the gift can't be wasted by using it. Using it only makes it stronger."

"I'm too tired," she said feebly.

"A true healer is never too tired to heal."

"You just made that up," she said hotly.

Jackery smiled for the very first time. "Get on with it."

"But I've lost my gift."

"No, you've just lost your confidence because Tobry turned you away. Don't *think* about healing your ankle—just *do* it because you must. Because you're a born healer and you can do nothing else."

Rannilt closed her hands around her throbbing ankle, mentally sought out the break in the bone and called on her healing gift to encourage the two pieces to re-join. This time she felt the strength in herself at once; she felt it rising into her hands. The golden radiance burst forth from her fingers and the pain faded as the break in her ankle bone began to fuse.

From behind her there came a great sigh. She whirled. Tobry was at the entrance. He'd been there all this time and there was a light in his eyes she had not seen in ages.

Rannilt swallowed, looked up at him and said, "If you really, *truly* want to be healed, come here."

And he came.

CHAPTER 89

When Tali roused several days later it seemed as though half of Garramide was gathered around her bed. Rix and Glynnie, Benn, Nuddell, Thom in his wheeled chair, the women from the healery and Glynnie's kitchen militia, and many others. Even Gummy Ned, who had lived for ninety-seven years and was accounted the wisest fellow in the fortress, especially by himself, was there.

"Garramide survived then?" said Tali.

"Most of it," said Glynnie. "We've had a few roof collapses from wind and the weight of ash, and the south cistern is full of sludge. And it's going to take weeks to clear the ash out of the yards and gardens ... but it could have been worse."

"What about Hightspall?"

"The northern half of the Red Vomit is gone," said Rix, who held his binoculars in his lap as if he'd come straight from the lookout. "Blown to bits. And the level of Lake Fumerous has dropped by a hundred yards."

"It could have been worse, I suppose," said Glynnie. "The whole of the Red Vomit might have blown up, instead of only half of it."

Tali shuddered. "And Caulderon?"

"I couldn't see it through the dust," said Rix. "Though the force of the eruption went north, not east. The city would have been spared the worst."

"But Stonespell, and the earthquakes, would have toppled the old stone buildings."

"I dare say. Though most people live in wooden houses. Caulderon survived a huge eruption back in 1133. It may have survived this one."

"And where the land collapsed?" said Tali.

"It's a steaming pit ten miles by five, fringed by a hundred waterfalls. No one could have survived, and the surrounding land is buried under ash fifty feet deep. Even in Togl, only the tops of the towers are visible. There must be thousands dead. Tens of thousands."

"Eruptions are the curse of Hightspall," Gummy Ned said thickly. He clapped his empty gums together, a pulpy, irritating sound that he repeated every few minutes.

"What about Cython?" Tali cried. "What about the Pale? It's not far at all from the Red Vomit."

"I can't guess," said Rix. "It'll be days before it's safe for people there to send out carrier birds—maybe weeks. But ... maybe people living underground are better off. Stonespell wouldn't have hurt Cython, in any event, since it's not made from stone mortared together, but excavated out of solid rock."

"What if ash blocked the air vents? Or an earthquake cracked the water storages and flooded the place?"

What terror her people must have felt when the land was shaking itself to pieces. Cython appeared safe, deep underground, but Tali knew how vulnerable it was. How could the Pale, who had only taken over two months ago after a thousand years of ignorance and slavery, know how to look after their home in such a crisis? Was Cython still that marvellously engineered and cultured realm, or had it collapsed into anarchy?

"And the Three Spells?" said Tali.

"The first did a lot of damage," said Rix, "though probably not as much as Grandys intended."

"How do you know, Lord Deadhand?" said Thom, who was sitting in his wheeled chair with his plaster-encased legs stretched out in front of him. The left leg was healing well but his right leg had been badly broken. No one knew if he would ever walk again.

"I've had lots of carrier bird messages, lad. Stonespell only knocked down buildings made from mortared stone, but the Cythonians mostly build with unmortared stone, keyed together. Stonespell wouldn't have affected their buildings."

"How come Garramide didn't fall down?"

"Grandys built it, and he protected his own."

"What about Writspell?" said Glynnie.

"It failed. No one knows why."

"The number was wrong," said Tali.

"How do you mean?" said Rix.

"Grandys put the *Immortal Text* into the furnace, and your father's portrait, so when he cast the spell, nineteen documents burned."

"So what?"

"The spell required seventeen—no less, no more."

"What's happened to Grandys' army?" said Thom. "Will it come back?"

"No, lad," said Rix. "Everything they believed in is gone and that army will never fight again."

"So it's over," said Tali.

"I hope so, because life is going to be a struggle for years to come."

"Life *is* struggle," said Glynnie. "It's also hope."

"But what if the disasters keep coming until there's nothing left? Will the creeping ice finally cover us all?"

Not even Gummy Ned could answer that one.

CHAPTER 90

When they had gone, Tali lay back on her pillows, thinking about her quest over the past half year. Had justice been done for her mother? And if so, had the price been worth it: the price she had paid; and the price paid by all those people she had used in her reckless pursuit of justice at all costs.

Tali had not been *totally* responsible for Mia's beheading, but she was to blame for Lifka's cruel death. She had also used Rix at one time or another, and Tobry, and her thoughtlessness had led to gentle Rannilt being attacked by Lyf in his caverns months ago, and almost dying. That had been unforgivable. As was taking advantage of Benn to track down Lyf. How could she have risked the lives of a ten-year-old girl and boy?

In enumerating her crimes, Tali had saved the worst betrayal until last. She could not begin to imagine how Rannilt had brought Tobry back from the rabid state he had been in, the day Rix and Tali had chained him to the tree to put him down. But somehow Rannilt had surpassed all the healers in the land and, with love, devotion and sheer persistence, she had found the man inside the beast and brought him to the surface.

Tali could still see the desperate yearning in Tobry's eyes the night Rannilt had brought him to her—and his terrifying plunge into madness after her rejection. How could she have spurned him so coldly when he needed her most? What kind of a monster was she?

Radl had been right; Tali's justice was thinly disguised vengeance, and she had used most of her friends in pursuit of it. She wasn't much better than Lyf himself, and to claim otherwise was rank hypocrisy.

She had to make amends. She had to reach out to everyone she had harmed, and show them how deeply sorry she was ... though it wasn't that simple. Mia and Lifka were dead; those debts could never be repaid. And Tobry was scarred for life. She did not see how she could make it up to him, either.

It brought her back to her quest for justice. What did it really mean? Whenever Tali relived the murders of her four closest ancestors for their ebony pearls, her rage was as strong as ever and the oath sworn on her mother's body felt as binding as the day she had made it. Lyf had not paid!

He had regained king-magery, and the power that came with it—overwhelming power. Could his statement that the war was over be believed? Or would he march out to complete his conquest of the devastated land?

He had achieved his goal. And yet, she realised, Lyf had failed in the most vital way of all—in the king's primary duty to heal the land. She had seen how crushed he was by that failure, and how aged. Had he suffered enough, or must she follow the oath she had sworn on her mother's body to the bitter end? Must she bring Lyf to justice no matter what? Could she ever let go?

She roused from her self-excoriation to the realisation that someone was knocking on her door. No, pounding on it.

"Tali, Tali?"

It was Benn. She wrapped a blanket around herself and went to the door. She had spent so much time in bed that for a minute she felt light-headed. He kept pounding. It was making her head throb.

"I'm coming!" she snapped, then bit her tongue. Benn was one of the many she had injured; she had to start making amends right now.

"Sorry I snapped, Benn. What's the matter?"

He hadn't noticed. "It's Rannilt."

"What about her? She ... she's not dead?"

"She's come back," said Benn. "*With Tobry!*"

The light-headedness worsened. Tali clung to the door handle, afraid she was going to faint.

"Can—can you bring them here, when they're ready?"

"Rix said you've got to come down to the gates to meet them."

In public? Panic overwhelmed her—she was a wreck and she couldn't let him see her in such a state. Neither could she bear to see the servants' knowing looks, and their self-righteous judgement of her.

"I'd rather not," said Tali.

"Rix said you'd say that. He said you've got to come—*right now*."

"Um, I'll just have a wash and get dressed. I'll be twenty minutes."

"Rix said you'd say that, too. He said if you don't come immediately, he'll kick the door in and carry you down to the gates, even if you're—if you're *in the nuddy*." Benn's expression was a mixture of embarrassment and scandalised delight.

"All right!" Tali put on some slippers, pulled her tattered dressing gown around herself and went with him.

At least a hundred people jammed the gates, and almost all of them were taller than her; she could not see anything. She wriggled and pushed her way through, though she was so shockingly weak that the effort exhausted her.

She reached the front of the crowd. Rix was out ahead with Glynnie. Benn slipped in beside her. Rix was shaking hands with a tall man on crutches. Tali did not recognise him. He had a week's growth of black beard and his left leg had recently been amputated above the knee—she could see the outline of the bandages on his stump. He appeared to be in considerable pain, but he was smiling.

Rix moved and she saw Rannilt. And Tobry! He was even thinner than before; no, gaunt, and it made his hollow eyes appear huge, but thankfully they weren't cat eyes. They were Tobry's familiar grey eyes, a little bloodshot in the corners.

Rix shook hands with Tobry, embraced him, then shook hands with the one-legged man again and embraced him as well. Rix bent and hugged Rannilt, turned, and Tali saw that tears were flooding down his face. He made no effort to hide them. She had never seen him so overcome.

Benn pushed Thom's wheeled chair forward. Rix introduced the two boys to the one-legged man, who shook their hands, and she caught the name, "Jackery". Rix lifted Rannilt high; he was beaming, laughing and crying. He called for three cheers for her, and the throng roared.

Benn whispered in his ear. Rix turned, put Rannilt down and his eyes picked out Tali, standing there with a desperate look on her face.

"Guard house!" said Rix coolly.

She went inside. It was empty. She sat in one of the plain chairs behind the rectangular table and pushed the other three chairs as far away as possible. What was Tobry's mental state? Could he be healed? No, that was impossible. She leaned back and stared at the water-stained ceiling. She wanted to see him, but she dreaded it as well. What a curse love was; it caused nothing but pain.

The door opened. Her hands flew to her hair, but encountered only stubble and a bandage that must have been changed while she was asleep. What would Tobry think of her shaven head? What if he couldn't care less?

Rannilt entered, taking some time to locate Tali in the dim room. Tobry followed, slowly, warily.

"Tobry," she whispered. So many emotions were flooding her— hope, fear, guilt and shame among them—that it was all she could think of to say. Hope rose above the others but she forced it down. She could not take that path again. "Are you—?" She turned to Rannilt. "Is he—?"

"He's still a *shifter*," said Rannilt coldly. "But he's much better. Aren't you, Tobry?"

Tali reached over and patted the chair closest to hers, a yard and a half away. He sat down gingerly. Was he afraid he'd break it? No— it was as if he had to re-learn what a chair was for, and how to use it.

He looked into her eyes and she saw that the madness was gone. All she could see was Tobry, though he was not the old Tobry, any more than she was the old Tali. But still . . .

"I'm glad you're better," she said. Her heart was racing and she felt a desperate urge to run, but she had to begin to make amends. "Tobry, I'm sorry. I pushed you away when you needed me most. Betrayed you. I . . . I was too afraid of reaching out to you, and losing you again. I just couldn't bear it."

He stared at her without reacting. Did he understand what she had said? Did he care?

"You ... couldn't bear it," he said after a pause that seemed hours long.

What was he saying? She reached for his hand. He allowed her to take it. His hand was warm, but when she squeezed it, he did not squeeze back. His hand simply lay in hers. Fear stabbed through her. Something was wrong. Did he not want her? Had he only come back to reject her, the way she had rejected him?

Their eyes met and Tali saw through his eyes into the agony within. It wasn't her—it was the shifter curse. Rannilt had partly healed him, and he was no longer mad, but that only heightened the pain. Death was the only release from the emotional agony of a shifter's final phase, *and he longed for it*.

Chills spiralled up her arms. If he had reached out to her in love or friendship she could have come to terms with it; all her life she had yearned for the kind of love her mother and father had. She could even have coped with a cold rejection, bitter though it would have felt.

But his indifference burned her. It was as if she were no more than a detail from the past that had to be tidied up before he departed—and that she could *never* come to terms with.

"Not long ... to go," said Tobry. "Will you ... will you stay by me ... to end?"

Tali wiped her eyes, swallowed, then looked away, directly into Rannilt's anxious eyes. Tali looked down at her hands. She could not do this.

Rannilt let out a hiss of rage.

CHAPTER 91

"How is she?" said Rix to Glynnie.

Everyone who was able-bodied was out in the yard, shovelling muck into carts and barrows, because the whole fortress was covered in a thick layer of fine volcanic ash and it all had to be cleaned away while it was still damp. Once the sun dried it out it would set like rock. And even if they cleared it away today, there would be more ash to be moved in the morning.

"Her head wound is much better," said Glynnie carefully.

"I was talking about Tali's emotional state."

She sighed. "I know. One minute she's raging against the world, and Lyf, and herself—mostly herself. The next time I see her she's just sitting vacantly in her bed, as though she's lost her wits. I'm worried, Rix."

"What about Tobry?"

"He's just waiting for the end."

Rix shovelled furiously. "There's got to be something we can do."

"I've tried everything I can think of." Glynnie leaned her shovel against the wall and went inside.

Rix laboured on until he had filled the waiting cart and the sweat was pouring down his face. He looked back, with a degree of satisfaction, at the small area he had cleared. It was honest work, he could see the results immediately, and it was something he could control. There weren't many such things in his life right now.

And Lyf wasn't one of them, he thought when Lyf turned up at Garramide that afternoon, along with Errek, Moley Gryle and a small escort.

"Time to put aside old enmities," Lyf said when Rix challenged him at the gates. "And time for explanations, too. Errek has regained the last of the memories he lost when he invented king-magery."

"I don't see that what happened in his lifetime has much bearing on ours."

"If I hadn't invented king-magery," said Errek, "you would not exist, and neither would this land."

"It was that dire?"

"It was. If you don't understand the past, you're liable to make the same mistakes in the future."

"And if we *do* understand the past," Rix said, "we make different mistakes." He ordered the gates opened.

"Benn," he said to the lurking lad, "run to the kitchens and tell Catlin we have guests. And who they are, and how many."

That afternoon, after they had dined and repaired to the best sitting room, along with Tali and Glynnie, Rannilt and an ever-silent Tobry, Rix poured wine for those who wanted it and sat back in his chair.

"Begin," he said to Lyf.

Lyf was sitting, head bowed, deep in thought. Moley Gryle sat beside him. He did not look up, merely signed to Errek. Errek took Lyf's untouched goblet of red wine, held it under his nose and wafted the air above it with his fingers.

"Ahh!" he sighed. "If only wrythens could drink."

"I didn't know they—you—had a sense of smell," said Rix.

"Some don't. I do. It's one of my few pleasures." He sniffed again and put the goblet aside.

"Get on with it," said Lyf without looking up. "I don't have long left."

Errek bestowed a kingly glare on him. "The tale begins long before my time—indeed, before Cythe had kings. Our land was placid in its isolation then, until the wyverin came through."

"Came through *what*?" said Tali. "Where did it come from?"

"It was created in the terrible void between the worlds, long ago, by members of a betrayed and exiled race."

"To what purpose?" said Rix.

"The noblest purpose of all. They were desperate to get back to their own world," said Errek. "And when that failed, to reach *any* habitable world—"

"What's the wyverin got to do with it?"

"It was an experiment begun with good intentions—a beast created solely to produce, dissolved in its tears, an incredibly rare alchymical element called *gueride*. That's why the wyverin was called the Chymical Beast. And *gueride*, since Glynnie is about to ask, has the unique property of being able to create portals between one world and another. If you know how, and have enough of it, that is."

"But something went wrong," said Glynnie, sipping her wine.

"The Chymical Beast could be used, or rather, *reshaped*, to extract other alchymical elements from traces in its food," said Errek. "Almost all of the elements, in fact. But of course that offered limitless power, and it corrupted those who made use of it. Such power could not do otherwise.

"The ruling council of the exiles ordered the work abandoned and the Chymical Beast, and all the records, destroyed. This was done, but Herox, Axil Grandys' distant ancestor who was the leader of a clan of reckless alchymical sorcerers, smuggled out an egg. He also took copies of the most vital secrets, and kept on with the forbidden work in a distant part of the void."

"*I* began my quest for justice with noble intentions," said Tali in a monotone. "And I corrupted myself when I chose to pursue justice at any cost." She avoided Lyf's eyes, meeting Errek's instead.

"And you can't let go," said Errek.

"My quest has been the mainstay of my life since I was eight. If I give it up, what do I have left?"

"You must give it up," said Errek, kindly. His eyes flicked to Lyf, whose head was still bent, his face invisible, then back to Tali. "If you don't it will consume everything good in your life, and finally you as well."

He bent his wrinkled old neck for a moment, then continued.

"The wyverin we saw the other day is a greatly twisted version of a noble creature, a fire-breathing wyverin. Wyverins can create, or rather *liberate*, the light, gaseous element called hydrogenium inside them. However Herox reshaped the wyverin, internally, to separate *gueride* and almost all the other precious alchymical elements."

"Why?" said Glynnie.

"Once they had enough *gueride* to open a portal to a suitable world, Clan Herox wanted the power to take that world for themselves, and hold it."

"Why would anyone want to own a whole world?"

He shook his head at her naïvety. "Herox's greed was insatiable. He realised that pain greatly enhanced production of these elements, so he shaped the wyverin to be in perpetual pain. To increase the production of *gueride* he gave it over-sensitive eyes that were constantly producing tears. And to heighten its alchymical abilities, whenever it woke he fed it with a live sorcerer."

Rix stirred, not liking the way this story was going. "How did it end up here?"

"One day, tormented beyond endurance, the wyverin devoured Herox and the next two greatest sorcerers in the clan. It assimilated their genius for magery and went on a rampage. By now it was too big and powerful to deal with, so the ruling council drove it, and the surviving members of Clan Herox, into the most empty part of the void to starve."

"But it didn't starve."

"They didn't realise it could now feed on anything, even rock, dust and icy comets. It survived there, and Clan Herox subsisted nearby, hiding from the beast which so hated its creators. The clan found a way—a deadly dangerous way—to collect its tears in the hope that, one day, they would have enough *gueride* to make a portal and reach a real world . . . which they called their Promised Realm."

"And one day they did," said Glynnie.

"It finally formed enough *gueride* for Clan Herox to crystallise out the Waystone, *Incarnate*, a forbidden artefact."

"Why was it forbidden?"

"Because with a Waystone, even a minor adept can make a portal to almost anywhere, without leaving a trace. And that allows any crime or depravity or wickedness to be committed, anywhere, *and gotten away with*."

"Ah!" said Glynnie.

"Clan Herox used the Waystone to locate and widen a dimensional weakness—a portal to another world. Our world!"

"When was this?" said Rix.

"Twelve thousand years ago," said Errek. "The Heroxians were determined to have our world at any cost, but the starving wyverin also saw the dimensional weakness. It clawed a way through first and ended up in ancient Cythe. Here it fed ravenously on a rich seam of pitchblende ore, which was refined internally, and the metal from that ore was taken up into its scales.

"But those heavy metal scales gave out heat and irritated its skin, so it continually shed them and formed new scales. Eventually the great beast, consumed by the urge to lay eggs, began to carry its cast-off scales down into a deep cavern, where it arranged them in stacks to form a gigantic, self-warming nest. Soon the nest grew too warm, so it created channels to funnel groundwater through the cavern and carry the excess heat away.

"The eggs never hatched—perhaps that infernal radiance killed them—but the wyverin kept laying them; it kept hoping some would produce young. For two thousand years it continued to feed on the pitchblende ore, and carry down its scales, by which time it had deposited millions of them in the vast arrays of stacks you saw—"

"Creating the Engine at the heart of the land," said Glynnie.

"But it doesn't have metal scales now," said Rix.

"There's no pitchblende ore in the chamber where I put it to sleep," said Errek. "I made sure of that. But as I was saying, the metal extracted from pitchblende heated up everything around it, and bathed everything in that infernal luminosity.

"With time the drainage channels began to clog and the stacks of scales grew ever hotter until they formed the Engine, which woke the sleeping Vomits and caused them to erupt ever more violently. Vast ash clouds blocked out the sun, allowing ice to spread across the oceans . . . you see the picture, I'm sure."

"What about Clan Herox?" said Rix.

"Here the story is less clear," said Errek, "bound up as it is with lies and legends. However it appears that they followed the wyverin through the portal, intending to take our world, but things went wrong."

"Why?"

"Objects carried between worlds are transformed in unpredictable ways, and that included the Waystone. Halfway through, it went dead and the Heroxians ended up on the far side of the world, in a cruel land called Thanneron. Without the use of the Waystone they had no way to escape and were immediately enslaved.

"Because they looked so different from the other peoples of Thanneron, they were kept as slaves and serfs for thousands of years. Eventually they gained their freedom, though they were still oppressed and despised. When the chance came to join the First Fleet, many of them took it, determined to create a Promised Realm solely for themselves."

"What about king-magery?" said Tali. "It's said you invented it to heal the troubled land."

"A half-truth and a cover story to conceal the deadly reality," said Errek, "but let's back-step a bit. Ten thousand years ago the Engine overheated and caused a catastrophic eruption. A fourth Vomit, north-east of the present three, blew itself to bits so violently that a vast chasm was left where it had stood, the abyss that became Lake Fumerous.

"In central Hightspall nothing survived, and no one. After it was over the land was covered hundreds of feet deep in lava and ash. It rained acid for weeks, and then the overcast was so thick that everything froze. Hundreds of years passed before people dared to come over the mountains from east and west to move into that devastated but fertile land.

"I became Cythe's first king, and I worried that it would happen again. The wyverin was often seen in the sky then, and it always presaged dire events. I tracked it to its lair, discovered what it was, and I knew it could create more Engines. If it did, our land could not survive.

"After great labour I invented king-magery to put the wyverin into an enchanted sleep, then set my stone Defenders to watch over it and attempted to heal the land. But the strain was too great. I burned out my life force at the age of forty-two . . . I lived just long enough to pass on king-magery to my successor.

"The Engine could not be stopped or broken, because it proved deadly to everyone who approached it. Only by 'healing the land'— that is, using king-magery to keep the cooling water channels flowing freely—could a balance be maintained between stability and destruction."

"And this was done," said Tali, "until, two thousand years ago, Grandys walled Lyf up to die alone."

"King-magery was lost," said Lyf, still looking down, "and the balance tilted towards disaster."

"Which Mad Wil made so much worse a few months ago by walling off the cooling water channels," said Errek.

He sat for a moment in silence, then turned to Lyf. "And so we come to today, and what you must do to ensure the land can be healed."

Only now did Lyf raise his head, and Rix was astounded at the change in him. In the hour it had taken Errek to tell his tale, Lyf had changed from a relatively young man to a wrinkled ancient. The simmering rage that had always characterised him was also gone. He looked like a little, sad old man.

"My time is over," said Lyf. "Through my own corruption I lost my healing gift, and Cython is no more. The past I sought to recreate is gone forever and the urge for vengeance has been burned out of me." He looked into Tali's eyes as he said it, and she was the first to turn away.

"I cannot heal my land," he continued. "It's time to make amends for the many wrongs I've done, then leave this world so king-magery can pass to someone more suited to the task. Someone untainted."

Lyf's gaze passed across each of their faces, in turn, though he could not have been considering them. Only a Cythonian could inherit king-magery.

"Would that *I* could make amends for the terrible wrongs I've done," said Tali, to no one in particular.

Tobry let out a sharp breath. There was a long silence.

"But I'm afraid to go on that terrible journey . . ." said Lyf.

"And he cannot go alone," said Errek. "A living soul always accompanies the dead king—a sacrifice to make sure his soul does not go astray, but passes through the Abysm so king-magery can choose the new sovereign."

He paused again, longer this time.

"But no one should pass through the Lower Gate while still alive. The sacrificial soul suffers the most agonising death imaginable."

Another pause, then Errek went on.

"Who would go willingly to such a fate?"

CHAPTER 92

Tali stared at her fingers, which were still raw and blistered from crushing the master pearl. She did not know what to make of

Lyf's statement. He had not paid for his crimes, and now he was planning to take the final escape. Could she allow it?

Was her quest over, or must justice still be served? And did she, burdened with so many crimes of her own, none of them atoned for, have any right to act as its agent?

Tobry rose stiffly. "I will go with you, and gladly."

Rannilt sprang up, slapped him and tried to push him down into his chair. "*You won't!*" she said shrilly. "I'm not lettin' you sacrifice yourself just to get away *from her*." She glared at Tali, who looked away.

Errek bestowed a paternal smile on Rannilt. "The sacrificial soul must be fully human, in command of his or her faculties, and choose freely. Tobry, your offer is appreciated, but not accepted."

Tobry sat. Rannilt took hold of his hands and hissed something in his ear. He bent his head, meekly accepting her chastisement.

No one else spoke. The minutes passed. Lyf rose like the old man he now was.

"Thank you for listening. I must return to Turgur Thross to prepare myself for the Abysm."

He bowed to each of them in turn and began to shuffle out.

Tali sat, watching him, then realised that it could not be left like this. The business between them had to be ended. She went across to him, and despite her history and her oath she felt compassion for the troubled old man.

Tobry let out an inarticulate, howling cry and sprang to his feet. Rannilt held him back.

"Our fates were linked long ago," Tali said to Lyf, "by our shared drives for vengeance—whatever else we may have called it—and for justice. More and more, in your ruined shell, I see the decent young king of ancient times, and how he was driven by his barbaric fate to become the avenger."

Lyf turned, looked up and met her eyes. She could not read his.

"Now that the master pearl has been cut from me," she touched the top of her head, gingerly, "and the dreadful thing has been destroyed, I understand how you were driven to do the things you did. And why. And I've realised that I'm not so different. Driven by seeing my mother killed, and discovering that her ancestors were also murdered, I too have done terrible, shameful things. I have many evils to atone for, more than I care to think about … but I have to number the worst of them publicly, here, now—

"In Cython my double, Lifka, was tortured and executed because I used her identity to escape. I knew at the time I had treated Lifka badly. I did not know how badly I had wronged her until it was far too late.

"At one stage or another I've used every one of my friends—Mia, Rix, Tobry, Holm—" She closed her eyes for a few seconds, remembering. "And even Rannilt and Benn." She met their eyes, each in turn. "For what I did to you I am truly sorry. Especially for the reckless way I risked the lives of innocent children."

Finally she turned to Tobry. "Most of all, I'm sorry for what I've done to you. You came when you needed me desperately, and I rejected you. I betrayed your love, not because I did not love, but because I could not allow myself a hope that would inevitably be dashed, more cruelly than before."

Tobry gave her a stiff nod, as if in acknowledgement, though not necessarily forgiveness.

But Rannilt leapt to her feet, picked up her chair, swung it around her head as if she planned to smash it across Tali's face, then hurled it through the window. Glass went everywhere. She was red in the face and her eyes were bulging. Tali felt a stabbing pain in her belly.

"You're a stinkin', rotten liar," Rannilt said in a hoarse screech. "This ain't about makin' up for nothin'. You just want to make sure Lyf's dead, and punished, and you'll sacrifice anyone for it—even Tobry who loves you desperately though I'll never understand why—just to see your enemy dead. I hate you! I hate you! I hate you to bits!"

Rannilt collapsed in front of Tobry's chair, sobbing desperately. He picked her up and rocked her in his arms. He was looking Tali's way but his eyes were unfocused, gazing towards infinity.

The pain spread to Tali's head, then her heart. Her knees began to shake and tears welled in her eyes.

"That's not true," she whispered. As she reached out to Tobry, the tears flooded her hot cheeks.

"From when I was a little girl," said Tali, "I dreamed of the kind of love my mama and papa had for each other. Their love was pure, absolute, but all too brief—Papa was killed when I was six, and Mama when I was eight."

Tobry's head tilted down a little, though his eyes did not move. She could not tell if he was listening or blocking her out.

"I thought—no! I *had* the same kind of love, with Tobry. A love I expected to be eternal. But the shifter curse and my own folly broke it, and now I see in Tobry's eyes that it can never be repaired. He's leaving our world, and I have to atone for my crimes the only way I can.

"All this time, in selfishly pursuing my quest, I knew I was doing wrong by my own code. How could I require justice be done to Lyf, yet avoid it for myself? I have to pay."

"It was war," said Rix. "We all did things we regret now, but then it was kill or be killed. We did what we had to do to survive—and protect the people we cared about."

"I did what I did in the name of justice, yet what I really sought was revenge. I wanted to see Lyf suffer the way Mama had suffered."

"Lyf has suffered more than any man alive," said Moley Gryle.

"And it's enough," said Tali. "But the price of vengeance must be paid. I've got to end the cycle here, *now*. As Radl did, and Rix, and even Lyf. As Grandys and the Heroes could never do."

"What are you saying?" said Lyf.

"I will be your sacrificial soul," said Tali. "If you will show me the way."

CHAPTER 93

Lyf had to die and be given the proper kingly rites, but it could not take place on Touchstone, as of old. The crucible was broken and Touchstone utterly defiled.

Lyf would be given the rites at Turgur Thross, at the edge of the real, concealed Abysm. Once that was done his dead body, and Tali's live one, would make the journey from which there was no return. She already regretted her choice but would not repudiate it. Her debts had to be paid.

On the way they diverted to Touchstone to check on the crater where the wyverin had fallen. The portal was still whirling above it but the rubble was covered in a foot-deep layer of ash and there was no sign that it had ever been disturbed.

Hundreds of Cythonians, who had come via Lyf's gate, were gathered at Turgur Thross. It was still raining but they did not seem to be troubled by it. They met the intruders with hostile eyes, until Lyf explained what the people from Garramide were doing at this sacred ceremony.

A team of fifty men and women fastened ropes around an ancient, circular monument whose sides and top were intricately carved in the Cythian manner. The carvings, eroded by time and weather, were hard to make out. Another ten burly men and women levered the base of the monument up a few inches with long crowbars. The rope teams heaved, and slowly the monument ground to the side, exposing a circular shaft five yards across.

The Abysm.

Tali had seen it before, once at Lyf's caverns under Precipitous Crag, and another time when Rix, partly under Grandys' thrall, had attempted to raise his opalised body from the place where Lyf's wrythen had cast it in ancient times. Neither Abysm, it had since emerged, was the real one—they were merely displaced echoes of the true Abysm which had always been concealed here.

Everyone assembled around the shaft, to bear witness. Lyf's ancestor gallery was there too, one hundred and six spirit kings and queens. Moley Gryle stood by the canister containing king-magery.

Tali stood apart from everyone else, looking down, because every Cythonian eye was on her and she did not like being the focus of attention. She had spent too much time as a slave trying to avoid attention.

What did they make of her decision? Her life story, her incredible escape from Cython, her bouts with Lyf, and the tale of the rebellion she had led in Cython, were known to them all. Did they accept her decision to be the sacrificial soul, or did they, like Rannilt, think she planned to avenge herself on Lyf at the last moment? Whatever they thought, it did not show in their black eyes.

Her friends were also watching her. Tali could feel the pressure of their combined gazes. She kept looking down the Abysm. It seemed easier, somehow. She had once seen multi-coloured loops and whorls in its walls, patterns that held vast power. She had even tapped a tiny amount of it, months ago, but with the master pearl gone she could neither see the patterns nor draw upon the power. When she looked down the Abysm now, she saw only black.

Had Tobry appealed to her to live, she might have repudiated her offer to Lyf. Tobry's agony was evident on his face. He had begged her to stay until his end, and she had not even been able to do that for him.

But whatever Tobry was thinking, he stayed mute.

Lyf and Errek walked among the Cythonians, those who had been brought here from Caulderon because they were the best, strongest, cleverest or wisest. From these they selected fifteen possible candidates for the new king.

"Doesn't the old king select the new one?" said Rix.

"The choice is too important to be left to one man, no matter his rank," said Lyf.

Errek smiled at that. "King-magery itself selects the new king— the one judged most suited to the task."

"When? Now?"

"Once king-magery has been released, after Lyf passes the Lower Gate."

"And it selects the new king from those fifteen?" said Rix.

"Often, but not always. Sometimes it selects another. And occasionally it selects none."

"What happens then?" said Benn, who was studying the proceedings, wide-eyed. The end of the war had released him from his burdens and he was happily being a boy again.

"More of our people must be brought to the Abysm," said Errek, "and sometimes even a third lot, until king-magery touches one and its work is done."

He raised his hands. The low hum of talk died away. Wind

sighed through the overgrown ruins. Tali expected an oration, or perhaps a eulogy, but Lyf had asked that there be none.

"It is time," Errek said simply. "All hail the king."

The Cythonians cheered, as did the Hightspallers, and Tali too. This was no time to be churlish. The ovation echoed up and down the shaft, then died away.

Lyf accepted the potion from his weeping adjutant. Moley Gryle had prepared it lovingly, according to the ancient formula. He raised it to his people, to his ancestor gallery and then to his former enemies. All saluted him. He drained the cup, lay back, closed his eyes, and in a minute he was dead.

His ancestor gallery faded with his death, save only Errek First-King, who as a wrythen had an independent existence. He reached out to the body, intoned the rites of shriving he had written in the impossibly distant past, then raised his hand.

"Come."

Lyf's body drifted across until it was floating above the Abysm. Lyf's wrythen separated from it and waited there until Errek joined him. He reached out to Tali.

"Do you still cleave to your offer to be Lyf's sacrificial soul?"

Tali dared not look at her friends' faces. It would have undermined her resolve.

"I—I do," she said.

"Then come."

She found herself lifted up and drifting across the Abysm. When she joined Lyf and Errek, they began to sink. Now, as she looked on her friends' faces for the last time, she saw the pain she was causing them, even Rannilt. Too late!

Lyf, Errek and Tali sank down the Abysm. Tobry cried out in anguish. Tali could not bear to look up.

"I thought I would escape the pain in death," said Lyf after a minute or two, "yet still my shins throb from Grandys' cruel blow two thousand years ago."

"Soon you will be free of all pain," said Errek.

Down they went, and ever down, until the Abysm was black above and below, and its top became a tiny circle of white no bigger than a dot. Tali had no idea how far they had gone. It could have been miles. She could see the relief on Lyf's face as his pain was progressively lifted from him. Her pain, however, physical and mental, grew ever worse.

"The Lower Gate," said Errek.

Tali saw no gate, merely a point where the Abysm changed from uniform black to pure, dazzling white. Her pain was almost unbearable, and it would be much worse when she passed, alive, through the Lower Gate. What happened after that she did not know, save that she would die. She hoped it was quick.

Lyf's body passed through the Lower Gate and disappeared. His wrythen stopped above it. "It's gone!" he cried in wonderment. "All pain is gone."

He looked young and whole again, as he must have before his murder. Even his feet were restored.

"Come," said Errek. "We have both endured far beyond our allotted span, and I long for surcease."

"There is one final task," said Lyf.

"You astound me." Errek was smiling.

"I did Tali, her family and the women of her line a great wrong."

"Yes, you did," said Errek.

"Before I pass through the Lower Gate I have to atone. At least, I must do all I can to atone."

"That would be the action of a true king."

"But what I propose to do has never been done before. And I don't think I can do it alone."

"I doubt that you can," Errek said blandly.

"But with your help—"

"It will strain you to your limits. And if you take her pain upon yourself, it will not be lifted when you pass through the Lower Gate."

"I know," said Lyf, "but that's the price I must pay."

"What—what are you talking about?" said Tali. "Whatever it is, don't I get a say?"

"No," said Errek.

"Why not?"

"There's no democracy after death."

And precious little before it, she thought.

Lyf and Errek reached out and touched her, Lyf on the right shoulder, Errek on the brow. They strained for a few seconds, then all pain lifted from her. It came as such a relief that she floated up a few feet.

"There will be a cost to you, too," said Errek. "Before Lyf could take your pain upon himself, he had to give you a little of himself."

"What cost?" said Tali.

"You may outlive all your friends and everyone you know."

"Since I'll be down here, and they're in the real world, I hardly see that it matters."

"Ah," said Errek. "There's something Lyf neglected to tell you."

"What's that?"

"In ten thousand years of king-magery it has never been done before."

"Yes?" said Tali, still not understanding.

"We're sending you back."

She drifted for a few seconds. "Back?" she croaked.

Lyf nodded.

Tears formed in her eyes and she did not wipe them away. "Thank you."

"There may come a time," said Errek, "when you will long for release as much as I do. If that time comes you, alone among your kind, may take our Abysm."

"Thank you," she repeated, bowing to each of them.

"There is no nobler act than being a king's sacrificial soul," said Lyf.

He gestured and Tali began to drift upwards.

"I too have one final task," said Errek. "To pass on king-magery."

"But . . . " said Lyf. "Who are you passing it to?"

Errek smiled enigmatically but did not reply. He raised his right hand and pointed past Tali, up the shaft.

They drifted through the Lower Gate and vanished into white. Tali gave a great sigh.

Surely, now, the best justice that could be done had been done.

CHAPTER 94

"Had enough," muttered Rannilt. "Want to go home.'
Rix did too. They had been standing at the edge of the Abysm for hours, waiting for the sign that king-magery had anointed the new king, but no sign had yet come. He was cold, tired, wet and hungry, and he just wanted to go back to Garramide, close the door to his chambers and be alone with his grief.

"We can't," he said as patiently as he could. "It would be a great insult to the Cythonian people to walk away at such an important time."

"Bugger the Cythonian people!" Rannilt muttered.

"Rannilt!" hissed Glynnie. "Where did you learn such language?"

"We've just ended a war that began two thousand years ago," Rix said to Rannilt. "Insulting the Cythonians would not be a good way to begin the peace."

Rannilt scowled across the Abysm. They were laughing, joking, and loudly debating which of the candidates would be the next king. Whoever it was, he would inherit a devastated land, and his choices would either heal it or destroy it.

An argument broke out between two rival candidates, each loudly stating his own qualities and decrying the qualities of his rival.

Moley Gryle came running across, her black hair flying. "How dare you!" she cried, pushing them apart. "It will certainly be neither of you."

The rivals grinned, shook hands and walked off cheerfully. Rannilt made that seething sound again and went to Tobry, who was standing by himself, staring down into the Abysm with a desolate look on his face.

"It's all right," she said gently. "You've still got us."

He clutched at her hand and dragged his other hand across his eyes.

Rix swallowed the lump in his throat and went looking for Glynnie. Before he reached her there came a dazzling explosion of golden light from the canister of king-magery, a fountain that rose up from the centre and rained light beams down over all.

The core of the fountain continued rising. It drifted around over the heads of the Cythonians, then the fifteen candidates, and on, then finally swooped and settled.

On Rannilt.

Who was staring around her as if she had no idea what was going on.

There was utter silence for twenty seconds, then a deafening clamour as everyone, Cythonians and Hightspallers, started talking at once.

"Who the hell is she?" said an unidentified voice from the throng.

"Why her?" said one of the young men who had been fighting several minutes ago. "She's not even one of us."

"She's just a grubby little kid," said the second young man. "It's got to be a mistake."

Moley Gryle stepped forward. She held a parchment envelope in one hand.

"King-magery has spoken. The girl named Rannilt has been gifted with king-magery. She is our child-queen."

"But she's a *girl*!" said a third candidate.

"Queens generally come from girls," Moley Gryle said with evident sarcasm.

"But . . . she's not one of us. She's a Pale."

Moley Gryle held up the envelope. "This was given to me by Errek First-King, before he passed down the Abysm." She unsealed it and began to read.

"Rannilt's mother was a Pale," she read, "and her father was Cythonian. She is the best choice to unite our two peoples in the troubled times that lie ahead. But Rannilt has been chosen for other, finer qualities. She is the only *gifted* person never to use her great gift for herself, but only to help others.

"And because, when Lyf stole *quessence* from this innocent child five months ago, she lost her magical gift but gained Lyf's healing gift to enhance her own. No one but a future sovereign could have gained, and so wisely used, the healing gift of a king of Cythe."

Again there was silence. The radiance was slowly dwindling above Rannilt, shrinking as if it was passing into her. She kept turning around and around. She had no idea what to say, nor what to do.

Tobry stepped forward and put his arm around her.

"Rannilt!" he said thickly. "Queen of Cython; Queen of Hightspall."

"The land's gunna need a new name," said Rannilt. "Not Cythe or Cython, nor Hightspall neither." She looked up at the glow above her. "I'm gunna call the land Radian."

Rix smiled. It was a good start.

The Cythonians flooded around her. Rannilt clung to Tobry for a moment, before stepping forward, spraying her own golden radiance from her fingertips, to accept the congratulations of her people. And despite her ragged clothing, which was no cleaner than it should have been, in the golden light she did look like a little queen.

Rix pushed his way through the throng to Moley Gryle and shook her hand.

"Will your people challenge her?" he said anxiously.

"Oh, no," said Moley Gryle. "The choice made by king-magery can't be challenged. It's the only way a new king—or queen—can be appointed."

"What will your people do now? Caulderon must surely be uninhabitable—and much of Central Hightspall."

"Our numbers here are only a few hundred, but we'll clean out Turgur Thross and make it habitable again, then send out search parties to find out where the rest of our people—the survivors—have taken refuge. I think some may have gone back to Cython, begging for sanctuary, though whether they gained it . . . "

"Miracles have happened lately," said Rix.

"Yes, they have. But until we know what's happened to them, and can plan for the troubling future, it might be best if Rannilt remained with her own people. She has much to get used to."

Rix offered Moley Gryle whatever help in men and supplies he could spare, including the vast quantities of goods, wagons and food

Grandys' fleeing army had abandoned outside Garramide. She thanked him, gravely, and turned away to her people.

Then she turned back, surreptitiously withdrew a small, heavy parcel from inside her coat and handed it to him.

"She'll need this," Moley Gryle said quietly. "Best if it's always kept secret."

Rix put it in an inner pocket. She picked up the empty canister and turned away.

"Let's go," said Rannilt. "I'm starvin'.."

As they were heading to the horses, and the Cythonians prepared to close off the Abysm again, Tobry stopped dead, making a whimpering sound in his throat. Light was flooding up. He stumbled to the edge, his arms outstretched, as Tali rose out of the top of the Abysm and settled on the ashy, trampled grass.

She opened her eyes, looked around, and he was the first person she saw. She went to him. Knelt before him. Bowed her head.

"I'm sorry for being such a fool," she said, her voice muffled. "Can—can you ever forgive me?"

He looked down at the top of her head, which was covered in golden stubble. The bandage was gone, and so was the wound, save for a small round scar.

"We'll see," said Tobry gruffly.

"I don't deserve you."

"No, you don't."

He lifted her to her feet and they walked off, together but separate.

CHAPTER 95

No one said a word in the time it took to ride back to Garramide. Even Rannilt was unaccountably silent.

Tali was free of the pain in her head, the hot and cold flushes from her fever, and the nausea in her belly. Lyf had lifted all that from her when he had taken her pain on himself. But she was still tired, still weak and still worried about Tobry. She had no idea how he felt about her, or if he could ever forgive her, though she felt sure he still wanted to die.

His own pain had not been lifted, nor the shifter curse.

After a late lunch they assembled upstairs, in an octagonal room below the old dame's observatory. It had been one of Tobry's favourite places and Rannilt had adopted it on their return, refusing to let him reoccupy the grim Black Hole far below.

Tali looked out the west-facing window. Volcanic dust had reduced the sun's light to a feeble glow and it was almost as chilly as the endless winter that had only recently ended. Was it coming back—a volcanic winter?

"The harvest will be poor this year," said Rix, as if to break the silence, "and perhaps for years to come. Life will be hard. And the ice closes in faster than ever."

"I thought," said Glynnie, "if the land was healed, the ice might be turned back."

"Queen-magery won't be easy to learn, much less to master, and nor will it be quick. The kings of old Cythe were trained from birth, but who will train Rannilt? Magery has always been forbidden among the Cythonians, and with Lyf and Errek gone, who can teach her?"

Rannilt looked up from a pamphlet on magery she was studying, then down again.

"Not many on our side, either," said Tali. "Lyf targeted our magians as soon as the war began. Most of them are dead and I dare say the rest have gone into hiding. They won't be easy to coax out."

"But we did it!" cried Glynnie. She stood up. "When I look around the room, all I see is long faces. What's the matter with you? *We did it!* We fought for our land and our people. We fought against overwhelming odds—*and we won!*"

No one spoke, though one or two people were smiling.

"Yes, the future looks gloomy," Glynnie went on. "Yes, we're probably going to be hungry, and cold, and afraid a lot of the time over the next few years. But that's for tomorrow to worry about. For tonight, let's celebrate that we're alive, that we beat Grandys, that we have food in our bellies and a safe place to sleep. *And that the war is over!*"

"And Rannilt—queen," Tobry said unexpectedly. "Rannilt—make world—better place."

Rannilt did not look up this time.

Rix jumped up. "Stir up the fire, Glynnie, and fetch out the best goblets. Benn, run down to Catlin and declare a feast, *for everyone*. I'll bring up a barrel of our finest wine—we've got a whole world to celebrate."

When the needs of the servants and soldiers had been taken care of, and the children on the far side of the room, Rix pulled the shutters, drew the chairs closer to the fire, and handed around brimming goblets of a mature red that his great-aunt had laid down in the first year of her marriage, more than fifty years ago. They clinked their goblets and raised them.

"To a better world—Radian."

Tali settled back in the shadows and sipped her wine, rather tentatively. She had never had a head for drink but, perhaps because the master pearl was gone, found that she could tolerate this wine very well. She drank the whole goblet and closed her eyes, thinking about the future Errek had laid out for her: the possibility that she might outlive everyone she knew. A long, lonely life seemed more a curse than a blessing.

"It's time," Tobry said after an hour had gone by and everyone was feeling mellow.

Fear shafted through her and her eyes sprang open. "Time for what?"

"Shifters end—with world that's ended."

"No!" cried Rannilt. "Tobry, you can't go!"

"Shifter curse," said Tobry. "Hurts too much. Never be free."

He leaned back in his chair, and Tali saw that not even Rannilt could stop him this time. Tobry was in emotional torment from the shifter curse, the residue of the shifter madness, and perhaps her rejection too. He just wanted it to end.

Tali sat beside him and took his hand. To her surprise, Rannilt gave way to her.

"We don't want you to go," said Tali. "*I* don't want you to go."

"Holding you back," said Tobry. "Need—move on."

"I don't want to move on. I failed you badly, but the best times of my life were spent with you, and I want to be with you."

"What best times?"

"When Rannilt and I met you out in the Seethings and you were kind to me after—after Rix was not. When we saved each other, also in the Seethings. When you carried me to the ruins of Torgrist Manor that time. When we fought Lyf and the facinore in the wrythen's caverns. When you took me to the Honouring Ball. What a night that was! I couldn't dance a step," Tali said dreamily, "yet when I was in your arms I was the belle of the ball."

Tobry favoured her with the lopsided smile that lit up his face and took years off him. "Yes," he said softly. "That was—best time."

"I loved you," she said. "Love you. Yet I failed you, over and over."

"Don't want—talk," said Tobry.

"I have to tell you. I've got to acknowledge how terribly I let you down."

"No!" said Tobry.

"But—"

"Forgive you."

"But you can't . . . I haven't—"

"Forgive you," he repeated. "Shut up—arms around—last time."

Tali shuddered. Was this it? She could not speak; fear rose up her throat until it was choking her. She hugged him tightly and did not ever want to let go.

After a minute he pulled away and lay back in his chair. The deeply etched lines on his face seemed to dissolve as the tension drained from him. Rannilt laid her twisted hands on him but it did not seem to help.

He began to breathe shallowly. A flush developed on his face and throat. He went redder and grew hotter until he was drenched in sweat. He cried out, gasped, and fell silent.

The minutes passed into an hour, two, three. Tali did not move from his side. She was afraid to turn away in case it turned out to be his last moment, and when she turned back he would be gone.

Rannilt came and went with damp cloths and mugs of water. The fever passed, as quickly as it had come. His breathing was shallow now, the flush fading to grey. He breathed out, but did not breathe in.

"*No!*" Tali wailed.

Rannilt leapt over her and shook Tobry. His head lolled from side to side.

"Queen-magery!" said Rannilt.

She laid her hands on his head. "No," she said, shaking her head. She moved her hands to his heart, frowned, pursed her lips, then lowered them to the region of his liver.

"The twin livers!" she shrieked. "That's the true core of a shifter cat. It's gotta be. That's why no one's ever healed a shifter—they were healin' the wrong place."

She pressed her hands down hard, trembled, and the golden light that had so characterised her ever since she came into her gift exploded from her fingers.

"Queen-magery," she repeated, as if trying to call it when she did not know where it was—or perhaps *what* it was.

The golden light bathed Tobry's midriff; it seemed to pass into him. His face went red. He jerked convulsively and Tali saw a bulge grow under Rannilt's hands. Another bulge grew, a smaller one.

"It ain't workin'," said Rannilt. "What's wrong?"

Rix started, then ran across the room and took the wrapped package from the coat he had been wearing at the Abysm. He unwrapped the circlet and put it on Rannilt's head. It slipped down to her ears. He tilted it up at the front and down at the back so she could see.

Rannilt pressed down again. Tobry groaned; he thrashed and howled. His fingers hooked and clawed at her. The shifter side was fighting her all the way.

"A king's magery was used to create shifters," said Rix. "So queen-magery, in the hands of the rightful ruler, ought to be able to heal him from the shifter curse."

The smaller bulge under Rannilt's twisted fingers shrank and shrank again. The howling died away. Tobry's eyelids fluttered. The red washed from his face, replaced by jaundice yellow that deepened until even his empty eyes and lips were that colour. Rannilt pressed harder.

"Queen-magery," she called for the third time.

The second, smaller bulge continued to shrink until it disappeared. The larger bulge also shrank, though only a little. Tobry gave another jerk. A twitch. The yellow began to fade, first from the whites of his eyes, then from his lips and fingernails, and finally from the rest of his skin.

He slept for ten minutes, then his eyes opened, and this time they weren't empty. They were the old familiar grey, and the whites were white, with those little bloodshot patches Tali remembered in the corners.

Rannilt lifted her hands. "Not lettin' you die," she said to Tobry. "I need you for my teacher."

"There are far better teachers than I, child," said Tobry, a trifle haltingly, though in the old, familiar voice. "Cleverer teachers. Harder-working and more knowledgeable."

"And less sarcastic," Rix said with feeling, remembering his own youth.

"But I want *you*," said Rannilt.

Tobry smiled weakly, then raised his open hands, palms upward, as if to say, *What can I do? She's beaten me.* "Then you shall have me, my little queen."

He sat up and the strain was gone from his face, the tension that came from the shifter constantly attacking the man.

"Is the curse gone?" said Tali, suddenly feeling so light that she could have been weightless again, as she had been in the Abysm. It did not seem possible—no one could heal a shifter. She knew. She had tried. *Really gone?*

"I told you I could heal him," said Rannilt. "After we met at Glimmering, at the peace conference, I told you."

"Yes, you did," said Tali. "And lots of times after that. But I never believed you."

Rannilt looked down at her hands, which were red and swollen. She looked up again and Tali saw that she looked older, at least thirteen. The others had noticed it, too.

"You've aged in the healing," she said, alarmed. "Rannilt, you look two years older."

"I know."

"You've got to hold back your gift. You're just a kid and you've got your whole life ahead of you."

"I'm never holdin' back from healin'," said Rannilt. "Never, ever."

"But if healing a shifter has aged you two years, how much more life will you lose if you try to heal the land?"

"It's gunna take years to learn enough queen-magery to heal the land." Rannilt was glowing, radiant. "Years and years."

"But . . . you're just a little girl."

"And since the night Mama died beside me, when I was three, all I've ever wanted was to heal."

CHAPTER 96

Despite yesterday's optimism, Rix knew they had to face up to some hard realities, and the sooner the better.

It was 9 p.m. and they were in his rooms again—the adults in the salon and the children, apart from Thom, out in the anteroom. Through the window he could see the eerily glowing portal in the distance. It was still spinning slowly in the air, high above the rubble-filled crater where the wyverin had fallen.

Tali was scrunched up against Tobry, her eyes closed. He was reading *The Wicked Lords and Ladies of Garramide*, a small book, of questionable taste, bound in cracked green leather. Rix noticed that he was squinting, as if he needed spectacles. Tobry's ordeal had aged him in other ways, too—his face held more lines than a man of twenty-five should have, and many more scars. His hair was peppered with grey and sometimes he moved like a man twenty years older.

As Tobry looked down at Tali, his face took on a wary expression. Rix had often seen it lately, as if he had been hurt too deeply and was afraid to give himself completely. Yet in other respects he was the old Tobry, the friend who had stood by Rix for the past ten years, and that was, unquestionably, a miracle.

He studied the others, in turn. Glynnie, his joy, was staring into the fire, her slender frame wracked by occasional shivers. He often heard her crying out in the night; sometimes he carried her to his bed and held her, and in his arms her nightmares eased, though he did not know how to heal what really ailed her—the murder she had committed to save his life. Only time could do that. At least, he hoped it could . . .

Jackery sat in a corner, beside Thom in his wheeled chair. They had become friends and Rix often saw them discussing the merits of various kinds of walking aids, and how the locomotion of people on crutches or in wheeled chairs might be improved.

Jackery was whittling a wooden lower leg out of a piece of timber. He also planned to carve himself a foot and upper leg, and he'd spoken to the master smith about designing knee and ankle joints. Rix did not see how an artificial leg could be made to work, but Jackery was determined to walk again. With brilliant craftsmanship and sheer persistence, aided by a touch of magery, perhaps he would.

Rannilt was visible through the doorway, standing at the far end of the anteroom. She was studying a primer on magery, practising it with sweeping hand gestures, knocking over lamps and cups and everything else in her way.

Thom wheeled his chair out the door and over to Benn, and they began playing a game of cards. Rix watched them for a while. Thom was laughing like any normal, carefree boy, and it gladdened Rix's heart.

He returned to his easel; he was trying to paint the wyverin while his right hand remained alive. He wanted to show it fighting, feeding and flying, and to capture its majesty and its ferocity while he could still remember it clearly, but his painting would not go right.

With a grimace, he dropped his brush on the table. "We need to talk," he said quietly. "We've got some tough decisions to make."

Jackery put his carving down, swept the wood shavings up in a dustpan, hopped to the fire and tossed them in. The fire flared; he hopped back to his chair and sat with a thud. Rix perched on the arm of the chair beside him.

"Go on," said Tali.

Rix glanced at Rannilt and lowered his voice further. "I don't want to undermine Rannilt . . . "

"But?"

"The land needs healing *urgently*, but king-magery takes years to learn—"

"And *many* years to master," said Tobry.

"Many years," Rix echoed. "How can she learn enough to heal it in time? What if it's already past the point of no return? What if we only have months left? Or weeks?"

"Or *days*," Tali said direly. "I don't see how we can find out, Rix. No one can approach the Engine without suffering Radl's fate, and we can't make a gate to look into it, either."

"Even so, we've got to plan for the worst."

"What is the worst?" said Jackery, kneading the muscles of his thigh above the stump, and wincing. "I'm not up on all this."

"The worst," said Tali, "is a far greater eruption than the one we've just been through. The worst is the Engine making Hightspall blow itself to bits . . . and if that happens, the end may come so quickly that there'll be nothing we can do—save die!"

"Since there's nothing we can do about that," said Tobry, "there's no point worrying about it. We've nowhere to go, anyway; there's nothing beyond Hightspall but endless ice."

"I haven't fought all this way to give up now," Rix snapped.

Out in the anteroom, Rannilt stopped in mid-gesture. She looked at Rix, smiled vaguely, then swept her arms out in an extravagantly uncontrolled gesture. *Crash!* Another of his great-aunt's porcelain statuettes broken.

"Sorry," she said.

No one spoke. After several minutes Rix rose heavily, clipped a piece of paper onto the easel and took a stick of charcoal. After touching the talon blade for inspiration he did a sketch at lightning speed. This time, though he had not planned it, it showed the wyverin in its vast and gloomy lair.

He took a sip of wine and moved back a few feet. The sketch was far from perfect but it was better than any of today's paintings. Not bad at all.

"What's that?" Tobry said sharply.

"Where?" said Rix.

"There." Tobry pointed to the area below the wyverin's elongated snout.

"It's just shading."

"No, it's not." Tobry levered himself to his feet like an old man. "*There!* The woman."

"I didn't draw a woman—"

Rix bent down and then he made her out. Though the figure was only strokes and squiggles, it was definitely a buxom woman. Lirriam! She was reaching up with a stone, holding it below the wyverin's open eye—and the stone had a spark in the centre.

"What's she doing?" Tali rose and stood beside Tobry, staring at the sketch.

He did not answer.

"We saw her fall to her death," said Glynnie.

"But she fell with the Waystone in her hand," said Tali. "The stone that can make *portals*. If she made one as she fell . . . and called the wyverin through . . . it could be alive too."

Rix considered that possibility and didn't like it at all. "We don't know that either her or it is alive."

"This drawing says they are," said Tali.

"It's just a bloody sketch," he said irritably. He tore it off the easel to cast it into the fire. "It doesn't mean anything."

Tobry extended an arm to block him. "Your father's portrait was just a painting, Rix. Yet it predicted the fate of the land—and the doom of two men."

"Bah!" Rix tossed the sketch on the table and turned away.

"Why don't you draw it again?" said Glynnie. She went to the window and stood there, looking out into the night.

"No, paint it," said Tali.

"We've been through this kind of thing before," Rix said irritably, thinking about his cellar sketch that had shown Tali's mother, or Tali, or possibly both of them, being killed for an ebony pearl. His divinations were never simple, never clear. "I'm not doing it again."

Tali picked up the sketch and examined it in the firelight. "The wyverin's eye is open! Lyf's sleep spell must have broken." She peered at the small figure. "What *is* she up to?"

Jackery leaned forward. "She's holding the Waystone under the wyverin's eye, letting its tears flow over the stone."

"She's trying to wake it!" Tali cried.

"But it's already awake," said Rix.

"Not fully. When the stone's fully awake it glows crimson all the way through ..." She glanced towards the window. "So *that's* why the portal is still out there."

"Why?"

"The Waystone must have been awake enough to *create* a portal, but not to open it all the way—"

"Open it to another world, you mean?" said Tobry.

"Lirriam said she wanted to go someplace where she could start afresh ... and there's nowhere in our world she can do that."

A red flash lit the salon through the window, then faded.

"It's gone," Glynnie said softly.

"The portal?" Rix and Tali said at the same time.

"It flashed crimson, shot down towards the crater and disappeared."

"Then Lirriam's gone," said Rix, "and she's not coming back." He went to the window. "I hope she finds what she's looking for."

"What is she looking for?" said Tobry.

"Her ancestral people, I suppose. The folk Errek said had been 'treacherously exiled from their own world'—whoever they are."

"I think Tobry knows who they are," said Rannilt, standing in the doorway.

"Do I, my little queen?" said Tobry, smiling fondly at her.

"You kept sayin' the same word when we were in the wyverin's lair. It sounded like a name. 'Khar—, Khar—' or somethin'."

"Did I?" He frowned. "*Kharoon!* The exiled people who cast Herox out were called Kharoon ... or was it Khar*on*?"

"How do you know that?" Tali said curiously.

"I must have got it from the wyverin," said Tobry, "when we communed mind-to-mind, two beasts in pain."

A pink flush crept up Tali's pale face. She looked away.

"If Lirriam does find her people," Rix said slowly, "I wonder what they'll make of her?"

There was a long pause.

"The wyverin created the Engine in the first place," said Tali. "And now it's awake again. We can't risk it making any more. We've got to put it to sleep."

"We don't know the spell," said Tobry, "and even if we did, we don't have the power to use it. The sleep spell was mighty magery—it exhausted Lyf, and he was a far greater magian than any of us, with the power of king-magery at his command."

"Then the wyverin has to be killed."

"How?" said Rix. "It eats rock, earth, metal, flesh—*anything!* And it can't be burned, frozen, trapped, starved or poisoned."

"No magery we have can touch it," said Glynnie in a remote tone, as if her mind was elsewhere. "No weapon can pierce its armour. No warrior can stand against it . . ."

Tobry picked up the sketch and studied the wyverin's cavern. "Then if Hightspall is doomed—and the wyverin is going to be hunting in the ruins—we'd better make plans to get away while we can."

"What are you talking about?" Rix snapped.

Tobry tapped the paper below the wyverin's head. "It spent ten thousand years asleep in this cavern, its sore eyes streaming tears all that time. There were twin stalagmites three feet high where they'd been falling."

"So?"

Tobry did not speak for a minute, then his words fell into the silence like an anvil onto an eggcup. "There might be enough *gueride* in them to make another Waystone . . ."

No, Rix thought. No, no, *no!*

"Herox put the wyverin in perpetual torment just to get enough *gueride* to make the first Waystone," he said. "Sneaking into its cavern to steal the stuff would make the past six months seem like a birthday party."

"And trying to use a perilous Waystone, untutored, would be even more reckless," said Tali.

"But if the land can't be healed," said Tobry, "and the wyverin can't be put to sleep, a Waystone may be our only hope of survival."

"No one's risking their life based on my damned sketch!" said

Rix. "It could mean anything, or nothing. And more likely nothing."

"Then do another sketch," said Tali. "See if it confirms the first one."

Rix squirmed. "I really don't want to, Tali. My art has caused too much trouble already."

"What's our other choice?"

"You don't have the faintest idea what you're asking," he said coldly.

"Please try."

He loaded his brush and made some enigmatic blue-grey marks on a fresh canvas. They might have represented the upper snout of the wyverin. He took a clean brush and had just picked up some red paint when the strength drained out of his right hand. The brush fell, spattering red paint across the carpet. His hand went numb, starting at the wrist, then turned blue, then grey. Then black.

"My gift's gone," said Rix, studying his black fingers, which were beginning to shrivel and hook into claws like a mummified hand. "Gone for good."

"Rannilt?" said Tali. "Can you heal Rix's hand?"

Rannilt glanced at it for a second. "Can't heal stuff that's dead. It'll have to be cut off." She looked down again.

Tali was staring at Rix as if expecting him to be devastated by the loss of his hand and his gift of divination, but all he felt was a vast relief, a lightness that lifted him onto the tips of his toes.

"I'm glad it's gone," he said. "No one should know in advance what life has in store, otherwise where's the joy in unexpected good fortune?"

"Or the hope when you know about the coming darkness?" said Glynnie.

He went to her side and they looked out the window, up at the windswept stars. Glynnie took his good hand. She was smiling.

"The future is a blank canvas, and that's the way it should be," said Rix. "Whatever is to come, we'll face it *when* it comes."

"And in the meantime, we'll live every moment to the fullest."

"Let's raise a glass to that." He turned back to the table and the last bottle of wine.

"And to absent friends," said Jackery.

"And forgiveness?" said Tali, taking Tobry's arm.

"Yes, forgiveness." He kissed her on the forehead. "And most of all," Tobry added, looking through the doorway at Rannilt, who was lost in her world of healing magery, "to the child who never gave up."

"To Rannilt," said Rix, and tears stung his eyes. She was the true hero of their story.

As they touched goblets, the earth gave a deep, warning shudder.

THE END

ENDNOTE ON THE ENGINE

Years ago, in *Scientific American*, I read a fascinating article on naturally occurring nuclear reactors. About two billion years ago, seventeen separate natural reactors formed in the vicinity of Oklo in Gabon, Equatorial West Africa, in areas where the geological conditions—very rich uranium deposits and a suitable groundwater regime—allowed self-sustaining chain reactions to develop. These reactors operated for a period of about a million years.

When I read the article it struck me as a fascinating idea for a story. But The Tainted Realm is epic fantasy, and it was not appropriate for the Engine to have a purely scientific explanation. Thus I created the wyverin, a gigantic, intelligent beast that had been formed by magically re-engineering a wyvern to feed on earth and rock, and concentrate within its own body certain rare and desirable alchymical elements.

This had unintended consequences after the wyverin ate its creator, Herox, and escaped, because it was also capable of concentrating elements that he had never heard of. When it ended up in Cythe, it fed on a rich seam of pitchblende ore (the main ore of uranium), and the uranium became concentrated in its foot-long, inch-thick scales.

The uranium scales irritated its skin, so the wyverin continually shed them and formed new scales. Eventually, consumed by the urge to lay eggs, it began to carry its cast-off scales down into a deep cavern, where it arranged them in intricate stacks to form a gigantic, self-warming nest. Soon the nest grew too warm, so it created channels to funnel groundwater through the cavern and carry the excess heat away—and so the Engine at the heart of the land was born. That is, a self-sustaining reactor.

Because of the radiation, its eggs never hatched, but the wyverin did not understand that. It kept laying, hoping some eggs would produce young. For two thousand years it continued to feed on the pitchblende ore, and carry down its uranium scales, by which time it had deposited millions of them in an enormous, intricate array. The Engine produced considerable amounts of heat; enough, in the highly volcanic landscape of Central Hightspall, to wake the sleeping Vomits and set off another round of catastrophic eruptions.

Whether or not the Engine would really be capable of doing this is a matter for conjecture. It's also not clear whether the Cythian kings' attempts to "heal the land" by maintaining the water flow through the Engine would actually do so, or would make things worse—that would depend on many factors including the precise structure of the Engine. But The Tainted Realm is fantasy, not science fiction, and that's an issue for another story.

For further information, Google "Oklo reactor".

GLOSSARY

Abysm: The conduit or shaft down which Cythonian souls are believed to pass after death.

Alkoyl: A deadly alchymical fluid used for a myriad of purposes by the Cythonians. It will dissolve anything, even stone and flesh, and can only be kept in platina-ware.

Ancestor Gallery: Spirit versions of the 106 most important kings and ruling queens of old Cythe, recreated by Lyf as advisors, though they're more prone to lecture him about morality.

Banj: Tali's overseer when she was a slave in Cython. She killed him during her escape, with an uncontrollable blast of magery.

Bastion Barr: One of Grandys' fortresses, in the mountains of Nyrdly.

Benn: Glynnie's little brother, lost somewhere in Caulderon.

Bloody Herrie: An angry shade, one of Lyf's ancestor gallery.

Bombast: A barrel-shaped explosive weapon hurled by a catapult.

Caitsthe: The most powerful and savage of all shifters, a cat or cat-man, seven feet tall, which can heal wounds quickly by partial shifting. The one sure way to kill a caitsthe is by burning its twin livers on a fire fuelled with powdered lead. Tobry became one in order to save Rix and Tali at the end of Book 1: *Vengeance*.

Castle Rebroff: Grandys' strongest fortress north of Lake Fumerous.

Castle Swire: The first castle taken by Grandys after his return from opalisation.

Caulderon: The capital city of Hightspall, on the south-eastern shore of Lake Fumerous. Caulderon was built on the site of the Cythian city of Lucidand, which the Hightspallers largely tore down.

Caverns, the: The uncanny chambers deep below Precipitous Crag where Lyf's wrythen dwelt and plotted for almost two thousand years after his death.

Chancellor, the: The leader of Hightspall, a small, twisted, cunning man. He died at the end of Book 2: *Rebellion*.

Chuck-lash: A chymical device like a thick bootlace. When thrown at someone, it explodes against the skin leaving a burn wound like a whip lash. Heavier versions, such as death-lashes, can blast a limb off, or kill outright.

Chymical or Alchymical Art: An art practised with considerable mastery by the Cythonians, lately used to create many new kinds of weapons of war.

Chymical Beast: The wyverin.

Command: A powerful compulsion spell.

Cythe: The name of the Cythians' island realm in ancient times.

Cythian: Pertaining to Cythe, the name of the land and the kingdom in ancient times.

Cython: The underground city of the Cythonians. After losing the Two Hundred and Fifty Years War, the surviving *degradoes* went into the mines of Cythe fifteen hundred years ago and built a great city there. Cython lies under part of the Seethings, a thermal wasteland. Cython fell in the slaves' rebellion at the end of Book 2: *Rebellion*.

Cythonian: Pertaining to Cython; also, the people of Cython.

Deadhand: Rixium Ricinus.

Defenders: Tall stone statues of stern old women which guard the passage to the wyverin's lair.

***Degradoes*:** The Cythians who survived the Two Hundred and Fifty Years War were herded into filthy camps, and became known as *degradoes*. Several hundred years later Hightspall burned the camps and the *degradoes* were killed, save for a group of innocent children who disappeared underground, led by three matriarchs, who founded Cython following the instructions set down by Lyf in the Books of the Solaces.

Deroe: A magian possessed by Lyf's wrythen over a hundred years ago and used by him to cut out the first ebony pearl. Deroe subsequently rebelled and stole the next three pearls. He was killed by Lyf in Book 1: *Vengeance*.

Engine, the: At the lower end of the Hellish Conduit, in the deep heart of the land, Cythonians believe that a great subterranean Engine powers the workings of the land itself, causing volcanic eruptions, earthquakes and other phenomena. The Engine has to be kept in balance by the king's healing magery, but since king-magery was lost on Lyf's death two thousand years ago, the land has not been healed and the Engine is increasingly out of balance.

Errek First-King: The legendary inventor of king-magery, recreated as a spirit by Lyf.

Facinore: A vicious shifter-beast created by Lyf, and subsequently cannibalised to give him a body again, so he would be able to leave his caverns and take charge of the war.

First Fleet: The original fleet that came from ancestral Thanneron to Cythe, two thousand years ago, bearing the Hightspallers (and some Herovians, including those later known as the Five Heroes). Three more fleets came, though the Third or Herovian Fleet was wrecked by a storm and only one person out of seven thousand survived, a girl said to be Grandys' daughter, but actually adopted by him.

Five Heroes, the: The Five Herovians—Grandys, Syrten, Rufuss, Lirriam and Yulia who killed Lyf two thousand years ago. They were subsequently turned to opal and cast into the Abysm, but recently escaped and are bent on turning Hightspall into their Promised Realm.

Fortress Rutherin: A grim old fortress on the cliff-top above Rutherin, where the chancellor took refuge after fleeing from Caulderon.

Garramide: A vast, strong fortress on a high plateau in the Nandeloch Mountains, built by Grandys for his daughter nearly two thousand years ago. Rix's great-aunt left it to him on her death.

Gate: An instantaneous opening from one place to another.

Gauntlings: Humanoid, winged shifters created by Lyf for spying and for carrying his human spies. Gauntlings are prone to insubordination, vengeful malice and madness.

Gift, the: Magery.

Gift, Healing: The ability to heal by the laying on of hands. It is related to magery, though many people consider it separate from magery. This kind of healing is unrelated to the kind of healing that the kings of Cythe could do, which *was* a form of magery.

Glimmering-by-the-Water: An ancient temple site on the southern tip of the Nusidand Peninsula in Lake Fumerous; site of the peace conference.

Glowstone: A kind of rock, mined in Cython, which emits a feeble bluish glow. Used for lighting in Cython, and elsewhere.

Glynnie: A heroic maidservant who rescued Rix from Grandys. Benn's big sister.

Grandys, Axil: A great warrior and leader; a brutal and treacherous man who was the first of the Five Heroes and the legendary founder of Hightspall. Most of all, he wants the power of king-magery so he can create the Herovians' Promised Realm.

Grasbee: A general of Hightspall's army, sacked for incompetence.

Grenado: A hand-thrown exploding weapon.

Grolik: A gauntling in Lyf's service.

Healing blood: Tali's blood, and perhaps the blood of some other Pale slaves, has the virtue of healing. It can even heal some people who have been turned to shifters, if given soon enough. This virtue may be due to exposure to emanations from heat-stone.

Hellish Conduit: A winding, exotic passage that leads down from Cython towards the subterranean Engine.

Herovians, the: A persecuted minority who came to Hightspall on the first fleets, seeking their Promised Realm, two thousand years ago. Due to their fanaticism and brutal excess they fell from power and many now conceal their true heritage.

Hightspall: The nation founded by the people who came on the First Fleet, after taking Cythe from the Cythians.

Hillish: One of Lyf's generals.

Holm: An oldish man, very clever with his hands, Tali's friend. He was once a brilliant surgeon.

Hramm: Lyf's supreme commander, an acerbic, impatient man.

Ice, the: Ice sheets spreading up from the southern pole, and down from the north, are steadily cutting Hightspall off from the rest of the world. The ice is thought to be due to the Engine at the heart of the land getting out of balance. Many Hightspallers also believe that the land is rising up against them because of the evil way they took it from the Cythians two thousand years ago.

Immortal Text, **the:** The sacred book of the Herovians. It sets out the guiding beliefs of their faith, tells them where to seek the Promised Realm, and how to take it. Other people believe the *Immortal Text* to be a pernicious, racist tract which should be destroyed.

Incarnate: A perilous stone, now dead, carried by Lirriam. She is trying to wake it. Also called the Waystone.

Iron Book, the: A book, *The Consolation of Vengeance*, written by Lyf for his people; the final book of the Solaces. He etched the words of the book onto sheet iron pages, using alkoyl. The book's appearance in Cython was a call to war, though the iron book was not yet complete when Tali stole it from Lyf. It was subsequently stolen by Mad Wil, a blind Cythonian seer and killer who is obsessed by completing the story in the book.

Iusia (vi Torgrist): Tali's mother, murdered in front of Tali by Lord and Lady Ricinus for her ebony pearl, at the beginning of Book 1: *Vengeance*. They on-sold the pearl to Deroe.

Jackery: A highly competent sergeant in Hightspall's army.

King-magery: Magery used by the king or ruling queen of Cythe to heal the land or the people. No one else in Cythe was permitted to use magery. King-magery was only passed on to the new king on the death of the old king. But because Lyf died alone and his body was never found, the death rituals could not be enacted, his king-magery was never passed on, and it was lost. King-magery is different from, and far more powerful than, other forms of magery.

Krebb: A colonel of Hightspall's army, sacked by the former chancellor.

Lady Ricinus: Rix's late mother, a cold, manipulative woman, obsessed with raising the social position of House Ricinus at any cost. She was executed at the end of Book 1: *Vengeance* for high treason, and the murder of Tali's mother and grandmother for their ebony pearls.

Libbens: A choleric general, sacked by the former chancellor.

Lirriam: One of the Five Heroes, an enigmatic woman and Grandys' bitter rival.

Lord Ricinus: Rix's father, and lord of House Ricinus, formerly one of the wealthiest and most powerful Houses in Hightspall. Also a foul drunkard, sick with guilt at the crimes his wife forced him to commit. Executed at the end of Book 1: *Vengeance* for high treason and murder.

Lyf, King Lyf: The eighteen-year-old king of Cythe at the time the first war began. He was betrayed in his own temple by Grandys and the other Heroes, maimed and walled up to die in the catacombs. But after death Lyf's soul could not pass on, and he used the last of his king-magery to become a wrythen, so as to protect his people and take revenge on the enemy. Later Lyf wrote the Solaces, a series of books which showed his people how to live underground. As a wrythen, he spent the next two thousand years harrying Hightspall, and trying to get his king-magery, and a body, back. Now reincarnated from his wrythen, Lyf leads the Cythonian people in a war of vengeance. Lyf needs all five ebony pearls in order to recover king-magery, so as to do his kingly duty and heal the troubled land.

Magery: Wizardry, sorcery. Magery was brought by the Hightspallers from Thanneron, but has been failing ever since. This is believed to be due to the land they conquered rising up against them. Magery has a different origin to king-magery.

Magian: A wizard or sorcerer.

***Maloch*:** An enchanted sword made from titane. Originally wielded by Axil Grandys, it was lost for almost two thousand years after he was cast into the Abysm. Rix inherited *Maloch* but later Grandys took it back. Its enchantment protects him.

Matriarchs: When the king-magery was lost, Cythe could no longer have a king, and after the Cythonians took refuge in Cython they were ruled by a trio of matriarchs, who were themselves advised by the Solaces. They died in the slaves' rebellion.

Mia: Tali's best friend, executed in Cython for using magery. Tali blames herself and swore a blood oath to make up for failing Mia. This subsequently became a blood oath to save her people, the Pale which she did in *Rebellion*.

Moley Gryle: Lyf's adjutant, a striking young woman and a brilliant *intuit*.

Mulclast: A natural fortress in between the Vomits.

Nandelochs, Nandeloch Mountains: A high and rugged range of mountains in north-east Hightspall. A Herovian stronghold.

Nuddell: Rix's sergeant at Fortress Garramide.

Pale, the: A thousand years ago, a host of noble Hightspaller children were given to the enemy as hostages, but, oddly, never ransomed. Their enslaved descendants are known as the Pale because, having lived underground in Cython all their lives, their skin has never been exposed to the sun.

Pearl, Ebony: Black, marble-sized objects that have grown inside the heads of certain Pale women in Cython, due to radiance from the heatstone deposit. Ebony pearls can enhance a gift for magery many times over, and are beyond price. Only five can exist at any one time. Four of Tali's ancestors were killed for their ebony pearls and Tali bears the fifth, the master pearl, though few people know this deadly secret.

Portal: A gateway that can be used both within and between worlds.

Promised Realm: The legendary land the Herovians came to Cythe in search of, but have not yet found (or created).

Radl: Commander of the Pale army. She has been Tali's enemy since childhood.

Rannilt: A little slave girl who escaped with Tali. She wants to be a healer.

Red Mesa: A mesa in southern Reffering, used as a lookout by Grandys.

Ricinus: A fabulously wealthy house in Hightspall, toppled by the chancellor after the discovery that the basis of its wealth was the depraved trade in ebony pearls. The name comes from the deadly poison ricin, obtained from the castor oil plant, which was the symbol on the family crest.

Rixium (Rix): Formerly heir to the vast estates of House Ricinus, he was stripped of this inheritance by the chancellor due to the high treason of Rix's parents. Rix is a brilliant swordsman, and also a masterful artist, though some of his paintings have been disturbingly divinatory. His right hand was amputated on the chancellor's orders, though Glynnie re-joined it with some of Tali's healing blood. Rix is now Lord of Fortress Garramide and reluctant commander of Hightspall's army. He's also known as Deadhand.

Rufuss: One of the Five Heroes, a tall, gaunt man full of murderous rage.

Sacred Beast: The wyverin.

Salyk: A compassionate female Cythonian soldier who found Rix's brilliant portrait of his father, and saved it, disobeying Lyf's order to burn it. She later rescued Tobry but was put to death by her own people for aiding the enemy.

Seethings, the: A thermal wasteland of boiling pools, chymical lakes and deadly sinkholes.

Shifters: Vicious, bastard creatures created by Lyf with the blasphemous art of *germine*, in order to harry the Hightspallers. Shifters come in a number of kinds, such as hyena and jackal shifters, caitsthes and gauntlings. All are prone to insanity. Exposure to their bite or blood can cause others to become shifters.

Shillilar: A foreseeing. It was Wil's foreseeing that identified Tali as the one who would change the story Lyf had written in his iron book, *The Consolation of Vengeance*, and thus change the world.

Solaces: A series of books written by Lyf, detailing various aspects of living underground, which he sorcerously transmitted to the matriarchs of Cython. They were held in the Chamber of the Solaces. There, Wil was the first to glimpse the iron book. He had a *shillilar* or foreseeing about the one (Tali) but the book burned his eyes out, and he never told the matriarchs the truth about her.

Stink-damp: Rotten-egg gas that seeps up from underground. It is used for lighting in Caulderon though it's both poisonous and explosive.

Sunstone: A kind of rock, mined in Cython. After exposure to sunlight, sunstone emits a bright light for days or weeks. It is used to provide "sunlight" in the underground green farms in Cython. Breaking a sunstone releases all its stored power at once, which is deadly to those directly exposed, and Cythonians (but not Pale) nearby but not directly exposed will be knocked unconscious.

Syrten: One of the Five Heroes, an inarticulate, golem-like warrior.

Tali: The familiar name of Thalalie vi Torgrist, a Pale slave. She was the first person in a thousand years to escape from Cython. Tali's mother and three other female ancestors were murdered for magical ebony pearls grown inside their heads, and Tali is being hunted because she bears the fifth pearl, the master pearl.

Temple, Lyf's: In ancient times it was the Cythian kings' private temple, but it was defiled by Grandys' treachery there, and his assault and abduction of King Lyf. It was subsequently preserved as a skull-shaped chamber deep beneath Palace Ricinus, and was where Tali's ancestors were killed for their ebony pearls. Lyf has recently rebuilt it.

Thanneron: The ancestral homeland of the Hightspallers, on the far side of the world. They came from Thanneron in four fleets, two thousand years ago. All contact with Thanneron was lost after the Fourth Fleet, and it is believed to have disappeared under the ice long ago.

Thermitto: An alchemical powder which burns so hot that it can melt rock; used for mining in Cython by the technique known as *splittery*.

Thom: A wood boy in Garramide.

Tirnan Twil: A remote tower, a kind of museum to the Five Heroes and their heritage; it was burned by gauntlings in Book 2: *Rebellion*.

Titane: A light, immensely strong metal. The secret of how to forge it has been lost.

Tobry Lagger: Rix's brave, clever but disreputable friend, Tobry lost everything when House Lagger fell when he was about thirteen. Tobry had a mortal fear of shifters, and of becoming one himself, because his maternal grandfather became one and stalked the house, and Tobry was forced to kill him to save his father. At the end of Book 1: *Vengeance*, Tobry became a caitsthe because it was the only way to save his friends. The chancellor ordered him hurled from the top of Rix's tower to his death. Tobry survived but is now a mad, dying shifter.

Tonklin: A loyal sergeant, rescued from a crevasse by Rix.

Touchstone: A holy peak with three carved platforms, near Turgur Thross, where king-magery was first used.

Turgur Thross: Sacred ruins at the northern edge of the plateau of Garramide.

Two Hundred and Fifty Years War, the: The war that Grandys began a couple of years after the arrival of the First Fleet. It ended two hundered and fifty years later (1750 years ago) with the utter defeat of Cythe.

Vi Torgrist: Tali's family name. Vi Torgrist is an ancient house which first came to Hightspall on the Second Fleet, but is now extinct except in the Pale.

Vomits, the: A trio of immense active volcanoes, the Red, Brown and Black Vomits, south-west of Caulderon. Cythonian legend holds that a fourth Vomit blew itself to bits in ancient times, creating the vast crater now filled by Lake Fumerous.

Wil, Mad Wil, Wil the Sump: A lowly, blind Cythonian who has *shillilars*, and is addicted to sniffing *alkoyl*. Wil is obsessed by the story set down in the iron book; but the story has gone wrong and he wants to set it right, but in trying to do so he has interfered with the Engine.

Wrythen: A semi-solid spirit or ghost.

Wyverin, the: A legendary beast whose appearance is said to forecast the doom of Hightspall.

Yulia: One of the Five Heroes, she is sick with guilt at all they have done.

ACKNOWLEDGEMENTS

I would like to thank my Australian publisher, Bernadette Foley, my UK editor Jenni Hill, my editors in the US, Will Hinton and Tom Bouman, and in Australia, Kate Stevens and Abigail Nathan, plus all the other people at Orbit Books who have worked so hard and so long on this series. I would especially like to thank Tim Holman for advice, assistance and encouragement since I first became an Orbit author way back in 1999. To my agent, Selwa Anthony, thank you for your support over the past seventeen years and twenty-nine books.

extras

www.orbitbooks.net

about the author

Ian Irvine was born in Bathurst in 1950, and educated at Chevalier College and the University of Sydney, where he took a PhD in marine science. After working as an environmental project manager, Ian set up his own consulting firm in 1986, carrying out studies for clients in Australia and overseas. He has worked in many countries in the Asia–Pacific region. An expert in marine pollution, Ian has developed some of Australia's national guidelines for the protection of the oceanic environment and still works in this field.

To date, Ian has written twenty-nine novels, including epic fantasy, eco-thrillers and books for children. The eleven books of his Three Worlds epic fantasy sequence, The View from the Mirror quartet, The Well of Echoes quartet and The Song of the Tears trilogy, have been bestsellers in Australia and the UK and have been published in many countries and languages. He is currently working on the long-awaited sequel to The View from the Mirror quartet.

Ian can be contacted at ianirvine@ozemail.com.au.

His website is www.ian-irvine.com.

His Facebook author site is www.facebook.com/ianirvine.author.

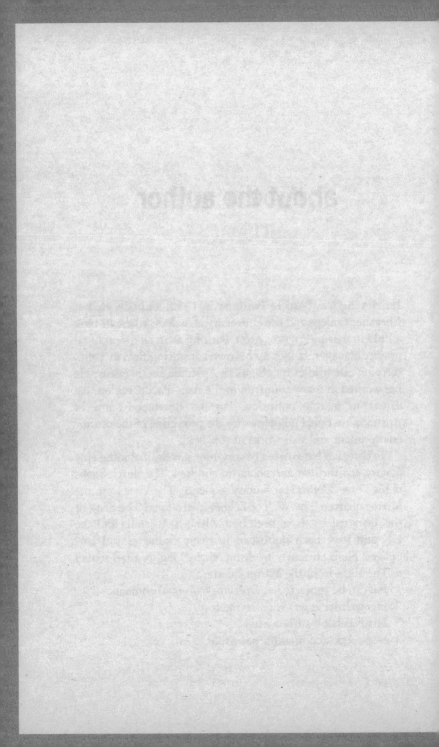

if you enjoyed
JUSTICE
look out for

THE CROWN TOWER
Book One of the Riyria Chronicles

by

Michael J. Sullivan

CHAPTER 1

PICKLES

Hadrian Blackwater hadn't gone more than five steps off the ship before he was robbed.

The bag—his only bag—was torn from his hand. He never even saw the thief. Hadrian couldn't see much of anything in the lantern-lit chaos surrounding the pier, just a mass of faces, people shoving to get away from the gangway or get nearer to the ship. Used to the rhythms of a pitching deck, he struggled to keep his feet on the stationary dock amidst the jostling scramble. The newly arrived moved hesitantly, causing congestion. Many onshore searched for friends and relatives, yelling, jumping, waving arms—chasing the attention of someone. Others were more professional, holding torches and shouting offers for lodging and jobs. One bald man with a voice like a war trumpet stood on a crate, promising that The Black Cat Tavern offered the strongest ale at the cheapest prices. Twenty feet away, his competition balanced on a wobbly barrel and proclaimed the bald man a liar. He further insisted The Lucky Hat was the only local tavern that didn't substitute dog meat for mutton. Hadrian didn't care. He wanted to get out of the crowd and find the thief who stole his bag. After only a few minutes, he realized that wasn't going to happen. He settled for protecting his purse and considered himself lucky. At least nothing of value was lost—just clothing, but given how cold Avryn was in autumn, that might be a problem.

Hadrian followed the flow of bodies, not that he had much choice. Adrift in the strong current, he bobbed along with his head just above the surface. The dock creaked and moaned under the weight of escaping passengers who hurried away from what had been their cramped home for more than a month. Weeks breathing clean salt air had been replaced by the pungent smells of fish, smoke, and tar. Rising far above the dimly lit docks, the city's lights appeared as brighter points in a starlit world.

Hadrian followed four dark-skinned Calian men hauling crates packed with colorful birds, which squawked and rattled their cages. Behind him walked a poorly dressed man and woman. The man carried *two* bags, one over a shoulder and the other tucked under an arm. Apparently no one was interested in *their* belongings. Hadrian realized he should have worn something else. His eastern attire was not only uselessly thin, but in a land of leather and wool, the bleached white linen thawb and the gold-trimmed cloak screamed *wealth*.

"Here! Over here!" The barely distinguishable voice was one more sound in the maelstrom of shouts, wagon wheels, bells, and whistles. "This way. Yes, you, come. Come!"

Reaching the end of the ramp and clearing most of the congestion, Hadrian spotted an adolescent boy. Dressed in tattered clothes, he waited beneath the fiery glow of a swaying lantern. The wiry youth held Hadrian's bag and beamed an enormous smile. "Yes, yes, you there. Please come. Right over here," he called, waving with his free hand.

"That's my bag!" Hadrian shouted, struggling to reach him and stymied by the remaining crowd blocking the narrow pier.

"Yes! Yes!" The lad grinned wider, his eyes bright with enthusiasm. "You are very lucky I took it from you or someone would have surely stolen it."

"*You* stole it!"

"No. No. Not at all. I have been faithfully protecting your most valued property." The youth straightened his willowy back such that Hadrian thought he might salute. "Someone like you should not be carrying your own bag."

Hadrian squeezed around three women who'd paused to comfort a crying child, only to be halted by an elderly man dragging an incredibly large trunk. The old guy, wraith thin with bright white hair, blocked the narrow isthmus already cluttered by the mountain of bags being recklessly thrown to the pier from the ship.

"What do you mean *someone like me*?" Hadrian shouted over the trunk as the old man struggled in front of him.

"You are a great knight, yes?"

"No, I'm not."

The boy pointed at him. "You must be. Look how big you are and you carry swords—three swords. And that one on your back is huge. Only a knight carries such things."

Hadrian sighed when the old man's trunk became wedged in the gap between the decking and the ramp. He reached down and lifted it free, receiving several vows of gratitude in an unfamiliar language.

"See," the boy said, "only a knight would help a stranger in need like that."

More bags crashed down on the pile beside him. One tumbled off, rolling into the harbor's dark water with a *plunk!* Hadrian pressed forward, both to avoid being hit from above and to retrieve his stolen property. "I'm not a knight. Now give me back my bag."

"I will carry it for you. My name is Pickles, but we must

be going. Quickly now." The boy hugged Hadrian's bag and trotted off on dirty bare feet.

"Hey!"

"Quickly, quickly! We should not linger here."

"What's the rush? What are you talking about? And come back here with my bag!"

"You are very lucky to have me. I am an excellent guide. Anything you want, I know where to look. With me you can get the best of everything and all for the least amounts."

Hadrian finally caught up and grabbed his bag. He pulled and got the boy with it, his arms still tightly wrapped around the canvas.

"Ha! See?" The boy grinned. "No one is pulling your bag out of *my* hands!"

"Listen"—Hadrian took a moment to catch his breath—"I don't need a guide. I'm not staying here."

"Where are you going?"

"Up north. Way up north. A place called Sheridan."

"Ah! The university."

This surprised Hadrian. Pickles didn't look like the worldly type. The kid resembled an abandoned dog. The kind that might have once worn a collar but now possessed only fleas, visible ribs, and an overdeveloped sense for survival.

"You are studying to be a scholar? I should have known. My apologies for any insult. You are most smart—so, of course, you will make a great scholar. You should not tip me for making such a mistake. But that is even better. I know just where we must go. There is a barge that travels up the Bernum River. Yes, the barge will be perfect and one leaves tonight. There will not be another for days, and you do not want to stay in an awful city like this. We will be in Sheridan in no time."

"We?" Hadrian smirked.

"You will want me with you, yes? I am not just familiar with Vernes. I am an expert on all of Avryn—I have traveled far. I can help you, a steward who can see to your needs and watch your belongings to keep them safe from thieves while you study. A job I am most good at, yes?"

"I'm not a student, not going to be one either. Just visiting someone, and I don't need a steward."

"Of course you do not need a steward—if you are not going to be a scholar—but as the son of a noble lord just back from the east, you definitely need a houseboy, and I will make a fine houseboy. I will make sure your chamber pot is always emptied, your fire well stoked in winter, and fan you in the summer to keep the flies away."

"Pickles," Hadrian said firmly. "I'm not a lord's son, and I don't need a servant. I—" He stopped after noticing the boy's attention had been drawn away, and his gleeful expression turned fearful. "What's wrong?"

"I told you we needed to hurry. We need to get away from the dock right now!"

Hadrian turned to see men with clubs marching up the pier, their heavy feet causing the dock to bounce.

"Press-gang," Pickles said. "They are always near when ships come in. Newcomers like you can get caught and wake up in the belly of a ship already at sea. Oh no!" Pickles gasped as one spotted them.

After a quick whistle and shoulder tap, four men headed their way. Pickles flinched. The boy's legs flexed, his weight shifting as if to bolt, but he looked at Hadrian, bit his lip, and didn't move.

The clubmen charged but slowed and came to a stop after spotting Hadrian's swords. The four could have been brothers. Each had almost-beards, oily hair, sunbaked skin, and angry faces. The expression must have been popular, as it left permanent creases in their brows.

They studied him for a second, puzzled. Then the foremost thug, wearing a stained tunic with one torn sleeve, asked, "You a knight?"

"No, I'm not a knight." Hadrian rolled his eyes.

Another laughed and gave the one with the torn sleeve a

rough shove. "Daft fool—he's not much older than the boy next to him."

"Don't bleedin' shove me on this slimy dock, ya stupid sod." The man looked back at Hadrian. "He's not that young."

"It's possible," one of the others said. "Kings do stupid things. Heard one knighted his dog once. Sir Spot they called him."

The four laughed. Hadrian was tempted to join in, but he was sobered by the terrified look on Pickles's face.

The one with the torn sleeve took a step closer. "He's got to be at least a squire. Look at all that steel, for Maribor's sake. Where's yer master, boy? He around?"

"I'm not a squire either," Hadrian replied.

"No? What's with all the steel, then?"

"None of your business."

The men laughed. "Oh, you're a tough one, are ya?"

They spread out, taking firmer holds on their sticks. One had a strap of leather run through a hole in the handle and wrapped around his wrist. *Probably figured that was a good idea*, Hadrian thought.

"You better leave us alone," Pickles said, voice wavering. "Do you not know who this is?" He pointed at Hadrian. "He is a famous swordsman—a born killer."

Laughter. "Is that so?" the nearest said, and paused to spit between yellow teeth.

"Oh yes!" Pickles insisted. "He's vicious—an animal—and very touchy, very dangerous."

"A young colt like him, eh?" The man gazed at Hadrian and pushed out his lips in judgment. "Big enough—I'll grant ya that—but it looks to me like he still has his mother's milk dripping down his chin." He focused on Pickles. "And *you're* no vicious killer, are ya, little lad? You're the dirty alley rat I saw yesterday under the alehouse boardwalks trying to catch crumbs. You, my boy, are about to embark on a new career at sea. Best thing for ya really. You'll get food and learn to work—work real hard. It'll make a man out of ya."

Pickles tried to dodge, but the thug grabbed him by the hair.

"Let him go," Hadrian said.

"How did ya put it?" The guy holding Pickles chuckled. *"None of your business?"*

"He's my squire," Hadrian declared.

The men laughed again. "You said you ain't a knight, remember?"

"He works for me—that's good enough."

"No it ain't, 'cause this one works for the maritime industry now." He threw a muscled arm around Pickles's neck and bent the boy over as another moved behind with a length of rope pulled from his belt.

"I said, let him go." Hadrian raised his voice.

"Hey!" the man with the torn sleeve barked. "Don't give us no orders, boy. We ain't taking you, 'cause you're somebody's property, someone who has you hauling three swords, someone who might miss you. That's problems we don't need, see? But don't push it. Push it and we'll break bones. Push us more and we'll drop you in a boat anyway. Push us too far, and you won't even get a boat."

"I really hate people like you," Hadrian said, shaking his head. "I just got here. I was at sea for a month—*a month*! That's how long I've traveled to get away from this kind of thing." He shook his head in disgust. "And here you are—you too." Hadrian pointed at Pickles as they worked at tying the boy's wrists behind his back. "I didn't ask for your help. I didn't ask for a guide, or a steward, or a houseboy. I was just fine on my own. But no, you had to take my bag and be so good-humored about everything. Worst of all, you didn't run. Maybe you're stupid—I don't know. But I can't help thinking you stuck around to help me."

"I'm sorry I didn't do a better job." Pickles looked up at him with sad eyes.

Hadrian sighed. "Damn it. There you go again." He looked back at the clubmen, already knowing how it would turn out—how it always turned out—but he'd to try anyway. "Look, I'm not a knight. I'm not a squire either, but these swords are mine, and while Pickles thought he was bluffing, I—"

"Oh, just shut up." The one with the torn sleeve took a step and thrust his club to shove Hadrian. On the slippery pier it was easy for Hadrian to put him off balance. He caught the man's arm, twisted the wrist and elbow around, and snapped the bone. The crack sounded like a walnut opening. He gave the screaming clubman a shove, which was followed by a splash as he went into the harbor.

Hadrian could have drawn his swords then—almost did out of reflex—but he'd promised himself things would be different. Besides, he stole the man's club before sending him over the side, a solid bit of hickory about an inch in diameter and a little longer than a foot. The grip had been polished smooth from years of use, the other end stained brown from blood that seeped into the wood grain.

The remaining men gave up trying to tie Pickles, but one continued to hold him in a headlock while the other two rushed Hadrian. He read their feet, noting their weight and momentum. Dodging his first attacker's swing, Hadrian tripped the second and struck him in the back of the head as he went down. The sound of club on skull made a hollow thud like slapping a pumpkin, and when the guy hit the deck, he stayed there. The other swung at him again. Hadrian parried with the hickory stick, striking fingers. The man cried out and lost his grip, the club left dangling from the leather strap around his wrist. Hadrian grabbed the weapon, twisted it tight, bent the man's arm back, and pulled hard. The bone didn't break, but the shoulder popped. The man's quivering legs signaled the fight had left him, and Hadrian sent him over the side to join his friend.

By the time Hadrian turned to face the last of the four, Pickles was standing alone and rubbing his neck. His would-be captor sprinted into the distance.

"Is he going to come back with friends, you think?" Hadrian asked.

Pickles didn't say anything. He just stared at Hadrian, his mouth open.

"No sense lingering to find out, I suppose," Hadrian answered himself. "So where's this barge you were talking about?"

～

Away from the seaside pier, the city of Vernes was still choked and stifling. Narrow brick roads formed a maze overshadowed by balconies that nearly touched. Lanterns and moonlight were equally scarce, and down some lonely pathways there was no light at all. Hadrian was thankful to have Pickles. Recovered from his fright, the "alley rat" acted more like a hunting dog. He trotted through the city's corridors, leaping puddles that stank of waste and ducking wash lines and scaffolding with practiced ease.

"That's the living quarters for most of the shipwrights, and over there is the dormitory for the dockworkers." Pickles pointed to a grim building near the wharf with three stories, one door, and few windows. "Most of the men around this ward live there or at the sister building on the south end. So much here is shipping. Now, up there, high on that hill—see it? That is the citadel."

Hadrian lifted his head and made out the dark silhouette of a fortress illuminated by torches.

"Not really a castle, more like a counting house for traders and merchants. Walls have to be high and thick for all the gold it is they stuff up there. This is where all the money from the sea goes. Everything else runs downhill—but gold flows up."

Pickles sidestepped a toppled bucket and spooked a pair of cat-sized rats that ran for deeper shadows. Halfway past a doorway Hadrian realized a pile of discarded rags was actually an ancient-looking man seated on a stoop. With a frazzled gray beard and a face thick with folds, he never moved, not even to blink. Hadrian only noticed him after his smoking pipe's bowl glowed bright orange.

"It is a filthy city," Pickles called back to him. "I am pleased we are leaving. Too many foreigners here—too many easterners—many probably arrived with you. Strange folk, the Calians. Their women practice witchcraft and tell fortunes, but I say it is best not to know too much about one's future. We will not have to worry about such things in the north. In Warric, they burn witches in the winter to keep warm. At least that is what I have heard." Pickles stopped abruptly and spun. "What is your name?"

"Finally decided to ask, eh?" Hadrian chuckled.

"I will need to know if I am going to book you passage."

"I can take care of that myself. Assuming, of course, you are actually taking me to a barge and not just to some dark corner where you'll clunk me on the head and do a more thorough job of robbing me."

Pickles looked hurt. "I would do no such thing. Do you think me such a fool? First, I have seen what you do to people who try to *clunk you on the head*. Second, we have already passed a dozen perfectly dark corners." Pickles beamed his big smile, which Hadrian took to be one part mischief, one part pride, and two parts just-plain-happy-to-be-alive joy. He couldn't argue with that. He also couldn't remember the last time he felt the way Pickles looked.

The press-gang leader was right. Pickles could only be four or five years younger than Hadrian. *Five*, he thought. *He's five years younger than I am. He's me before I left. Did I smile like that back then?* He wondered how long Pickles had been on his own and if he'd still have that smile in five years.

"Hadrian, Hadrian Blackwater." He extended his hand.

The boy nodded. "A good name. Very good. Better than Pickles—but then what is not?"

"Did your mother name you that?"

"Oh, most certainly. Rumor has it I was both conceived and born on the same crate of pickles. How can one deny such a legend? Even if it isn't true, I think it should be."

Crawling out of the labyrinth, they emerged onto a wider

avenue. They had gained height, and Hadrian could see the pier and the masts of the ship he arrived on below. A good-sized crowd was still gathered—people looking for a place to stay or searching for belongings. Hadrian remembered the bag that had rolled into the harbor. How many others would find themselves stranded in a new city with little to nothing?

The bark of a dog caused Hadrian to turn. Looking down the narrow street, he thought he caught movement but couldn't be sure. The twisted length of the alley had but one lantern. Moonlight illuminated the rest, casting patches of blue-gray. A square here, a rectangle there, not nearly enough to see by and barely enough to judge distance. Had it been another rat? Seemed bigger. He waited, staring. Nothing moved.

When he looked back, Pickles had crossed most of the plaza to the far side where, to Hadrian's delight, there was another dock. This one sat on the mouth of the great Bernum River, which in the night appeared as a wide expanse of darkness. He cast one last look backward toward the narrow streets. Still nothing moved. *Ghosts*. That's all—his past stalking him.

Hadrian reeked of death. It wasn't the sort of stench others could smell or that water could wash, but it lingered on him like sweat-saturated pores after a long night of drinking. Only this odor didn't come from alcohol; it came from blood. Not from drinking it—although Hadrian knew some who had. His stink came from wallowing in it. But all that was over now, or so he told himself with the certainty of the recently sober. That had been a different Hadrian, a younger version who he'd left on the other side of the world and who he was still running from.

Realizing Pickles still had his bag, Hadrian ran to close the distance. Before he caught up, Pickles was in trouble again.

"It is his!" Pickles cried, pointing at Hadrian. "I was helping him reach the barge before it left."

The boy was surrounded by six soldiers. Most wore chain

and held square shields. The one in the middle, with a fancy plume on his helmet, wore layered plate on his shoulders and chest as well as a studded leather skirt. He was the one Pickles was speaking to while two others restrained the boy. They all looked over as Hadrian approached.

"This your bag?" the officer asked.

"It is, and he's telling the truth." Hadrian pointed. "He is escorting me to that barge over there."

"In a hurry to leave our fair city, are you?" The officer's tone was suspicious, and his eyes scanned Hadrian as he talked.

"No offense to Vernes, but yes. I have business up north."

The officer moved a step closer. "What's your name?"

"Hadrian Blackwater."

"Where you from?"

"Hintindar originally."

"Originally?" The skepticism in his voice rose along with his eyebrows.

Hadrian nodded. "I've been in Calis for several years. Just returned from Dagastan on that ship down there."

The officer glanced at the dock, then at Hadrian's knee-length thawb, loose cotton pants, and keffiyeh headdress. He leaned in, sniffed, and grimaced. "You've definitely been on a ship, and that outfit is certainly Calian." He sighed, then turned to Pickles. "But this one hasn't been on any ship. He says he's going with you. Is that right?"

Hadrian glanced at Pickles and saw the hope in the boy's eyes. "Yeah. I've hired him to be my ... ah ... my ... servant."

"Whose idea was that? His or yours?"

"His, but he's been very helpful. I wouldn't have found this barge without him."

"You just got off one ship," the officer said. "Seems odd you're so eager to get on another."

"Well, actually I'm not, but Pickles says the barge is about to leave and there won't be another for days. Is that true?"

"Yes," the officer said, "and awfully convenient too."

"Can I ask what the problem is? Is there a law against hiring a guide and paying for him to travel with you?"

"No, but we've had some nasty business here in town—real nasty business. So naturally we're interested in anyone eager to leave, at least anyone who's been around during the last few days." He looked squarely at Pickles.

"I haven't done anything," Pickles said.

"So you say, but even if you haven't, maybe you know something about it. Either way you might feel the need to disappear, and latching on to someone above suspicion would be a good way to get clear of trouble, wouldn't it?"

"But I don't know anything about the killings."

The officer turned to Hadrian. "You're free to go your way, and you'd best be quick. They've already called for boarders."

"What about Pickles?"

He shook his head. "I can't let him go with you. Unlikely he's guilty of murder, but he might know who is. Street orphans see a lot that they don't like to talk about if they think they can avoid it."

"But I'm telling you, I don't know *anything*. I haven't even been on the hill."

"Then you've nothing to worry about."

"But—" Pickles looked as if he might cry. "He was going to take me out of here. We were going to go north. We were going to go to a university."

"Hoy! Hoy! Last call for passengers! Barge to Colnora! Last call!" a voice bellowed.

"Listen"—Hadrian opened his purse—"you did me a service, and that's worth payment. Now, after you finish with their questions, if you still want to work for me, you can use this money to meet me in Sheridan. Catch the next barge or buckboard north, whatever. I'll be there for a month maybe, a couple of weeks at least." Hadrian pressed a coin into the boy's hand. "If you come, ask for Professor Arcadius. He's the one I'm meeting with, and he should be able to tell you how to find me. Okay?"

Pickles nodded and looked a bit better. Glancing down at the coin, his eyes widened, and the old giant smile of his returned. "Yes, sir! I will be there straightaway. You can most certainly count on me. Now you must run before the barge leaves."

Hadrian gave him a nod, picked up his bag, and jogged to the dock where a man waited at the gangway of a long flat boat.